D0522265

BY MAEVE BINCHY

Light a Penny Candle
Echoes
London Transports
Dublin 4
The Lilac Bus
Firefly Summer
Silver Wedding
Circle of Friends
The Copper Beech
The Glass Lake
Evening Class
Tara Road
Scarlet Feather
Quentins
Nights of Rain and Stars
Whitethorn Woods

Aches & Pains (non-fiction)

Maeve Binchy was born in County Dublin and was educated at the Holy Child Convent in Killiney and at University College Dublin. After a spell as a teacher in various girls' schools, she joined the *Irish Times*, for which she wrote feature articles and columns. Her first novel, *Light a Penny Candle*, was published in 1982, and since then she has written more than a dozen novels and short-story collections, each one of them bestsellers. Several have been adapted for cinema and television, most notably *Circle of Friends* in 1995. She was awarded the Lifetime Achievement award at the British Book Awards in 1999. She is married to the writer and broadcaster Gordon Snell. Visit her website at *www.maevebinchy.com*

Maeve Binchy

NIGHTS *of* RAIN *and* STARS

WHITETHORN WOODS

Nights of Rain and Stars
First published in Great Britain by Orion in 2004

Whitethorn Woods
First published in Great Britain by Orion in 2006

This omnibus edition published in 2009
by Orion Books Ltd
Orion House, 5 Upper St Martin's Lane
London WC2H 9EA

An Hachette UK Company

A CIP catalogue record for this book is available
from the British Library.

ISBN 9781407221236

Printed in Great Britain by Clays Ltd, St Ives plc

www.orionbooks.co.uk

NIGHTS *of* RAIN
and STARS

For dear good Gordon
who has been such a supportive and kind person
that nobody would believe it if I were to
write him into a book!
Thank you with all of my heart.

CHAPTER ONE

Andreas thought he saw the fire down in the bay before anyone else did. He peered and shook his head in disbelief. This sort of thing didn't happen. Not here in Aghia Anna, not to the *Olga*, the little red and white boat that took visitors out to the bay. Not to Manos, foolish headstrong Manos whom he had known since he was a boy. This was some kind of dream, some trick of the light. That could not be smoke and flames coming from the *Olga*.

Perhaps he was not feeling well.

Some of the older people in the village said that they imagined things. If the day was hot, if there had been too much *raki* the night before. But he had gone to bed early. There had been no *raki* or dancing or singing in his hillside restaurant.

Andreas put his hand up to shade his eyes and, at the same time, a cloud passed overhead. It wasn't as clear as it had been before. He must indeed have been mistaken. But now he must pull himself together. He had a restaurant to run. If people came all the way up the hilly path, they would not want to find a madman, someone crazed by the sun fancying disasters in a peaceful Greek village.

He continued fixing the red and green plastic-covered cloths with little clips to the long wooden tables on the terrace outside his taverna. This would be a hot day, with plenty of visitors at lunchtime. He had laboriously written the menu on the black-board. He often wondered why he did it . . . it was the same food every day. But the visitors liked it; and he would put 'Welcome' in six languages. They liked that too.

The food was not special. Nothing they could not have got in two dozen other little tavernas. There was *souvlaki*, the lamb kebabs. Well, goat kebabs really, but the visitors liked to think they were lamb. And there was *moussakas*, warm and glutinous in its big pie dish. There were the big bowls of salad, white squares of salty feta cheese and lush red tomatoes. There were the racks of *barbouni*, red mullet, waiting to be grilled, the swordfish steaks. There were the big steel trays of desserts in the fridge, *katáifi* and *baklava*, made from nuts, honey and pastry. The chilled cabinets of retsina and local wines. Why else did people come to Greece? People came from all over the world and loved what Andreas, and dozens like him, could provide.

He always recognised the nationality of any

visitor to Aghia Anna and could greet them in a few words of their own language. It was like a game to him now, after years of studying the way people walked and reading their body language.

The English didn't like it if you offered them a *Speisekarte* instead of the menu, the Canadians did not want you to assume they were from the United States. Italians did not like to be greeted with a *Bonjour* and his own fellow countrymen wanted to be thought of as important people from Athens rather than tourists from abroad. Andreas had learned to look carefully before he spoke.

And as he looked down the path he saw the first customers of the day arriving.

His mind went on to automatic pilot.

A quiet man, wearing those shorts that only Americans wore, shorts that did nothing for the bottom or the legs, but only pointed out the ridiculous nature of the human figure. He was on his own and stopped to look at the fire through binoculars.

A beautiful German girl, tall, tanned, with hair streaked by the sun or a very expensive hairdresser. She stood in silence, staring in disbelief at the scarlet and orange flames licking over the boat in Aghia Anna bay.

A boy, also in his twenties, small and anxious-looking with glasses that he kept taking off and wiping. He stood open-mouthed in horror, looking at the boat in the bay down below.

A couple also in their twenties, exhausted after the walk up the hill; they were Scottish or Irish, he thought – Andreas couldn't quite make out the accents. The boy had a sort of swagger about him, as if he were trying to tell some imaginary audience that the walk had not been difficult at all.

In their turn, they saw a tall man, slightly stooped, with grey-white hair and bushy eyebrows.

'That's the boat we were on yesterday.' The girl had her hand over her mouth in shock. 'Oh, my God, it could have been us.'

'Well, it isn't, so what's the point in saying that?' her boyfriend said firmly. He was gazing in disdain at Andreas's laced-up boots.

And then, there was the sound of an explosion from down in the bay and, for the first time, Andreas realised that it was true. There *was* a fire. Not just a trick of the light. The others had seen it too. He could not put it down to an old man's failing eyesight. He began to tremble and hold on to the back of a chair to support himself.

'I must telephone my brother Yorghis, he is in the police station . . . maybe they don't know about it, maybe they cannot see the fire from down there.'

The tall American man spoke gently. 'They see it, look, there are lifeboats already on the way.'

But Andreas went to make the phone call anyway.

Of course there was no reply from the tiny police station up the hill from the harbour.

The young girl was peering down at the innocent-looking blue sea where the ragged scarlet flames and the black smoke seemed like a grotesque blot in the middle of a painting.

'I can't believe it,' she said over and over. 'Yesterday he was teaching us to dance on that very boat, *Olga*, he called it, after his grandmother.'

'Manos – that's his boat, isn't it?' asked the boy with the glasses. 'I was on his boat, too.'

'Yes, that is Manos,' said Andreas gravely. *That fool Manos with too many people on the vessel as usual, with no proper catering facilities but insisting on pouring drink into them and trying to make kebabs with some out-dated gas cylinder.* But none of the people of the village would ever say any of this. Manos had a family here. They would all be gathered now, down by the harbour, waiting for news.

'Do you know him?' asked the tall American with the binoculars.

'Yes, indeed, we all know everyone here.' Andreas wiped his eyes with a table napkin.

They stood as if transfixed, watching the distant boats arriving and trying to douse the flames, the bodies struggling in the water hoping to be picked up by the smaller craft.

The American lent his binoculars to anyone who

5

wanted to see. They were all at a loss for words; too far away to go and help, there was nothing they could do, but still they couldn't stop looking at the tragedy unfolding below on that innocent, beautiful, blue sea.

Andreas knew he should make some move to serve them but somehow it seemed crass. He didn't want to leave what was left of Manos and his boat and the unsuspecting tourists who had gone out for such a happy holiday cruise. It would be too insensitive to start telling these customers about stuffed vine leaves and seating them at the tables he had been preparing.

He felt a hand on his arm. It was the blonde German girl. 'It's worse for you – this is your place,' she said.

He felt tears come to his eyes again. She was right. It *was* his place. He had been born here, he knew everyone in Aghia Anna, he had known Olga, the grandmother of Manos, he knew the young men putting their boats out into the tide to rescue the victims. He knew the families who would be standing waiting at the harbour. Yes, it was worse for him. He looked at her piteously.

Her face was kind but she was practical too. 'Why don't you sit down? Please do,' she said kindly. 'There's nothing we can do to help them.'

It was the spur he needed. 'I'm Andreas,' he said. 'You're right, this is my place, and something terrible has happened here. I will offer you all a Metaxa brandy for the shock and we will say a prayer for the people in the bay.'

'Is there nothing, *nothing* that we can do?' asked the English boy with the glasses.

'It took us about three hours to get up this far. By the time we got back I guess we'd only be in the way,' said the tall American. 'I'm Thomas, by the way, and I think we'd better not crowd the harbour. See – there are dozens of people there already.' He offered his binoculars so they could see for themselves.

'I'm Elsa,' said the German girl, 'and I'll get the glasses.'

They stood with tiny glasses of the fiery liquid in their hands and raised a strange toast in the sunshine.

Fiona, the Irish girl with the red hair and a freckled nose, said, 'May their souls and all the souls of the faithful departed rest in peace.'

Her boyfriend seemed to wince slightly at the expression.

'Well, why not, Shane?' she asked him defensively. 'It's a blessing.'

'Go in peace,' said Thomas to the wreckage. Now the flames had died down and they were in the business of counting the living and the dead.

'*L'chaim*,' said David, the English boy with the glasses. 'It means "To life",' he explained.

'*Ruhet in Frieden*,' said Elsa with tears in her eyes.

'*O Theos n'anapafsi tin psyhi tou*,' said Andreas, bowing his head in grief as he looked down on what looked like the worst tragedy that Aghia Anna had ever known.

They didn't order lunch, Andreas just served them. He brought them a salad with goat's cheese, a plate of lamb and stuffed tomatoes, and afterwards a bowl of fruit. They spoke about themselves and where they had been. None of them was a two-week package tour visitor. They were all in it for the long haul – several months, at least.

Thomas, the American, was travelling and writing articles for a magazine. He had a year off, a proper sabbatical from his university. He said that they were much sought after . . . a whole year with their blessing to see the world and broaden his mind. Teachers of every kind needed a chance to go out and talk to people of other countries, otherwise they could get caught up in the internal politics of their own university. He looked somehow a little far away as he spoke, Andreas thought, as if he were missing something back in California.

It was different with Elsa, the German girl. She seemed to miss nothing she had left behind. She said she had grown tired of her job, she realised that what she had once thought of as important was in fact shallow and trite. She had enough money saved to finance a year's travel. She had been on the road for three weeks and never wanted to leave Greece.

Fiona, the little Irish girl, was more uncertain. She looked at her moody boyfriend for confirmation as she spoke of how they wanted to see the world and find somewhere to settle where people wouldn't judge them, want to improve them, or try to change them. Her boyfriend said nothing either to agree or disagree, just shrugged as if it were all very boring.

David spoke of his wish to see the world while he was still young enough to know what he liked and maybe join in. There was nothing sadder than an old man who found what he was looking for decades too late. Someone who had not shown the courage to change because he had not known what opportunities for change there were. David had only been a month on his road of discovery. His mind was filled with all he had seen.

But even as they talked and told each other a little of their lives in Düsseldorf, Dublin, California, and Manchester, Andreas noted, they said nothing of the families they had left behind.

He told them of life here in Aghia Anna and how the place was rich today, compared to his childhood when no tourists ever came by and a living was earned in the olive groves or minding goats on the hills. He spoke of brothers long gone to America, and his own son who had left this restaurant after

9

an argument nine years ago and who had never come back.

'And what did you argue about?' asked little Fiona, with the big green eyes.

'Oh, he wanted a nightclub here and I didn't – the usual thing about age and youth, about change and not changing,' Andreas shrugged sadly.

'And would you have had a nightclub if it meant he would have stayed at home?' Elsa asked him.

'Yes, now I would. If I had known how lonely it would be to have my only son in Chicago, far across the world and never writing to me . . . then, yes, I would have had the nightclub. But I didn't know, you see.'

'And what about your wife?' Fiona asked. 'Did she not beg you to get him back and open the club?'

'She had died. Nobody left to make peace between us.'

There was a silence. It was as if the men were nodding and understanding completely and as if the women didn't know what he was talking about.

The afternoon shadows grew longer. Andreas served them little coffees and none of them seemed to want to leave. From high on the hill here at the taverna they could see down below at the harbour a hellish scene was unfolding. A sunny day had turned into death and disaster. Through the binoculars, they saw bodies on stretchers, and crowds gathering and people pushing to see if their loved ones were alive or dead. They felt safer here, up the hill, and even though they knew nothing of each other, brought together like this they talked as if they were old friends.

They were still talking as the first stars came into the sky. Now, down in the harbour they could see the lights of flashing cameras and of television teams recording the tragedy to tell to the world. It hadn't taken long for news of the disaster to get to the media.

'I suppose they have to do it,' said David with resignation. 'But it seems so ghoulish, monstrous, preying on people's lives in a tragedy.'

'It is monstrous, believe me, I work in it. Or worked, anyway,' Elsa said, unexpectedly.

'A journalist?' David asked with interest.

'I worked on a television current affairs show. There's somebody like me now, at my desk in the studio, asking questions at long distance of someone down there in the harbour: how many bodies have been recovered, how did it happen, are there any Germans among the dead? What you say is true – it *is* monstrous. I'm glad to be no part of it now.'

'And yet people do have to know about famines and wars – otherwise how can we stop them?' Thomas asked.

'We'll never stop them,' Shane said. 'It's a matter of money. There's big money in this kind of thing, that's why it's done, that's why anything's done in the world.'

Shane was different from the others, Andreas thought. Dismissive, restless, anxious to be somewhere else. But then he was a young man, it was natural that he would want to be with his attractive little girlfriend, Fiona, just the two of them, rather than having a conversation with a lot of strangers high on a hill on a hot day.

'Not everyone is interested in money,' David said mildly.

'I didn't say you had to be, I'm just saying it's what gets things going, that's all.'

Fiona looked up sharply as if she had been down this road before, defending Shane for his views. 'What Shane means is that that's the system – it's not the God in his life nor in mine. I certainly wouldn't be a nurse if it was money I was looking for.' She smiled around at them all.

'A nurse?' Elsa said.

'Yes, I was wondering, would I be any use down there, but I don't suppose . . .?'

'Fiona, you're not a surgeon, you're not going to amputate a leg down there in a harbour café,' Shane protested. There was a sneer on his face.

'But, you know, at least I could do *something*,' she said.

'For God's sake, Fiona, get real. What could you

do, tell them in Greek to keep calm? Foreign nurses aren't in high demand at a time of crisis.'

Fiona flushed darkly.

Elsa came to her rescue. 'If we were down there I'd say you'd be invaluable but it would take us so long I think we're better off to be up here, out of people's way.'

Thomas agreed. He was looking through his binoculars again. 'I don't think you'd even be able to get near to the wounded if you were there,' he said reassuringly. 'See, there's such confusion.' He passed her the glasses and with trembling hands she looked down at the distant harbour and the people jostling each other.

'Yes, you're right, I see,' Fiona said in a small voice.

'It must be wonderful being a nurse, I guess it means that you're never afraid,' Thomas said, trying to make Fiona feel better. 'What a great career. My mother is a nurse, but she works long hours and doesn't get paid enough.'

'Did she work while you were a kid?'

'Still does. She put my brother and me through college and we got careers out of all that. We try to thank her and give her a rest, a place to live, but she says she's programmed to keep going.'

'What career did you get out of college?' David asked. 'I have a degree in business studies but it never got me anything I wanted to do.'

Thomas spoke slowly. 'I teach nineteenth-century literature at a university.' He shrugged as if it weren't a big deal.

'What do you do, Shane?' Elsa asked.

'Why?' He looked back at her directly.

'Don't know, probably it's because I can't stop asking questions. It's just that the rest of us said. I suppose I didn't want you to be left out.' Elsa had a beautiful smile.

He relaxed. 'Sure, well, I do a bit of this and a bit of that.'

'I know.' Elsa nodded as if this were a reasonable answer.

The others nodded too. They also knew.

Just then, Andreas spoke very slowly. 'I think you should all call and tell them back at home that you are alive.'

They looked at him, startled.

He explained what he was thinking. 'As Elsa says, this will be on the television news tonight. They will all see, they may know you are here in Aghia Anna, they will think that you might be on the boat of Manos.' He looked around him. Five young people from different families, different homes, different countries.

'Well, my mobile phone doesn't work here,' Elsa said cheerfully. 'I did try a couple of days ago and I thought, so much the better, now it's a real escape.'

'It's the wrong time of day in California,' Thomas said.

'I'd get the answering machine, they'll be out again at some business function,' David said.

'It would only be another earful of "Dear, dear, look what happens when you leave your nice, safe job and go gallivanting round the world,"' said Fiona.

Shane said nothing at all. The notion of phoning home had just never occurred to him.

Andreas stood up at the table and addressed them. 'Believe me, when I hear there has been a shooting in Chicago or a flood or any disaster, I wonder to myself, could my Adoni be caught up in it? It would be so good if he were to ring . . . just a short message to say that he is safe. That's all.'

'His name was Adoni?' Fiona said in wonder. 'Like Adonis, the god of beauty.'

'His name *is* Adoni,' Elsa corrected.

'And *is* he an Adonis, with the women, I mean?' Shane asked with a grin.

'I don't know, he doesn't tell me.' Andreas had a sad face.

'You see, Andreas, you're the kind of father who *does* care. Some fathers don't,' David explained.

'Every parent cares, they just have different ways of showing it.'

'And, of course, some of us have no parents,' Elsa

said in a light voice. 'Like me, a father long disappeared, a mother who died young.'

'But there must be someone in Germany who loves you, Elsa,' Andreas said, and then thought perhaps he had gone too far. 'I tell you, my telephone is there in the bar. Now I will open a bottle of wine to celebrate that we were here tonight, with all our hopes and dreams still left to us as we sit in another night of stars.'

He went inside and could hear them talking out on the terrace.

'I think he really *does* want us to use his phone,' Fiona said.

'Well, you just said what you'd be letting yourself in for,' Shane objected.

'Perhaps it's making too much of it all,' Elsa wondered.

They looked down again at the scene below. And there was no argument, this time.

'I'll call first,' said Thomas.

Andreas stood polishing glasses and listening to their calls. They were a strange little group gathered today in his taverna. None of them seemed at ease with the people they called. It was as if they were all running away from something. Each of them sounded like someone escaping from a bad situation.

Thomas's voice was clipped. 'I *know* he's at day camp. I just thought . . . no, it doesn't matter . . .

believe me, I had no agenda. Shirley, please, I'm not trying to make trouble, I was just ... All right, Shirley, think what you like. No, I haven't made any plans yet.'

David sounded apprehensive. 'Oh, Dad, you're at home, yes, well, of course you should be. It's just that I wanted to tell you about this accident ... no, I wasn't hurt ... no, I wasn't on the boat.' A long silence. 'Right, Dad, give my love to Mum, won't you. No, tell her there's nothing definite about when I'm coming back.'

Fiona's conversation was hardly about the boat tragedy at all. No one seemed to let her talk about it. It was, as Shane had predicted, some kind of plea for her to come home. 'I can't give you a date yet, Mam, we've been through this a million times. Where he goes I go, Mam, and you must make your own plans for that – it would be much better that way.'

Elsa's conversation was a mystery. Andreas spoke German, and he understood perfectly. She left two messages on answering machines.

The first was warm: 'Hannah, it's Elsa. I am in this glorious place in Greece called Aghia Anna and there was a terrible accident today. People died in a boat tragedy. In front of our eyes. I can't tell you how sad it was. But in case you wondered was I involved in it, I wanted to tell you I'm one of the lucky ones ... Oh, Hannah, I do miss you and your kind shoulder to weep on. But I weep a lot less now, so possibly I did the right thing to come away. As usual I'd prefer you not to say that you heard from me. You're such a friend – I don't deserve you. I'll get in touch soon, I promise.'

Then she made a second call and this time her voice was ice cold. 'I wasn't killed on that boat. But you know that there are times I would not mind if I had been. I don't pick up e-mails so save your energy. There is nothing you can say, nothing you can do. You've done and said it all. I only called you because I imagine the studio is hoping that I was either burned in that pleasure-boat fire or that I am standing on the harbour waiting to give an eye-witness account. But I am miles away from it, and even more miles away from you, and that's all I care about, believe me.'

And Andreas saw the tears on Elsa's face as she replaced the receiver.

CHAPTER TWO

Andreas knew that none of them wanted to leave his place. They felt safe here on his terrace, far from the tragedy unfolding below. And far from their own unhappy lives back home.

He wondered, as he had wondered so many nights before, about families. Was it just the argument about the nightclub that had driven Adoni away? Was it a need to be free, away from the old ways? If he had to do it all over again, would he have been more open and giving, supported his son to go and see the world before he settled down?

But then these young people were all doing that and yet they were still having problems at home. He had heard that in all their conversations. He left their wine on the table and sat in the shadows with his worry beads moving from hand to hand while they talked. As the evening came and more wine was poured they grew relaxed and seemed to want to talk. They were no longer secretive about their home lives.

Poor little Fiona was the most eager of all.

'You were right, Shane ... I shouldn't have called, it just gave them another chance to tell me what a mess I was making of my life, and how they can't get their silver wedding plans organised until they know where I am going to be. Five months left, and my mother, who thinks that a take-away Chinese meal is entertaining, is now worrying about a party! I told her straight out that I hadn't a notion of where we'd be then, and she starts to cry. She's actually *crying* about a party, and here we are with all those people down at the harbour who really *do* have something to cry about. It would make you sick.'

'Told you.' Shane inhaled. He and Fiona were smoking a joint; the others didn't join in. Andreas didn't approve, but now wasn't the time to make heavy rules.

Thomas spoke up. 'I had no luck either. Bill, my little boy, who might actually care about me, was out at day camp. My ex-wife, who would love to think that I had perished on Manos's boat, was less than pleased by the call. Still, at least the boy won't look at the news and worry about me.' He was philosophical about it.

'How would he know that you were even in this

area?' Shane obviously thought the phone calls home were a waste of time for everyone.

'I sent a fax with my telephone numbers. Shirley is meant to put it up on the bulletin board in the kitchen.'

'Does she?' Shane asked.

'She *says* she does.'

'But has your son called?'

'No.'

'Then she doesn't, does she?' Shane had it all figured out.

'I guess not, and I don't imagine she'll call my mother either.' Thomas's face was set in hard lines. 'I wish I had thought of calling Mom instead. But I wanted to hear Bill's voice, and then Shirley got me so upset . . .'

Finally David spoke quietly. 'When I called, I was getting ready to leave a nice calm message on the answering machine – but they were at home and it was my father . . . And he said . . . he said that if nothing had happened to me, what was I ringing about?'

'He didn't really mean that, you know,' Thomas said, soothingly.

'You know the way people always say the wrong thing, just because they're relieved,' Elsa added.

David shook his head. 'But he *did* mean it, he really didn't see the point, and I could hear my mother calling out from the sitting room, "Ask him about the award, Harold, is he coming home for that?"'

'Award?' the others asked.

'It's a pat on the back for having made so much money, like the Queen's Award for Industry. That sort of thing. There's going to be a big reception and a ceremony. Nothing else on earth matters to them except this.'

'Is there anyone else at home who could go to the ceremony in your place?' Elsa asked.

'Well, there's everyone in Father's office and his friends from Rotary and the golf club, and Mother's cousins . . .'

'You're an only child then?' Elsa said.

'That's the problem. That's the whole problem,' David replied sadly.

'It's *your* life, do what you want to,' Shane shrugged. He couldn't see what the problem was.

'I suppose they just wanted to share the honour with you,' Thomas said.

'Yes, but I wanted to tell them about the tragedy and people dying, and all they could do was to start talking about this function and wanting to know if I would be home in time for it. It's monstrous.'

'It might be a way of saying, "Come home", mightn't it?' Elsa suggested.

'Everything's a way of saying, "Come home", but "Come home and get a good job and help your father in his business", and that is not what I am going to do, not now, not ever.' David took off his glasses and wiped them.

Elsa had said nothing about herself. She sat looking far out to sea over the olive groves at the coastline of the little islands where all those people thought they would be spending a sunny holiday afternoon. She felt everyone looking at her, waiting for her to talk about the phone call *she* had made.

'Oh, what response did I get? Well, I think that there's nobody at home in Germany! I called two friends, got two answering machines, and they'll both think I'm mad, but what the hell?' Elsa gave a little laugh. There was no hint that she had left a vague, cheery message on one machine and tense, almost hate-filled words on the other.

From the shadows Andreas looked at her. The beautiful Elsa, who had left her job in television to find peace in the Greek Islands, had certainly not found it yet, he told himself.

They were quiet again on the terrace now, thinking about their phone calls and wondering how they would have played the scene if they had to do it all over again.

Fiona *might* have said to her mother that there were so many anguished mothers and daughters looking for each other down at the harbour it had made her need to talk to home, and that she was sorry for all the anxiety she was causing, but just because she was a grown-up woman and had to lead her own life it didn't mean that she couldn't love her mam and dad as well. They couldn't have got so upset if she had said that, if she had talked about her mother's plans and just said over and over that she *did* care about them and that she would try to be home for the silver wedding. They would have to wait and see.

David thought he *might* have said that he was visiting many places and learning a lot about the world. He could have told them that today there had been this sad tragedy on a beautiful Greek island, and it had certainly made him stop and think about how life was so short and how it could end so unexpectedly.

His father enjoyed proverbs and sayings. David might have told him that there was a proverb that said, 'If you love your child, send him on a journey,' and he could have said that his plans weren't firm yet but he felt every day was a learning experience which would make him a better person. It might have worked: it couldn't have been worse than the empty chasm he had created.

Thomas realised that he should have called his mother, not Shirley. It was just that he had been so hoping to talk to Bill and hadn't been able to resist the possibility that the boy might be there. Mom was the one he should have phoned. He would have told her that he had not been involved in the tragedy and asked her to tell Bill. He could have told his mother that, as he sat with people he had never met, he had told them what a great woman she was and how grateful he was that she had paid for his education by taking on extra night work. Mom would have loved that.

Elsa alone thought that she had handled her calls well. They both knew she was in Greece, but they did not know exactly where and she had left them no way of getting in touch with her. She had said exactly what she wanted to say to each of them. She had been vague and gentle to one; she had been curt and cold to the other. She would not have changed a word.

The phone rang and Andreas started. It might be his brother Yorghis, calling from the police station. Maybe he was calling to let him know about the dead and the casualties.

But it wasn't Yorghis, it was a man speaking German. He said his name was Dieter and he was looking for Elsa.

'She is not here,' Andreas said. 'They all went back to the harbour a while ago. Why do you think she is here?'

'She can't have left,' the man said, 'she only called me ten minutes ago. I have traced the number she called from . . . where is she staying, please? Forgive me for sounding so urgent, but I really do need the information.'

'I have no idea, Herr Dieter, no idea at all.'

'And who was she with?'

'A group of people – I think they leave this village tomorrow.'

'But I must find her.'

'Sincerest regrets at not being able to help you, Herr Dieter.' He hung up, and turned to find Elsa standing looking at him. She had come in from the terrace when she heard him speaking German on the telephone.

'Why did you do that, Andreas?' Her voice was steady.

'I thought it was what you would want me to do, but if I was wrong the telephone is still here – please telephone him again.'

'You were not wrong. You were absolutely right. Thank you very much, very much. You were very right to turn Dieter away. Usually I am strong but tonight I could not have had that conversation.'

'I know,' he said gently. 'There are times when you will say too little or too much. It's best then not to have to say anything at all.'

The phone rang again.

'You still don't know where I am,' she warned.

'Of course,' he said with a bow.

This time it was his brother Yorghis.

Twenty-four people dead.

Twenty from abroad and four from Aghia Anna: not only Manos but also his little nephew who had proudly gone out for the day to help his uncle. A

26

boy of eight. And the two local boys who had worked on the boat, young men with their lives ahead of them.

'It's a very dark time for you, Andreas,' Elsa said, her voice full of concern.

'These are not bright days for you either,' he answered.

They sat there, each thinking their own thoughts. It was as if they had always known each other. They would talk when there was something to say. Elsa spoke eventually.

'Andreas?' She looked outside; the others were talking together, they couldn't hear.

'Yes?'

'Will you do one more thing for me?'

'If I can, yes, of course.'

'Write to Adoni. Ask him to come home to Aghia Anna. To come back now. Tell him that your village has lost three young men and a boy, that you all need to see the face of someone who left, someone who *can* come back.'

He shook his head. 'No, my friend Elsa, it would not work.'

'You mean you won't try to make it work. What's the worst that can happen? He can write and say no, thank you. That's not the end of the world, compared to all that has happened here tonight.'

'Why do you want to change the lives of people you don't know?'

27

She threw back her head and laughed. 'Oh, Andreas, if you knew me in my real life, that's what I do all the time, I'm a crusading journalist – that's what the television station calls me, my friends say I'm just interfering, meddling. I'm always trying to keep families together, get children off drugs, get litter off the streets, get integrity into sports . . . It's my nature to change the lives of people I don't know.'

'And does it ever work?' he asked.

'Sometimes it works. It works enough times for me to want to keep at it.'

'But you've left?'

'Not because of the work.'

He looked at the telephone.

She nodded. 'Yes, you're right, it's because of Dieter. It's a long story. Some day I will come back here and tell it all to you.'

'You don't need to.'

'I do, oddly, but I'd also love to know you had written to Adoni in Chicago. Tell me that you will.'

'I was never a great letter-writer.'

'I'd help to write it for you,' she offered.

'Would you?' he asked.

'I could try to speak with your voice, though I might not get it right.'

'Well, neither might I.' Andreas looked sad. 'Sometimes I think I know the words and I imagine myself putting my arms around him and he says,

28

"Papa" – other times I imagine him being very stiff and hard and saying that what has been said cannot be unsaid.'

'If we were to write a letter then it has to be one that will make him say "Papa",' she said.

'But he would know it was not from me, he knows his old father does not have the power of words.'

'It's often the timing that's most important. He will read in the newspapers, even in Chicago, of this tragedy, this disaster back home in Aghia Anna. He will want to hear from you. Sometimes things are bigger than we are, more important than our little fights.'

'And could that be the same for you and Herr Dieter?' he asked.

'No.' She shook her head. 'No, that's different. Some day I'll tell you, I promise you I will.'

'No need to tell me your business, Elsa,' he said.

'You are my friend, I want to tell you.'

But they heard the others approaching.

Thomas was the spokesman. 'We must let you sleep, Andreas, tomorrow will be a long day,' he said.

'We think we should go back down the hill, back to where we are staying,' David began.

'My brother Yorghis is sending a truck up this way for you soon. I told him I had friends who would need a lift; it's a long way.'

'And can we pay you now for our meal – our long day and night with you?' Thomas asked.

'As I told Yorghis, you are friends, and friends do not pay for their food,' he said with dignity.

They looked at him: old, slightly bent, poor, working hard in a place where they had been the only customers today. They *had* to pay him yet they couldn't insult him.

'You know, Andreas, it would make us feel bad to go away from here without sharing in the cost of our meal together, as if we were all friends in a way,' Fiona began.

Shane saw it differently. 'You heard the man say he doesn't want the money.' He looked around at them all, people who couldn't see a free day's eating and drinking when it was staring them in the face.

Elsa spoke slowly. She had a way of capturing their attention. The others all stopped to listen. She seemed to have tears in her eyes.

'What do you say that we make a collection for the family of Manos and his little nephew and the other people who died in front of our eyes today? There will undoubtedly be a fund for them. We can gather what we think our food and drink here would have cost in another taverna, and then get an envelope and put on it, "From the friends of Andreas".'

Fiona had an envelope in her shoulder bag. She took it out and without a word they poured their euros on to a plate. The sound of the police truck was heard coming up the hill.

'You write the message for the people, Elsa,' Fiona suggested.

And Elsa did with a steady hand.

'I wish I could write in the Greek language,' she said to Andreas, and looked at him as if they shared a secret.

'It's fine – your generosity, all of you, is very fine in any language,' he said, sounding very choked. 'I was never good at writing any sort of letter.'

'It's just the first words that are always the hardest, Andreas,' she persisted.

'I would begin "*Adoni mou*,"' he said haltingly.

'Now you're halfway there,' Elsa said, and held him to her for a quick moment before they climbed into the truck to go back down the hill to the little town which had changed so much since the night before, even though the stars looked exactly the same.

CHAPTER THREE

They travelled in silence as the little van bumped its way down the hill. They all knew that they would never forget tonight. It had been a deep and emotional long day. In a way they had learned too much about one another to feel any sense of ease and comfort with each other. But they all hoped that they would indeed see the old man Andreas again. He had told them that he had a putt-putt bike with a trailer attached to it and that he came down the bumpy road to what he called The Town every day to buy supplies.

None of them slept well that night. The only thing that united them was that they could not lie under warm, dark Mediterranean skies and find sleep. They tossed and turned, the starlight too bright somehow and seeping into their bedrooms. A million little pinpoints up there preventing them from getting the sleep they needed.

Elsa stood on the tiny balcony of her apartment

hotel and looked out at the dark sea. She was staying at the Studio Apartments, run by a young Greek man who learned the property business in Florida and had returned with the idea of having six little self-contained units here: simply furnished, Greek rugs on the wooden floors, colourful Greek pottery on the shelves. No one balcony overlooked the others. He charged a lot by Aghia Anna standards but his apartments were always full.

Elsa had seen an advertisement for them in a travel magazine and had not been disappointed.

From her balcony the dark sea looked so safe and comforting, even though twenty-four people had perished outside that very harbour earlier and that same water had not been able to rise and douse the flames.

She understood for the first time why someone very sad and lonely might want to end their life in the arms of the sea. It would be foolish, of course, there was nothing romantic about drowning. Elsa knew that it wasn't just a matter of closing your eyes and being swept gently away from the problems of life. You would thrash about and struggle for breath and panic. She wondered had she meant what she said in the message to Dieter . . . that she wished she too had died today?

No, she hadn't really meant it. She didn't want to fight with all her strength against overpowering torrents of water.

But yet in a way, in one way, it would have solved everything. It would have sorted out the terrible situation she was running fast away from but which was following her everywhere. She knew she wouldn't sleep for hours. There was no point in lying down. She pulled out her chair and sat with her elbows on the little wrought-iron balcony, looking at the patterns the moonlight was making on the water.

David's little room was too hot and stuffy. It had been fine up to now but tonight was different. The people in the house were wailing too loudly for anyone to sleep. Their son had died on Manos's boat today.

When David had walked into the house and discovered the family and friends comforting each other he had been stricken. He had shaken hands awkwardly and fumbled for the words to express what could not be said. They spoke little English, and they looked at him wild-eyed as if they had never seen him before. They hardly noticed when he came downstairs again to walk in the night air. Their grief was too great.

David wondered what would have happened if he had died on the boat. It could so easily have been. He had just chosen one day for a tour rather than another. People's lives are changed or destroyed by casual choices like that.

Would there have been wailing like this in his home? Would his father have rocked forward and back in misery? Or would he have said grimly that the boy had chosen his life and he had to live with that choice and die by it.

Suddenly David felt very anxious as he walked around the sorrowing town. He wondered if he might meet some of the people he had spent all that time with. Not Fiona's awful boyfriend Shane, of course, but any of the others.

He thought he would go to a small taverna where people were still sitting talking about the terrible events of the day. He might even meet and speak to Fiona about Ireland, a place he had always wanted to go.

He could have asked her about nursing, and if it really was as rewarding as people said. Did you get a glow of pleasure as patients got better? Did they remember you and write and thank you? Were English people welcome in Ireland as tourists or as workers, had all that hostility died down? Were there any crafts courses in the west of Ireland? David had often thought he would like to be a potter. Do something with his hands, anything far from the world of making money.

Or he could have asked Thomas about his writing: what kind of thing he wrote, why he was going to be so long away from his university, how often he got to see his little boy.

David loved to listen to people's stories. It was why he was so useless in his father's investment broking business.

Clients needed him to tell them what to spend and how. David was much more interested in asking about their houses as homes rather than investments. He unsettled them by wanting to know would they have dogs or an orchard when what they really wanted to talk about was a quick turnover.

As he walked he saw Elsa on her balcony but didn't call out to her. She was so calm and in control, the last thing she needed was a bumbling fool like him in the middle of the night.

Thomas had booked himself for two weeks into a little apartment over a craft shop. It was owned by an eccentric woman called Vonni – in her late forties or so, always dressed in a different floral skirt and a black shirt. She looked like someone you would have to give money to for her next meal, Thomas had thought – but in fact she owned this splendid luxury apartment which she let out to visitors. It was expensively furnished and had some valuable little figurines and pictures.

Vonni was Irish originally, he gathered, though she didn't want to talk about herself. She was a perfect landlady in that she left him alone. She offered to take his clothes to a local laundry and she left an occasional basket of grapes or a bowl of olives on his doorstep.

'Where do you live while I stay here?' he had asked at the start.

'I sleep in an outhouse,' she had replied.

Thomas was unsure if she was joking or was in fact somewhat simple in the head. And he asked her no more – he was happy in Vonni's place.

He would have been happy in somewhere one-tenth of the price, but he needed a phone in case Bill wanted to call him.

Thomas had always resisted the cellphone back in the States. Too many people were slaves to it. He felt it would be intrusive on his travels, and anyway people were always complaining that they couldn't get a signal in remote places. And what did it matter how many euros he spent on an apartment with a telephone? He had nothing else to spend his professor's salary on, and even his poetry was beginning to earn him money.

A prestigious magazine had paid for him to go abroad and write travel articles, in his own style from wherever he wanted. It had been the perfect assignment when he'd realised that he needed to get away. And he had badly needed to get away. He had wanted to write about Aghia Anna, but the world's press would be arriving tomorrow and Aghia Anna would already be notorious.

Once he had thought it would be easy to go on

living in the same town as his ex-wife, seeing his son Bill as often as possible, keeping a civilised and non-combative relationship with Shirley. After all, he didn't love her any more so it was easy to be polite.

People had even admired them for being so non-judgemental, so unlike the other bitter couples who had separated and who revisited the scenes of their resentment over and over.

But now things were different.

Shirley's new boyfriend was Andy, a car salesman she had met at the gym. When Shirley announced that she was getting married to Andy it changed everything.

It meant that things would be easier if Thomas were not around.

She explained that she had found a real and permanent love. She hoped that Thomas would remarry also.

Thomas remembered how he had filled up with bile at the patronising way she spoke. As if she were rearranging the furniture.

Thomas had been surprised to find how much he had resented it. Andy wasn't a *bad* guy, it was just that he'd moved too easily into the house which Thomas had bought for himself, Shirley and Bill.

'Because it's all so much *easier*,' Shirley had explained.

Bill had said that Andy was okay, and that's just what he was: *okay*. But he was a bit of a jock and not into reading, not into holding a book with Bill at night and saying, 'Come on, you choose what to read and we'll read it together.'

And, to be fair, Andy had sensed the awkwardness of it all. He had suggested that Thomas visit Bill between five and seven when he, Andy, was in the gym.

It had been reasonable, sensible, sensitive even, but that had annoyed Thomas even more. As if he were being tidied away to a place that didn't impinge on their lives. Every time he visited he had come to hate the house more: the jars of vitamins and health supplements all over the kitchen and bathrooms, the rowing machines in the garage, the magazines about health and fitness on the coffee tables.

When the chance to get away came Thomas was sure he was right in taking it. He could keep in touch with his boy by phone, by letter, by e-mail. There would be less chance of getting annoyed or resentful.

He had convinced himself it was better for everyone.

And for the first few weeks it had worked well. He didn't wake up angry any more, nor drive himself crazy thinking about his son's new household. The break had been a good thing.

But the events of today had changed everything. All those people dead, a village plunged into mourning. He could hear the sounds of their crying floating up to him over the harbour.

There was no way he could sleep, and his thoughts kept buzzing round like angry insects.

Thomas paced Vonni's apartment all night. Sometimes he looked down at the hen-house at the end of the tangled, vine-filled garden. Once or twice he thought he saw her tousled head at the old window – but then again, it might have been an elderly hen.

Fiona too was awake in their room in a cramped little house outside town.

It belonged to a thin anxious woman called Eleni, who had three little boys. There didn't seem to be any sign of a husband. She didn't normally take guests. Fiona and Shane had found the place by knocking at various doors and offering a small handful of euros in return for overnight accommodation. Shane had been adamant. They had no serious money to throw away on luxuries like a bed for the night. They must get the cheapest on offer.

Eleni's simple house proved to be the cheapest around.

Now Shane lay sprawled in the chair asleep, the only one of them who had managed to get a night's rest. Fiona couldn't sleep because Shane had said out of the blue that they should move on next day.

She had been startled.

They had both thought Aghia Anna the kind of

place where they might stay a while. But now Shane had changed his mind.

'No, we can't stay. It's going to be a creepy place after all this,' Shane had said. 'Let's get out, we'll get a boat to Athens tomorrow.'

'But Athens is a big city . . . it will be so hot,' she had protested.

But Shane said that he had a fellow to see, someone there he just had to meet.

Nothing at all had been mentioned about this fellow they were to meet when Fiona and Shane had set off a month ago. But Fiona knew from experience that it was not wise to upset Shane over something so trivial.

And in a way it was trivial whether they were here or in Athens after all.

It was just that she had wanted to go to the funeral for Manos, the handsome, sexy Greek who had pinched her bottom and said she was *orea*, which meant wonderful, *beautiful*.

He was a silly guy, but good-tempered and cheerful, he thought all ladies were *orea*, he drank wine from the bottle and he danced Zorba-like dances for them, revelling in the pictures that were taken of him for albums all over the world.

But there had been no harm in him, he didn't deserve to die with his little nephew and his work-mates and all those tourists who had been having such a great time.

And Fiona would have liked to see the people from today again. The old man, Andreas, had been so gentle, so generous. Thomas, the college professor, was a wise, good person, and she might even have encouraged David a little to be more outgoing.

And as for Elsa . . .

Fiona had never admired anyone so much, for knowing exactly what to say and when to say it. No wedding ring, and yet she must be about twenty-eight. Fiona wondered who she had telephoned in Germany.

Shane was still asleep in the chair.

Fiona wished that he had not brought out the pot in front of Andreas and the others today, and that he had been a bit nicer to them all. He could be so prickly and difficult at times. But then he had lived a confused life with no love in it.

Not until he had met Fiona, that was. And she alone knew how to reach the real Shane.

The room was very hot and poky.

She wished they could have stayed somewhere a little better. Then Shane might not want them to move on so quickly tomorrow.

During the night, as the stars shone down on the bay, Andreas wrote a letter. He wrote several versions and decided that the last one was the best. By morning he was ready to post the first and only letter he had written in nine years to his son in Chicago.

When the sun came up he got on his putt-putt bike and made the journey to the town.

When the sun came up on Aghia Anna, the phone rang in the tasteful apartment over the craft shop.

It was Thomas's son Bill calling him.

'Dad, you okay?'

'I'm great, son, just fine. Thank you for calling. Your momma gave you my number?'

'It's on the board, Dad. It's just Mom says it's always the middle of the night out there. Andy said I should try anyhow.'

'Say thanks to Andy.'

'I will, Dad. He got out a map of the world to show me roughly where you are, when we saw the fire on television. It must have been scary.'

'Well, it was sad,' he said.

'It's a long way away, where you are, Dad.'

Thomas yearned to be beside his boy. It was a real ache. But he had to remain cheerful otherwise what was the point of all this?

'Nowhere's a long way away these days, Bill, the phone is always there. Listen to you! You could be in the next room.'

'Yeah, I know and you always liked to travel,' the boy agreed.

'I do, and so will you one day.'

'Sure. And I called Gran to tell her you were okay and she said you are to take care.'

'I will, Bill, believe me, I'll take care.'

'I've got to go now. Bye, Dad.'

He was gone but the sun had come up and the day was beautiful. His son had called. Thomas felt alive and for the first time in a long time he felt how good everything was.

When the sun came up on Aghia Anna, Fiona went to the bathroom and suddenly realised that her period was six days late.

When the sun came up on Aghia Anna, Elsa walked down towards the harbour. She passed by the church, which had become a temporary morgue; then, as she rounded the corner, she saw with horror that among the crowds of people arriving from Athens was a German television crew from her own network setting up shots of the still-smouldering wreck which had been towed into the harbour.

She knew the cameraman and the sound man. And they would have known her had they seen her. And then Dieter would know where she was and would be here in a matter of hours.

She backed carefully into a little café and looked around wildly.

Inside were old men playing a form of backgammon – no help there. Then at a table she saw David, worried David from yesterday, the kind English boy who had said there was no pleasing his father.

'David,' she hissed.

He was overjoyed to see her.

'David, can you go and get a taxi and bring it here for me? I can't go outside. There are people out there I just don't want to see, can you do that for me, *please* . . .'

He seemed alarmed that she was so different from yesterday, so out of control by comparison. But, mercifully, he seemed to understand.

'Where will I tell it you're going?' he asked.

'Where were *you* going today?' she asked, wildly.

'There's a place about fifty kilometres away, a little temple and an artists' colony. It's called Tri . . . Tri . . . something. It's on a little gulf. I was going to get a bus there.'

'We'll take the taxi there,' she said firmly.

'No, Elsa, we'll go out and get on a bus, a taxi would cost a fortune, believe me,' David argued.

'And I *have* a fortune, believe me,' she said, handing him a wad of notes. 'Please, David, just be full of guts and act now, this minute, and take a chance this once . . .' She looked at him and saw his face fall. Why had she spoken so cruelly and harshly, as good as telling him she thought him a weakling?

'I mean that it's a crazy thing for someone you hardly know to ask, but I need your help, I'm

45

begging you. I'll tell you all about it when we get to this place. I haven't committed a crime or anything, but I am in trouble and if you don't help me now then honestly I don't know what I'll do.' She spoke from the heart, not acting, but with the same intensity she summoned up so well for the camera.

'There's a line of taxis in the square. I'll be back in five minutes,' said David.

And Elsa sat down in the dark café, unconcerned that every eye in the room was directed towards the tall blonde goddess who had marched into such an unlikely place, offered a nervous young man with spectacles what looked like a year's wages, and was now sitting, waiting, with her head in her hands.

CHAPTER FOUR

Fiona had quite a long time to wait until Shane woke up. He lay there in the chair with his mouth open, his hair damp and stuck to his forehead.

He looked so vulnerable when he was asleep. She longed to stroke his face but she didn't want to wake him until he was ready.

The room was hot and stuffy, the people of the house had left their clothes in it and it smelled like a second-hand shop.

Downstairs she could hear the tired Eleni, whose eyes were red with weeping over the tragedy, calling to her three little sons. Neighbours kept calling in, obviously telling the story over and over to each other, all of them shocked by the tragedy.

She wouldn't disturb these people by going down, not until Shane woke, until he was ready to go.

When he did wake he was not in good humour.

'Why did you let me sleep in the chair?' he asked, rubbing his neck. 'I'm as stiff as a bloody board.'

'Let's go and have a swim – that will make you feel better,' she tried to encourage him.

'Easy for you – you've been sleeping in the bed all night,' he grumbled.

This was not the time to tell him that she had been awake most of the night, thinking about poor Manos, whose body lay in the local church beside that of his little nephew and so many others who had died on his boat. And it was certainly not the time to tell him that she could very possibly be pregnant. That must certainly wait until he was awake, alert and not complaining of pains in his shoulders.

Anyway they were going to Athens today, so he had said. He had a man to meet, something to do.

'Will we pack before breakfast?' she asked.

'Pack?' he said, puzzled.

Perhaps he had forgotten the whole idea.

'Don't mind me, I don't know where I am half the time,' Fiona said with a laugh.

'You can say that again ... Here, I'm going to bed for a bit and you could go and get us a couple of coffees. Okay?'

'It's a long way to the café – it would be cold by the time I got back.'

'Oh, Fiona, ask them for it downstairs. It's only coffee, after all, and you know all those *please* and *thank you* words that they like.'

Words that most people like, Fiona thought to herself, but didn't say so.

'Sleep for a couple of hours, then,' she said to him, but he didn't hear her as he was asleep already.

She walked along the beach back towards the town, her bare feet kicking the warm sand at the edge of the water, and letting the Mediterranean tickle her toes. She could not believe that this was happening. Fiona Ryan, the most sensible of her whole family, the most reliable nurse on the whole ward, had thrown up her job to go off with Shane, the man they had all warned her against.

And she might now very possibly be pregnant.

It wasn't just her mother who had rejected Shane as the other half of her life, it was all her friends, including Barbara, her best pal since they had been six years of age. And her sisters, and her fellow nurses.

But what did they know?

And anyway love was never meant to be uncomplicated, think of any of the great love stories and you realised that. Love had nothing to do with meeting a nice *suitable* person, someone who lived nearby, who had a good job, who wanted a long engagement and to save a deposit on a house.

That wasn't love, that was compromise.

She thought about the possible pregnancy and her heart lurched. There had been a couple of times, fairly recently, when they had not been careful. But there had been times like that in the past too and nothing had happened.

She felt her flat stomach. Was it possible that a speck which could become a child was growing there, someone who would be half Shane and half her? It was too exciting to imagine.

In front of her on the beach she saw the strange baggy shorts and over-long T-shirt of Thomas, the nice American man that they had spent the day with yesterday.

He recognised her and called out, 'You look happy!'

'I am.' She didn't tell him all the reasons, and the way her mind was filling up with wild wonderful plans, for living here in Aghia Anna, bringing up a child with these people, Shane working on the fishing boats or in the restaurants, she helping the local doctor, maybe even as midwife. These were all dreams for the future, dreams that would be discussed later when Shane had his coffee, she would tell him then.

'My son called me from the States. We had a great conversation.' Thomas couldn't help sharing his own good news.

'I'm so very glad.'

This man seemed to care about only one thing: the little boy called Bill whose picture he had shown them during their long time together. A little boy like any other with blond hair and a toothy grin but the most special child in the world to Thomas, as to any parent.

She dragged herself back from that train of thought. 'You know I *thought* he might call you back last night – I felt it when you were telling us about him.'

'Let me buy you a coffee to celebrate,' he said, and they walked together along to a small taverna near the beach. They talked easily as they had yesterday, about the tragedy, about how hard it was to sleep, and to believe that all those people had begun yesterday with coffee in a taverna like this and now were lying dead in the church.

Fiona explained that she had walked into town to buy bread and honey for their breakfast, and she would give some to the people in the house where they were renting a room so that in return she could make a cup of coffee for Shane when he eventually woke up.

'We were meant to be going to Athens today, but I think he's too tired,' she said. 'In some ways I'm actually rather glad he's too tired. I like this place. I want to stay on.'

'So do I. I'm going to walk up in those hills, and I want to stay for the funeral for some reason.'

She looked at him with interest. 'So do I, and it's not just ghoulish wanting to see it all first hand, I wanted to be part of it.'

'Wanted? Does that mean you'll not stay?'

'Well, we don't know what day it will be and, as I said, Shane says that he wants to go to Athens.'

'But surely if *you* want to . . .' His voice trailed away.

Fiona saw the look on his face. The same look that eventually came over everyone's face when they met Shane. She stood up.

'Thanks for the coffee. I'll go now.'

He seemed disappointed, as if he had wanted her to stay. She too would like to have stayed talking to this nice, easy man, but she couldn't risk Shane waking up and not finding her there.

'Thomas, do you think I could give you some money for flowers in case . . . well, in case people do have flowers for them all.'

He put up his hand. He knew she didn't have much money. 'Please – I'd love to get the flowers and I'll put "Rest in peace" from Irish Fiona.'

'Thank you, Thomas, and if you see the others, David and Elsa . . .'

'I'll say that you and Shane had to go to Athens and you said goodbye,' he said very gently.

'They were very nice, you were all great people to be with . . . I wonder where they are now?'

'I saw them both heading out of town in a taxi together this morning,' Thomas said. 'But it's a tiny place. I'll see them again.'

He watched her go and buy the great warm bread and the little pot of local honey to take back to that selfish young man and he sighed. A professor, a poet, a writer – and he didn't understand the smallest thing about life and love.

Like why Shirley found him cold and distant and found the empty-headed Andy a delightful companion. Thomas remembered their conversations as the sun had set yesterday; he hadn't understood the lives that were being described there, either. Like why David's father, who should be so proud and happy to have such a son, kept the boy at arm's length and managed only to say the wrong thing, the hurtful thing.

Thomas had no idea what could have happened to that gorgeous German girl Elsa that had her running away from her homeland with haunted eyes.

He would never begin to understand such things, he told himself with resignation. Better not to attempt it.

He looked up and saw Vonni crossing the street.

'*Yassu*, Thomas,' she said.

'*Yassu* – isn't it such a tragedy? I expect you knew him, Manos?'

'Yes, I knew him as a toddler, a schoolboy, he was wild then, wild always. He would steal things from my garden so I gave him a job working in it. That sorted him out.' She seemed pleased with the memory.

Thomas felt an urge to talk to her, ask her why

she had come to this island – but there was something about Vonni that discouraged any intimacy. She was always too quick with a jokey remark that headed you off.

'Anyway he has to deal with God tonight and, knowing Manos, he'll get by on charm.' She shrugged and moved away.

Thomas knew that was the end of the conversation. He watched Vonni continue down the street towards her craft shop. There would be little business today. He wondered if she would even open her little shop.

He saw her shake hands with passers-by, easy and at home in this place.

Elsa bent down in the taxi and hid her head under a scarf until they had left the town. Only then did she straighten up. Her face looked strained and anxious.

'Why don't I tell you what I know about this place we are going to?' David offered.

'Thank you. That would be perfect.' She lay back and closed her eyes while his words rolled over her. Apparently it was the site of a minor temple that had had some excavation work but the money had dried up so it had been left in a semi-exposed state. Nobody knew all that much about the temple, the excavations had yielded little in the early stages. But there were those who said it was well worth a tour.

And an artists' colony had started there years ago,

which was still going strong. Even today, silver-smiths and potters came there from all over the world. It wasn't at all over-commercialised, and the artists brought their wares to town to sell.

David looked at her from time to time as he spoke.

Her face was relaxing. Obviously, she didn't want to tell him what she was frightened of so he wouldn't ask. Better to go on burbling away about this place they were visiting.

'Am I boring you?' he asked her suddenly.

'No, why on earth do you think that? You are restful and soothing,' Elsa said with a wan smile.

David was pleased. 'I often bore people,' he said frankly. He wasn't self-pitying or asking to be contradicted. He was stating a matter of fact.

'I doubt it,' Elsa said, quickly. 'I think you are a very peaceable person to be with. Is that the right word or should it be "peaceful"?'

'I like peaceable,' David said.

She patted his hand and they sat back companion-ably in the taxi, looking up to one side of them where goats clambered on the rugged hillside, and down at the sparkling blue sea on the other. The sea that looked so friendly and inviting now but had taken the lives of so many yesterday.

'When will the funeral be?' Elsa suddenly asked the taxi driver.

He understood the question but didn't know the words to reply.

'*Avrio?*' he said.

'*Avrio?*' she repeated.

'Tomorrow,' David said. 'I just learned fifty words,' he added apologetically.

'That's forty-five more than I learned,' Elsa said, with a trace of the old smile coming back to her face. '*Efharisto*, David my friend, *efharisto poli*.'

They drove on along the dusty road. Friends indeed.

Shane felt a lot better after the coffee, bread and honey. He said that they would have one last day in this crazy place and leave for Athens on the following day. Boats to Athens left the harbour every couple of hours, it was no big deal.

He wondered where they would find a place with some action.

'I don't think there'll be much action today or tonight – the whole town is full of press and investigators and officials. You know the funeral is tomorrow, the people downstairs told me.' Fiona longed to ask if they could leave after the funeral. But she had so much to tell him during the day she could let that question wait a while. 'There's a lovely little place I saw out on a point – they catch fish and grill them straight from the sea, will we go there, do you think?'

He shrugged. Why not? The wine was probably cheaper there than in the fancy places by the harbour anyway. 'Come on, let's go there then, Fiona, and don't spend hours and hours struggling to say "Me going – you staying" to all these people downstairs.'

She laughed at herself good-naturedly. 'I don't think I'm quite as bad as that, I just try to say thank you to Eleni for being so nice to us and that I'm sorry about what happened to their friends.'

'It's not *your* fault. For *Christ's* sake.' Shane was in one of those moods where he would fight about anything.

'No, of course it isn't, but it doesn't hurt to be polite.'

'They're being well paid for our staying here,' he grumbled.

Fiona knew they were paying practically nothing – if the family had not been so poor they wouldn't have moved out of their bedroom. But this was not the time to argue the point with Shane.

'You're right, we should go now before it gets too hot,' she said, and they walked down the shabby stairs and through the crowded kitchen past the family who sat bewildered by the scope of the tragedy. She longed to stop and sit there with them, to murmur consoling phrases to them, little Greek sentences she had heard everywhere: *Tipota, Dhen pirazi.*

But she knew that Shane was anxious for his first cold beer of the day. She had so much to tell him today, this was no time for delay. It would soon be noon and it was very hot. They should go to the taverna on the sea straight away.

The day was indeed becoming very hot.

Thomas decided against going up into the hills, he should have left much earlier in the morning for that kind of trip. He looked into the craft shop. He had been right. Vonni had not opened for business. She had put a notice in the window in Greek. Black-edged and short, he had seen similar ones in other places. He had been told that it said: 'Closed out of respect'.

Vonni was asleep in her chair. She looked tired and old. Suppose she really slept in the hen-house? When there was an empty bedroom in the apartment? She could easily sleep in there – but he knew better than to ask her.

The shops were closed but there was plenty to see. And if the truth be told he didn't want to move far from the little town that was shrouded in grief. He would walk along the coast to a simple place on a point which he had seen last week. There had been a wonderful smell of grilling fish when he had passed it a few days back, and it would be just the spot to sit and look out to sea and think. He was glad that he had remembered it.

There had been some raggedy umbrellas there that would protect him from the sun, and a cool breeze coming in from the sea. Just the place to go.

Elsa and David's taxi arrived in the old square that was the centre of Kalatriada.

The driver wondered where to leave them.

'Here is just fine,' Elsa had said, paying him handsomely. David had wanted to share the cost but she insisted it was her treat. They stood and looked around the village where they had arrived up twisty, perilous roads. It was not a popular tourist spot. A place that most certainly had not been discovered by developers.

The sea was far below, down another narrow track. Half the buildings around the square seemed to be tiny restaurants or cafés, and there was a selection of pottery shops.

'I'm sure you want to go and find your temple,' she said to him. 'This is a good safe place you brought me, I can hide here.'

'I'm in no great rush to see the temple,' David said. 'I can sit with you for a while.'

'Well, after all those turns and corners, I must say I would love a coffee,' Elsa smiled. 'But truly this is a fine place to come to, I can breathe properly here. You really are my hero, you know.'

'Oh, hero, you say!' David laughed at the idea. 'Not my usual role, I'm afraid.'

'Now don't try to tell me that you're normally cast as a villain.' Elsa was cheerful again.

'No, nothing as dashing. The buffoon more often,' he admitted.

'I don't believe it for a moment,' Elsa said.

'That's because you don't know me, you haven't seen me in my real life where I just mess everyone up.'

'That's not so. You told us that you don't see eye to eye with your father. That's not a hanging offence, half the men in the world feel the same way.'

'I've let him down in everything, every single thing, Elsa. Honestly, if he had been given any other kind of son it would have worked. A ready-made business, a position of honour in the community. A lovely home – but it all choked me and made me feel trapped. No wonder he despises me.'

'Shall we sit here, do you think?' Elsa indicated the nearest place and sat down on a broken-looking chair in a very basic café.

The waiter came and spread a piece of waxed paper on another chair.

'Better chair for the lady,' he said.

'They're all so nice here,' she marvelled.

'Everyone's nice to you everywhere, Elsa, you are so full of sunshine.'

David ordered two *metrio*s, the medium-sweet coffees. They sipped them companionably.

'I didn't *know* my father, David, he left us early but I had many, many arguments with my mother.'

'You see, that's probably more healthy. In my case there aren't any real arguments at all, it's all sighs and shrugs,' David said.

'Believe me, I said far too many things to my mother, far, far too much criticism, if I had my time over I would have said less. But that's women and their mothers, they always say!'

'What kind of things did you argue about?'

'I don't know, David. Everything. I used to say that my way was right and hers was wrong. Her clothes were awful, her friends, you know, the usual destructive things.'

'I don't know, you see. Because we don't talk at all.'

'If you had it all over again what would you do?' Elsa asked.

'The same, mess it up I imagine.'

'That's so defeatist. You're young. Much younger than me, your parents are alive, for you there is time.'

'Don't make me feel worse, Elsa, please.'

'Of course not, I just think it's fair to tell you we share something but I don't have a chance to put it right. My mother's dead.'

'How did she die?'

'In a car crash with one of her unsuitable friends.'

David leaned over and patted Elsa's hand. 'It was quick and I am sure it was painless for her,' he said.

'You are such a kind boy, David,' she said in a shaky voice. 'Finish your coffee and we'll go and investigate Kalatriada. And then at lunch I'll tell you my problems and you can give *me* advice.'

'You don't have to, you know,' he said.

'Peaceable David,' she said with a smile.

'Where's this place you said was so good?' Shane grumbled. His attention was drawn by a noisy bar they passed. 'Maybe this place would be fine,' he suggested.

It wasn't at all the kind of place where she could have told him the news so Fiona refused to consider it. 'Much too expensive – tourist prices,' she said. And that settled it. They moved towards the fish restaurant on the point.

Andreas sat with his brother in the police station. Yorghis's desk was piled high with reports about the accident. His phone had been ringing constantly. Now there was a lull.

'I wrote to Adoni today,' Andreas said slowly.

'Good, good,' Yorghis said after a little time.

'I didn't say sorry or anything.'

'No, of course not,' Yorghis agreed.

'Because I'm *not* sorry. You know that.'

'I know, I know.' Yorghis did not need to enquire

why his brother had written to the long-estranged son in Chicago. He knew why.

It was because the death of Manos and all the people on the boat had shown them how very short life was. That was all.

Thomas passed the television crews and photographers in the square beside the harbour. It was a job like any other, he supposed, but they did seem somehow like a swarm of insects. They didn't gather where people were having a good time and getting on with life, only where there had been a disaster. He thought about Elsa, that golden handsome German girl. She had been fairly dismissive of her own role in it all. He wondered where she had been going today in the taxi. Perhaps she even knew these German television crews who were gathered around the harbour. Greece was a popular destination for Germans, there were even two German visitors said to have lost their lives on Manos's boat. But even though he looked, she was nowhere to be seen. She must not have come back from her taxi ride. He walked on to the restaurant on the point.

David and Elsa walked around the ruins of the temple. They were the only visitors.

An elderly guide asked them for half a euro and gave them a cloakroom ticket in return, also an ill-written and near incomprehensible account of what the temple had once been.

'There could be a fortune made from writing a proper leaflet in German,' Elsa said.

'Or even in English,' David laughed. They wandered back to the square.

'Let's see about this great lunch I'm going to take you to,' she said.

'I'm easy, Elsa . . . look, the waiter where we were before is waving at us, I'm happy to go back there if you are.'

'Of course I am – I'd prefer to, as it happens. But then I wanted something more grand because I have to ask another favour of you.'

'You don't have to pay me with an expensive lunch, and I don't think Kalatriada has a posh restaurant anyway.'

Their waiter ran out, delighted to see them. 'I knew you come back, lady,' he said, beaming all over his face. He brought a dish of olives and little bits of cheese, he indicated the kitchens where they could see dishes kept warm in the big heated cabinets. Proudly he opened up each dish so that they could choose what they would eat.

They sat companionably and talked as if they were old friends.

They wondered what it would be like to have grown up in a small hill village like this instead of in big cities as they had.

They marvelled at the tall blond Scandinavians who had come from the northern cold to work here as jewellers and potters. It was only when they were sipping the dark sweet coffee that Elsa said, 'I'll tell you what this is about.'

'You don't have to, we're having a lovely day.'

'No, I have to tell you, because, you see, I want us not to go back to Aghia Anna tonight. I want us to stay here, stay until tomorrow when the funeral is over.'

David's mouth opened. *'Stay here?'*

'I can't go back to the town, David, my television crew is there, people will recognise me, they'll tell Dieter, our boss back home, and he'll come and find me. I couldn't bear that.'

'Why?'

'Because I love him so much.'

'So that's bad – if the man you love comes to find you?'

'If it were only as simple as that,' she said, and she took his two hands and held them to her face. He felt the tears splash down over his fingers and on to the table.

'I understand that of course we have to stay here in Kalatriada tonight,' said David, who felt that he was indeed becoming more like a hero every hour of this day.

It was early. Fiona and Shane were the only people in

the restaurant. The waiter left them alone with the fish and the wine by the dark blue sea and white sand. Shane had drunk two beers and a glass of retsina very quickly. Fiona watched him, waiting for the right time to tell him her news. Finally, when she could wait no longer, she put her hand on his arm and told him that she was six days overdue. She said that since she had been twelve years old she had never been one day late. And with whatever medical knowledge she had as a nurse she felt sure that this was not a false alarm and that it really did mean they were pregnant. And she looked hopefully into his face.

She saw disbelief written all over it.

He drank another glass of wine before he spoke. 'I can't take this in,' he said. 'We took precautions.'

'Well, we didn't ... all of the time. If you remember . . .' She was about to remind him about one particular weekend.

'How could you be so stupid?' he asked.

'Well, it wasn't only me.' She was hurt.

'God, Fiona, you really have a way of spoiling everything and wrecking everyone's life,' he said.

'But we *did* want children, we said, you said . . .' Fiona began to cry.

'One day, I said, not now, you're such a fool, not now that we're only a month out on the trip.'

'I thought ... I thought ...' She struggled to speak through her tears.

'What did you think?'

'I thought we might stay here, you know, in this place and we could bring up the baby here.'

'It's not a baby, it's a six-day-overdue period.'

'But it could be a baby, *our* baby, and you could get a job in a restaurant maybe, and I could work too . . .'

He stood up and leaned across the table to shout at her. She could hardly hear the things he was saying, so hurtful and cruel were they all. She was a whore, like all women. Scheming and plotting to get him tied down with a brood of children and make him work as a *waiter*. A waiter in a god-forsaken place like this.

She must get rid of the baby and never think of coming up with this kind of fairy story again. Never. She was a stupid, brainless fool.

She must have argued with him, none of it was clear, but then she felt the stinging blow on her face with such a shock that she had begun to reel back as he was coming at her again with his fist clenched.

The ground was coming up at her, she felt sick, she was shaking all over. Then she heard the running and shouting behind her and two waiters held Shane back and Thomas, who had arrived from nowhere, was pulling her away, guiding her to a chair.

She closed her eyes as he dabbed her face with cold water.

'You're all right, Fiona,' he said as he stroked her hair. 'Believe me, you're all right now.'

CHAPTER FIVE

The restaurant gave Thomas the number of the police station. Fiona heard Shane laugh when he heard that the call was going to be made.

'Waste of time, Thomas, she's not going to press charges, and even if she does, it's only a domestic. That's what they'll say. Even worse, a *foreign* domestic, no chance of anything holding up.' He reached for another glass of wine.

The two waiters looked at Thomas as if for advice. Should they let Shane drink or should they restrain him?

But Thomas just nodded slightly. The drunker Shane got, the worse the impression he would make when Yorghis, the brother of Andreas, turned up to deal with things.

He went into a back room to make the call privately and introduced himself to the policeman on the phone, who immediately knew who he was.

'You were one of the generous people who gave such a donation to the family of Manos.'

'It was really your brother who did that, he didn't charge us for the meal.'

'He said you were friends.' It seemed clear to Andreas's brother.

'And we are proud to be his friends, but, sir, we have a problem ...' Thomas explained it all to Yorghis who understood the situation instantly. There was remarkably little red tape. Then Thomas quietly asked the waiters to take Shane into a back room and lock him in. Shane didn't even put up a struggle.

'It's a waste of time, a waste of police time, believe me, you'll be sorry when they've been and gone. Know-it-all Thomas bleating on yesterday about not being able to communicate with your son. You couldn't communicate with a cat, Thomas, you don't have the style.'

'And you do, of course, and with the fists,' Thomas said.

'Very droll, very droll indeed.'

'They don't take kindly to hitting women here, you'll discover that shortly.'

'I'll walk out of here with that girl on my arm, it's happened before, it will happen again.' He looked cocky and confident.

Thomas felt the bile of anger rise in his throat and

he realised that his hand had turned into a fist without his intending to do it.

Shane saw and laughed. 'Don't tell me you're going to behave like a man at last,' the boy sneered at him.

But the anger had left Thomas almost as soon as it arrived. He was calm again. 'Leave him some wine, I'll pay,' he said to the waiters, and went to sit down beside Fiona, whose tear-stained face showed someone still in shock.

'It will be fine,' he said, stroking her hand.

'It will never be fine,' she said with a terrible finality.

'We survive, you know, that's why we're all here roaming the earth instead of being extinct.'

And then he didn't say any more while they waited for the police van to arrive. They sat there listening to the waves crashing against the rocks under the restaurant. Her face looked sad and empty, but Thomas knew that he was some kind of strength and company for her just by being there.

When Yorghis arrived he told Shane that an assault had been seen by three independent witnesses, that he would be locked up in the police station for twenty-four hours.

'But she didn't mind.' Shane's voice was slurred now and nervous. 'Ask her. I love her, we're together, we might even be going to have a baby – right, Fiona? Tell them.'

She still had her eyes closed.

'That's not important,' Yorghis explained. 'The complaint has not been made by this lady, what she says is irrelevant.' Then he handcuffed Shane and helped him into the police van.

The van had driven off in the sun when people started to arrive for their lunch. The waiters were relieved. They were young and inexperienced, it had all been disturbing, a fracas, the arrival of the police van, an arrest, but order had been restored and trade had not been interrupted. It had been a busy morning so far.

Fiona had said nothing during the whole time but now she started to cry. 'I wish I had a friend, Thomas,' she said.

'I'm your friend.'

'Yes, I know, but I meant a woman friend like Barbara back home, she'd tell me what to do, she'd advise me.'

'Do you want to call her? I have a telephone in my apartment,' he suggested.

'It's not the same now. Too much water under the bridge, too many times when she offered to help and I didn't listen, she couldn't understand how much has changed. How much has happened.'

'I know, you'd have to start too far back.' He was sympathetic.

'I *could* talk to Elsa, but we don't know where she

71

is, and anyway, she might not want to listen to all my complaints,' Fiona said sadly, wiping her eyes with a napkin.

'We could find out where she is, I saw her getting into a taxi this morning with David. I don't know where they were going. But why don't we have something to eat to build you up a little?'

'You sound like my mother.' She gave a weak little smile.

'I'm good at mothering skills,' he said. 'When you are strong enough to walk we'll go and ask the taxi drivers. They won't have forgotten someone like Elsa.'

'It's a bit feeble of me really.'

'She's very warm and sympathetic . . . she's just the person to talk to,' he reassured her.

'Do you think so?'

'Yes, I do. Oh, Fiona, another thing?'

'What?'

'Is it true what he said that you might be pregnant?'

'He said that? I didn't realise.' There was a pathetic hope in her face again.

'He only said it hoping to get out of trouble.'

'I thought he might have been pleased.'

'No. I don't want to be cruel but he didn't sound pleased. Might it be true?'

'It might.' She sounded glum.

'We'll have an omelette and then we'll go interrogate the taxi drivers. If they can't remember Elsa then they're certainly not worthy to be called men.'

He was right. They all remembered the German blonde and the small man with glasses. The man who had taken them to Kalatriada said it was a wonderful fare.

'Let's go there,' Thomas said, and offered the startled taxi driver his second great fare of the day.

It was certainly a twisty road up through the hills. Once they got to the small town of Kalatriada it was easy to find Elsa and David. The place was not very much more than a big square ringed with cafés and craft shops. Elsa's blonde hair was hard to miss as she bent over some pottery plates in a little shop. There was hardly any need for explanations. It was obviously not a coincidence. And Elsa panicked.

'Anyone looking for me?' she asked urgently. Her eyes looked wild and frightened.

Thomas went straight to the point. 'In a way, Elsa. We were hoping that you and Fiona could have a talk. She's been a bit upset, you see.'

'I can see that,' David said, looking at the livid red mark on Fiona's cheek.

'Next one would have broken her nose,' Thomas said grimly.

'Well, certainly we'll have a talk.' Elsa had her

hand on Fiona's arm. 'Sorry for immediately thinking it was about me but I have a few problems, which is why David and I are staying here tonight.'

'Staying?'

'Staying here?' Fiona and Thomas spoke together, amazed.

'Sure, it's a nice place, isn't it, and there's a lovely little hotel over there on the other side of the square. We have two rooms. Fiona can share with me and you men can share a room. Is that suitable, do you think?' Elsa's confident smile was back, and it seemed the most natural thing for four people who had never met until yesterday to be having a mini holiday that none of them had expected in a tiny village called Kalatriada. A place that only David had ever heard of. They all agreed that it was very suitable indeed.

This time yesterday they had barely met. Today they were involved in each other's lives.

They talked easily about everything. It was as if they were old friends who had grown up in the same neighbourhood instead of four strangers from four different lands.

It would not be like last night when they were all so emotional about the accident and the effect of their phone calls home. Last night when they had begun to talk intimately as soon as the stars came into the night sky. Tonight was different. A storm was coming.

The family who ran the little hotel seemed to show no surprise at the ill-assorted group of people with no luggage who had turned up so unexpectedly. They all seemed pleasant easy-going people, a little strained, but then they had been in Aghia Anna where that terrible tragedy had happened. Maybe they knew people on the boat that had been lost.

Irini was the woman who ran the hotel. She looked tired and bent as she got them towels and a little cake of soap. Her smiles warm but weary, she appeared to do all the cleaning and cooking while three men sat playing a board game in the corner; not one of them helped her.

'A lot of work to be done by the women's movement here in this house, I think,' Elsa whispered to Fiona as they went upstairs to claim their room.

'You could probably start with me, Elsa,' Fiona said humbly. 'You don't need to look much further than at me to see a victim.'

Elsa's face was full of sympathy. 'Sleep for a little,' she urged. 'Everything is better after a couple of hours' sleep.'

'I want to tell you about him, and why he does what he does,' Fiona began.

'No, you don't. You want to hear me say you're perfectly right to go back to him, and that he didn't mean it.'

Fiona's eyes opened wide.

'Maybe I *will* say that but not now, Fiona, you are too tired and upset to hear anything at all. Rest now. We'll talk later, there's all the time in the world.'

'And you?'

'I'll sit here and look at the mountains,' Elsa said.

To her amazement Fiona felt her eyelids become heavy and soon she was breathing deeply.

Elsa sat in the little cane chair and watched the shadows come down over the valley.

There was rain tonight, covering the blanket of stars.

'Do you play chess, Thomas?' David asked.

'Badly,' Thomas admitted.

'Me too, but I have a little chess set, would you care for a game ... no expectations of high standards.' The boy looked drained but he didn't look as if he wanted to confide or talk. Chess could be a substitute.

They set up a little table by the window, and as the night shadows fell and the downpour began they played chess together happily.

Irini knocked on both bedroom doors.

They could not eat out of doors, too much rain, but they could sit inside and see the square in Kalatriada, she said. She made no comment on the great bruise starting to emerge on Fiona's face.

They all came down to the table with its blue and yellow check cover. And with the background of old men clicking dice and counters from the backgammon game in the corner, they all began to eat the kebabs and salad that Irini proudly produced for them.

'*Orea*,' David said. '*Poli poli kala!*'

Irini's tired face smiled a big toothless smile. She might only be forty, Elsa thought, less even. It was no life here for her, but she was surrounded by the people she knew and liked, and now four guests were praising the simple food and saying it was beautiful.

Once Elsa had been so sure and confident about everything. She would have *known* what was wrong with Irini's life. Now she was not so sure. Possibly it was better for Irini to live here in this beautiful village between the mountains and the sea, one of those men at the backgammon tables might be her husband, another her father. There were children's clothes flapping on the line. She probably had a family, little children who knew everyone in the village.

There was a case to be made that she might be much better off here than if she had gone, like Andreas's son, looking for brighter lights in Chicago.

Elsa sighed. It had been much easier when things had been certain. Once Elsa would have urged Fiona to look hard at Shane and realise that he would never love her, and was probably incapable of loving anyone. She would have said that although no woman should advise another to have a termination, Fiona should consider all aspects of carrying Shane's child to term. But nowadays Elsa was not at all certain about what was the right thing for anyone to do.

She realised that she had been daydreaming and dragged herself back to the conversation at the table. She had come away to clear her mind, not to sit confused and brooding as she had a few weeks ago in her apartment until she bought her ticket to Athens.

She must pay attention and not allow herself to drift off like this again. Thomas was talking about his landlady.

'She's a real character, Vonni, been here for years apparently, she never talks about herself, but she speaks Greek like a native. She knows this place Kalatriada well, she said, she comes every few weeks or so to buy pottery to sell in her craft shop.'

'She's from Ireland, Andreas told me yesterday,' Fiona said. 'I was thinking about her only today . . . you know if she could stay here, maybe I could.' Her small pale face looked very sad.

'Did she come here with anyone, do you think?' Elsa wanted to inject some reality back into the discussion before Fiona started living in some fantasy world where she and Shane might raise a family here in the purple Greek mountains.

Thomas didn't know. He told them that although Vonni was so open and friendly you didn't ask her questions.

David had been in Vonni's craft shop and talked to her, she had chosen a good range of items, he thought ... she had to walk that difficult line between stocking touristy things for visitors and good taste.

'I really like the fact that she doesn't seem obsessed by money and I wouldn't say she has much,' David said.

'No, I think she's fairly pushed for a living,' Thomas agreed. 'She teaches English, and she sleeps in a sort of shed out back so that she can let me rent her place.'

'How old is she?' Elsa asked.

'Fifty to sixty,' David said.

'Forty to fifty,' Thomas said at the same time. They all laughed.

'Well, so much for dressing ourselves up to please men,' Elsa said with a wry smile.

'No, Vonni doesn't dress up, she wears a T-shirt and a coloured skirt, and open sandals. I don't expect she ever wore makeup.' Thomas was thoughtful. 'It's oddly restful, somehow.' He seemed miles away, as if thinking of some other woman who did dress up and applied a lot of makeup regularly.

'Do you fancy her then, this restful woman of uncertain age?' Elsa teased him.

'No, not remotely, but she does interest me. I called her before dinner tonight in case she saw no lights in her place and wondered whether I'd disappeared on her.'

'That was thoughtful of you,' Fiona said in wonder. It wasn't the kind of thing Shane would have thought of.

'She told us not to dream of getting a taxi again, that we should take the bus from the square, one leaves every two hours. I told her that I thought we would all probably go back tomorrow for the funeral, I checked that we wouldn't be in the way. She told me that it would be appreciated. Is that okay with everyone?'

'It's fine with me,' David said.

'Yes, and I can go to the police station and talk to Shane,' Fiona said eagerly. 'He will be so sorry and upset by now, now that he's had time to think it all through.'

The others didn't catch her eye. Elsa was the only one who hadn't spoken.

'Elsa?' Thomas spoke gently.

'I might just stay on here for a couple of days, you know, I could join you all later.' It seemed to need an explanation. She hesitated and then decided to speak. 'It's a little bit awkward, you see, I'm trying to avoid someone, and I would prefer to hide out a little until he has gone away.' She looked at three blank faces. 'I know it sounds stupid but it's just the way things are. I ran away from Germany, from my friends, from a good job that I loved . . . just to get away from him. It would be stupid to meet up with him again in a tiny place like Aghia Anna.'

'And you are certain he's there?' Thomas asked gently.

'Yes, this is just his sort of story. No one does human interest better than he does. That's why I ran away here with David.' She looked at David gratefully.

'We could all keep him away from you.' David was busy living up to his heroic role in all this.

'We could tell Yorghis, you know, Andreas's brother . . . he would warn him off if he tried to stalk you or harass you.' Thomas was reassuring.

Elsa looked from one to the other. 'No, it's not that, I'm not afraid of him, I'm afraid of myself, that I might go back to him and then all this – all the business of coming here – would have been such a waste of time.' Her lip was trembling. Elsa the cool, confident Elsa.

They were perplexed.

'I'd stay with you, Elsa,' Fiona began. 'Only I have to go to the police station and check about Shane.'

'You don't *have* to, Fiona, you just want to,' Elsa said.

'Well, I love him, *you* must understand that.' Fiona was stung by this remark. 'Seriously, Elsa. You have to be in love with this fellow otherwise you wouldn't be so afraid of meeting him.'

Thomas intervened. It was getting too serious between the women.

'We've all had a long day . . . suppose we meet here for breakfast at eight. We could get the nine o'clock bus . . . those of us who want to go. Is that okay?' He had a gentle voice, but from years of teaching students he had an air of authority.

They realised he was right, and started to move off.

'Just a moment,' Elsa said. 'I'm very sorry, Fiona, I was rude to you, you have every right to go and see the man you love. And I apologise for putting my own selfish affairs before other people's tragedy. Of course I'll come to the funeral with you and I would be delighted to have the protection of kind friends like you.' She looked from one to the other, her eyes over-bright, as if the smile was hiding a lot of tears.

CHAPTER SIX

In the holding cell at the back of the police station, Shane sat with his head in his hands. He needed a cold beer very badly but he was highly unlikely to get one from that ignorant Greek policeman, the brother of the tiresome Andreas up in the taverna.

Where *was* Fiona? He would have thought that she would be here by now. He could send her down to the fish bar at the harbour to get him three cold cans. Of course he would have to do the *sorry, sorry* bit, explaining that he had been so upset by the way she had sprung things on him, he couldn't help his reaction.

He banged the plate which had held hard bread against the door.

Yorghis pulled back the shutter and peered in. 'Yes?'

'My girlfriend, I'm sure she's been to see me, have you kept her away from me? You can't get away with this, you know, people in custody have a *right* to see family and next of kin.'

Yorghis shrugged. 'Nobody came.'

'I don't believe you.'

'Nobody came.' Yorghis began to move away.

'Look – I'm sorry, I didn't mean I didn't believe you exactly, it's just that, you see, we are very close and I expected . . .' His voice trailed away.

'It didn't look as if you were very close yesterday,' Yorghis said.

'No, you don't understand, we have a very passionate relationship, naturally it explodes from time to time.'

'*Endaxi*,' Yorghis said.

'What does that mean?'

'It means right, or okay, or whatever you say.' Yorghis moved off.

'Where is she?' Shane cried.

'I heard she left Aghia Anna yesterday,' Yorghis called over his shoulder.

'I don't believe you!' Shane shouted.

'Believe what you like, I was told she took a taxi and left the place.'

Shane sat there in disbelief. It couldn't be true. Fiona would never leave without him.

'*Kalimera sas*, Yorghis, you look worried.' Vonni stopped to lean on the wall of the police station.

'Well, we have all these crowds of cameramen

trampling on everyone for the funeral, the station is full of accident investigators and insurance officials, I have eleven different reports still to compile and I have this young pup in a cell. I don't know what to do with him.'

'The boy who hit the Irish girl?' Vonni asked. Nothing happened that she didn't know about.

'Yes. I wish he were hundreds of miles from here.'

'Well, export him so.'

'What?'

'That's what we used to do in Ireland years ago: if some tearaway was causing trouble the judge or the guards would say that if he was on the mail-boat to England that night no further action would be taken.'

Yorghis smiled in disbelief.

'No, it's true, terrible thing to do to England, send our dregs over there, but we thought, well, England is bigger, it can cope.'

'I see.'

'Suppose you put him on the eleven o'clock boat to Athens. Seriously, Yorghis, he'd be out of here before the funeral starts, it would be an ease to everyone.'

'And indeed Athens is big enough to cope with him.' Yorghis stroked his face thoughtfully.

Vonni's lined, tanned face broke into its wide smile. 'True, Yorghis, Athens is well big enough,' she agreed.

*

85

'You can't order me off the island,' Shane said.

'Take it or leave it. We have no time to deal with you now. Locked up here until next week then a prosecution – maybe jail. That's on the one hand. On the other, you get a free trip to Athens. You choose. You have ten minutes.'

'What about my things?' Shane asked.

'One of my boys will drive you past Eleni's house. You can pack your rucksack and be on the boat at ten-thirty.'

'I'm not ready to go yet.'

'Suit yourself,' said Yorghis, turning to leave the cell.

'No – wait a minute, come back. I think I'll go.'

Yorghis ushered him out to the police van. Shane got in sulkily.

'Bloody strange way of running a country,' he said.

Back in Eleni's house he noticed that Fiona's things were still there in the room.

'I thought you said she had gone away.'

Eleni explained in Greek that the girl would be back that day. The young policeman knew better than to translate. His boss wanted this violent boy aboard the 11 a.m. ferry and out of his jurisdiction. No point in delaying things because that foolish girl was coming back and it wasn't as if he had been asking much about her anyway.

He watched while Shane stuffed his clothes into

his bag. He made no attempt to pay Eleni for the room. He didn't even say goodbye as he left in the police van.

The bus from Kalatriada wound its way through the little hill villages as it headed slowly towards Aghia Anna.

Old women in black got on and off, saluting everyone: some of them carried vegetables which they might be going to sell at a market, one woman had two hens. A young man played the bouzouki.

At one stage they stopped at a wayside shrine with a statue of Mary the Mother of God. Bunches of flowers had been laid around it.

'This is amazing,' Thomas said. 'It looks as if it was all set up by central casting somehow.'

'Yes, or the Greek Tourist Board,' Elsa agreed.

But apart from that they said little. They were all lost in their own thoughts and concerns about the day that lay ahead of them.

Elsa wondered what were the odds against Dieter and his television team turning up in this tiny village where she had run to flee from him.

Fiona hoped that Shane would feel much calmer now. Perhaps she could persuade that nice old man Andreas to put in a word for Shane, maybe they would let him out for the funeral.

Thomas worked out how he could ask Vonni to sleep in the spare bedroom of her own apartment rather than in that terrible shed. He did not want to patronise her, just to make her see sense.

David looked out at the families of children who waved at the passing bus. He wished he could have had brothers and sisters who would have shared the load. If he had a brother who had trained as an accountant, a sister who had read law and another brother who had not been academic but who had gone into Dad's business when he was sixteen and learned it from the ground up – then he, David, would have been properly free to go and learn about pottery somewhere like Kalatriada.

He sighed as he looked out at the hills covered in olive groves. Instead of that, here he was, tortured with guilt. Last night Fiona had mentioned Catholic guilt. She didn't even begin to know what Jewish guilt was like!

Vonni gave English lessons to the children in the big room behind her craft shop. She suggested that she would teach them a verse of an English hymn which they could sing at the funeral. It might be a small consolation to the English-speaking relatives who had been arriving on every boat for the past thirty-six hours, coming to the scene of the tragedy. She might even find something in German too. She would enquire.

Everyone thought it was a good idea.

And it would distract the children too, take them

away from weeping households for a while. The families were grateful to Vonni as they had been for years and years since first she had come to Aghia Anna as a young girl. She had grown older with them all, spoke their language, taught their children, shared the good times and bad. A lot of them could not even remember why she had come here in the first place.

As Thomas went up the whitewashed steps to the apartment above and let himself in, he paused, unbelieving.

He heard the voices of little children singing: 'The Lord's my shepherd, I'll not want . . .'

It had been a long time since he had been in church. Possibly at his father's funeral. That was the last time he had heard it sung. He paused, stricken, in the sunshine. This funeral was going to be even sadder than he had thought.

Andreas and his brother Yorghis stood beside the ferry.

Shane avoided their eyes.

'Is there anything you would like to do before you leave?' Andreas asked.

'Like what? Like congratulate you on your legendary Greek hospitality for example?' Shane sneered.

'Like write a letter to your girlfriend.' Andreas was curt.

'I don't have any paper or pen,' Shane said.

'I do.' Andreas offered both.

'What am I to say? That you and your Gestapo brother threw me out? That's not going to cheer her much, is it?' Shane looked very belligerent.

'She might like to know that you are safe and well, and free . . . and that you'll contact her when you are settled.'

'She knows that.'

The pen and paper were still in Andreas's hand. 'A few short words perhaps?' the old man urged.

'Oh, for God's sake.' Shane turned away.

They blew the whistle to show the boat was about to leave. The young policeman escorted Shane on deck and came back to Andreas and Yorghis.

'It's better he doesn't write to her,' he said to the older men.

'Possibly,' Andreas agreed. 'In the long term certainly, but in the short term it will break her poor little heart.'

David and Fiona walked with Elsa back to her apartment.

'Look, nobody around,' David said. It was true. The streets which had thronged with press and bureaucrats were quiet now.

'I wish I could stay longer, I just have to check Shane is all right,' Fiona apologised, as she went up the hill towards the police station. From down in the harbour they all heard the hooting of the 11 a.m. ferry as it left for Athens. At midday another boat would arrive carrying even more people coming to attend the funeral.

'Would you like me to stay with you here, Elsa?' David asked.

'Just for five minutes so that I don't run away again,' she laughed.

'You won't do that.' He patted her hand.

'I hope not, David. Tell me, did you ever in your life love anyone obsessively, foolishly?'

'No. I never loved anyone at all,' he said.

'I'm sure that's not so.'

'I'm afraid it is, it's not something to be proud of at twenty-eight.' He was apologetic.

'You're exactly the same age as I am!' she exclaimed in surprise.

'You put your years to better use than I did,' he said.

'No, you wouldn't say that if you knew. I'd prefer never to have loved. Maybe I can get back to where I was before all this. That's what I'd choose more than anything.' Her eyes were far away.

David wished he knew what to say. It would be wonderful to be able to say the right thing, to make this sad girl smile. If only he knew a joke or a funny story to lift the mood. He racked his brains. He could only think of the golf jokes his father told.

'Do you play golf, Elsa?' he asked her suddenly.

She was startled. 'A little,' she said. 'Were you thinking of a game?'

'No, no, I don't play, I was actually thinking of a golf joke to try to cheer you up a little.'

She seemed touched. 'Tell it to me then.'

David sought the joke and sort of retrieved it. It was about a man whose wife had died out on the golf course. His friends had sympathised and the man had said no, it wasn't too bad, the worst thing was picking her body up and carrying her on to the next hole as he played each shot.

Elsa looked at him expectantly.

'That's it, I'm afraid.' David was miserable. 'You see, golfers are meant to be so obsessed . . . that he sort of carried the corpse rather than give up on the game . . .' He stopped, appalled at himself. 'Look, I'm so sorry, Elsa, on the day of a funeral to tell such a stupid story . . . I'm such a fool.'

She reached out and stroked his cheek. 'No, you're not, you are a dear gentle person, and I'm so happy to have you here. Let's make ourselves a little lunch together?'

'Or I could take you out for an *omeleta tria-avga* . . . they love you to ask for that . . . you know, stressing you want three eggs.' He looked enthusiastic at the thought of it all.

'I'd prefer not to be out there if you don't mind, David. I feel safer in here. We could eat on the terrace and see without being seen. Would you hate that?'

'Of course not, I'd love it,' said David.

And he went to Elsa's fridge happily to take out feta cheese and tomatoes and make them lunch.

'Hallo, I wonder if I could speak to the police chief, please.'

Yorghis stood up wearily.

Fiona stood there in a little blue cotton dress with a white wool shoulder bag. Her hair falling over her face didn't hide the bruise. She looked frail and unable to cope with the hand that life had dealt her.

'Come in, *Kyria*, sit down,' he said, offering her a chair.

'You see, my friend stayed here with you last night,' she began, as if Yorghis ran some up-market bed and breakfast instead of Aghia Anna's jail.

Yorghis spread out his hands in front of him. She looked so anxious to see this boy, so forgiving of what he had done. How did young pigs like that get good women to love them? And now he had to tell this girl that he had gone an hour ago on the ferry without a backward glance. He found it hard to select the right words.

'Shane is very sorry, he may not sound it to you but he *is*,' she began. 'And in a way a lot of it was my fault, I told him something all the wrong way instead of explaining it properly . . .'

'He has gone to Athens,' Yorghis said baldly.

'No, he can't have, not without me, not without

93

telling me. No, no. It's not possible.' She looked at him with a distraught face.

'On the eleven o'clock ferry.'

'Did he not leave me a note? Tell me where he's going? Where I should meet him? He *can't* have gone just like that.'

'He will get in touch when he's settled, I'm sure he will.'

'But where? Where will he write to me?'

'He could write a letter here, I suppose,' Yorghis said, doubtfully.

'No, you know he wouldn't do that!'

'Or maybe to the place where you and he were staying.'

'No, he wouldn't be able to remember Eleni's house, or where it was. No, I must go on the next boat, I'll find him,' she said.

'No, my dear girl, no, Athens is a huge place. Stay here. You have good friends here, stay until you are stronger.'

She was weeping now. 'But I have to be with him . . .'

'There will be no more boats leaving today, because of the funeral. Please, please be calm. It's better that he left.'

'No, no, how could it be better?'

'Because otherwise he would be in jail, locked up. At least he is free.'

'Did he leave me any message?'

Yorghis said, 'It was all in a great hurry you see.'

'Anything at all?'

'He *did* ask about you, wondered where you were.'

'Oh, why did I go away? I'll never forgive myself for the rest of my life . . .'

Yorghis patted her shoulder awkwardly as she sobbed. Over her shoulder, down at the foot of the hill, he saw Vonni passing by with her little troupe of children and he had an idea.

'Andreas tells me you are a nurse?' he said.

'I was. Yes.'

'No, you are always a nurse . . . could you do something to help? Do you see Vonni down there, she's looking after the children during the funeral, I know she'd love you to give her a hand.'

'I'm not sure I could help anyone just now . . .' Fiona began.

'That's often when we help best,' Yorghis said. He called out something in Greek. Vonni called something back. Fiona looked wistful.

'You know, if we could live here and have our child, we would learn Greek and be part of the place like she is.' She spoke almost to herself but Yorghis heard her and felt a lump in his throat.

Thomas felt restless; he wished that the funeral would begin soon and end soon. There was a heavy air of expectancy hanging over the little town. He couldn't settle until these people had been laid to rest. And indeed he was anxious that the television teams and journalists should leave. And things could go on like they had before.

Well, not exactly as before.

Not for the family of Manos and the other boys who had died. Some of the visitors were going to be buried here, some would be put into coffins and taken back to England and Germany.

But it would be better for everyone when this day was over.

He had promised to collect Elsa at her apartment and walk with her to the little church. He hoped that she would not meet this man she was avoiding and seemed so afraid of. There was too much pain in her face when she talked about him.

It would be very crowded there. Whoever he was, he might not see Elsa.

'I'm Fiona,' she said to the lined, tanned woman.

'A Dub?' the woman asked.

'Yes, and you? They told me you were Irish too?'

'I'm from the west,' Vonni said. 'But a long, long time ago.'

'And what are you doing with the children?'

'Their families are all at the house of Manos.' Vonni spoke English with an Irish accent but in a slightly foreign way, as if it were her second language. It probably was by this stage. 'I thought we would go a little outside the town and pick some flowers on the hill, will you help me?'

'Yes, of course, but I'm useless – what will I say?'

'They're meant to be learning English. Keep saying *very good* and *thank you*. I think they've mastered that much.' Vonni's lined face cracked into a huge smile that lit up everything.

'Sure,' said Fiona, brightening up for a moment and stretching out her hands to two five-year-olds. They all walked together in a straggling line down the dusty road out of town to pick flowers for the church.

Thomas saw the priests walk together in twos. Tall men with long robes with their grey hair tied back in little buns under their black headgear. They looked pale and solemn, and Thomas wondered what would make a young Greek man from this sunny island choose a life in religion. But then, back in sunny California he knew people, even in the faculty, men who were in Holy Orders – that young priest who taught mystic poetry, the Methodist preacher who also lectured in Elizabethan literature. These men were strengthened by their faith. It could be exactly the same for these Greek Orthodox dignitaries.

Thomas knew it was now time to go to the church. He went to Elsa's apartment as he had promised and was surprised to hear voices inside. Perhaps she had met her friend after all.

He was disappointed, but cheered up when he realised that of course this guy wouldn't be with Elsa, he would be out filming the funeral.

He knocked on the door and was surprised when David opened it.

'It's only Thomas,' David called out. It wasn't much of a welcome.

'Well, I *did* tell Elsa that I'd walk with her to the church,' Thomas said huffily.

'Lord, I'm sorry, Thomas, I don't know what's wrong with me today, I can't say the right thing to save my life. It's just that we thought . . . we were afraid that . . .'

Elsa came out to join them. She was wearing a smart cream linen dress with a navy jacket. She had dressed formally for the ceremony.

Thomas had a tie in his pocket in case it would be appropriate. Now he realised that it would.

'Thomas, I asked David to answer the door for me because I am so paranoid – I still think that Dieter will come calling. Forgive me.'

'What's to forgive?' Thomas was putting on his tie at the little mirror in the hall.

'I should have gone home for a tie too.' David was worried.

'No, you look fine, David,' Thomas said, and they set out together following the crowds to the little church. The people stood on both sides of the street winding up from the harbour. Their heads were bowed, the conversation low.

'I wonder where Fiona is?' David whispered.

'Up there at the precinct feeding lover boy biscuits through the bars,' Thomas said.

'She *does* love him,' Elsa said, as if offering some sort of excuse.

'You should have seen him hit her,' Thomas said.

'If she's up at the station, she's there on her own, all the police are here,' David observed.

Then a great hush came over the crowd and they stood in silence at the approach of the funeral party. Lines of men and women walked behind the coffins in a little procession. Their tear-stained faces and black clothes seemed totally wrong for the bright sunshine, the blue sea and the whitewashed buildings.

Behind them walked the English and German families who had come so unexpectedly to this Greek village to bury their loved ones. They looked around them bewildered and confused, as if they were taking part in a play where they hadn't learned their parts.

Every shop, taverna and business in Aghia Anna had closed. The fishing boats stood idle, all of them flying a flag at half mast. Bells tolled from the monastery in the valley beyond. The television cameras of half a dozen countries filmed the scene. There was room in the little church for only a tenth of the people gathered to sympathise. Crackling speakers relayed the service to the people outside. And unexpectedly, in the middle of the Greek prayers and music, came the sound of children singing 'The Lord's My Shepherd'. The sound of the English people sobbing in the church could be heard. Thomas wiped a tear from his face.

Then there was a verse from the German hymn '*Tannenbaum*', and Elsa too cried openly.

'It was my friend Vonni who taught them that,' Thomas whispered.

'Well, you must tell her that she's done a fine job in breaking our hearts,' David whispered back.

When the congregation came out of the church and prepared to walk the short journey up to the graveyard, Elsa spotted Fiona. She was with Vonni and the children, all of whom had armfuls of wild flowers. Fiona was holding tight the hands of two little boys.

'Another day, another surprise,' Thomas said. 'Who would have thought she would have got her act together.'

'It's probably to take her mind off him,' Elsa decided.

Yorghis made an announcement. The families would like to go alone to the burial service in the graveyard. They thanked people for coming to the church to sympathise, but now they wanted to be alone. They had asked the café owners and restaurants to open again and for life to carry on. They were sure everyone would understand.

Reluctantly the television teams agreed. This was not a situation where arguing would do any good. The children marched with Vonni and Fiona towards the small graveyard. Open graves waited among the old stones and the crumbling walls.

'This is an unreal day and we haven't even lost anyone,' Thomas said.

'I don't really want to be alone just now,' Elsa appealed.

'I could treat you to a glass of retsina and a little plate of *kalamari* and olives down at the harbour. Look, they're all putting out chairs,' Thomas said.

'I think Elsa would feel happier out of the public eye,' David countered.

'Sure, I forgot. Listen, I have some nice cold retsina in my place, you know, over the craft shop.' They were reluctant to leave each other and so they thought it would be a good plan.

'Is there a way we can tell Fiona where we are?' Elsa wondered.

'It might mean involving what Thomas calls "lover boy".' David was doubtful.

'No, I'd say he's still well locked up,' Thomas said. 'So is that an okay plan then?'

'Very okay,' Elsa smiled. 'I'll just go back home

and get a scarf for the evening breeze then I'll go get some olives in Yanni's on the way back and see you at your place.' She seemed happy with what had been arranged.

Thomas was soon tidying up his sitting room, and getting out glasses. David walked around looking at the books.

'Did you bring all these from California?' he asked, astonished.

'No, a lot of them are Vonni's. I do really wish that she'd sleep here, you know.'

'What?'

'She sleeps down there at the end of the yard, it's a shed and there are hens and the Lord knows what else in it.'

'I don't believe you.' David looked in surprise at the dilapidated building. They chatted easily for a while as they set out paper napkins and little plates.

Eventually David said what they were both thinking. 'Elsa is a very long time getting the olives, isn't she?'

There was a long pause.

'I suppose she met him,' Thomas said.

'And went off with him,' David said.

Elsa saw Dieter as soon as she came out of Yanni's delicatessen. He was talking to Claus, the chief cameraman, and looking at his watch. Elsa knew they would have hired a helicopter if they had felt they could not wait for slow ferries to take them back to Athens.

The pictures and commentary would be in Germany already, sent by modem.

She moved back into the doorway of Yanni's shop but not quickly enough.

Dieter had seen her.

She could see him running towards her.

'Elsa! Elsa!' he called, pushing past the people in the narrow street. His face was flushed and his eyes were bright. She had forgotten how handsome he was, like Robert Redford in his early years.

There was no escape: he was beside her.

'Dieter?' she said uncertainly.

'Darling Elsa, what are you *doing* here, what did you mean by running away?' He stood with his hands on her shoulders, admiring her and drinking her in.

Any attempt at discretion had been abandoned. But then Claus had probably known anyway. Like half the television company had probably known.

She said nothing, just looked into his very blue eyes.

'Claus heard you were here, someone from the other networks saw you yesterday, but I didn't believe them. Oh, my dearest lovely Elsa – how very, very good to have found you.'

She shook her head. 'You haven't found me, you've just met me by chance. Now I must go.'

She saw Claus move back discreetly: he wanted no part of this lovers' quarrel.

'Elsa, don't be ridiculous – you leave your job, you leave me, no explanation for either . . . you think there is nothing to discuss?'

His face was working with emotion; she had never seen him so upset. He called out to the cameraman, 'Claus, I'm going to stay the night here, you go back with the others and I'll call you tomorrow.'

'Don't stay for me, Dieter, I beg you. And if you try to force me or threaten me, I swear I'll get the police. They've locked up one man yesterday for threatening a woman here, they'll have room in his cell for another.'

'Threaten you, Elsa?' He was astounded at the idea. 'As if I would! I *love* you, Elsa, is it so demanding and mad that I ask you to tell me why you left me? With no explanation?'

'I wrote to you,' she said.

'Twelve lines,' he said, reaching into his jacket. 'I carry it everywhere, I know it by heart, I am always hoping one day I will read it and it will make sense.' He looked so confused she felt herself softening.

'It's all there,' she said.

'Nothing is there, Elsa. I'll go away, leave you alone, I swear, if you tell me. Just tell me why you threw away two years like that. You know why . . . I don't. We have always been fair with each other. Be fair now. You owe me that much.'

She was silent. Perhaps she did owe him more than a twelve-line letter.

'Where are you staying? Let me come to your place,' he asked quickly, seeing her hesitation.

'Not my place, no – where are you staying? The Anna Beach?'

It was the one vaguely touristy, comfortable place. She would have expected him to stay there.

'Yes, exactly,' he agreed.

'Right, I'll go there with you, we can talk in a corner of the café, the sort of veranda looking over the sea.'

He seemed to expel a sigh of relief.

'Thank you,' he said.

'First I have to leave a message.'

He produced his mobile phone.

'No, I don't know the number.' She went to the counter and gave the olives back to Yanni. There was some discussion and it was agreed. Yanni's little brother would take the bag of olives and a note to the apartment over Vonni's craft shop. She scribbled something on a piece of card.

'You didn't even write this guy twelve lines – I suppose I should be flattered,' Dieter said.

She smiled at him. 'No, it's not a guy, well, it's two guys actually, but you know what I mean.'

'I love you, Elsa,' he said with great intensity.

*

'You were so helpful today, Fiona, the parents said to thank you very much.'

'It was nothing, I love children.' Her voice was sad.

'You will have your own one day.'

'I don't know, Vonni, I really don't. Did you have children?'

'One,' Vonni said. 'A son, but it wasn't what you'd call straightforward.' Her tone meant that the subject was now closed. But she was not shutting Fiona out. She was prepared to talk, but not about her son.

'I meant it, you *are* good with children, it doesn't matter that you don't speak their language.' Vonni was praising.

'Vonni, I could be pregnant now,' Fiona said in a rush. 'In fact I'm certain I am and . . . well, it's not what you'd call straightforward either.'

'And the young man who has gone to Athens – does he know?'

'Sort of, I told him badly, you see.'

'You shouldn't be on your own now,' Vonni said. 'I'd ask you home but I'm living in what Thomas calls the hen-house.'

'I'll go to Elsa's place,' Fiona said. But there was no reply there.

The people in David's house said he had not come home, either.

Vonni escorted her to the craft shop.

'I'll wait here until I see you have someone to be with,' she said, and stood in the street as Fiona went up the steps to the apartment.

Vonni saw Thomas open the door and welcome her in, then she went back to the harbour. She was going to go to help in the kitchen of Manos's family, where there was plenty of food but nobody to serve it or wash up afterwards. Vonni would stay there as long as she was needed.

'They sent him away to Athens, before I could see him,' Fiona wept.

'Maybe it was all for the best,' David said. Then he saw the expression on Fiona's face. 'What I mean is, it gives a cooling-off period for everyone, then he'll be back or something,' he finished lamely.

'Or he'll write,' Thomas added doubtfully.

'Where's Elsa?' Fiona asked suddenly. Elsa might say something helpful, unlike these well-meaning men.

There was a silence.

Then Thomas said, 'She was coming back here but she met someone . . .' he began.

'The German guy,' David said.

'And she went off with him?' There was naked envy in Fiona's voice.

'Apparently,' Thomas and David said at exactly the same time.

CHAPTER SEVEN

At the Anna Beach most of the journalists were at the checkout desk. Another job was over, another disaster recorded, and now they were heading off to the next one. They'd pick up the story again when the investigators had reached their official conclusions and produced their report.

Dieter and Elsa went over to the big rattan chairs and low tables of the conservatory. Below them the dark blue sea lapped innocently against the rocks. It was impossible to believe that this very sea had taken the lives of so many people in the bay this week.

Dieter ordered coffee for two.

'Sorry,' Elsa called the waiter back. 'He is having coffee, I'm not, he ordered for me by mistake . . . I would like an *ouzo* and water, please.'

'Please don't be difficult,' Dieter begged her.

'Difficult? Choosing what I want to drink?' she asked, perplexed.

'No, you know, scoring points,' he said.

'Oh, I'm way beyond that now. Anyway, Dieter, you wanted to talk, so here I am. Talk to me.'

'No, I wanted *you* to talk, I wanted you to tell me why you disappeared, ran out on everything . . . to hide secretly in a backwater like this.'

'I'm not hiding,' Elsa said indignantly. 'I resigned from my work formally, I am here under my own name, when you asked me to come and meet you I came, so where's the secrecy bit? And why do you call it a backwater? Look over at that desk – half the world's media is here . . . plenty of action I'd say.'

'I hate it when you're flippant, Elsa, it's an act, and it doesn't suit you.'

The waiter arrived. Elsa poured some water into the aniseed drink and watched it go cloudy. Then she drained it in one gulp.

'That was fast!' He was startled and amused as he began to sip his coffee.

'Well, why don't you finish yours too – then we can go to your room?'

'*What?*' he looked at her in astonishment.

'Your room,' she repeated as if he were a little deaf.

He stared at her, uncomprehending.

'Dieter, isn't this what it's about? You said talk, but you don't mean talk, do you? You mean screw.'

He looked at her, open-mouthed.

'Well . . . I . . . oh, come on, Elsa, there's no need to be crude about it all. That's not what we had.'

'Sorry, I thought that's just what we had every night you came to my apartment, and lunchtime too, when it could be managed.'

'Elsa, I love you, you love me, why on earth are you reducing it all to such coarse words?'

'So you don't want me to go to bed with you?' She looked at him innocently.

'You know I do.'

'Well, finish your coffee and get your key,' she said.

'Thank you, Vonni, nobody but you would think of coming here to wash dishes on a night like this.' Maria, the widow of Manos, stood in her kitchen looking at all the clean dishes and the polished glasses.

'How are you managing in there? Are the relations being a help?'

'Most of them, yes, but some say he was irresponsible and that's no help.'

'Oh, there are always people who say the very wrong thing, they sort of specialise in it,' Vonni assured her.

'You sound as if you have had experience of it.'

'I could write a book about it. Who has upset you most?'

'My sister, I think. She told me I should look for a

new husband soon, before I lose my looks. Manos is not cold in his grave and she tells me this.'

'This is the sister married to the miser on the other side of the island?'

'Yes.'

'Well, she's hardly a world authority on love, ignore her. Who else?'

'My father-in-law, he says I'll never manage to raise his grandchildren here, that we should all go to Athens to live with him. I'd hate it, Vonni, really I would. I couldn't go.'

'Of course you couldn't. Tell him you'll think about it for a year. Say you heard that no one should make a decision for twelve months after a bereavement, say it's an old custom.'

'Is it?' Maria asked.

'It is back in Ireland, but you don't need to tell him where the tradition came from, just say it's well known.'

'He'll start making plans if he thinks I might.'

'No, be very firm, say no plans until a year from now. In a year you can say the children can't leave their school or whatever.'

'Did you really have things like this to worry about, funerals where they say the wrong thing? You always look so calm.'

'After my mother's funeral, my sister wrote and told me that I was a scourge and a lash for my mother's back, that she never slept easy in her bed because of me.'

'Oh no, Vonni, that can't have been true.'

'I was wild when I was young, much more irresponsible than your Manos ever was. I was very hurt, I thought for a long while that it might indeed be true, but then I remembered that I made my mother laugh too, something my boring, serious sister never did, so I cheered up then.'

'And do you stay in touch with your sister? I would like to go back into the other room and slap *my* sister's face,' Maria said.

'Yes, so did I for a long time, but life is much easier if you don't slap them. Believe me. I send her a birthday card and a Christmas card every year.'

'And does she reply?'

'She sends me cards when she goes to the opera in Italy, or a classical tour of Spain, just to show me how cultured she is. But she is lonely, she has no real friends. I am a million times better off in this warm, welcoming place. I can afford to send her polite greetings. You too, Maria, you are so lucky not to be married to that miser your sister chose, rejoice in it every day, and hang on in there. She'll be back with him counting coins in two days. Don't slap her this time.'

Maria laughed. 'You make me feel much better – I didn't think I would laugh again,' she said, putting her hand on the older woman's arm.

'Yes, you will,' Vonni promised her. 'Cry a lot, but laugh as well. It's how we survive.'

David didn't want to go back to the house where he was staying. The family were wiped out with grief over their dead son, he felt in the way. Fiona didn't want to walk all the way out to Eleni's house to sleep there alone in the knowledge that Shane had left her with no explanation, no letter, no message.

'Why don't you both stay here?' Thomas suggested suddenly. 'Fiona can have that room at the back, David can have the sofa bed.' He looked at their faces, both of them very grateful and relieved.

They nodded their acceptance, it was a great idea, they said.

It wasn't a night to be alone.

'Can I stay here in the station?' Andreas asked his brother Yorghis.

'I was just going to suggest it.'

'It's just that it seems a long way to go the whole way up that mountain road tonight, I'm not quite sure why.'

'Nobody wants to be alone on a night of such a sad funeral,' Yorghis said, reaching out and patting his brother's hand. 'I don't want to be alone either. I'm glad you want to stay.'

Neither of them mentioned the reason why they were alone.

They talked about the people who had come out today to mourn. They talked about their sister Christina and how she would have come to the funeral but she had to look after her family far away. No word was spoken about Andreas's son Adoni who lived in Chicago and was in contact with neither his home town nor his father. Adoni who would have gone to school along these roads with Manos.

No mention was made of Yorghis's wife who had left him over an incident many years ago. His wife always said that she was just being friendly to a tourist. Yorghis had seen it as being a great deal more than friendly. Words had been said that could never be taken back. She had long since gone back to her own people in Crete.

Yorghis went to one of the filing cabinets and brought out a bottle of Metaxa brandy and then he got some clean sheets and pillows.

'Are you giving me a cell?' Andreas asked.

'No, brother, you and I have spent enough years as boys sharing a room, it won't hurt us to do it again, two lonely old men, on a sad night.'

Vonni had served coffee and *baklava* to the family of Maria and Manos, and she was preparing to leave quietly when Maria came back into the kitchen.

'Vonni, can I ask you a favour?'

'Anything, Maria.'

'Could you stay here for the night, just one night? I don't think I can manage on my own tonight.'

'Of course I will.'

'You are such a good friend, the bed is too big, too empty for me.'

'I snore a bit, I'd better warn you,' Vonni apologised in advance.

'So did Manos, every night, even though he denied it loudly.'

'Dear Manos,' Vonni said fondly. 'I'm sure he would be pleased if I snored for a night or two in his place.'

The Hotel Anna Beach had little bungalows facing the sea. Dieter opened his bungalow door with his key and stood back to let Elsa go in first.

She didn't sit down but stood looking at the pictures on the walls, big blown-up photographs of the coast along Aghia Anna.

'Very cool,' she said admiringly.

'This is not what I had expected,' he said.

'But we have agreed that it's what you'd like,' she smiled.

'That's not a real smile, Elsa,' he began.

'You taught me to smile for television. Teeth and eyes, you said. Teeth and eyes. I remember it well.'

'Please, my love, you *are* my love. Please don't be brittle.'

'No, indeed, and let's not waste time either.' Elsa had already taken off her navy jacket. Now she drew the cream linen dress over her head and laid it neatly on the back of the chair.

He was still very unsure.

She removed her lace bra and pants and placed them on top of her dress, then finally she stepped out of her smart navy sandals.

'You are so beautiful, and to think I believed I'd never see you again.' He looked at her in open admiration.

'Not you, Dieter, you get everything you want.' She put her arms around his neck and kissed him. And suddenly it was as if they had never been apart.

In the apartment over the craft shop, Fiona had gone to bed in the small white room that Vonni had furnished with a turquoise bedspread and a bright blue chair. The little white chest of drawers had a blue-framed mirror and some shells and pottery on top. It was cool and welcoming.

Fiona was weary and sad.

It had been a nightmare of a day, and further nightmares were ahead. She didn't think she would sleep. Too much had happened and the future was too frightening. How wonderful it would have been if Shane were still here and they might both have been able to stay with Thomas for a few days in this wonderful apartment. But even as she thought it

Fiona knew she was fooling herself. Shane would have fought with Thomas about something. The way he always did with people. Out of insecurity.

She gave a little sob.

It was such a tragedy that people misunderstood Shane and brought out the worst in him.

She lay on the bed with its blue cover and cried herself to sleep.

In the room next door Thomas and David played chess. They heard the sounds of weeping through the wall.

'She's crying over that bastard!' David whispered in amazement.

'I know, it's beyond comprehension,' Thomas whispered back.

And they sat there and waited until the sobs had died down. Then they smiled at each other in relief.

'Do you know what we're like?' David said. 'We're like the parents of a toddler who won't go to sleep.'

Thomas sighed. 'Yes, there was always that moment of not wanting to leave the room until you were *sure* he was asleep, and then just when you crept to the door he'd call you back. They were great days really.' He looked sad, thinking about his son.

David thought hard about what to say. He so often got it wrong.

'It's hard to understand women, isn't it?' he said eventually.

Thomas looked at him thoughtfully. 'It sure is, David, the exact same thought was going through my mind. Fiona crying over that drunken brute who would have beaten her senseless, Elsa going off with the man she had run a thousand miles to escape, my wife who used to tell me she loved poetry and literature and art living with a bonehead who has some exercise machine in every room of my house.' He sounded very bitter.

David looked at him, stricken. It had not been a good thing to say after all.

Thomas shrugged. 'And you probably have your own women-are-unfathomable story, David,' he said.

'No, that's just the problem. I was telling Elsa before, I never really loved anyone. That makes me superficial, cold and shallow.'

Thomas smiled at him. 'No, you're a good guy, and I'm glad to have your company tonight. But you are *not* a skilled chess player. You didn't free up the squares around your king. He has no egress, poor fellow, it's checkmate, David, that's what it is.'

And for some reason they both found that very funny and laughed as loudly as they could while keeping the volume low enough so as not to wake the sleeping Fiona in the next room.

*

Dieter stroked Elsa's face.

'I must have been mad to think I had lost you,' he said.

She said nothing.

'It will all be fine again,' he said.

Still no reply.

'You could not love me like that and not mean it?' he said, just a little anxiously now.

Elsa lay there saying nothing.

'Speak to me, tell me this has all been nonsense, that you'll come back with me and it will all be fine again . . .'

She still said nothing at all.

'Please, Elsa . . . please?'

She got up slowly from the bed and put on the big white fluffy robe that was hanging on the bathroom door. She picked up Dieter's packet of cigarettes and lit one.

'You gave up!' he said accusingly.

She inhaled deeply and sat in the big bamboo chair looking at him.

'You'll come home with me, Elsa?'

'No, of course I won't. This is goodbye, you know this and I know this, so let's not be foolish, Dieter.'

'Goodbye?' he asked.

'Yes, goodbye. You are going home, I am going to go to . . . well, somewhere. I haven't decided exactly where yet.'

'This is insane, we were meant for each other, you know that, I know it. Everyone knows it.'

'No. Everyone does *not* know. A few people at work know and say nothing, because they take their lead from you. And because you do not want us to go public we have lived a secret life for two years. So less of the *everyone knows we are meant for each other* line.'

He looked at her, startled. 'We went into it, eyes open. Both of us,' he said.

'And I'm walking out of it, eyes open,' Elsa said calmly.

'You aren't the kind of woman to hold out for an engagement ring,' he said with scorn in his voice.

'Of course not. I didn't exactly hold out, did I? I slept with you the third time I met you. That's hardly playing games, withholding favours.'

'So what are we talking about then?' He was genuinely bewildered.

'I told you. I wrote it all down before I left.'

'You did like hell, you scribbled twelve jumbled lines that I still can't make head nor tail of. Life is not meant to be a guessing game, Elsa, we are both far too old for this sort of thing. What do you want? Tell me. If you're holding a gun to my head and saying we must be married, then all right. If that's what it takes, all right, that's what we'll do.'

'I've heard of better proposals,' she said with a smile.

'Stop playing the fool. If it's the only way I can have you with me, I'll marry you. Be *proud* to marry you,' he added as an afterthought.

'No, thank you, Dieter. I don't want to marry you.'

'So what *do* you want?' he cried, in near despair.

'I want to get over you, to forget you, to make you no longer any part of my life.'

'You took an odd way to show all that.' He looked down at the bed she had so recently left.

Elsa shrugged. 'I told you. I no longer trust you, I don't admire you or respect you any more. Sex has nothing to do with those things. Sex is just sex, a short amount of pleasure, excitement. You told me that yourself, if you remember.'

'I do remember, but it was in totally different circumstances. I wasn't talking about us, not about you and me.'

'Still, the principle is the same, isn't it?' She was ice calm now.

'No, it's not in my case, we were talking about a totally meaningless drunken encounter at a film festival with some very silly girl whose name I can't even remember.'

'Birgit. And she remembers you.'

'Only well enough to tell you and upset you over something that couldn't have mattered less.'

'I know, I realise that.'

'So tell me, Elsa, if you realise this, what in God's name is all this drama about? Why did you leave?'

'I wrote it in my letter.'

'You did *not* write it, you wrote some rubbish about responsibilities and lines having to be drawn. I swear I didn't know what you meant. I still don't know.'

His handsome face was working with emotion and his thick hair was tousled.

'Birgit told me about Monika,' Elsa said.

'Monika? Monika? But she was ages before I met you. We agreed that the past was past. Didn't we?'

'Yes.'

'So why bring her up? I swear I never saw her since I met you. Not even once.'

'I know.'

'So explain to me. I beg you. If you know I haven't seen or thought of Monika in years . . . what is this about?'

'You haven't seen or thought of your daughter either.'

'Ah,' Dieter said. 'Birgit really went to work, didn't she?'

Elsa said nothing.

'It was never meant to happen. I told Monika I wasn't ready to be a parent, to settle down. She knew that from the very start. There were no grey areas.' He was beginning to bluster now.

'How old is she, Dieter?' Elsa's voice was level.

He was genuinely confused. 'Monika?'

'Gerda. Your daughter.'

'I don't know, I told you I have nothing to do with them.'

'You must know.'

'About eight or nine I suppose. But why do you keep probing it, Elsa? All that has nothing to do with us.'

'You fathered a child. That has something to do with you.'

'No, it has not. That was a long past incident in my life and not my fault. Monika was in charge of contraception. I have nothing to do with her child, never had and never will. We all began again.'

'But Gerda began with no father.'

'Stop calling her by her name, you don't know her, you're only repeating tittle-tattle from that bitch Birgit.'

'You should have told me.'

'No, if I had that would have been wrong too. You would have said I was always hanging around a child from a previous relationship. Be fair, Elsa, you would not have liked that either.'

'I'd have liked it a hell of a lot more than a father who opted out and left a child hoping and wondering.'

'That is fantasy talk, you don't know *anything* about that child.'

'It's my own story all over again. My father left home and I spent years waiting and hoping and wondering. Every birthday, every Christmas, every summer. I was so sure he would write or call or come to see me.'

'It was different in your case: your father *had* lived at home with you. You had a right to think he would always be around. In my case I had nothing to do with Monika's child. Not ever. There were no expectations.'

Elsa gave him a long look.

'What do you want me to do?' he asked eventually.

'Nothing, Dieter.'

'You'd come back to me if I made some kind of link to this totally strange child?'

'No, I will not come back to you ever.'

'But all this . . .' Again he looked at the bed where they had made love. 'Did it mean nothing to you?'

'You know it did. It meant goodbye,' she said, and put on her dress and her sandals. Slipping her underwear in her bag, she walked to the door.

'You *can't* do this!' he cried.

'Goodbye, Dieter,' she said and walked through the manicured little rock gardens of the Anna Beach towards the gate. Her navy jacket she had slung over her shoulder.

From his bungalow Dieter called after her. 'Don't

go, Elsa, please don't go. I love you so much. Don't leave me . . .'

But she walked on.

Vonni had realised there was no milk in Maria's house and that everyone would want it in the morning. As soon as Maria's breathing became regular Vonni slipped out of the big double bed and found a pottery jug. She would go to the Anna Beach where the kitchen would be open all night.

She was returning with the jug that they had willingly filled for her when she saw the beautiful German girl walking alone. There were tears on her face. Vonni pulled back behind a big bougainvillaea so as not to encounter her.

Then she heard a man calling and shouting. Vonni didn't speak much German but she could understand what he was saying. And if she was any judge at all, he meant it, whoever he was.

But Elsa did not look back.

CHAPTER EIGHT

Thomas had gone out for hot fresh bread and figs for their breakfast. He made a large pot of coffee and rattled the cups.

Fiona emerged pale and tired-looking but with a grateful smile. David had folded the light rug Thomas had given him, and plumped up the cushions.

He came eagerly to the breakfast table.

'He spoils us, Fiona, weren't we lucky to find a benefactor?'

'Oh, I know.' Fiona too was fervent. 'I feel much, much stronger today, I'm full of plans now, so I am.'

Thomas smiled at her. 'Tell us your plans,' he said.

'I'm going up to the station to see the chief of police, now that I'm calm and not hysterical. I'll ask him to help me find Shane, he might know where he would head for. We were only in Athens for twenty-four hours on the way here, but he loved Syntagma

126

Square, perhaps Yorghis might know some police-men there who could get him a message. Then I'll go back to Eleni's and change my clothes. I've been wearing this dress for days, then I'm going to find Vonni and ask her does she need any help with the children.' Her eyes were bright and enthusiastic and the dead, defeated look had gone.

David too seemed to be energised. 'I'm going to walk up to that taverna and see Andreas again, he was such a gentleman, if that isn't too stupid a word.'

'That's exactly what he is and he'd be so happy to see you again. Give him our best, won't you?'

'I'll do that,' David promised.

'And I too have several things to do today. Later on, when they're all awake in California, I'll call my son. But first I'm going to find Vonni – she didn't come home to her shed last night.'

'How on earth do you know?' David was sur-prised.

'Because normally she pokes around in there with her torch, she didn't do that last night. But when I find her, this time I'm going to *insist* that she stays in her own bedroom, I'm getting tetchy and antsy just having her living in that place in the yard.'

'*Antsy?*' Fiona asked.

'I know, it's a great word, isn't it. Means something irritates you, gives you ants in your pants.'

'Shane will love that,' Fiona said happily.

And neither of the men could think of anything to say.

Elsa was in her apartment. She knew that she would not sleep so she sat on her balcony and watched the dawn come up in Aghia Anna.

She saw the little town come to life. Then, as if she had finally accepted that the night with all its fears and nightmares was over, she went in, had a long shower, washed her hair. She put on a fresh yellow cotton dress and sat down with a cup of coffee to watch the ferry getting ready to leave.

He would leave on the 8 a.m. for Athens. She was utterly certain of this. Dieter knew she wasn't coming with him, so why wait for the 11 a.m.? He wasn't a person to hang about. He had sent Claus and the others ahead of him by the chartered helicopter yesterday. He knew there was no point in searching the town for her. He would never see her on this balcony, but she would be able to see him and know that he had gone.

She couldn't pick him out in the crowd that lined up before the brightly coloured gangplank. Yet she knew he would be there. They knew each other very well despite everything.

And then she saw him, his hair tousled, wearing an open-necked shirt, and clutching that leather grip bag which she had seen so often.

His eyes were raking the crowds around as if he were going to see her in their number. He saw nothing, nobody he recognised, but he knew her well enough to assume that she was watching. He put down his bag and raised both his arms in the air.

'I love you, Elsa,' he called out. 'Wherever you are I will always love you.'

Some of the young men near him clapped him on the back approvingly. Declaring love was good.

Elsa sat like stone as the little ferry sailed across the sea to Piraeus, the harbour of Athens. The tears dropped slowly down her face and splashed into her coffee and on to her lap.

'David, my friend, welcome, welcome.' Andreas was delighted to see him.

David wished that he could have a father like this, a man whose face lit up when he approached, not a man whose features had set in discontent and disappointment over his only son for as long as David could remember. They talked easily about the sad funeral yesterday and how Aghia Anna would never be the same again.

'Did you know Manos well?' David asked.

'Yes, we all know each other here, there are no secrets, we know everyone's history. Manos used to come here to play with Adoni and another boy when he was a child. They made a swing on that tree over there, he used to come up here to escape from his family – there were eight of them. Adoni was an only child so we were so happy to have people come up here and play with him. When my wife, who has now gone to God, was cooking she could look out the window and see the boys playing with the old dog and the swing and she knew he was safe. I wonder if she can see from heaven, David . . . see poor Manos buried . . . see Adoni over in Chicago cutting himself off from everything here. If hearts can be heavy in heaven her poor heart will be like a lump of lead.'

David wished so much that he had the gentle insights of someone like Thomas. Thomas would have said something thoughtful and helpful, he might even have found a couple of lines of poetry that would be appropriate.

David could think of no quotation that was remotely suitable.

'I only know about Jewish heaven, and I actually don't know all that much about that,' he said apologetically.

'Well, do the people in Jewish heaven see what's going on down here, do you think?' Andreas asked.

'Yes, I think so, but I believe that they have a broader view of things, like they see the whole picture. That's what I heard, anyway.'

Oddly, it seemed to give Andreas some comfort. He nodded several times.

'Come, David, share a lunch with me, we won't see many visitors today.'

David looked at the open cabinets of food the old man had prepared and he felt a lump in his throat. To have got all this ready and then nobody to arrive.

'I never tried that big pasta dish,' he began.

'David, if you don't mind, I can freeze that one. I only made it this morning. Could I persuade you to have the *moussaka* or the *kalamari*? It's not great hospitality asking you to eat only the items that have to go today.' Andreas laughed at himself, embarrassed.

'I'd prefer the *moussaka*, I only said the pasta because it was big. I didn't want to see all your hard work go to waste,' David said.

'What a kind person you are. Sit here in the sunshine and I will get the glasses and plates . . .'

And David sat wondering what that foolish young man was doing in Chicago when he could be here.

Eleni welcomed Fiona back. It was a shock to see all Shane's things gone, his crumpled shirts and jeans, his canvas bag, his tin of tobacco and whatever else it might contain and papers for rolling cigarettes. She had hoped desperately that he might have left a note for her here with this family. But it hadn't happened.

She felt very dizzy suddenly. Perhaps it was the stuffy room or the realisation that Shane really had gone out of her life.

It would have been so simple for him to scribble her a note and leave it here even if he didn't want to do it at the police station. She felt light-headed and as if she might faint. But she steeled herself in front of the kindly Eleni, whose face was sympathetic and pitying.

Then she felt a hot, wet sensation on her thighs.

It must be sweat.

It was such a hot day.

But as she looked down at her sandals she knew only too well what it was.

And Eleni knew too, as she saw the blood.

The Greek woman helped her to a chair. '*Ela, ela, ela,*' she said and ran for towels.

'Eleni, could you find Vonni for me please, Vonni, you know?' She put her hand to her face to show lines and wrinkles as if to describe Vonni.

'*Xero* Vonni, yes, I know Vonni,' Eleni said, and shouted down to the children.

Fiona closed her eyes.

Vonni would be here soon and would know what to do.

Vonni was sitting opposite Thomas in the apartment over the craft shop.

'I've told you before, I'm telling you again, you

are paying me an enormous number of euros so that this is your place. Because of you I am a rich woman, I will *not* take your pity and sleep in your house.'

'Have you no concept of friendship, Vonni?' he asked.

'I think I have, but then we all think that.'

'Then apply it here. I am asking you, not as my landlady but as my friend, sleep in that little room you decorated so beautifully, sleep there, not where chickens are crapping all over you.'

Vonni pealed with laughter. 'Oh, Thomas, you are *so* Californian, so hygienic, there are no chickens crapping on me. A couple of hens in a different part of the building certainly . . .'

'Stay in that room, Vonni, please. I hate my own company. I'm lonely, I need someone in the place.'

'Oh, come on, Thomas, you love peace and time to yourself. You are a sensitive man, don't offer me charity. Please.'

'You are a sensitive woman, don't throw my offer of friendship right back in my face. Please.'

Just at that moment, they heard children shouting something urgently up the staircase.

'I must go,' she said, standing up.

He reached out and grabbed her wrist. 'Vonni, you are not going anywhere unless you agree to what I offer. Do you hear me?'

'I hear, I agree,' she said to his surprise.

'Good, well then, okay you can go.'

'Come with me if you like, you can help, get us a taxi from the square.' To his even greater surprise she snatched some towels from his bathroom and ran down the steps to talk in Greek to two little boys.

'What's happening?' he asked as he ran after her.

'What's happening is ... that with any luck, Fiona is losing the baby of that little shit who beat her up, but that's not exactly how we are going to phrase it when we get there.'

Thomas ran for a taxi and Vonni bundled Eleni's two little sons into the back seat, congratulating them for having found her. A taxi ride was a rare treat and they were beaming with pleasure. Thomas had been about to ask if he was really necessary on this particular expedition, but he realised Vonni would not have asked him to come unless she thought so. So he smiled at her and climbed in after her.

'Life is never going to be uneventful with my new room-mate,' he said.

'Good man yourself, Thomas,' she said, with a huge wide smile.

They asked the taxi to wait in case they might need him to go to the doctor's. Thomas stayed downstairs watching the little boys play and make occasional journeys to stroke the car in which they had travelled.

They were not very much younger than his boy Bill who had travelled in a car since he could remember. How different people's lives were.

Vonni had gone upstairs and he could hear the women's voices as they spoke in English and Greek. From what he could make out, Fiona would be all right.

Then Vonni came down and reassured him.

'She's going to be fine, she's lost some blood but she's a nurse after all and she's a sensible little thing about everything except that fool. She thinks he'll be upset when he hears. God protect us! Anyway I'll ask the doctor to have a look at her, give her something to sedate her.'

'Is she all right staying here?'

'I don't think so, they don't speak English in any real sense . . . what I was thinking—' Vonni began.

'That she might come and stay with us,' Thomas interrupted.

'No, not that at all. I was going to suggest she spent a couple of days with Elsa, the German girl.'

Thomas shook his head. 'I think Elsa's a bit tied up with her own affairs just now, better if she comes to us,' he said.

'You might find she's not tied up any more,' Vonni said.

'But . . .'

'I hear her German friend left on the eight a.m. ferry,' Vonni said.

'I imagine she must be very upset then.' Thomas was pessimistic.

'No, I think it was her doing, but we needn't necessarily say that we know all this?' Vonni suggested.

'I expect you know where she lives?' Thomas said, smiling.

'I know the apartment building, but perhaps you could take the taxi that's outside and ask her?'

'Would I be the right person?' He was doubtful.

'Nobody better. I'll wait here until you come back.'

A moment later he turned and looked behind. He could see Vonni staggering out with sheets and towels – she was going to wash them there and then. What an extraordinary woman! He wished he knew more about her but he knew she would reveal very little and then only when she wanted to.

'Vonni?'

'You're all right.'

Fiona held out her hand. 'I wanted to say sorry for all the trouble, the blood, the mess and everything.'

'It doesn't matter a bit, you know that. You, of all people, a nurse, know about cleaning up, it's of no importance. What is important is that you are all right, that you recover and get strong again.'

'I don't care if I do or not.'

'Terrific,' Vonni said.

'What?'

'That's terrific. Eleni and I are both worried sick about you, she sent her sons to find me, Thomas brought us all here in a taxi, he's gone to find Elsa to ask if you can stay in her house, we have sent for Dr Leros who is coming to see you here, everyone who has met you and even people who haven't care about you, but you, you don't care. Great.'

'I don't mean that, I meant it's not really important to me what happens now. It's all over, I've lost everything, that's what I meant . . .'

She looked wretched.

Vonni pulled up a chair beside her.

'Very soon Dr Leros will be here, he's a kind man, a real old family doctor person. But you are not meeting him at his best, Fiona, his heart is broken over the accident, and having to pronounce dead, young men whom he delivered into this world. He has been stumbling for hours talking as best he can in English and German to the families of the foreigners who died here, telling them that their loved ones did not suffer much. He doesn't want to hear that a perfectly healthy young girl who has had a miscarriage at a very early stage doesn't care if she lives or dies. Believe me, Fiona, this is not the time to tell him this. Of course it's sad, of course you are upset, but think of other people as you have done all your life as a nurse, as you do about that fellow you claim to love. I will always be here – you can tell me how you may want to die, but don't tell Dr Leros, not today. He has been through just as much as you have.'

Fiona was sobbing. 'I'm sorry, it's just that everyone says Shane was awful, they'll say this was all for the best. It's *not* all for the best, Vonni, truly it isn't. I would have been happy to have his child, I would have loved to have his son or daughter, now it's all gone.'

Vonni held her hand and stroked it. 'I know, I know,' she said meaninglessly, over and over.

'You don't think it was all for the best?'

'Of course I don't! Losing what was on its way to being a person is terrible. I'm so sorry for you. But if the child had lived, you would have had to be strong. All I am saying is that you still have to be strong. And you have friends here, you are not alone. Elsa will be here before too long.'

'Oh, no, why should she take me in, she has her own life, her own fellow, she thinks I was weak to love Shane in spite of everything. She won't want anything to do with me.'

'Mark my words, she will,' said Vonni. 'And I hear Dr Leros arriving.'

'I'll remember what you said,' Fiona said.

'Good girl,' Vonni nodded approvingly.

Eleni's little boys had never known such a day.

A trip in a taxi, people coming and going, sheets and towels being pinned on the line in great numbers to wave in the sunshine. The tall American man with the funny trousers had brought them a big watermelon to share when he came back the second time.

'*Karpouzi!*' he had said proudly, as if delighted that he knew the name of something so ordinary as a melon. They went behind the house and ate it all, then planted the seeds in the earth.

The American man, who was waiting near the taxi until the women came down, watched them with a pleased expression on his face. Then the woman who had been sick came down with Vonni and their mother and the smart woman in a yellow dress who looked like a film star. Dr Leros was with them, and he kept saying the sick woman was fine but she must rest.

The sick woman's bag had been packed for her, so she must be leaving for good.

She kept talking about money and their mother kept shaking her head. Eventually the man with the mad trousers, who must be a millionaire, travelling all day in a taxi, insisted their mother take some notes and then they were all gone.

Except Vonni, who sat down to have coffee with

their mother, but there was something about their faces that made it clear small boys weren't welcome at the kitchen table.

'I'll only stay a couple of days until I get myself together,' Fiona promised when she saw the beautiful apartment that Elsa had.

'I'll be glad of your company,' Elsa assured her as she took out Fiona's clothes from the canvas bag, shook them and hung them up. 'There's an iron here, we can get all domestic later on.'

Fiona looked at Elsa's cream linen dress and navy jacket drying on hangers out on the balcony.

'Aren't you disciplined, Elsa, that's what you were wearing at the funeral yesterday, and look, you have it all laundered already.'

'I'll never wear either of them again but I wanted to give them away to someone, so I washed them first.' Elsa spoke calmly.

'But, Elsa, that's your best outfit – it must have cost a fortune! You just *can't* give it away!' Fiona was aghast.

'Try it on later, and if it fits you, Fiona, and suits you, then you are more than welcome to it, it's just that I'm *never* putting it on again.'

Fiona lay back against the pillow and closed her eyes. It was all too much to take in.

'I'm going to sit and read. It's too hot outside so

I'll be here in the room with you. Try to sleep if you can, but if you want to talk then I'm here.'

'There's not much to talk about now, honestly, is there?' Fiona spoke in a small voice.

'You might feel like it later.' Elsa's smile was warm. She pulled a curtain to darken the room.

'Will you be able to read in the dark?' Fiona asked.

'Sure. There's a nice beam of light coming in here.'

Elsa settled in a chair by the window.

'Did you meet him, Elsa?' Fiona asked.

'Yes. Yes, I did.'

'And are you glad you did?'

'Well, it was just to say goodbye, really. It had to be said, it wasn't easy, but it's finished now. What is it you say . . . onwards and upwards?'

'Dead easy to say, but not to do.' Fiona's voice sounded sleepy. The sedative was beginning to work. Soon she was asleep, breathing regularly. Elsa looked at her as she slept. She must be about twenty-three or twenty-four, but she looked even younger. Hadn't it all been a great mercy? But Elsa had heeded well Vonni's whispered advice that whatever she said she must not even hint that it had all been for the best.

Thomas had worked out when best to call his son, Bill. It would be when the boy was having breakfast.

He dialled the number, wondering what the chances were that he would get straight through to his son. Three to one probably, or maybe the odds were stacked even more against him since he couldn't expect a child to answer the phone when there were two adults there.

As it happened it was Andy.

'Well, hi, Thomas, good of you to call the other night, one helluva scene that must have been.'

'Yeah, it was very tragic.' Thomas felt his voice becoming clipped and curt. There was a silence between them.

'But apart from that, everything else okay?' Andy asked.

The man was insufferable, to call a catastrophe that ripped the soul out of a small town *one helluva scene*.

'Hunky-dory,' Thomas said scathingly. 'Is Bill around?'

'He's helping his mother do the dishes,' Andy said, as if that's all there was to it.

'Sure, and could you perhaps tell him he might dry his hands and come talk to his father phoning from the other side of the world?'

'I'll see if he's through.' Andy was genial about it all.

'Perhaps his mother might risk letting him leave even if he hasn't *quite* finished.' Thomas realised that his fists were clenched with fury. In the distance he was aware that Vonni was watching him from the kitchen door. It didn't help his mood.

'Hi, Dad.' Bill always sounded delighted to hear from him.

'How are things, son? Good?'

'Yeah, fine. Is your island in the Dodecanese, Dad?'

'No, but if you have your big atlas handy I'll tell you where it is . . .'

'No, not beside me, Dad, the books have been put upstairs on the landing,' Bill explained.

'But not the atlas surely, not the dictionary? You *need* these things when you are looking at television, Bill, you can't let him stow away any signs of culture from your life to make room for another rowing machine or whatever.' There was real pain in his voice as he spoke.

At the other end there was a silence as the child tried to think of something to say.

'Get me your mother, Bill, put Shirley on the phone.'

'No, Dad, you and she would only fight, that's what happens. Please, Dad it doesn't *matter* where the atlas is, I can run and get it if you hold on.'

'No, you're right, it's not important where the atlas is. I'll send you an e-mail with a drawing attached and you can look it up. That is if the computer also hasn't been filed away where no one can get at it.'

'No, Dad, of course it hasn't.' He sounded reproachful.

'So what are you going to do today, it's only morning there, isn't it?'

'Yes, well, we'll be going to the shopping mall first, I'm getting new sneakers, and then Andy is going to take me for a run to try them out.'

'Sounds great,' said Thomas in a voice that sounded sepulchral as it went across the thousands of miles between them.

'I miss you, son,' he said eventually since Bill had said no more.

'Yeah, Dad, and I miss you too, a lot, but it *was* you who went away,' the child answered.

'Who told you that? Was it your mother? Andy? Listen to me, Bill, we discussed this endlessly, better for me to go and give you space together as a family—'

'No, Dad, she doesn't say that,' Bill interrupted. 'And Andy doesn't either, I just said I missed you, and that I was still here and you were the one that was gone.'

'I'm sorry, Bill, we're all upset here. So many people died. Please forgive me. I'll call again soon.' He hung up, as low as he had been in years.

Vonni came towards him with a brandy.

'You made a right dog's dinner out of that,' she said.

'You don't understand what it is to have a son,' he said to her, willing the tears away from his eyes.

'Why the hell do you assume I don't have a son?' she asked him, her eyes blazing.

'You do?' He was astonished.

'Yes, so you don't have a monopoly on being a parent.'

'And where is he? Why isn't he with you?'

'Because like you I made a mess of things.'

He knew she would say no more. And yet critical though she was of him it was somehow comforting to have her there. Much better than four walls to cry to, and rail against what was happening to his beloved Bill.

Yorghis drove up to the taverna. Someone had given him a big leg of lamb. He thought maybe Andreas could cook it for his customers. Andreas explained sadly, nobody but David had come to the taverna today and it didn't look likely that anyone would come tonight. But then Andreas had an idea. Why didn't they cook it at the police station, give all those young boys who had worked so hard at the funeral a real dinner?

They would ask David and his friends to join them, and Vonni. Andreas scraped up all the salads into a big bowl. He was pleased and excited at the thought of cooking for people rather than sitting alone in his empty taverna.

'It's not very comfortable, of course, in the police station,' Yorghis said doubtfully. 'Not very welcoming.'

'We'll get those long red cushions. We can put them on benches.' Andreas would not let the idea die. 'David, run up to Adoni's room and get them, will you?'

David looked at him in surprise. Adoni had been gone for years in Chicago yet he still had his own room in this house.

'At the top of the stairs on the left,' Yorghis advised him and David hastened up the narrow steps.

The room had pictures of Panathinaikos, the Athens football team, and posters of a Greek dance troupe; it had images of the Panayia, the Virgin Mary. He was a man of varied tastes, the missing Adoni.

His bed was made as if he were coming back that night, with a bright red rug folded at the end. On the window seats were long narrow red cushions.

David looked out of the window. The afternoon sun shone down on the hills, over the olive groves to the blue bay of Aghia Anna. What *could* that boy be looking at in Chicago, Illinois, that would be one-tenth as beautiful as this? He grabbed the cushions and went down to help them pack Yorghis's van.

'This will cheer us all up, brother Yorghis,' Andreas said with a happy smile.

David looked at him longingly. Imagine having a father who was so easily satisfied with simple things.

They called first to Thomas and left David there. Thomas sounded very pleased at the thought of the feast. He said he would go out and get some wine. Vonni said she'd check out the situation with Elsa and Fiona. She explained admirably briefly to David what had happened and how Fiona might not feel like joining them.

'That's terrible,' David said. 'But maybe when you think of it, it might be all for the—'

'You know the expression *don't go there* . . . David, this is the very occasion that phrase was invented for. You might think it, I might think it, but Fiona most definitely does *not* think it. I thought I'd warn you.'

'Very wise,' David agreed, 'I always say the wrong thing anyway. But what about Elsa? I thought that she had gone off with her German friend?'

'I know I sound like some manifestation of the Sphinx,' Vonni said. 'But to be very honest I wouldn't go there either!'

The young policemen were delighted with the great smells of cooking meat, basted with garlic and oregano. It had been an exhausting and draining time. It was good to relax with their boss, his brother, Vonni and the four tourists. One of the girls looked like a beauty queen, the other very washed out, as if she had been ill.

The two men were very different: one tall and lanky in ludicrous baggy Bermuda shorts with pockets, the other small and serious with spectacles.

All the visitors made attempts to speak a few words of Greek. They knew wine was *krassi*, so the young police officers taught them *aspro* and *kokkino* for white and red, and how to say *yassu* with exactly the right pronunciation.

In return they were taught how to say *cheers*, *prosit*, *l'chaim* and *slainte*.

Andreas carved proudly and the moonlight made patterns on the sea as the clouds raced across the sky.

'It seems so long since we were in Kalatriada,' Fiona said.

'When the night was full of rain beating against the roof and the walls. It was only two nights ago,' Elsa said. 'And so much has happened since!' She reached out and held the hand of Fiona as a gesture of solidarity.

Fiona's eyes filled with tears, and David flashed a glance at Vonni. How wise she had been to mark his card.

Down near the harbour they saw a group of young men gather in front of the little house that belonged to Maria and Manos. And soon they saw other people leave the cafés and restaurants to come and join them.

'What's happening?' Thomas asked, anxious in case anything was wrong.

Yorghis was peering down. 'I can't see, one of you boys go down and see is everything all right,' and he pointed at one of the policemen. It was possible, unlikely but possible, that someone might have wanted to blame Manos for the whole tragedy. They had better be prepared.

Vonni spoke gently. 'It's no problem. Some of the young men said they would like to dance tonight in honour of Manos and his friends, outside his house, in memory of how he used to dance *Syrtaki* and other dances.'

'There isn't usually dancing after a funeral here,' Yorghis said.

'This isn't a usual funeral,' Vonni said quietly.

And as they watched, twelve men with black trousers and white shirts lined up, arms on each other's shoulders. The bouzouki players played a few chords and then they began. Bending, swooping, leaping in the night, as Manos and his friends had done until a few short days ago.

Maria and her children sat on chairs outside their little house. When all this was a long-distant memory, perhaps the children would recall the night that Aghia Anna had come out to dance for their father. The crowd grew ever bigger and even from a distance they could see people wiping tears from their eyes.

Then the crowd began to clap in time to the music and dancing, every single person joining in.

From their veranda at the police station, the group watched too. All of them were wordless, watching the scene. It was so different to anything they had ever seen before.

Then Elsa began to clap in time to the music, and Thomas immediately after her. David and Fiona exchanged glances and joined in, as did Vonni, the young policemen and Andreas and Yorghis. They too had tears on their faces as they encouraged the young men in a dance of homage.

Elsa passed a paper table napkin to Fiona who was crying openly.

'What a wonderful thing to do,' Fiona said when she could speak. 'I'll never forget this night as long as I live.'

'Nor I,' Thomas agreed. 'We are privileged to be able to share it.'

The others didn't trust themselves to speak.

And in an unexpectedly clear voice Fiona said, 'Those same stars are shining on Athens and on all our homes. I wonder what everyone is doing and if they have any idea on earth what we are all doing here just now.'

CHAPTER NINE

In Fiona's home they were talking about her as they did almost every evening. Her mother was looking at the pictures of Aghia Anna in the *Evening Herald*.

'Imagine Fiona being in that very place!' she said in surprise.

'Imagine!' her husband grunted.

'But, Sean, it *was* good of her to ring in case we'd be worried about her. At least she thought that we might be concerned.'

'Why would we be concerned? We didn't know where the hell she was except joined at the hip to that lout.' Fiona's father found very few silver linings in the whole situation, very little cause to see the bright side. He picked up the remote control and turned on the television deliberately to end the conversation.

His wife went over to the set and turned it off.

'Maureen! Why did you do that? I wanted to watch that.'

'No, you didn't want to watch anything, you just didn't want to talk about Fiona.'

'I'm sick to death of Fiona,' Sean said. 'And I couldn't care less if she comes back for the silver wedding.'

'Sean! How can you even say that?'

'I mean it. What's the point of her being here for any celebration, moping, hanging on to the arm of that spaced-out fool, telling us we don't understand him?'

'She's your child as much as mine.'

'She's not a child, according to you . . . she's a woman of twenty-four. She is entitled to make her own decisions, that's what you said when you were standing up for her.'

'Sean, I said that we were only going to alienate her by attacking Shane, that she was old enough to know the choices she was making. I didn't say that any of them were right.'

'Huh,' he said.

'I want you to listen to me. I invited Barbara around tonight to talk to her about everything. They've been friends for fifteen years, since they made their First Communion, and she's as upset as we are.'

'She is not. She's just as bad as Fiona. If a drug-crazed drunken loser like Shane turned up for her, she'd be off too. They're all the same these days.'

'This is *not* the way we must talk, we must try to

keep a lifeline open to Fiona, tell her that we are here when she wants us.'

'I'm not sure that I am here if she wants us. She said some very hurtful things to you as well as to me, remember.'

'That's because we said to her things that she thought were hurtful about Shane.' Maureen struggled to be fair.

'She gave up her family, her home, her good job – for what? For a foul-mouthed drug addict!'

'We can't help who we fall in love with, Sean.'

'Yes, we can. We don't all go out looking for lunatics like Fiona did.' He was unbending.

'She never intended to fall in love with a lunatic, wouldn't it be much easier for her if she'd found a nice banker, or a doctor or a fellow who ran his own business? But that didn't happen.'

'You've got very forgiving all of a sudden.' He was confused.

'I'll tell you something, I was touched that she thought to ring us when this terrible thing happened, whether we knew she was there or not doesn't matter.'

The doorbell rang.

'That's Barbara, be nice, be reasonable please, Sean, she may be our only link with Fiona, our only hope.'

'She's heard nothing from Madam either,' he scoffed.

'Sean!'

'All right,' he said.

In David's house in the smart suburbs of Manchester they had been looking at a television documentary on the events in Aghia Anna and were talking about their son.

'It must have been a terrible thing to see,' David's mother said.

'It must indeed have been terrible if he telephoned us,' his father agreed.

'He has been away for six weeks, Harold, we have had ten letters from him. He does keep in touch.'

'Some of them were only picture postcards,' David's father said.

'But he goes and finds a stamp and a postbox,' his mother defended him.

'Miriam, this is the twenty-first century, the boy could find an Internet café, send an e-mail, behave like a normal person.'

'I know, I know.'

They sat in silence for a while.

'Miriam, should I have been different, please tell me?' He looked at her begging for the truth.

She reached for his hand and stroked it. 'You have been a wonderful husband, a wonderful father,' she said.

'So why is our son out in this one-horse town in Greece if I was so wonderful? Tell me that.'

'Perhaps it's my fault, Harold, maybe it was I who drove him away.'

'No, of course not, he adores you, we know that. It's the business he doesn't want. Should I have said something like *be* an artist, *be* a poet, *be* whatever you want to be? Should I? Is this what was needed? Tell me!'

'I don't think so, he always knew you wanted him to run the company, he knew that since his bar mitzvah.'

'So why was that such a crime? I built up this business for my father. He came to England with nothing. I worked day and night to try and show him that his suffering had all been worth while in the end. Where was the problem? I try to hand over to my only son a thriving business, that's bad?'

'I know, Harold, I know all this.' She was trying to soothe him.

'If you understand it, why can't he?'

'Let me tell him, Harold, please let me tell him.'

'No, a thousand times no. I will not have his pity. If I can't have his love and respect, nor even his company, I will not settle for his pity.'

Shirley and Bill came back from the shopping mall. Andy had gone up to the university where he and other athletic members of the community gathered to motivate some of the students training for a marathon. They thought it was cool that old guys, who must be well into their thirties, still liked running.

Bill helped his mother to unpack the shopping and stack it away.

'You're a great kid,' she said unexpectedly.

'Am I?'

'Sure you are. I've never loved anyone on earth more than I love you.'

'Aw, come on, Mom . . .' He was embarrassed.

'No, I mean it. Truly I do.'

'But your own mom and dad? What about them?'

'No, they were fine but it wasn't nearly as strong as the love I feel for you.'

'And what about Dad when you loved him? And Andy now?'

'That's different, Bill, believe me. There's something absolutely earth-shaking about the love you have for your child, it's unconditional.'

'What's that?'

'It means that there are no ifs and buts. You are this special kind of person, nothing can get in the way of it. I wish I could explain properly, but when you love a guy or a woman I guess you actually can stop loving them. You don't intend to but it happens, but never with your child . . .'

'And would Dad feel the same about me as you do?'

'Totally the same, Bill, your dad and I didn't see eye to eye about a few things, you know that, but we both thought and do think you were the best thing that ever happened to us. We never argue about you. Never. We just want the best for you.'

'Does Dad still love you, Mom?'

'No, honey, he still respects me and likes me I think, but love, no. We just share our love for you.' She smiled at him encouragingly, hoping he would agree.

Bill thought about it for a while. 'So why doesn't he act like that?' he asked.

'I think he does,' Shirley said, surprised.

'I don't think he does,' Bill said. 'I think he wants me to miss him and be sorry he's not here, and that's very unfair. *He's* the one who went away. I didn't. I stayed right here.'

Birgit saw Claus coming into the newsroom.

'You're back from Greece!' she said, delighted.

'Hi, Birgit.' Claus, the chief cameraman, had no illusions that Birgit was happy to see him. If he were back, then Dieter would be back too. That was what interested her. And interested most of the women in the television network.

Claus sighed.

Dieter didn't even try, and the women just fell over themselves for him.

He waited until Birgit asked about Dieter. He assumed it would be thirty seconds. He was wrong: it was even sooner.

Birgit didn't waste time on preliminaries such as saying it all must have been very sad. 'Dieter back too?' she asked casually.

'No, actually.' Birgit was a hard woman. Claus actually savoured telling her the bad news. 'No, he stayed on a bit. He met an old friend out there. Amazing coincidence, wasn't it?'

'An old friend? Some guy he knew in the press corps?'

'No, it was some woman who used to work here actually. He met Elsa.'

It was a pleasing moment to see her face.

'But it's all over between them,' Birgit said.

'I wouldn't hold your breath, Birgit,' Claus said and moved on.

Adoni looked at the newspaper pictures of the village where he had grown up. He saw the face of his friend Manos whom he had known all his life. There was a picture of Maria too. Adoni had danced at their wedding.

How extraordinary that newspapers all over America would have pictures and stories of his home town. But he wouldn't tell anyone here in Chicago. He had come here all those years ago because Eleni back in Aghia Anna had given him a contact. One of her cousins worked here, he gave a job to a boy who had come with a personal recommendation.

The cousin had moved on but Adoni had stayed. He liked it here, even though he was sometimes lonely. But he would say nothing about the tragedy having taken place in his home town. Why bring grief on himself?

The people here in the greengrocer's where he worked knew little about him and his background. If he told them then they would have to know why he didn't stay in touch, they would learn about his fight with his father, the years of silence. They would never understand. These people that he worked with just lived for family, their fathers were in and out of their houses all the time. What would they think of a father and son who hadn't spoken to each other for nine years?

Of course he could call his father to offer sympathy over what had happened to Aghia Anna. But then his father would take this as some sign of weakness, a giving in, an admission that Adoni had been in the wrong. His father knew where he was. If he wanted to say something then let him say it.

Shane didn't know how to use the Métro in Athens. When they had been here before Fiona had worked it out. The whole thing was called the *Ilektrikos* or something. Had she bought tickets in a kiosk? Or was that for the trolley buses? He couldn't remember.

Shane knew that he wanted to go to the Exarchia

area, he had heard on the ferry that it was full of *ouzo* shops and tavernas. He still had plenty of grass in his bag, he could sell it there. Then he would sit down, work out what he would do. He was free now, free as a bird. Nobody would be coming at him with cracked notions that he should be a waiter for the rest of his life in a backwater. Fiona must have been soft in the head to suggest it.

In the end, of course, like everyone else she had let him down. But then Shane had learned to expect that of people. And she wasn't really pregnant. He knew that. If she had been she wouldn't have gone off and left him when he was in the police station. She could well be on her way home to her awful family in Dublin. They would certainly kill a fatted calf for her once they realised that Shane was no longer around.

He worked out that he needed the Métro stop called Omonia. God, they had really ridiculous names here, and writing that nobody could read as well.

'Come in, Barbara.' Fiona's mother ushered her in.

'You're out late in the evening.' Fiona's father didn't sound very welcoming.

'You know how it is, Mr Ryan, eight a.m. to eight p.m. and we're an hour from the hospital.' Barbara was cheerful and taking no nonsense from anyone. She threw herself into an armchair as she had done for years in this house, her red hair tousled, her face tired after a long day's work.

'Will you have tea, Barbara, or something stronger?'

'Oh, I could murder a gin, Mrs Ryan, specially if we are going to talk about Shane,' Barbara said apologetically.

'Sean?'

'Well, if we're going to have to talk about him then I need an anaesthetic, too,' he said.

'I was wondering if we could write to Fiona and say that we sort of misunderstood the situation.' Fiona's mother served the gin and tonics and sat down looking from one to the other.

Her husband glowered at her. 'I think we understood the situation only too well. Our daughter is infatuated with a bog-ignorant criminal. What else is there to understand?'

'But it hasn't worked, our saying that. She's hundreds of miles away. And I miss her, Sean, every moment of the day. I'd love her to be coming in, like Barbara now, telling us about the kind of day she had. We've only driven her away by our attitude. Don't you think, Barbara?'

'I agree with Mr Ryan, actually, we didn't misunderstand anything. Shane is a real out-and-out bastard because he manipulates her, he makes things seem to be her fault, not his. He plays the victim card, the rest of the world has a down on him, that's the hardest bit to deal with.'

'What I find the hardest is that they say they *love* each other.' Maureen Ryan's face was troubled.

'He's never loved anyone but himself. He'll only stay with her for as long as it suits him and then she'll be alone, miles away with no friends and humiliated. She won't want to come back to us. She'll know that we'll all be thinking, I told you so, even if we manage not to say it.'

'You miss her as much as we do.' Fiona's father sounded surprised.

'Of course I do, I miss her at work every day and I miss going out with her in the evening. I think of a dozen things to tell her and then remember she's gone . . . I was wondering if we could try to build some kind of a bridge?'

'What kind of bridge?' Sean Ryan didn't hold out much hope.

'Well, could you write her a letter sort of implying that we all know now she and Shane will be together in the long run? And I could do the same, like asking would she and Shane be home for your silver wedding or Christmas, something like that?'

'But we can't assume that she's going to be with him for ever, Barbara. What kind of message are we giving the other children if they think we accept Shane as part of their sister's life?'

'Listen, Mrs Ryan, he *is* part of her life, they've

gone off to live together, for God's sake, but deep down I've a feeling it's not going to last that long, and if we pretend that we think it's normal then we stop being part of the Bad Cruel World that's beating up on Poor Misunderstood Shane.' Barbara looked from one to the other.

Fiona's father was shrugging helplessly as if to say it was all beyond him. Her mother's face was working as if to try and stop the tears.

Barbara gave it one more go. 'Believe me, I don't like it either, and I don't like sitting here talking about my friend Fiona behind her back, but I think that we've got to do something or else we've lost her entirely.'

The letter was pushed through the door and fell to the floor. Miriam Fine went to see who could possibly be delivering something by hand at this time of night.

It was a big thick envelope addressed to them both. It contained some kind of heavy card. She brought it in to her husband and they opened it together.

It was the confirmation that Harold Fine had won the coveted Businessman of the Year award and details of the ceremony. It would be presented in November at the Town Hall before an invited audience. They hoped that he would ask a group of family and friends to join them for drinks first with the Mayor and dinner later.

'Oh, Harold, I'm so pleased for you, to see it there in black and white,' she said, tears in her eyes.

'It's amazing.' He looked at the document as if it might fall away or crumble in his hands.

'David will be so proud and pleased, we'll tell him the actual invitation has arrived. It will make it real for him too. I know he will come home for it all,' Miriam said.

'Let's not be too confident, Miriam, from where David stands, businessmen are bad enough. A Businessman of the Year would be the worst thing he could encounter.'

'Hi there, Bill.'

'Hi, Andy.'

Andy sat down beside him on the swinging seat in front of the house.

'You down about something, kid? Want a run?'

'No, running doesn't solve everything.' He didn't even look up.

'You're so right there, kid, but it kind of blocks bad things out for a bit.'

'You don't have bad things, Andy.'

'I don't, huh? Then I've been doing a pretty good job hiding things.' He punched Bill affectionately in the arm, but this time the boy winced and withdrew from him.

'Sorry, kid.' Andy looked at a loss.

'It's okay, it's not your fault.'

'So whose fault is it?' Andy asked.

'I don't know, I think it's mine. I wasn't enough for them. Mom and Dad. I didn't make them happy enough.'

'They're both crazy about you, kid, it's the one thing that they really see eye to eye about.'

'So my mom says, but maybe she just wants me to think that.'

'Your dad says it too, he told me so before he went away.'

'But he went away, Andy.'

'He did it for you, kid, to give you space, so that you could get used to me being around and feel part of your mom's life and mine together. It was good of him to do that.'

'I don't want space,' Bill said.

'What do you want, Bill?'

'I suppose I want him and Mom to love each other still, but I can't have that so I guess I want him to be living nearby. You and Mom don't mind if I see him a lot. That's right, isn't it?' He looked anxiously at Andy.

'Sure it's right, you know it is.'

'And does he know, does Dad know that?'

'Ah, Bill, you know he does.'

'Then if he knows this, why did he have to go so far away?' Bill asked simply.

*

Hannah, a secretary in the television centre, had overheard the conversation between Claus and Birgit. She could hardly credit it. Elsa had gone so far away to leave what had been the love of her life and this catastrophe had brought them together.

'Claus, excuse me, can I have a word?'

'Of course!' Everyone liked Hannah, a bright, helpful, confident young woman. She had been Elsa's friend.

'I just wanted to ask is she coming back?' Hannah asked. She too spent no time beating about the bush.

'Would you like her to come back?' Claus asked gently.

'For me, I would. I would like to have my friend back home again. But for her, I think she might be better to stay away.' Hannah spoke from the heart.

'I wish I could tell you what has happened, but truthfully I don't know,' Claus said. 'Dieter told us to go home ahead of him. So of course we did. But she looked different. She wasn't the same Elsa that we know. She was changed somehow, as if she had made up her mind.'

'I see.' Hannah was doubtful.

'I know you probably think that men are hopeless about reading the signs but, believe me, you would have found it difficult to know what was happening.'

'Oh, I know, Claus, it's not easy. Thank you for telling me. We can only wait and hope.'

'And what are you hoping for, Hannah?'

'I'm much more hopeless than you! I actually don't know what I hope. I suppose I hope things turn out for the best,' said Hannah truthfully.

Adoni decided he would telephone his father. He would do it quickly before he changed his mind. It would be evening in Greece, his father would be at the taverna. It would be busy so his father would not be able to talk for long which was just as well. Adoni would say that he was very sorry about the tragedy and that he sent his sympathies. They would not talk about what had passed between them.

He could hear the telephone ringing.

It rang and rang and there was no reply. He must have dialled the wrong number. He dialled again. But in the empty taverna the phone rang and nobody answered.

Before he had left Aghia Anna, he had installed an answering machine for his father. Evidently the old man had never learned to switch it on.

Adoni eventually hung up. In many ways it was probably all for the best.

Shane found exactly the place he was looking for. This was his clientele. It was just the kind of place he would have gone if he had been looking to score. It didn't matter that he didn't know the language. There was an international language over this sort of thing. He spoke to a guy who was some kind of thicko, who understood nothing, then to another who shrugged at him.

The third man looked more promising.

'How much?' the man asked. He was small and round with quick dark eyes.

'How much do you want?' Shane asked.

'Well, how much do you have?' the man wanted to know.

'Enough,' said Shane.

At that moment there was the flash of a Polaroid camera and then another. Right in his face.

'What the hell . . .?' Shane began. Then he felt a hand on his collar, almost choking him. The round face of the man with the quick dark eyes was an inch from Shane's own face.

'Listen to me good. We have two pictures of you, one in this bar, one we will show to the police. If they see you trying to deal again it will be very, very bad for you.'

'You *said* you wanted to buy.' Shane choked the words out somehow.

'This is my father's bar, my family runs this place. I would go very far from here very quickly. That is my uncle holding you. He is expecting you to apologise and leave. In twenty seconds from now.'

'I don't know how to apologise in Greek.'

'*Signomi* will do.'

'*Sigomi*, is it?' Shane stuttered.

'*Signomi* . . . learn to say it, you little shit, and be pleased you got away so easily.'

'I could come back,' Shane threatened.

The man laughed.

'You could, of course. Ten seconds.'

'*Signomi!*' Shane cried over his shoulder to the older man who was holding him. Then the grip was released and Shane staggered out of the door into the warm Athens night.

CHAPTER TEN

Thomas woke with a slight headache. It didn't take him long to remember why. The red wine they had drunk last night at the police station had not been allowed to age for any respectable time. Yorghis said it could well have been made last month.

Still, a couple of cups of good coffee would cure that. Maybe he would go out and get fresh oranges and hot crusty rolls for breakfast. Possibly Vonni would have a hangover too. There would be solidarity in the cure.

But when he got up, he saw the door to the spare bedroom was open. The bed was neatly made. No sign of any personal possessions around the place. She was truly using it only as a bed for the night. He wondered where she was now. Back in the henhouse? Or like the Pied Piper with a group of children at the harbour?

She was such a self-sufficient little figure, hair braided around her head, suntanned lined face with its broad smile, that made it impossible to know what age she was. Forty? Fifty? Sixty? Hard to know from anyone how long she had been in Aghia Anna. And she told little or nothing about herself, so you would be a long time guessing.

Thomas yawned and went into the kitchen. She had beaten him to it. There were four large oranges on the table and, wrapped in a little check cloth to keep them warm, some fresh bread rolls. Thomas sighed with pleasure and sat down to his breakfast.

Fiona was still asleep.
Elsa left her a note.

Gone down to the harbour. Didn't want to wake you. Why don't you come and meet me at noon. Bring a swimsuit if you feel like it and we can have something in that nice place with the blue and white tablecloths. I can't remember its name. I'd like that.
   Love,
   Elsa

She looked at Fiona as if she were a younger and more foolish sister. To think that, back in the real world, this girl was a competent nurse and yet she was still so foolish as to believe that Shane was somewhere in Athens, worried and concerned about her.

Elsa walked slowly through the narrow streets looking around her at the way life went on. The people washed the pavements in front of their little shops, and laid out their wares. In the cafés and restaurants they were laboriously writing their menus on big blackboards.

There wasn't the same carefree, cheerful way as before the accident. But at least they were getting on with it. Or pretending to. Like Elsa herself.

She felt she was making a fairly good job of hiding the fact that she was numb and empty inside. She thought she was managing quite well, all things considered. She had talked well to the others last night, she had been a rock of strength to Fiona who had cried on her shoulder when they came back.

She was able now to nod and smile at people she passed, saying, '*Kalimera*,' here and there.

But she felt very light-headed and unreal.

She wished that she belonged somewhere, that there were people who cared about her. She had never felt so isolated. No family, no love, no job, and since she had left Germany . . . no home. A father who had abandoned her, a mother who had only been ambitious for her, not loving, a lover who had lied and wanted to go on lying for ever.

Somebody in a shabby, broken-looking van hooted at her. Elsa put up her hand to shield her eyes from the sun and see who it was.

It was Vonni with a load of children.

'We're going for a swim on a really fantastic beach you might not know. Would you like to come?'

'Great, I said I'd meet Fiona at noon in the harbour but I'd be back by then, right?'

Elsa was glad that she had her bathing suit and straw hat in her basket. She was now prepared to go anywhere.

Vonni nodded at her in agreement. 'Oh certainly, we'll be back by then. I can't expose children to the midday sun.' She said something in Greek to the five- and six-year-olds in the back of the van and they all smiled at her and chorused, '*Yassu*, Elsa!'

Elsa felt a sudden lump in her throat as if suddenly her wish had been answered. As if in a small way she did belong somewhere. Just for a while.

David had hired a bicycle and travelled five kilometres to where the family he stayed with had told him there was a wonderful beach. He would love to have met the others from last night and talked about the evening, the dancing, the way people had shown respect. But nobody had suggested it and David hated the thought of being a hanger-on.

He puffed up some hills and sailed down the slopes on the other side. The countryside was so beautiful. Why would anyone want to live in a crowded city? Spending hours commuting, breathing in diesel fumes, when they could have this?

He came to where the beach must be and to his disappointment he saw first a parked van. And then he saw Elsa and that strange older woman Vonni, already down on the sand with eight or nine children.

He watched as Vonni lined the children up at the water's edge. She was making great signs with her arms. The children were nodding in agreement. She must be explaining that she would go in first with Elsa, and that nobody must go out any further than the grown-ups.

David lay on a grassy mound and watched them all. Elsa was so beautiful in her elegant turquoise swimsuit, her short blonde hair reflecting the sun; she had a light suntan and moved gracefully in and out of the sea, playing with the children.

Vonni, small and swarthy, her hair in plaits over her head, wore a functional black swimming costume that would not have been in fashion twenty years back. She too ran in and out of the little waves calling and encouraging the youngsters to join her and helping the more timid ones by holding a hand under the chin.

David longed to join them but he felt he would be intruding. Just then Elsa saw him.

'*Ela, ela*, David, come and swim, it is total magic!'

Awkwardly he went to join them. He had his

swimming trunks on under his shorts. He took off his glasses and left them on top of his neatly folded clothes.

He greeted the children. '*Yassas, ime Anglos.*'

'As if they ever thought you were anything but English!' Vonni said, teasing him.

'I suppose so,' David said ruefully.

'Come on, David, you're better than ninety per cent of the tourists, you take the trouble to learn a few words of Greek. People are so delighted with that, you wouldn't believe it.'

'Are they?' He was childishly pleased.

One of the children splashed him with a handful of water. 'Very good, *poli kala*,' he said.

'I hope you have six children, David, you'll be a wonderful father,' Vonni said unexpectedly.

Thomas walked down to the harbour. Everything was nearly back to normal. Many of the fishermen had already set out to sea, others were there mending their nets.

They nodded at him. He had been here now for many days, he wasn't a stranger, someone passing through.

One of the men said something which Thomas could not understand. He wished now that he had studied a phrase book like David had, he might have been able to get some hint as to what they were saying.

175

'I'm sorry, *signomi*,' he apologised.

A man with many tattoos and the appearance of a sailor said, 'My friend said you and your friends are good people, that you have shared our tragedy.'

Thomas looked at him, puzzled. 'We are all so sad for what has happened here and we were so very touched by the dancing last night. We will never forget it.'

'When you go back to your land you four will talk about it, you and your friends?' The sailor man obviously knew them and was going to translate for the others.

Thomas spoke slowly. 'We are from four different countries – Germany, England, Ireland and the United States – but we will all bring this memory back to our lands when we go,' he said eventually.

'We thought you had been friends for ever,' said the man with the tattoos.

Fiona woke up and read the note. Wasn't life so odd that she should meet by accident such a kind and generous girl? Elsa was almost as good a friend to her as Barbara had been. What an amazing chance! Shane would be so glad when she told him.

He *would* get in contact soon, no matter what they all thought. Fiona washed her hair and used Elsa's hairdryer. She didn't look too bad. Pale, a bit wishy-washy but nothing that would frighten the birds off the trees, as her father used to say about people who didn't look well.

Fiona thought about her father for a while. He had been such a loving, marvellous father until she had brought Shane home. She wished in many ways that she could be there for her parents' silver wedding party.

But that was her father's mistake.

He had been so definite about Shane. No time must be spent thinking about it now. She must get on with her life until Shane sent for her. She would dress as well as she could and then walk slowly down to the harbour. She did not want Elsa to think she was some kind of pathetic loser.

She would show her best face.

They left David sitting on the beach learning his ten phrases for the day, then Vonni let the children off in the square and dropped Elsa off from her van at the harbour shortly after 11 a.m.

'Thank you for your company,' Vonni said.

'How do the people in Aghia Anna hand over their children to you, Vonni?' Elsa asked.

'I don't know, they've seen me here for many years now, they believe that I am fairly reliable, I suppose.' Vonni was not at all certain.

'How many years, Vonni?'

'I came here over thirty years ago.'

'What!' Elsa said in shock.

'You asked me. I told you.' Vonni looked impassive.

'Indeed. Forgive me. I am sure you are a person who does not want people to intrude,' Elsa apologised.

'As it happens, I don't at all mind people asking reasonable questions. I came to Aghia Anna when I was seventeen to be with the man I loved.'

'And were you with him?' Elsa asked.

'Yes and no. I'll tell you another time.' Vonni revved up the van and drove away.

'Thomas!'

He looked up at her from where he sat on an old wooden box looking out of the mouth of the harbour to sea where the wind was lifting the waves.

'Good to see you, Elsa, would you like a nice easy chair?' He pulled over another old box for her.

She sat down as elegantly as if she really were in a drawing room.

He realised suddenly what a good television presenter she must be. Or have been. Never fussed or at a disadvantage, always in control.

'Your hair is damp, were you swimming?'

'Yes, there's a truly beautiful beach in a little lagoon about five kilometres away. Up that coast,' she pointed.

'Don't tell me you've walked ten kilometres today!' He was disconcerted.

178

'No, shamefully, Vonni drove me both ways. We met David there, he's the fit one, he has actually rented a bicycle. Am I imagining it, Thomas, or is the sea much more attractive here than anywhere else?'

'It sure beats my part of California anyway, very flat where we are. Nice sunsets, but no surf, no changing colours like this.'

'You don't want to think about the sea in Germany, freezing cold up there by Holland and Denmark. Certainly not like this. No wonder people get inspired by the place. I mean, I know it's meant to be a reflection of the sky, but don't tell me that water isn't dark blue.'

'Roll on, thou deep and dark blue Ocean – roll!' Thomas quoted.

To his astonishment Elsa continued:

Ten thousand fleets sweep over thee in vain;
Man marks the earth with ruin – his control
Stops with the shore . . .

He looked at her open-mouthed. 'You can quote English poetry. How dare you be so well educated!'

Elsa laughed, pleased at the praise. 'We had an English teacher at school who loved Byron. I think she was in love with him actually. If you had picked another poet I wouldn't have done so well!'

'But I mean it. I couldn't quote you one verse

179

of German poetry, not a line. What am I talking about, German poetry? I can't even speak a word of the German language.'

'Yes, you can, you said *Wunderbar*, and *Prosit* last night,' she consoled him.

'I think I said *Prosit* a little too often last night as it happens . . . oh, I've remembered another German word. *Reisefieber*.'

Elsa pealed with laughter. 'What a marvellous word to know . . . how on earth do you know that?'

'It means "journey fever", doesn't it? Being in a panic at airports and railway stations?'

'That's exactly what it means, Thomas. Imagine you knowing that!' She was impressed.

'There was a guy in the faculty who kept coming up with great words like that, we all took them over.'

They sat companionably together as if they had known each other all their lives.

No wonder the fishermen had thought they had been friends for ever.

Vonni drove the van back to Maria's house.

Maria was sitting at the table in front of an empty coffee cup.

'It's getting harder, not easier,' she said. 'I thought that was Manos coming back in his van.'

'Of course it's getting harder, it's sinking in and that's what hurts so much.' Vonni hung up the keys on a hook on the wall and then produced a pot of hot coffee she had bought at the taverna across the road and some flaky *baklava*.

Maria looked up with her tear-stained face. 'You always know what people want,' she said gratefully.

'I don't indeed. Me? I get it wrong and make more mistakes than the whole of Aghia Anna put together,' Vonni protested.

'I can't remember any,' Maria said.

'That's because you're too young. My more spectacular mistakes were made before you were born.'

Vonni moved around the kitchen, picking up things here and there, rinsing cups, restoring order without seeming to.

Then she sat down.

'The dancing was beautiful last night. He would have loved it,' she said.

'I know.' Maria was weeping again. 'And last night I felt strong and as if his spirit was still here. That feeling has gone today.'

'Well, it might come back when I tell you my plan,' Vonni said, passing her a piece of kitchen paper to dry her tears.

'Plan?'

'Yes, I'm going to teach you to drive.'

Maria actually managed a weak watery smile. 'Drive? Me drive? Vonni, stop joking. Manos wouldn't even let me hold the keys of the van.'

'But he would want you to drive now, I know he would.'

'No, Vonni, he wouldn't, he'd think I'd kill myself and everyone in Aghia Anna.'

'Well, we'll have to prove him wrong then,' Vonni said. 'Because you'll have to drive for your new job.'

'Job?'

'Oh, yes, you're going to help me in the shop, aren't you? And a lot of your work will involve driving to places like Kalatriada and collecting stuff. Save me trekking for miles on buses.'

'But you can drive there in the van, Vonni, it's just standing there . . .'

'No, I can't. Manos would hate that, he saved long and hard for that van, he wouldn't want you just handing it away. No, he'd be so proud of you if you used it for your work.'

And, magically, Maria smiled again. A real smile this time. It was as if she saw his spirit back in the house again and she was squaring up to him as she had done so often when he was alive.

'Right, Manos, this is going to amaze you,' she said.

David came across them during the driving lesson up on a big patch of waste ground at the top of the town.

'*Siga, siga,*' Vonni was screaming as the van jerked and shuddered.

'What does that mean, *siga*? I've often heard it,' David asked, interested.

'Well, you never heard it said with such fervour as this time.' Vonni had got out of the van, mopped her brow and taken some deep breaths. Maria sat gripping the steering wheel as if her hands had been glued to it.

'It means "slow down" but the lady doesn't get the concept.'

'That's the wife of Manos, isn't it?' David peered at the woman still clutching the wheel.

'God knows I never thought of myself as in any way co-ordinated but compared to herself there I could be a Formula One driver,' Vonni said, closing her eyes momentarily.

'Does she need to drive?' David asked.

'I thought so this morning, now I'm not so sure. But of course I had to open my big mouth and suggest it so now we have to keep at it.' Vonni sighed.

'I taught my mother to drive when no one else could. Three driving schools gave up on her,' David said slowly. 'Perhaps I could give it a go?'

'How did you do it?' Vonni said, with hope beginning to show in her eyes.

'I was very patient, I never raised my voice once and I spent hours on the clutch,' he said.

'Would you, David? Oh, dear good kind David, please would you?'

'Sure. If it would help. You'll have to tell me the words for brake and accelerator and gears, though.'

He wrote them down in his notebook and went over to the van. Maria looked at him doubtfully as he sat in beside her.

'*Kalimera*,' he said formally and shook hands.

'How do you say, "Let's go"?' he asked Vonni.

'*Pame*, but don't say it yet or she'll drive you splat into that wall.'

'*Pame*, Maria,' David said gently and with a lurch they moved forward.

Vonni looked on, amazed. She watched as he taught Maria to stop the van. He really did have a gift. The look of terror was leaving Maria's face.

'Drive her home when you've finished, will you?' Vonni said.

'What about my bike?'

'I'll cycle down on it and leave it for you at Maria's house.'

Before he could answer she had swung her leg over the man's bicycle and was heading off down to the town.

David turned back to his pupil. '*Pame* again, Maria,' he said gently, and this time she started the van without stalling it.

Fiona sat at a table outside the little café and was surprised to see Vonni streaking by on a bike. Vonni saw her and did a wheelie turn to come back.

'All on your own?' she asked.

'I'm meeting Elsa here at midday.'

'Oh yes, Elsa did tell me. She helped me take the children for a swim.'

'Did she?' Fiona sounded envious.

'Yes, and David came by on his bicycle, he lent it to me, I'm just leaving it at Maria's house for him. David's taking his life in his hands and teaching her to drive.'

'Lord, everyone's really settling in.' Fiona was wistful.

Vonni leaned David's bike against one of the empty tables.

'I'll sit with you until Elsa arrives,' she said.

Fiona was pleased. 'Will you have an *ouzo*?' she asked.

'No, just a *metrio kafethaki*, little coffee,' Vonni said.

They sat there peacefully watching the life of the harbour around them. That was an interesting thing about Vonni, Fiona observed. She had a great sense of stillness. She knew that you don't need to talk all the time. It was very restful.

'Vonni?'

'Yes, Fiona?'

'I was wondering, could I get some kind of a job here, here in Aghia Anna? I could learn Greek. I could help Dr Leros. What do you think?'

'Why do you want to stay here?' Vonni's voice was gentle.

'It's beautiful here and I want to be sort of settled when Shane comes back for me.'

Vonni said nothing at all.

'You think he might not come back, don't you?' Fiona cried. 'Like everyone else you judge a book by its cover, you don't know him like I do.'

'True.'

'Believe me, Vonni, he has never in his whole life had anyone who understood him until he met me.'

Vonni leaned forward and moved Fiona's hair gently from her face to reveal the bruise. 'And he took a fine way to show you how much he appreciated that you understood him,' she said.

Fiona pulled back angrily. 'That's not the way it is, he is heartbroken that he raised his hand to me, I know that.'

'Sure.'

'Don't be so lofty and patronising, I've had enough of that from everyone at home.'

'Everyone who loves you, I imagine.'

'It's not real love, it's choking claustrophobia, and wanting everyone to settle down and marry a civil servant or a bank clerk and get a mortgage and have two children.'

'I know.' Vonni sounded sympathetic.

'So if you know why don't you believe that Shane will come back for me?'

'You really believe he will?'

'Well, of course I do. We love each other, we went away together for ever. Why wouldn't he come back?'

Vonni swallowed and looked away.

'No, please, tell me. I'm sorry I shouted at you, Vonni, I just get so upset when people come out against Shane, I keep thinking that this is going to go on for ever until we're an old, old couple. Perhaps you know something I don't.'

She looked so anxious, she had her hand on Vonni's weather-beaten arm, her eyes were wide, wanting to know more.

Vonni paused.

After all, she was responsible for Shane going to Athens, she had advised the police chief Yorghis to ship him away from Aghia Anna, she did therefore owe Fiona some kind of explanation. But what could she tell her but bad news?

Yorghis had given Shane a card with the address and phone number of the police station.

Eleni had said she offered Shane a pencil and paper to write a note as he was packing his case, and he had refused it. None of this would bring Fiona any cheer.

'No, I don't think I know anything that you don't,' she said slowly. 'But I was going to suggest that Shane might not expect you to stay on here, you know, without him. If he does contact you . . .'

'He will, of course he will.'

'When he does contact you then, he might contact you back in Dublin. Isn't that a possibility?'

'No, he'd know I'd never go back there, back to them, and admit they were right. Shane knows me too well, he'd never think of ringing me back there. No, one day he'll get off one of those ferries. I want to be here and settled when he does.'

'It's not realistic, Fiona, this is a holiday place. Not a place to settle down in.'

'You did,' Fiona said simply.

'It was different then.'

'Why was it different then?'

'It was, that's all, and I came here not on my own like you are but to live with a man from Aghia Anna.'

'You did?'

'I did indeed, years and years ago, there were hardly any tourists here then, I was considered very unusual, a slut of course. In those days people here, as well as at home, got engaged and married and everything.'

Vonni looked out to sea remembering it all, a different time.

'So then you know it's possible to leave Ireland and come to a beautiful place like this and be happy?' Fiona was trying desperately to find similarities between them.

'In a way,' Vonni said.

'You're not going to tell me you regret it,' Fiona said. 'You're part of the place here, it must have been the right decision.'

'No, heavens, no, what a waste of time regret is, it must be the most useless emotion of all time.' Then she fell silent again.

'And what happened to the . . . er . . . man . . . from Aghia Anna?' Fiona felt daring and asked her a direct question.

Vonni looked her straight in the eye. 'Stavros? I don't know really,' she said and closed down the conversation.

Vonni said she had a hundred things to do and she wanted to thank God above that one of them was not giving Maria a driving lesson.

'Are you all right here on your own?' she asked Fiona.

'I'm fine, and thank you so much for being so kind,' Fiona said politely.

She was glad that the older woman was leaving. She should not have asked Vonni what happened to her man. She saw Elsa coming towards her and waved.

'I'll leave you in good hands then,' Vonni said, and left.

Elsa sat down and told Fiona about the morning on the beach. They ordered a salad and talked easily about life on this island. Just as they were finishing they saw an old van come sputtering past them. It was being driven somewhat erratically by Maria, and David was in the passenger seat. They watched as he opened the van door for her, patted her encouragingly on the back, and finally bent over and kissed her hand.

'God, isn't he going to make someone a wonderful husband!' Elsa said admiringly.

'Yeah, isn't it a tragedy that we can't in a million years fall for people like that,' Fiona said with a heavy sigh. For some reason they both found it funny and were still laughing when David cycled by. He came in to join them.

'Was she dreadful? Vonni said she was a nightmare.'

'Vonni exaggerates. She's okay, just nervous and naturally very upset about everything. Vonni's going to give her a job when she can drive. She's one amazing woman.'

Fiona was going to tell them about the man, Stavros, all those years ago. But then she decided against it. Vonni was very private about things.

The sun was setting and there was a gold-red light over the harbour. Thomas saw that Vonni was still working in her craft shop. He thought about going in to invite her to come up for an evening drink with him. But he remembered how much she liked to be left alone.

She had only agreed to sleep in the spare bedroom

after a lot of reassurance that they would not intrude on each other's lives. Yet he did not want to go up to that apartment and be by himself.

He wanted to call Bill. It had been left so awkwardly hanging in the air the last time. He still felt stung by Vonni overhearing him and saying that he had made such a mess of it all. This time he would say the right things.

Thomas sat down in a small street café and made a list of things he would talk about. Like that he had dinner in a police station beside prisoners' cells, like the men coming out to dance after the funeral, like the Germans learning English poetry even though we don't know any of theirs.

He looked at the headings. What dull, odd things he had picked to talk about. A child would not be interested in these things. Maybe he would think it odd that his father was eating dinner beside prisoners' cells. He would be startled to hear that men danced together and particularly at a funeral. What did Bill care about poetry in English or German?

Thomas sat with his head in his hands, thinking how pathetic he was not to be able to find something to say to the boy that he loved with all his heart.

'Vonni?'
'Come in, Yorghis, sit down.'

'You have nice things here.' The policeman looked around.

'Some of it is nice, yes. Thank you again for your hospitality last night, Yorghis, they all loved it.'

'It's not a time to be alone. I hear you've given up on teaching the widow to drive.'

'I turned it over to that nice English boy but it was meant to be a secret!' Vonni laughed.

'In this town?'

'I know, I know.' Vonni stayed still. He would tell her eventually what business brought him here.

'We got a call from Athens, that boy we exported, the Irishman you know . . .'

'Oh, yes?'

So he *had* called after all. Fiona had been right. Vonni didn't know whether to be pleased or disappointed.

'What did he say?'

'He said nothing. We got a call from a police station in Athens. He had been taken in for dealing in a bar. They found my card on him and wondered what I knew.'

'And what did you know, Yorghis?' she asked.

'Nothing as yet. I wasn't there to take his call. I wanted to discuss it with you. She's such a nice little girl.'

'I know, so nice she'd probably get on the next ferry and go to Stand by Her Man.'

'That's what I thought,' Yorghis said.

'You know the phrase about locking people up and throwing away the key?' she asked.

'I know the phrase and I'm often tempted. I think I'll just tell them that we had a bit of girlfriend battering and drunkenness here. I don't think I'll say anything specific about Fiona, do you?'

'I think you're right and we might not say anything *to* Fiona either. Do you agree?'

'Is that playing God, do you think?' Yorghis wondered.

'Even if it is, let's do it. God was never around to help when that lout was beating the pulp out of Fiona. Maybe the Almighty needs a hand now and then,' said Vonni with a grim smile of satisfaction.

Much later that night when Vonni went upstairs she found Thomas sitting in his chair in the dark.

'Holy St Joseph, you put the heart across me,' she said.

'Hi, Vonni.' He was very down.

'Did you ring your son and annoy him again?' she asked.

'No, I sat here for hours wondering what to say and I couldn't think of anything so I didn't call him at all,' he confessed.

'Probably wiser in the long run,' Vonni said approvingly.

'What kind of a horse's ass does that make me,

not able to find things to say to a nine-year-old?' he asked.

'I'd say it makes you like every father and son in the world, unable to communicate.' She wasn't as unsympathetic as the words might have sounded.

'He's not my son,' Thomas said flatly.

'What do you mean?'

'What I say. Nearly ten years ago when Shirley and I were trying for a baby I went for a medical. Childhood mumps had made me sterile apparently. I walked around all day wondering how to tell Shirley. But when I got home *she* had something to tell me. Wasn't it wonderful – she was pregnant.'

'Did you tell her?'

'No. I needed time to think. I had no idea that she was playing away. Not a clue. And because I didn't speak then I couldn't later.'

'So you never spoke?'

'I love him as much as if he *were* mine.'

'He is yours in every real sense,' Vonni said.

'Yes, that's true. I raised him with her, I got his formulas in the night, I taught him to read, to swim. He's mine as much as anyone's. His natural father must have disappeared from the face of the earth. It wasn't Andy, he only turned up years later. Andy thinks he's mine.'

'Did you raise it during the divorce?'

'What, and lose any chance of access to Bill?'

'Of course,' she nodded.

'He's a wonderful boy, Vonni.'

'I'm sure he is. I'm very sure he is.'

There was a long silence.

'Go back to him, Thomas, it's breaking your heart to be so far away.'

'I can't. We all agreed it was for the best this way.'

'Agreements can be changed, plans can be rewritten,' Vonni said.

'I'd be worse back there than here. Suppose I had to look at that fool every day, posturing, pretending to be his father.'

'You are his father in every way that counts.' Vonni looked at the floor as she spoke.

'I wish I could believe that,' he said.

'You should believe it, Thomas.' She spoke with quiet certainty as if she knew what she was talking about. His eyes met hers and suddenly it was crystal-clear to Thomas that Vonni really did know what she was talking about.

The night she had told him that he had made a dog's dinner of his conversation with Bill, she had said that she too had a child. A son that she had lost for ever by making the wrong decisions.

Thomas closed his eyes. He had not prayed for a very long time, but tonight he prayed with all his heart. Please may he decide the right thing. Oh, please may he not lose that little boy.

CHAPTER ELEVEN

Vonni and David were drinking coffee at the café with the check tablecloths. Maria would be out shortly to have her driving lesson.

'She says you are a very good man and you don't shout at her,' Vonni said approvingly to David.

'Poor Maria, did she expect people to shout at her?' David asked.

'Well, I did for one, and Manos did too, a lot, so I think she did expect it, yes.'

'It doesn't get you anywhere, shouting,' David said.

'I told Maria that you taught your mother to drive. She said your mother was fortunate to have such a son.'

'*She* doesn't think so.'

'Why do you say that?' Vonni asked.

'Because it's a fact. She sides with my father over everything. She parrots him all the time: I have a ready-made business to walk into, I can be my father's right-hand man, his eyes and ears. I am so lucky, most men would love to have a business that they could walk into, a company built up by his hard work.'

'And can you not tell her that you love them but you don't love the work?'

'I've tried and tried, but it ends in recriminations and arguments every single time. I've told them that I feel uneasy and as if I'm having a panic attack or something just as soon as I go in the office doors . . . but you might as well talk to that harbour wall.'

'When you go back you'll find that they have softened,' she began.

'I'm not going back,' he said.

'You can't run away, stay here for ever.'

'You did,' David said simply.

'I'm weary of telling people that those were different times.' Vonni sighed.

'I'm taking Maria up some of those mountainy roads today,' David reported to Vonni.

'God, you're brave as a lion.' Vonni was admiring.

'She's fine on her own where you don't meet too much traffic, she doesn't get fussed.'

'But, David, those awful hairpin bends, those bits where the road sort of crumbles away . . .'

'I know, but aren't these the very roads she'll have to drive to hill villages if she's going to work for you?'

'Yes, but in months or weeks not days.'

'No, she's better away from the town, huge trucks reversing at her out of that big ugly petrol station.'

'Tread softly on that petrol station because you tread on my dreams,' Vonni warned.

'What do you mean?'

'That was my petrol station, I worked there day and night for years.'

'Never!'

'Oh, yes, it was.'

'Did you sell it or what?'

'No, it was sort of taken away from me, too long and complicated a story to tell you now. What area are you and Maria driving in today? Just so that I'll know to avoid it.'

'I thought we'd go up to see Andreas, that's a windy road.'

'You like him, don't you?' Vonni observed.

'Who wouldn't like him? He's so kind and gentle. He doesn't pressurise people into doing what they don't want to do.'

'He's set in his ways of course,' Vonni said.

'But good ways,' David said. 'His son must be a real fool, not to come back from Chicago and help him.'

'Maybe.' Vonni shrugged doubtfully.

'Why maybe? The boy works in a vegetable shop miles and miles away in the middle of a big noisy neighbourhood, Andreas says, when he could be here in this wonderful place, helping his father.'

Vonni stood looking at David quizzically, her head on one side.

'What is it?' he asked eventually.

'You *know* what it is, David. Couldn't someone say exactly the same about you, you have a father and in your case a mother too who miss you and wonder what *you* are doing miles and miles away.'

'It's different,' David said mutinously.

'Oh yes?'

'It's totally different. My father isn't reasonable, he's just never wrong. No one could live with him.'

'There were ways that Adoni found the very same thing in his father. Andreas wouldn't get lights on the taverna roof, he wouldn't have live bouzouki music to draw the people up the hill in the evening. Adoni could suggest nothing, change nothing. Andreas was always right.'

'I don't see that in him, not a bit,' David said a little coldly.

'No? Well, of course he's polite and respectful to you, people often are not courteous to their own sons.' She looked thoughtful.

'You have a son, Vonni?'

'Yes. Stavros, like his father.'

'And are you courteous and polite to him?' David asked.

'I don't see him, to be courteous or discourteous.'

'You must see him sometimes?' David was startled.

'No. Not at all. But in the days when I did see him
I was going through a rather odd period when I was
polite to nobody, least of all to him. So he has no
way of knowing how much I miss him and how
respectful and warm I could be to him these days.'

She straightened herself up and looked purposeful
again. 'Right. I'm taking those children with me so
that you can take their mother up the Wall of Death
or wherever you want to go with her.'

She stood up, calling out something in Greek to
the children, who sounded delighted.

'What did you tell them?' David asked.

'I brought up the topic of ice cream, it seemed to
appeal,' she said.

'I bet you were always courteous to everyone.' He
smiled at her.

'No, David, it would be wrong to think that, but
don't go asking about me, they'll tell you nothing.
The only person who can explain my troubled life is
me.'

At that point Maria came out of her door ready
for her driving lesson. She greeted Vonni and then
turned to David.

'*Pame*, David,' she said.

'*Pame*, Maria,' said David.

Vonni watched amazed as she got into the van in

the driver's side, looked in the rear-view mirror and slid the van out easily on to the Harbour Road.

If this boy was going to stay in Aghia Anna maybe he had a career ahead of him in teaching everyone to drive.

Andreas and his brother Yorghis were having a game of backgammon in a café near the police station. They saw the familiar van that Manos had hurtled around Aghia Anna drive by.

'That's Maria! Someone's teaching her to drive!' Yorghis explained.

'That will be Vonni, I expect,' Andreas said.

'No, it looks like a man.'

'It's that boy David Fine. Such a good young man,' Andreas said, pleased.

'Yes, isn't he,' Yorghis said. They sat silently for a while.

'Was there any word from . . .' Yorghis began.

'No, no word,' Andreas said quickly.

'Of course they might not have heard over there,' Yorghis said.

'No indeed.' Andreas clicked the pieces on the board.

There would be no more talk about Adoni far away in Chicago. They spoke about their sister Christina, who had had a troubled youth but was happy now living with a kind man on the other side of the island. They didn't talk about her past nowadays. Nor indeed did they talk about Yorghis's former wife who would have known Manos and his friends when they were children. She had not got in touch either.

Thomas found the bookshop.

'*Vivliopolio*,' Vonni had told him earlier.

'Really?' Thomas said. 'It sounds like a vitamin drink.'

'You know the V in Greek looks like a mad B with a sort of leg hanging out of it. When I came here one of the first things I wanted was a bookshop and when I found it I thought that it was *biblionwakyo* or something, like the French word *bibliothèque*.'

'Aren't you funny?' he said to her affectionately.

'I'm a scream,' said Vonni. 'What are you looking for in the bookshop?'

'German poetry as it happens. Do you think they might have any?'

'They might,' Vonni said. 'You never know.'

And she was right. The bookshop had a small section, including a book of Goethe's work, German on one side and English on the page opposite. He bought it and took it outside and sat on a bench near the store.

Thomas studied it carefully until he found something appropriate. Then he took out his notebook and wrote it down.

Kennst du das Land, wo die Zitronen blühn,
Im dunkeln Laub die Gold-Orangen glühn.

He wrote the translation beside it:

Do you know the land where the lemon-
trees blossom,
Where the golden oranges glow in the dark
foliage.

He would learn it by heart and quote it to Elsa. She must not be allowed to think that he didn't know German writers.

He was just beginning to copy the next bit, which was all about soft winds, myrtles and laurels standing tall, when he felt a shadow fall over the page. It was Elsa looking over his shoulder to see what he was reading. Then she moved back and spoke the lines to him.

Kennst du es wohl? Dahin! Dahin
Möcht ich mit dir, o mein Geliebter, ziehn.

'All right, I give in,' he said. 'I haven't read the translation. What does that bit mean?'

'It means ... let me see ... it means: Do you know it perhaps? It is there, there that I would like to go with you, my beloved.'

And as she said it they looked at each other,

slightly embarrassed, as if they had accidentally uncovered something too intimate.

'Did he come to Greece, Goethe? Is this the land where the lemon-trees blossom?' Thomas asked, to move the conversation into safer waters.

'It was the Mediterranean certainly but I think it was mainly Italy he travelled in, he was mad about Italy. But of course he could have come to Greece as well. This is where I am showing my ignorance.' Elsa looked apologetic.

'What about mine? Until now I never read a word he wrote in any language,' Thomas confessed.

'And why are you reading it now?'

'To impress you,' he said simply.

'You don't have to, I'm impressed already,' Elsa said.

Andreas got a phone call from Ireland.

'Is that a taverna in Aghia Anna?' the voice asked.

'Yes it is, can I help you?'

'Fiona Ryan called her family from your taverna on the day of your terrible tragedy.'

'Yes, yes, I remember.'

'I'm Fiona's best friend at home, Barbara. Fiona gave your number in case she got cut off so I rang because . . . well, I was wondering, are they still in Aghia Anna?'

'Yes, is there any problem?'

'No, not a problem really . . . excuse me, who am I speaking to?'

'My name is Andreas, this is my taverna.'

'Oh good, and have you seen her since?'

'This is a very small place, we see almost everyone every day.'

'And Fiona's all right, is she?'

Andreas paused. All right?

The girl looked wretched, she had been beaten by her boyfriend, who had then abandoned her, and gone to Athens where he was now in jail awaiting trial for drug dealing. Fiona had suffered a miscarriage; she still thought that Shane was coming back to find her.

All right? Hardly.

But even though his instinct was to tell this pleasant woman Barbara all that had happened he knew it wasn't his story to tell.

'They all seem to like it here,' he said lamely.

'All? You mean she's been able to make friends with Shane in tow? Usually people avoid them like the plague.'

'Very nice people. German, American, English,' he said to reassure her.

'Well, that is a surprise. Listen, Andreas, is there anywhere I could send her an e-mail or a fax do you think?'

'Certainly.' He gave her the numbers of the police station.

'And we were all very sorry about what happened there. It must have been a nightmare.'

'Thank you. You are very kind and sympathetic,' he said. And she *was* kind and sympathetic, unlike his cold-hearted son in Chicago.

Andreas wished over and over that he had not written that letter to Adoni.

But he had promised Elsa. And it was too late now, the letter was nearly there.

Fiona had gone to see Dr Leros for an examination and a checkup as she had promised.

'Everything is fine,' he said. 'You are a healthy young woman. Plenty more chances of babies.'

'Oh, I hope so some day,' Fiona said.

'Are you going back to your country?'

'No. I have to wait until Shane comes back here to find me, I was hoping to get a job here. I'm a qualified nurse. Is there anything I could do for you, for example, in your practice here?'

'Well, not really, my dear girl, you see my patients only speak Greek for one thing.'

'Oh, I'm going to learn it,' Fiona promised. 'It would be such a marvellous thing for Shane to come back and find me settled.'

'And will he be upset that you miscarried?' Dr Leros had heard something of Shane's behaviour before he left Aghia Anna. He knew that the general opinion was that Shane would not return.

Poor soft-hearted mistaken girl.

But there was really no way he could give her a job.

'He will be upset in a way, but maybe it will be better when it's properly planned. He will be so pleased to know your good news that I am healthy.'

'Good. Good girl.'

'And about a job?'

'It's not possible, believe me. Could you try the hotel? The Anna Beach.'

'Yes, but they close in the winter,' Fiona said.

'You're going to live here all year round?' His eyes were wide.

'Vonni did,' Fiona said defensively.

'Ah, that was different.'

'Why was it different?' Fiona cried.

'You didn't know Stavros,' Dr Leros said.

'You knew him?'

'Yes, he was my best friend.'

'And where is he now?'

'I don't know, he left the island.' His face was grim.

Fiona was desperate to know. 'And will he ever come back, do you think?'

'Not now, too much has happened.'

'But no one talks about it?' she asked.

'It was too long ago. Too much has happened since then.' And he stood up to shake her hand and let her know that the consultation was now over.

*

Yorghis was driving around Aghia Anna, he knew he would see Fiona or one of her friends somewhere along the way. He saw her with a straw basket buying vegetables.

'Oh, great, Yorghis, just the man I need. What's the Greek for watermelon?'

'*Karpouzi*,' he said.

'Good! *Karpouzi, karpouzi*,' she said happily.

'I have a letter for you,' Yorghis said.

'Shane! I just *knew* he would get in touch.' Her face was radiant.

'No, it's from your friend Barbara in Ireland.' He handed over the printed-out e-mail.

She barely looked at it, she was so disappointed. She just put it in her basket.

'You can always come up to the station and send an e-mail back,' he offered.

'No, thank you, Yorghis, but is there any way we could find out what's happened to Shane in Athens?'

He bit his lip as he looked at her.

It surely couldn't be right to keep from her the fact that Shane was in detention and would not be coming back for her. But there were pens and paper and telephones in Athens, he could get in touch if he wanted to, and he hadn't wanted to.

Leave things as they were.

'*Karpouzi*,' he said, leaving.

'Is that Greek for goodbye?' she asked glumly.

'No, it's watermelon.' He laughed. 'You'll have to try harder.'

She sat down at a café and pulled out the letter.

You must wonder how Sherlock Holmes Barbara tracked you down, but it was easy: your mother had the number you phoned from, and Andreas told me his brother ran the cop shop. He said you and Shane had nice friends from all over the world. That's great news.

Oh, I miss you in the hospital, Fiona, really I do. Carmel is unbearable as Ward Sister. Frightening the patients, terrifying the nurses, upsetting the visitors, stamping round the place like a mad woman on speed. We have two new Filipino nurses, gentle little things, they nearly fled back to Manila until we told them that we were all equally horrified by her.

They were looking for more staff nurses in Orthopaedic, I thought I might apply. It's great working with the new knees and new hips. Any news at all on when you and Shane are coming back? It's just that if it were going to be at the end of the summer there are some really great flats coming on the market, you and Shane could easily get

one of them, it would only be a ten-minute
walk to the hospital. I'd just love one myself
but you'd need two to pay for it.

In fact, I was telling your mam and dad
about them, I said that was probably the
kind of place the two of you would want to
live when you came back. They didn't even
flicker an eyelid. Remember when they
wouldn't hear his name mentioned? You've
certainly laid down the ground rules okay.

They were very pleased you called about
that awful tragedy. It must have been
terrible.

Anyway, you have my e-mail address now,
do tell me how you are and how you both
like Greece. I always wanted to go there but
never got any further than Spain. Remember
that time we went to Marbella and met the
two English guys who got burned to a crisp
and gave us the keys of their car? Weren't
we reckless then? You still are of course!
Love to you both,
Barbara

Fiona sat there stunned.

Barbara sending her love to Shane? Her mother
and father accepting the fact that she was going to
live with Shane for ever? The world was tilting
slightly.

She read the letter again and went back to Elsa's apartment to make soup and a fruit salad.

Elsa stopped by Vonni's craft shop and invited her to join them for an evening meal.

'Fiona is cooking for us, we can have a Ladies' Dinner,' she suggested.

'No, thank you, Elsa, very kind of you both, but I have to work.'

'Work? What on earth do you do?'

'Every week I go to a group of blind people who make rugs. I choose the colours of the wool for them. Then I try to sell the rugs.' She shrugged as if this was everyday work anyone might do.

'Did you always know about rug-making?' Elsa asked.

'Not at all.'

'So why did you take it up, particularly with the blind?'

'Oh, I had to give something back and I realised that the blind could weave with the best – they just needed someone to mark out which was pink and which was orange.'

'What do you mean, you had to give something back?' Elsa asked.

'This place was good to me. I was nothing but a nuisance for years, upsetting them all, howling and frightening their children. They put up with me until I recovered.'

'I can't believe this . . . *you* howling and frightening people?' Elsa laughed as if it were a joke.

Vonni looked very serious. 'Oh, I did, believe me. But I had an excuse. My husband betrayed me, you see. He played *tavli* in the restaurants and tavernas – that I didn't mind. It's the way. But then he saw beautiful Magda and he forgot everything we had. He was entranced by her. He would not come home to me. I had a little boy and the people here helped me look after him while I worked up in the petrol station. I'll never forget that . . . and it was hard for them to take my side. I was the foreigner – they would have been tempted to side with him rather than me.'

'And what happened?'

'A lot happened,' Vonni said. 'Well, one big thing that happened was that Stavros moved out of our house and into hers.'

'No! In this small place!' Elsa was aghast.

'The size of the place was unimportant, truly it was. It would have been as bad in a big anonymous city. He just would not return. I did a lot of stupid things – that's when the people here were so tolerant and good.'

'What kind of stupid things?' Elsa wanted to know.

'Another time possibly.' The shutters came down in Vonni's face.

'It's just that *I've* done some very stupid things

recently. It's comforting to know others did and survived,' Elsa said.

'Is this the man who was staying in the Anna Beach calling out to the stars that he loved you?'

'You know everything!' Elsa exclaimed. 'Yes, it is of course, it is. And I still love him so much, that's the problem.'

'Why is it a problem?'

'Well, it's complicated.'

'It's always complicated,' Vonni said sympathetically.

'I suppose it is, we forget that. His name is Dieter, he runs the television station where I work . . . used to work. He taught me everything and I became a sort of star there, presenting the big news programme at night. And anyway we fell in love, got together, whatever you'd call it, and have been together for over two years.'

'You live together?' Vonni asked.

'No, it's not as simple as that.'

'Is he married to someone else?'

'No, it's not that. It's just awkward in the Network if people know.'

Vonni raised her eyes and looked at Elsa levelly. Somehow Elsa felt slightly flustered and defensive.

'You don't know what it's like back there, Vonni, very hot-house. People would think I only got my good job because I was living with him. Easier for him to have his place and me to have mine.'

'Sure.' Vonni was clipped. 'So what are you doing here then?'

'I discovered something very cold and unfeeling about him.'

'More than the fact he just wouldn't commit to you publicly?' Vonni asked.

Elsa was annoyed now. 'You really don't understand, that was a mutual decision.'

'Yes, of course,' Vonni said. 'So what was the cold unfeeling thing?'

'I discovered that he has a child by a woman he knew years back.'

'So?'

'What do you mean – So? He has a child that he has never acknowledged, he's no part of her life. You don't think that's bad?'

'I think it happens all over the world every day of the week. People survive.'

'It happened to me,' Elsa said. 'My father walked away, didn't give a damn.'

'And look at you! Didn't *you* survive, Elsa? So very beautiful, confident, successful at everything. It proves my point.'

'It proves nothing. You don't know what I feel, have always felt. I feel that I must be so utterly worthless that even my own father couldn't be bothered with me.'

'Grow up, Elsa. In the end we all have to rely on ourselves. Ourselves and the friends we make if we are lucky enough to make them. We are not tied to our children, nor they to us. There's no huge law that says *Thou shalt love thy child* and that *Thy child shalt love thee* in return. Happy Families is a game people play with cards, it's not any kind of reality.'

'I don't know what made you so bitter and cynical but I'm glad I don't feel like that,' Elsa said.

'You want him to play Saturday Father to some child he probably never intended should exist.'

'But she *does* exist and that's exactly what he should do.'

'That's not why you are leaving him,' Vonni said.

'I beg your pardon?'

'You're leaving him because you don't trust him. You thought that he would eventually admit that he needed you as part of his life. You are such a beautiful young woman, you are accustomed to getting your own way. If you truly loved him you could put this child out of your mind. But no, you can't be sure that he loves you at all. That's why you are seizing on this episode of his life which took place long before he met you. You are making it the excuse, aren't you?'

Elsa felt her eyes stinging at the injustice of the attack. 'You're so wrong, he *does* love me. You heard him yourself shouting it aloud. And he cried out to me again next morning as he got on the ferry. And I have such a huge, lonely hole in my heart without him. I've decided that I'm going back to Germany as soon as I can to tell him that I love him too.'

Vonni leaned forward. 'You are never in your whole life going to get such good advice as this. Don't go back there, keep going, leave him be. Remain a beautiful golden memory for him. He's never going to love you the way you want to be loved.'

Elsa stood up, not trusting herself to speak. She thought she saw Thomas going up the side stairs in his silly baggy trousers. She didn't want to talk to him. Or anybody. She wanted to get back to her own apartment. Fast.

'You're very quiet, Elsa,' Fiona said. 'Don't you like that lovely healthy soup I made you?'

'It's very good. I'm sorry, I just don't feel too cheerful tonight. Don't worry, I'll get over it, I hate moody people.' She smiled a very bright smile.

'Did something happen?' Fiona asked.

'Well, yes, as it happens I had a row with Vonni of all stupid things,' she said.

'*A row with Vonni?*'

'I know it sounds impossible but that's what happened.'

'But what about?' Fiona was astounded.

'She knows about me and Dieter, she wants me to leave him alone, stay away from him.'

Elsa had mentioned nothing to Fiona about her situation up to this point. Fiona was wordless.

'So we saw things a bit differently, if you see what I mean?'

'But you still love him, don't you?'

'Oh yes, most definitely, and he feels the same,' Elsa said.

'Well, there's no question about it then.' Fiona was matter-of-fact and businesslike about it. 'You have to go back to him, Vonni or no Vonni.'

They had all agreed to meet at the harbour café after dinner and the four of them talked about their day.

'Do any of you get the feeling that we are just marking time here – that we should be doing something else?' Thomas asked.

'I'm happy here. I like it,' David said.

'And I do too,' Fiona agreed. 'Anyway, I have to stay here until Shane gets back.'

'I'll probably go back to Germany next week,' Elsa said. 'I'm just thinking it through. What about you, Thomas?'

'Well, Vonni thinks I should go back to California to see my son. I haven't worked it out either,' he said.

'Vonni's busy dispatching us all home! Once Maria can drive that van, Vonni wants me out too, back to make peace with my parents and work with my father.' David sounded gloomy.

'She doesn't think Shane is coming back, she says there are no jobs here, I'd be better to go back to Dublin.'

'She's actually more of a policeman than Yorghis is. She says I should end my relationship with a man who doesn't really love me,' Elsa said, giggling.

'She never put it like that?' David said.

'Almost precisely like that – anyway I'm different to the rest of you, she wants me to keep on the move and *not* to go home.'

They pooled what they knew about her: she came from the west of Ireland over thirty years ago because she loved a man called Stavros. Somehow she managed to buy him a petrol station, where Vonni worked night and day. She had one son, Stavros, whom she didn't see now. Stavros senior had left the island, possibly with Vonni's young son. Vonni had gone through a troubled time but the people of Aghia Anna had looked after her and she felt she owed them in return.

'What kind of a troubled time?' Fiona wondered. 'Maybe she had a breakdown when Stavros left?'

'I think she was an alcoholic,' David said softly.

The others were startled. That quiet, capable, together woman a slave to drink? Impossible.

'Why do you say that?' Elsa asked.

'Well, have you noticed she never drinks any wine or *ouzo* or anything?' David said.

They looked at him with respect. They had all been with Vonni around many a table. Only the gentle, sensitive David had noticed what was now so obvious to everyone.

CHAPTER TWELVE

Vonni had been right when she said that the people of Aghia Anna would close ranks about her. The four of them could get no information at all.

'I believe that Vonni used to run that gas station over there,' Thomas said casually to Yorghis.

Yorghis said something that was neither yes nor no.

'Did she hate giving it up?' Thomas asked.

'I don't really know,' Yorghis said.

'Or it might have been a relief.'

'You live in Vonni's house, I'm sure that you could ask her all about it,' Yorghis said politely.

David got nowhere with Andreas either. 'You must have known Vonni's husband, Stavros?'

'Everyone knows everyone here.'

'And I suppose you knew Magda, too?'

'As I say, it's a very small place.'

'Their son, was he friendly with your son and with Manos?'

'In a village, every child knows every other child.'

'You think I'm asking too many questions, don't you, Andreas?'

'You are interested in this place and the people who live here, that's good,' Andreas said, but told no more.

Elsa tried talking to Yanni in the delicatessen when she went in to get olives and cheese. He was a man of about sixty; he would have been around for all the drama.

'It's wonderful how Vonni is so much a part of this town, isn't it?' Elsa began.

'Vonni is a very good woman, yes,' Yanni said.

'I expect you knew her when she was married to Stavros?' Elsa said.

'Does she talk to you about Stavros?' Yanni asked.

'A little, yes.'

'Then I suppose she tells you all she wants you to know about him,' Yanni said with a huge smile showing many gold teeth, but giving nothing away.

And Elsa, who had been able to interview politicians, business tycoons, authors and actors on German television and make them reveal their stories, had to admit defeat.

Fiona walked out to Eleni's house with sweets for the children. 'I wanted to thank you for being so kind when I was sick,' she said to Eleni.

'Are you good now?' The woman was concerned.

'Yes, I'm fine, but I'm a bit sad because I'm waiting here for Shane,' she said. 'If he comes back for me, you'll be sure to tell him where I am staying.'

'Shane, yes. I tell him, yes. If he comes back.'

'Oh, he will come back, Eleni. He loves me.'

'Yes.' There was an awkward silence between them.

Fiona didn't want to protest any more. She changed the subject. 'Did you know Stavros, the husband of Vonni, long ago?'

'I don't speak English good, I tell this Shane where you stay if he comes back. Thank you for the *karameles* for the children. You are kind, good girl.'

'Vonni, come upstairs for a *portokalatha* when you're through. Okay?'

'So you've finally noticed I only drink soft drinks,' she laughed at Thomas.

'I didn't, David did, he's the one who notices things. Anyway, what you drink isn't important – I want your advice.'

'No, you don't, you want me to tell you that it's all going to turn out fine without you having to lift a finger. Isn't that right?'

'If you could tell me convincingly, I'd sure love it,' he said.

'I'll be up in ten minutes,' she said. He noticed she was wearing a clean, fresh, yellow blouse with little embroidered roses on it. She must keep her clothes in the craft shop.

'That's pretty,' he indicated the stitching. 'Did you do that?'

'No, it was done by someone else. It's thirty years old.'

'Really? Who did it?'

'It doesn't matter now, Thomas, she could sew like an angel.'

Thomas swallowed. He had been too intrusive. 'I guess I ask too many questions, Vonni, forgive me, you don't have to talk about it.'

'Well, I do, really. You four are all anxious to know about me . . . you are asking everyone else in Aghia Anna about me.' She smiled at him innocently.

Thomas looked at the floor. 'They told you?' he said ruefully.

'Of course they did!' To her it was obvious.

'I'm sorry, it looks very nosy, but I tell you, Vonni, you're special. We are all fascinated by you.'

'I'm flattered, and astonished. But anyway, I'll tell you whatever you want to know.' She smiled at him encouragingly.

'I don't know. Now that I'm in a position to ask questions, I honestly don't know what to ask. I suppose I want to know if you are happy?'

'Yes, I think I am fairly happy, as it happens. Are you happy, Thomas?'

'No, I'm not, you know that, I've messed up on Bill, you told me yourself. But we're meant to be talking about you.'

'And what will we talk about?' she asked.

'I suppose we wanted to know what your husband was like, and what happened to him,' Thomas said uneasily.

He felt awkward asking probing questions, but Vonni was totally at ease with it all.

'Very hard questions to answer, both of them. His name was Stavros, he was very dark, big brown, almost black eyes, black hair, long always, whether it was fashionable or not. His father was the barber here, he used to say he was ashamed of his wild and woolly son, and that Stavros was no advertisement for his father's barbering skills. He wasn't exactly tall, he was . . . I suppose you'd call it stocky. The moment I saw him I knew I never wanted any other man.'

'And where did you see him? Here in Aghia Anna?' Thomas asked.

'No, I met him somewhere very different. The most unlikely place,' Vonni said, almost dreamily.

'Are you going to make me beg or will you tell me?' he asked.

'I met Stavros in Ardeevin, a small village in the west of Ireland in the spring of 1966, before you were born, Thomas.'

'True, but I was born four years later so it was touch and go,' he said.

'He came to work in a garage on the main street. We had never seen anything quite so exotic. A real live Greek man in our main street, well, our only street. Ardeevin didn't run to more than one. He was learning English, he said, and the motor trade, and seeing the world . . .' Vonni sighed at the memory. 'We didn't think Ardeevin was the right place to start seeing the world. What about Paris? London? Even Dublin? But he said he liked it, it reminded him of his home town, Aghia Anna. It felt familiar, comfortable.' She paused to think about it.

Thomas didn't encourage her to say more. Either she would or she would not, it had nothing to do with his promptings.

'I was still at school, in my last year. My family hoped I would get what was described as a Call to Training. It meant a place in a college where you became a primary teacher. A Call to Training was like winning the Irish Sweepstakes, you were educated free into a grand career and a permanent job and a pension.'

'But the call never came?' he said gently.

'I don't know whether it did or not. I never heard because I was so much in love with Stavros nothing else mattered. I had stopped going to school, abandoned studying, examinations had no meaning for me. My only purpose each day was to hide from my sister, to sneak into the back of Ardeevin Motors. I didn't care about anything but being with him.'

Thomas listened enthralled at the calm way she told the story of her first love.

'So Jimmy Keane, who ran the garage, began to think Stavros wasn't concentrating fully on his work and started making sounds that he was going to sack him. I could neither eat nor sleep with the worry of it all. What would I *do* if Stavros had to move on? I went in and sat my school examinations. I could barely understand the questions, let alone answer them.'

'And what kind of results did you get?' Thomas, ever the teacher, wanted to know.

'I have no idea. You see, the most marvellous event occurred in Ireland that summer. There was a bank strike!' Her eyes shone at the memory.

'The banks went on strike? Never!'

'Oh, they did,' she said happily.

'And how did people manage?'

'On trust, mainly, a series of IOUs – they even printed blank cheque-book forms to try and make it seem more normal.'

'And?'

'And what happened then was nothing short of a miracle,' Vonni said. 'Supermarkets would have a lot of cash and no banks to lodge it in, so they cashed these "cheques" for people they knew. The big town ten miles away had a supermarket where I was known, because the manager was a cousin of my mother. So I cashed a cheque for two and a half thousand pounds. And that day Jimmy Keane said he'd have to let Stavros go.' Vonni began to pace the room at this stage, but she continued the story.

'He told me he would miss me, that I was his true love and that one day we would meet again, that he would go back to Aghia Anna, open up a petrol station and send for me to come and join him. And I asked what was wrong with going right now, that I had the funds to set him up. I told him that it was my savings.'

'Tell me he was pleased.'

'Oh, he was, but my parents weren't. I told them that day that I was seventeen and a half, in six months I could marry without their permission anyway. What were they going to do? Lock me up? They cried and shouted a lot, they talked about the waste, the bad example to my sister, about not being able to raise their heads in Ardeevin. My father was a teacher, a man of considerable importance in the community, my mother was related to big important shopkeepers all over the place. Oh, the shame of it all.'

'But you wore them down.'

'I told them I was leaving that very night, and we did, on the seven-thirty bus.'

'And the money?'

'Ah yes, the money. We were well in Aghia Anna by the time the bank strike ended. A wonderful journey by train and boat, we saved the big money, you see, didn't touch it until we got here. We travelled through Switzerland and Italy, and ate bread and cheese. I was never so happy in my life. *Nobody* was as happy as I was then.'

'And you arrived here?'

'And it wasn't so great. There was this girl, you see, very pregnant with Stavros's child. She thought he had come back to marry her. She was Christina, the sister of Andreas and Yorghis. When she discovered he had *not* come back for her, she tried to kill herself. It turned out that she killed the child she was carrying, not herself. It was a terrible time for everyone.'

'What happened to Christina?'

'She went to the hospital on the hill, you know, on the Kalatriada road.'

'Yes, I know it. And – what happened to you then, Vonni?'

'Me? I learned to speak Greek, I bought the petrol station. I learned how to change wheels, pump up tyres. I went to see Christina every week. She didn't speak to me for forty-five weeks then one day she did. And soon she got better and she married a good man. She has children and grandchildren. They live on the other side of the island. I see her often.'

'You married Stavros?'

'In a civil ceremony in Athens. No one thought it was a real wedding – not my family back in Ardeevin, not his family here in Aghia Anna.'

She had begun to sound tired and weary. Thomas knew he must not push her.

'And in 1970, the very same year that you were born in California, our son Stavros was born. By this time, people were used to me. We had a christening at the church, and even Stavros's father relaxed and sang songs. And Christina came and gave me all the baby clothes she had made when she had thought *she* was going to have Stavros's baby.'

'How amazing,' Thomas said.

'I know. No word from Ireland, of course. I wrote and told them they had a grandson. No reply at all.'

'They must have been very bitter.'

'Well, the money was the final straw that broke the camel's back.'

'Ah, the money,' Thomas smiled.

'Well, I was always going to pay it back.'

'Sure,' he said, with no conviction.

'And I did,' she said, as if it was the most obvious thing in the world.

David opened the letter. It was the first time his parents had written to him. He sat and read unbelievingly of their pride and delight in the actual invitation to this award his father had won. They had sent him a photocopy but described how the wording was embossed on the thick card.

David knew those awards; businessmen patted each other on the back every year. It was a reward for nothing except making money. No achievement, philanthropy, no research, no generosity to charity was being praised. No, it was only the huge god *profit* that was being worshipped here.

His mother wrote on and on – about seating in the Town Hall, what they would all wear, that there would be a table plan. She wondered how soon he would come home for it.

He would calm himself and write a courteous letter explaining why he would not be there. A letter was wiser than a phone call. No danger of anyone losing their temper.

Fiona went to the Anna Beach Hotel and sent an e-mail to her friend Barbara in Dublin.

It was good to hear from you, really it was. Lord, but it's beautiful here, Barb, I'm so glad we chose this place. The accident was terrible, but the people are full of courage, they would do your heart good. Shane's gone to Athens for a few days on work. He'll be back any day now. I keep watching the ferries. Thanks for telling me about the

hospital. Imagine Carmel-the-cow being
Ward Sister.

I'll write again when I know our plans.
Love,
Fiona

'There is a fax for your friend the German woman,' the man at the reception desk said as Fiona was leaving the Anna Beach.

Fiona marvelled at how everyone knew who they all were.

'I'll take it back to the villa,' she said.

She was becoming very familiar with Aghia Anna by now, even knew little short cuts from one side to the other. She laid the piece of paper on the table in front of Elsa.

'I'd have read it but it's in German,' Fiona said.

'Yes.'

'Aren't you going to read it? You don't have to translate it,' Fiona said.

'I know what it says,' Elsa said.

'That's pretty psychic of you,' Fiona said in surprise.

'It's telling me to pull myself together and come back to where I belong, which is in bed with him two nights a week, and no more gestures of independence.'

'Maybe it's not that,' Fiona encouraged her.

'All right – I'll translate . . .' She picked up the paper. 'It's fairly short anyway.'

Darling Elsa,

The decision is yours. Come back to me and we will move together into an apartment openly for all to see. We will even be married. If that's what you want. I will write letters and send gifts to that child if it makes you feel better. We were intended for each other, you know that and I know that. What is the point in playing games? Fax me yes, soonest.

Love until the world ends,
Dieter

In Chicago, Adoni took the letter with the Greek stamp. If the kindly Italian family who employed him thought that it was odd he never heard from Greece they didn't say anything. He took the letter to the men's room and sat down to read his father's spidery handwriting.

'*Adoni mou*,' it began and told simply of the boat that had burned in full sight of the town with people unable to get to it in time.

'It makes everything else that has happened seem very unimportant,' his father wrote.

Arguments about the taverna are so small compared to life and death. It would give me great pleasure, my son, if you were to come back to Aghia Anna and see me before

my *death. I assure you that I would not*
speak to you in that tone of voice that I did
when you were here. Your room is always
there if you come for a visit, and of course
bring anyone you like. I hope there is
somebody to bring.

And Adoni took out a big blue handkerchief to wipe
his eyes. And then he cried again because there was
nobody to bring.

There was no bail for Shane in Athens so he was
brought back to the cells after the initial hearing.

'I'm allowed to make a phone call!' he shouted.
'You're meant to be in the bloody European Union,
one of the reasons we let you in was for things like
this, so as you'd pay some attention to human
rights.'

They passed the phone to him without comment.
He dialled the police station in Aghia Anna. He
wished he could remember that old guy's name. But
what the hell.

'I'm trying to get in touch with Fiona Ryan,' he
said.

'I'm sorry?' Yorghis said.

'I'm phoning from a police station, or jail, or
some hell-hole in Athens,' he began.

'We told you before, she is not here,' Yorghis lied
smoothly.

'She *must* be there, she's expecting my child, she'll have to get the bail money . . .' He sounded frightened.

'As I say, sorry we can't help you,' Yorghis said and hung up.

Shane begged for a second call. He was so anxious, the policemen shrugged.

'Not too long if it's Ireland,' they warned.

'Barbara! They took a hell of a time to find you, it's Shane.'

'I was on the wards, Shane, it's called work,' she said.

'Very droll. Listen, has Fiona gone back to Dublin?'

'What? Have you two split up?' She couldn't keep the pleasure out of her voice.

'No, don't be ridiculous, I had to go to Athens . . .'

'For work?' Barbara suggested dryly.

'Sort of – and those half-wits in Aghia Anna say she's left there so it's been a bit of a breakdown in communications, you might say.'

'Oh dear, Shane, I'm so sorry.'

'No, you're not, you're thrilled.'

'How can I help you, Shane, exactly?' Barbara asked.

'You could tell her to contact me at . . . no, don't bother, I'll find her.'

'Are you *sure*, Shane? I'd love to help,' Barbara

purred. She had never heard better news since the day her friend Fiona had taken up with the dreaded Shane.

Thomas looked at Vonni, who was quietly telling him the story of her life. Now she had told him that she had paid back that huge debt. How many more secrets did she have?

'You paid the supermarket back?' he said.

'It took some time – like nearly thirty years,' she admitted. 'But they got every penny. I started at a hundred pounds a year.'

'Did they thank you? Forgive you?'

'No, not even remotely.'

'But the guy who was your mother's cousin, didn't he say the money was returned?'

'Not in any way that made any difference. No.'

'And do you keep in touch with your family?'

'Cold little note every Christmas. Done out of Christian charity, proving to themselves they are big-hearted, capable of *forgiveness*, that went on for a time. I wrote long letters, sent them pictures of little Stavros. But it was a bit one-sided. And then of course things changed.'

'Changed? They came round?'

'No, I meant *I* changed. I went mad, you see.'

'No, Vonni, you, mad? This I can't see.'

She looked tired. 'I haven't talked about myself so much for ages, I'm a bit weary.'

'Lie down then, in your own room in there.' He was gentle.

'No, Thomas, I have to feed the chickens.'

'Let me do that for you.'

'Thank you, but no, and Thomas – you can tell the others what I told you. I don't want them bothering people here for my story.'

He looked embarrassed. 'They don't need to know, none of us needs to know anything about your business.'

'I'll tell the rest another time . . . you know, like *New readers start here* . . .' She had a wonderfully infectious smile.

He found himself grinning back.

She did not return to the apartment that night.

When Thomas looked out of the window later on he saw her torch moving around the hen-house.

Thomas told them the story next day down by the harbour. They had got into the habit of turning up at the place with the blue check tablecloths around noon.

David had reported on the latest driving lesson: they had stopped and given some of Maria's neighbours a lift. David couldn't be sure what they had said but it appeared to be great cries of approval.

Elsa and Fiona said nothing about their messages from home but they told how they had spent the morning helping an old man to paint some wooden chairs. He had wanted them all white until Elsa had suggested painting one blue and another one yellow. He had been delighted with them. Or at least they *thought* he had been delighted.

And Thomas told them Vonni's story.

'She did want you to know, it's as if she were going to take it up with one of the three of you.'

They wondered at the notion of a country where the banks went on strike.

'I remember my father talking about it, he said that the country ran perfectly well without them. There were a few loose cannons like Vonni who went off with small fortunes, but not many,' said Fiona.

'I wonder who she'll tell the next episode to,' Elsa said.

It turned out to be David. Later that afternoon.

Thomas and Elsa had gone for a walk down the coast, Fiona had gone to ask Yorghis had there been any news from Athens. David sat on the harbour wall with his Greek phrase book. Vonni came to join him. She helped him with some pronunciation.

'You'll be speaking like a native soon,' she encouraged him.

'Hardly. But I do like it here, people have proper values, they're not obsessed with making money.'

'Scratch them and you'll find that a fair few of them are,' Vonni said.

He told Vonni about the invitation to his father's award back home, how ludicrous it would all be. He took the invitation from the little music case he always carried with him and she read it carefully. Then he handed her his mother's letter to read as well. To his surprise she had tears in her eyes.

'You'll go back, of course?' she said.

'No, I can't. Six months later it would be something else. I'd never escape, I'd be sucked back in. No, Vonni, you of all people understand how important it is to get away. You never went back to Ireland, did you?'

'No, but I wanted to, a thousand times I wanted to go back and see them. Like for my sister's wedding, like for my father's retirement party, when my mother was in hospital, all those times and many more. But I was never welcome, so I couldn't go.'

'How do you know that you would not have been welcome?' David asked. 'Did you have friends you kept in touch with?'

'No, my friends were all furious with me, I had done all the things they would love to have done – had sex with a grown-up man, abandoned school, cashed a rocky cheque in the bank strike, run off to the isles of Greece. No, they didn't keep in touch – but, oddly, Jimmy Keane did. I think he felt guilty. If he hadn't sacked Stavros, none of this might have happened. So he and he alone replied to my letters. I told him that I was *delighted* he had sacked Stavros, I think that made him feel better. Anyway, he told me all that was going on and I knew something about Ardeevin – not much, but something.'

'And he kept writing, then?'

'Yes, but, you see, I went mad then and that sort of changed everything.' She spoke as casually as if she was saying that she'd gone somewhere on the bus instead of out of her mind.

'It wasn't *really* mad, was it?' David asked.

'Oh, I think so. It was because of Magda, you see. She had a terrible husband, very violent over nothing, always imagining that Magda was flirting with people. But the truth was that she tidied her house, cooked her husband's meals and kept her head down, bent over her embroidery. That's what we thought the truth was anyway. And it might well have been. Possibly she didn't raise her head from her embroidery until Stavros was kind to her. Who will ever know now?'

'And you liked her at first?'

'Oh yes, indeed, she was a lovely gentle woman with a beautiful smile; she had a hard life – no children and a man who was unreliable. Sometimes she had bruises or a cut but she said she was clumsy or tired and had fallen. Stavros played *tavli* in the café with her husband like the other men. He didn't really want to hear stories of what went on in that house. "It's their life, Vonni, their marriage, we should not interfere . . ." And I suppose because I was so busy working long hours and looking after little Stavros . . . Well, I went along with it. Until one day I went to collect a tablecloth, and she was sitting there, the blood dripping down on to the white material. I ran for old Dr Leros, the father of Dr Leros who is here now. He patched her up and he said that this could not go on, we needed a strong man, someone like Stavros, to do something. So I told Stavros what he had said. And for once he listened to me and brought two of his friends with him. I don't know what happened but I gather they held Magda's husband down on the floor for a while and told him what would happen to him if there was another incident.'

'And did he take them seriously?'

'Very seriously, apparently, and Magda stopped being *clumsy*, as she called it, and walked with her head high and looked people in the eye for the first time. That was when people realised that she was very beautiful. Up to then we just thought she had beautiful hair,' Vonni explained in a small sad voice.

'Did you suspect that Stavros was . . . well . . . interested in her?' David asked gently.

'No, not at all. I was the last to know, the very last person in Aghia Anna. I had heard it's often the way, but I didn't believe it. Or if it happened, I thought the wife must be a spectacular thicko. Anyway it finally dawned on me.'

'How?'

'Well, not the best way really. Little Stavros was at the petrol station – he was four then, going on five. He asked why was Magda always so tired. I said I didn't think she was and little Stavros said she must be, she always had to go to bed when she came to our house, and Papa had to go and sit with her. I remember that moment as if it were this morning. I felt so dizzy and faint. Magda and Stavros? In our house? In my bed? It must be a misunderstanding. It *had* to be a mistake.'

'So what did you do?'

'I closed the petrol pumps and went home early the next day. Little Stavros was playing in the garden. We had a house over there behind Maria's. I took him by the hand across to a neighbour, then I went back. I opened the door very quietly and went in. It was very quiet, then I heard them laughing. He was calling her his little furry rabbit, something he used to call me when we made love. I opened the door and stood and looked at them. She was beautiful with her long dark curls and her olive skin. I caught a reflection of myself in the mirror. Not good. Not the right thing to do.'

There was a silence between them. Then Vonni spoke again.

'And I thought, *why* had I come home and

disturbed them? Now it was all out in the open. If I hadn't come back we could have gone on for ever, pretending everything was all right. All of us. But as I looked at her, and how beautiful she was, I knew I had lost. Of course he would want her not me. So I said nothing, just looked from one to the other for what seemed a very long time. Then Stavros said, "Please don't make a scene, Vonni, you'll upset the child." That's what he thought of first, not upsetting little Stavros! To hell with upsetting me! I had left my family and my land to be with him. No worry about upsetting Vonni who had stolen money to buy him a garage and worked in it from dawn to dusk every day to make it a success ... Suddenly things seemed as if they had tilted, like a picture being crooked on a wall. Nothing was right any more ...'

David listened, chilled by her intensity.

'I walked away. Out of the door of our bedroom, out of our house. Past where little Stavros was playing with other children. I walked up to the top of the town and into a little bar. A place where normally only the old men sat and drank. I ordered *raki*, you know, the very rough spirit they have – it's like *poitín* back home. I drank until I could forget the way her round beautiful shoulder had snuggled against his chest. I drank until I fell on the ground.

'They carried me home, I remember nothing of it. I woke up next day in our bed. There was no sign of

Stavros. I remembered her there in the bed and I got up to be very sick. There was no sign of little Stavros either. I went to work, but the smell of the petrol and the exhaust of the cars made me very sick again. I went to the bar where I had been the previous day, apologised for my behaviour, asked them how much I owed them. They all shook their heads, they were not going to charge me for becoming incapable on their terrible and probably home-made liquor. Nervously I enquired what had been the reception when they took me home.

'Magda had taken my child, *my* child, to his grandfather the barber. Stavros had just pointed them to the bedroom and left. They couldn't help me further. I had brandy this time, good Metaxa brandy to get me over the shock, and then I sort of crawled back to the petrol station but couldn't talk to anyone so I went home. Home! Huh! There was nobody there. Four days and nights of drinking, then I realised they had taken my child away from me. I heard like in a dream that Magda's husband had gone away on a fishing boat to another island. And then I remember waking up in the hospital on the Kalatriada road. Christina, who had been Stavros's first love, came to see me. "Pretend to be calm, pretend to be better, then they'll let you out," she said. So that's what I did, pretended.'

'It worked?' David said.

'Only for a bit. Stavros would not speak to me,

wouldn't tell me what he had done with my son, and I knew I must not raise my voice again or I would be back in that hospital where they locked every door behind them.'

'And Stavros?'

'Had gone across the road, was living with her. I knew they were all watching me, so I couldn't drink in the place at the top of the town. I bought a bottle here, a bottle there, I drank until I passed out. I never slept in that bed again, apart from the night when they carried me home, always on the sofa. I don't know how long it went on.

'Then Christina came and helped me pull myself together. And so a lot cleaner, tidier and relatively sober, I went up to see him. Politely he asked me to go away, to leave him. I could stay in the house. He had changed all the locks on the petrol pumps, the whole place, taken my name off the accounts, cheque books. He said that our son was living in Athens with his aunt and that I would never see him again. He explained as if he were talking to someone with mental problems that soon he would sell the garage, *his* garage, and that he and Magda would go and find little Stavros, settle somewhere new and build some kind of a life for him again.

'And suddenly I realised that this was exactly what would happen. I would be here alone, without my son, without my love, without my garage. Unable to go home, owing two thousand pounds

. . . I had managed to pay five instalments of one hundred pounds a year, which was hard enough going when I was working nine hours a day. How was I going to find that money now?'

'But in fairness, Stavros knew about the debt, surely he must have said he'd help you?' David was shocked.

'No, he never knew about it. I never told him. He thought it was my money, my inheritance, my savings,' Vonni said.

Then she moved away, and left David sitting on the harbour wall with his Greek phrase book unopened as he thought about the story he had just heard.

'Do you know what I don't understand,' Fiona said the same day as they were putting together the jigsaw pieces of Vonni's story.

'Why she didn't get a lawyer?' Thomas suggested.

'She was in no position to do that. Stolen money in her background, he *did* give her the house, and she didn't really know their customs and their ways here in a foreign community,' Elsa said.

'No, wait, I don't understand why Andreas said that little Stavros came up to the taverna on the hill to play with his son Adoni and climb trees, he couldn't have done that at four.'

'Maybe Stavros and Magda stayed for a while longer, even a good time longer,' David suggested.

'That would have been even harder for Vonni to bear if her child just lived across the road.'

'Well, she'll tell one of us, she promised that she would,' Thomas said.

'I didn't want to push her any more,' David apologised.

'You're an easy person to talk to, David, I would not be at all surprised if she came back to you,' Elsa said to him with her wonderful smile.

Vonni came back to David sooner than he had expected.

'Can you do me a favour?'

'I'd love to,' he said.

'I have to deliver some potting clay and moulds to the hospital, for their rehab classes. Will you come with me? You see, I just hate going there on my own. I keep thinking that they'll lock the door behind me as they did before.'

'But you weren't there very long?' David said. 'Didn't Christina get you out by telling you to pretend?'

'Oh yes, that was the first time. But I went back, I was there for years really,' Vonni said casually. 'Will we go and pick up Maria's van now and head off?'

'We will, we will.' David smiled.

'Are you imitating my accent, young fellow?'

'Imitate you, Vonni? I wouldn't dare!' he said.

'There's a very nice part of the garden, I'll show

you,' she said when the goods had been handed over. And they sat together looking down from one of the many hills that surrounded Aghia Anna and she picked up her story as if there had been no interruption.

This time she filled in some of the painful gaps.

'Once I knew I had lost everything I didn't see any point in pretending. I sold things out of the house, *his* house I always considered it, and bought drink. So I was back in here and out like a yo-yo. Stavros explained to everyone that I was an unfit mother. We didn't have courts or laws or social workers then . . . or if we did I wasn't sober or sane enough to understand them. I saw little Stavros once a week on a Saturday for three hours. There was always someone else there, not him, not Magda, but Stavros's father sometimes or his sister, or Andreas, they trusted him.'

'Everyone would trust Andreas. You did too?'

'Of course. But the visits were not a success. I used to cry, you see, cry over all I had lost. All that could never be. And I would clutch at little Stavros and tell him how much I loved him and needed him. He was terrified of me.'

'No, no,' David murmured.

'Truly he was, he hated the meetings. Andreas used to drive him up the hill to his place to the swing on the tree to cheer him up after he had to deal with me, then I would get bladdered with drink to get over it. It went on for years. I mean years. He was twelve when they took him away.'

'They?'

'Stavros and Magda. I was in here then, and oddly it was when they were gone I decided that there was still a life to be lived. A man here killed himself that year and it shocked us all, particularly the drunks. That had been his little problem, too, you see.

'So I got sober. Sounds simple. It was far from simple but I did it. But it was too late.

'My son the teenager was gone. No point in my trying to find out where. The boy's grandfather, the old barber, was even kind to me in the end. But he wouldn't tell me. I wrote to him, young Stavros – letters on his birthday through his grandfather and later through his aunts, every year. Even this year when he was thirty-four.'

'And no answer ever?' David asked.

'No answer, ever.'

'Does Andreas not know? He's such a kind man, he'd tell you or he'd let your son know what you are like now.'

'No, Andreas doesn't know.'

'He'd understand, too, his own selfish son won't come back to him from Chicago, Andreas knows what it feels like.'

'David, listen to me.'

'Yes?'

'There are two sides to everything. I was a pig of a mother when young Stavros was growing up, so how does he know I am mellow and easy-going now? If he were ever to get in contact, it would only be out of pity.'

'Someone might tell him,' David said.

Vonni brushed it away. 'Listen to me, David, Andreas knew everything about running a taverna when Adoni was growing up, how does Adoni know that his father is lonely and sad, and wants him to come home?'

'As I said, Vonni, someone could tell him. Like you, for example?'

'Don't be ridiculous, David, why would Adoni listen to a mad old fart, nearly as old as his father? He has to discover for himself that it might be worth while.'

'Well, they are *so* foolish, these young men, Adoni in Chicago and Stavros wherever he is, why they can't see sense and come back to you both is beyond me,' David said.

'There are probably many people in England who wonder the same about you,' Vonni suggested.

'It's totally different.'

'Do you still have that letter with you?'

'Yes, but that doesn't mean anything,' he said.

'David, you fool, I do like you hugely, but you are such a fool. That letter from your mother, she's *begging* you to come home.'

'Where does she say that?'

'In every line. Your father's ill. He may be dying for all you know.'

'Vonni!'

'I mean it, David,' she said, and looked out to sea as she had so many times from this place when her mind was gone.

CHAPTER THIRTEEN

Elsa had written nothing back to Dieter. She still needed time to think about it.

There was no doubt that Dieter meant it. If he said he would marry her then he would be prepared to do that. It would not be easy for him, after years of being on his own. He would get a lot of stick from his friends. He would hate the guilt of admitting that he had abandoned his own child. Which he would have to admit if he opened up a lifeline to little Gerda. He was prepared to do that for Elsa also, he had said as much.

Up to now he had genuinely believed that their lives could run easily together and that there was nothing about the situation that needed to be altered. But when forced to make a choice he had made it. It was up to Elsa to tell him when she would be back home and he would be there, waiting for her.

So what was holding her back?

Elsa walked on her own up one of the windy roads away from town. She had not been this way before, and since she would be leaving soon, she wanted to imprint the whole place on her mind.

No smart restaurants, traditional tavernas or craft shops on this road. Small poor dwellings, sometimes, with a goat or two outside, children playing amongst the hens and chickens.

Elsa stopped and looked at them.

Would she and Dieter have children? A little blond boy and girl, different from these dark-eyed Greek children in every way except for the smiles.

Would that take away some of the pain? Would her children grow up knowing that they had a half-sister Gerda who didn't live with them?

She was smiling to herself at being so fanciful when, unexpectedly, Vonni came out of a house.

'Heavens, Vonni, you're everywhere!' Elsa exclaimed.

'I could say the same about all of you! I never move but I fall over one of you,' Vonni said with spirit.

'Where does this road lead? I just came up this way to explore.'

'It doesn't really lead anywhere – just more of the same – but I have to deliver something a bit further on, come and walk with me, I could do with the company.'

Vonni looked uncharacteristically downhearted.

'Is something wrong?' Elsa asked.

'That house I was in just now, the woman is pregnant. The father was one of those who drowned on Manos's boat. She doesn't want the child. It's just such a mess. Dr Leros won't hear of doing a termination, so she's going to go to this woman who "manages things", as she puts it, in a village about fifty kilometres away. She could die, she could certainly get septicaemia. Why she can't have this child and love him or her is not clear. I've been there for an hour saying we'll all help her to look after the baby. But will she listen? No.'

'That's an unusual position for you to be in, Vonni. People not listening to you,' Elsa teased her.

'Why do you say that?'

'Well, we all listen to you, and take great notice of everything you say, believe me. We spent hours talking to David about your theory that his father might be ill.'

'Not might be ill, *is* ill,' Vonni said. 'And what did he decide? He wasn't too pleased with me, I can tell you that.'

'Well, he thinks it's all a trap, a way to get him home, and then it will be harder for him to get away again. But you've unsettled him.'

'I didn't want to do that,' Vonni said.

'Yes, you did in a way, you wanted to shake him up, make him think. And you've succeeded – he's going to call his home today.'

'Good,' Vonni nodded her approval. She stopped at a small ill-kept building. 'I'm going into this house – come with me. I have to give Nikolas some magic medicine.' She took a small clay pot from her woollen shoulder bag.

'You make magic medicines too?' Elsa gasped.

'No, it's an antibiotic cream actually, but Nikolas doesn't trust doctors and modern medicine so Dr Leros and I have this little ruse.'

Elsa watched as Vonni moved around the old man's simple house, picking up things here, arranging them there, talking away effortlessly in Greek; and then she produced the magic ointment and applied it solemnly to the sore on his leg.

When they left, the old man smiled at them both.

Elsa and Vonni continued to walk companionably down the windy road. Vonni pointed out landmarks and told Elsa the names of the places they passed and what they meant in English.

'You love it here, don't you?' Elsa said.

'I was lucky to find this place. Maybe I would have found another place, a different place, but Aghia Anna was good to me, I'd never live anywhere else.'

'I'll be sorry to leave, I really will,' Elsa said.

'But you are leaving? Going back to Germany?' Vonni did not sound best pleased.

'Yes, of course, I have to move on,' Elsa said.

'Move back, more like, move back to what you ran away from.'

'You don't know—' Elsa began.

'I know what you told me, how you made up your mind to escape a bad situation, and how he came here, found you and changed your mind.'

'No, *he* didn't change my mind – I changed my mind,' Elsa said, stung.

'Oh yes?'

'Really, Vonni, you of all people should know what it is to love someone and cross a continent to be with him. You did it, for heaven's sake. You should understand.'

'I was a child when I did what I did, a schoolgirl, you are a grown, sophisticated woman, with a career, a life, a confident future. We are not comparing like with like.'

'We are, it's exactly the same, you loved Stavros and gave up everything to be with him because you loved him, I'm doing the same thing for Dieter.'

Vonni paused in her walking and looked at Elsa in astonishment.

'You *can't* believe that it's remotely the same. What are *you* giving up? Nothing. You're getting everything back, your job, your man whom you still don't trust. You are returning to all that you ran from, and you think that's a victory . . .'

Elsa was angry. 'That's not true, Dieter wants to marry me. It will all be out in the open now. We'll live together as man and wife, no more hiding, and then, in time, we will *be* man and wife.' Her eyes flashed.

'And the reason you ran away in the first place . . . that was all about forcing him to propose, was it? I thought you said you felt guilty because he had abandoned his daughter and thought it didn't matter. Has all this disgust with him vanished?'

'We only have one life, Vonni. We have to put out our hands and take what we want.'

'No matter who we take it from?'

'You took what you wanted, didn't you?'

'Stavros wasn't promised to anyone else, he was free.'

'What about Christina?'

'I didn't *know* about Christina until I got here, and he had left her, and the baby died, so it was different.'

'What about the money? You took that money. You can't claim to be whiter than white!' Elsa blazed.

'It was only money and I paid it all back, every single penny!'

'You couldn't have, Vonni, that's a fantasy – you earned nothing. You were in and out of that hospital. How could you have raised that money?'

'Well, I'll tell you how. By cleaning floors in the police station, by chopping vegetables up in Andreas's taverna, by cleaning the kitchens in the delicatessen, by teaching English in the school – once I got sober enough for them to trust their children to me.'

'You did all these jobs? Washing floors?'

'I didn't have your qualifications, Elsa . . . or your confidence or your looks. What other way could I raise the money?'

'You got over Stavros in the end, didn't you? Didn't you?'

'Why do you ask?'

'I don't know. I need to know in case I make a different decision.'

'Oh, no, Elsa, you've made your decision: go back and stretch out your hands and take what you want.'

'Why are you so cruel and destructive?' Elsa cried.

'Me cruel and destructive? *Me?* Oh, catch yourself on, Elsa, for God's sake. Just listen to yourself speaking. I told you before that you were too used to getting your own way. And I mean it. There's a careless selfishness about beauty. Magda had it, you have it. It's a lethal thing to have because it gives you too much power for a time. For a time.'

'Did Magda lose her looks? Is this what you're telling me?'

'How would I know?'

'You'd know, someone would have told you,' Elsa said grimly.

'Well, funnily enough, someone did tell me – a

few people told me in fact. And she *did* lose her looks, and she has lost quite a lot of Stavros too. Apparently there's a younger woman who works in their business and Stavros sees a lot of this woman.' Vonni smiled at the thought.

'What kind of people tell you these stories? Vindictive people carrying tales?'

'Let me see what kind of people ... Possibly people who think I deserve *some* reward for losing everything and clawing my way back to a position of respectability again.'

'You don't care about respectability,' Elsa scoffed.

'Oh, but I do, we all need respect to be able to live with ourselves and make sense out of the whole thing.'

'You're a free spirit, you don't care what other people think,' Elsa insisted.

'I care what I think of myself, oh, and by the way – I did get over Stavros, though I think of him from time to time. I know his hair is white now, but I would like to see him come up 25th March Street if we could talk as normal people talk. But it's not going to happen.'

'All right, back to my situation.' Elsa was business-like. 'Why should I not go back to Dieter? Just tell me calmly without us arguing about it. Please.'

'It doesn't matter, Elsa.' Vonni sighed. 'You're not going to take any notice of what I say. You are going to do what you want to. Forget I spoke.'

And they walked in awkward silence until they reached the town.

'Shirley?'

'Yes, Thomas?'

'Is Andy there?'

'You don't really want to talk to Andy?'

'No, I was just hoping that I might be able to talk to my son without Andy-the-athlete hopping a ball and getting him away to more training, more workouts.'

'Are you picking a fight, Thomas?'

'No, of course I'm not, I'm telling you straight, I just want to talk to my kid. Okay?'

'Well, hold on, I'll get him for you.'

'And without Muscle Man Andy breathing down his neck, please.'

'You are grossly unfair as usual. Andy always makes himself scarce when you call, then he asks Bill whether he had a good chat with his dad. The only one making any trouble is you.'

'Get him, please Shirley, this is long distance,' Thomas said.

'Well, whose fault is that?'

He could almost hear her shrug.

'Hi, Dad.'

'Bill, tell me about your day,' he said and half listened as the boy went on about a track and field event for families at the university. He and Andy had won a three-legged race.

'Father-son race, was it called?' Thomas asked bitterly.

'No, Dad, they don't call them that now – you know so many families have sort of re-formed themselves.'

'Re-formed themselves?' Thomas gasped.

'Well, that's what our teacher calls it, it's got to do with so many people being divorced and everything.'

It wasn't such a bad word, but it didn't begin to hint at the whole story.

'Sure, so what do they call it?'

'A Senior-Junior race.'

'Great.'

'Are you upset about anything, Dad?'

'Are you on your own now, is it just you and me?'

'Yes, Andy always goes out to the yard when you call and Mom's in the kitchen. Why do you want to know?'

'I wanted to say that I love you.'

'Dad!'

'It's okay, I've said it now. I won't say it any more this call. I got you a wonderful book today, there's a bookshop here in this tiny place. It's stories from Greek myths but written for the modern day. I've been reading it myself all afternoon. Do you know any Greek stories?'

'Is the one about the kids who flew off to find the Golden Fleece a Greek story?'

'Sure it is, tell me a bit about it,' Thomas said, pleased.

'It was about this brother and sister and they rode on the back of a sheep . . .'

'Did you read it at school?'

'Yes, Dad, we have a new history teacher and she keeps making us read stories.'

'That's great, Bill.'

'It'll be great when I have a brother or sister next year.'

His heart felt like a lump of lead. Shirley was pregnant again. And of course she hadn't had the courtesy or courage to tell him. Now she and Andy were starting a family and she had said nothing. Thomas had never felt so alone in his life. But he must keep every door and channel open to Bill.

'That's *great* news, certainly,' he heard himself say through gritted teeth.

'Andy's painting a nursery for it. I told him how you made one for me and put in bookshelves even before I was born.'

And Thomas felt the tears in his eyes as he waded in with his two big feet and broke the whole mood.

'Well, I guess Andy will be busy putting up shelves for trainers and trophies and sports gear for the poor little kid. To hell with books this time round.'

He heard Bill gasp.

'That's not fair, Dad.'

'Life's not fair, Bill,' said Thomas, and hung up.

'Tell me about it,' Vonni said when she saw Thomas's face a couple of hours later.

Thomas didn't move from the chair where he had sat motionless. All day.

'Come on, Thomas, you messed it up again with that kid, didn't you?'

'I got out of his hair, gave him space, did all the things you *should* do, what would you have done?'

'Gone back there, claimed my territory, been a presence for him.'

'Shirley is pregnant,' Thomas said, bleakly.

'He'll need you all the more now if his mother is pregnant. But no, you have to be noble and distant and break that child's heart by giving him space he doesn't want at all.'

'Vonni, you of all people know how hard it is to do the right thing for a child. You've spent a lifetime regretting that. You should understand.'

'Do you know, I *hate* that expression "you of all people" must know this or that. Why should I, of all people, know anything?'

'Because you had a child taken away from you, you know that pain, others only guess at it.'

'I get impatient with people like you, Thomas. Very. I know I am a different generation, my son is your age but I have *never* indulged in self-pity like you do. Especially since the solution is in your own hands. You love this child, nobody but yourself is putting any distance between you and him.'

'You don't understand, I'm on sabbatical leave.'

'They're not going to get out the FBI if you go back to your home town to see your own son.'

'Would that it were so simple,' he sighed.

Vonni went towards the door as if to leave.

'Your bedroom is that way, Vonni.' He nodded his head towards the spare room.

'I'm going to sleep with the hens tonight,' Vonni said. 'They are oddly comforting in a way, just clucking and gurgling. They don't complicate their lives unnecessarily.'

And then she was gone.

Fiona was talking to Mr Leftides, the manager at the Anna Beach Hotel, about a job.

'I could mind the guests' children for you, take them off their parents' hands. I'm a qualified nurse, you see; they would be safe with me.'

'You don't speak any Greek,' the manager objected.

'No, but most of the visitors here are English-speaking, I mean even the Swedes and Germans all speak English.'

She saw Vonni across the foyer, stacking the shelves of the hotel's tiny craft shop.

'Vonni will speak for me,' Fiona said. 'She'll tell you that I can be relied on. Vonni!' she called out. 'Can you tell Mr Leftides that I'd be a good person to work here?'

'As what?' Vonni sounded curt.

'I'm going to need somewhere to live when Elsa goes back, I was asking Mr Leftides if I could work here in exchange for board and lodging and a very little money.' Fiona looked pleadingly at the older woman.

'Why do you need a job – aren't you going home?' Vonni was terse.

'No, you know I can't leave here until Shane comes back.'

'Shane is not coming back.'

'That's not true. Of course he's coming back. Please tell Mr Leftides that I'm reliable.'

'You're not reliable, Fiona, you are deluding yourself that this boy is coming back to you!'

Mr Leftides, who had been looking from one to the other as if he were at a tennis match, decided he had had enough. He shrugged and walked away.

'*Why* did you do that, Vonni?' There were tears of annoyance in Fiona's eyes.

'You are being ridiculous, Fiona. Everyone was sorry for you and kind when you had the miscarriage and all that upset. But surely by now you have come to your senses? You must know there's no future for you here, waiting foolishly for a man who will never return. Go back to Dublin and take up your life.'

'You're so cruel and cold – I thought you were a friend,' Fiona said in a shaky voice.

'I'm the best friend you ever had, if you had the intelligence to see it. Why should a friend try to help set you up in a non-job in this hotel and prolong the agony for yourself? What would you do on your own?'

'I wouldn't be on my own. I have friends, Elsa, Thomas, David.'

'They're all going back. Mark my words you'd be on your own.'

'Would it matter if I were on my own? Shane will come for me, despite what you think. Now I have to find somewhere else to work, to live.' She turned away to hide the fact that she was crying.

'Vonni, you want a Morning Glory?' Andreas often looked into the craft shop and treated her to a little metal dish with three colours of ice cream across the road in Yanni's delicatessen.

'No, I'd prefer a bottle of vodka with a lot of ice,' she said.

Andreas was startled. Vonni never joked about her drinking, and did not refer to her alcoholic past.

'Is there a problem?' he asked.

'Yes, there is. I've fought with every one of those foreign kids, every single one of them.'

'I thought you liked them, they're all very attached to you.' Andreas was very surprised.

'I don't know what it is, Andreas, I'm like a weasel, nothing would please me these days. Everything they say annoys me.'

'That's unlike you, you are always keeping the peace, smoothing things down . . .'

'Not these days, I'm not, Andreas, I feel like stirring everything up. I suppose it was the boat and all the unnecessary waste of life, it makes everything seem pointless. I can't see any sense in anything.' She was pacing around her little shop.

'There's a lot of sense in your life,' he said.

'Is there? Is there really? Today I can't see any. I think I'm a foolish woman perched here in this faraway place until I die.'

'Vonni, we are all perched here until we die.' Andreas was bewildered.

'No, you don't understand, there's a sense of uselessness about it all somehow. I used to feel like this years back, and then I would go up to the top of the town and hit the *raki* until I was senseless. Don't let me go down that road again, Andreas, my good friend.'

He laid his hand on hers.

'Of course I won't. You've fought so hard to get out of that pit you fell into, nobody is going to let you fall in again.'

'But what a stupid life I've lived – people having

to mind me, look after me, rescue me. I think telling those young people all about it over the past couple of days made me realise how stupid I've been, how selfish. That's why I suddenly want to drink and forget it all.'

'You normally forget problems by helping other people, that's what gets you by, that's why they all love you so much here.'

'If that's true then it's stopped working for me, and, do you know, I don't want to help anyone any more, I want to blank things out. And people certainly don't love me any more. I think everyone is running a hundred kilometres away from me at the moment.'

Andreas made a sudden decision. 'I need your help, Vonni, my hands are stiff, can you come and help me make *dolmadhes*? I can't bend the old fingers to stuff the vine leaves. Please close your shop here and come up to the taverna with me. As a favour, will you?'

'And of course you'll have plenty of coffee and ice cream to distract me and keep me away from the demon drink.' She gave him a weak smile.

'Certainly. That was my very plan,' he said, and they went out of the door together.

Thomas was running down the whitewashed outdoor stairs, but he couldn't have seen them as he ran by without saying hallo.

*

They sat and discussed her at midday by the harbour.

'I can understand her attacking me, because, to be very honest, a lot of people have a problem with Shane,' Fiona said. 'But the rest of you? I don't get it.'

They thought about it for a while.

'It's easy to see where she's coming from with me,' Elsa said. 'I'm a tramp who has somehow blackmailed a poor innocent guy into proposing to her.'

'And did he?' Thomas asked.

'Yes, but it's much more complex than that. Why has Vonni turned on you?' Elsa changed the subject.

Thomas rubbed his chin thoughtfully. 'I truthfully don't know what annoyed her so much about my situation, but she went on about how I had a choice over my son, and she didn't. I felt tempted to say that at least I didn't lose my senses in a vat of alcohol like she did. But I didn't want to offend her, I just wanted her to agree I was trying to be responsible and do the right thing.'

David tried to stand up for Vonni. 'You can see why she envies you though. If she had been allowed anywhere near her son she'd have been there. She knows it's her own fault – that's what makes her so enraged.'

'You're very forgiving, David, after all, she lit into you unmercifully as well,' Fiona said.

'Yes, but she got that all wrong, you see, she

doesn't know what kind of people my parents are, she doesn't begin to understand. I've read that letter over and over and there's nothing in it to suggest that my father isn't well . . .'

'But David, why did she get angry with you exactly?' Elsa asked.

'Because I was saying what a good man Andreas was and how selfish his son was not to come back and help him. She said I was putting Andreas on some kind of pedestal and that a lot of people might say I was exactly the same as Adoni, staying away instead of helping my father. But, of course, it's a totally different thing.' He looked around the table and thought he saw a look on their faces that suggested it might not be so different after all.

'I have to go and give Maria her lesson,' he said a little stiffly and went over to the house where the black-clad young widow was waving at him from the door.

David could manage a feeble conversation in Greek with Maria by now. It was halting and stumbling, but he managed to understand that she thought he was leaving the island soon. Vonni had told her that his father was ill back in England.

'No!' David cried. 'He is well! Very well!'

'Vonni say you telephone home,' Maria said.

It was hard enough to explain the situation to people who could speak English. With Maria it was impossible.

'No telephone home,' David stammered in Greek.

'*Yiati?*' she asked. It was the Greek word for why. David had no answer.

Vonni rolled up the vine leaves neatly around their little packages of rice and pine nuts. She was very quiet.

Andreas looked at her from under his big bushy eyebrows. She was right to be concerned. She had the same sense of unease and restlessness that had led her to those frightening drinking bouts all those years ago.

He wondered if he should contact his sister Christina. She and Vonni had been good friends and a huge mutual support. But then, he would do nothing without consulting Vonni.

Her face was lined as always, but today she had a deeply worried look. She frowned and gnawed at her lip.

They worked on the open-air terrace looking down over the town. Twice she got up and went into his kitchen for no reason. He watched her without appearing to do so. Once she reached up to where bottles of brandy and olive oil stood on a line on the shelf.

But she took her hand away.

The second time she just went in and looked. She touched nothing. She was breathing fast as if she had run in a race.

'What can I do for you, Vonni? Tell me,' he begged.

'I've done nothing of any use in my life, Andreas. What can anyone do for me? Ever?'

'You've been a good friend to my sister, to me, to all the people in Aghia Anna. That's worth while, isn't it?'

'Not particularly. I'm not looking for pity, I hate that in a person, it's just that I actually can't see any point in the past, the present or the future.' Her voice was flat.

'Well, then, you'd better open the brandy,' Andreas said.

'Brandy?'

'Metaxa brandy. It's on the shelf in there, you've been looking at it all morning. Take it down, drink it, then none of us will have to worry about *when* you're going to do it, it will be done.'

'Why are you saying this?'

'Because it's one way to go. You can throw away the work and discipline and denial of years in an hour or so. Because it will bring this oblivion you want. It will probably bring it quite quickly since you're not used to it.'

'And you, my friend, would stand by while I did this?'

'If you're going to do it, better it's up here, away from all the eyes of Aghia Anna,' he said philosophically.

'I don't *want* to,' she said piteously.

'No, I know that. But if you see nothing in the past, the present or the future, then I suppose you have to,' he said.

'And do *you* see any point in anything?' she asked.

'Some days it's harder than others,' Andreas said. 'You have good friends everywhere, Vonni.'

'No, I end up driving them away.'

'Who are you thinking about?'

'That foolish little Fiona, I told her her boyfriend won't come back. She was in tears. But then, I know where he is. She doesn't know.'

'Hush, hush, don't you get upset too.'

'I had no right to do it, Andreas. I'm not God.'

'You did it for the best,' he soothed her.

'I must tell her where he is,' Vonni said suddenly.

'I wonder if that's wise?'

'Can I use your telephone, Andreas?'

'Please . . .'

He heard her dial the number and then speak to Fiona. 'I called to say I had no right to shout at you today. To say that I'm sorry. Very sorry.'

Andreas moved away to give her privacy. He knew how very hard it was for Vonni to admit that she was wrong.

In Elsa's villa, Fiona looked at the telephone in her hand, mystified. Whatever she had expected it wasn't this. She was at a loss to know what to say.

'That's okay, Vonni,' she said awkwardly.

'No, it's not okay as it happens. The reason he didn't get in touch is because he's in jail in Athens.'

'Shane in jail! Oh, my God, what for?'

'Something to do with drugs.'

'No wonder I haven't heard from him. Poor Shane – and would they not let him get in touch and tell me?'

'He did try to get in touch eventually, but only so that you'd get him bail, and we said—'

'But of course I'll get him bail. Why did nobody tell me?'

'Because we thought you'd be better without him,' Vonni said lamely.

Fiona was outraged. '*We* thought, who is *we*?'

'Yorghis and I, but mainly me,' Vonni admitted.

'How dare you, Vonni! How dare you meddle in my life? Now he thinks I haven't bothered to get in touch with him. All because of you.'

'That's why I'm getting in touch now,' Vonni said. 'I'll take you to him.'

'What?'

'I owe it to you. I'll go with you on the ferry to Athens in the morning, take you to the jail, find out what's happening.'

'Why are you doing this?' Fiona was suspicious.

'I suppose I realised that it is your life,' said Vonni. 'I'll see you at the harbour for the eight o'clock ferry tomorrow morning.' Then she came back and sat down with Andreas.

'Did that work?' he asked.

'I don't know, tomorrow will tell. But I feel stronger somehow. You know the way you said a while ago that some days are better than others? How is it for you today?'

'Not great. I wrote to Adoni in Chicago and he would certainly have got the letter by now. But there's no word from him. It was hard to write, and it's even harder to bear that there's no reply. But I think we have to keep struggling on, Vonni. Manos and those boys on the boat didn't get a chance to, so I'm going to keep going until the end.'

'You wrote to Adoni?' Her eyes were bright and interested.

'Yes, nobody knows but you and Yorghis.'

'I'm so glad; you are great to do that. He'll get in touch. Believe me.'

'Why should I believe you? Seriously, you don't believe in anything yourself. Why should anyone heed what you say?'

'I know he'll ring. Is your answering machine switched on? You're always forgetting. Adoni will come back, I know he will. Suppose he comes back soon? Is his room ready?'

'It's as he left it,' Andreas shrugged.

'But we should paint it, make it smart for him.'

'He may never come back, we are only storing up more heartbreak.'

'We must not be defeatist, that's the worst crime, let's do it today. I've finished the bloody *dolmadhes* – stick them in the refrigerator and get out some paint. Have you got brushes?'

'Yes, in the shed at the back – they may be a bit hard and stiff, I'll see if we have paint remover.'

'Right, but keep a beady eye on me, one whiff of that and I could be on the slippery slope.'

He looked at her in astonishment. She truly had turned a corner. There was life and enthusiasm in her face. It was worth painting the bedroom with her just to keep it going.

Even if that boy never came, it would be worth it.

CHAPTER FOURTEEN

'Mother?'

'David!' The delight in her voice was hard to take.

'Mother, I got your letter. About the award.'

'Oh, David, I just knew that you'd call. I knew it. You're such a good boy to phone so quickly.'

'Well, you see, I'm not certain yet what's happening . . .' He did not want to be railroaded into dates of return, times of flights, seating plans and what he would wear to the function.

'Your father will be so pleased when he hears you called. It will make his day.'

Already he felt the familiar heavy weight that their pressure always created, it was in his chest and around his shoulders.

His mother was still talking excitedly. 'He'll be back in about an hour and that will really cheer him up.'

'He's not in the office on a Saturday surely?'

'No, no, just . . . um . . . out . . .'

David was surprised.

His father did not go to synagogue every week, only at the High Holidays. Saturdays were always spent at home.

'What's he doing?' David asked.

'Oh, you know . . . this and that . . .' His mother was evasive.

David felt suddenly cold. 'Is Father ill?' he asked suddenly.

'What makes you think that?' He could hear the fear in her voice.

'I don't know, Mother, I sort of got the idea that he might have an illness and that he wasn't telling me, neither of you were.'

'You got that feeling suddenly, far away in Greece?' She spoke in wonder.

'Sort of.' He shuffled. 'But is it true, Mother?'

He felt that time was standing still as he waited for her to answer. It could only have been seconds but it felt like an age. He watched from the phone box by the harbour as the day's work went on, crates being loaded and unloaded on boats, crowds going about their business normally as he waited.

'Your father has cancer of the colon, David, they can't operate. They've given him six months.'

There was a silence on the line as he caught his breath.

'Does he know, Mother? Has he been told?'

'Yes, that's what they do these days, they tell people. He's very calm.'

'And is he in pain?'

'No, amazingly, he has a lot of medication.'

David gave a gulping sound, as if he were trying to stifle a sob.

'Ah, David don't get upset, he's very resigned, he's not afraid.'

'Why didn't you tell me?'

'You know your father, he is such a proud man, he didn't want you coming back just out of pity, he wouldn't let me tell you.'

'I see,' David said miserably.

'But he didn't bank on your knowing by telepathy, David. Imagine you sensing that from all that distance away. It's uncanny, but then you were always sensitive.'

David had rarely felt so ashamed in his life.

'I'll call again on Monday,' he said.

'With your plans?' his mother said eagerly.

'With my plans,' he said wretchedly.

Thomas called his mother.

'Don't call me from so far away, son, wasting all the money on me.'

'It's okay, Mom, I get my full salary, I told you, plenty to live on like a millionaire out here, and to pay support for Bill.'

'And to send me treats too. You're a good boy, I

love those magazines you send me every month. I'd never go out and buy them for myself.'

'I know, Mom, everything for us, nothing for you. That was always your rule.'

'It's what most people do when they have children, not that it always works. I've been blessed with you and your brother, it's not always the way.'

'It's not easy being a parent, is it, Mom?'

'I didn't find it too bad, but then my spouse went and died on me rather than take up with someone else like yours did.'

'It takes two to break up a marriage, Mom, it wasn't all Shirley's fault.'

'No, but when are you finding yourself a partner?'

'One day, I assure you, and you'll be one of the first to know. Mom, I called to ask you about Bill. Do you talk to him at all?'

'You know I do, son, I call him every Sunday. He's doing fine at school, playing lots of games – he loves sport now.'

'Sure he does, now that his boring old father isn't there to annoy him with books and poetry and things.'

'He misses you like hell, Thomas, you know that.'

'Hasn't he got Golden Boy Andy and a new brother or sister on the way? What does he want me for?'

'He told me you didn't feel good about the new baby,' his mother said.

'I was meant to dance with joy about it, I suppose,' Thomas said bitterly.

'He said he thought you would love the new baby, like Andy loves him even though he's nothing to him.'

'He honestly thought I'd love the new baby?' Thomas was astounded.

'He's a child, Thomas. He's just nine years of age, his father has left him, left America. He was clutching at straws. He thought that maybe you would come back if there was a new baby for you to be stepfather to, like Andy is to him.'

'Andy is a horse's ass, Mom.'

'He may well be, son, but he's a kind horse's ass, Thomas,' his mother said.

'*I'm* kind, Mom.'

'I'm sure you are, in fact I know you are, but I'm not entirely sure Bill knows that.'

'Come on, Mom, I've done the right thing, given him his freedom, not crowded him out. I've let him adjust to his new life.'

'Yeah, and at the age of nine a child will understand all that?'

'What do you think I should do?'

'I don't know, be near him, not thousands of miles away, I guess.'

'You think that would sort it?'

'I don't know, but at least Bill wouldn't think

you, who are his flesh and blood, had abandoned him.'

'Sure, Mom, I hear what you say.'

Elsa read the second fax from Dieter.

> *I know you read what I wrote last week.*
> *They told me in the hotel that the message*
> *had been given to you. Please stop playing*
> *games, Elsa; just tell me when you are*
> *coming back. You are not the only player on*
> *the stage, I have my life to lead too. Why*
> *should I tell anyone anything about us until*
> *I know that you are coming back and when.*
> *Please answer me today.*
> *I love you for ever,*
> *Dieter*

She read it over and over and tried to hear his voice as if he were speaking the words. She could hear it very well. Dieter speaking quickly, decisively and urgently. *Please answer me today.*

It was he who was playing the central figure on the stage. Had he forgotten that this was all about her life, her future? How dare he ask her for such a speedy answer. She went to the little business centre in the Anna Beach where you could send e-mails.

> *It's a big decision. I need time to think.*

Don't hassle me. I'll write in a few days.

I love you for ever also, but that's not the only consideration.

Elsa

Fiona woke very early, she saw the dawn come up over Aghia Anna. She could hardly believe the conversation that she had had with Vonni last night.

She was still furious with Vonni and Yorghis for having lied to her. How dare they tell her that Shane had not been in touch? How dare they leave her with this sick feeling that Shane might possibly have abandoned her, left her because she was too stupid, too thick? But he *had* tried to contact her and these old busybodies had interfered.

They said his motive was only to get her to raise the bail money. Well, of course he had to get bail first to get out, to get on with life. What did they expect?

She was so glad that she would see him today.

She was not relishing the thought of the ferry trip with Vonni as a companion. She wished too that she hadn't told it all to Elsa last night. Elsa had been less than supportive.

Fiona wished mightily that she could turn the clock back. Why had she asked Elsa to help her raise the money? To lend her a thousand euros, just for a few days until Barbara could send it to her from Dublin.

'Lend you money to get him out to finish off your face?' Elsa had scoffed.

'That was different,' Fiona began. 'He was in shock, I told him the news all wrong you see.'

Elsa had lifted Fiona's hair. 'The discoloration and the bruises are still there,' she had said softly. 'Nobody on earth, Fiona, is going to lend you money to get that guy out of a place where he should be kept permanently.'

Fiona must have looked desolate because Elsa had become contrite immediately.

'Look, I'm as bad as Vonni lecturing you, I know it's hard, I *know* this. But I'll tell you what I'm trying to do, I'm trying to stand outside myself to look at things, my own situation, I mean, objectively. Look in on it rather than be a part of it. That might help you too.'

Fiona had shaken her head. 'I don't think it would do anything except make me see from the outside poor Shane, who loves me and who tried to contact me, languishing in a Greek prison. That's all I can see, Elsa, Shane thinking I've abandoned him. And it isn't helping me at all.'

Elsa had looked at her with the kind of look you might give to a picture of a starving orphan in an advertisement for famine relief. It was a look of pity, concern and bewilderment that such things were allowed to happen in the world.

*

When Vonni and Fiona met at the harbour, Vonni had bought the tickets. Two day returns. Fiona opened her mouth to say that she would not be coming back today. But closed it again.

'You've brought a big bag with you?' Vonni said, surprised.

'Well, you never know.' Fiona was vague.

The ferry pulled out of the harbour and Fiona looked back at Aghia Anna. So much had happened since she came here such a short time ago.

Vonni had gone downstairs to where they were serving coffee and drinks. Suppose she suddenly went back on the drink. Here on this boat. It could happen. Andreas had told David that Vonni was very low and for the first time in years had actually mentioned the possibility of drinking. Please God may it not happen when they were out on the high seas.

To her relief she saw Vonni returning with coffee and two sticky-looking cakes.

'*Loukoumadhes*,' she explained. 'They're honey fritters with cinnamon. They'll give you great energy for the day.'

Fiona looked at her gratefully. The woman was making every attempt at an apology. Fiona knew she must be gracious.

'You have been kindness itself,' she said, patting Vonni's hand.

To her surprise she saw tears in Vonni's eyes. And they sat companionably and ate their honey cakes.

'Yorghis?'

'Andreas! I was just thinking of you, come in, come in!' The chief of police pulled up a chair for his brother.

'Yorghis, something has happened . . .'

'A good thing or a bad thing?' Yorghis asked.

'I don't know.'

'Come on, you must know.'

'No, I *don't* know. There was a message on the answering machine in English. It was from the store where Adoni works. They said that as soon as I saw him I was to ask him to telephone about the keys to a storeroom which none of them could find. It was a complicated message but it was as if they thought . . . as if they believed he might be . . .'

Yorghis grasped his brother's hand. 'Do you think that means he might be coming home?' he asked, almost afraid to get the words out.

'It might mean that, Yorghis, it might,' said Andreas, his face alive with hope.

In the newsroom, Elsa's friend Hannah saw Dieter sitting alone and went up to him. Normally people didn't approach the great Dieter unless it was very important indeed. But she judged that this was fairly urgent. Hannah had just got an e-mail. Very short and to the point.

I feel very safe and peaceful in this small town. It's a good place to make decisions. But everything moves slowly here including my brain. If Dieter does ask about me, can you please say that I'm not playing games. I am thinking things through and will be in touch. *He probably won't ask you, but I wanted you to be prepared.*
    Love, Elsa

Hannah laid it on Dieter's desk.

'I know you didn't exactly ask ...' she said hesitantly.

'But I am very pleased to read this. Thank you, Hannah.' He had remembered her name, which was unusual for Dieter.

Vonni pointed out the places the ferry passed by. This was an island where there had once been a leper colony; that was a place which had suffered in an earthquake; this was a place where they had a festival in the springtime; here was a headland where a whole village left overnight and went to Canada, no one knew what made them leave.

'Weren't you lucky that you came to this land, Vonni? You love it so much.'

'Lucky?' Vonni said. 'I sometimes wonder about luck.'

'What do you wonder about it?'

'I don't think there's any such thing really. Look at all the people hoping for luck, buying lottery tickets, all the thousands going to Las Vegas, the millions reading their horoscopes, people hunting for four-leafed clovers or not walking under ladders. It's all fairly pointless, isn't it?'

'But people need to have some hope,' Fiona said.

'Sure they do, but we *make* our own luck, we make decisions which turn out well or badly, there isn't anything outside us that works like a black cat crossing our path or being born under the sign of Scorpio.'

'Or a prayer to St Jude?' Fiona suggested with a smile.

'You're surely too young to have heard of St Jude!' Vonni said.

'My gran relied on him entirely to find her spectacles, for her numbers to come up at bingo, for her horrible little yapping Jack Russell terrier to get over his fits. Anything at all, St Jude was called on. And he always obliged.'

'Always?' Vonni was sceptical.

'Well, maybe not in the case of her eldest granddaughter! Gran had St Jude on standby to find me a nice rich doctor to marry. That one didn't take.'

Fiona grinned proudly as if single-handedly she had defeated St Jude, the famed patron saint of hopeless cases, and thwarted his plans by sticking resolutely to Shane.

'Are you looking forward to seeing him?' Vonni asked.

'I can't wait, I hope he won't be angry that it took me so long.' The sense of accusation and outrage was still there.

'I told you, I'll explain, I'll tell him it wasn't your fault.'

'I know you will, Vonni, thank you . . . it's just . . . you know . . .' Fiona was twisting her hands awkwardly, trying to explain something.

'Tell me,' Vonni encouraged her.

'Well, you've met Shane, he can be a bit difficult you know, say things that sound much more aggressive than they are. It's just the way he reacts. I wouldn't want you to think . . .'

'Don't worry, Fiona, I won't think anything,' said Vonni through gritted teeth.

'Elsa! I'm delighted to see you,' Thomas called.

'Well you must be the only person on this island who is,' Elsa said.

'You can't mean that. I was going to rent a rowing boat and go out for a couple of hours, would you trust me enough to come with me?'

'I'd love it. Shall we go now?'

'Sure. David's not coming to the café, his father is ill, Vonni was right about that anyway. He's going to arrange a ticket home.'

'Poor David.' Elsa was sympathetic. 'And Fiona's gone to Athens with Vonni. She left this morning, very angry with me, because I wouldn't lend her money to bail Shane out of prison.'

'So we're on our own,' Thomas said.

'I'd love a farewell boat journey, I'll help with the rowing if you like.'

'No, lie back and enjoy it. A farewell journey? You *are* going back to Germany then?'

'Oh yes, I don't know exactly what day, but I am going.'

'Is he very pleased, Dieter?'

'He doesn't know yet,' she said simply.

Thomas was surprised. 'Why haven't you told him?' he asked.

'I don't know, there are a few things I haven't sorted out in my mind,' Elsa said.

'I see,' said Thomas, in the voice of one who didn't.

'And you, Thomas, when will *you* go back?'

'It depends a bit,' he said.

'On what?'

'On whether I really believe Bill wants me there.' He spoke candidly.

'Of course he does, that's obvious,' Elsa said.

'How is it so obvious to you?' he wondered.

'Because *my* father left us when I was young. I would have given anything to have had a phone call saying that he was on the way home to live near our street and I could see him every day. That would have been the best thing that could have happened. But it never did.'

Thomas looked at her, astounded. She made it seem so simple, so easy. He put his arm around her shoulder and headed down to where they hired out the brightly coloured boats.

In the crowded harbour of Piraeus, Fiona followed, lugging her heavy bag with her, as Vonni led the way to the *Ilektrikos* and bought the tickets.

'It's a fine place on its own apart altogether from being beside Athens,' Vonni explained. 'Full of marvellous little fish restaurants, and there's a great big bronze statue of Apollo – but we've no time for any of that now.'

'Do you know, I'm a bit afraid of seeing him again,' Fiona said, as they got on the Métro for Athens.

'But he loves you, he'll be delighted to see you, won't he?' Vonni asked doubtfully.

'Yes, yes of course. It's just that we don't know how much the bail will be, and really I'm not sure how I'm going to get it when we *do* know. It's not the kind of thing that they're going to help me with from Dublin. I might have to tell them back home that it's for something else.'

Vonni said nothing.

'But of course he'll be very pleased to see a friendly face.'

'You're not really afraid of seeing him, are you?' Vonni asked.

'Well, I think you're always a bit nervous of someone you love,' Fiona said. 'It sort of goes with the territory, doesn't it?'

Yorghis had phoned ahead to let them know that Vonni and Fiona were on their way. He had given a short thumbnail sketch of who they were. The policeman at the Athens station listened to him until he finished.

'Well, if this foolish girl can somehow raise the bail and get him out of our sight there will be nobody more pleased than us,' he said grimly. 'We'd nearly give her the money ourselves to be rid of him.'

As they went into the police station Fiona paused to take out her compact and comb. Vonni watched stricken as the girl applied makeup to the yellowed bruise on her forehead and arranged her hair so that it disguised it still further. She put on some lipstick and sprayed cologne on her wrists and behind her ears.

She smiled at her own reflection to give herself confidence.

'I'm ready now,' she said to Vonni in a shaky voice.

They only told Shane ten minutes before the visit that Fiona was on her way.

'Has she got the money?' he asked.

'What money?' Dimitri, the young policeman, asked.

'The money you bloodsuckers want, to give me back my human liberties!' Shane shouted, kicking at the side of his cell.

'Do you want a clean shirt to wear for her visit?' Dimitri was impassive.

'You want it all to look good and squeaky clean – no, I don't want a bloody fresh shirt, I want her to see things as they are.'

'They'll be here very shortly.' The policeman was curt.

'They?'

'She has another woman from Aghia Anna with her.'

'Another lame duck, that's just typical of Fiona, she takes her time getting here and then she drags someone else in on the act.'

As he closed and locked the door, Dimitri reflected on the nature of love. He himself was engaged to be married. He was a solid, reliable person, and sometimes he worried that he might be too dull for his glamorous-looking fiancée. They often said that girls liked a whiff of danger. That old policeman in Aghia Anna had said that the young woman who was coming to see Shane was a nurse, a gentle soul, an attractive girl ... Heigh-ho as they said. He must not make generalisations.

'How old are you, Andreas?'

'I am sixty-eight years old,' Andreas said.

'My father is sixty-six, and he is dying,' David said.

'Oh, David, I am so very sad to hear that, really so very sad.'

'Thank you, Andreas, my friend, I know that is the truth.'

'You will go home to be with him?'

'Yes, I will, of course I will.'

'And he is going to be so pleased to have you there. Believe me. Can I advise you on something? Be very kind to him. I know you were all upset when Vonni tried to give you advice . . .' Andreas sounded hesitant.

'Yes, I was annoyed, but it turned out that she was right, I tried to find her and tell her, but she's not here . . .'

'No, she went to Athens today, but she will be home tonight.'

'Suppose you were ill, Andreas, what would you like your son to say to you?'

'I think I would like him to tell me that I had been a reasonable father to him,' Andreas said.

'I'll say that when I get home,' David said.

'He will be happy to hear that, David.'

They led Vonni and Fiona to the holding cell to see Shane.

Dimitri opened the door. 'Your friends are here,' he said tersely.

'Shane!' Fiona cried.

'You took your time.'

'I didn't know where you were until yesterday,' she said, moving towards him.

'Huh,' Shane said, not responding to her arms held out to him.

'I was responsible for all that, I did not pass on the fact that you had been in touch,' Vonni said.

'Who the hell are you?' Shane asked.

'I'm Vonni, from Ireland originally, but I've lived in Aghia Anna for over thirty years. I'm sort of a local there by now.'

'What are you doing here?' he asked.

'I came with Fiona to help get her here to see you.'

'Okay, thank you. Can you piss off now and leave me with my girlfriend?' he asked with darkened brow.

'Up to you, Fiona,' Vonni said pleasantly.

'Not up to her actually. Up to me,' Shane said.

'Perhaps you could wait for me ... a bit ... outside, Vonni?' Fiona begged.

'I'll be there when you need me, Fiona,' Vonni said and left.

Dimitri was waiting outside the door.

'*Dhen pirazi*,' she said to him.

'What?' he said, alarmed.

'I've lived here for years,' she said in his own language. 'I am married to a Greek, I have a Greek son older than you are, I was saying, *Dhen pirazi*, it doesn't matter, nothing matters, that fool of a girl is going to forgive that horrific boy everything.'

'Perhaps women *like* those kind of men.' Dimitri had misery written all over his face.

'Don't believe it. They do not love nor even like people like that. For a time, they might think it's love. But it passes, women can be foolish but they are not idiots. Fiona will soon realise what a horror that boy in your cell is. It's only a question of when.'

Dimitri seemed pleased with her confidence in this matter.

'Who's that old bat you brought with you?' Shane asked.

'She was very kind.'

'Sure,' he scoffed.

Fiona moved towards him to kiss him, to hold him to her, but he didn't seem to be interested.

'Shane, it's so great to see you,' she said.

'Did you bring the money?' he asked.

'Sorry?'

'The money, to get me out!' he said.

'But, Shane, I don't *have* any money. You know that.' Fiona's eyes were enormous. Why was he not reaching out to hold her?

'Tell me you didn't eventually turn up here with nothing to say?' he asked.

'I have plenty to say, Shane . . .'

'Say it then.'

Fiona wondered why were they still not embracing, but she knew she must keep talking. She didn't know whether to tell him the good news or the bad news first.

'Well, the good news is that I heard from Barbara. There are lovely apartments very near the hospital and we could easily get one and go back there.'

He looked at her uncomprehending.

Fiona spoke quickly. 'But the sad news is that we lost our baby. It was awful but it happened. Dr Leros said that there are no problems – as soon as we want to try again . . .'

'What?'

'I know you're upset, Shane, I was too, desperately, but Dr Leros said—'

'Fiona, shut up talking rubbish about Dr this and Dr that. Do you have the money or do you not?'

'Sorry, Shane, what are you saying?'

'Have you the money to get me out?'

'Of course I don't have the money, Shane, I told you, I came to see you, to talk about it, to tell you that I love you and it will all be all right . . .'

'How will it all be all right?'

'Shane – I'll borrow it and we'll get this flat back in Dublin and we'll pay the money back . . .'

'Oh, Fiona, stop wittering on, for Christ's sake. Where are we going to get the bail?'

He still hadn't touched her, held her or talked about their dead baby.

'Shane, aren't you sad about the baby?'

'Shut up and tell me where on God's earth we're going to find the *money*!' he said.

'I lay in a bed and our baby drained away,' Fiona said.

'That was not a child, it was a period. You *know* that, Fiona, so just tell me where we are going to get the money?'

'We'll ask them, Vonni and I will, how much it is they want and then I'll try and raise it – but that's not the most important thing, Shane . . .'

'So what's the most important thing?' he asked.

'Well, that I've found you and that I love you for ever.' She looked at him waiting to see a response.

There was nothing.

'I adore you, Shane . . .' she said.

'Sure,' he said.

'So why don't you kiss me?' she asked.

'Oh God, Fiona, will you shut up about love and think who might get us the money,' he said.

'If we are able to borrow it, then we'll have to get a job to pay it back,' she said anxiously.

'*You* get a job if you want to, as soon as I'm out of here I have people to meet, contacts to make. I'll have plenty of money then.'

'You're not coming back to Aghia Anna?'

'That dump? No way.'

'So where will you go, Shane?'

'I'll hang round Athens for a bit and then I might move up to Istanbul. It depends.'

'What does it depend on?'

'On who I meet, on what they say.'

She looked at him levelly. 'And am I to go with you to meet people and go to Istanbul and everywhere?'

He shrugged. 'If you want to, but you're not to nag me about settling down and getting jobs and dragging me back to that one-horse town. We left Ireland to get away from all that kind of shit.'

'No, we left Ireland because we loved each other and nobody understood it, they kept putting difficulties in our way.'

'Whatever,' Shane said.

She knew that tone of voice. It was his switch-off voice. He used it when talking to people who bored him rigid. When they had escaped from such people, Shane would sigh with relief and say that there were so many laws and restrictions in place, why wasn't there a law against bores?

Fiona knew now that she bored Shane. She began to understand that he had never loved her.

Never at all.

It was staggering and almost impossible to take in but she knew she was right. It meant that all this had been for nothing, all her hopes and dreams. All the fears and anxieties of the last few days when she had been sleepless in case he would not get in touch. He would never have got in touch if he hadn't wanted the money for bail.

She knew that her mouth was open and her eyes widening. She knew that from the way he was looking at her.

'What are you gawping at?' Shane asked her.

'You don't love me,' she said in a shaky voice.

'Oh, Lord God above, how often do I have to play the record? I *said* you could come with me if you wanted to. I just begged you not to nag me. Is that a crime? Tell me.'

There was a wooden chair in the corner. Fiona sat down and buried her head in her hands.

'No, Fiona, not now. Not when we have to think what to do. This is not the time to go all weepy and emotional on me. Leave it off, will you . . .'

She looked up at him, her hair was back from her face. Despite the makeup, the bruising was still very visible.

He stared at her.

'What happened to your face?' he asked, as if somehow repelled by it.

'You did it, Shane. In the restaurant out on the point.' She had never before referred to his having beaten her. This was a first.

He began to bluster. 'I did *not*,' he said.

Fiona was calm. 'You've probably forgotten. It's not important any more.'

She stood up as if to leave.

'Where are you going? You've only just got here, we have to work this out.'

'No, Shane, *you* have to work it out.'

'Stop threatening me.'

'I'm not threatening you, nor nagging you. I've seen you and now I'm leaving.'

'But the money? The bail?' His face was distorted. 'Look, I'll say all that stuff about love if it's what you want ... Fiona, don't go!'

She knocked on the door and Dimitri opened it for her. He seemed to have taken in the situation. There was a smile on his face.

This drove Shane into a frenzy. He leaped towards Fiona and caught her by the hair.

'You are *not* coming in here playing games like this with me!' he roared.

But Dimitri was more speedy than anyone would have thought. He had his arm across Shane's throat, forcing his chin upwards. It meant he had to let go of Fiona in order to fight off the policeman.

It was no contest.

Dimitri was big and fit. Shane was no match for him.

Fiona stood at the door for a moment, watching, then she moved out into the corridor and walked to the front office.

Vonni was sitting there with a senior policeman.

'They're talking about two thousand euros,' she began.

'Let them talk about it, he's not getting it from me,' Fiona said. Her head was high, her eyes were bright.

Vonni looked at her, hardly daring to hope. Could it really be over? Could Fiona be free? It looked very like it indeed . . .

CHAPTER FIFTEEN

Thomas rowed the little boat back to the harbour. It seemed like coming home.

They looked up towards the hills and pointed to the places they knew. That was the hospital in the Kalatriada road. And that was the road up to Andreas's taverna.

And there, finally, was the harbour and the café with the check tablecloths. It was all so different from California and Germany. They sighed as they came into the arms of the harbour.

It was as if the escapism were over.

Thomas and Elsa had returned the little boat.

'It was good, your voyage?' the old man asked.

'Very good voyage,' Elsa said with a smile.

'*Avrio*? You come again for the boat tomorrow?' Business had been slow and the old man wanted to secure as many bookings as he could.

'Possibly, but not certainly,' Thomas said. He didn't want to promise something that could not be delivered. He knew that Elsa would be spending tomorrow getting ready for her trip back home. They hadn't talked about it but they both knew the leisurely row along the coastline had been a form of goodbye.

They walked up the harbour road towards the town.

'I wonder if we'll forget this place eventually,' Thomas said.

At exactly the same moment, Elsa said, 'Imagine all this busy world going on without us!'

They laughed at thinking almost the same thought, and as they were passing a café, Thomas indicated that they should sit down.

'Why not?' Elsa was pleased. 'By this day next week there'll be very little chance of dropping into a café, let's make the most of it.'

'Ah, you speak for yourself,' Thomas said. 'I'll still be here dropping into cafés, rowing boats, reading in the sunshine.'

'No, you'll be on your way back to California,' she said with a great sense of being right about it.

'Elsa! You're as bad as Vonni. I told you I'm only three months into my sabbatical, I'm not going back until the year is over. And even if I could, it would only make things worse.' He was puzzled at her certainty.

'I'll send you a postcard, you'll be there to get it,' she laughed.

'You are so wrong. Why should I go?'

'Because the great goddess of this island Vonni has said you should go, and when she speaks, things happen. And look, David is leaving tomorrow . . .'

'But he's the only one, and his father *is* dying – he *has* to go, she was right about him. The rest of us aren't taking any heed of her. Fiona's gone to Athens to find her madman, you're leaving, I'm staying. One out of four – that's not a great strike rate.'

'The game isn't over, I'd say she'll have a much higher strike rate in the end.'

Andreas came over to their table.

'May I join you? I have some good news to share.'

'Adoni?' Elsa gasped with excitement.

Andreas shook his head. 'No, not as good as that, alas, but still good. The little Fiona has turned her back on Shane, she has walked out on him, straight out of the police station. She and Vonni are on the last ferry, they will be back by sunset.'

'How do you know?' Thomas asked.

'One of the police telephoned Yorghis with the news. She did not even try to raise his bail – just left.' Andreas spread out his hands at the mystery of it all.

'But why? Why on earth did she go to all that trouble and then walk out on him?' Elsa was mystified.

'Apparently he hit her, or hurt her somehow,' Andreas said hesitantly.

'Well, he sure did that before and it didn't worry her,' Thomas said grimly.

'This must have been different. Something happened there to make her see him as he is.' Elsa was thoughtful.

'Well, it is all very much for the best,' Andreas said. 'And David is coming up to dinner in my taverna tonight to say goodbye, he is leaving Aghia Anna tomorrow afternoon. I wanted to ask you to join us. Yorghis will pick up Fiona at the ferry and take her there. Say yes?'

Thomas asked, 'And will Vonni join the dinner too?'

'I hope so, yes indeed.' Andreas's smile was warm at the thought of cooking for so many friends.

Thomas spoke quickly. 'You are so kind, Andreas, but alas Elsa and I have to meet someone tonight for dinner. What a pity, we would have much preferred to have gone to you.'

Elsa picked it up quickly. 'Yes, that's such bad timing,' she said. 'Can you tell David we'll see him at the harbour at midday?'

Andreas understood.

He understood more than they realised. Of course, it was very last-minute, he reassured them. But he could read signs as well as anyone. These two wanted to be alone.

He didn't say it, however, he left them courteously.

They watched as he saluted the waiters and many of the customers.

'Amazing to be so centred, so rooted in a place like he is,' Thomas said admiringly, watching the old man leave.

'Why did you say that, about us having dinner?' Elsa asked.

Thomas was silent for a moment. 'I don't really know, Elsa, but I knew you didn't want another run-in with Vonni, and as it happens I share your view. Neither do I. I also didn't want to hear one word tonight about Shane. And . . . and . . .'

'And what?'

'And I'll miss you when you go. I wanted some more time together before you left, just the two of us.'

She gave him one of her extraordinary smiles.

'Those were all very good reasons, Thomas, and as it happens – to use your phrase – I share every one of them!'

Fiona and Vonni walked through Piraeus. Such a busy place, a city in its own right. They were jostled by the crowds as they walked together, Fiona dragging her large bag.

But she was very cheerful.

'You were right, Vonni, about all those fish

restaurants. Can I treat you to a meal? I don't know what we'd call it, late lunch, afternoon tea?'

'Oh, I'd love some *barbouni*,' Vonni said, clapping her hands like a child being offered an ice cream.

'That's red mullet, I know that much. Here, does this place look all right to you?'

'It looks fine, shall I tell him it's *barbouni* and fries for two?' Vonni asked.

'Great, and I could murder a bottle of retsina.'

'Sure,' Vonni said in a clipped voice.

Fiona bit her lip. What a thoughtless thing to have said to a woman who must never touch alcohol.

'Or fizzy water,' she said lamely.

'Oh, for God's sake, Fiona, drink the retsina, you're entitled to it, and if I'm going to break out, it won't be because my dining companion has her snout in that paint stripper of a wine. Even in my worst days I couldn't swallow it. So you're not putting me in any temptation.'

They talked companionably of the life of a big port like this, sailors coming and going, fishermen unloading their catch. Students with backpacks getting off boats, and the rich yachting set driving to their berths further on.

It was a lively scene.

At no stage did Vonni mention what had happened at the police station. Nor the future for Fiona without Shane. Fiona would bring the matter up when and if she wanted to, and they were both easy with that.

When it was time to leave for the ferry that would take them back to Aghia Anna, Fiona asked for the bill.

'*O logariasmos!*' said the waiter, presenting it to her.

'You know, it's like the word for those logarithms we did at school . . .'

'Do they still have those? Here, let me pay half,' Vonni said.

'They may be gone since my time,' Fiona agreed. 'No, put your money away, you bought the ferry tickets.'

'I have a job, which is more than you do,' Vonni protested.

'Look at it this way: I'm actually two thousand euros to the good because of today's events. I call that as good as winning the lottery.' And the two women smiled at each other. In many ways it was better than winning the lottery.

On the boat back to Aghia Anna, Vonni saw Fiona gripping the boat rail and looking out to sea.

Her lips were moving. She might be praying. Or crying. Or just working something out. Whatever it was, Vonni didn't think she needed any assistance, or even conversation.

David helped Andreas in the kitchen.

'I'll miss all this so much,' he said.

'Perhaps you could cook for a while for your father.'

'It's not the same.'

'No, but it won't be for very long and he might like it. Take out your notebook and write this down. I tell you how to make a good *moussaka*. Do you have *melitzanes* in England?'

'Aubergines? Yes, we do.'

'Then I'll show you, it will please him to see you cook for him.'

'Do you think so?' David was doubtful.

'I don't think so, I *know* so,' said Andreas.

Yorghis telephoned from the harbour. He had waylaid Fiona and Vonni, they would be at the taverna in fifteen minutes.

'Yorghis says that Fiona is in great form,' Andreas said.

'She must have got that fool out of jail then,' David said glumly.

'No, on the contrary, I was about to tell you. She turned her back on him. Left him there.'

'For the moment. She'll go back for him.'

'I think not, but I suggest that we let her tell us herself. Do you agree?'

'Oh yes, that's always my policy,' David said. 'And is she speaking to Vonni still?'

'The best of friends apparently, according to Yorghis.'

David laughed. 'Aren't you a wonderful pair of old gossips!'

'If you can't gossip with your own brother, I ask you, then who is there to gossip with? Where is your notebook? Right, a kilo of best minced lamb, next . . .'

'Would you like to go to the Anna Beach?' Thomas suggested to Elsa.

'No, it's too . . . I don't know . . . too full of chrome and opulence. Besides, it doesn't have good memories for me. What about that little place out on the point where the waves break?'

Thomas didn't want to go there. 'It reminds me too much of the day that savage hit Fiona. He came at her with his fist – he could have broken every bone in her face . . .'

'But it didn't happen and now she has left him,' Elsa soothed. 'So where should we go? It can't be too public, we did say we were meeting some-one . . .'

'Why don't we get some kebabs and wine and go back to my place?' Thomas suggested.

'Sure, that's great. And if Vonni sees us we can say something . . .'

'She's on hen-house duty at the moment, she won't come in. But just suppose she does, we'll tell her that our friend, an unreliable German, didn't turn up.'

'No! She'd never believe that. A German unreliable? Not in a million years,' Elsa laughed. 'Let's make it an unreliable American . . .'

'How grossly unfair and racist of you. No, I won't have such a slur on my people. An unreliable Irishman maybe?'

'No, Vonni's Irish, she'd know him – reliable or unreliable. It had better be something else. English, I think.'

'That's so unfair on poor David, who is by far the most reliable of the four of us. But these are desperate times needing desperate measures. English he is then, the bad man who let us down.'

'I'll leave a note for Fiona saying I'll be back later and then let's go buy supper.'

There was a definite change in Fiona, they could all sense it. She held her shoulders back, she smiled more readily. She had lost that stooped and slightly defensive tone. Suddenly you could see the kind of girl she had been before.

She ran around helping to get things organised for the evening dinner.

There were three tables of customers, all of them English-speaking. Fiona translated the menu and advised them all to start with *dolmadhes*, which, she explained, were little fat packets of stuffed vine leaves. They were made on the premises, Fiona assured them, and were excellent. She suggested the house wine, which was inexpensive and good. Soon she had them so well organised that little Rina, the girl who helped in the kitchen, could serve them.

That meant that Andreas could sit down with his party and look at the lights going on down in the heart of Aghia Anna.

'A pity Thomas and Elsa couldn't join us,' David said.

'Oh well, you know,' Andreas shrugged.

The others didn't know, but it wasn't something to argue about.

'I'll never forget this place, never,' David said with a catch in his voice.

'You'll come back and visit us again often.' Andreas spoke quickly before David became emotional.

'Oh, I will, it won't be the same, but I will,' he promised.

'And you, Fiona, you are very good with people, you look after them well, would you like to work here?' Andreas said unexpectedly.

'Work? Here?' She was disbelieving.

'I watched you with the customers – you were just what I need. You could even stay here in Adoni's room. You'll need somewhere to stay when Elsa leaves.'

Fiona laid her hand on his. 'If you had asked me this last night or even early this morning I would have cried with gratitude. But now, now I say thank you from my heart, but I will not be able to come and work here.'

'It is too far up from the town?' Andreas asked.

'No, Andreas, not too far. It's just that I'm going home. Back to Dublin.'

She looked around the table at their astonished faces.

'Yes, I thought about it all the way back from Athens on the ferry. I just came back to say goodbye.'

Hannah wrote an e-mail.

Dear Elsa,
 I don't quite know what you want to hear. But anyway I showed Dieter your last e-mail. He read it carefully and thanked me. Very politely. That's not his usual form. I thought you should know. Also you should know that Birgit has done everything except strip in front of his desk to attract his attention and he is only greatly irritated by her.
 I tell you these things, Elsa, so that you should be in full possession of the facts before you make whatever decision you do.
 Naturally I would love you to come home.

But wherever you are we will always be friends.
    Love,
    Hannah

Thomas and Elsa finished their meal and sat on the balcony looking out over the rooftops.

'You have a nicer view from your place,' Thomas said.

'You can still see the stars from here, that's all that matters,' Elsa said.

'What is the stars, Joxer?' Thomas quoted in a heavy Irish accent.

'Will you say that I am showing off if I say I know where that's from?'

'Go on, tell me, shame me, put me down!' he laughed.

'It's by Sean O'Casey,' she said.

'Top of the class, Elsa. Another devoted teacher?'

'No, Dieter and I went to London, on a secret trip, and we saw it there. It was brilliant.'

'Are you looking forward to being back with him again?' Thomas asked.

'There's a problem,' she said.

'Isn't there always?' he sympathised.

'I suppose so. This problem is an unusual one: he has promised that there will be no more deception and hiding and sneaking away from people. It will all be out in the open.' She sounded doubtful.

'That's better, isn't it, in the open?' Thomas asked, surprised.

'Well, I think so, but in a way it might not be.' She chewed her lip.

'You mean you get a kick out of it being secret, clandestine?' he asked.

'No, I don't mean that at all. It's just that he never owned up to something else. Like the fact that he and another woman had a child.'

'Since you and he were together?' Thomas asked.

'No, years before, but the point is that he never acknowledged that little girl.'

'Is that what you ran away from?'

'I did not run away, I left my job and went to see the world. But I did think less well of him. Anyone who has a child, either deliberately or accidentally, must be there for that child.'

'And he didn't agree?'

'No, and somehow I was revolted by it. I felt I could never trust him again. I felt ashamed of loving him. I told him all this.'

'And so what has changed? What makes you think that it's right to go back to him now?'

'Meeting him here, knowing he loves me and will do anything for me.' She looked at him, hoping he understood.

Thomas nodded. 'Yes, I would have believed him, too. If you love someone you'll pretend anything to keep that person. I did, I know.'

'What did you pretend?' she asked gently.

'I pretended that I believed Bill was my son, I

loved Shirley then so much I couldn't face her with the absolute proof that he couldn't be.'

'He's not your son?' Elsa was astonished.

Thomas told the story simply and without emotion. The tests that had proved him to be sterile, the joyful announcement of Shirley's pregnancy, and the totally unexpected bonus that when Bill arrived Thomas discovered that he adored the boy, and biological parenthood was not important any longer.

He hadn't bothered to find out who the real father was, it was irrelevant anyway.

And looking back he had been right not to create a drama. If Thomas had disputed the paternity of Bill then he would have been denied access to the child after the divorce.

'Do you still love her? Shirley?'

'No, it sort of passed like influenza does, or a summer storm. I don't hate her either. She irritates me, and now she and Andy are having a child together and that irritates me too. Greatly. The fact that they *can* for one thing, and for another that Bill is so excited about it . . . his new brother or sister.'

'Did you ever think Shirley was having an affair?'

'No, not remotely. But let's put it this way, the very existence of Bill meant that Shirley was not exactly the faithful type. I guess I thought it was just one fling.'

'It probably was,' Elsa said.

'Yes, I think so, but for whatever reason we found less and less to say to each other. And then we got divorced.' He looked gloomy.

'And did you find anyone else?'

'No, I guess I didn't really look. I cared so much about Bill, you see. And I was really very surprised when she brought Andy to meet me so that they could tell me their plans. Shirley said she wanted things to be "civilised". She said she just hated secrets and pretence. I swear she sounded positively virtuous about it all. Said she wanted us to be up-front about everything.' He was scornful.

'Well, what was wrong with that?' Elsa asked.

'Oh, there had been months of secrets and pretence there! People in love can be so smug, and they expect everyone else to fit in with their plans.'

Elsa was silent. She was thinking hard, working something out.

'Sorry for droning on,' Thomas said.

'No, not at all, you've just clarified something for me.'

'I have?'

'Yes, if Dieter is to be any kind of a worthwhile human being, he must accept the fact that he has a daughter, and recognise her.'

'Even if it means losing you?' Thomas asked.

'He wouldn't lose me over it, if he could really believe that this girl needs a father. The problem is that he might just put on some kind of an act. He

316

thinks that what I want is a diamond ring, respectability, commitment. All that sort of thing.'

'He doesn't know you very well then, does he?' Thomas said.

'How do you mean?'

'I mean, you have been with him for over two years and he doesn't understand your values.'

'That's completely true, he doesn't understand me at all, but it never mattered. The love part of it pushed all that under the carpet. And what you just said about people in love being smug and uncaring about others – that is *so* true. I never thought of it before.'

'Well, what is a friend for except to come up with an idea now and then?' Thomas laughed.

'But you think I should give him up, don't you?'

'What I think doesn't matter.'

'It matters to me.'

'All right then, I think you should be with someone who does understand you ... as well as the other thing.'

'What other thing?' she laughed.

'You well know what I mean, sex, love, attraction. All of those are very fine but if you held out for the understanding as well then you'd be very happy.'

'And where would I find all that in one package, Thomas?' Elsa asked.

'Ah, if I knew the answer to that I'd run the world,' he said, raising his wine glass to her.

At the table in Andreas's taverna they were still stunned by Fiona's news. Rina cleared away the dishes and they sat with their little cups of coffee.

'Do your parents know yet?' David asked.

'No, I only just know myself, nobody else knows except all of you, my friends here,' Fiona said.

They murmured approval, agreeing on the need to get back to real life and nursing. Nobody mentioned Shane. Andreas said he felt sure that her mother and father would be overjoyed. Yorghis asked would she get her job back in the hospital. David asked would she continue to live at home.

Again, nobody mentioned Shane.

The only person who didn't join in the conversation was Vonni. Very unusually for her, she sat and stared ahead of her.

Eventually Fiona spoke to her.

'You were right all along, Vonni, I'm the first to admit it. Aren't you pleased you were right?'

'It's not a game where you score points or lose points, it's your whole life, it's your future.'

'All the more reason to be pleased then,' Fiona said. 'To say "I told you so." You deserve to say it.'

'I don't want to say it, I've said enough to all of you. And I managed to annoy you all. That was always my trouble, knowing what was right for everyone except myself. Andreas and Yorghis here will confirm this. Stupid, bossy Vonni, who could run the world but couldn't run her own life.'

There was a silence. Then Yorghis spoke.

'You certainly knew how to run our sister Christina's life for her, she would never have recovered without you,' he said.

'And every day of the year you do something to make someone's life better here, getting Maria to drive, minding the children, visiting the sick. That doesn't seem stupid and bossy to me,' Andreas said.

'I would never have known my father was dying if it hadn't been for you, Vonni,' David said. 'Think of the guilt for the rest of my life if I had not discovered.'

'And you came with me today and never once did you try to influence me. I don't think you were interfering at all. You just happened to be right,' Fiona said. 'And you left me to my thoughts. I'll never forget that.'

Vonni looked from one to another. Her heart was so full she didn't trust herself to speak. Finally she managed two words in the Irish language.

'*Slan abhaile*, Fiona,' she said unsteadily.

'What does that mean?' David asked.

'It means "Safe home",' Fiona said.

Thomas and Elsa talked on the balcony, as old friends talk. It was impossible to believe that they had known each other not for years but only a dozen or so days. They knew the secrets of each other's heart.

'So you will go back long before the year is over, before Shirley's baby is born?' Elsa asked.

'You think I should?' He looked at her.

'Hey, I'm not telling anyone what to do, remember how angry we all were with Vonni when she told us what we should and should not do. You didn't tell *me* what to do.'

'That's different,' Thomas said. 'I'm asking you and I really do want to know what you think.'

'Okay . . . I think that you love Bill, and that he loves you, and in life it's so hard to find a good generous love like that so I believe it's a great waste for you not to be near him. It's not as if you are putting him out of your mind and getting on with your own life. You worry about him all the time. So why not be near him, have a home he feels welcome to visit. He'll be jealous when the new baby arrives, he'll need a place where he is king.'

Thomas listened to her carefully.

'It *was* a good generous love once, but I became mean-spirited about Andy. I diminished that love.' He looked very sad.

'Then maybe you should try to stick it back together, firm it up before it all trickles away,' Elsa suggested.

'In my head I agree with you, but in my heart I

fear I'd make such a mess of it that I'd truly be better off out of his way . . . for his sake just as much as for mine.'

'Well, Thomas, you'll come to the right conclusion. I know you well enough. Now come on, before you leave, and you will leave, are you going to tell me what to do with my messy life?'

'I suppose I could tell you that we can and do get over loving people and I hope you might contemplate getting over him.'

'But why, why do you want it to be over? You're my friend, you're out for my good as I am for yours. You know that Dieter is quite simply the love of my life.' She was confused.

'You asked me what I thought, I told you.' Thomas spoke simply.

'But I can't think why you would want me to give him up, get over him . . .'

'I could comfort you.'

She looked at him open-mouthed. 'Thomas, this is not true!' she gasped. 'You and I are mates, friends. You don't fancy me, as you put it, it's only the wine and the stars.'

'You never thought of me in that way at all?' he asked, his head on one side.

'I did think that it would be very easy to love a gentle, thoughtful person like you rather than a restless urgent man like Dieter. But then I've often wished idly for things that didn't happen. Couldn't happen.'

'All right, then I think you should go back to him tomorrow. Why hang around?' he said.

'You give up pretty easily,' she said flirtatiously.

'Come on, Elsa, everything I say is wrong. I did you the courtesy of considering what you said. You are not doing that.'

'I'm only playing with you,' she said.

'Don't,' said Thomas.

She was contrite. 'I know I'm like those feminists who get annoyed if a man stands up to give them a seat and get annoyed if he doesn't. I'm only playing games because I don't know what else to do. I know what you should do. It's so obvious and easy. And what everyone else – Dieter, David, Fiona, Andreas, Vonni – all of you, should do. It's just my own decision that isn't clear.'

'What should Vonni do?' Thomas asked with interest.

'She should get Andreas and Yorghis to find her son and tell him what kind of person she is now. Young Stavros would come home if they told him.'

Thomas smiled at her. 'Elsa the Crusader,' he said affectionately, and patted her hand.

In the taverna they talked about Fiona's journey home and when she should leave.

'Perhaps you could come on the last ferry with me

tomorrow,' David said. 'We would be company for each other, and you might even fly to London with me.'

'That's not a bad idea, it would make it much less hard to say goodbye.'

'For a while,' Vonni said. 'You'll come back again, you've both got many friends here.'

'Tomorrow I'll go and say goodbye to Eleni and thank her for everything and call on Dr Leros as well.'

'And I'll give Maria a last driving lesson and tell her that Vonni will take over now. Is that right, Vonni?'

'Has she *any* co-ordination these days?' Vonni asked.

'Much improved,' David soothed. 'And she's great if you can manage not to shout at her but to build up her confidence.'

'Aren't we all great when people don't shout at us and build up our confidence,' Vonni grumbled.

'Have you told them, yet, in Ireland that you are going back?' Andreas asked Fiona.

'Not yet, I'll call from the Anna Beach tomorrow.'

'Go in and use my phone,' he said, as he had said all that time ago on the day that Manos had perished with his boat.

'Just a quick call then to my friend Barbara. Thank you so much, Andreas.' And Fiona ran into the kitchen.

'Isn't it unusual that you young people don't have mobile phones?' Yorghis wondered.

'Yes, it is odd. Not one of the four of us has one that works here,' David said.

'It's not unusual at all,' Vonni said. 'You're all running away from something. Why would you want a phone so that you could be tracked down?'

'Barbara?'

'God Almighty, it's Fiona!'

'Barbara, I'm coming home!'

'Well, that's *great* news, when will the pair of you be back?'

'Not the pair of us. Just me.'

There was a silence at the other end.

'Shane is staying there?' Barbara said eventually.

'In a manner of speaking, yes.'

'Well, that's a pity,' Barbara said neutrally.

'Don't be such a hypocrite, Barbara, you're delighted.'

'That's not fair – why should I be delighted that my friend is upset?'

'I'm not upset, Barbara – could you and I share a flat, do you think?'

'Of course we could, I'll start looking right away.'

'Great, and Barbara, could you sort of tell my ma and da?'

'Sure, what exactly will I tell them?'

'That I'm coming home,' Fiona said, surprised that there should be any question about it.

'Yes, but you know the way people of that generation always want to ask questions . . .' Barbara began.

'Oh, head them off at the pass,' said Fiona casually.

Thomas walked Elsa back to her villa and kissed her on the cheek.

'*Schlaf gut*,' he said.

'You're learning German just to impress me?' She smiled at him.

'No, I think I'd have to do much more than say, "Sleep well", to impress you, Elsa,' he said ruefully.

'Like what?' she asked.

'I'd have to be restless and urgent. I could try but it might take a long time.'

'You're better the way you are, believe me, Thomas. See you midday tomorrow at the harbour.'

'You won't have gone back to Germany by then?'

'Nor you back to California?'

'Goodnight, beautiful Elsa,' he said and turned away.

Fiona was in Elsa's villa already packing her suitcase.

'Before you say anything, I want to apologise, I

was completely out of order with you, trying to borrow money and everything,' Fiona said.

'It doesn't matter a bit, anyway I was very short and harsh with you, I am the one to be sorry.'

'It doesn't matter now. I'm over Shane. I'm going back to Dublin. I suddenly looked at him and saw what the future would be like with him, and that it wasn't worth it. I suppose you'll say or think anyway that it can't have been real love if it vanished so quickly.'

'No, it was real love all right,' Elsa consoled her. 'But as you say it has ended, and that will make life easier for you.'

'I didn't give him up to have an easy life,' Fiona explained. 'I just suddenly saw him in a different light, like you all saw him in, I suppose, and then it was quite easy to walk away. I'm sorry of course that he wasn't the person I thought he was. It's not like your situation.'

'Why do you say that?'

'Well, Shane only tolerated my attaching myself to him. In your case, Dieter writes begging you to come back to him, promising to change for you. That's real love.'

Elsa ignored this. 'What was it that finally made you choose to walk away from Shane?' she asked.

'I think there was a kind of indifference in his tone, he didn't care.'

'I know what you mean,' Elsa nodded slowly.

'You can't know! Your guy is down on his knees beseeching you to come back to him. That's utterly different!'

'Something you said there about a tone of voice seemed fairly relevant to me. I'm going out on the balcony to look at the sea, do you want to join me?'

'No, Elsa, I'm exhausted. I've been to Athens and back in one day, changed the whole direction of my life. I'm going to have to sleep.'

Elsa sat for a long time looking out at the moonlight on the sea then she went back into the sitting room. She took some paper and began to write a letter which she would fax the next day.

My dear Hannah,

You have been such a good unselfish friend. Asking nothing and always ready to listen. It was, as it turned out, a very good decision for me to come here. And it was even better that I met Dieter again as now I can make a decision based on the facts as they are, not on some fantasy world. I'm still not sure what I am going to do. But a few more days on this peaceful island will make it all clear to me. I heard two things tonight, one from an American man who told me that we can get over people. He just said it casually, like you can get over whooping cough. I don't know if he's right.

Then an Irish girl said to me that I was lucky because Dieter had promised to change for me. And I have been wondering why we should want to change people. Either love them as they are or move on.

It's late at night and I am writing this by moonlight. I've been thinking in a way I never did before about my life with Dieter. I went into it as an escape. I had a fair amount to escape from. My father left home when I was a child and I always hoped he would get in touch when he saw me on television, but he never did. My mother and I were never close, possibly we were too alike, always striving for perfection.

But in the weeks I have been travelling I have learned that there really is no perfect life, so we must stop seeking it. I have met many people on this voyage whose problems are much greater than mine. Oddly it has calmed me down.

And I thought of you, Hannah, and your happy marriage to Johann. On the day you married five years ago, you said there was nothing about him you would change.

I envy you that, my dear, dear friend.

Love from Elsa

CHAPTER SIXTEEN

Miriam Fine had prepared David's room for him, bought a new lilac-coloured duvet cover and matching curtains, laid out dark purple towels.

'They look nice and manly, somehow. I hope he'll like them,' she said.

'Don't fuss over him, Miriam, he hates fuss,' David's father said.

'You tell me not to fuss? What will you do, yes, tell me what will you do the very moment he comes in the door?'

'I'll do nothing to upset him.'

'You'll start talking to him about responsibility. If there is anything guaranteed to fuss him it's that!'

'No, I won't talk about responsibility, at least he's seen sense and decided to give up these mad ideas.'

'He's coming home because you're ill, Harold. He worked that out for himself, you saw the letter I sent. I never mentioned it. Not once.'

'I don't want his sympathy, I will not have his pity.' The man's eyes filled with tears.

'But you might want his love, Harold, after all, that's why he's coming home, because he loves you.'

Fiona's father turned the key in the lock. It had been a long tiring day in the office. It was a week from his fiftieth birthday. He felt eighty-five. His shoulders were stiff and cramped. There were young fellows in the office snapping at his heels. He might well be passed over for the next promotion.

He had been tempted to go and have three pints in his local pub, but realised that Maureen would have his supper ready. It wasn't worth the hassle.

As soon as he opened the door she ran out to meet him.

'Sean, you just won't believe this! Fiona's coming home. This week!' Maureen Ryan was overjoyed.

'How do you know?'

'Barbara rang when you were out.'

'Could that lout not draw his dole money out there? Is that what happened?' Sean grumbled.

'No, wait till you hear, she dropped him – she's coming home on her own!'

Sean put down his briefcase and his evening paper and sat down. He put his head in his hands. 'Someone asked me at lunch today did I think there was a God,' he said. 'I told the lad to grow up, of course there wasn't. What kind of a God would allow all this mess and confusion to go on? But now I may have to rethink my answer. There might well be something out there. She's really coming back?'

'Tomorrow or the day after, she asked Barbara to tell us, she's looking for her old job back.'

'Well, isn't that great – do the girls know yet?'

'No, I waited to tell you first,' Maureen Ryan said.

'And I suppose you've been doing up her room?' He smiled wearily.

'No, and I'll tell you why, she wants to live in a flat with Barbara.'

'Well, that's all right, isn't it?'

'I think it's all for the very best, Sean,' said Fiona's mother with tears in her eyes.

'Big surprise, Bill, I'm going to take you and your mom on a little trip!' Andy said.

'Hey, that's great, where are we going?'

'Your grandma is going with a group to the Grand Canyon, remember she told you?'

'Yeah?' Bill looked very excited. Dad had often told him about the Grand Canyon, showed him pictures of it. Told him that they would go there some day. 'Do you mean we might go there too?' Eagerness shone in his face.

'Well, I said to Shirley we always intended to go there and why not do it when you could meet your gran as well?'

'And what did Mom say?'

'Well, she said I was a kind man, and that pleased me, but I didn't do it to be kind, I suggested it because I thought it would be good for all of us.'

'You are kind, Andy,' Bill said.

'I'm very fond of you, Bill, you know that, and when the new baby comes I'll be as lucky as you are. I'll have two children to love.'

'How does that make you as lucky as me?'

'You have two dads, don't you? And talking about that, you should call your dad in Greece and tell him you're going on this trip.'

Bill dialled the number in Greece but there was only an answering machine.

He left a message.

'Dad, Andy is driving us to Arizona to see the Grand Canyon, we're going to cross the Sierra Nevada and we're going to meet Gran there, she's going with her book club. Andy says I can call you when we get there so that Gran and I can both say hallo.'

Then Andy took over the phone.

'Thomas, just in case you don't get this message before we leave and you want to call Bill, this is the number of my cellphone. I'll try and show things properly to your boy; we have the atlas out now looking at the journey, but I guess there'll be a lot I miss out. Maybe he could go again with you some time when you get back.'

'That's if he *ever* comes back,' Bill said before Andy had hung up the telephone.

Because Andy had not yet hung up when Bill said this, it was there on the message when Thomas came back from walking Elsa home and turned on his answering machine.

He sat up for a long time wondering about the world. He saw the torchlight moving around in the hen-house. He had been right in assuming that Vonni would not come to sleep in the guest room tonight. He thought of the strange tortured life she had lived amongst these people in Aghia Anna.

He thought of the beautiful, bright Elsa going back to that selfish German who only looked on her as a trophy. He thought of the simple, decent Andy, the man whom he had always demonised.

Who was only doing his best.

He thought of his Bill who believed he might never come home. He sat there thinking until the stars faded from the sky and the early light came up over the hills.

They met for a last lunch at the restaurant with the blue check tablecloths.

'Imagine, we have been coming here so often and we don't even know its name,' Fiona said meditatively.

'It's called Midnight,' David said. 'Look at the letters.' And he spelled it out slowly: *Mesanihta*.

333

'How on earth do you work that out?' Elsa asked.

Painstakingly he went over the Greek letters again: the thing that looked like a V is actually an N.

'You would be a great teacher, David,' Elsa said, very sincerely.

'I don't know, I don't have all that many certainties,' he said.

'All the better for a teacher,' Thomas said.

'I'll miss you all, I don't have very many friends back home,' David said.

'Me neither, but I'd be very surprised if you were without friends for long,' Thomas said. 'And don't forget, you'll make a whole new circle through your driving lessons!'

'It's easy here, a bit different with motorways in England,' David said. 'I don't think I'll set up my own school.'

'Do you have a lot of friends back in Germany, Elsa?' Fiona asked.

'No, hardly any, a lot of acquaintances but only one good friend, Hannah. When you're in the fast track, or think you are, and have to keep yourself ready and available, then there's no real time for friends.' She spoke regretfully.

They all nodded, it was easy to understand.

Fiona announced that she was going on the train to see David's parents with him, help smooth over the homecoming, try to explain something about the life on this magical island and how it had seduced them.

'Like the Lotos-eaters,' Elsa said.

'Elsa is showing off how much English literature she knows.' Thomas looked at her affectionately.

'It's Tennyson,' she smiled, ignoring him. 'When they all arrived where the Lotos-eaters lived and ate nectar, in a land in which it seemed always afternoon, one of them said, "Oh rest ye, brother mariners, we will not wander more." This place has that effect on all of us, I think.'

'Except Fiona and I are leaving,' David said sadly.

'But you'll be back here again one day. It's different now from Tennyson's time, he was back in the nineteenth century with no cheap air tickets, or indeed any air tickets then.' Thomas was cheering them up.

'I'd love my friend Barbara to come out here with me one day, but it won't be the same without you,' Fiona said.

'Vonni will always be here, and Andreas, Yorghis, Eleni – loads of people.' Thomas was still looking on the bright side.

'Will you be here for much longer yourself, Thomas?' Fiona asked.

'No, I don't think so. I think I'll go back to California fairly soon,' Thomas said. His eyes had a faraway look. They didn't want to ask him any more. It was clearly a decision not fully made.

'And when are you going back to Germany, Elsa?' David asked gently, to change the subject.

'I'm not going back,' she said simply.

'You're staying here?' Fiona gasped.

'I'm not sure, but I'm not going back to Dieter.'

'When did you decide this?' Thomas leaned forward and looked at her very intensely.

'Last night, on my balcony, looking out at the sea.'

'And did you tell anybody, like Dieter for example?'

'I wrote to him. I posted the letter this morning on the way to meet you all. He should get it in four or five days. So now I have all that time to make up my mind where to go.' She smiled at Thomas, one of those slow warm smiles which had made her the darling of television all over Germany.

'You're not going to go down to *Mesanihta* to say goodbye to them, Vonni?' Andreas asked as he called into the craft shop.

'No, I annoyed them all enough while they were here. I'll let them go in peace,' she said, not looking up.

'You are a difficult woman, Vonni, prickly like a thorn bush. Both David and Fiona said last night how grateful they are to you.' Andreas shook his head, mystified.

'Yes, they did, they were very polite, as were you

and Yorghis and I thank you. And by the way, the urge to drink seems to have passed over like a summer cloud. But it's the other two, Thomas and Elsa, I really upset them, I don't want to sit there pontificating like some old bat. You and I heard plenty of advice years ago, Andreas, but did we ever take it? The answer is no.'

'And what would you have changed if you could have your life all over again?' he asked.

This was unfamiliar territory for Andreas. Normally he left things as they were, without question or analysis.

'I'd have fought Magda for Stavros. I wouldn't have won then, but I might have won later. He might have come back when he tired of her. And of course I should have fought Stavros for the petrol station. The people here are fair, they would have known I bought it for him. I could have raised my son. But no, I thought the solution was somewhere at the bottom of a *raki* bottle. So it didn't happen.' She looked around her despondently.

'Did anyone give you any advice like that at the time?' he asked gently.

'Yes, Dr Leros's father did, and your sister Christina, but I had my face so far into drink I couldn't listen to them.'

'You haven't asked me what I would change if I were given the chance,' he said.

'I suppose you'd have managed to keep Adoni here. Am I right?'

'Yes, of course I should have done that. But would I listen to people who told me that? No, I would not.' His eyes were sad. 'And also I should have asked you to marry me twenty-five years ago.'

She looked at him, astounded. 'Andreas! You don't mean that. We never even remotely loved each other.'

'I didn't love my wife either, not in any real sense, that is. Not like people read about and sing about, we got on all right and we were company for each other. You and I could have been fine companions.'

'We *are* fine companions, Andreas,' she said in a weak voice.

'Yes, but you know . . .' he muttered.

'No, it would never have worked, not for five minutes. Believe me. You did the right thing there. You see, I loved Stavros exactly the way you read about, sing about and dream about. I could never have settled for any other kind of love.'

She said it in a matter-of-fact way which brought normality back to their conversation.

'So it was all for the best,' Andreas said.

'Definitely. And listen to me, Andreas, I meant it when I said Adoni will come back to see you. I *know* it.'

He shook his big head. 'No, it's only a wish, a fairy tale.'

'The man is thirty-four, you wrote to him, of course he'll come back.'

'Why has he not called or written then?'

He didn't want to tell Vonni about the mysterious phone call which seemed to assume that Adoni was already here. It could have all been a mistake, a misunderstanding, he didn't want to raise her hopes like he had raised his own and his brother's. But even though she knew nothing of the call, Vonni's faith was unshaken.

'He needs a little time, Andreas. Chicago is a long way. He'll need to get his head around it. But he'll be here.'

'Thank you, Vonni, you are indeed a good companion,' Andreas said, and blew his nose very loudly.

'Hey, Dimitri?'

'Yes?' Dimitri's voice was cold. He had never seen such a violent attack on a gentle girl who had come to visit this Shane in love and good faith.

'Can I write a letter?'

'I'll get you paper.'

He looked in from time to time and Shane was writing and thinking and writing again. Eventually it was finished and he asked for an envelope.

'We'll put it in an envelope. Just tell me where it's to go.' Dimitri wasted little time with him.

'Like hell you will, I'm not having you read my letter,' Shane said.

Dimitri shrugged. 'Please yourself,' he said and left.

A few hours later Shane called out to him.

Dimitri wrote down the address ... Andreas's taverna, Aghia Anna.

'How strange!' Dimitri said.

'You asked for the bloody address, don't start criticising it,' Shane said.

'No, it's just that I know that man's son, Adoni, he and I are friends.'

'You are, huh? Well, his father doesn't think much of him,' Shane said.

'They had a difference of opinion, it's something that happens to many fathers and sons,' said Dimitri with a great sense of dignity.

They agreed to meet at the ferry half an hour before departure. And they all headed off from the café they now knew was called Midnight, in their different directions.

Fiona and David went to say their goodbyes and collect all the gifts that were being offered to them.

Maria had made a cake for David to take home to his parents. Eleni had made a lace collar for Fiona.

Yorghis had got them worry beads made of amber-coloured glass.

Andreas had a photograph of himself and David framed in a little carved wooden frame.

Dr Leros had given Fiona some coloured tiles she could put on her wall to remind her of Greece.

They couldn't find Vonni. She was not at home.

'She'll come to wave us off,' David said.

'She's very sad these days, she's lost her sparkle somehow,' Fiona said.

'Maybe she's envious with you going back to Ireland . . . something she was never able to do,' David speculated.

'Yes, but she says herself it turned out all right, her love affair, for quite a time, and she did have a son to show for it, which is more than a lot of people do.'

'But where is he now?' David asked.

'She claims she doesn't know, but I bet she does,' Fiona said.

'Wouldn't it be wonderful if he came back? If he met Adoni somewhere out in Chicago and they decided to go back and swing again on the old tree up at the taverna,' David said.

'Ah, David, and they say the Irish are the sentimental ones believing in fairy tales.'

Fiona pealed with laughter and patted him on the arm to show she was laughing with him, not at him.

'You're a dark horse, Elsa, all these plans and you

never told me.' Thomas tut-tutted in disapproval as they walked together up in the little town.

'I did tell you.'

'But when everyone was there?'

'Well, that's where we were, with everyone else, when the subject came up.' Elsa was totally unrepentant.

'But I thought you and I had sort of discussed things fairly intimately . . .' He was hesitant.

'We did, and I enjoyed it,' she said.

'Where are you off to now? I was thinking of having a siesta personally.'

Elsa laughed. 'Where am I going? I'm going to find Vonni.'

Vonni wasn't in her hen-house, nor in her craft shop nor at the police station.

Elsa decided she would go out on the road to the old man who didn't believe in modern medicine. She might find her there.

The sun was high in the sky and she wore her white cotton sun-hat against the heat. The road was dusty. Children came from the tumbledown buildings and saluted her, opening and closing their little fingers.

'*Yassas!*' they called out to her as she passed by.

Elsa wished she had brought some candy, *karameles*, they called it. But she hadn't thought that there would be this reception committee.

She remembered the old man's house and gathered together some sentences in halting Greek to say she was looking for his friend Vonni. But they weren't necessary. Vonni was there, sitting by the old man's bed holding his hand.

She didn't look remotely surprised to see Elsa.

'He's dying,' she said in a matter-of-fact tone.

'Should I go and get the doctor?' Elsa was practical.

'No, he wouldn't let a doctor cross the door, but I'll tell him that you are a herbalist and he'll take what you give him.'

'You can't do that, Vonni.' Elsa was shocked.

'You'd prefer he died in pain?'

'No, but we can't play games with someone's life . . .'

'He has about six or seven hours more of life, if that. If you want to help go to Dr Leros, you remember where he lives from Fiona that time. Tell him the situation here, ask him for morphine.'

'But won't I need . . .'

'No, you won't need anything, call into my shop and get a pottery bowl as well. Go quickly now.'

On her way back down the dusty road an old van came along. Elsa stopped it and said she needed to go to the doctor for medicine. The two men looked at her admiringly and drove her willingly to the doctor's. As Vonni had predicted there was indeed no problem getting the drugs, the men in the van waited while she picked up the bowl and then drove her back.

'That was very speedy,' Vonni said approvingly, and Elsa held the old man's thin hand and repeated to him over and over, '*Dhen ine sovaro, Dhen ine sovaro*. It's not serious, it's not serious.'

Vonni ground up the morphine tablets, mixed them with honey in her pottery bowl and spooned the mixture into the old man's mouth.

'It would be better if we could inject it, more instant relief, but he wouldn't hear of that.' Vonni was grim.

'How long will it take for him to feel it?'

'A matter of minutes. It's really magic this stuff,' Vonni said.

The old man mumbled something.

'What did he say?'

'He actually said that the herbalist is very beautiful,' Vonni said wryly.

'I wish he hadn't said that.' Elsa sounded sad.

'Come on, these are the last things he's going to look at – your face and mine. Isn't it good he has yours to concentrate on?'

'Vonni, *please*.' She had tears in her eyes.

'If you want to help, keep smiling at him, Elsa, he'll start feeling less pain quite soon.'

And indeed, his face began to relax a little, his grip on her hand was less frantic.

'Think of him as if he were your father, put love and warmth in your eyes,' Vonni instructed her.

Elsa felt that this wasn't the time to remind Vonni that she hardly remembered the father who had abandoned her. Instead she looked at this poor old Greek man and thought of him and his strange odd life that ended with an Irishwoman and a German woman at his deathbed, giving him a very large dose of morphine . . .

'Yorghis, it's Dimitri here in Athens, remember, we've talked a few times . . .'

'Of course I remember you! How are you, boy, it's good to hear from you! Are you getting ready for your wedding?'

'Yes, don't women go to a great fuss about one day? I mean it's the life afterwards that matters, isn't it?'

'For us, yes, but for them the day itself is very important.'

'You know that Irish dope pusher?'

'Shane? Indeed I do, but the most important thing was that the girl left him. Walked out on him in front of you, didn't she?'

'That's right, how did you know?'

'Vonni told us, the woman from here who went with her. She said you were quite a hero.'

'Oh, you know the old woman? No, I was nothing like a hero, I'm afraid. But I wanted to tell

345

you he's written a letter to your brother, sent to the taverna. It was in English and I can't read English very well, but I wondered what it was about.'

'He probably thinks Andreas is a soft touch, but it's not going to work. Little Fiona is going back to Ireland, Andreas and I are going down to the ferry tonight to say goodbye to her. So whatever he writes to Andreas it will be too late.'

'Good,' said Dimitri. 'And while I'm talking to you, did Adoni ever come back to Aghia Anna? Remember I knew him here in Athens and I've been thinking about him today.'

'No, he never did.'

'Making too much money over there I suppose?'

'Not that I heard, and we *would* hear if anyone from here did well in the United States. But there you go! Funnily, a day or so ago I thought he might be coming back, but it was a false alarm.'

'How do you mean?'

'Oh, some garbled message came through from Chicago wanting to know where he had put some set of keys. I thought . . . I hoped he might be on his way here but, alas, no.'

'I suppose we all do what we want to do in the end,' Dimitri sighed.

'You are a philosopher, Dimitri my boy. And old men go on hoping that the world will become easy and people will remember that life is short, and no row is worth prolonging.'

*

A queue was forming to get on the last ferry from Aghia Anna.

Fiona and David stood in the middle of a crowd of well-wishers. Maria and her children were there, Eleni from the house where Fiona and Shane had stayed was there with her children. Vonni and Elsa both looking tired and anxious, but obviously friends again. Thomas was there in his ridiculous trousers. He had bought a little book about the island for each of them, and a copy of a photograph of the four of them at their café.

He had written 'Midday at the Midnight' on the pictures. Andreas and Yorghis were there with promises of more roast lamb when they came back.

Vonni could see that the two who were leaving were becoming quite emotional.

She spoke authoritatively. 'Now you can't leave us all here clinging to this rock in the Mediterranean without knowing what happened when you got home,' she said sternly. 'You can write it to me and I'll come down to the *Mesanihta* and read it to the others.'

They promised her faithfully that they would indeed write.

'Twenty-four hours after you get back, remember,' Vonni said fiercely. 'We want to know what happens.'

'It will be easy to write to you lot, we don't have to tell you any lies,' David said.

'Or put on an act,' Fiona agreed.

And just on cue at that moment the ferry hooted aggressively and they went up the gangplank amongst the people carrying baskets, and some that looked like bags of washing. A few definitely had hens and geese in boxes with holes punched in them for the air to get in.

They waved until the boat had left the harbour and turned along the coast and they were out of sight of their friends.

'I feel desperately lonely,' Fiona said.

'Me too. I could have lived there happily for ever,' David said.

'Could we? Or are we just fooling ourselves, do you think?' Fiona wondered.

'It's different for you, Fiona, truly it is, you love your job, you have friends, your family aren't going to overpower you, suffocate you.'

'I'm not sure quite *how* they're going to react, I'm the eldest of the family, I didn't show much example to my sisters by running off with a certifiable lunatic.'

'But at least you have sisters, I'm the only one. I bear the whole brunt of it. And my father is dying. I have to look at him every day and tell him I'll be proud to work in his company.'

'Maybe it won't be as bad as you think.' Fiona was hopeful.

'It will and worse since I let go of the reins as he

calls it. You're very good to come and help me break the ice.'

'Will they think I'm your girlfriend, a frightening Catholic coming to destroy your tradition?'

'They already do,' he said gloomily.

'Well, it'll cheer them up enormously when I hare off to Ireland next day,' Fiona said cheerfully. 'They'll be so relieved they'll gather you to their bosoms.'

'We were never slow on the bosom gathering – that's part of the problem,' David said.

And for some reason they both found this incredibly funny.

Elsa and Thomas watched until the ferry was out of sight. Then they walked slowly back up to the town.

'Where were you this afternoon?' he asked. 'I was looking for you, I thought we could take off in the boat again.'

'Tomorrow would be lovely,' she said. 'That's if you're free.'

'I'm free.'

'I'm interested that you really are going back to California,' she said.

'And I'm very interested that you're really not going back to Germany,' he said.

'So let's make the most of what time we have here,' Elsa said.

'How do you mean exactly?' Thomas enquired.

'I meant by renting a boat tomorrow, having a picnic, another day taking the bus to Kalatriada, I'd love to see that place again when I'm not so stressed. That's what I meant.'

'There, that's settled,' he said. And they both smiled conspiratorially.

To change the subject he asked, 'You didn't tell me what you were doing all afternoon.'

'I was in a small cluttered house with Vonni, watching an old man die. An old man with no family, no relations, only Vonni and me. I never saw anyone die before.'

'Oh, poor Elsa.' He leaned towards her and stroked her hair. 'Poor Elsa.'

'Not poor Elsa, I am young, I have my life ahead, he was old and lonely and frightened. Poor old Nikolas. Poor old man.'

'You were kind to him, you did what you could.'

Elsa pulled away from him. 'Oh, Thomas, if you could have seen Vonni. She was wonderful – I take back everything I ever said about her. She fed him honey on a spoon and made me hold his hand. She was like a sort of angel.'

They walked together back to her place.

'Tomorrow we'll take out a little blue boat and go to sea,' he said and as she turned to leave, she gave him a big hug.

'Andy, is this an okay time to call?'

'Sure, Thomas, for me it's fine, but I'm afraid Bill and his mother aren't in the car, they've gone exploring.'

'Exploring?'

'I mean shopping really, they call it exploring. Could you call in thirty minutes, or make it forty-five? You know what shopping can turn into, I don't want to waste your nickel just talking to me.'

'I'm happy to talk to you, Andy, because I want to ask you something.'

'Sure, Thomas, ask what you want.' He could hear the slightly wary note in Andy's voice.

'I was wondering, if I came back, like a bit sooner than anyone thought, do you think that would be a good thing?'

'Came back? Sorry, Thomas, I'm not entirely with you. You mean come back here to town?'

'Yes, that's what I meant.' Thomas felt cold. The guy was going to say that it would be a bad idea. He knew it.

'But you leased your apartment for a year, didn't you?'

'Yeah, but I thought I'd get a place, a bigger place, with a yard for Bill to play in.'

'You're going to try and take Bill back?' Andy's voice was choked.

'Not back to live, of course not, just a place he could visit.' Thomas tried not to sound impatient.

'Oh, I see.'

God, Andy was slow. It took for ever for an idea to sink in and another age for him to answer.

'So what do you think? Andy, do you think it would be something Bill would like . . . to have me down the street from him? Or would it confuse him? You're the guy on the spot. Tell me. I just want to do what's best.'

Across thousands of miles, Thomas could almost hear the slow smile crossing Andy's handsome, empty features.

'Thomas, that boy would love it, it would be like Santa Claus and all his birthdays coming together!'

There was no doubting the utter sincerity of the man. Thomas could hardly stumble out the words. 'I won't tell him just yet, if that's okay with you, I'd like to set it up and give him a definite date before I begin talking to him about it. Does that make sense to you, Andy?'

'Sure it does, I'll say nothing until we hear from you.'

'Thanks for understanding,' Thomas mumbled.

'Understanding? That a man should want to be near his own flesh and blood? What's to understand?'

Thomas hung up and sat for a long time in the dark. Everyone believed that Bill was his flesh and blood. Everyone except Shirley. And indeed for all he knew she might believe it too. After all, he had never told her about the doctor's report. It had been too late to tell her.

She might well not know.

Vonni settled herself down in the shed that Thomas called her hen-house. She had seen him talking on the telephone. And earlier she had seen him holding Elsa's hand. They had so much ahead of them, those two.

She sighed with envy.

It would be wonderful to have years and years ahead. Time to make decisions, to go places, to learn new things. To fall in love again. She wondered what they would do. She wondered about Fiona and David taking a late plane tonight to London from Athens.

Would their homecomings be stormy, awkward or emotional? She hoped they would let her know. She had terrorised them into writing to her when they got back!

She looked back on the long hot day and how she had closed the eyes of Nikolas and wiped the honey from his chin before sending for Dr Leros to pronounce what she knew already. She thought about Yorghis up in the police station. Yorghis whose wife was never mentioned.

She tried to imagine what Magda looked like now and if she cried from those huge dark eyes over Stavros paying attention to another woman. She wondered about Andreas announcing that they should have married long ago. He had been quite wrong of course. But if they had married he might have got Adoni back. It would have been so very easy. The boy was aching to be asked. Unlike her own son, who would never come back.

The boy who had once sent a message to say that she had stolen his childhood and he never wanted to see her again. In all her confessions and recitals of her story she had never told any of them that. It was too hurtful to say, even to think about. And as she had done every night for over thirty years she said a prayer for her son Stavros. Just in case there might be a God out there and the prayer might do some good.

CHAPTER SEVENTEEN

Elsa had the picnic ready when Thomas came by to pick her up next morning. It was in a basket with a cloth tucked in to cover the food.

'I was wondering . . .' Thomas began.

'What were you wondering, dear Thomas?'

'Don't mock me, I'm a frail poor creature!' he begged.

'I wasn't mocking you, I swear.'

'I was wondering if we might row up the coast to Kalatriada, and stay there. For the night. That's what I was wondering.'

'I think you should wonder no more, it's a great idea.' She began to go back into the villa.

'Where are you going?' he asked anxiously.

'To get a toothbrush, an extra pair of panties, a clean blouse. Okay?' she asked.

'Very okay.' He had been expecting some kind of resistance. She was out in thirty seconds.

'Will the man with the little boats let us take it away for so long?' she asked.

'I've been down there to check, well, in case you said yes, and he said it would be fine.' Thomas looked slightly embarrassed.

'Go on, Thomas, what did he really say?' She laughed at him affectionately.

'He kept talking about you as . . . my *sizighos* or something . . .'

'What on earth is that?'

'I looked it up, it's a partner or a spouse or something in that area, I'm afraid.'

'Well, all right, *sizighos*, let's hit the high seas!' Elsa said cheerfully.

They took the little boat and rowed out of the harbour. The old man who cast them off kept explaining that if the weather was bad anywhere they must just go ashore and tie the boat up. Too many people had come to harm.

The sea was calm outside the arms of the harbour and they went up the coast identifying places as they passed. That was the hospital where Vonni had stayed for so long, that was the bathing place where Elsa had been with the children. That must be the wayside shrine where the bus had stopped the morning they had all come back for the funeral. It seemed so long ago now, so very long ago.

About halfway there they found a big wooden platform about a hundred yards from shore. The kind of place that people might swim out to. Thomas could tie their little boat to one of the posts. It was ideal for their picnic. Elsa climbed out of the boat and spread the cloth out between them.

She spread the taramasalata and hummus on the pitta bread, arranged the figs and watermelon on a plate. Then she poured a glass of wine and held it out to him.

'You know you really are quite dazzlingly beautiful,' he said.

'Thank you, that's very kind of you, but it's not important,' she said in a matter-of-fact voice. She wasn't putting him down. She was just stating a fact.

'All right, it's *not* that important, but it's true,' he said and spoke of it no more.

Kalatriada didn't have a real harbour so they tied up to a jetty and walked up the steep road to the little village.

Irini remembered them from the last visit. She took their hands in hers and greeted them warmly. She seemed to think it in no way unusual that this happy, handsome couple asked for two rooms.

'We only have one room free, but it has two beds – one for each person,' she said.

'I think we could survive that, don't you, Elsa?'

'Certainly,' she agreed.

Irini might not have travelled far from her home

357

village but she was wise in the ways of the world. She knew that you must never be surprised by anything.

'Did he say anything at all about this girl he's bringing with him?' Harold Fine asked for the third time.

'Only what I told you, that she and he and two others were friends on the island and they are travelling back together.'

'Hmm,' said David's father.

'I don't think it's a romance,' David's mother said.

'He's never brought a girl home before, Miriam.'

'I know but I still don't think so. She's Irish for one thing.'

'Why would that stop him? Hasn't he been living out in the furthest wildernesses of Greece for the summer?'

'She's only staying one night, Harold.'

'That's what they say now,' David's father said darkly.

'And what in the name of God is she stopping off in Manchester for?' Sean Ryan asked Barbara.

'There wasn't much time to explain but apparently it's someone she met whose father is dying and so Fiona is going to spend a night with the family to ease the situation,' Barbara said.

'Another lame duck,' Fiona's father grumbled.

'Just Fiona being kind,' Barbara said.

'Look where being kind got her before,' he muttered.

'But that's all over now, Mr Ryan.' Barbara sometimes felt that life was all about being relentlessly cheerful both on and off the wards. 'She'll be home tomorrow at six o'clock and without Shane. Isn't that all we ever wanted?'

'And she really doesn't want any of us to come to the airport?' Maureen Ryan was puzzled.

'Yes, she says she hates emotional scenes in front of strangers. Her plane lands at four, she'll be here before six.'

'I wonder, Barbara, if you were free could you ever . . .' Fiona's mother began.

'Like, be here when she arrives . . .' Fiona's father finished for her.

'To ease the situation?' Barbara asked.

'To stop me saying the wrong thing,' Sean Ryan said bluntly.

'Sure, I'll get them to let me change my shift,' Barbara said.

'It's just that words were said when she was leaving,' Maureen explained.

'Oh, words are always being said, believe me.' Barbara wondered if she should hand in her notice and apply to run the world officially. It seemed to be what she was doing in her spare time.

'And do you think she should stay here or spend the night with you?'

'Do you know, Mrs Ryan, I think it would be great if we could all have a lovely welcome home supper here and then she came off with me . . . that way, Rosemary wouldn't have to leave Fiona's old room where she's settled now, and there would be no danger of more words being said.'

As Barbara ran for the bus she wondered whether she should take over the United Nations this month or wait for a little bit longer.

'Dimitri?'

'Yes?'

'Did you post that letter?' Shane asked.

'It was posted. Yes.'

'Well, why hasn't that stupid old man replied?'

'I have no idea,' Dimitri shrugged.

'Maybe he can't read anyway, mad old fellow wearing laced-up boots in the middle of summer.'

Dimitri turned to leave. Shane put his hand on Dimitri's sleeve.

'Please don't go . . . I'm . . . Well . . . I'm a bit frightened and lonely here to be frank.'

Dimitri looked at him. He remembered the way Shane's face had contorted when he had held that girl's hair and was about to beat her against the walls of the cell.

'We're all frightened and lonely from time to time,

360

Shane. We have arranged for a lawyer to represent you in court,' he said, shaking off the hand and locking the cell behind him.

Dimitri's telephone rang.

It was Andreas, he had got the number from his brother Yorghis in the police station.

'It's about the young Irishman.'

'Oh, yes?' Dimitri sighed.

'He wrote to me for news of Fiona, he said he was very sorry and could I explain that he didn't mean to hurt her.'

'He meant to hurt her,' Dimitri said.

'Yes, you know this and I know this but he wanted me to tell her. I wanted to send him a message that I can't tell her, she has gone. Back to her country.'

'Good,' said Dimitri.

'So will you pass him that message?'

'Could you send a letter, a fax, an e-mail? Something? He's not going to believe me.'

'I'm not good at writing in English.'

'Is there someone there who could do it for you?'

'Yes, yes there is, thank you, I know who to ask.'

'Before you go I wanted to ask you how is your son Adoni? I knew him when we did military service together.'

'He is well, I think, he lives in Chicago now.'

'And does he come back?'

'Not really, why do you ask?'

'Because I would like to see him again. And I am getting married. I wanted to ask him to our wedding.'

'Well, if I hear from him I'll ask him to contact you,' Andreas said with a heavy heart.

Dimitri sat looking at the phone for a long time. People did extraordinary things. Adoni had been a great fellow when they had been together at military camp, spoken lovingly about his father and the taverna on the hill. Dimitri sighed. Nothing got easier to understand.

It was their second night in Kalatriada and, unlike the time that they had been here with David and Fiona, it was a clear starry night.

Irini set a little table for Thomas and Elsa out in the open air where they could see the square and the people walking up and down. She had put two little sprays of bougainvillaea in a white china vase as a decoration on their table.

Thomas took Elsa's hand and stroked it.

'I feel very happy here, calm somehow, as if the storms had died down.'

'I feel the same,' Elsa said.

'Which is, of course, ridiculous,' Thomas said. 'The storms haven't really gone away at all. They're round the corner for both of us, to be dealt with sooner or later.'

'But maybe we feel calm because we think we can deal with them now,' Elsa suggested.

'How do you mean?'

'Well, you are going back to Bill – the only question is when? And I'm not going back to Germany, so the only question is where?'

'You've a quick, bright mind, Elsa. You can sum things up very well.'

'Not all that quick, this is something I should have seen a long time ago.'

'We'll waste no time on regrets though, will we?' he enquired.

'No, I agree, regrets are useless. Destructive even.'

'Would you like coffee?' he asked.

'Maybe – I'm a little nervous actually, Thomas,' she admitted.

'So am I, but I don't think coffee ever calmed anyone down. Shall we go, do you think?' She held his hand as they walked up the wooden stairs.

Irini smiled at them and seemed to understand that this was an important night.

In the bedroom they both felt awkward. Elsa pointed out the mountain peaks, naming this one and that.

'It's a beautiful place to be,' she said softly.

He went towards her, held her to him and kissed her neck gently. She gave a little shiver.

Thomas drew away.

'Was that gross or something?' he asked, irresolute.

'No, it was exciting and lovely. Come here,' she said.

And first she stroked his face and then she kissed him, holding him close. Her hands went up and down his back and gently he opened her blouse.

'Elsa, I don't know . . . I hope . . .' he began.

'I don't know either, and also I hope,' she murmured. 'But remember, no looking back, no regrets, no comparisons.'

'You're beautiful, Elsa.'

'Hold me,' she asked him. 'Please love me, Thomas. Love me in this beautiful island and let's not think about anything beyond tonight . . .'

Vonni sat down with Andreas and wrote to Shane.

I am replying to your letter about Fiona Ryan. She left this island two days ago on her way back to Ireland where she hopes to resume her nursing career. I could not therefore give her your message of apology but I presume you know how to contact her in Dublin.

I hope that you will co-operate with the authorities in Athens in the matter of your detention. They view all drug infringements very seriously.

Yours faithfully,
Andreas

She translated it for Andreas.

'Is it a little cold, do you think?' he wondered.

'It's very cold,' Vonni agreed. 'Would you prefer to have paid his bail and invited him to stay here for six months?'

'No, I know all that. It's just he is in jail and he did apologise.'

'Andreas, you have a soft heart over everything . . . everything except your son.'

'I have a soft heart for him too now, Vonni, but alas it's too late. No, don't tell me you have a feeling, I don't believe in feelings any more.'

'Right. No more on the subject, I swear. Will we mail this letter or ask Yorghis to fax it, do you think?'

'You want it sent as it is, even though you agree it's cold?' he asked.

'My opinion, and of course I could be wrong, is that there's a time in life for coldness and this is one of those times.'

'You, wrong, Vonni? Never!' He smiled. 'Let's fax it and put the poor fool out of his misery.'

'I'll drop it in to the police station on my way home,' she said.

'Where's home tonight? Is it your apartment or your hen-house?' Andreas asked.

'Now you are worse than Thomas! Making fun of my domestic arrangements no less! But since you are so curious, tonight I will sleep in the little guest room. Thomas and Elsa have gone to Kalatriada together, I will have the place to myself.'

'They have gone back there together.' He stroked his cheek. 'I see . . .'

'I know. Imagine,' she said.

'And when will they come back?' Andreas asked.

'Thomas left a note; he said if it all went well it might be a few days.'

'Let's hope it goes well for them,' Andreas said.

'You are a dear man,' Vonni said.

'You never said that before.'

'No, but over the years I said a lot of rubbish. You always had the wisdom to know what I meant and what I didn't mean. I *do* mean that you are a dear and good person. I hope you know that.'

'I do, Vonni, and I'm happy you think of me like that,' he said.

David sat and talked to his father along the lines that he and Fiona had rehearsed. Nothing about the illness that was ending his life but a lot about the office and the upcoming award.

'I didn't think you'd care about that kind of thing,' Harold Fine said.

'But they are honouring you, Father, why should I not care and be very proud?'

His father nodded and smiled. 'Well, I'll tell you frankly, son, it wouldn't have been the same if you weren't here to take part in it. What's the point of these things if your own flesh and blood isn't there to share it?'

In the next room, Fiona talked with David's mother.

'Mrs Fine, you are very kind to put me up for the night. I so appreciate it.'

'Well, of course, any friend of David's is most welcome.'

'He told me all about your lovely home but he didn't do it justice, it's gorgeous.'

Miriam Fine was pleased and confused in equal measure.

'And you live in Dublin, David tells me?'

'Yes, I've been away for many weeks now, I'm so looking forward to seeing them all again.' Fiona's smile never faltered.

'And it was a nice place, this island you were all visiting?'

'Oh, it was lovely, Mrs Fine, they were very simple, very kind people. I'd love to go back there again, and I will, I know I will.'

'And what exactly were you doing there?'

'Having a career break,' Fiona said blithely. She and David had agreed there was no need to mention Shane, miscarriages, drugs arrests. Anything that would disturb the even lives of the Fine family.

'And you're a nurse in Dublin?' Miriam Fine was beginning to breathe more easily. This was not a girl with designs on her only son.

'I spent six months on an oncology ward before I went away, and let me assure you that these are the days to be living in, Mrs Fine.'

'I'm sorry?'

'They can do so much to help people nowadays, you'd be amazed. Let me tell you . . .'

And to her amazement Miriam Fine found herself sitting down and talking to this girl with an Irish accent who was extraordinarily helpful on many different levels. She could not have asked for a better visitor to her home.

At the desk of the Anna Beach Hotel they held several faxes for Elsa. They were increasingly urgent, asking her to pick up her e-mail. But Elsa was nowhere to be found.

The desk clerk spotted Vonni in the foyer craft shop.

'I wonder could you advise me about these messages? The German woman hasn't come in for a while . . .'

Vonni looked at them with interest. 'I can't read German – what do they say?'

'Some man in Germany saying she can't play games like this, can't leave him. That sort of thing.'

'I see.' Vonni was pleased.

'Do you think we should fax him back saying she isn't around?' the clerk asked, anxious that the Anna Beach should not be blamed for inefficiency.

'No, I'd leave it really. Better not get involved. If he calls, of course, you could say that you heard she has gone away.'

'And has she?'

'For a few days, yes, she won't want to be disturbed.'

Dublin

My dear Vonni,

I swore to you that I'd write when I was home for twenty-four hours. So here goes.

The journey was fine, a plane full of tourists, holidaymakers. David and I felt very superior because we knew the real Greece, not just beaches and discos. We took the train up to David's place. He is seriously rich, by the way, his family have this huge house full of lovely antiques and valuable ornaments. His mother is very innocent and fussy and obviously gave in to her husband all her life. Mr Fine looks very badly, he only has a few months to live. Very few. He was quite frightened but actually he was able to talk to me about palliative care. He didn't really know what they did and didn't want to ask. David and I cried at Manchester Airport – people thought we were lovers saying goodbye.

Barbara was at home when I got there, to take the edge off things. Dad was walking on eggshells trying not to say anything that would offend; Mam was like some kind of TV commercial about gravy and home cooking, you'd think I'd been in some gulag or other rather than on an island full of wonderful smells and tastes. I still yearn for the smell of charcoal at the Midnight Café or the roast lamb and pine nuts up in Andreas's.

Do give him my love, I'll write when I start my job and when Barbara and I get our new flat. At the moment I'm sleeping on her sofa and I'll go round to see Mam and Dad every second day. They're fine, actually, and hardly ever mention the bloody silver wedding at all. My two sisters have turned into horrors. I thought it best not to dwell on things like the miscarriage and Shane being in jail. Well, more than not dwelling on them, I didn't really mention them at all.

I can never thank you enough, Vonni, particularly for that day in Athens. I have a hope, a dream that you find your husband and son again. You deserve to.

Love,
Fiona

Dear Vonni,

Oh, I miss you and Aghia Anna every hour of every day. How good it would be to wake up to that bright sky and spend a day without care until the stars came out. I suppose there are stars here, it's been overcast so I don't seem to see them.

My father looks awful. Fiona was wonderful with him, by the way. Talking to him as if she had known him all her life and telling him how great the drugs were to take the edges off pain. Even my mother loved her and, having bristled at the thought that I was bringing a gentile girl into the house, she was quite sorry to realise that we actually were just friends. They made her promise to come back nearer the end and I know she will. We cried at the airport. It symbolised the end of everything – the summer, Greece, friendship, hope.

Am I glad I came back? Well, put simply, I had to come back. I feel weak at the thought that I might not have done so if it hadn't been for you. You were so clear-sighted, and strong in making me see what was happening. The awful thing is that I keep getting praised by uncles and aunts and friends for my great 'intuition' in knowing

that something was wrong. Some intuition,
Vonni! It was you! But as we agreed, I
don't tell them that.

The days are dreary, and I will soon be
starting to work in the office. I have to
concentrate because my father wants to talk
about it each evening. The man who was
running the show naturally hates me, and is
very resentful. He keeps wanting to know
when I start. I so want to tell him how I
feel about it all. But of course I can't. The
award is next week. More fuss and
preparation than for a moon landing. I'll
write and tell you about it. Can you write to
me? I long to know about Maria's driving,
about the people in the Midnight, about
whether Thomas and Elsa stayed or went, or
even got together, which is what I thought
might happen.

I dreamed the other night that your son
came back. Right into the harbour in a boat
with an outboard engine. It could happen,
couldn't it?

Love,
David

'When should we go back to the real world?' Elsa
asked after days spent wandering around the hills
and coves of Kalatriada.

'Do you mean back to Aghia Anna or points further west?' Thomas had picked wild flowers for her and was busy making them into a posy with a length of string.

'I suppose Aghia Anna as a base camp,' Elsa said. They had been living a strange life here, totally disconnected from the real world. They had gone shopping in the markets and bought cheese for their lunch on the hills. There was a bookshop where they had found some English books. Thomas had asked a potter to make a plate with his mother's name on it.

Because they hadn't really packed for such an extended visit, they bought a couple of extra garments at stalls on market day. Thomas looked splendid in his colourful Greek shirt; Elsa had bought him a pair of elegant cream-coloured trousers in a desperate attempt to get him to abandon the three-quarter-length shorts with all the pockets which he seemed to love.

'*Orea,*' Irini said when she saw him dressed up.

'Yes, indeed, he is beautiful,' Elsa agreed.

'I miss my other trousers,' Thomas grumbled.

'You're the only one that does – they're quite terrible!'

'Oh, Elsa, indulge me, let me wear them, they're familiar like a comfort blanket. Please,' he begged.

'A blanket would be more elegant,' Elsa said. 'Hey, I'm talking like a wife. This will never do. Wear what you like,' she laughed at him.

'Shall we row back to Aghia Anna tomorrow?' he suggested.

'Yes, it's not as if it were goodbye, we can still be together there,' Elsa consoled herself.

'Of course we can, we're in no hurry to go anywhere,' Thomas agreed.

Maria and Vonni knew that they were back from Kalatriada, as they had just seen them returning the rowing boat at the harbour.

'The American looks very well, he doesn't wear those foolish trousers any more,' Maria said approvingly.

'Well, thanks be to the Divine Lord for that,' Vonni said devoutly. 'The Divine Lord helped and ably assisted, I'd say, by a very bright young German woman.' Vonni watched as she saw them kiss each other goodbye, Elsa heading for the Anna Beach, Thomas for the town. They looked relaxed and at ease with each other. The trip had obviously been a success.

'Heigh-ho, Maria, *pame*, let's go. Lots of three-point turns today, and where better than up in the square? I got a message that I have to go to see Takis, the lawyer, he has a message for me apparently.'

'What about?'

'I have no idea. It's hardly a court summons, I've been well behaved now for a couple of decades. But we'll hear.' Vonni was giving nothing away. Maria had no idea that Vonni had been up half the night wondering if the message had anything to do with Stavros. Either Stavros – her husband or her son.

Elsa sat in the Anna Beach with her big organiser diary beside her. For the first time in months she looked up contacts back in Germany, people who worked in the media.

The desk clerk brought her a sheaf of faxes plus four telephone message dockets. The last one said that Dieter would come out in two weeks' time to find her.

Elsa calmly ripped all the faxes in half without reading them and threw them into the wastepaper basket with the telephone messages. Then she went to the business centre where she could log on to her e-mail; and there she began to work.

Her first e-mail was to Dieter.

I have written a long letter explaining why I am not coming back. Come out to Greece if you like, Dieter, but I will be gone. It will be a wasted journey.
Elsa

'Andy, am I disturbing you, it's Thomas.'
'No way. We're down in Sedona today, another canyon, it's real pretty here, Thomas.'

Thomas could hear Bill calling out excitedly.

'Is that Dad? Can I talk to him?'

'Sure, Bill, he called to talk to you. Take the phone and go off to have a real good chat with him.'

'Dad? Is it really you?'

'Nobody else, Bill, just me.'

'Dad, if you could just *see* this place. We've had a great time here, the colours keep changing all the time. And Gran's got all these friends, old, old people, she calls them the girls. And I said they were girls with wrinkly faces and they all laughed.'

'I bet they did.'

'What have you been doing, Dad?'

'I went to a little village, a tiny little place, real old-fashioned. One day I'll take you there.'

'Will you, Dad?'

'I don't ever say things I don't mean. One day I'll have a holiday with you on this island.'

'Was it lonely for you in this little village all by yourself?' Bill asked.

'Um, no, not lonely no . . .'

'So you don't miss us or anything?' the boy asked, sounding disappointed.

'Oh, I do, Bill, I miss you every single day, and do you know what I'm going to do about it?'

'No.'

'I'm going to come back there in ten days' time and we'll have a great time.'

'Dad, that's *fantastic*! How long are you coming back for?'

'For good,' he said.

And as he heard the boy who would always be his son shouting out, 'Mom, Andy, Dad's coming home. In ten days' time and he's going to stay for ever', Thomas felt the tears falling down his face.

'Takis! How are you?'

'I'm fine, Vonni, and you?'

'I'm keeping a slightly beady eye on Maria in case she ploughs through us and knocks down your office.'

'Let's watch her from inside the office, we won't be directly in the line of fire,' he said, leading her in. 'Do you know what I want to talk to you about?' Takis asked.

'No, not a clue.'

'Can you guess?'

'Is it something about Stavros?' she asked hesitantly.

'No, not at all,' he said, taken aback.

'Well then, you'll have to tell me, Takis,' she said. The light had gone out of her face.

Takis spoke quickly. 'It's about Nikolas Yannilakis. As you know, Nikolas died last week.'

'Poor Nikolas.' Vonni looked slightly worried. There surely couldn't be any trouble, any inquiry about giving him the morphine – Dr Leros had been aware of everything and co-operated all the way.

'He left you everything.'

'But he didn't have anything to leave!' Vonni said, wide-eyed.

'He had enough. He came in here six months ago and made a proper will. Left it all to you. His little house, his furniture, his savings . . .'

'Well, imagine him thinking of doing that!' Vonni was stunned. 'I suppose we should give the house to his neighbours, they have a lot of children, they could do with more space. I could sort of clear it out for them.'

'You haven't asked about his savings,' Takis said gravely.

'Sure, poor Nikolas didn't have any savings to speak of,' Vonni said.

'He left you over a hundred thousand euros,' Takis said.

Vonni looked at him in amazement. 'That can't be, Takis, the man had nothing, he lived in a hovel . . .'

'He had it all in the bank, some of it in shares, some in cash, I had to wait until it was totalled before I told you.'

'But where on earth did he get that amount of money?'

'Family apparently.'

'But why in the name of God didn't he use it to

give himself some comfort?' She was angry with the dead man for denying himself what he could have had.

'Oh, Vonni, don't talk to me about families, the most extraordinary institution ever invented. Somebody insulted somebody somewhere along the line. Don't ask me because I don't know. But it meant that Nikolas didn't touch the money. So now it's all yours.'

She said nothing.

'And rightly so, Vonni. No one deserves it more than you, you looked after him in a way no one else could have.'

She sat very still, looking ahead of her.

'What will you do, will you travel, go back and visit them in Ireland?'

She still sat in shocked silence.

Takis wasn't used to Vonni being like this.

'Of course, you don't have to make any decisions yet. I'll arrange all the transfers when you've had time to think about things and feel like giving me instructions.'

'I feel like doing it now, Takis, if that's all right.'

'Certainly.' He sat down opposite her, his face to the window looking on to the square.

'Tell me first, is that madwoman Maria obstructing traffic or anything?'

'No, she's fine, she's doing rather big loopy turns but she's fine, everything is steering well clear of her,' Takis said, pulling a pad of paper towards him to write down the instructions.

'I don't intend to touch any of that money. Just leave it where it is. I will as I said give the little house to the family next door, but I would like them to think it came directly from Nikolas. And I want to make a will . . .'

'Very sensible, Vonni,' Takis said in a low voice. He didn't think it was sensible at all, but it wasn't his business.

'And I would like to leave everything, my craft shop, my apartment and this legacy from Nikolas to my son Stavros.'

'I beg your pardon?'

'You heard me.'

'But you haven't seen him in years. He never came back to you despite all your pleas.'

'Are you going to make this will for me, Takis, or do I have to go and find another lawyer?'

'I'll have it drawn up by tomorrow at this time. And I'll have two people here to witness your signature.'

'Thank you – and I presume this is all just between us?'

'It is, Vonni. Just between the two of us.'

'Right, I'll go save Aghia Anna from Maria,' she said.

She walked out shakily, Takis noticed, as he stood

at the door and watched her as Maria came running over.

'I understand it now, you turn the wheel exactly the wrong way to what you think! In the opposite direction!' she cried triumphantly.

'Whatever you think, Maria . . .'

'And what did Takis want?' she asked.

'To help me make my will,' said Vonni.

'I missed you,' Thomas said to Elsa when she came up the whitewashed steps to his apartment.

'And I you. The lazy days of Kalatriada are no more.' She kissed him lightly and walked into the sitting room. 'That's beautiful,' she added, pointing to a little vase of wild flowers.

'I'd love to say that I went out and gathered them for you on the hills, but actually Vonni left them there. She left a note to welcome us both back.' He passed her the little card.

'So she knows then?' Elsa said.

'I expect she knew before we did,' Thomas said ruefully.

'I wonder what she thinks?'

'Well, look at the flowers! That's a seal of approval, isn't it?' Thomas said.

'That's true, and of course it does also mean we've signed up for her own kind of messy, complicated lifestyle,' Elsa agreed.

'Messy?'

'Well, look at us! They say the secret of the universe is timing. We timed things spectacularly badly, didn't we? You going in one direction and me going in the other!'

Thomas reached for her hand. 'We'll work it out,' he promised.

'I know,' she said doubtfully.

'Honestly, we'll work it out together,' Thomas said.

'We will,' said Elsa with greater conviction.

Dublin

My dear Vonni,

Thank you so much for the letter. I got so homesick for Aghia Anna when I read it. I was right to come back here, but that doesn't mean I can't ache for the sunshine and the lemon trees and all the marvellous people I met out there.

The Ward Sister here, Carmel, is horrific; she used to be a mate of ours, but all power corrupts . . . She thinks I should be punished for having left the hospital and is dreaming up ways. Barbara and I have a terrific flat, we are having a housewarming party on Saturday, so wish us luck.

Mam and Dad have been great, Shane's name is never mentioned, it's as if he has become a family secret never to be spoken of. Which is probably for the best. They've decided to have a much simpler silver wedding, no place names and all that bullshit. Which is a great relief. I telephoned David and he was a bit grim. It was the day of his father's award. He just hates being back. But he'll stay there until his father dies.

Fancy Thomas and Elsa being a number! I never saw that coming. But it's perfect!

Loads of love to all pals,
Fiona

Manchester

Dear Vonni,

You are wonderful, telling me all the things I want to hear. I'm so pleased about Maria's progress. Imagine her driving alone all the way to Kalatriada!

That's wonderful news about Thomas going home, but what about Thomas and Elsa? How will they manage to sort it out?

I am too close to it to write and tell you in any balanced way about my father's award. It was a truly awful day. Worse than I had feared, because my father looked so frail and my mother so ludicrously proud, and everyone there, businessmen of every type, just worshipped the God of money and profit.

I'll write when it's less raw, but it was awful. My father made a speech where he announced that I was to be head of his company from next January. Everyone clapped and I had to look so pleased. But I did hate it, Vonni, and I know it's just self-pity of a high order but I feel my life is over at twenty-eight. I know you'll say something positive to keep me going. I think of you so often, and in a dream life I wish that you were my mother and Andreas my father. I'd never let either of you down. It's just so hard in my own family.

Love from a disgustingly morose,
David

The days went by. Elsa spent a lot of time at the Anna Beach on e-mail.

'Who on earth are you writing to?' Thomas asked her.

'I'm examining the job situation,' she said crisply.

'But I thought you weren't going back to Germany?'

'It's hard to accept but there *are* other countries,' she laughed.

Thomas spent those hours beside her at another computer. He was in touch with the university. If he did come back early could he have access to his rooms on campus? All these things had to be worked out.

It was two days before Thomas would leave for Athens.

'I want you to come up to Andreas's tonight for dinner,' Elsa said. 'We have a lot to talk about.'

'Is that the right place to talk about it?' Thomas wondered. 'We always seem to be part of a huge crowd up there.'

'No, I'll see that we have a quiet table,' she promised.

She wore a simple white cotton dress that night and had a flower clipped in her hair.

'You look lovely and so dressed up. I'm so pleased I wore my smart new Kalatriada pants,' he said when he saw her.

'I got this dress today to impress you and I have a taxi to take us to the restaurant. How about that for style?'

They went up the windy road to Andreas's taverna, pointing out places to each other, and watching the usual starry sky unfold out over the sea.

They had indeed been given a little table for two right at the edge of the terrace with an uninterrupted view.

Little Rina served them. Andreas was indoors.

Yorghis, Vonni and Dr Leros were in there with him too. They all waved. They would talk to them later. When it was time for the second coffee.

'I need to talk to you about my looking for a job,' Elsa said.

'Yes, I didn't ask too much.'

'Why didn't you ask?'

'Because even though you said there are other countries I was afraid you would be offered a big position back there in Germany. And I suppose, to be honest, I was afraid you might meet Dieter again and . . . and . . .' He rushed on before she could say anything. 'I've been working out just how soon you can come out to see me, and then I'll come and see you. I can't bear to let you go now that I've found you. Maybe I'm mad to risk losing you by going back to Bill.'

'I got a job, Thomas.'

'Where?' he asked in a very shaky voice.

'I'm almost afraid to tell you.'

'Then it *is* Germany,' he said with a defeated face.

'No.'

'Where, Elsa? No games, I beg you.'

'Based in Los Angeles, but roaming up and down the west coast. A weekly column for a big magazine, interviews, politics, features. Whatever I can come up with really.' She looked at him anxiously for a reaction.

'Where?' he asked, dumbfounded.

386

'California,' she said nervously. 'Is it too soon, too much of an assumption? I mean I just couldn't bear to lose you . . . but if you think . . .'

A slow smile began to broaden across his face.

'Oh, Elsa darling, isn't that wonderful . . .' he began.

'I don't have to live with you or anything, I don't want to crowd you out, but I thought we could be together a lot . . . you see, I know that we haven't been together long but now I couldn't exist without you . . .'

Thomas stood up and went to her side of the table, he pulled her to her feet and kissed her. He didn't care about the other guests. Someone took a photograph of them but they didn't care, they stood locked in each other's arms as if they were never going to be able to draw apart. Then of course the group in the kitchen came out to join them, and many toasts were drunk. To the couple.

'That man who took your picture, he was German, he recognised you, Elsa, from the television.'

She couldn't have worried less.

'He asked who Thomas was,' said Vonni. 'I explained you were a high-powered American academic and you were Elsa's fiancé.'

'*What!*' Thomas and Elsa spoke at the same time.

'Well, I wouldn't have told them anything, Thomas, if you had been wearing those terrible shorts with all the pockets. Once I saw you in a decent pair of trousers, then I thought it doesn't matter for Elsa if some fan sells the picture to a German newspaper!'

They talked on easily as always, looking down on the harbour way below. The last ferry had come in an hour ago but Andreas's taverna hadn't expected any guests coming from that sailing. It was too late and too far a walk. So they were surprised when they saw someone toiling up the windy path.

It was a man of about thirty. He must be fit because he had a pack on his back and carried a suitcase in each hand.

'There's a dedicated diner,' said Elsa admiringly.

'Maybe he's heard of Vonni's stuffed vine leaves,' said Thomas with a smile. He loved Vonni for calling him Elsa's fiancé even though he was bewildered that everyone had hated his lovely shorts with the pockets.

'It's late for anyone to come up here,' Dr Leros said, mystified.

'Unless they really intended to,' said Yorghis in an odd sort of voice, peering at the gateway.

Vonni had stood up to look at the man hesitating at the entrance.

'Andreas!' she said in a choked voice. 'Andreas, my friend, it *is*, it really is!'

Elsa and Thomas looked from one to the other without any idea what was happening. Andreas had stood up and was staggering towards the gate with his arms out. Everyone watched as his laced boots faltered across the terrace.

'*Adoni* . . .' he cried. '*Adoni mou!* You came back. *Adoni ghie mou.* My son, you came back to see me.'

'I came back to stay, Father, if you'll have me?'

The men embraced in a grasp that looked as if it would never end. Then they drew away from each other and stroked each other's faces in wonder. The two men kept saying the same words.

'*Adoni mou!*' Andreas said over and over.

'*Patera!*' Adoni said to his father.

Then Yorghis moved forward, and Vonni and Dr Leros. And they were a little group talking excitedly in Greek and embracing.

Thomas and Elsa held hands very tight.

'We'll never forget this night,' Thomas said.

Elsa said, 'Was I too forward, too pushy? Tell me, Thomas?'

Before he could answer, Andreas and his son came over.

'Adoni, this is the wonderful young woman who told me that I should write to you, when I wondered if you would care. She said everybody loves a letter . . .'

Adoni was tall and handsome. He had a great shock of black hair which would one day go grey-white like his father's, but not for a long time and then possibly here in Aghia Anna. Elsa, who could summon words at will on television in front of millions of viewers, was without words now. Instead she stood up and hugged Adoni tight as if they were old friends.

'Aren't you just beautiful,' Adoni said admiringly to the blonde girl in the white dress and the flower in her hair.

'Elsa and Thomas are together,' Andreas said hastily, lest there should be any misunderstanding.

Adoni shook Thomas by the hand. 'You are a very lucky man,' he said with great sincerity.

Thomas agreed. 'I am a very lucky man.' And then he stood up to address the group of friends. He looked straight at Elsa as if to answer her question about whether she was too pushy, too forward.

'I want to tell you all that Elsa will be leaving with me. We will be going to California together.'

'Yet another reason to celebrate tonight,' Andreas cried out, tears in his eyes.

Thomas and Elsa kissed again, and then they sat with his arm around her shoulders as they watched the homecoming unfold.

Andreas, Yorghis and little Rina ran to get food and wine for the prodigal son. The feeling was that he had never eaten properly in all those years in Chicago.

Vonni sat beside Adoni, her eyes sparkling.

'And your son Stavros?' Adoni asked.

'Has his own life somewhere . . .' she said hastily.

'But why can he not find it in his heart to . . .'

'Let's not talk about that now, the important thing is that *you* are back, Adoni! And by the way, your father has changed; he won't be like he was . . .'

'Neither will I be as I was, Vonni.'

Then Adoni was borne away by more well-wishers.

Vonni sat flanked on either side by her friends Andreas and Yorghis as she had been for so long.

'One night Stavros will come into that harbour,' Andreas said.

'And it will be a night like this,' Yorghis encouraged.

'Yes, yes, I'm sure,' Vonni said, eyes bright, face hopeful.

They knew she was putting on a cheerful manner. At the same time they each stretched out a hand to hold hers. Now her smile was genuine.

'Of course he will come back one day,' she said as she gripped their hands. 'We only have to look at tonight to know that miracles happen. And there is no point in going on if you don't believe that.'

Dr Leros came out of the kitchen excitedly.

'There are two bouzouki players out there, they want to play to welcome you home, Adoni,' he begged.

'I'd love that,' he laughed.

And as the music rang out into the night and the people in the restaurant began to clap to the beat, Adoni stood up and went into the centre of the terrace. And in front of everyone he began to dance. Adoni danced in front of forty people, some of them customers who knew nothing of what was happening, some like Thomas and Elsa who knew part of the story, and some like his father, his uncle, the doctor and Vonni who knew everything.

His arms high in the air, he swooped and bent and danced, overjoyed to be back where he belonged.

And a little light rain came down but nobody cared.

It didn't get in the way of the stars.

WHITETHORN
WOODS

For dear good Gordon.
Thank you for the great happy life
we have together.

Contents

CHAPTER I

The Road, the Woods and the Well – 1

Father Brian Flynn, the curate in St Augustine's, Rossmore, hated the Feast Day of St Ann with a passion that was unusual for a Catholic priest. But then as far as he knew he was the only priest in the world who had a thriving St Ann's Well in his parish, a holy shrine of dubious origin. A place where parishioners gathered to ask the mother of the Virgin Mary to intercede for them in a variety of issues, mainly matters intimate and personal. Areas where a clod-hopping priest wouldn't be able to tread. Like finding them a fiancé, or a husband, and then blessing that union with a child.

Rome was as usual unhelpfully silent about the well.

Rome was probably hedging its bets, Father Flynn thought grimly, over there they must be pleased that there was *any* pious practice left in an increasingly secular Ireland and not wishing to discourage it. Yet had not Rome been swift to say that pagan rituals and superstitions had no place in the Body of Faith? It was a puzzlement as Jimmy, that nice young doctor from Doon village, a few miles out, used to say. He said it was exactly the same in medicine: you never got a ruling when you wanted one, only when you didn't need one at all.

There used to be a ceremony on 26 July every year where people came from far and near to pray and to dress the well with garlands and flowers. Father Flynn was invariably asked to say a few words, and every year he agonised over it. He could not say to these people that it was very near to idolatry to have hundreds of people battling their way towards a chipped statue in the back of a cave beside an old well in the middle of the Whitethorn Woods.

From what he had read and studied, St Ann and her husband St Joachim were shadowy figures, quite possibly confused in stories with Hannah in the Old Testament who was thought to be for ever childless but eventually bore Samuel. Whatever else St Ann may have done in her lifetime, two thousand years ago, she certainly had *not* visited Rossmore in Ireland, found a place in the woods and established a holy well that had never run dry.

That much was fairly definite.

But try telling it to some of the people in Rossmore and you were in trouble. So he stood there every year mumbling a decade of the rosary, which couldn't offend anyone, and preaching a little homily about goodwill and tolerance and kindness to neighbours, which fell on mainly deaf ears.

Father Flynn often felt he had quite enough worries of his own without having to add St Ann and her credibility to the list. His mother's health had been an increasing worry to them all, and the day was rapidly approaching when she could no longer live alone. His sister Judy had written to say that although Brian might have chosen the single, celibate life, she certainly had not. Everyone at work was either married or gay. Dating agencies had proved to be full of psychopaths, evening classes were where you met depressive losers; she was going to come to the well near Rossmore and ask St Ann to get on her case.

His brother Eddie had left his wife Kitty and their four children to find himself. Brian had gone to look for Eddie – who had now found himself nicely installed with Naomi, a girl twenty years younger than the abandoned wife – and had got little thanks for his concern.

'Just because you're not any kind of a normal man at all, it doesn't mean that the rest of us have to take a vow of celibacy,' Eddie had said, laughing into his face.

Brian Flynn had felt a great weariness. He thought that he *was* in fact a normal man. Of course he had desired women, but he had made a bargain. The rules, at the moment, said if he were to be a priest then there must be no marriage, no children, no good normal family life.

3

Father Flynn always told himself that this was a rule that would one day change. Not even the Vatican could stand by and watch so many people leave the ministry over a rule that was made by Man and not by God. When Jesus was alive all the Apostles were married men, the goalposts were moved much later.

And then all the scandals in the Church were surely making the slow-moving conservative cardinals realise that in the twenty-first century some adaptations must be made.

People did not automatically respect the Church and Churchmen any more.

Far from it.

There were hardly any vocations to the priesthood nowadays. Brian Flynn and James O'Connor had been the only two ordinations in the diocese eight years back. And James O'Connor had left the Church because he had been outraged by the way an older, abusive priest had been protected and allowed to escape either treatment or punishment by a cover-up.

Brian Flynn was hanging in there, but only just.

His mother had forgotten who he was, his brother despised him and now his sister Judy was making a trip from London to visit this cracked pagan well and wondering, would it work better if she came on the saint's Feast Day.

Father Flynn's parish priest was a gentle elderly man, Canon Cassidy, who always praised the young curate for his hard work.

'I'll stay on here as long as I can, Brian, then you'll be considered old enough and they'll give you

4

the parish,' Canon Cassidy often said. He meant very well and was anxious to spare Father Flynn from the indignity of having some arrogant and difficult parish priest brought in over the curate's head. But at times Brian Flynn wondered would it be better to let nature take its course, to hasten Canon Cassidy to a home for the elderly religious, to get someone, almost anyone, to help with the parish duties?

Admittedly attendance at church had died off a great deal since he was a young man. But people still had to be baptised, given first communion, have their confessions heard; they needed to be married and buried.

And sometimes, like when in the summer a Polish priest came along to help him, Brian Flynn used to think he might manage better alone. The Polish priest last year spent *weeks* making garlands for St Ann and her well.

Not long ago he had been in the junior school at St Ita's and asked if any of the pupils wanted to become nuns when they grew up. Not an unreasonable question to ask little girls in a Catholic school. They had been mystified. No one seemed to know what he meant.

Then one of them got it. 'You mean like the movie *Sister Act*?'

Father Flynn felt that the world was definitely tilting.

Sometimes when he woke in the morning, the day stretched ahead of him, confused and bewildering.

Still he had to get on with things, so he would have his shower and try to pat down his red hair which always stood in spikes around his head. Then he would make a cup of milky tea and a slice of toast and honey for Canon Cassidy.

The old man always thanked him so gratefully that Father Flynn felt well rewarded. He would open the curtains, plump up the pillows, and make some cheerful comment about how the world looked outside. Then he would go to the church and say a daily Mass for an ever-decreasing number of the faithful. He would call to his mother's house, heart in his mouth about how he would find her.

Invariably she would be sitting at her kitchen table looking lost and without purpose. He would explain, as he always did, that he was her son, a priest in the parish; and he would make her a breakfast of porridge and a boiled egg. Then he would walk down Castle Street with a heavy heart to Skunk Slattery's newsagents where he would buy two newspapers: one for the canon and one for himself. This usually involved some kind of intellectual argument with Skunk about free will or predestination or how a loving God could allow the tsunami, or a famine. By the time he got back to the priests' house, Josef, the Latvian carer, had arrived and got Canon Cassidy up, washed and dressed him and made his bed. The canon would be sitting waiting for his newspaper. Later, Josef would take the old man for a gentle walk to St Augustine's Church where he would say his prayers with closed eyes.

Canon Cassidy liked soup for his lunch and sometimes Josef took him to a café but mainly he took the frail little figure back to his own house where his wife Anna would produce a bowl of something home-made; and in return the canon would teach her more words and phrases in English.

He was endlessly interested in Josef and Anna's homeland, asking to see pictures of Riga and saying it was a beautiful city. Josef had three other jobs: he cleaned Skunk Slattery's newsagents, he took the towels from Fabian's hairdressers to the Fresh as a Daisy Launderette and washed them there, and three times a week he took a bus out to the Nolans' place and helped Neddy Nolan look after his father.

Anna had many jobs too: she cleaned the brasses on the doors of the bank, and on some of the office buildings which had big important-looking notices outside; she worked in the hotel kitchens at breakfast time doing the washing up; she opened the flowers that came from the market to the florists and put them in big buckets of water. Josef and Anna were astounded by the wealth and opportunities they found in Ireland. A couple could save a fortune here.

They had a five-year plan, they told Canon Cassidy. They were saving to buy a little shop outside Riga.

'Maybe you'll come to see us there?' Josef said.

'I'll look down on you and bless your work,' the canon said in a matter-of-fact tone, anticipating the best in the next world.

7

Sometimes Father Flynn envied him.

The old man still lived in a world of certainties, a place where a priest was important and respected, a world where there was an answer for every question asked. In Canon Cassidy's time there were a hundred jobs a day for a priest to do. And not enough hours to do them. The priest was wanted, expected and needed at all kinds of happenings in the lives of the parishioners. Nowadays you waited to be asked. Canon Cassidy would have called uninvited and unannounced to every home in the parish. Father Flynn had learned to be more reticent. In modern Ireland, even in a town like Rossmore, there were many who would not welcome the appearance of a Roman collar on the doorstep.

So as Brian Flynn set out down Castle Street, he had half a dozen things planned to do. He had to meet a Polish family and arrange the baptism of their twins the following Saturday. They asked him, could the ceremony take place at the well. Father Flynn tried to control his annoyance. No, it would take place at the baptismal font in the Church of St Augustine.

Then he went to the jail to visit a prisoner who had asked for him. Aidan Ryan was a violent man whose wife had finally broken the silence of years and admitted that he had beaten her. He showed no sorrow or remorse, he wanted to tell a rambling tale about it all being her fault as many years ago she had sold their baby to a passer-by.

Father Flynn brought the Blessed Sacrament to an

old people's home outside Rossmore with the ridiculous name of Ferns and Heathers. The owner had said it was nicer in a multicultural Ireland not to have everything called by a saint's name. They seemed pleased to see him and showed him their various gardening projects. Once upon a time all these homes were run by Religious, but this woman Poppy seemed to be making a very good fist of it.

Father Flynn had an old battered car to take him on his travels. He rarely used it within the town of Rossmore itself since the traffic was very bad and parking almost impossible. There had been rumours that a great bypass would be built, a wide road taking the heavy trucks. Already people were in two minds about it. Some were saying that it would take the life out of the place, others claimed that it would return to Rossmore some of its old character.

Father Flynn's next call was to the Nolans' house.

The Nolans were a family that he liked very much. The old man, Marty, was a lively character full of stories about the past; he talked about his late wife as if she were still here, and often told Father Flynn about the miracle cure she had once got from St Ann's Well that gave her twenty-four years more of a good life. His son was a very decent man, he and the daughter-in-law Clare always seemed pleased to see him. Father Flynn had assisted the canon at their marriage some years back.

Clare was a teacher in St Ita's and she told the priest that the school was full of gossip about the new road that was coming to Rossmore. In fact she was asking her class to do a project on it. The extraordinary thing was that from what you heard or could work out, the road would be going right through here, through their own property.

'Wouldn't you get great compensation if it did go through your land?' Father Flynn said admiringly. It was pleasing to see good people being rewarded in this life.

'Oh, but Father, we'd never let it go through *our* land,' Marty Nolan said. 'Not in a million years.'

Father Flynn was surprised. Usually small farmers prayed for a windfall like this. A small fortune earned by accident.

'You see, if it came through here it would mean they'd have to tear up Whitethorn Woods,' Neddy Nolan explained.

'And that would mean getting rid of St Ann's Well,' Clare added. She didn't have to say that this was the well that had given her late mother-in-law another quarter-century of life. That fact hung there unspoken.

Father Flynn got back into his little car with a heavy heart. This insane well was going to become yet again a divisive factor in the town. There would be still more talk about it, more analysing its worth, claims and counter-claims. With a deep sigh he wished that the bulldozers had come in overnight and taken the well away. It would have solved a lot of problems.

He went to call on his sister-in-law, Kitty. He tried to visit at least once a week, just to show her that she hadn't been abandoned by the whole family. Only Eddie had left her.

Kitty was not in good form.

'I suppose you'll want something to eat,' she said ungraciously. Brian Flynn looked around the untidy kitchen with its unwashed breakfast dishes, the children's clothes on chairs and a great deal of clutter. Not a home to welcome anyone.

'No, I'm great as I am,' he said, searching for a chair to sit on.

'You're better not to eat, I suppose, they feed you like a prize pig in all these houses you visit – it's no wonder you're putting on a bit of weight.'

Brian Flynn wondered had Kitty always been as sour as this? He couldn't recall. Perhaps it was just the disappearance of Eddie with the sexy young Naomi that had changed her.

'I was in with my mother,' he said tentatively.

'Had she a word to throw to you?'

'Not many, I'm afraid, and none of them making much sense.' He sounded weary.

But he got no sympathy from Kitty. 'Well, you can't expect me to weep salt tears over her, Brian. When she did have her wits, I was never good enough for her marvellous son Eddie, so let her sit and work that one out for herself. That's my view.' Kitty's face was hard. She wore a stained cardigan and her hair was matted.

For a fleeting moment, Father Flynn felt a little sympathy for his brother. If you had the choice of all the women around, which apparently Eddie had,

Naomi would have been an easier and more entertaining option. But then he reminded himself of duty and children and vows, and banished the thought.

'The mother can't manage much longer on her own, Kitty, I'm thinking of selling up her house and moving her into a home.'

'Well, I never expected anything out of that house anyway, so go ahead and do it as far as I'm concerned.'

'I'll talk to Eddie and Judy about it, see what they think,' he said.

'Judy? Oh, does her ladyship ever answer the phone over there in London?'

'She's coming over here to Rossmore in a couple of weeks' time,' Father Flynn said.

'She needn't think she's staying here.' Kitty looked around her possessively. 'This is *my* house, it's all I have, I'm not letting Eddie's family have squatters' rights in it.'

'No, I don't think for a moment that she'd want to ... to ... um ... put you out.' He hoped his voice didn't suggest that Judy would *never* stay in a place like this.

'So where will she stay then? She can't stay with you and the canon.'

'No, one of the hotels, I imagine.'

'Well, Lady Judy will be able to pay for that, unlike the rest of us,' Kitty sniffed.

'I was thinking about Ferns and Heathers for our mother. I was there today, the people all seem very happy.'

'That's a Protestant home, Brian, the priest can't send his own mother to a Protestant place. *What* would people say?'

'It's not a Protestant home, Kitty.' Father Flynn was mild. 'It's for people of all religions or no religions.'

'Same thing,' Kitty snapped.

'Not at all, as it happens. I was there bringing them Holy Communion. They are opening a wing for Alzheimer's patients next week. I thought maybe if any of you would like to go and look at it . . .' He sounded as weary as he felt.

Kitty softened.

'You're not a bad person, Brian, not in yourself. It's a hard old life what with no one having any respect for priests any more or anything.' She meant it as a kind of sympathy, he knew this.

'Some people do, just a little bit of respect,' he said with a watery smile, getting up to leave.

'Why do you stay in it?' she asked as she came to the door.

'Because I joined up, signed on, whatever, and very occasionally I do something to help.' He looked rueful.

'I'm always glad to see you anyway,' said the charmless Kitty Flynn, with the heavy implication that she was probably the only one in Rossmore who might be remotely glad to see him anywhere near her.

He had told Lilly Ryan that he would call and tell her how her husband Aidan was getting on in prison.

She still loved him and had often regretted that she had testified against him. But it had seemed the only thing to do, the blows were so violent now that she had ended up in hospital and she had three children.

He didn't feel in the mood to talk to her. But since when was all this about feeling in the right mood? He drove into her little street.

The youngest boy Donal was in his last year at the Brothers School. He would not be at home.

'Aren't you a very reliable man, Father?'

Lilly was delighted to see him. Even though he had no good news for her it was at least consoling to be considered reliable. Her kitchen was so different to the one he had just left. There were flowers on the window sill, gleaming copper pans and pots; there was a desk in the corner where she earned a small living by making up crosswords: everything was in order.

She had a plate of shortbread on the table.

'I'd better not,' he said regretfully. 'I heard in the last place that I was as fat as a pig.'

'I bet you did not.' She took no notice of him. 'Anyway can't you walk it all off you in the woods above? Tell me, how was he today?'

And with all the diplomacy that he could muster, Father Flynn tried to construct something from his meeting with Aidan Ryan that morning into a conversation that would bring even a flicker of consolation to the wife he had once beaten and now refused to see. A wife that he seriously believed had sold their eldest baby to a passer-by.

Father Flynn had looked up newspaper accounts over twenty years ago of the time that the Ryan baby girl had been taken from a pram outside a shop in town.

She had never been found. Alive or dead.

Father Flynn managed to keep the conversation optimistic by delivering a string of clichés: the Lord was good, one never knew what was going to happen, the importance of taking one day at a time.

'Do you believe in St Ann?' Lilly asked him, suddenly breaking the mood.

'Well, yes, I mean, of course I believe that she existed and all that . . .' he began blustering and wondering where this was leading.

'But do you think that she is there listening at the well?' Lilly persisted.

'Everything is relative, Lilly, I mean, the well is a place of great piety over centuries and that in itself carries a certain charge. And of course St Ann is in heaven and like all the saints interceding for us . . .'

'I know, Father, I don't believe in the well either,' Lilly interrupted. 'But I was up there last week and, honestly, it's astonishing. In this day and age all the people coming there, it would amaze you.'

Father Flynn assembled a look of pleased amazement on his face. Not very successfully.

'I know, Father, I felt the same as you do, once. I go up there every year, you know, around Teresa's birthday. That was my little girl, who disappeared years before you came to the parish here. Usually it's just meaningless, but somehow last week I looked at it differently. It was as if St Ann really was listening to me. I told her all the trouble that had happened as a result of it all, and how poor Aidan had never been right since it happened. But mainly I asked her to tell me that Teresa was all right wherever she is. I could sort of bear it if I thought she was happy somewhere.'

Father Flynn looked mutely at the woman, unable to summon any helpful reaction.

'But anyway, Father, I know people are always seeing moving statues and holy pictures that speak, and all that kind of nonsense, but there was something, Father, there really was something.'

He was still without words but nodding so that she would continue.

'There were about twenty people there, all sort of telling their own story. A woman saying so that anyone could hear her, "Oh, St Ann, will you make him not grow any colder to me, let him not turn away from me any more . . ." Anyone could have heard her and known her business. But none of us were *really* listening. We were all thinking about ourselves. And suddenly I got this feeling that Teresa was fine, that she had a big twenty-first birthday party a couple of years ago and that she was well and happy. It was as if St Ann was telling me not to worry any more. Well, I *know* it's ridiculous, Father, but it did me a lot of good and where's the harm in that?

'I just wish that poor Aidan could have been there when she said it or thought it or transferred it to my mind or whatever she did. It would have given him such peace.'

Father Flynn escaped with a lot of protestations about the Lord moving in mysterious ways and even threw in the bit of Shakespeare about there being more things in heaven and earth, Horatio, than are dreamed of in your philosophy. Then he left the little house and drove to the edge of Whitethorn Woods.

As he walked through the woods he was greeted by people walking their dogs, joggers in tracksuits getting some of the exercise he obviously needed himself according to his sister-in-law. Women wheeled prams and he would stop to admire the babies. The canon used to say that a playful greeting of 'Who have we here?' was a great get-out when you came across a child in a pram. It covered both sexes and a failing memory for names. The others would fill you in and then you could take it up from there – grand little fellow, or isn't she a fine little girl?

He met Cathal Chambers, a local bank manager, who said he had come up to the woods to clear his head.

He had been flooded by people wanting to borrow money to buy land round here so that they could sell it at a huge profit once the new road was given the okay. It was very hard to know what to do. Head Office had said he was the man on the ground so he should have a feel for what was going to happen. But how could you have a feel for something like that?

He said that Myles Barry the solicitor was in exactly the same predicament. Three different people had come into him asking him to make an offer to the Nolans for that smallholding they had. It was pure greed, speculation and greed, that's what it was.

Father Flynn said it was refreshing to meet a banker who thought in such terms, but Cathal said that was not at all the way they looked at things in Head Office.

Skunk Slattery was walking his two greyhounds and came up to sneer at Father Flynn.

'There you go, Father, coming up here to the pagan well to hope that the gods of olden times will do what today's Church can't do,' he taunted the priest, while his two bony greyhounds quivered with what seemed like annoyance as well.

'That's me, Skunk, always one for the easy life,' Father Flynn said through gritted teeth. He nailed the smile to his face for the few minutes it took before Skunk ran out of rage towards him and moved the trembling dogs onwards.

Father Flynn also went onwards, his face grim as he headed for the first time ever on his own to visit St Ann's Well. He had been here as part of parish activities, always resentful and confused but never voicing his opinion.

A few wooden signs carved over the years by pious local people pointed to the well, which was in a big, rocky, cavernous grotto. The place was damp and cold; a little stream ran down the hill behind and around the well and it was muddy and splashed where many of the faithful had reached in to take scoops of the water with an old iron ladle.

It was a weekday morning and he thought that there would not be many people there.

The whitethorn bushes outside the grotto were festooned, yes, that was the only word Father Flynn thought suitable, literally festooned with bits of cloth and notes and ribbons. There were medals and holy cures, some of them encased in plastic or cellophane.

These were petitions to the saint, requests for a wish to be granted; sometimes they were thanks for a favour received.

'He's off the drink for three months, St Ann, I thank you and beg you to continue to give him strength . . .'

or

'My daughter's husband is thinking of getting the marriage annulled unless she gets pregnant soon . . .'

or

'I'm afraid to go to the doctor but I am coughing up blood, please, St Ann, ask Our Lord that I be all right. That it's only some kind of an infection that will pass . . .'

Father Flynn stood and read them all, his face getting redder.

This was the twenty-first century in a country that was fast becoming secular. *Where* did all this superstition come from? Was it only old people who came here? A throwback to a simpler time? But many of the people he had met even this very morning were young and they felt the well had powers. His own sister was coming back from England to pray here for a husband, the young Polish couple wanted their babies baptised here. Lilly Ryan, who thought she heard the statue tell her that her long-disappeared daughter was all right, was only in her early forties.

It was beyond understanding.

He went inside the grotto where people had left crutches and walking sticks and even pairs of spectacles as a symbol of hope that they would be cured and able to manage without them. There were children's bootees and little socks – meaning who knew what? The desire for a child? A wish to cure a sick baby?

And in the shadows, this huge statue of St Ann.

It had been painted and refurbished over the years, making the apple cheeks even pinker, the brown cloak richer, the wisp of hair under the cream-coloured veil even blonder.

If St Ann existed she would have been a small dark woman, from the land of Palestine and Israel. She would *not* have looked like an Irish advertisement for some kind of cheese spread.

And yet kneeling there in front of the well were perfectly normal people. They got more here than they ever did in St Augustine's Church in Rossmore.

It was a sobering and depressing thought.

The statue looked down glassily – which was a bit of a relief to Father Flynn. If he had begun to imagine that the statue was addressing him personally he would really have given up.

But oddly, even though the saint was not speaking to him, Father Flynn felt an urge to speak to her. He looked at the young troubled face of Myles Barry's daughter, a girl who had failed to get into law school to her father's great grief. *What* could she be praying for with her eyes closed and her face so concentrated?

He saw Jane, the very elegant sister of Poppy who ran the old people's home. Jane, who, even to Father Flynn's untutored eye, seemed to be wearing high-fashion designer clothes, was mouthing something at the statue. A young man who ran an organic vegetable stall in the marketplace was there too, his lips moving silently.

As he gave a last look at what he considered an entirely inappropriate representation of the mother of the mother of Jesus, he wished he could ask the saint through the statue whether any of these prayers were ever heard and ever answered. And what did the saint do if two people were seeking conflicting favours?

But this way fantasy lay, and madness. And he was not getting involved.

He stroked the walls of the cave as he left the grotto, damp walls with messages carved on them. He made his way past the whitethorn bushes crowding the entrance, bushes that no one had cut back to give easier access because they felt the hopes and prayers and petitions of so many people were attached to them.

Even on the old wooden gates there was a note pinned:

'*St Ann, hear my voice.*'

All around him Father Flynn could almost hear the voices. Calling and begging and beseeching down the years. He heard himself make up a little prayer.

'Please let me hear the voices that have come to you and know who these people are. If I am to do any good at all here let me know what they are saying and what they want us to hear and do for them . . .'

CHAPTER 2

The Sharpest Knife in the Drawer

Part 1 – Neddy

I've heard people say about me, 'Oh, Neddy Nolan! He isn't the sharpest knife in the drawer . . .' But, you see, I never *wanted* to be the sharpest knife in the drawer. Years ago we had one sharp knife in the kitchen and everyone was always talking about it with fear.

'Will you put the sharp knife up on a shelf before one of the children cuts the hands off themselves,' my mam would say, and 'Make sure the sharp knife has the blade towards the wall and the handle out, we don't want someone ripping themselves apart,' my dad would say. They lived in fear of some terrible accident, and the kitchen running red with blood.

I was sorry for the sharp knife, to tell you the truth. It wasn't its fault. It didn't set out to frighten people, that's just the way it was made. But I didn't tell people how I felt, they'd just say again that I was being soft.

Soft Neddy, they called me.

Because I couldn't bear to hear a little mouse squealing in a mousetrap, and I had cried when the hunt came near where we lived and I saw the eyes of the fox as it fled by and I shooed it into Whitethorn Woods. Yes, I suppose other fellows thought it was soft but the way I looked at it, the mouse hadn't asked to be born in the scullery instead of out in a field where he could have lived peacefully to be an old happy mouse. And the lovely red fox certainly hadn't done anything to annoy all those hounds and horses and people dressed up in red who galloped after him with such fury.

But I'm not quick and clear at explaining things like that, so often I don't bother. And nobody expects too much from Soft Neddy so I more or less get away with my way of looking at things.

I thought it would be different when I grew up. Adults didn't get all silly about things and sorry for them. I was sure this would happen to me too. But it seemed to take a very long time.

When I was seventeen a crowd of us – me, my brother Kit and his pals – all went off from Rossmore in a van to a dance, oh, miles away beyond the lakes, and there was this girl. And she looked very different to the others, like they were wearing dresses with straps over their shoulders, and she was wearing a thick polo-necked jumper and skirt, and she had glasses and frizzy hair, and no one seemed to be asking her to dance.

So I asked her up, and then when the dance was over she shrugged and said, 'Well, at least I got one dance out of tonight.'

So I asked her again, and then again; and then I said at the end, 'You got fourteen dances out of tonight now, Nora.'

And she said, 'I suppose you want the going home.'

'The going home?' I asked.

'A court a ride,' Nora said in flat resigned tones. This would be the price she would pay for having been asked to dance fourteen times.

I explained that we were from the other side of the lakes, from near Rossmore, and we'd all be going home together. In a van.

I couldn't work out whether she was relieved or disappointed.

The others were slagging me in the van.

'Neddy's in love,' they kept singing all the way home.

There was very little singing four months later when Nora and her dad turned up at our place and said that I was the father of the baby she was carrying.

I could not have been more shocked.

Nora didn't look at me, she just looked at the floor. All I could see was the top of her head. Her sad frizzy perm. I felt a great wave of pity for her. Even more pity when Kit and my other brothers laid into Nora and her dad.

There was no way, they said, that their Neddy

had spent ten seconds alone with Nora. They had a hundred witnesses for this. They were going to get Canon Cassidy to come to the house as a character witness. Red-faced, they confronted Nora's dad and swore that I hadn't even kissed the girl goodbye when they were bundling me into the van. This was the greatest scam they had ever heard.

'I never made love with anyone,' I said to Nora's dad. 'But if I had, and it resulted in a child being conceived, then I'd certainly live up to my responsibilities and I would be honoured to marry your daughter, but you see . . . that's not the way things happened.' And for some reason everyone believed me. Everyone. And the situation was over.

And poor Nora raised her red, tear-stained face and looked at me through her thick glasses.

'I'm sorry, Neddy,' she said.

I never knew what happened to her.

Somebody once said that it was all the fault of her grandfather, but because he was the money of the family, nothing had been done about him. I didn't know if her child got born and if she brought it up. Her family lived so far away from Rossmore, there was never anyone to ask. And our family didn't encourage me to enquire.

They were very scathing about it all.

'A bold rossie,' my mam said.

'Palming off someone else's bastard on our Neddy,' my granny said.

'Sure, not even Soft Neddy could fancy that poor ibex,' my dad said.

And I felt a lump in my throat for the poor young woman, who had said so proudly that at least she had got one dance out of the night and offered herself to me in abject thanks for having had the luxury of fourteen dances.

It was all very sad.

Not long after this, I left Rossmore and went off to London in England to work on the buildings with my eldest brother Kit. He had found a flat over a shop, there were three of them there already and I made the fourth. It wasn't very clean or tidy or anything but it was near the Tube station and in London that's all that mattered.

At first I just made the tea and carried things for people on the site, and they had such cracked, broken old mugs that on the day I got my first wages I went to a market and got a dozen grand new ones. And they were all a bit surprised at how I washed the mugs properly and got a jug for the milk and a bowl for the sugar.

'A real gent is Neddy,' they said about me.

I'm never quite sure whether people are praising me or not. I think not. But it's not important anyway.

But there was this way they had of doing things on the site, like every sixth dustbin wasn't filled with rubbish at all – there were bags of cement and bricks and spare tools. Apparently it was some kind of system, an arrangement, but nobody told me, so naturally I pointed out to the foreman that perfectly good stuff was being thrown away and I thought everyone would be pleased.

But they weren't.

Far from it.

And Kit was the most annoyed of all. I was ordered to stay in the flat next day.

'But I'll be sacked if I don't go into work,' I begged him.

'You'll be flayed alive by the other fellows if you *do* go in.' Kit was very tight-lipped. It was better not to argue with him.

'What will I do here all day?' I asked.

Kit always knew what everyone should do. Not this time.

'Jesus, I don't know, Neddy, do some bloody thing, clean the place up a bit. Anything. Just don't come near the site.'

The other lads didn't speak to me at all which made me realise how serious this whole dustbin thing had been. I sat down to think. It wasn't working out nearly as well as I had thought it would.

I had been planning to save lots of money in London. So that I could get my mam a holiday and my dad a good overcoat with a leather trim. And here I was being ordered not to go into work.

Clean the place up a bit, they said. But with what? We had no cleaning stuff. No bleach for the sink or the bath. No polish for the furniture. No detergent to wash any sheets. And I only had nine English pounds left.

I got an idea and I went down to the shop where the Patels worked hard day and night.

I picked out cleaning stuff and a tin of white paint

28

worth ten pounds in all and put them in a box. Then I spoke to Mr Patel.

'Suppose I was to clear up your yard there for you, sweep it, stack all your boxes and crates. Would you give me those cleaning things as a wage?'

He looked at me thoughtfully as if adding up and weighing the cost and the amount of work I would do.

'And would you clean the shop window as well?' he bargained.

'Certainly, Mr Patel,' I said with a big smile.

And Mr Patel smiled too. A slow unexpected smile.

Then I went to the launderette and asked them if I could paint their door which looked a bit scruffy.

'How much?' Mrs Price, the woman who ran the place and, they said, had many gentlemen friends, was wise in the ways of the world.

'I want to have two loads of washing and extra drying,' I said.

It was a done deal.

When Kit and the lads came back from the site they couldn't believe the transformation.

They had clean beds, the shabby linoleum on the floor was polished, the steel sink was gleaming. I had painted the cupboards in the kitchen and the bathroom.

There were more jobs I could do for the Patels next day, I told them, and they would give me a thing that restored the enamel on baths. And there was more painting to be done in the launderette and that meant we could have loads of things washed there – shirts, jeans, anything – and I'd take the bags of stuff and pick them up again, what with not being able to go to the site and everything.

And because they all seemed to have calmed down and become so admiring of the nice new clean flat, I felt I could dare to ask them about the other business. Had the foreman cooled off any?

'Well, he has apparently,' Kit said. 'He can't believe that you would shop me, your own brother! I put it to him that no one would do a thing like that, nor the lads you lived with. That he'd have to look elsewhere for the culprits. So now he is looking elsewhere.'

'And do you think he'll find them?' I asked, excited. It was like living in a thriller.

They looked at each other confused. There was a silence.

'Probably not,' Kit said after a time.

'And will I come back to work next week?' I wondered.

Another silence.

'You know, you're doing such a great job here, Neddy, making this a real smart place for us to live, maybe *this* is what you should do. Do you know?'

I was very disappointed. I thought I'd be going out to work with them every day like mates.

'But how will I earn my living, my deposit on a house, if I don't have a job at all?' I asked in a low voice.

Kit leaned towards me and spoke to me man to man.

'I think we should regard ourselves as a company, Neddy, and you could be our manager.'

'Manager?' I said, feeling overawed.

'Yeah, suppose if you were to cook us a breakfast, even make us a packed lunch and keep this place looking shipshape. And of course handle our finances, put our money in the post office for us. Then you'd be taking a load off our backs and we'd all kick in with a wage for you. What do you think, lads? Nice clean place for us to live in, we could even bring people back here once Neddy puts his mark on the place.'

And they all thought it was a great idea and Kit ran out for fish and chips for everyone to celebrate the day I became their manager.

It was a great job altogether and much less confusing really than working on the site because I made my own arrangements and knew what I was doing. I wrote all this on my weekly letter home and I thought Dad and my mam would be pleased. But they sent me warning letters telling me to be sure that Kit and the others didn't work me too hard and make use of me.

'You're such a decent, gentle boy, Neddy,' my mam wrote, 'you must look out for yourself in this life. You'll promise me that, won't you?'

But actually it wasn't hard at all because everyone was so nice and I could make everything fit in. After serving a good, cooked breakfast for the lads, I'd take the Patel children to their school. Then I'd open up the launderette because Mrs Price who had a lot of men friends wasn't good in the early morning.

Then I'd go back to the Patels and help them stack shelves and take their rubbish down to a dump. Then I'd get to work on the flat, clean it all up, and every day I tried to do something new for them, like put up a new shelf or do a bit of cleaning in the television repair shop in exchange for a second-hand telly. Then Kit found a video that had fallen off a lorry but hadn't got broken so it was like having our own cinema in the kitchen-sitting room.

I'd pick up the Patel children from school; do the shopping for Christina, an old Greek lady who made our curtains in return.

And every year I would organise the tickets back to Ireland. Kit and I went back home to the little farm outside Rossmore to see the family.

The place changed all the time, the town was growing and spreading out very far. There was even a bus now that came to the corner of our road. I never heard a word about that poor girl Nora and her problems. Kit said it was wiser not to ask.

I always did a bit of work in the house when we came home for the two weeks. Well, Kit would be out at dances, and he didn't really notice anything wrong, like the place getting shabby and needing a coat of paint here, a few shelves there. Dad was out with the cattle and he hadn't the time or the energy to do it.

I would suggest to Kit that we get them a nice television set or maybe even a washing machine, but Kit said we weren't made of money and to stop pretending we were returned millionaires, which was enough to give everyone the sick.

I used to worry about our mam. She had been delicate always, but she always said that St Ann had given her those extra years to watch her family grow up and she was very grateful. One summer I thought she looked very frail, but she said that I was not to worry about her as everything was fine and they lived comfortably now that Dad had sold off a field and had fewer cattle so he was at home more often to hand her a cup of tea. She had no worries about anything except would Dad be all right when she eventually did go.

And then Kit and I went back for Mam's funeral.

And all our friends in London sent flowers because I had told them about Mam. People said that Kit must be very well thought of over in London to have so many friends. Actually they were *my* friends, but it didn't matter anyway.

Poor Dad looked like a bloodhound. His face was all set in lines of sadness as he waved us goodbye.

'You look after young Neddy now,' he instructed Kit at the railway station. Which was odd really as I did all the looking after.

'Wouldn't you think he'd have given us our fare,' Kit grumbled. But I had our fare so it didn't matter.

And then because I fixed up all Mr Patel's out-houses for him to give him more storage, the Patels let us have another entire room included in the same rent, and one of the lads had moved out and got a girlfriend and a real shacked-up relationship so now we were only three in the flat and we had a room each.

The others brought girls back sometimes, nice girls all of them, and they'd have breakfast and be very nice to me.

And honestly it was all so very busy that the time just passed by and I was thirty-seven years old but I'd been saving for nearly twenty years so I had a fortune in the building society. I mean, if you're putting away twenty pounds a week at first and then that goes up to thirty and fifty, well, it all adds up to a huge sum.

I managed to get Kit to come back home with me every year, which wasn't always easy. He said being in Rossmore was like spending time with the living dead. So this particular year, anyway, when we went back home our dad really wasn't well. He hadn't mended the fences of the chicken run and the fox had all the hens. He wasn't able to go to the market any more and relied on people coming to him and making an offer for the beasts, which broke his heart.

He'd grown very in on himself and wasn't keeping the place right at all. I said to Kit that he couldn't live much more on his own like this. Kit said that he'd hate to be sent to the County Home. As if I'd send our dad to the County Home!

No, I said, I thought I should come back and mind him. Try to run the place for him.

'And take all our inheritance for yourself?' Kit said in a horrible voice.

'Oh no, Kit, I'd get someone to value the place, maybe Myles Barry the solicitor in town, and then give you and the others your share. Wouldn't that be fair?'

'You'd live here with Dad?' Kit was open-mouthed.

'Someone has to,' I explained, 'and anyway, I might get married soon if I could find a nice girl.'

'Buy this house? Give us all a share? In your dreams,' Kit laughed.

But I could buy it and I did, the very next day, and my dad was delighted but Kit wasn't pleased at all.

He had no savings, he said, and yet I, who had never done a day's work in my life, was able to put my hand in my pocket and draw out enough to buy a small farm and a gentleman's residence. It was a strange state of affairs.

'But what do you mean I've never done a day's work in my life, wasn't I your manager?' I cried, very upset at the false accusation.

He didn't seem to accept that explanation.

'I *was* your manager,' I insisted. Because I was. I had been a great manager, made a smashing flat for them all to live in. I would have put their money away every week like I put my own, if they'd only have given it to me. It had to go into post office accounts with a whole lot of different names, something to do with accounting apparently. But I couldn't snatch the money from them on a Friday if they were going up west to clubs or taking girls out or buying classy gear.

The reason I was able to save was because I didn't

35

drink. I bought my clothes in Oxfam and anyway I worked so many hours that I didn't have *time* to go out and spend money – so I saved it for a house.

And I told all this to Kit patiently and explained it to him carefully in case he hadn't understood. I watched his face and he stopped being angry. You could see it. His face got all soft and kind like it was the night he had made me manager. The night he had gone out for the fish and chips. And he put out his big hand and laid it over mine.

'I'm sorry, Neddy, I spoke out of turn. Of course you were our manager and a very good one. And I don't know how we'll replace you if you come back here. But then we'll have a lump sum from this place and we'll know Dad's being looked after and that will be a great relief in itself.'

I smiled with relief. It was all going to be all right again.

'You know, the getting married bit might be harder, Neddy, you won't get upset if that isn't as easy for you as everything else. Women are very difficult to understand. Hard to work out. You're a great fellow but you're not the sharpest knife in the drawer and you wouldn't be up to what women want these days.'

He was being kind so I thanked him as I always thanked people for advice whether I understood it or not. And I set about finding a girl to marry.

It took seven months. Then I met Clare.

She was a schoolteacher. I met her when she came home to our parish church outside Rossmore for her father's funeral. I thought she was very nice indeed.

'She's too bright for you,' they all said.

Well, my dad didn't say that because he loved living with me, and he didn't want to say anything that would annoy me. I made him porridge every morning, and I employed a man to look after the few cows we had. I minded the chickens and the ducks. I went for walks with him up to the woods to keep his legs mobile. Sometimes he went to the well to thank St Ann for all those extra years he had with my mam. And I brought him to the pub every day to meet his friends and have a pint and a hot lunch.

Dad used to say about me, 'Neddy's not as soft as you all think . . .'

And Dad thought Clare would be fine for me. He said I should spend money on a few nice shirts and get my hair properly cut in the salon in Rossmore. Imagine Dad knowing words like 'salon'.

Clare was ambitious, she told me this from the start. She wanted to get on in teaching and maybe become a principal sometime, and I said that would be fine because the way I saw it I could be the manager in the house and have everything done when she got home. And suppose, just suppose, we had a little baby, I could look after the baby while Clare went out to work. And to my delight she said it all sounded very good and very restful and she'd be honoured to be my wife.

Kit wasn't able to come to the wedding, because he was in jail in England over some misunderstanding. The real culprits weren't found this time either.

And Dad was much stronger and better now. All it had been really was loneliness and neglect that had him feeling so low.

So we got in a great builder and fixed a price and he did a marvellous job dividing up the house so that Clare could feel that, when she came to live here when we were married, she would have her own home for herself and myself and not that she had come to live with Dad and me. And this way everybody would be happy.

I encouraged Dad's friends to come and see him of an evening. And I bought him a great big television which they all loved when the sport was on.

Our wedding day in Rossmore was just great.

Canon Cassidy did the actual wedding bit, but the new curate Father Flynn was very helpful too. And we had a reception in the hotel where people made speeches.

My dad said that as far as he was concerned his beloved wife who had been cured by St Ann was in this room with us to celebrate the day and I was the best son in the world and would be the best husband and indeed father too when that time came.

I made a short speech and said that I wasn't the sharpest knife in the drawer. I wanted people to know that I *knew* that's what they said. But I was the luckiest knife. I had got everything I wanted all my life and I could ask for no more.

And Clare said that she would like to make a speech. She knew it wasn't usual for the bride to speak but there was something she wanted to say.

I had no idea what it was going to be.

She stood up in her beautiful dress and said to everyone in the room that the drawers were full of sharp awful old knives. So many that she had almost despaired of opening a drawer again. And that then she had found me and her whole life turned around. And as I looked around the big room in the hotel I saw everyone was half crying as they clapped and cheered and it was simply the happiest day of my life . . .

Part 2 – Gold Star Clare

When I was at school at St Ita's, Rossmore, I used to get the gold star every week.

Once when I had flu, another girl, my friend Harriet Lynch, got it but otherwise it was always mine.

I used to take it off my school tunic every Monday morning and lay it back on the Principal's desk and then an hour later, when the gold stars in each class were being read out, I would get it back again.

It was a reward for a combination of good marks, good behaviour and school spirit. You couldn't just get one for studying hard. No, you had to be an all-rounder, a balanced person, as they saw it.

And it was easy really to make them see it like that. Because I liked being at school. I was in early and I left late. They had plenty of time to see me and my good school spirit in their environment. I mean, if you came from *my* home, any environment was preferable. Who wouldn't prefer to be at school than at home?

It wasn't entirely my mother's fault. Not entirely.

Women were different then, they did literally everything not to rock the boat, no matter how dangerous and unpleasant that boat was. Any marriage was better than no marriage, any humiliation was better than the ultimate humiliation of being an abandoned wife. They went up to St Ann's Well to pray that things might get better but they didn't try to make them better themselves.

And I wasn't the only child in the school that had trouble like that at home. There was a poor girl – Nora Something – who was a bit soft in the head. In her case it was her grandfather who bothered her. And she got pregnant and she said that it was some fellow she had met at a dance, but apparently the fellow brought all his brothers and proved that he was never alone with her. And poor Nora went to the nuns, had her baby and gave it up for adoption and her grandfather went on living in that home. And they all knew. All the time. And said nothing.

Like they knew about my Uncle Niall in our home. And said nothing.

I put a lock on my bedroom door and no one asked me why. They knew too well that my father's brother fancied me. But he owned most of the farm, so what could they do?

I asked God a lot if he could stop Uncle Niall from trying to do these things. But God was busy back in those days or there were a lot of cases worse than mine, I suppose. The really hard thing was that they all knew and did nothing. They knew why I did my homework up at the school lest he approach me when the house was empty, and why I didn't come back until I was certain that my mother had come back from the creamery where she worked and my father in from the fields and that there would be other people to protect me. Sort of, anyway.

I was both proud and ashamed when I was a schoolgirl. Proud that I was able to stay out of my uncle's messy clutches. And ashamed because I came from a family that wouldn't look after me but left me to fight my own battles against things I didn't understand.

And I suppose it did make me grow up quickly. And then when I passed my exams I announced firmly that I was going to university miles away.

There was a bit of grumbling about this. Where would they get the money to pay for all this? my father wondered. He had wondered about money all his life, it was his greatest curse.

Why couldn't I stay at home and do a secretarial course and mind my sister? my mother said, as well she might.

My sister Geraldine *did* need to be minded and I would warn her well before I left. Maybe I'd go to the bad in a big city? Uncle Niall said that, even though he knew and I knew and my parents knew. I'd go to the bad much quicker here had I not got a lock on my bedroom door.

But I was much tougher than they all thought.

I was really quite grown up for my years.

I'd survive, I told them, I'd get a job to pay for a flat and my fees. I was a gold star girl. An all-rounder. I could turn my hand to anything.

And I did. I went to Dublin two weeks before term started and I fixed myself up in a flat with three other girls, and got a job in an early-morning breakfast place, which was terrific because I had nearly a day's work done and a huge breakfast eaten by the time I went to my 10 a.m. lectures, and then I worked a shift in a pub from six to ten every night, which kept me out of the way of spending money and I had the whole day to myself.

And because of Uncle Niall and all that sort of thing I wasn't all that keen on fellows like my flatmates were, so I could put my mind to my studies as well. And at the end of the first year I was in the top five of the whole group, which was an achievement.

I never told them any of this when I went back home to Rossmore. Except for my sister Geraldine because I wanted her to know we could do anything, *anything*, if we wanted to.

Geraldine thought I was wonderful and she told me too that she was well able to deal with Uncle Niall now by shouting aloud, 'Oh *there* you are, Uncle Niall, what can I do for you?' at the top of her voice, alerting the whole house and he would slink away. And she had announced one day in front of everyone that she was putting a giant padlock on her door.

And then in the middle of my second year at

university a lot of things went wrong. My mother got cancer and they said they couldn't operate. My father coped with it all by drinking himself senseless every night.

My sister went to stay with my friend Harriet Lynch's younger sister in order to study and to get away from Uncle Niall since there was no one to protect her.

Back in Dublin they put up the rent on our flat. Seriously high. And just then I met Keno who ran a nightclub down a little cobbled street in Dublin and asked me to dance there. I said, nonsense, I couldn't dance, and he said there was nothing to it. And I said it would be dangerous, wouldn't it be sort of flaunting yourself at people and then not letting them touch you?

But Keno had bouncers who looked after all that sort of thing.

And then my mother died.

Yes, it was awful, and I tried to mourn her properly but I could never forget that she had turned aside and left Geraldine and me to our fate. And shortly after the funeral Uncle Niall sold the farm over my father's head and Geraldine hadn't done any work at school because she was so upset about everything and if I did do the bloody dancing it meant I could have my own flat in Dublin, finish my university degree, put Geraldine into one of those sixth form Leaving Certificate colleges and keep an eye on her. So I said okay to Keno and wore this ludicrous thong and danced around a pole every night.

It was silly. Just mainly silly and a bit sad really.

And the music sometimes would do your head in.

But the tips were enormous, and the bouncers were great and there was always a taxi home at 3 a.m. and God, why not?

I told Geraldine that it was a gambling club, and I was a croupier taking in the money, and that the law said she was too young to come in, and that was fine. And then one night of course, wouldn't you know, Harriet Lynch's father and some friends were there and recognised me. They nearly dropped dead.

I went to their table to have a drink and said very sweetly that everyone earned their living and took their pleasures in an entirely individual way and I didn't see any need to inform Harriet Lynch's mother or daughters back in Rossmore of the nature of these business trips to Dublin. They got the message and Keno told me afterwards that I was the brightest girl he ever had in his stable. I didn't like the word 'stable'. I felt we were all like performing prancing horses or something. But I did like Keno. A lot. He was very respectful to us all and he was doing all this because he had a very poor family who needed support back in Morocco. He would really like to have been a poet but there was no money in poetry. His little sisters and brothers wouldn't have had an education if he were busy writing verses, so he had this club instead.

I understood so well.

Sometimes we'd have a coffee, Keno and myself – my friends from college thought he was gorgeous.

He always talked about poetry so they thought he was some kind of student. He never told any actual lies, I noticed, but he never told the whole truth either.

But I wasn't going to criticise him for that, I didn't want him to tell my friends from the BA honours group that he knew me from my dancing nearly naked five nights a week in his club.

He was the same with Geraldine, who was now also at university, and mercifully having too good a time to want to investigate my so-called life as a croupier in a casino. I didn't fancy Keno and he didn't fancy me, but we often talked about love and marriage and what it might be like. He was cynical that any romance ever really lasted. His business experience told him so much the contrary.

He said he would like children and in fact he had a child, a daughter in Marrakesh. But she was being brought up by her grandmother. Her mother was an exotic dancer in one of his clubs there. That was the first time I knew he had any other establishments than the one where I worked in Dublin.

But I said nothing and never brought the matter up again.

'You're a great girl, Clare,' he said to me often. 'A real star.'

'I was a gold star at school,' I explained and he thought that was very endearing.

'Little Gold Star Clare! Give up this nonsense of becoming a teacher and manage my club for me instead,' he begged.

But I told him that in fact when I did become a teacher I'd actually give up the club. Too much danger that the pupils' fathers might see me!

'Well, as you said yourself, they shouldn't be there,' he laughed.

He came to my graduation and sat at the conferring ceremonies with Geraldine. I smiled as I took my parchment in my hand. If they knew that the girl with the First Class honours was a topless dancer . . . Only Keno knew and he was clapping loudest of all.

A year later I was a fully-fledged teacher with my diploma and I got into exactly the kind of school I wanted to. I took Keno out to lunch to say goodbye. He didn't believe it when I told him what I was going to be earning. For me it was plenty.

Geraldine had won a scholarship, I had my savings and hardly any outgoings.

I thanked him from the bottom of my heart for having made it all possible. He was dark and moody looking, and he said I was ungrateful.

'Over the years, Keno, if there's anything I can do to help you I will,' I promised and I meant it.

I didn't hear from him for three years. And by the time he got in touch again a lot had changed.

After years of drinking my father eventually died and at the funeral I met an old man in a wheelchair called Marty Nolan, who had known my father once. Like back in the days when it had been possible to talk to my father. A long time ago. A nice old man. His son, who was pushing the chair, was a really good-natured fellow called Neddy. Neddy had worked in England on the buildings, he said, well, more as manager for his brother and their friends, and now he had come home and looked after his father.

He was an oddly restful person and I liked talking to him.

Harriet Lynch said to me, I should see his elder brother Kit, a real hunk. Take the sight out of your eyes, he would. And where was he now, I wondered? Apparently he was banged up in jail for something, Neddy was the one who had the decent streak in that family.

Not the brightest mind, a bit slow, a minute late, she said. Harriet Lynch was always sorry she had volunteered this information to me.

Very sorry.

I saw Neddy again because I came back to Rossmore over and over to get what I considered were Geraldine's and my just portions of my father's estate. If you could use a word like 'estate' to describe what was owing to a drunk who had died in the County Home. Over the years I had tried to contribute to my father's keep from my earnings in Keno's club, but the doctor told me to save my breath. He said that my father didn't know where he was and would only spend any money that came his way on cider. People had been discouraged from giving him anything at all.

I faced my Uncle Niall after the funeral when he was busy accepting sympathy about his unfortunate poor brother. The one with the drink problem, people said, shaking their heads sadly.

I asked for his attention for a moment.

He looked at me witheringly.

'And what can I do for you on this sad day, Miss Clare?' he said.

'Just a third of what you got for the family farm,' I said to him pleasantly.

He looked at me as if I were mad.

'One third is fine. I have written down the bank account number.'

'And what makes you think I am going to give you one single Euro?' he asked.

'Let me see, I think you won't want Geraldine and myself to tell the local doctor, the priest, half of Rossmore and, even more important, a top lawyer the reason why she and I had to leave home at a very young age,' I said.

He looked at me, unbelieving, but I met his stare and eventually it was his eyes that moved away.

'It will be no problem, there's a new young curate here who would give Canon Cassidy the courage to stand up to you. Mr Barry would get us a hot-shot barrister from Dublin, the doctor will confirm that I asked his help to get Geraldine away from your clutches. The world has changed, you know. The days are gone, Niall, when the uncle with the money can get away with anything he likes.'

He spluttered at me. I think my calling him Niall was about the clincher.

'If you think for one moment . . .' he began.

I interrupted him. 'One week from now, and a decent gravestone for my father,' I said.

It was surprisingly easy. He lodged it.

It was blackmail, of course, but I shrugged. I didn't see it as that.

Then I was going out with Neddy. He came to Dublin once a week to see me. And I went down to see him once a week. And we hadn't slept together because Neddy wasn't like that.

And in the middle of things in Dublin, which were always a bit pressurised, he was very restful indeed.

And then I heard from Keno.

They really needed me back at the club, he wouldn't ask if he wasn't desperate. He'd been having a bit of trouble with some of the girls from abroad. Visas and red tape and form filling. He needed someone reliable to be in there, dancing, yes, and keeping an eye on things for him.

I explained how impossible it was for me, or I tried to explain. I even told Keno about Neddy and the kind of man he was. I shouldn't really have told Keno about Neddy.

When he put the pictures down on the table, he mentioned Neddy.

I hadn't known there were any pictures being taken, and it was very obviously me, and the positions were very suggestive indeed. It was sickening, looking at them.

It didn't bear thinking what the board of the school or dear innocent Neddy would make of them.

'It's blackmail,' I said.

'I don't see it as that,' Keno said, shrugging.

'Give me a week,' I said. 'You owe me that.'

'Right.' Keno was always agreeable. 'But you owe me too. For your start in life.'

During the week, of course, wouldn't you know, Neddy asked me to marry him.

'I can't,' I said. 'Too much baggage.'

'I don't care about the past,' Neddy said.

'It's not just the past. It's the future,' I said.

And I told him. Everything. Every single thing – like my awful Uncle Niall and Geraldine and how boring and tiring the dancing had been. I had left the envelope of pictures on the table and he just threw it into the fire without opening it.

'I'm sure you are very beautiful in the pictures,' he said, 'and why shouldn't people pay to look at you?'

'He'll have more,' I said in a despairing kind of voice.

'Yes, of course he will, but it won't matter.'

'Ah, come on, Neddy, these are nice respectable girls I teach – do you think anyone would let me near them if they saw those pictures?'

'Well, I was hoping that if you married me you'd come back to Rossmore and teach near by.'

'But he could still show them,' I said. I wondered if Neddy might really be soft in the head.

'But you could tell them in advance. You could say at the interview you had to pay your way through college by doing various jobs including exotic dancing,' he said.

'It won't work – we won't get away with it, Neddy.'

'It will work because it's true.' He looked at me with his honest blue eyes.

'I wish things had been different,' I said to him.

'Would you have said yes and married me if it weren't for this little problem?' he asked me.

'It's a big problem, Neddy.' I sounded weary.

'Would you, Clare?'

'Well, yes, I would, Neddy. I would have been honoured to marry you.'

'Right then – we'll sort it out,' he said.

And he came with me to Keno's that night. We walked right through the dancers and the punters to the office at the back. To say Keno was surprised is putting it mildly.

I introduced them formally and then Neddy spoke.

He told Keno that he sympathised with the situation, and how it must be hard running a business with all the staff problems and everything, but it wasn't fair to take away my dream, as I had *always* wanted to be a teacher ever since I was a schoolgirl.

'Clare was a gold star at school,' Keno said, more to make conversation, I think, than anything else.

'I'm not at all surprised,' Neddy said, beaming at me proudly. 'So, you see, we can't make Clare do anything else except concentrate on her teaching. Neither of us can.'

Keno pulled a big brown envelope from his desk drawer.

'The pictures?' he said to Neddy.

'They're very beautiful, Clare showed them to me earlier tonight,' he said.

'She did?' Keno was amazed.

'Of course, if we are to be married we must have no secrets. I have told Clare about my brother Kit who has been and still is in prison. You can't keep quiet about things that are part of you. And I know that Clare is very, very grateful for the start you gave her. So that's why we are here.'

'Why exactly are you here?' Keno was totally bewildered.

'To know was there any *other* way we could help you.' Neddy spoke simply as if it were obvious.

'Like what way, in God's name?'

'Well, I have a great friend who does wrought iron, he could do you really nice windows outside which would look well and also be good and strong against unwelcome visitors. And let me see, what else could we do? If the dancing girls were tired and wanted somewhere to stay, it's very peaceful by the woods where we live . . . Perhaps some of your dancers might need a nice restful holiday. They could come to stay with us. There's lots to see in Rossmore. There's even a wonderful well in the woods. People can wish there and it comes true.' His good-natured face was straining with good ideas for Keno.

I begged God not to let Keno mock him, or tell me I was marrying a simpleton. I spoke to God very strongly in my mind. 'I never bothered you about things, did I, God? I didn't go up to that well rabbiting on to your grandmother, St Ann, now did I? No, I sorted out my own problems and looked after my little sister. I didn't go round doing much sin, unless the dancing is a sin? But it's so silly, it can't really be a sin, can it? And now I want to escape from all this and marry a good man. So that's the kind of thing you're meant to be *for*, isn't it, God?'

And God listened. This time.

Keno turned on the shredder and put the pictures into it.

'There aren't any more,' he said. 'Get your wrought iron man to give me a ring, Neddy. And now get the hell home, the two of you, to plan your wedding. I have an ailing business to run here.'

And we walked out of the club together hand in hand and down the cobbled street.

CHAPTER 3

The Singles Holiday

Part 1 – Vera

It was very clear from the moment I saw the advertisement:

> Holiday for Singles
> *fun, sun, sea and relaxation*

That was exactly what I wanted.

And they were so slow back at the Active Retirement Association, and they were so scornful at the cardiac exercise class. They were positively hostile at the Gardening in Later Years Group. My cousins back in Rossmore were the most disapproving of all. They said that sort of holiday was only for young people. Undesirable young people who would probably have sex on the plane on the outward journey, and be drunk for fifteen days when they got there.

But where did it say anything about that in the advertisement?

Nowhere.

I paid my two hundred Euro deposit and then the rest when they sent the invoice. At no time did anyone ask me my age. And proper order too. I had not asked them *their* ages. I turned up at the airport with my little purple and yellow label saying *Holiday for Singles*.

That's what I was, single.

I could easily have married Gerald, and quite possibly I could have married Kevin. But Gerald was very, very dull. So I didn't marry him. And the woman who *did* marry him went sort of mad from the tedium of it all. And I didn't try to make Kevin infatuated with me or anything because truly he was very unreliable. I wouldn't have had a moment's peace with him.

And I never regretted being single. Never for one moment – except sometimes on holidays.

You had to pay a single room supplement. You were often given a very small, poky table away from other people's eyes. It was a bit lonely not having anyone to talk to like other people had, someone to laugh over the day with. That's why I was thrilled to see a holiday that catered for exactly what I needed.

At the airport I saw lots of those purple and yellow labels and, yes, the fellow travellers did seem to be very young, like about forty years younger than me, but then that was just who I saw now. The older crowd would turn up later.

55

They didn't as it happened. And as I stood in the line waiting for check-in, I got a few odd glances. But then I have always had a few odd glances. A sixty-something woman in jeans and a big floppy sun hat does often attract a second look. People often look again just to check that they haven't imagined all those lines and wrinkles under a floral, cotton hat and over a trim pair of jeans.

The check-in girl asked me if I was sure I had booked the right holiday and I assured her that I was indeed single and greatly looking forward to it. On the plane they were all introducing themselves to each other, so I joined in too.

'I'm Vera,' I said and shook hands heartily with those nearest to me. They were nice young people called Glenn and Sharon and Todd and Alma. None of them had ever been on a singles holiday before, and neither had I, so we had that in common anyway.

'Where did you go last year, Vera?' Glenn asked.

I told them about the Active Retirement Association's walking holiday in Wales, and the year before the bus tour of Scotland for the cardiac exercise class. I had been planning to go on the Gardening in Later Years Group trip to Cornwall and the Eden Project but suddenly I had seen this advertisement and decided that it had everything I really wanted.

Sharon, who was a very pretty girl with a lovely smile, asked did I have family at home and I said sadly, no, I had been an only child, I had never married but I had lots of good friends. And plenty of time to see people nowadays since I had retired.

Todd wanted to know where I was from. I explained Dublin nowadays, but originally from Rossmore – they probably wouldn't have heard of it. It turned out they all had.

There had been some kind of documentary on television about it. There was what they called a cool kind of wishing well, which gave you whatever you wanted. Alma said maybe we should all be going there on holiday rather than Italy, imagine getting what you wanted from a holy well. I thought of telling them that the well wasn't really holy, it had been there for years before St Patrick ever came to Ireland. But it was a mistake to give young people too much information.

Glenn asked had I been to Italy before and I told them a bit about Rome and Florence and Venice but said that I'd never been to this place, Bella Aurora, where we were heading. In fact I had never heard of it until I got the brochure which said it was full of places of interest. I was eager to see what they were.

'Mainly clubs, I think,' Alma said. Her friend had been here last year, and said it was great, that she had been locked day and night.

Locked? I wondered but didn't say. Young people get so irritated if you sound bewildered.

'Sounds good,' I said with a bright smile and maybe it was only my imagination but they seemed to look at me with more interest.

After we arrived and got our luggage at the airport, two almost naked girls with purple and yellow

57

bikinis checked us all off on clipboards and put us on a bus. We went through several very big resorts until we got to Bella Aurora. All had huge white hotels facing the sea, lines of cafés, pizzerias, ice cream parlours, bars. And Bella Aurora looked just the same.

Hard to see where all the interesting things were. But I never start by complaining. Hard to know how it could be exactly relaxing either – very loud music blaring everywhere – but no point in finding fault before you have settled in. There might well be fun, though not much room for it, the beach looked very crowded. But they had promised fun and no doubt it would be delivered.

Three more near-naked courier girls with clip-boards were waiting for us at the hotel to assign us our rooms and we were told we had half an hour to unpack and then there would be welcome drinks by the pool.

So I hung up my clothes and had a shower, put on a nice clean T-shirt with my jeans and down I went.

To my surprise almost all the people who had travelled on the plane were almost naked too, like the courier girls. A lot of them were very white-skinned but some, like Alma and Sharon, had been on electric tanning beds. Sharon looked very beautiful, like someone from Hawaii. They looked as if they had been here for weeks.

There was a kind of fruit punch served and very nice and refreshing it was too; and we were all quite thirsty what with the heat and the travelling and everything. And the almost naked courier girls told us of all the interesting things to do, which was mainly a list of clubs that opened at midnight and were lively, and cool, and full of action. And then I began to feel a bit odd and as if the swimming pool had started to slide away so I lay down for a while and closed my eyes.

When I woke up it was much darker and the others seemed to be dancing beside the swimming pool. There was very loud music.

Todd was lying on one of those slatted wooden sunbeds beside mine.

'They put a fair whack of vodka in that punch all right,' he said appreciatively.

Vodka? I had been drinking vodka in the afternoon, in this heat?

'You're a great old stayer, Vera, I'll give you that,' said Glenn who was holding his head. 'I like a woman who can hold her drink. Personally I think I'm going to have to pace myself a bit. See you at dinner . . .'

Dinner? I thought I had slept through it. I thought it was bedtime. But maybe food was what I needed.

The dining room was decorated with paper flowers and you could sit where you liked. I sat beside Sharon, who was depressed and didn't want to eat. She told me that she fancied Glenn. But in the way of things, he didn't seem to see her. Only that noisy Todd came on to her and then he had passed out at the cocktails. Life was very hard, wasn't it?

I said it was, but that it was early days yet, maybe

59

she was better off not to be fancied too soon. She brightened up at this and ate a huge dinner.

Just after midnight they all headed off to one of the interesting clubs down the road and I went to bed and passed out again.

Next morning I went down and swam three lengths of the pool and felt much better. I looked around for my new friends but none of them showed up. So I went back to the pool and read. I would normally have taken a walk and found an old church or museum but I didn't want the Singles people to think I was being aloof. So I waited and waited and nobody turned up at all.

Then I thought there must have been Something Interesting arranged and I had missed it when I had sort of passed out from the vodka fruit punch the night before. One of the near-naked courier girls had given us her card in case of any problems, so I phoned her and wondered had I missed anything Interesting.

The near-naked girl sounded upset, annoyed almost, to be woken so early. Early? It was past midday, I had been up since eight. No, of course nothing was planned for the morning, she said. People didn't want anything in the *morning*. There would be a seafood buffet lunch any time after two-thirty, which would be followed by water polo. It was all written up on the hotel notice board. And now if I would excuse her, she had to get back to sleep.

So I read my book and waited for the seafood buffet lunch. About 3 p.m. everyone started to appear, very tired still and hung-over. They all had about three cups of black coffee and an occasional orange juice, which must have been breakfast, then they moved on to cold beers and ate mountains of prawns, squid and mussels. And then amazingly they all had the energy to play water polo. I don't think there were many real rules, it had a lot to do with removing the tops of other people's bikinis.

I watched it and said that I didn't usually take exercise for two hours after a meal. It used to be the way in the olden days. And they listened, interested, as if I were telling them news from the planet Mars.

And Sharon said that Glenn did fancy her a bit now, which was terrific, and I had been right to tell her to hang in there. And Todd told me that Sharon was a proper little slapper. And Alma said she thought that Todd was divine. And Glenn said to me that he thought this was a fantastic holiday and wondered, was I enjoying it? And because I was brought up to be polite and always to say that things were great even when they weren't, I said that I was loving it.

But the truth was that I didn't think there were all that many interesting things to do, and I was a bit too old for their kind of fun. Still there was the sea and the sun and nice people to have meals with, so while they were playing what they called water polo I went off and got postcards and sent them back to my friends in the Active Retirement Association, and to my cousins in Rossmore, to the Gardening in Later Years Group and the cardiac exercise class, saying it was all delightful. Which it mainly was.

I watched the fruit punch carefully the second evening and at dinner Sharon confided that Glenn wanted to be with her even when they got back home. Todd said that Sharon was a tease, Alma said that Todd was only loud because no one had understood him. They all went to another cool club this time and I went off to bed.

I realised of course that I had the whole morning to do my kind of interesting things. Just as long as I was back for the seafood buffet lunch at three no one would miss me. I went to the museum in the Old Town, which was delightful, and I saw a really old-fashioned hotel, completely unlike the rest of Bella Aurora. It was so different from all the very noisy places along the seafront, full of near-naked people, that I decided to go in and have a cup of coffee.

They served it in a big shady garden. This was much more my sort of place really, except that it would have been lonely here. And there would be nobody's lives to get involved in as I had on my Singles holiday.

In the hotel garden there was an older man in a sun hat doing a sketch. He nodded at me graciously and I nodded back hoping that I was being gracious in return. Forty-eight hours with these wild young people had made me speak differently, think differently almost. Eventually he came over and showed me the drawing.

'What do you think?' he asked.

I said it was excellent and that he had a great sense of detail.

He said that he was called Nick and he had been here for two days. It was a lovely hotel but quiet, and then of course everyone else was a couple. I sighed with him and said it was always a problem. He told me he was a widower with no children, he quite liked his own company but was not entirely happy as a retired person. I told him I had never married, and that because of discrimination against solo travellers I had signed up for a Singles holiday.

He was astounded.

'Aren't they for much younger people than us?' he said.

'It didn't say in the advertisement,' I explained and this seemed to please him. He laughed and said I was a fine person.

I explained that of course they didn't get up until 3 p.m.

'And what are they doing?' Nick wondered.

I said that I honestly didn't know. I couldn't believe that they would *all* be having sex all morning, I assumed that they must stay up so late all night at these clubs that they were all exhausted.

Again Nick said I was a very interesting person and he wondered if I would have a late lunch with him. I explained that I had to be back for the seafood buffet lunch at three.

And he patted my hand as if I were an old friend.

'Well, please say you'll come back here tomorrow morning and we'll explore somewhere while the Singles all sleep on?' he asked.

I said that would be great.

At the buffet lunch, Alma said she and Todd had got together last night and it was great. I didn't enquire exactly what 'got together' might mean. I just nodded enthusiastically. Sharon didn't know whether she should be easy or hard to get with Glenn. It was so difficult to know. I advised them as best I could. There was a wet T-shirt contest instead of water polo but it seemed more or less the same. At dinner Todd said that Alma was a slapper and Glenn seemed to have eyes only for one of the near-naked courier girls. They went off to another club and I went to bed and listened to the music coming from all over Bella Aurora.

I was looking forward to meeting Nick next day. And then the days got into a very nice easy rhythm.

Nick and I went out every day together. Sometimes we took a bus to various inland villages and on two occasions I skipped the 3 p.m. buffet lunch but I never missed the dinner.

'Could I come to the dinner one night?' he asked.

Nobody had ever brought a guest in so I said I'd have to enquire.

'I'd pay, of course, and bring some wine,' he said.

'I'll tell them that,' I reassured him.

One of the near-naked courier girls said it was not normally allowed but that it was no problem in my case. So I invited Nick.

'I'm a bit nervous, as if I were meeting your family,' he said. I had told him about Todd and Glenn and Sharon and Alma and their complicated lives. I had told them nothing about Nick.

The night he came to dinner Glenn was kissing the near-naked courier girl instead of eating his dinner, Sharon was crying, Alma was telling everyone that Todd was a toe-rag.

'What is that exactly?' I asked.

'A scut,' Alma said, which didn't make things any clearer.

Nick took it all in.

'It's the climate and the drink,' he told Sharon. 'Get Glenn away from the booze and the heat for a day, up to a nice shady village where you can talk without all this flesh around. You'll be fine.'

And he told Todd to stop behaving like a horse's ass or he'd end up going home a total loser, and that that nice girl was only calling him a toe-rag because she fancied him. And Nick came to dinner all the nights except the last one when we went out by ourselves and discussed all the things we had in common.

He had a little car but he was nervous of motorways and only liked driving on back roads. Maybe he could drive me down to Rossmore and I could show him these famous woods that everyone was getting excited about.

'And I could meet your cousins,' he said tentatively.

'They will disapprove of you, they disapprove of everyone and everything,' I told him.

He thought this was great.

'What will I talk about to them?' he asked.

'They will interrogate you,' I explained. 'And then when they have found out enough they will blind you with their views about a new bypass being a

65

National Disgrace, and they will ask you to write letters to the papers about it.'

'And is it a National Disgrace?' Nick asked.

'No, it's totally necessary, Rossmore is like a car park except you can't get in or out of it. Should have been done years ago.'

'But this holy well?'

'It's a pagan shrine. The whitethorn is meant to have some kind of magic about it – farmers never want to cut it down. The whole thing is hysterical rubbish of the highest order.'

Nick said he found me very entertaining. And wasn't it great that he only lived a short bus ride away from me in Dublin, and how he had always wanted to learn about gardening but thought it might be too late and how I had always wanted to sketch but didn't know how to begin, and how liking your own company was good but liking someone else's was better.

The next day when we were leaving, Glenn and Sharon were arm in arm, and Todd was carrying Alma's suitcase for her.

When the near-naked courier girl was checking us back on to the bus she asked me would I be coming back on another Singles holiday. I looked at her from under my flowery sun hat and said that next year I might well not qualify for a Singles holiday at all.

Part 2 – Chez Sharon

Well, I just hated coming home from that holiday. Hated it, I tell you. When we were pushing the trolleys through Dublin airport I had a big knot in my stomach. I was dead sure it was all over now, a summer romance kind of thing. He'd say, 'See you around,' or he'd call me and then it would be finished. No lovely places to go like in Bella Aurora. Only desperate work and rain, and I'd never liked anyone as much as Glenn, not in my whole life, and I'm twenty-three now so that's been a fair old life.

Anyway they were all shouting goodbyes and kissing each other and swearing that they'd see each other in this club or that, and Glenn just stood there looking at me. I wished to God I could think of something to say instead of what was racing through my head, things like *don't dump me, please, Glenn*, or *we will be all right even back home when we have to go to work and all* . . . I could only think of awful tying-down things – the things fellows dread to hear.

So I said eventually, 'Here we are then,' which wasn't very bright. I mean, of course we were here. Where else would we be?

Glenn just smiled. 'Indeed we are,' he said.

'So it was great fun.' I hoped I didn't sound too intense, too tying down.

'Yeah, but it's not over, is it?' Glenn asked anxiously.

'No way,' I said and I knew I had this big silly grin all over my face.

Just then Vera came up to say goodbye.

'Nick will be coming back next week, he had a week longer than we all did, and I was going to have a few people round for a get-together in my house – a sort of a reunion. You will come? Todd and Alma are coming. You have my address so it's Chez Vera, Friday of next week then? About eight o'clock?'

'Shay Vera?' I asked foolishly.

She's dead nice, Vera, she'd never make a fool of you.

'It's a silly expression. It means . . . at the house of someone, Chez Moi at my house, Chez Vous at your house . . . It's just something we used to say a hundred years ago.' She was apologetic under her ridiculous hat and with her faded jeans.

She waved as she went off to catch her bus. Funny little figure, yet everyone was mad about her – *and* she'd pulled on the holiday, too.

Glenn said that his brother and some mates were coming in from Santa Ponsa in an hour's time and he was going to meet them in the bar. They'd give him a lift back to Chez Glenn. Would I like to wait and they'd drive me to Chez Sharon too?

I would have liked to wait very much, to have given our holiday romance some kind of base in Ireland as well as out there under the blue skies. But there was no way I could let him see Chez Sharon. Now Glenn isn't posh, it's nothing like that, but there's about a month's work to be done tarting up our house before I'd even let him see it. This is not putting on airs or anything, this is survival.

The garden is full of dandelions and bits of old metal that can never be thrown out. The kitchen window is boarded up after the last time Dad started throwing things, and they're unlikely to have got any glass in it since I went away. The paintwork is all peeling. Whatever chance I had with Glenn it would be wiped out if he saw Chez Sharon.

So I said no, that I had to run and that I'd hear from him soon, and I sat on a bus and cried the whole way home.

My mam was getting the supper. She looked tired, as she had always looked tired for as long as I could remember.

'Don't upset your dad tonight,' were her first words.

'Is he on the piss again?' I asked.

'He had a bit of bad luck, Sharon, be a good girl now and don't upset things, you've just had a lovely holiday, what have the rest of us had?'

It was unanswerable.

My mam had had nothing but dog's abuse, and a desperate job cleaning offices from 4 a.m. until 8 a.m. and then turning round and going out to be a washer-up in a place that did all-day breakfasts. I had just had fourteen days of sunshine and sangria and great laughs and I'd met a fabulous fellow. I wasn't going to upset things.

I nailed a smile on my face when my dad came in, fulminating about some horse and some false friend who had told him wrong things about this horse.

'Well for you, Sharon, out in foreign parts,' he said, looking at me resentfully.

'I know, Dad, I was very lucky,' I said and saw my mam's face relax. In fact I wasn't lucky at all, I was just hard working. I had saved twenty Euro a week from the money I earn at the dry-cleaners for thirty-seven whole weeks! All to pay for this holiday and a few outfits to wear on it.

Dad had never saved anything. Mam saved all right, but then she spent it all on us and the house and getting him a few decent shirts in case he ever had an interview and might ever get a job again.

My young brothers came in for their tea and I gave them all the big box of Italian biscuits I had brought home and my dad dipped them into his tea because his teeth weren't good and he hated chewing things.

Suppose I had brought Glenn home here? To this room draped with clothes drying on the backs of chairs with newspapers open at the racing page thrown around the floor. With no cloth on the table. I gave a shiver at the thought.

Next day it was back to work in the dry-cleaners in my uniform and it was as if I had never been on holiday. The girls who worked there did comment on my tan all right but the customers never noticed. They only cared about getting a red wine stain out of a white lace blouse without leaving a trace, or how to get tar out of an expensive skirt where someone had sat on something that couldn't be shifted.

Then I looked up and Glenn was standing there at the counter.

'You look beautiful in yellow,' he said, and suddenly I thought it might well be all right. He hadn't forgotten me, he wasn't going to dump me.

He worked for his uncle who was a builder and had a job which was quite near by. We could meet every day, he said. The question of where we might meet every night was one that could be dealt with later. He was one of six children so no space in his house, and there was no way he was going to be let within a mile of Chez Sharon.

And then even the customers began to notice me – they said I was all smiles and good cheer. The girls who worked with me told them I was in love, and they loved to hear that. In a world of grease-based stains, water stains and fabrics that crumpled up as soon as you looked at them, it was pleasant and distracting to think about love, just for a moment or two.

We went to Vera's on the following Friday. It was in a very smart part of town, I don't suppose the residents had ever seen people like Glenn and me and Todd and Alma visiting that area before. Vera had a three-storey house, much too big for her and Rotary the ginger cat who lived with her. Of course Nick might be going to live with her too the way things were working out. They got on together like a house on fire and he had obviously been visiting her every day since his return. He laughed so much at her jokes and told us that she was a wonderful woman. He closed his eyes when he said 'wonderful'.

Nick, it appeared, lived in rented accommodation

a bus ride away. Surely he would come and live in this big place. They would be company for each other and they might even get married.

Vera had made us a big spaghetti bolognese, and Nick had made a great pavlova full of strawberries, and everyone had a great time except Alma, who whispered to me that Todd had suggested they cool it a bit, which was bad news. And then when Todd said he had to leave early, Alma said she'd go with him, which I thought was a bad idea, it looked clinging. You could see that he was annoyed and that made poor Alma more anxious than ever.

Anyway Vera and I were doing the washing up and Glenn was helping Nick to cut back some of the worst briars and brambles that were threatening to take over the back door of the house.

'You two look nice and cosy together,' I said as I dried the plates.

'Yes, he's a very, very good man,' Vera said, pleased with it all.

'So will you be moving in together?' I asked. You could ask Vera that sort of thing even though she's nearly ninety or something.

'No, no, that wouldn't do at all,' she said unexpectedly.

I was sorry I had asked now. 'I didn't mean for *sex*,' I said, trying to take the harm out of it. 'I meant for companionship.'

'No, there's no problem with the sex part of it, we'll probably have sex again after you've gone,' Vera said matter-of-factly.

I wondered what the problem was. Could he have a wife, another woman hidden away somewhere? Did he have a rake of children who wouldn't let him get together with Vera?

Apparently not. It had all to do with being set in their ways. When you get old it seems that you don't want to change your way of going on, in fact you can't change it, much as you would like to. It has to do with space, and having your own things where they've always been.

'I wouldn't mind *where* my things were if I was with a fellow I was mad about,' I said.

'Yes, but then you probably don't *have* all that many things and they haven't been in place as long as ours have.'

'What sort of things?' I wondered.

'Oh it's all cracked, Sharon, there's things I couldn't bear Nick to touch, like my collections of pressed flowers, and my boxes of things I'm going to put into a scrapbook one day. And he is very odd about his tubes of paint, almost worn out with hardly a squeeze of anything left in them, and torn sketchbooks and boxes of letters and cuttings that he will throw out sometime but not now. We couldn't merge all that, Sharon, we'd be fighting in a week. What we have is much more important. We can't risk losing that by moving in together.'

Glenn and I talked about it when we left. It seemed a waste of two nice people not getting together for the time they had left. We sighed. No one had everything. We were just dying to live together and no problems about being set in our ways. It was just that we had no money, and we'd never find a place to live.

'Could I not move into your house, Sharon? Share your room? At least you *have* a room – I have to share with my brother,' Glenn pleaded.

'No, Glenn, believe me, no. It won't work. My dad's a wino and a gambler.'

'Well, sure, mine is a religious nutter, I told you, it doesn't matter.'

'It would if you were living there.'

'I could bring in some money, couldn't I?'

'Ah, no, Glenn, it would just go towards getting more drink for my dad.'

'So what will we do then?' He seemed defeated.

'We'll think of something,' I said, sounding much more confident than I was. I watched my mam's life and was determined I would never settle for anything remotely like it. She cooked and washed and cleaned up around my dad and the boys every hour that she wasn't working cleaning office floors or washing greasy plates.

'I'm happy enough, Sharon,' she would say if I questioned it. 'I mean, I love him and we've got to remember that he didn't walk away when I was expecting you.'

A lifetime of gratitude that he had acknowledged what was after all *his* child too. Twenty-four years of saying thank you and calling that love.

I met Alma from time to time. She said that Todd

was definitely seeing someone else, but she loved him and would do anything to get him back. He was seeing another woman and she *knew* it but whatever she felt for him she called love.

And then I would talk to Vera as well and she talked about loving Nick and what a delightful person to meet in the late afternoon of her years, yet at the same time she was prepared to lose it all over books of pressed flowers or his tubes of paint. It seemed a very peculiar definition of love to me. And there were Glenn and myself who really *did* love each other and wished the best for each other and we hadn't a chance of getting a place to live together.

It didn't seem fair or just somehow. But there was some old wan on the radio going on about how we have to *make* our own luck, that it doesn't come by magic and she had known people whose life turned out fine – they had got whatever they wanted. So I said to Glenn that's what we'd have to do. Make something happen.

I wish I could say that he was full of ideas – but then neither was I.

I asked Vera, did she think this holy well thing in Rossmore might work. She said it wasn't very likely. If there was a St Ann, and St Ann was listening, which was more problematical still, then she might be slow to bring about a situation where a couple could live in sin and have lots of extramarital sex. I said that I was desperate and might try it so Vera said she'd come with me to point me to the

75

Whitethorn Woods and go and visit her hatchet-faced cousins.

It was a lovely walk up to the well but once I got there I felt kind of ashamed. I mean, it's not as if I knew who this St Ann was or went to Mass or anything. And there were nearly a hundred people there. Some of them had children in wheelchairs or on crutches and some didn't look in good shape at all. And they were all asking desperately for favours. I felt I couldn't ask for a place for Glenn and me to . . . well . . . it didn't seem right.

So I sort of said, 'If you get a chance and the matter comes up it would be nice. But to be fair maybe you should deal with these people first . . .'

And I told Vera this on the way home and she said I might well get what I want because I was far nicer than lots of people including herself.

I asked her about the cousins, and she said they were like weasels. Weasels with small minds, pointed teeth and horrible voices. All they could talk about was the price of land and what compensation people would get when their homes were disturbed. When we got off the bus Glenn and Nick were waiting for us, Glenn with his motorbike and Nick with his little car.

'We missed you girls,' Glenn said, and I hoped that St Ann was listening. Glenn was so decent, any old saint would want you to be living with him. I must look St Ann up and see what kind of a private life she had herself.

I asked Glenn what kind of things he and Nick

had talked about when the four of us went out for a pint together. Apparently it was all about the basement in Vera's house.

Nick said he thought that despite the looming presence of Rotary the ginger cat, there might well be an r–a–t in it, and Glenn had said there were probably dozens of them. Nick wondered, was it the kind of place that could ever be done up to live in, and Glenn said he'd ask his uncle to look at the place and give an estimate.

So I realised that they were still mulling over the possibilities of it all. But that crashed to the ground eventually because apparently it would cost a small fortune to get it done up right and Vera didn't really like the notion of Nick living below stairs and they were both droning on about being so old and maybe needing someone to look after them in even later years. When they got older still.

God, they'd make you sick. The two of them have twenty times more life in them than people half their age and now suddenly they start talking like geriatrics. It was the thought of change that had done it, they were fine as they were with their old paint tubes and books of pressed flowers.

It's only the thought of the merger that has unhinged the pair of them. The waste, the sheer waste of it all.

And there, looking us all in the face, was a perfectly good rat-filled basement which Glenn and his uncle could clean up in three weekends for *us* to live in. We wouldn't be picky – we'd do it up in time.

It was hard to concentrate on work in the dry-cleaners when there were so many things churning through my head. I realised that this woman was going on and on about something and I hadn't been paying any attention at all. It was about this outfit she had borrowed from her sister to wear to a wedding and some eejit had spilled an Irish coffee over it. Was there *any* way of getting the stain out completely? Her sister was like a lighting devil about most things but in particular about clothes that would be described as ruined.

'And you wouldn't mind, only that's what I do, solve problems for a living, I'm an agony aunt and I don't even know how to face my own sister.'

I did a deal with her there and then, I'd get the manager on the case, we'd get the stain out if she could solve *my* problem. I told her about Vera and Nick who loved each other but hated each other's possessions, and about Glenn and me who wanted to get into the rat-filled basement and live there.

She asked how many bedrooms were in the house. Four, I explained.

'Far too many for them, they're not going to be hearing the patter of tiny feet at their age. Give them a study each, get your fellow to put up shelves and things for all the paint tubes in one and the pressed flowers in the other. Do up the basement, tell them you'll mind the house, scare away the burglars, give Rotary the cat a bowl of something and fresh water when they go on holidays, and look after them when they're old. It's obvious, isn't it?'

And amazingly it was.

And even more amazingly there was some kind of terrifying solvent that got the stain out of the borrowed dress.

Glenn and his uncle shelved the two studies in no time, and as the wise agony aunt realised, Vera and Nick had no objection to sharing bedroom, bathroom, sitting room or kitchen as long as their precious belongings were safe.

Then they attacked the basement with Rotary looking on loftily as some rodents were removed. Rotary was the kind of cat who didn't exert himself unnecessarily. Why attack something big and menacing when you had humans who could do it for you? And I asked Vera about St Ann's private life, and she said that St Ann was married to a fellow called Joachim.

Happily, I asked?

'No better or worse than anyone's marriage, I'd say,' said Vera who had never tried marriage at all.

I think she saw I was disappointed at that. I wanted a better ending.

'Oh, go on then,' Vera said grudgingly. 'Happily, I'd say. If there had been any sacrificing the children or pestilence, we'd have heard about it.'

There was plenty of room for us in the basement. It was just gorgeous, so we made a grand little nest for ourselves. Mam gave us some old saucepans from home and some cleaning materials which she came across when doing the offices in the early mornings. Glenn's mam gave us some curtains. My dad gave us a lawnmower so that he would never have to use it again, not that he had ever used it much. Glenn's dad gave us a tip for a greyhound, which won at five to one.

Nick gave us his bed, since he would be sharing Vera's now. Alma gave us a bunch of flowers and a lecture about there being No Good in Men. Todd had gone his way.

Glenn is terrific when he comes up to my parents' house, once called Chez Sharon. He gives my dad a hand with all the work my dad didn't do during the week. Glenn and I are getting married next year when we have enough saved to have a nice wedding day. Vera said if it was in the summer we could have it in the garden and she could be my bridesmaid. She said she only meant it as a joke but I said that it would be great, I'd love it. I said I could be *her* bridesmaid, maybe at St Ann's Well when she and Nick finally got it together. But she laughed at the very idea of it.

She and Nick aren't going to get married at all, apparently. That's oldies for you. And people laugh when we say we met Vera and Nick on a Singles holiday.

'You *are* funny, you and your fancy tales,' they say.

As if you could make up something like that.

CHAPTER 4

Friendship

Part 1 – Malka

I met Rivka Fine, let me see, oh, it was years and years ago now, back in the 1960s. We were on a kibbutz in the Negev desert for the summer. I was the first person from Rossmore to do such an adventurous thing, head for the Middle East and pick oranges and pluck chickens. I remember that way back then poor Canon Cassidy said that though it was a great thing to go to the Holy Land and walk where Our Lord had walked, I would have to be careful that I didn't lose my faith when I met so many people of other beliefs.

I didn't know that Rivka and I would be friends at first – she seemed a bit sulky, moody even, while I was delighted with everyone and talked to them all. They came from so many countries: Morocco, Romania, Turkey, Germany. They had all learned to speak Hebrew. There were only a few English speakers around, so we had to manage, Rivka and I, learning that *tapoosim* meant oranges and *toda raba* meant thank you. I tried to learn ten words a day but actually with the heat and the hard work in the kitchen and everything, it was too much and I settled for learning six.

We had to share a hut so we learned quite a bit about each other. She was there because her parents back home in New York felt guilty about not emigrating to Israel, so they wanted to be able to say, 'Our daughter is out there as a volunteer in the desert.' I was there because I had taught Latin to two little Jewish boys back in Rossmore and their parents, Mr and Mrs Jacobs, had given me a trip to Israel to thank me. It was the holiday of a lifetime, they had even found me this kibbutz to work in because a cousin of Mrs Jacobs had been there one summer and had enjoyed it.

And I thought it was really great. I fell in love with Shimon who was originally from Italy and he loved me too and we were going to set up our own business growing gladioli when his National Service was over.

I suppose Rivka may have been a little bit jealous because Shimon was always coming and hanging round our hut. Not that we slept with each other or anything. I know, I know, but we just didn't in those days. Afraid, I suppose. Anyway that's the way it was.

Rivka asked me was I *really* going to work in a

gladioli farm, and I said I sure hoped so, all I had to do now was go back home to Rossmore and sort of soften up my family for the whole idea, which wasn't going to be easy. There was bound to be interference from Canon Cassidy about marrying a non-Christian. Then we'd have to deal with *his* family – which was going to be another day's work, what with the Jews believing that the line sort of passed down through the woman and they wouldn't care for him bringing a non-Jewish girl back to them.

And then Rivka fell in love with Dov who was Shimon's friend and that made everything more cheerful and the four of us could go off for drives. Rivka had no long-term plans to live with Dov in Israel back then. She said she had to go back to New York and marry a dentist or a doctor. It was as simple as that. No, she couldn't take Dov with her when he had finished his National Service. Dov was from Algeria. His people lived in a hut. No, Rivka didn't mind that – but her mother would. Big time.

It was a magic summer. We were busy taking oranges from trees, and feathers from chickens, and stray hairs from our eyebrows. We rinsed our hair in lemon juice, we both lost tons of weight because we hated the margarine they used so we just ate oranges and pieces of grilled chicken. If they could see me now, all those people back in Rossmore, I kept thinking.

Then, quicker than we could have imagined, it

was all over and time for me to go back home, back to being a teacher in St Ita's in Rossmore, and it was time for Rivka to go back to working in a travel agent's office in New York. We were firm friends by then and hated saying goodbye. No one else would understand the summer we'd had and how we loved the Friday night dance and the red rock of the desert. We both knew that tales of Shimon and Dov would sound like foolish holiday romances to our friends and would be like a red rag to a bull if mentioned to our parents.

We swore that we would keep in touch and we did.

I wrote a tear-stained letter to Rivka when I heard from Shimon that there was no future in gladioli. Or anything else. Rivka wrote in rage to say that Dov's brother had been in touch to say that Dov couldn't read English writing and please to stop pestering him. I told Rivka about how my mam had offered to pay for golf lessons in the hopes that I would meet a lawyer or a banker at some golf resort. Rivka explained that *her* mother was taking her for a week to this mountain place which was like a marriage market. She must look her very best, it was make or break time.

It must have been break time. It certainly wasn't make time.

Rivka was promoted to become office manager but there was nothing moving in the marriage stakes. This was a heavy stress factor at home apparently. It was stress time with my mam too. Several serious rows, with fairly unforgivable things said: 'When I was your age, Maureen, I was married and pregnant,' and, 'You don't think you are going to get *better* looking once you've passed twenty-five, do you?' I said that I'd prefer to die wondering than to put myself up to be chosen by these bog-ignorant, so-called professional men of her choice who preferred drink and golf to female company anyway. My dad just said that it would be very nice to have Peace in his Time, which was all he asked.

Back in Rivka's place things were getting really serious, she told me.

Her mother was now advertising for a husband for her in some suitable magazine. I knew that if I had to spend the summer vacation at home this year I would go mad.

My mam would be sending me up to St Ann's Well in Whitethorn Woods to pray for a man and I would probably kill my own mother with my bare hands and go to jail, and this would not be Peace in his Time or anyone's time for my quiet gentle dad. So I applied for a summer job teaching in a children's camp in America.

First I was going to stay with Rivka for a week in New York.

'What kind of a name is that? *Rivka?*' my mam asked.

'It's her name,' I heard myself say mutinously, as if I were a six-year-old.

'But where does it come from? I mean, was she baptised Rivka?' My mam was in one of those moods. I was too weary to explain that Rivka was very unlikely to have been baptised at all.

'I don't really know,' I said glumly.

I allowed my mind to drift away while my mam went on about the fact that for all my great education I actually never really knew anything. Men liked a woman who was alert, awake, alive – not dreamy and drifty like I was.

I thought it was a small miracle that my mam didn't know just how alert and alive I had been out in the Negev desert with Shimon. For all the good it had done me. Anyway I would be out of here soon in New York with Rivka.

She met me at the airport and we hugged each other in delight. On the way to her house she told me that she was very sorry to lay all this on me but she had implied to her mother that I was Jewish and would I mind pretending that I was? Just for a week?

It was idiotic, I said. It wasn't as if Rivka was going to marry *me*!

'It's just for an easy life, just for one less battle to fight,' she begged. *Snap!* It was the same situation at home for me. We sighed over mad mothers.

'So I said your name was Malka,' she confessed.

'*Malka?*' I shouted.

'It's the Hebrew for queen,' Rivka explained, as if that made any difference.

'Right,' I said.

The 1960s were meant to be a decade of change, of looking forward. Not for me, not for Rivka. I couldn't be Maureen for her mother, she had to have been baptised for mine.

Heigh-ho.

It was a great help having worked for Mr and Mrs Jacobs, and having been in Israel. At least I knew about Seder, and Pesach, and High Holidays. I knew about Hanukkah instead of Christmas, I knew about milk and meat dishes being separate, even the plates they were served on, and about not eating things that had cloven feet.

Mrs Fine was beautifully dressed and very pretty. She fussed a lot, as Rivka had warned me. But one thing I hadn't been told. She absolutely adored her daughter.

I said this to Rivka when we were alone up in the amazing frilly bedroom.

'Maybe,' Rivka said, 'but what's the use if it's only a suffocating kind of love? I'd prefer not to be loved at all.'

We got through the first days without too many problems. Mrs Fine wanted to know did my mom keep a kosher kitchen. So I said she did and I even heard myself describing the synagogue that the Jacobs family went to when they went up to Dublin, not that I had ever been inside it. I had to excise from my conversation the fact that I taught with nuns in St Ita's convent and make the school into a secondary school for the small but active mythical Jewish community in Rossmore. In fact there were only three Jewish families in Rossmore, but no need to burden Mrs Fine with this.

They were pleased with me, and they were happy that I, like their Rivka, lived with my parents at home. They thought it was fast for young girls to live in apartments, they said.

Young girls! – Rivka and I sighed to each other when we were on our own. As if we were young! Pathetic old maids, nearly a quarter of a century on this earth and no sign of a husband or even a fiancé.

When they addressed me as Malka or called out that name, I feared that I never responded quite quickly enough, but Rivka told me I was doing so well, and she apologised again for what was even in those days a totally ludicrous farce.

And then it was time to go and I took a long, tiring train journey to the summer camp where I was called Maureen again, not Malka, which I had begun to get accustomed to. It was all much more sporty than I had thought, lots of hikes and field trips with the kids and baseball, and endless consoling of girls who thought their mothers hated them because they had been sent away for the summer.

'Mothers don't hate us,' I explained over and over. 'They just think they are doing the best for us. It's always wrong, but honestly they don't know that.' I think I mended a few fractured relationships and calmed down a few troubled hearts but then teachers are always thinking they do that anyway. Maybe they didn't take a blind bit of notice.

And I was doing it by mail too.

Rivka wrote constantly to say that her mother had really admired me and it was Malka this and

Malka that since I had left. Malka had such a sunny disposition and Malka never ate between meals and was interested in all the people who lived near by instead of dismissing them like Rivka did.

I wrote back saying that I had decided life was mainly an act. There was I, a complete fake, passing myself off as a member of their community. They had been taken in. There was a lesson there somewhere. We must put on a show for people, pretend that we were calmer, happier, more in control than we really were.

Rivka wrote back to say that she had thought about this a great deal and that I might indeed have found the Secret of the Universe.

And about a week later, when our camp was playing a series of games against another camp, I met Declan who was a teacher from a small country place a few miles outside Rossmore and we fell madly in love.

So much so that he said he wanted to come and meet my parents the moment we got back to Ireland. And even though he wasn't a doctor or a lawyer, only a teacher like myself, he was everything my mam wanted: a Catholic, from a nice family, and had really good manners.

By Christmas he said he wanted to marry me.

I wasn't too sure about wanting to go and live in the wilds of the country and maybe getting absorbed into his huge family network; but they were all very welcoming and in those days no self-respecting man made any lifestyle changes for a wife or anything.

So that's what I did – marry him and go to live in the wilds of the country. I kept Rivka informed every step of the way and, as luck would have it, she had met Max who was not exactly a dentist but was a very successful businessman who owned travel agencies, and *her* mother was utterly delighted with him, and *she* would be getting married too. So she came to my wedding in Ireland first and it was lovely to have her, and my mother was so excited about what she would wear and the fact that Declan had an uncle who was a judge coming to the wedding that she managed not to interrogate Rivka about her odd name, and didn't even notice that Rivka's mother had sent a wedding gift addressed to 'Dear Malka'.

Rivka got everything wrong in Rossmore. She kept calling the statue in the church the Holy Heart instead of the Sacred Heart. She was astounded by the length of the nuptial Mass and the papal blessing, and the fact that a lot of the women wore headscarves and mantillas on their heads during the ceremony rather than splashing out on hats.

She couldn't take in the amount of drink served at the wedding, and the number of people who had songs that they insisted on singing . . .

But it was all a great occasion and Declan kept squeezing my hand and I had never believed I could be so happy.

Declan and I went to Spain for two weeks for a honeymoon and then came back to live in his part of the world, which was a sort of mountainy place where nothing much happened. Because I was a married woman I couldn't teach any more so time hung heavy on me. Days seemed very much the same except that we went to lunch with his mother every Sunday and his sisters called around every week to enquire whether or not I was pregnant.

My letters from Rivka were a lifeline in this odd backwater. She told me what books to read, she suggested that I set up a kind of amateur mobile library and drive around to people who were housebound. And everyone liked my doing that. Declan went so far as to say that I was inspired.

But he wouldn't come to Rivka's wedding with me. It was too far, too expensive, he wouldn't know where to put himself with all these Jewish people and their customs. No, really he wanted to pass on this one. Well, you know when you're not going to win. I cheered myself up, I told myself that if I were to be Malka there again it would be easier to be without Declan. And indeed it was.

It was all so different – the canopy in the Fines' huge garden and the singing and chanting in Hebrew, and the smashing a glass which was something to do with the destruction of the Temple or something, but I couldn't really ask, what with my being Malka and meant to know all this already.

Max was very cheerful and friendly and whispered to me that he knew my little secret. I had no idea what he was talking about. Did he know that I had gone to a doctor in Dublin to get the contraceptive pill because I didn't want to get pregnant until

I had the library up and running? Did he know that I found Declan's mother and three bossy sisters a hundred times worse than my own mother had ever been and that I went to huge lengths to avoid meeting them?

No, it turned out that he knew I wasn't really Malka, that I wasn't even a little bit Jewish.

'Rivka and I have no secrets, never will,' he said.

And for some reason I felt a bit uneasy. Which was ludicrous, of course. Why should I be uneasy about Max? He was gentle and kind, he loved Rivka. In fact he was a pussycat.

Rivka and I still wrote to each other. For a while. Then she began to call me from the office from time to time. She said it was easier, more immediate, one to one. Well, it was, of course, but it was also much more expensive. I mean, there was no way I could afford transatlantic calls. But Rivka said it didn't matter, she could call free from her office where she was manager. She didn't mind that I wasn't able to make calls from my end.

I missed our long rambling letters, but it wasn't that she was keeping anything from me, she told me every heartbeat of what seemed to be an exhausting life. Rivka seemed to be permanently on some crucifying diet. She was always wasting a long-distance call telling me about some big benefit night that was coming up and she had to drop twelve pounds in fourteen days to get into a dress. She said she was always tired these days.

And I told her how horrific Declan's sisters were

and that I should be canonised in my own lifetime for not telling him what a trio of mad bats they were.

'Will you?' she asked with interest.

'Will I what?' I said.

'Be canonised in your own lifetime?' Rivka asked. She must have been *very* tired. Even Jewish people should know that was a joke and that you can't be made a saint until you're dead.

And then we both had a crisis at the same time.

Rivka's wasn't that big a crisis as it happens, she was just desperately tired at some travel conference they went to in Mexico and fell asleep when everyone thought she was getting dressed for the awards banquet where they were giving Max a lifetime achievement award, and she had to be woken up and arrived flustered and looking terrible. And it was somehow an insult to Max, and to the travel industry, and to Mexico. God, you'd think the Third World War had begun.

Compared to what had happened to me it was nothing. *Zilch*, *nada*, as they say in Mexico.

My beautiful sister-in-law felt that she had to tell Declan what she found in our medicine cupboard in the bathroom where she just *happened* to be looking. Poor Declan wouldn't have known that these pills I was taking were *abortifacient*. That was her word: they prevented conception and killed the incipient baby. They wouldn't tell their mother – she would be too shocked, she might not survive hearing the information. Declan was very upset and said

I had been holding out on him. I said my fertility was *my* business and he said, no, it was *our* business and he should have been consulted, and what kind of fairness and equality in marriage and the future did we have if I behaved in this secretive way?

And there was a bit of me that agreed that he had a point, but sadly I didn't say that: I said instead that his sisters were a pack of interfering hyenas and that I hated them with a passion almost equal to that which I felt against his mother. This was not a sensible or good thing to say, and things were very cool between us for a long time. The sisters smirked all over the place. I threw the pills into the fire but Declan said he didn't want to force a child on me so we didn't have sex and the sisters seemed to guess this and smirked even more.

So I spent more and more time driving the mobile library up into the mountains, and Declan spent more and more time talking about hurling and firing pints into himself down in Callaghan's with that awful fellow Skunk Slattery, and to be honest times weren't great at all.

And I tried to tell Rivka about all this, but she thought with some reason that Declan's sisters were from the funny farm and even though she tried to understand she just didn't.

And I tried hard to understand why Rivka simply had to go to all these functions when she was so tired. It was a rulebook that I had somehow missed, and I knew she wanted to explain it but there weren't any words.

When we talked on the telephone I just kept on advising her.

'Tell him you're really tired.'

And she kept advising me.

'Tell him you're really sorry.'

Eventually Declan came back to our bed. It wasn't the same as before but it was less lonely and the atmosphere wasn't hanging around the house any more. Meanwhile Rivka found some marvellous vitamin supplement that gave her more energy, and amazingly we both got pregnant at the same time.

They had a girl called Lida, after Max's mother, and I hoped we would have a girl too and we would call her Ruth and that she and Lida would be friends for ever. Declan said it was a bit far-fetched as an idea, and anyway he'd prefer a son who would play hurling for the county.

Brendan, named after Declan's father, was born two weeks after Lida, and now that Rivka wasn't in the office any more she and I began to write to each other again about labour pains, about breastfeeding, about disturbed nights, about tiny fingers and toes. We seemed in a veiled way to be telling each other that life wasn't quite as good as we had hoped it might be.

But we never said that. Why would we say such a thing? We had our children.

I suppose I *should* have noticed how late Declan came home at night and how he wasn't drunk, which he ought to have been if he had spent four hours in Callaghan's, and I *should* have noticed that

Skunk Slattery often asked me how Declan was, which was odd since he was meant to be drinking every night with him, but I didn't because I was so taken up with little Brendan who was an angel. I spent busy days putting toddler Brendan into the mobile library van and driving him round to meet all the readers in small villages and to be admired. I was also concentrating very hard on keeping him well away from his awful aunts.

The months went on and on. We still went to see Declan's mother every Sunday, each of us bringing a dish as she became more frail. It made her happy to see all her children around her, so I went along with it. Rivka often sent me recipes from America. When Declan's mother eventually died it was very peaceful and she sort of slipped away.

On the evening after her funeral Declan told me in a very calm voice that of course I must know he was seeing someone else. Her name was Eileen, she was the school secretary and they were going to England at the end of term. Brendan was seven then. Quite old enough to come and visit his dad regularly, Declan said casually. And he added reassuringly that Eileen would be like a second mother to Brendan.

I looked at Declan as if I had never seen him before. It felt very unreal, like fainting or the sort of shock you get if you bang your head suddenly. I said that Brendan and I had to go to Dublin on the train the next day and we could talk about the visits and everything when I came back. I had put Brendan on my passport two years ago when I thought we might be going to America to see Rivka and Lida, but Max had something on that time and we couldn't go.

I left a note for Declan saying that I had taken enough money from our bank account to go to New York and for a little spending money when we were there; he could make the arrangements about the house and telling people about the situation. He wasn't to think I was taking his child away for ever, I would be back.

No need to call Interpol.

I didn't mention what a rat he was, how upset I was, or even a word about the lovely Eileen.

Rivka had said she would be delighted to see me. 'What about Max?' I asked fearfully.

'He's hardly ever at home, he won't notice if you are there or not,' she said.

We cried in each other's arms when we met, big heaving sobs. It was the first time I had cried since the night that Declan had told me. I wept for all that there might have been. But no, I wouldn't take him back now even if he were to beg me. Possibly he was right, it was over, long over.

The two seven-year-olds played happily with Lida's toys. My blond boy and her beautiful little girl with the dark ringlets. We gave each other advice as we had always done: Rivka said I must get him to sell the house, and I should move. My father was dead now, Rivka said I should live with my mother.

'But I can't go back to her house, I spent so long trying to get out of it,' I heard myself bleating.

'Well, you can't stay *there* in that place way out of Rossmore, with all the sisters, and the dreadful Eileen, and the whole place talking about you. This is the time for courage, Malka, up and out. Go back to Ireland, you could even move to Dublin, and take your mother, find a place of your own. Start again.'

Yes, it was all very well for her, Americans are accustomed to doing that, new frontiers and covered wagons, but not in Ireland. Living with my mam and all the I-told-you-sos? Not really.

I advised *her* to throw in the job at the office, which was cutting across her busy social life, and to go into the travel business like Max, build up an aspect of the holiday business that he hadn't yet done. Let her mother help more in looking after Lida. Her marriage wasn't over yet but it could be, the way she was going.

Of course she resisted that terribly too but we laughed over it.

As the days went on, I felt stronger and better than I had for years. Brendan loved it all there.

'Why do they all call you Malka out there, Mammy?' he asked on the plane coming home.

'It's American for Maureen,' I explained.

And he was perfectly satisfied. As he was when we moved to Dublin, and when my mam turned out to be miles better than we all thought, and never said I told you so once.

I got a job teaching in a school where I set up a real library and Brendan grew up big and strong. I did make sure he went from time to time to see his dad in England, and learned with some pleasure that Eileen was very sharp-tempered and told Declan that he drank too much, and then the Principal of the school told him he drank too much.

I wrote to Rivka every week, and then she got a fax machine, which was quicker still.

And finally e-mail.

She was in Europe four times a year now because she ran an art tours section of Max's business and brought people to galleries and exhibitions. They included Ireland in the itinerary so that Rivka could come and see me. Well, there *were* nice art things to visit too, I suppose.

Rivka talked less and less about Max and more and more about Lida. Max went to a lot of business meetings and came home only rarely. We didn't *think* he had another woman but we agreed that he had lost interest in Rivka. Somehow it didn't really matter all that much, any more than Eileen with her sharp temper mattered, nor the fact that Declan had been sacked from his job in England and was back in his place outside Rossmore, helping out his brothers-in-law where he earned so little that he had to ask Eileen for drinking money to go to Callaghan's every night. But Lida mattered to us and Brendan mattered to us.

They were our future.

When Lida was seventeen she came to me for a holiday in Dublin. She wanted to be away from her mother for a bit and, well, Rivka and I understood *that*. We could write the textbook on that sort of thing.

She said that her mother and father hadn't slept in the same room for as long as she could remember; she wondered whether that was natural? Normal?

I said I hadn't a clue about America, it was probably different there. And that maybe it was all for the best anyway. I had slept in the same bed as my husband for years and it hadn't done me all that bit of good since he left me for another woman.

She was very sympathetic. She sat and stroked my hand. She said men were hard to fathom. That a man had said to her she was frigid when she wouldn't have sex with him. Then he had said she was queer like her father. She hadn't said it to anyone.

I told her she was right, best to forget it, the guy was obviously just mad to have sex with her and was flailing around because she wouldn't.

We kept in touch over the years, but she never mentioned it again and neither did I.

Now Lida was in her twenties and headstrong, dark and beautiful. She had studied law. And then this summer she announced that she was going to Greece for two months before she settled down in a big law firm. Nothing her mother said would make her go to Israel. Oh no, she objected to this about the place and that.

Rivka and I were very disappointed.

My Brendan was also in his twenties: fair-haired, leisurely and, I thought, very handsome.

He was almost qualified as an engineer but before

his career began properly he would take a long holiday in Italy.

How Rivka and I would have liked them to go to the Negev desert, to 'our' kibbutz. They could have checked whether the gladioli farm had ever come to anything and what kind of women Shimon and Dov had married in the end. They could have fallen in love with each other, Brendan and Lida, against the romantic backdrop of those red cliffs and valleys. They would marry and give us three grandchildren, which Rivka and I could share. The young couple and their family would live six months of the year in America and six months in Ireland.

Well, stranger things have happened, you know. Like both our own mothers turning out to be quite reasonable in late middle age, people you could talk to, not automatically lie to. That had never been on the cards.

And though we sometimes sighed wistfully when we heard the radio play tunes for couples whose thirtieth wedding anniversary it was or saw a big celebration in a hotel, mainly we were fairly contented with the way things had turned out for us.

We were fiftyish, trimmer and better dressed than when we were twenty-five and not too bad looking. If we were to put ourselves out in the marriage market again we might not do too badly. But we didn't need to, we each had jobs we enjoyed, we each had a child we adored and for decades we had shared a friendship with no secrets, no disguises, and the wisdom to know that such a great friendship was rare.

I remember reading once that your enjoyment of something doubled if you realised how lucky you were to have it. If everyone had a huge diamond on their fingers, or if sunsets were universally scarlet and gold, then we wouldn't value them at all. It was like that with us.

Part 2 – Rivka

I sometimes give little talks, nothing too demanding, but you know the kind of thing – either for charity or to get publicity for Max's company. Or both, even. Anyway I have learned over the years that there are two subjects that never fail to hold an audience. One is how to drop five pounds painlessly before your vacation, and the other is the positive power of friendship.

The five pounds one is easy, it's got to do with having exotic fruits for breakfast and supper, mangoes, papayas and the like. And small portions of grilled fish or chicken for lunch. I sort of intersperse it with funny stories about times things went wrong, and I ate a box of chocolate chip cookies or a tub of ice cream. They love that.

But they love even more my stories about my great friend Malka. I call her that, even though her real name is Maureen. I tell them how we met on a kibbutz and remained friends for a lifetime, and how love could come and go but friendship survived. That friendship was *better* than love in a way, it was more generous. You didn't object if your friend had other friends, you even encouraged it. But you did object violently to your love having other loves and did everything possible to discourage it.

I could see the audience nodding in recognition.

I always smiled when I talked about Malka.

We had great times together after that chance meeting on a kibbutz. My mom thought she was a nice Jewish girl and didn't realise that she came from a town of mad Catholics who all worshipped some well in the middle of the woods. I mean, if you only *saw* it. Cherish friendship, I advised them, and then I gave them the hard sell about going on vacation with a friend rather than a spouse.

If your spouse didn't want to visit art exhibits, go shopping, and sit in a piazza or a square watching strangers and making up stories about them – your girlfriend would.

When I started working for his family firm, Max always admired the way I built up this side of the business: the art tours, the painting classes and the ladies' bridge clubs or reading groups. But he admired this and indeed admired me very distantly and objectively.

You see, looking back on it all, Max never really loved me, not *loved* as people write about and sing about and dream about. I never thought that he loved anyone else. I told myself that possibly he didn't have a high sex-drive, not like Malka's husband sure did over in Ireland. No, I am sure that he didn't love anyone else, he just thought of what we had as a sort of business partnership. That's the way he was made.

For a while I thought that if I tried harder, dressed better, got thinner, developed more sparkle, he would grow to love me. But oddly it was my friend Malka who convinced me that this was not really the way it worked. Otherwise all thin, groomed, sparkly people would be very happy and we all knew – because we saw them all round us – that most of them were totally miserable.

And Malka told me I was a scream, and as bright as a button, and sharp as a tack, and a dozen other insane Irish phrases, and I started believing it all and became unreasonably confident about almost everything. And I was happy, most of the time, when I look back on it.

I wasn't happy in those years when my mom was on my case screeching at me about getting married. And there was that time when I was wearing myself out, eating nothing and putting in a ten-hour day at the office followed by social functions: I wasn't happy then.

But when Lida was born, my beautiful, beautiful daughter, I was happy then and never stopped being happy. And I had a notebook where I wrote down all the things my mom had done to irritate me and break my heart, and I tried not to do any of them myself.

But the world had changed.

Imagine my asking Lida to consider her marriage options before she lost her looks.

I mean, *imagine* it! It would be like living on a different planet.

And oddly, my mom had changed around that time too, she became normal and knew a lot of the world's wisdom. She certainly had not been normal or wise when I was young and could have done with it, still it was nice that she had discovered it in later life.

Malka said the same thing about her mother too, that she had calmed down since she had a grandchild. But I had never thought that Mrs O'Brien was all that bad. Very superstitious, of course, and caring about what other people in Rossmore thought or would say, like all people of her age. But basically a nice person.

Yet Malka said Mrs O'Brien had been quite horrific when she was younger, so I guess that generation just improved with age.

Malka's little boy Brendan was a darling, which was just as well since her husband turned out to be a lot less than we had all hoped he would be. I loved it when she brought Brendan over to stay with me for a few weeks that time, the time that Declan, the roving husband, had roved off with Eileen the school secretary. Malka was very depressed when she first arrived, she cried a lot. She said she hadn't cried back home – she wouldn't give her sisters-in-law nor her own mother the satisfaction of seeing her down. But she cried in my kitchen, and in my garden as we watched our children playing in the pool, and she cried when we went out to a piano bar one evening, she and I, and the pianist played 'Blue Moon', which had been their song, hers and Declan's.

'I never thought he'd fancy another woman,' she wept. 'He always said I was the only one. I thought that if I ever lost him it would be to the drink, I believed it was a battle between Callaghan's licensed premises and myself for his attention.'

I patted her hand in the piano bar, and passed her tissues. This was not the time to tell Malka that her intended had tried to jump me for three evenings before their wedding.

If I hadn't told her back then just on the eve of her wedding day when it might have been helpful, useful, wise, then there was no point in telling her any time afterwards.

I had told myself that maybe it was just high spirits. I didn't know these people and their culture, did I? Maybe for him and his friends it was just meaningless to press me, the bride's best friend, up to a wall in a grip I couldn't get out of and to kiss me. So I either spoke then and ruined her wedding and our friendship, or I shut up.

You might have done it differently but I made my choice and was stuck with it.

And I always told myself that if I had said anything that time, then maybe Brendan would not exist and her life would have been greatly the less.

Brendan has been a fine son for her – won't listen to advice, of course, but then what young person does listen these days? He was never any trouble to her, all that time he grew up in Dublin, with his father away from home. He always got himself a holiday job to help to pay his tuition fees. One summer Max gave him a position in one of the travel agencies and he worked so hard they were prepared to offer him a full-time post. But I said, no way, imagine if my friend Malka were to be deprived of saying, 'My son the engineer'!

Unfortunately he didn't get to know my Lida that summer; she was in Ireland of all places. She and Malka had loved each other from the word go, but then I knew they would so that didn't surprise me a bit. And I liked her Brendan too, very much, when he came to stay here at weekends. He was easy and relaxed and had no hang-ups about his father.

'Dad was over-interested in women always, one was never enough for him,' Brendan told me. 'I think he felt he had to try it on with everyone to prove he was alive or something.'

I nodded in agreement, he had it right. That's exactly what Declan was doing, proving something.

'And are you the same?' I asked. Sort of joking.

Apparently not, it's like the children of a wino being teetotal. Brendan told me that his mates said someone would have to light a fire under him to get him going.

'I expect my father made a pass at you, Rivka?' he said.

'Way back, it wasn't important,' I heard myself say.

'Did you tell my mam? You know, later, when they split?' he asked.

'No,' I told him. 'As I said, it didn't seem important.'

He nodded approvingly.

It was the only secret we had, Malka and I, that's a fact. We told each other everything. I don't think she had any secrets from me. I don't think so, but then if she were to be asked had I kept anything back, she would have said no.

And what could she have known or experienced that she couldn't tell me? Max certainly never leaped at Malka like her husband-to-be had leaped on me. Max has a low libido, that's what my mom says to explain his long absences. It might be true. She says I should be grateful. I suppose that tells me more about her life with Father than I want to know.

It was never great sex with Max by my reckoning but I realise that he felt that it was never great with me.

Malka always said that she had loved it with Declan but had always been nervous in case she got pregnant. His sisters had five children each and these were regarded as *small* families.

Malka was the only person I ever talked to about sex and not very often. When you think of wars starting over sex, and murders being committed, and people breaking up families and getting publicly disgraced, it's really very hard to understand.

Lida, I gather, has had plenty of sex so far in her young life. She told me a long time ago that she went to a women's clinic to get herself sorted out.

When I imagine myself saying that sort of thing to my own mom, well, I almost feel faint. But times change.

And who would have thought that I, Rivka Fine-Levy, would have my own specialist art tours agency and be highly thought of as the wife of the great Max Levy. Unlike so many women I knew, I never had a day's worry about Max being unfaithful to me, I just sort of knew. It was the way he was with women, not interested, not like Declan who was always up for it, as even his own son recognised.

Who would have known that I would become someone who loved my mom instead of hated her, and that I would really enjoy going shopping with her? That I would love my own daughter more than life; that I would still remain such a friend of Malka whom I had met plucking chickens all those years ago when she was going to convert to Judaism, marry Shimon and run a gladioli farm? The time when I was too timid to let that Algerian boy, Dov, get to first base.

I do wish Lida had gone to Israel, but of course there was no point in mentioning it.

She was proud of Israel, she explained, but she disapproved of something or other they were doing out there at the moment and she wouldn't lend support by visiting.

Lida was like that, taking stands, concerned about issues, standing up and being counted.

Very laudable, admirable even. But it didn't always make for an easy life.

Max was hardly ever there to discuss it with. If I tried he just kept repeating that he was astounded to have a daughter at all, which wasn't much of a help, and a bit repetitive.

After nearly a quarter of a century you'd think he might have got used to the fact by now.

So this summer I planned a little trip for Malka and myself. We would go for a week to Florence and a week by the sea in Sicily to recover from all the sightseeing and the pounding round art galleries. It was so odd to think that our two children would be also on the Mediterranean, swimming in the same sea. But we knew we must make no plans to meet them, nothing claustrophobic that would make them resent us. We had been through enough of that in the old days when *our* mothers were bad, suffocating people. We knew all about the long rein and letting them be free. Don't let them know you miss them.

I was so busy getting ready for the trip, I really didn't miss Lida. I can pack two cases very quickly and scientifically now. Another of my talks on the breakfast or ladies' lunch circuit is 'intelligent packing'. People just love it.

I tell them about having the typed master list and adding items like a small torch, your own favourite pillowcase, and a little wooden wedge to keep doors open – you won't believe how useful that is.

Anyway, out of a clear blue sky when I was folding the dresses between sheets of tissue paper, this young man called to the house, about thirty-something. I wondered if he had called for Lida. But no, he was looking for Max.

Max was away, coming back tonight, I said. I was leaving for Europe next day, we would be having a rare dinner at home together – I could give him a message. What name would I say?

The man said I was to tell him that Alexander had called by, and that he was very sorry, he thought I was leaving for Florence today, not tomorrow. He knew I was going to Florence this week and yet I had never even heard of him. I felt alarmed somehow. He refused tea, gave no details of what his business was with Max, then left very quickly.

'Alexander came today,' I said to Max that evening. 'He thought I would already have left for Florence.'

Max looked at me levelly.

'I'm so very sorry you had to find out this way,' he said.

I had no idea what I had found out. None at all, as Malka would say. I looked at him blankly.

'About Alexander,' he said.

And then suddenly it was all clear. Everything made sense. The long absences, the discretion, the way I was worn on Max's arm for public occasions, the separate bedrooms.

Malka asked me afterwards, did I behave well, did I react as I would like to have done.

The answer is yes, I behaved perfectly out of sheer shock. I sat wide awake in my bedroom all night piecing things together. Of course that was the explanation. Why had I been so blind? But it's not something you'd expect.

Then I'm afraid I began to worry whether everyone else knew. Was I the only fool who didn't realise that my husband played for the other team? And as the clock ticked on and dawn came to the sky, I decided that it was *not* generally known, that I was *not* a laughing stock. And that helped. Perhaps it shouldn't have but it did. At least I wasn't a public fool.

I dressed carefully and did my face. My car was coming to pick me up at 10 a.m.

Max looked terrible, white faced and unkempt. He hadn't slept either. He looked at me like a puppy that knows it's going to be punished.

'What will you do?' he asked fearfully.

'I'll tell you my plans when I get back, Max.' I was cool, polite and slightly distant.

I left everything else, the weeping, the railing, the questioning, the rage, until I got to Florence, and to Malka.

She knew at once. You can't fool Malka. She poured some duty-free and I told her everything, left nothing out. I can't remember anything that we did on that holiday that didn't involve both of us bawling, crying, deciding to kill Max, to sue him, to take him for everything that he had. We were going to 'out' him, make him look ridiculous, or we were going to be noble and say it didn't matter.

By the time we got to Sicily we were completely exhausted. We rented a car and drove around the island. We swam in the bright blue sea, we drank more wine than I had ever thought possible.

'I'll have to go into detox when I get back to real life,' I said, not really wanting to think about getting back.

'Shouldn't you contact your office?' Malka suggested.

Normally I'm on my cellphone and picking up e-mails everywhere. The office was, of course and irritatingly, surviving fine without me.

There was an e-mail from Lida:

'Dad says he doesn't know where you are in Italy, your office says you'll call in but you haven't, so it's not my fault. I tried to find you everywhere to tell you my plans have changed and I am going to Israel after all. I met Brendan in Rome. We always planned to meet there, we've been in touch with each other for the past two years and meet a lot. We didn't tell you and Malka because you'd fuss so much, and we wanted to be sure before we said anything. And now we are. Very sure.

'And he asks me for you to tell his mom, because apparently she is hopeless about technology and expects a pigeon to come in carrying a letter. And there is to be none of this nonsense about culture and tradition and history and differences and all that kind of shit. You are to square it with Grandmother and Dad. You will, won't you? You've always been terrific about everything. Brendan says the same about his mom. Can you tell us where this bloody gladioli farm is and we'll go look for it and examine these guys who could have been our fathers if things had been different.'

Malka and I know the letter off by heart. Well, you would, wouldn't you? A letter that turned everything round and made sense of it all.

CHAPTER 5

The Plan

Part 1 – Becca

Mother was always saying to me, 'Becca, you could do simply anything in this world if you had a proper plan.' She would say this as we walked down Castle Street doing the shopping together or waited for the sheets and towels to dry at the Fresh as a Daisy Launderette or had coffee in the Jumping Bean.

Mother did have lots of plans as life went on. Like when I was twenty-one and Father wouldn't hear of paying for a big party, Mother developed a plan. She went to the new hotel that had just opened in Rossmore and showed them our guest list with lots of very important people on it. She insisted to the manager that they should give her half-price because of all the introductions she was giving them over her daughter Becca's party. And she eked this bit of money out of Father and that bit. And there you were. A stunning twenty-first with just *everyone* there! Just because she had a plan.

Dear Mother was so right about lots of things. Well, not always entirely right about Father, of course. But then, how could anyone have known what he was going to do? You'd need to have been some kind of mystic to have known. Father went off with Iris, this perfectly awful, common woman, when I was twenty-five and Mother was fast approaching fifty. The awful woman Iris wasn't even young. She was a woman who wore a cardigan and walked through the Whitethorn Woods with a mongrel dog. Mother said it wouldn't have been quite so bad if she had been a silly young girl with a huge bosom. But no, she was the same age as all of them. Humiliating.

I foolishly suggested to Mother that she might go to St Ann's Well, a lot of people got their wishes answered there. She was horrified at the very thought of it. Ludicrous place, pagan superstition, a place maids and women from cottages went. I wasn't even to mention it again.

Mother said that if she had the energy, she would kill Iris.

I had begged her not to. 'Please, Mother, don't kill Iris. You'll get caught, and arrested, and go to jail.'

'Not if I did it properly,' Mother said.

'But you wouldn't do it properly, Mother, and suppose for a moment that you did, imagine how terrible it would be if Father were to pine over this Iris. Think how terrible that would be.'

Grudgingly Mother agreed. 'If I were younger and could make a proper plan, then I could easily have killed Iris,' she said calmly. 'But, Becca darling, I should have started much earlier and it would all have been fine. I think you are right and that I'd probably be wiser to leave it now.'

Mercifully she did.

Father didn't really stay in touch. He wrote from time to time to say that Mother was bleeding him dry. Mother said that he and that terrifying Iris had taken every penny she was entitled to – all she had left was the falling-down house in Rossmore. She sighed and sighed, and said that to hire yet another lawyer on top of Myles Barry was like throwing good money after bad.

'When you grow older, Becca darling, I beg you to have a plan. Do nothing without a plan, and do it sooner rather than later.'

And it always seemed a very good idea because everything Mother did later, having waited around, had gone belly up, while all the things that had been done sooner had been fine. She must have been right about striking when the iron was hot.

So I tried to have a plan about most things. I worked in Rossmore's new fashion boutique that catered for rich clients and I planned to get to know these people socially. Sometimes it worked, sometimes it didn't. I also made a friend of Kevin the van driver, who drove a taxicab on the side, and he often gave me lifts to places – which was nice because I was fairly broke and I wouldn't have had money for taxis.

Kevin was nice. He had a terrible cough and he was a frightful hypochondriac, always thinking that a headache was meningitis, that sort of thing, but he was very fond of me and said that I could always ask him to come out and collect me on a wet night and he would. I never abused it but I did ask him from time to time.

Mother was in bad form a lot but to be very honest I didn't get too involved with Mother and her problems because there was so much going on in my own life. You see, I'd just met Franklin and everything changed then.

You know the way people find it impossible to describe some huge event in their life, like seeing a film star, or the Queen of England, or the Pope, or the President of the United States, or something earth-shaking? You can remember all kinds of unimportant details but not the thing itself.

It's as if it was too big to take in.

It was just like that when I met Franklin.

I remember the dress I was wearing: a red silk dress with a halter neck that I had got at a thrift shop. I remember the perfume I wore: it was Obsession by Calvin Klein. I couldn't afford it myself but amazingly a customer had left it behind her in the boutique.

I can't remember why I went to that particular party. It was to launch a new restaurant in Rossmore. The town was so big now and so different to the way it was when Mother was young. New restaurants, hotels, art galleries opening all the time. I hadn't been invited or anything but I knew that if you turned up looking well dressed they always let you in. So about two or three times a month I would show up at a party and mingle a little. It got me out from under Mother's feet and you never knew who you might meet.

Well, up to now I had only met a lot of frogs actually and was beginning to despair of meeting a prince at any of these dos and then that night I met Franklin. It was at 7.43 p.m. on the huge pink neon-lit clock. I had been thinking I might go home at eight. I wouldn't call Kevin tonight, there was a bus stop outside the door, and just then Franklin said hallo.

Blond, blue eyes, tousled hair, perfect teeth. He was startlingly good-looking. And so nice and easy. It began almost immediately between us. We discovered we had literally everything in common, just everything. We both loved Greece and Italy, we loved Thai food, and skiing, and re-runs of old movies on television. We liked big dogs, and tap dancing, and long brunches on a Sunday.

Mother had been going through a depressive stage at the time and she was very doubtful about my new romance.

'Everyone likes those things, Becca, you silly girl. Do stop getting your hopes up, darling, he's only stating the obvious. Imagine anyone not liking Italy, or *Sergeant Bilko*, or *Dad's Army*, or skiing! Be sensible, darling. Please!'

Then she met Franklin and like everyone else she was bowled over.

He was charming to her. She loved everything that he said.

'I see where Becca gets her wonderful cheekbones.' 'You must be fearfully intelligent to play bridge so well.' 'You *must* let me call you Gabrielle, you're much too young for me to call you "Mrs King".'

Now if I had been cynical, I could have said that it was just a line, he knew what to say to older ladies. But I'm not cynical – I'm sunny and optimistic and I said nothing. Just smiled.

And because Franklin, the poor lamb, had nowhere proper to stay at the moment, he came to stay with us. There was a fiction for a while that he stayed in the guest room, but actually we soon needed the spare room for all his gear so he moved into mine.

Franklin didn't have a job, not as such, but he and another man called Wilfred, a friend of his, were developing an idea, a concept. They were going into business together. It had to do with mobile phones and was very hard to explain and, indeed, to understand. But Franklin and Wilfred were like two bright schoolboys with a project. Their enthusiasm carried them along.

Mother said to me many times that I should have a plan to keep him because treasures like Franklin didn't come along every day of the week. I should be more domestic for one thing, and cook for him. Also I should dress up more, borrow clothes from the boutique, get them dry-cleaned and give them back. Show him what an asset I was and could be in life.

We were all so happy together. Mother taught us all, Franklin and Wilfred and me, how to play bridge, and then I would make us a supper. It was a wonderful four months.

Franklin and I had a terrific understanding. We were both twenty-nine years old so, naturally, we had a bit of a past but we had never ever loved anyone else in the past, not one tenth as much as we loved each other. And if for any reason our love began to diminish or we met someone else, there would be no deceit, no lies. We would tell each other straight out. We pealed with laughter at the very idea! It was so unlikely that it would ever happen.

Then one evening Franklin told me that he had met this girl called Janice and that they had feelings for each other, so true to our promise and our understanding he was telling me immediately. He smiled at me his heartbreaking smile.

He had a look on his face as if he should somehow be *praised* for telling me about this damn Janice. As if his honesty and trustworthiness had somehow been proved. I gritted my teeth and forced a smile on to my face. There was an ache at my cheekbones, so like my mother's cheekbones apparently.

'Maybe you only think you have feelings for her,' I said. 'Possibly, when you get to know her, you'll find it's quite different.' I admired myself so much for staying so calm.

But then he explained that he did know. He was very sure.

'Shouldn't you wait till you've slept with her to be sure?' I was so proud of how I was handling this.

'Oh, I have,' he said.

'That wasn't exactly part of our understanding, having sex before telling each other, was it?' I hoped my voice didn't sound quite as steely outside as it did from within.

'But you weren't there, I couldn't ask you,' he said, as if it was the most reasonable thing in the world.

'Wasn't where exactly?' I asked.

'In the hotel. Wilfred and I were there meeting some investors and there happened to be a bridge session on, so we joined it and that's where I met Janice.'

I realised that my own mother had delivered the weapon of destruction herself. Why couldn't she have left Franklin ignorant of how to play bridge? If she had, then he would never have met this Janice. Our lives would have been perfect.

But I knew that I must have a plan. And that until I had one I must remain calm.

'Well, if that's the way it is, that's it, Franklin,' I said with a huge smile. 'And I truly hope that you and Janice will be very happy together.'

'You are marvellous!' he cried. 'You know, I told Janice that you and I had this understanding but she said you'd never honour it. I knew you would, that we both would. So I was right.' He stood, beaming at me, delighted that his faith had been justified.

Was he insane? Could he not see what had happened to me – that the light had left my life? Did he not hear the sound that went click in my head and the rush like a great wind that seemed to be blowing all around me? Maybe it was shock. Or a breakdown. Or the beginning of madness. I had never felt that way before, it was like you feel before you faint. As if the world was advancing and receding at me.

But I couldn't faint, I must not show any signs of weakness. This was a turning point in my life. Now I still had to work out the plan to get him back, he must have no idea how my world was crashing down around me.

I told Franklin I had to rush, there was a late-night crisis at the boutique and that I simply had to leave. I wished him every happiness with this Janice and I fled. I hadn't smoked for five years but I bought a packet of cigarettes. Then I let myself into the boutique and sat down at a table and cried and cried.

Kevin was there. Always a heavy smoker, he joined me at the table and patted my hand.

Before I could tell him what was wrong he started to tell me his troubles.

'I'm not in great form myself, Becca,' he said and I noticed that his face was haggard and gaunt.

'What's wrong, Kevin?' I asked politely even though I couldn't have given a damn.

Something wrong with the van probably, not much work in the cab business, only two numbers off winning the Lotto – who cared? Who gave a blind damn about it, when Franklin was leaving me for Janice and the world was coming to an end?

'I've got really bad cancer, Becca. No point in operating, they say. I've got two months at the most.'

'Oh, Kevin, I'm so very sorry,' I said and I was. For thirty whole seconds I forgot Franklin and Janice and the plan. 'They're very good in hospitals nowadays,' I reassured him. 'They'll give you plenty of painkillers.'

'I'm not going to wait, Becca, I couldn't wake up every day wondering, is it going to happen today.'

'So what will you do?'

'I'll drive quickly in the van straight into a wall. Splat,' he said. 'Much quicker, no waiting, no worrying, no hanging about waiting for it to happen.'

And that's where I got my plan.

Suddenly my brain was working overtime – I felt I could cope with a hundred things at the same time. It was a daring mad plan. But it had a great deal going for it. It would solve everything in a stroke.

If he were going to kill himself, then he could take Janice with him.

If he were going to die anyway, and he was afraid of waiting, well then, why couldn't they both leave this life together?

I must be very, very clever, he must never know. He must not have an inkling what I was thinking.

'I think you're quite right, Kevin, that's just what

I'd do if it were me. Well, it will be me one day, of course. And I'll do just that. Leave at my own time, not someone else's.'

He was completely surprised. He had expected me to beg him not to.

'But do you know what I think, Kevin? I think you should do it in a cab rather than your own van. Cabs are always crashing. It would look more natural when people investigate it, better for your life insurance policy. For your mother or whatever.'

'I see,' he said slowly. 'So they wouldn't pay up if they thought it was suicide?'

'Apparently not.'

'You're very good to be so interested, Becca, but what has *you* so upset?'

'Oh nothing, compared to your problems, nothing at all, Kevin, a silly quarrel with my mother, it will blow over.'

'But everything's all right with you and Franklin?' he asked.

I think Kevin was always a little bit in love with me. Not, of course, that I showed any sign of noticing that. But he must never know what Franklin had done.

I reassured him. 'Oh, Franklin and I are fine, not a cloud on the horizon,' I said. Just thinking that made me stop crying. Kevin gave me a tissue and I wiped my eyes. It was all going to be all right.

I could afford to spend time being kind to Kevin. 'Come on, Kevin, I'll take you out for a Chinese supper,' I said, and he looked so pathetically grateful.

'Won't Franklin mind?' he asked.

'Franklin lets me do what I want to do,' I said.

'If you were mine I'd be just the same,' Kevin said.

And we went and had a long and terribly depressing meal where he told me about his diagnosis and his wish to end it all. I nodded sympathetically and told him he was absolutely right. I didn't listen to one word of what he said. I sat there thinking about my plan. Kevin would do it for me. Kevin would see it through.

I would pretend to be enthusiastic about this awful Janice, I would become her friend.

Then I would give her Kevin's number as a reliable taxi driver. Of course Kevin naturally wouldn't want to take a perfectly innocent passenger with him, kill her, so to speak. So I'd have to tell him some story that Janice was also suffering from a terrible incurable disease and she had asked me to arrange a swift exit from the world. It was going to be a challenging role for me. It was if I had to write it and act it. But it had to be done. It was the perfect plan. No one would ever suspect me because I was going to be Ms Nice Guy, full of human kindness.

'I don't know what I'd do without you, Becca,' Kevin said to me a dozen times during the Chinese meal.

'And I don't know what I'd have done without you, Kevin,' I said to him truthfully.

Wilfred, who was Franklin's friend and business partner, was astounded by me.

'You're really full of surprises,' he said. 'I thought we'd have the full hell hath no fury bit – but I was totally wrong.'

I laughed a tinkling laugh. 'Franklin and I always had an understanding, Wilfred,' and as I saw him looking at me in awe, I gave him a smile that I hoped would break his heart as well as Franklin's.

My mother was astonished when I told her that there was no point whatsoever in trying to hold on to Franklin if he didn't want to be held. She shook her head in wonder and said that I had always been even more unbalanced than she was, so it was amazing to see me so rational.

I told Franklin that he must be in no hurry to move out. But that, of course, he would sleep in the guest room now that things were different. I went out a lot myself. Often with Kevin. It seemed only fair. But of course the real part of the plan was getting to know Janice.

The first blow was that she was only nineteen.

Then she wasn't interested in clothes, so I couldn't offer her cheap things from the boutique. She didn't care about cookery so I couldn't give her recipes. *How* was I to get to know her?

As so often in life, the solution was to be found in the game of bridge. I asked the loathsome Janice to do me a favour and be my bridge partner at a ladies' social evening for charity. Since I'd been so nice to her and so desperately decent about handing her Franklin without any grumbling, there was really nothing she could do but accept.

We got on fine that first night and several times she told me that she admired me and my generation for our attitude to love. Some day she hoped she would be as mature as that.

I resisted choking her to death at the bridge table with my own hands. After all, I had a much better plan.

We actually won the competition and agreed to play together again the next week at another charity function at the Rossmore Hotel. In many ways she was a fairly pleasant companion. A university student with far too much money and time for her own good, but nice manners and, I have to say, a good bridge player. Very young and silly of course, like a niece or a neighbour's child.

And naturally I had a few pangs, a little remorse, a concern, I suppose you'd call it, about sending a nineteen-year-old girl to her death. I mean, I am human. Who wouldn't feel something? But then she had come between me and my one true love, there was no way he could be talked out of her or she of him.

It was this or nothing.

So on and on we played, Janice and I. We had been out together several times before I chose the night.

Franklin was talking about moving out of our home but I begged him to stay for a few more days. 'You can always go and spend nights with Janice,' I purred at him. 'But don't move all your gear yet.'

The plan would only work if he were still living with us when she died.

Kevin was very troublesome these days.

He was beginning to have second thoughts. He had become most concerned about taking another passenger with him. He thought he should discuss it with her first, ask her what preferences she had. Maybe she would like to be sedated before the crash, he suggested?

I said that I thought that she would very definitely not change her mind. As Kevin and I went through the details over and over again this was always his sticking point. Suppose she changed her mind at the last moment? He wouldn't be able to stop. It would be too late.

No, I said, this was definitely not going to happen. Again and again I explained that Janice had this terrible illness that was already beginning to take its toll, the pain would be unbearable. And in addition to this wasting disease she was developing a personality disorder. She had asked me to arrange it so that she wouldn't have to think about it or discuss it.

Well, he only wanted to do what was best, Kevin said. He really was such a kind and considerate man. Sometimes I allowed myself to think how much easier life would have been to love someone like that. But I didn't waste time going down that road of speculation. Since the incident when Franklin had told me about Janice I had become very focused.

Sometimes Kevin wondered was he right to take his own life. Was it his to take?

I dealt with that too. People preached about a

loving God who understood everything. If this was so, then this God would understand that Kevin couldn't hang about and wait for what was inevitable. That he was just speeding things up. For everybody. Usually it worked after about ten or fifteen minutes but it was utterly exhausting.

During this time, Mother, Franklin, Wilfred, people at work and even poor Kevin himself told me I was not looking myself. Wild, somehow. Unhinged, Mother said. But I put on more make-up and smiled a nightmarish grin.

The big night eventually came, the date that would be the night of the accident. I had met Kevin earlier that day and reassured him that he was doing the right thing about himself, and that we were both doing the right thing about Janice. He turned up just as we had planned outside the door of the hotel where the charity bridge function was taking place.

'Oh, here's a taxi for you, Janice!' I said, sounding pleased.

'You are marvellous, Becca, everyone else is rushing about looking for them and you find one immediately.' She looked genuinely admiring.

Kevin got out of the driver's seat and came to open the passenger door. He and I gripped each other's hands.

Janice was going back to her flat where Franklin would join her later. He and Wilfred were out at yet another business meeting. I said that I must run now as my bus was just coming and we were going in different directions anyway.

'Bye, lovely Becca,' Kevin said.

'See what I mean, Becca, everyone's mad about you,' Janice said enviously as she waved me good-bye.

And I went home and I talked to my mother for a long time and then went to bed. Franklin telephoned to know what time we had all left the bridge function because Janice wasn't back yet. I said I couldn't understand it, lots of people had seen her getting into a cab hours ago. And in the morning he telephoned again and said she hadn't come home all night.

I was so sympathetic but I had no idea what could have happened.

In the afternoon he rang to say that poor lovely little Janice had been killed and the taxi driver too, they had ploughed into a wall. Everyone was shocked. Franklin didn't move out because he was so shattered, and soon he began to love me again. The whole thing should have been perfect, it *would* have been perfect if it hadn't been for Kevin.

I was right.

He did love me.

And he had insured his life in my favour. I was going to get a small fortune. This of course destroyed the whole plan. No one would ever have connected it with me if it hadn't been for this policy.

That and the letter Kevin left thanking me for all I had done for him.

Now everyone was investigating it. Insurance people, police, everyone. And the whole of Rossmore is talking about me. They say that Janice's mother and sisters went up to that ridiculous well in the woods and a kind of procession went after them. As if that was going to bring her back!

People say I am as hard as nails. I never used to be, I was always as soft as a kitten.

Of course I may not get charged with anything. But Franklin is nervous of me. He didn't say so but he started to move all his things out last week.

It had been such a perfect plan – if only Kevin hadn't tried to be generous. Tried to give me something as he ended his life.

Instead of which he managed to take my whole life away.

Part 2 – Gabrielle

All my friends at the bridge club have been very kind. Very kind indeed.

They glare at each other if someone accidentally mentions prison, or murder, or convicts, or anything. They think I am very brave to go to visit Becca in jail every week and to hold my head up everywhere I go in Rossmore. It's not all that hard to have confidence actually. It depends really on how you look. I always knew that but I never had the money to look well.

My ex-husband, that bloody Eamon, left me penniless when he went off with that appalling, vulgar woman, Iris. The upkeep of the house was amazing, so I was always very stuck for cash when it came to it. Which, of course, was why I was so grateful to the tabloids.

Now I know we have to pretend to think they are terrible and that we only let them into the house for the maid sort of thing, but they were hugely interested in what poor Becca had done and in fact I was secretly delighted with them. One of them bought the story of Becca's childhood and the 'What Made Her the Woman She Became' angle. Another bought stuff about her life in the chic fashion boutique. I should have got a retainer from that hoity-toity madam who owns the place – I bet I doubled her business.

Then there was a piece about how Becca had changed after her father, bloody Eamon, had left home. I enjoyed helping to write that. Nowhere did they say that I was collaborating but I gave them all the information and all the pictures. It made a magnificent set of articles.

Of course I didn't like titles like 'In the Mind of the Murderess' but on the other hand it did sell papers, and in many people's minds that's exactly what poor silly Becca actually was.

Every time I visited, she would ask how had the reporters found out all these details. I reassured her that I had told them nothing new, they knew it all already. What they didn't know, they made up. Like all that silly business about poor Becca going up to the well in Whitethorn Woods to pray to St Ann that Franklin would love her.

'I never did, Mother, you know that,' she had wept at me.

I soothed her and patted her down. Of course everyone knew it was nonsense. They just made it up out of their heads . . .

I had been very well paid for that particular story. It gave the newspapers freedom to take pictures of the terrible shrine. And did that sell papers! Obviously Becca knew nothing of this and I reassured her and reminded her that I *had* managed to keep Franklin out of the story and she was naturally very grateful. When she came out of jail she would marry him, of course, so she didn't want him attracting unpleasant limelight and attention until then.

She had begged him to come and visit her until I told her that the reporters were outside the jail all the time and they would spot him and the careful privacy we had all been keeping would be blown. She saw the sense in that.

They're quite nice in the jail, really. Basically out for the prisoners' good – which must be quite hard when you think of the kind of people they have to deal with normally. Of course, Becca is different, and they see that, naturally they would. She's a lady for one thing and she hasn't the *mind* of a criminal for another. She's so far above everyone in the place and yet gets on perfectly pleasantly with them all, which is a true sign of good breeding.

She's learning embroidery at recreation time, from one of the warders, a nice woman called Kate. Becca says it's very restful, therapeutic even. She gave me a perfectly horrid little cushion cover she had made and I told her it has pride of place in the sitting room. Poor dear Becca! She thinks she'll be home any day to see it. She has risen above her whole terrible situation by refusing to acknowledge it. It's a way of coping and for Becca it's working very well.

She has started a huge coverlet for her bed with the words 'Franklin' and 'Rebecca' intertwined.

I have to remember not to wear my best finery going to see her because Becca can spot a designer outfit at half a mile, it was all those years working in the boutique. She would know I couldn't ordinarily afford Prada or Joseph jackets. I have what I call my prison visiting outfit, so that she won't make the connection between the publishing of the tabloid stories and her mother's new wardrobe.

Becca herself looks a lot better as the weeks and months go by. She walks straighter, she doesn't fuss about her hair and sort of twiddle with it like she used to, it's just straight now and classy looking. There's one of the warders, Gwen, who is a friend of Kate, the nice one, and apparently she trained as a hairdresser and still works part time in a beauty parlour and she gives them all a regular trim. They're not allowed to hold a pair of scissors themselves of course. Which is idiotic in Becca's case, I mean, what harm would she do to anyone with a pair of scissors?

She seems less anxious these days than when she was out in the real world, somehow much calmer. Very interested in shading and matching threads, and whether she'll be chosen for a netball team.

Becca! Interested in sports and embroidery! Who would have thought it? Well, who would have thought any of it really?

Sometimes the tabloid people ask me, do I have any sympathy for poor Janice who went unsuspecting to her death because of Becca, but I remind them that I cannot be quoted; my opinions and my natural, deep, deep sorrow cannot be entered into. And then before they start to turn against me I feed them another picture of Becca or titbit about the parties she used to go to, launches, receptions, to which she hadn't even been invited. They would run another story describing her as a good-time party girl.

Imagine!

You know the way they talk about people becoming institutionalised? Well, I think it's absolutely true. Becca has few interests now outside the terrible place where she is. She tells me of horrid lesbian affairs between the prisoners, and sometimes between prisoners and warders. The only thing that unites her to the world outside is her future with Franklin.

It's marvellous, of course, that she is so positive about everything but then she does seem to have lost touch with reality since she doesn't realise how long she is going to be in there. Nor did she ever refer to the enormity of what she had done. She sort of waves it away.

And yet it was a terrible thing. Killing Franklin's fiancée – or getting her killed, which was just as bad. 'A deliberate and cold-blooded killing,' as the judge said when he sentenced her after a unanimous verdict from the jury. She never once spoke of Janice or, indeed, that sad chap, Kevin, who did the driving, or anything at all about that night.

And I didn't want to distress her. Poor lamb, her life hadn't turned out at all as she had hoped.

So when she talked about Franklin and the future I did nothing to discourage her. Once she realised he couldn't come to see her, she stopped asking about him and what he was doing.

This was a great relief.

A huge relief in fact. It's been getting more and more difficult to field her questions about him. I tried to tell her about the bridge club but Becca had lost all interest – she barely reacted when I told her about the grand slam that I had got. I think she barely takes on board that Wilfred and Franklin and I play regularly together, getting a fourth where we can find one. But then I suppose bridge might have been a bit of a sore subject, what with Janice's having met Franklin there, being a bridge partner and everything.

So maybe better not mention bridge.

Trouble is that there are so many things it's better not to mention. I talk on about whether this thread is cerise or fuchsia, and how hard it is for Kate the warder to support two children on her wages, and I listen to stories about how Gloria's romance with Ailis is over, and how it's all political getting on the netball team.

And I listen to stories about women who are prostitutes, drug dealers, or have murdered their husbands in self-defence. It's such an uncanny sort of an existence. That bloody Eamon, my ex-husband, asked would Becca like him to visit and I said certainly not. He had been no help to her before all this business and he would only upset her further now. So that softened his cough.

Kate draws me aside from time to time when I visit and tells me that Becca is adapting very well and is very popular with the other prisoners. As if I would somehow be pleased that these terrible women liked my Becca or not! But Kate meant well, she couldn't help it if she had no advantages when she was growing up, and from what Becca said, Kate too had been a victim like I was, her husband had left her. Bastards, really, all of them when you think about it.

So I took to bringing Kate little presents as well when I visited. Nothing huge, just a nice soap or a glossy magazine, or a little jar of tapenade. Poor dear, I don't think she knew what it was, but she was pleased all the same. And as I say, it wasn't her fault that she didn't grow up in a proper home. And she was very kind to my Becca.

Franklin was relieved that I had sorted out that he shouldn't visit. Very relieved, I imagine. But Wilfred, who was so polite and always tried to do the right thing, asked, should he come and see Becca? I thought about it for a while but I said, not really, what would there be for him to say? And he too was frightfully relieved. I could see it. I didn't want Wilfred in there anyway, blabbing and saying the wrong thing. He was only offering to be polite.

He was still Franklin's partner in this mysterious mobile phone service they were doing, downloading or uploading or offloading something on to people's cellphones, impossible to understand.

Then the mother of that poor Janice asked could she visit Becca, but I told Kate to tell the authorities that this would be the wrong thing. This poor woman was Born Again or something very dubious and she thought Becca would find peace if she went to tell her she had forgiven her, but I think Becca has actually forgotten about Janice, to be honest, so I discouraged it and Kate must have passed the message on because she never went.

And life went on in the funny way it does, everything changed and yet finding a similarity in the days. We continued to play bridge two nights a week. Becca's father, bloody Eamon, would telephone me every time there was something new in the tabloids – his frightful wife apparently reads nothing else.

'How do they know these things?' he would cry at me into the phone.

I shrugged. I had no idea, I told him. I never saw him so he wouldn't know that I had such smart clothes and that I had bought a sports car. Or that there was a cleaner every day now and a gardener once a week. It was none of his business anyway. Little he had cared when he abandoned his wife and daughter.

I would take a taxi to the prison each week, and ask it to wait at the bus stop around the corner and then join the rest of the prison visitors, opening my bag for examination and accepting a body search before visiting my own daughter. I didn't want anyone to tell Becca that I kept a taxi waiting. She would wonder where I got the funds. And in the end it was all for her own good, her peace of mind, and enabled me to visit her every week without too much stress and strain.

'Kate is very good to me, Mother,' she said one day.

'Yes indeed.' I was wondering where this was leading.

'I was wondering if you could ask her for tea sometime on her day off, Mother?'

'No, darling, that wouldn't do at all,' I said.

'Please, Mother.'

Becca had lost touch with the real world. How could I ask such a sad, poor woman, who lived in a council flat and worked as a prison warder, to my house?

'Sorry, Becca, out of the question,' I said briskly.

Becca was very disappointed. I could see by her face. But the whole thing was totally impossible. She said no more, just resumed her stitching at a feverish pace. I wondered as I got back into my taxi why I had bothered to come and see her at all. She was really so ungrateful for all I had done. Wasn't it enough that I had bought all these little gifts for Kate? Not a word of thank you from Becca. Maybe the woman had never told her.

It was so hard to know! I mean, Kate was just a

prison warder. Imagine Becca thinking I could entertain her at home. I couldn't possibly let her see how we lived.

As the taxi pulled away, I thought I saw Kate standing there looking at me thoughtfully but it must have been my imagination. If she had seen me she would have come over and talked, not just stood there watching as she was. I hoped that she wouldn't say anything to Becca about my taking a taxi. But then I shook myself and told myself not to be fanciful. Being in that awful prison would make anyone fanciful, really.

When I got home the chaps were waiting for me with a scotch and ginger. Such dear boys. They always ask about Becca and I always say that it's too dreadful to talk about and that I must go and have a long bath. Just the very fact of *being* in that place makes you feel defiled. I lay in the warm scented bubbles and drank my long cool scotch and ginger. Life was a great deal better these days than it used to be. Amazing, really, how having enough money can take the edge off things.

I never worry these days about the roof slates, or getting a new handbag to tone in with a new outfit, or having good wine when we go out to dinner. I am beginning to accept as my right that I have a silk dressing gown and a redecorated bedroom. Tonight I would wear the really smart dress that had cost what we spent on our first car. It looked nice certainly but I needed better shoes. Perhaps I can come up with another little story for the ghastly papers.

Something like 'Stitching Her Way to the Future' and a description of the counterpane Becca is making. Yes, that would be good, it would throw suspicion on some of the people in the prison. That boot-faced Kate, for example.

I looked at myself in the mirror.

Not bad at all for my age. New shoes would make it perfect.

Franklin stood at the bottom of the stairs. Wilfred had gone ahead to be at the table to greet us. A special dinner out in a new restaurant. My treat. Always my treat. But then don't be all bitter and twisted, Gabrielle, I told myself. The boys' business is still in the foothills, it hasn't risen to great heights yet. They actually don't have any real money yet, poor darlings.

'You look lovely,' Franklin said. It really was a pleasure to get dressed for people who appreciated it. Bloody Eamon wouldn't notice what I was wearing.

'Thank you,' I purred at him.

'Does she not ask about me at all?' he said unexpectedly.

'No, well, you know, we all agreed that it was better for her not to get in touch until . . . you know . . . until she comes out.'

'But, Gabrielle . . .' he looked at me, astonished. 'She's not going to get out for years and years.'

'I know,' I said. 'But you'd be amazed at how strong she is. You and I would go under in a place like that, but not Becca, she's brave as a lion.'

He looked at me affectionately.

'You make all this so much easier for me,' he said, his eyes full of gratitude.

'Come on, Franklin, let's not be late,' I said, and we walked down the steps of our home, past the new wrought iron railings with the sweet peas and honeysuckle entwined. Just before we got into the car I thought I saw that Kate in our road.

But it must have been a hallucination.

What could she have been doing in our neighbourhood?

And then next day I thought I saw her there again. It couldn't have been, of course. But it made me uneasy for some reason and I decided to get her a little present and have a chat with her on my next visit. Possibly foolish Becca had already invited her to tea in my house. And now she was annoyed because the invitation had not been followed up.

Ridiculous, but who knows what kind of thoughts people like her have.

I brought Becca some roses from the garden, and some sweet peas for that Kate. Also a silly little lace-trimmed handkerchief with a letter K on it. She accepted the flowers and handkerchief silently with a nod of her head and left almost immediately without any little chat.

'Is everything all right, Kate?'

'Never better, thank you,' she said, reaching to the back of the door of her office for her overcoat and leaving immediately. It was very mystifying.

Becca looked just as usual but there was something watchful, wary about her. It was as if she were examining me.

'We are always talking about me,' she said. 'And really nothing much changes here. Tell me all about your days and nights, Mother,' she said.

I was a bit wrong-footed here. I hadn't expected this. Up to now I had been vague and she had never wanted to know.

'Oh, you know me, Becca darling, drifting from this to that, a little bridge here, a little reminding your bloody father to give me some support there. The days pass.' She reached for my hand and lifted it to admire my nails.

'Some of them must pass at the beauty parlour,' she said.

'Oh, I wish, darling, just cheap enamel I put on myself.'

'I see. Like your hairdo. Do it yourself with the kitchen scissors, do you?'

I was very annoyed. These were things I couldn't hide from her, the expensive styling and shaping of my hair every five weeks with Fabian. The weekly manicure at Pompadours.

'What are you saying?' I asked.

'Not very much, Mother. You learn not to say anything here until you're quite sure what it is you are trying to say.'

'That would make the world a very silent place,' I twittered at her.

'Not really, no, just a more certain place.'

I tried to change the subject. 'Kate seemed in a hurry today, she almost brushed past me.'

'It's her half-day,' Becca said.

'Yes and I know that you did want me to invite her to afternoon tea, darling, but you're a little out of touch, Becca. It would be so inappropriate. I hope you don't mind.'

'No, that's all right, I understood, and so did she.'

'Well, that's good,' I said doubtfully.

'Do you get lonely at all, Mother? What with Father having left you and my being in here and everything?'

I couldn't imagine why she was asking this question. 'Well, lonely isn't the right word. I don't ever think about that bastard Eamon these days. I miss you, darling, and wish you were at home. And you will be. One day.'

'Not for years and years, Mother.' She was matter of fact.

'I'll be there for you,' I said firmly.

'I doubt it very much, Mother, I really do.'

She still looked totally calm but this wasn't the way she normally spoke. A little silence fell between us. Then after what seemed a long, long time Becca spoke.

'Why did you do it, Mother?' she asked.

'I don't know what you're talking about,' I began. And I didn't really – there were so many things it could have been. Was it the taxi? Had that really been Kate in the road who would have told her about the house being all painted up? That there were definitely signs of money, ill-gotten money, around the place? Or had she told her anything else?

I stood up as if to leave but her hand shot out and pinned my wrist to the table between us. One of the warders moved towards us but Becca smiled and reassured her that everything was fine.

'My mother is just about to tell me something, she's finding it a bit difficult, but she will find the words.'

I rubbed my wrist. 'Well, you see . . .' I began.

'No, I don't see, Mother. I hear that you are living with Franklin. That's what I hear.'

I began to bluster a little.

'But I'm doing it for you, Becca darling. Wilfred and Franklin had to live somewhere, I live in a big falling-down house – why shouldn't they have rooms there?'

'Not so falling-down now, I hear,' Becca said.

'But, darling, they just have rooms there – don't be so silly.'

'Do you sleep with Franklin?' she asked calmly.

'Now how can you say that?' I began.

'Because Kate told me, and Gwen told me.'

'Gwen?'

'One of the warders here, you go to her every week for a manicure. Dressed very differently than you are dressed today . . .'

For once I was speechless. Becca wasn't speechless, however.

'It's disgusting, he's thirty years younger than you.'

'Nineteen,' I said with spirit.

146

'He'll move on,' she said.

'Maybe,' I agreed. 'One day, yes, maybe.'

'Sooner than you think,' my daughter said.

And Becca told me her plan. She reminded me that I had said everyone should have a plan. Becca's plan was to put Kate in touch with the tabloid papers. Kate and Gwen didn't think that it was fair, the way Becca had been treated, and had alerted tabloid photographers to lie in wait for Franklin and myself.

'Murderess Betrayed by Her Own Mother' was going to be a much, much better story than anything that I had sold them so far. They would really pay Kate well for this.

She looked very calm and in control as she spoke to me. I wondered suddenly whether, if I had put aside all my principles and invited the damn woman to afternoon tea, all this would never have happened. But we'll never know . . .

CHAPTER 6

Bank Holiday Party

Part 1 – Barbara

You see, I was always such fun and so much the centre of things in the office, I obviously assumed that I was part of the Bank Holiday party. It never occurred to me that they would all go off without me. Not without me, Barbara, life and soul of the party. I mean, I was the one who had told them about it in the first place, this hotel in a place called Rossmore, miles away in the country where they had a big swimming pool with a patio where they let you grill your own steaks or pieces of chicken. I found the website and I printed out all the information and showed it to them.

So naturally I thought I was part of it all.

Then I heard them all talking about it and who they were going to be sharing rooms with and what time they were all getting together to have a drink

148

before they set off to catch the train. And there was some kind of wishing well in the woods where a saint had kept appearing and they were going to investigate it and see could they catch her in mid-apparition.

And then suddenly it dawned on me that I wasn't part of it.

At the start, I thought it was a mistake, you know the way things are. Everyone thinks that someone else told me. They just couldn't be going without me. But you get a sort of gut feeling when you are being left out of things and this is what I had.

Well, at first I was totally furious. How dare they take my idea and not include me? Then I became upset. Why did they not like me? What reason could have made them leave me out? Tears of self-pity had to be beaten back. Then I started hating them all. People I had thought were my friends. Laughing behind my back. I hoped they would have a really awful Bank Holiday weekend, and that the hotel would be a disaster. I wished them downpours of rain, and wanted the patio to be crawling with awful beasts that would get into their clothes and hair.

They were leaving on Friday at lunchtime, catching a two o'clock train. They all brought their bags to the office that morning. What was really amazing was how they talked about it so openly in front of me. They weren't even embarrassed that they had stolen my holiday and then left me out of it. They didn't lower their voices or turn away, just discussed it as if I had assumed I would be no part of it.

On the Friday morning Rosie, who was one of the nicer ones, confided to me that she had great hopes of getting together with Martin from Sales during the weekend.

'Do you think I might stand a chance with him, Bar?' she asked.

'I don't know why you ask me,' I said coldly.

Rosie seemed surprised. 'Because you're so cool, you know everything, Bar,' she said. As far as I could see she wasn't mocking me. Which made it all the odder that she hadn't wanted me to join them.

'I think you have every chance of winning Martin's affections,' I said. 'Best keep him away from Sandra, though, she's meant to be a bit of a man-eater.'

'Oh Bar, you're just wonderful, I wish you were coming with us, you could advise me the whole time. Why will you not come? Just this once?'

'Wasn't asked.' I shrugged, trying not to show how much it mattered.

Rosie pealed with laughter. 'As if you would have to be asked,' she said. 'You just didn't want to come, we knew that from the word go, the way you talked about the place and sneered at it. We knew you had something much better to do.'

'I *never* sneered at Rossmore, I suggested it,' I cried, outraged.

'No, not sneered exactly, but, Bar, we all knew it wouldn't be your kind of thing. A bit beneath you. Not in a snobby way but that's the way it is.'

'I don't believe you,' I said.

'Well, ask anyone then,' said Rosie. And I did.

I asked the man-eating Sandra.

'I don't suppose it would be your scene,' Sandra said. 'All right for us ordinary folk but not for you, Bar.'

'Why not for me?' I asked in a voice of steel.

'You're sort of classier than we are, Bar, you know – no one could see *you* spending a weekend in jeans grilling sausages.'

I was astounded.

Well, yes, I do dress well. I take care of my appearance. I consider myself well groomed. I have had some elocution lessons to improve my accent. But too classy to go on an office outing? Come on. They couldn't all be so humble and in awe of me as not to include me? Surely?

But I wasn't going to let them see how startled and upset I was. No way.

'Have a good time anyway, Sandra,' I said cheerfully. 'Got your eye on anyone in particular for the weekend?'

'Not really. That Martin fellow in the Sales Department is a bit of a looker. But we'll see.'

Sandra could have any man she wanted, Rosie wasn't so fortunate. Even in the middle of my own disappointment I decided to even things up.

'I wouldn't waste my time on him, I heard he's as dull as ditchwater when you get to know him,' I said.

'Thanks, Bar,' Sandra said, putting on more lip

gloss. 'Good to have your card marked. What are you doing for the Bank Holiday by the way?'

'Me? Oh, I'm not doing much,' I said, confused.

'I bet you are,' Sandra said.

'I'm giving a big lunch party,' I heard myself say.

'Ooh, Barbara, aren't you something else? How many people?'

'Twelve, including me.' Was I mad? I don't *know* twelve people. I couldn't cook for them even if I did.

'Twelve people! You're fabulous, Bar, will you have photos next week?'

'Very probably,' I said miserably. I could always say the camera had jammed. Not only was I pathetic and unpopular . . . I was mad and dishonest as well. Great start to a Bank Holiday weekend.

I waved them all goodbye as they left the office for the two o'clock train. People I had thought were my friends – sexy Sandra, innocent Rosie, that nice, gentle Martin from Sales, and half a dozen others who all thought I was stuck up and superior. I looked at myself in the mirror in the ladies' room. A pale face, framed with an expensive haircut, a well-cut jacket, which I sponged and brushed every night. I wore cheap T-shirts underneath, a different colour every day. There was nothing upper class, snobby about me. Was there?

Two cleaning women came in with their buckets and mops. They greeted me pleasantly with big smiles and a lot of gold teeth. They weren't Irish but there are lots of overseas people working in Ireland now and I didn't know where they were from. They were remarkably good-humoured with three hours of scrubbing and polishing ahead of them.

And yet I dared to feel sorry for myself, I, who had a good job in marketing, a big garden flat, a flat-screen television and a designer jacket!

'Are you looking forward to the Bank Holiday weekend?' I asked them.

'Not very,' said one.

'Sunday often a sad lonely day in a big city,' said the other.

I knew how she felt.

'Would you like to come to lunch with me?' I heard myself say.

They looked at me open-mouthed.

'To eat a lunch with you?' they asked astounded.

'Well, yes. On Sunday at about one o'clock in my house. Look, I'll write down the address for you.'

I got out my little leather-bound notebook. The two women in their yellow working overalls looked on as if I were writing them an invitation to fly to the moon.

'Oh, and I'd better know your names, to introduce you to other people,' I said.

'There will be other people?' They looked alarmed.

'Oh, indeed, about twelve of us altogether,' I said cheerily.

They were from Cyprus, sisters, they told me. They had Greek names: Magda and Eleni.

Nobody had ever invited them to a home before, Eleni said, excited.

Magda was worried about it all. 'You like us to clean the house for you maybe?' she said.

I felt so ashamed I could hardly speak. 'No, no, as my guests,' I mumbled.

'We will make some baklava . . . beautiful Greek dessert,' Magda said, now that it had all been cleared up.

I left them talking excitedly in Greek, nothing so marvellous had happened to them before in their new country.

On the way back to my own office, before I had even time to think about what I had just done, I met my boss Alan, a tense, anxious workaholic of about forty-five, I suppose. We knew nothing about his private life except in bursts when he announced that he hated his ex with a great passion. This was one of these bursts.

'She is an evil vicious woman,' Alan told me in the corridor. 'A foul and very bad person.'

'What has she done now?' I asked. Alan was quite handsome and he could be good company apart from all this droning on about his ex.

'She's only gone and dumped Harry and two of his ten-year-old friends on me for the whole of the weekend, and instructions about no fast food. I'm to cook them proper meals apparently.'

'Oh, bring them round to my place on Sunday – about one o'clock,' I said, casually writing down my address.

'I can't do that, Bar,' he said, though it was obvious that he wanted to.

'Ah, why not?' I shrugged. 'There'll be twelve of us, and plenty of home-cooked food.' I began to wonder, was I going mad?

'I'll bring you some wine then,' Alan said, eagerly bursting with gratitude.

Back in my office and gathering up my things I took a last look at my diary. I would be away from it until Tuesday, better see was there anything I should remember. It was my Aunt Dorothy's birthday on Sunday – my father's elder sister. Disapproving of everyone, she had rarely been known to utter a pleasant remark.

There was still time to fling a birthday card into the post so that she couldn't accuse me of neglecting her when next she saw my parents. Then I thought, better still, I'd ask her to lunch. She couldn't make it any more ludicrous than the way it was shaping up to be.

Aunt Dorothy was in a black humour when I called. Her three bridge friends had forgotten her birthday, she always remembered *their* birthdays, but oh no, they hadn't said a thing about celebrating it.

'Why don't you return good for evil, Aunt Dorothy, and ask them all to lunch at my house,' I suggested. I was now completely insane, I realised. Aunt Dorothy liked the idea a lot. She would embarrass them, humiliate them even, make them feel ashamed.

'What can I bring with me for lunch, dear?' she asked in tones that almost approached civility. I thought for a moment. I hadn't even planned what we were going to eat but we'd need a salad. I suggested it.

'For five?' Aunt Dorothy asked.

'No, for twelve actually,' I said apologetically.

'You can't seat twelve,' she snapped.

'We'll eat in the garden,' I said. And hung up.

I did a count, we had now reached eleven. Only one more. Larry the security man came in. He was about to lock the place up for the weekend. So naturally I invited him to lunch and naturally he said he'd love to, and that he'd come over early in his van with some planks and set up a table in the garden.

So there was my party.

I went home by a bookshop where I looked up a book on very easy entertaining. On Saturday I went shopping and bought three cheap tablecloths, packets of crisps and dips, some brightly coloured balloons as well as the ingredients for an Easy Chicken Pie and an Easy Vegetarian Special. That and the Greek desserts, Aunt Dorothy's salad and Alan's wine should cover everyone.

I slept well on Saturday night and never thought at all about my colleagues on their patio in Rossmore, grilling their lamb chops and sausages amongst the mosquitoes and visiting walking statues in the woods.

Larry, true to his word, was round with the wooden planks, and he had put half a dozen folding chairs in the back of his van, borrowed from the office penthouse. I had no seating plan: let them sit where they liked.

At half past twelve I wondered whether any of them would come. At one o'clock sharp they all arrived and Alan had brought enough wine for half the neighbourhood. There was a roar of conversation from the moment they came in.

Magda and Eleni had brought olives as well as dessert.

Alan's son Harry and his two friends turned out to be hugely interested in money. 'How much will you pay us to be waiters?' they asked as soon as they arrived.

I looked at Alan helplessly. 'They're worth two Euro each, no more,' he said.

'Five,' I said, and then I settled back while they did all the work.

Aunt Dorothy lorded it over her friends very happily. 'Oh, Barbara has a wide circle of acquaintances,' she said proudly, and wept a little tear when I got everyone to sing 'Happy Birthday' to her.

Magda said that Eleni had always needed a strong helpful man like Larry and did everything to throw them together. Harry and his friends finished the washing up and wondered, would they be paid for weeding the flower beds.

'One Euro each,' Alan said.

'Three Euro each,' I said.

Magda and Eleni taught Larry to do a Zorba dance; Aunt Dorothy and her friends all sang 'Just a Song at Twilight'.

Alan said to me, 'You know, I always fancied you a bit but I thought you were rather toffee-nosed. I never in a million years thought you were like this. You are absolutely wonderful.'

So I forgot about the people who hadn't invited me to grill things on a patio on a holiday that I had more or less set up for them, and Alan forgot about his ex.

And I think somebody took some pictures but it didn't really matter. Because no one would ever forget the day.

Part 2 – Someone from Dad's Office

Lots of people at school have parents who are divorced. Well, it stands to reason, you don't always want the same thing all the time, do you? I mean, I don't like the things I liked when I was seven, not now that I'm ten. Those awful PlayStations that I liked then, well, of course they were fine then, but they are so boring now.

So I quite see why Mum and Dad got tired of each other and wanted different things. It's nothing personal. Or at least it shouldn't be. But that's not the way it is in this family. Mum never stops talking about how mean Dad is, how he keeps us in poverty.

I don't think we are in poverty but it doesn't do to say that so I don't say anything really.

Dad is always saying to me that that mother of mine will have us all in the workhouse before long and that can't be true either because Dad drives a big car and he is very high up in his office, but it's not a good idea to say that we don't look like the workhouse people you see pictures of in Charles Dickens' time. So I say nothing about that either.

They both keep telling me that they love me. Too much really.

Mum says, '. . . the one thing that can be said about that monument to selfishness is that he gave me you, Harry.'

Dad says, '. . . if there's one thing to be said about that dizzy self-obsessed woman it's that she gave me a fine son.'

I don't know why they think that, because I am always the problem, or the worry, or the person to be parked here or collected there.

George doesn't see his father at all, so he says I'm lucky compared to him. Wes says that his family are rowing all the time and we are both lucky compared to him. So obviously the whole family thing isn't really meant to work.

Anyway Mum has a new fellow. He's awful, of course, trying to be nice to me and pretending to be interested in me when he isn't a bit. His name is Kent, he's not from Kent in England or anything. Kent is what he is called.

George says that Kent has a very expensive car and so he must be loaded and that we should make as much money from him as possible while he lasts. He said I should say that I was saving for a new iPod, or a mobile phone, or computer updates. I should concentrate on something that sounded as if

I would get myself out of his hair and Kent would be likely to hand over a tenner or whatever.

I was nervous at first but it worked like a dream. I kept my part of the bargain: I stayed out of his way and was very polite to him when I was in his company. Mum asked me, did I like him and I opened my eyes very wide, which is a good thing to do if you're telling something not exactly true, and I said I thought Kent was just fine and Mum said I was a good son, a very good son indeed, and her eyes got watery so I took myself off.

George says that mothers go ahead and marry these kind of people anyway whether we like them or not, his mother certainly had. So George says, make life easy on yourself, say he's the greatest thing since sliced bread and make sure that he keeps contributing to various projects. Wes said that he would just love his parents to split up and he'd have someone to get him an MP3 player.

So anyway for this Bank Holiday we were going to work on Kent to take all three of us to a theme park. There were plenty of things for old folks to do there like sitting in restaurants and we could go on the rides. I had the spiel all ready to give him when suddenly he said to me in a very serious voice that he was going to take my mother away for a long weekend to a beautiful hotel by a huge whitethorn wood. I didn't want to go to a beautiful hotel by a wood. Not one bit. But I reminded myself to be very polite. I could hear George's voice as clearly as if he were standing beside me hissing warnings into my ear.

'Won't it be very expensive for you if we all come – Wes, George and me?' I asked.

A sort of shudder went over his face at the thought of taking us all to a beautiful hotel by a river and the Whitethorn Woods.

'Well, no, Harry, this is it, I'm going to take your mother by herself; I want to ask her a question, you see.'

I explained that she was in the kitchen and he could go out and ask her the question now, but no, it was a question that needed to be asked in the proper setting. I could see the theme park fading into the distance, theme parks weren't a place you could ask a question, apparently.

But I had invited Wes and George to stay. That had to be sorted. Was there any hope that they'd let us stay on our own? No, apparently that wasn't on. We were to go to Dad.

'But it's not his weekend,' I began.

'It will be,' Kent said.

From the kitchen I could hear Mum screaming down the phone. 'You were always selfish, Alan, that was never in dispute but unable to take your own son for a bonus weekend – most men would be delighted, but not you. It doesn't *matter* where I am going or with whom. I am not married to you, Alan Black, something I thank the Living God for every day of my life. Marriage is something that leaves me very cold indeed. So listen well. Harry and his friends will be dropped at your house on Friday. It doesn't matter about there being enough beds, they have sleeping bags, and they *must* have proper food, not takeaways, do you hear me . . .'

Half the neighbourhood must have heard her.

Kent was hovering nervously waiting for Mum to finish. He looked embarrassed. 'It's all right, Kent, they go on that way, it isn't important,' I explained.

'I don't like that – she says marriage leaves her cold. I don't like it one bit,' he said in a worried voice. I thought I understood about the holiday in the one-horse town called Rossmore.

I thought about it for a bit. He was better than any of the others.

'Oh, that's just marriage to Dad, I'd say. I don't think she's against it in general.' I nodded wisely as if I understood the problems of the world.

'It's just that Rossmore in this weather would be a perfect place – I don't want to say anything inappropriate.' He was biting his lip.

'Rossmore? Is that the place they have the big row about a road going through some woods? The teacher at school made us have a debate about it: some of us were to be for the road, some against it . . .' I was only saying this to distract him, but it seemed to please him.

'Yes, there was a big documentary about it on television. Your mother said it was a romantic place and I was hoping . . .'

'Okay, Kent, go on hoping, I'm sure it will all be fine,' I said cheerfully. 'Enjoy the hotel and the woods and the question and all that. Compared to us you'll have a great time. I'll have my dad grizzling and complaining from now until Tuesday,' I said with a real hangdog expression.

Kent gave me twenty Euro out of pure guilt to spend on anything I wanted.

When we arrived at Dad's house I thought Dad looked very grey and old and tired compared to Kent. Kent has a sort of permanent suntan and Dad looked as if someone had run over him with a garden roller. He cooked a chicken and we had frozen peas.

'It says *fresh* frozen peas on the packet,' he said defensively and we all said it was fine.

There was an apple tart, which he said was home-made at the local bakery, and ice cream.

Next day he agreed he would take us to the theme park.

'Do you have any current squeeze that you could bring to entertain *you*, Mr Black?' Wes asked politely.

'Current what?' Dad asked, mystified.

'Squeeze. Female companion is what Wes meant,' George explained.

'No, no, indeed,' my father said, embarrassed.

'Never mind – you might find one there,' Wes consoled him.

We didn't push Dad for as much money as we would have Kent but he was reasonably generous and of course I did have Kent's unexpected money so we had a great day.

Then on the Sunday it turned out that we had to go to lunch with someone from Dad's office. I asked, did he have a big house, this man, and Dad said it was a woman. Wes and George exchanged knowing glances. But I knew they were barking up the wrong tree. Dad goes off to work and comes back and fusses, and fights with Mum on the phone. Dad doesn't have lady friends. It must be business.

We wondered, might we skip the lunch, but it seemed that we mightn't. We asked, had this woman any children, would there be babes there, and Dad said he didn't know who would be there but he gravely doubted that there would be babes. So we set out without much hope.

Dad was bringing all the wine, boxes of it. They must be a fairly drinky crowd, we thought. It didn't bode well when we got there and saw a terribly old woman called Dorothy sitting on a chair. She had a face like a handbag that kept snapping open and shut and she had other old people beside her all full of disapproval. Then there were two foreign people putting out dishes of olives and a man called Larry laying out chairs who kept saying, 'Oh my God, Mr Black is here, he'll see the chairs.' I mean, why shouldn't my father have seen the chairs like everyone else? Where was he going to sit? Really, it couldn't have been a more crazy crowd.

Dad was busy setting up a bar with Larry on a side-table while Larry kept saying, over and over, that it was a surprise to see Mr Black.

'How are we going to be polite here all day?' I asked George who was very wise about the ways things should be done.

'We'd better find the hostess and start with her,' George said.

She was in the kitchen. Much younger than any-one else we'd seen but still old, if you know what I mean. She looked worried. Her name was Barbara.

'We'd like to help,' George said.

'We're not expensive,' Wes added.

'I thought you were guests,' Barbara said, con-fused.

'What my friends meant was that of course we are guests and delighted to be here but we won-dered, would you like any help with the waiting and serving, we're quite experienced in fact.' I saw George making awful faces at me but I didn't understand: I thought he was urging me on. 'We've done quite a few functions actually . . .' I went on. And then I realised my father was in the room.

'Illegally, I suppose,' he said.

'Informally, Mr Black,' George corrected.

'Not more than two Euro each then, and they have to work properly,' Dad said. A rate of five was suggested by Barbara, who said we would have to work like slaves. Dad went out to pour wine for people and we got our instructions.

We were to make a terrific fuss of that woman who sat upright in the chair. We were to tell her that this party was in her honour and to call her Aunt Dorothy.

'But she's not our aunt,' George said logically.

'I know, George, but it's what's called a courtesy title,' Barbara said. Which explained nothing.

'But she wouldn't want *Wes* to call her aunt, would she?' I wanted to get this clear, Wes was black.

Barbara seemed not to have noticed this or to think it was irrelevant.

'I don't exactly look like her nephew,' Wes said.

'None of you are her nephews. I told you it was a courtesy title. Now are you going to argue everything down to the bone or are you going to help?'

Aunt Dorothy said that we were extraordinarily nice, helpful boys and compared to the youth of today we were a delightful exception. Wes said that it was our privilege to be at this party and to get to know the guest of honour, and all Aunt Dorothy's awful friends sort of twittered with envy and rage at this. Back in the kitchen I reported all this to Barbara and asked, was there anything else that needed sorting, and she wondered, could I try to tell Magda and Eleni that we were the paid help and they weren't.

'Why do they think they are doing it?' I asked resentfully.

'Because people are mad, Harry, most of them stark raving mad. You'll realise that when you're older.'

'I realise it now,' I said and she laughed with me like a friend.

I went off to deal with these two mad women from Greece or wherever, and I sat them down and filled their glasses.

'You no work today, we work,' I said several times until I thought they understood.

George found an atlas and asked them to show us where they lived in Cyprus and apparently nobody had ever asked them this before and they were delighted. It turned out that nobody was vegetarian and Barbara seemed upset by this because she assumed that half the guests would be but I said we should ladle a bit of both dishes on every plate and that would mean plenty for everyone and she was very pleased.

'You're a complete treasure,' she said. 'What happened that your mother couldn't have you this weekend? I'm very glad about it by the way, but I just wondered.'

'She's gone to a place called Rossmore to be asked a question by Kent,' I explained. 'I don't know what the question is but it has to be asked by a river and a wood, it seems.'

She nodded as if she understood.

'He might be asking her to marry him,' she suggested. 'That's the kind of thing you might ask by a river.'

'It did cross my mind that it might be that, but if that's all it is, couldn't he have asked her in the kitchen at home?' I said. I was thinking that she was totally right – everyone was getting madder by the moment.

'Harry, would you do one more thing for me, could you tell Larry that Mr Black, I mean your dad, wouldn't recognise those chairs if they came up and bit him in the face – tell him to stop fussing.'

'It's hard to tell a grown-up to stop fussing,' I said. 'I've been trying to tell my dad to stop fussing for years and he won't and he says that it's impudence on my part even to say it.'

'All right, you keep chopping parsley and sprinkle it over these plates and I'll talk to Larry, while I'm getting them to sit down.'

Wes and George came into the kitchen. 'They're all mad,' Wes said.

'They're meant to be mad, she knows that, she talked about it. Stop eating that parsley,' I said.

'Maybe they're from a home.' George was thoughtful.

'What are we all doing here, and your dad, then?' Wes wanted to know.

It was unanswerable.

And the chicken pie was very good indeed, everyone praised it and said the sauce was delicious, and Barbara said that it was nothing really. I knew it was all cans of mushroom soup, a half-bottle of wine and frozen pastry because I had been helping her tie up the rubbish. But I said nothing. Dad ran round filling people's glasses and suggesting that he and Larry take off their jackets if the ladies didn't mind. Larry had stopped fussing and started fancying one of the Cypriot ladies. Aunt Dorothy had relaxed greatly and was telling everyone that there were no songs like the old songs. And when we were clearing the pudding plates away, George, who always says the right thing, said to Barbara that it was going very well and that she must be pleased with herself.

He reported that she took him by the lapels and for an awful sickening moment he thought she was going to kiss him so he shouted at her that the flower beds were in a terrible state and for an extra few Euro we would weed them for her. And then she released him and the deal was done.

Wes said that of course all these people must be from some kind of a home, Barbara included, and that my father was very decent to have spent the day looking after them. But I saw Dad sitting at the table in his short sleeves, singing 'Mad Dogs and Englishmen Go Out in the Midday Sun', and somehow I didn't *think* the whole thing was some massive work of charity.

Then the mad women began Greek dancing and Aunt Dorothy started singing old songs with her friends joining in the chorus, and we were all digging the flower beds with trowels and hoes that Barbara found for us. It was all pretty terrible, to be honest.

But we had eaten a good lunch and drunk all the dregs of people's white wine before they went on to red wine, and we were making a decent income out of the whole day. Dad wasn't fussing a bit and this woman, who apparently is called Bar, not Barbara, was very nice. She was drunk as all get out, of course, but very pleasant. Do you know, I saw her holding Dad's hand as he began another song, 'Bye Bye, Miss American Pie', and everyone joined in the chorus.

I said to Wes that Mum would never believe it.

'She won't be interested,' Wes said. That was odd because she was always interested in what Dad, or 'that bastard Alan' as she called him, did or said.

'Not now that she has had the question asked,' George explained. And I felt terrific for some reason. It might have to do with all the ends of white wine we had drunk. Or how we had washed up very well and left the kitchen tidy *and* done the flower beds. But I think the others might have been right all along about Bar being Dad's squeeze.

And that would be absolutely fine with me.

CHAPTER 7

The Last Word

Part 1 – Dr Dermot

I know everyone in the place, that's a fair enough thing to say. If they're thirty-five or under, then I delivered them into the world, and if they're any other age I listened to their chests and coughs and cured their measles and mumps, sewed up their torn ears, took glass out of their cut knees.

Doon is only a small place, twenty miles from Rossmore, along a narrow, bumpy road, but we don't need to go into the big town much. We have everything we want here, and it's just a small quiet country place where I know the story of every man, woman and child.

I've closed the eyes of their mothers and fathers and grandparents, I've told them good news and bad news, I've found the words that others don't find. These people owe me, for God's sake. That's why I was so betrayed and let down over the way they all flocked to this new young doctor.

Dr Jimmy White.

A young whippersnapper who called me Dermot as soon as look at me. Everyone here calls me Dr Dermot but, oh no, that's not good enough for Dr Jimmy White. Oh, very eager and anxious to please he is, running here and there. Of course he does house calls any time of the day and the night, and of course he has a mobile phone so you can find him anywhere. And he's thorough, sending people half-way across the country for scans, blood tests for everything, X-rays. These are simple people, they think that's a kind of magic in itself.

Even the hospital in Rossmore isn't good enough for Dr Jimmy White. Oh, no, he sends them to specialists, to teaching hospitals in Dublin, no less. Rather than relying on years of experience, and someone who has known them inside and out for generations.

Like myself.

Not that I let them see I was upset or anything. No indeed. I always spoke well of Dr Jimmy White. Very bright young man, I said, plays it by the book and, indeed, consults his medical books, he won't have to do that when he's older and more experienced, but very thorough, of course, always checking things out when he's not sure.

People thought I liked and admired him while I managed to sow the seeds of doubt, like why he was checking books, getting second opinions, sending blood to be tested and people to have scans.

There was an over-talkative American man called Chester Kovac – staying in the hotel, must have been made of money. His grandfather was called O'Neill, came from round here once, not that anyone remembers him or anything. Sure, the country's coming down with O'Neills. I told him several times that the young doctor had to learn his trade somewhere, but in a way it was hard to see him make his mistakes on the people of this parish. Chester said, surely he had to be a qualified medical man and I said yes, but that there was qualified and there was experienced. Chester nodded a lot as if the idea had sunk in.

Then he told me he was buying land in Doon and going to build. He wanted my advice about what kind of services this little town needed. What were we lacking, where were the gaps . . . He had a real over-concerned look on his face. It would sicken you. All that kind of sensitive stuff that has no place here. I pretended to be interested, you know, the way you have to in a small place like this. Some rambling on about social housing, affordable housing. You know the kind of thing they go on with, moaning over the past, saying that if his poor grandfather had only owned a house, then he wouldn't have had to emigrate.

I nodded and sipped my pint. And I thought to myself, if his grandfather hadn't got up off his arse and gone out to somewhere where he could find a living, Chester wouldn't be wearing designer suits and handmade shoes. But better not to say that. Let them live their dream. Oh and he was going to build a hall, and a centre of some sort. Here in Doon, no less! Terrific, I used to say to him, before going back to the subject of Dr White and the gaps in his learning.

For a while my way of coping with my rival worked and there was enough business for both of us. Well, for me anyway. But then things took a turn for the worse.

It was all to do with that stupid woman, Maggie Kiernan, who was having a baby, and let me tell you there was no baby ever born in the world except to Maggie. Her pregnancy was endless, no mammoth could have had a longer gestation period. She was in twice a week, she was sick and then she wasn't sick, the baby was moving – was that natural? or it wasn't moving – did that mean it was dead? What she needed was a private team, gynaecologists, obstetricians, all in a waiting room in her house.

Three weeks before she was due, she rang at two in the morning to say that the baby was arriving. So I told her to have a nice cup of tea and we'd talk about it in the morning. She kept on and on that the baby was definitely coming and wouldn't I come out. Four miles out, halfway up a mountain! Was she mad? I was soothing but she just slammed down the phone.

It wasn't until halfway through the next morning I heard the story: she called Dr Jimmy White and of course he went out there. And wouldn't you know?

The child was half born and there were complications and he got an ambulance up that mountainy road and if he hadn't accompanied her to Accident and Emergency in Rossmore, then the baby would have died, and Maggie would have died, and half the population hereabouts would have died out of sympathy.

I must have heard it fifteen times that morning, poor Maggie Kiernan and how frightened she must have been, and was not it the mercy of God that young Dr White had been able to attend her. And always the unspoken words that I had let Maggie Kiernan down.

I was annoyed of course, but I didn't show it: instead I showered praise on Dr Jimmy White and concern about Maggie, and said several times that babies had minds of their own and wouldn't life be easy if they'd only let us know. I never explained, never apologised. And I thought that eventually the message was getting over to them. I was still their wise, good Dr Dermot.

Now, every Saturday at lunchtime, Hannah Harty, a single lady, comes to do the books for me. She is a qualified bookkeeper, the soul of discretion, and does books for a lot of people in town. Just five Saturdays after all Maggie Kiernan's shenanigans, Hannah cleared her throat and told me straight out that I was losing a great many patients to the new young Dr White. And therefore a fair amount of income.

At first I didn't believe her. Hannah has always

been a bit of a gloom merchant. Word was that she had set her cap at me, long, long ago. But I don't think that can be true.

I certainly never gave her any encouragement. I had looked after her old mother for years. Well, Hannah actually looked after her old mother, but I would call and reassure them a lot, and if they were eating a supper I was made part of it.

I myself had never married. I had my heart set on a woman once but she told me I was too easy going, and that she could never settle down with a small-town doctor. Well, I am who I am. I'm not going to change for anyone, so I spent little time thinking back on her and what she had said.

I listened carefully to Hannah as she spoke and, indeed, less than half an hour after she had told me about our takings being down, I had begun to take action.

I called on the Foley family for a chat. Their old father was on his last legs; he wouldn't last much longer. But I was full of cheer about him, said he had the heart and constitution of a lion and that he was in fine fettle. When I left them the Foleys all felt vastly cheered. And I told myself as I so often do that *this* is what a doctor is meant to do, cheer people, buoy them up, carry them along. Not frighten the wits out of them with statistics and tests and scans.

On my way home I met the young Dr White.

'All that business about Maggie Kiernan . . .' he began awkwardly.

'Yes?' My voice was cold.

'Well, I wouldn't want you to think I was muscling in on your territory or anything like that . . .' he said, shifting from foot to foot.

'Do you feel you were?' I was still icy.

'Well, technically of course she is your patient, but I had to decide whether it was an emergency or not. And, well, I decided it was.'

'So you feel you did the right thing, Dr White?'

'I do wish you'd call me Jim, I call you Dermot.'

'I know, I've noticed,' I said with one of my smiles.

'There's plenty of work for both of us, Dermot,' he said with a familiar kind of leer. 'Neither of us will go hungry in this place.'

'I'm very sure of that, Dr White,' I said and went on my way.

When I got back home I sat and thought further and deeper. Hannah Harty telephoned and suggested that she bring me over a steak and kidney pie she had made. Since her mother died she had not asked me to supper in her house, which I missed, especially at weekends, which can get lonely.

I do have a housekeeper, a weary-looking woman, but she just keeps the place clean, washes and irons. She shops, of course, and prepares the vegetables but there's never anything tasty like Hannah makes. I said that I'd be honoured to eat the pie with her and would produce a bottle of claret. When Hannah came in bearing her dishes of food it was clear that she had been to the hairdresser since we had met in the morning. She was wearing a smart white blouse and a cameo brooch. She had even put on make-up, which was most unusual.

Could it possibly be true that she still had notions about the two of us?

Best thing possible was to ignore all the finery in case that was what was at the back of it all. No point in complimenting her or anything. That would be just asking for trouble. We talked about the famous Rossmore bypass and would it ever happen. It had been talked about for years. Would it make any difference to our little quiet backwater, or would they just ignore our bumpy little road to Rossmore? Nobody seemed to know.

We had a pleasant meal and since Hannah had brought a plate of rather good cheeses I opened a second bottle of wine.

'What in God's earth are you going to do about young Dr White, Dermot?' she asked me straight out. Her face was anxious. She really cared what was going to happen to me when most of the town had deserted and gone to the opposition. I reached forward and patted her hand.

'I wouldn't worry at all, Hannah my dear,' I re-assured her. 'It's always important to stay calm in a situation like this and wait until it all blows over.'

'But it might not blow over, Dermot. You know, I work in several different establishments around the place, and a lot of them are moving. Mr Brown in the bank is going to consult Dr White because of his father's pneumonia. Mr Kenny the solicitor is worried about his mother not being able to walk properly and he thinks young Dr White might get her some better drugs, newer, modern things. You can't just sit here, Dermot, and watch all your hard work setting up this practice trickle away into the ground.' She looked really upset on my behalf. Or maybe on her own behalf if she really saw a future with me.

'No, indeed, I won't sit here and watch, Hannah. I was thinking actually that I might take a little holiday.'

'A holiday? Now? In the middle of this crisis? Dermot, you must be going barking mad,' she gasped.

But I refused to respond or react. Just smiled at her.

'I know what I'm doing, Hannah,' I said over and over.

And over the next week I made several house calls. I decided that old man Foley had about two weeks to live; that Mr Kenny's mother should be allowed to live out her last months peacefully without any new medication, which would only unsettle her; that Mr Brown's father was entering his last bout of pneumonia, which would take him peacefully away from this world.

Then I announced that I was taking a little holiday. I encouraged the Browns, the Foleys and the Kennys to attend that nice young Dr White while I was away. No, of *course* I didn't mind, what was life about except give and take, and the young man was extremely well qualified. He would look after them perfectly.

Then I put my golf clubs into the back of the car and drove a hundred and fifty miles away to a nice quiet hotel by the sea. It was easy to find a four-ball so I played eighteen holes a day.

Every night I played bridge in the hotel lounge and at breakfast each morning, with my second cup of tea, I turned the pages to the Deaths column.

First I read of the death of old man Foley, then of Mrs Kenny, and finally of Mr Brown. I said a swift goodbye to my new golfing and bridge friends and drove straight back home to Doon.

I called on the homes of the bereaved, shaking my head in bewilderment over their great losses. I said I couldn't understand it – old man Foley had been in great form when I left, there had been plenty of life in him still; and in Mrs Kenny and Mr Brown. How sad and ironical that they should all die when I, who had known them for so much of their lives, was far away. Then I would shake my wise old head again and say it was a total mystery.

It didn't take long. In fact it all happened much quicker than I had expected. People began to talk.

They said that it was very odd that three perfectly well people had died during the ten days that Dr Dermot was on holiday. They said it was a pity to be hasty and to run to the new instead of staying with the tried and tested. With the man who had known them young, old, well and sick, all their lives. Little by little they came back to me, even those who had asked for their medical records to take to Dr White. Some of them had been annoyed about the scrappy nature of the records and had not accepted that it was all in my head. I knew which child had had mumps and which had had measles, for heaven's sake. No need for computers and print-outs in my case.

I was very generous, talking to them. I showed no hurt, not even a trace of sulking in my face. They were all so relieved that I was taking them back, they wanted to denounce Dr White. But here again I was noble. I wouldn't hear a word against the boy. I called him a boy, as I smiled about him forgiv-ingly, and said he was very young and that he had to make his mistakes somewhere. They marvelled at my great generosity.

He called on me before he left town, Dr White did. A courtesy call, he said, to tell me that he was moving on. I knew already but I pretended to be sur-prised. I wished him well and said I would be sorry to lose him as a colleague.

'You'll find somewhere more suitable,' I said.

'Yes, I'm sure I will,' he said.

'And you have a nice manner, which is what it's all about,' I added to praise him.

'Which is what *some* of it's about, certainly, Dermot,' he said.

I winced as I did every time he was familiar like that. But I don't think it showed. I offered him a drink but he refused.

'It won't last, of course, Dermot, it can't. Would you like a little bit of advice from me before I leave?'

To humour him I said that I would. After all I had

run him out of town. I could afford to be gracious.

'When the next young fellow comes in, Dermot, make him your partner, sell this house and take a room in Chester's clinic, go into semi-retirement, marry Hannah Harty, go and live in that big house of hers. It's better that way than a big malpractice suit or one of your old friends thinking you had been negligent.'

He stood up, impudent young pup, and left without looking back.

I thought for a little while about what he had said. There was no wisdom in it. None at all. And what was this that he was babbling about – Chester's clinic? Chester had been organising some kind of a medical centre, a ludicrous place with expensive machinery where people could waste time and money. They were even going to have rooms for aromatherapy or some kind of New Age nonsense. And what a mad time he had chosen to do it! Just when a new road would come to take the patients straight into Rossmore from here. As a project, it was doomed before it even began. That was nothing for me to worry about.

People round here had their feet on the ground, they wouldn't go for this kind of nonsense all in the name of Danny O'Neill, some loser whom none of them could remember. But one thing was definitely clear and was much more important: my name was definitely up with poor Hannah Harty's. That was something that must be nipped in the bud. She was meant to be making me a fancy salmon dish in pastry tomorrow. Better ring her now and tell her I wasn't free.

Everything was going so well now, it would be a pity to complicate things.

Part 2 – Chester's Plan

I had always promised my Irish grandpa Danny O'Neill that I would go to Ireland but I didn't make it while he was alive. He used to tell tales of his home in Doon, which was some miles from Rossmore. And of the huge Whitethorn Woods and how there was a holy well there where miracles had happened. But somehow I never got to Ireland when he was alive. There was too much else to do like get an education, and make a living.

My own father, Mark Kovac from Poland, had been a carpenter but he had TB and was never strong, and so as the eldest I had to support the family. I used to say to my mom that life would have been a bit easier if they hadn't felt it necessary to have nine children. But she only laughed and asked which of them would I send back? We worked hard, got good grades at school, and we each got a job from the moment we were high enough to stack shelves in a supermarket or collect cardboard and fold it in neat piles.

And I had a bit of luck and met a banking guy who offered me money to start my own building contractor's business, and then I was able to give jobs to all the brothers and sisters, and I put my father on the board. He was so delighted to see 'Mark Kovac & Family Building Contractors' on the trucks.

I didn't need to put my own name on the company, I *knew* it was mine, and it looked more established somehow to have the father of the family on it anyway. Gave us credibility, a pedigree.

My father's people had all left a village in Poland that didn't exist any more but my mother's father went on and on about this lovely place in Ireland. So when I was fifty I decided to reward myself with three months' vacation.

I had never married. No time really. It sounds a bit hopeless, I suppose, but I never thought of it like that. I was too busy getting everything up and running in the business and now that was done I found I had left it a bit late. My brothers and sisters were all well married with children and so I had plenty of family life around me if I needed it.

But then my doctor said that I was suffering from hypertension and therefore should take it easy. After Grandpa died, and there was all the Irish music at his funeral and the chat about Rossmore and the woods and everything, I got thinking about his country and I decided it might be a good time to go to Ireland and have a rest there, away from the business.

But at the same time, since I wasn't a person who was used to doing nothing, I could investigate this idea I had of building a tribute to Grandpa O'Neill. Something that would show to the people of his native place that his life and his travelling to America had all been worthwhile.

Everyone thought this was a good idea, and they assured me that Mark Kovac & Family Building Contractors could manage to stagger along without me.

'And maybe you might even find an Irish colleen over there,' my mother said. I thought she'd have to be a fairly long-in-the-tooth colleen to fancy me, but I said nothing like that. Over the years I got used to smiling at people and agreeing with them rather than having to have the last word. The last word isn't all that important really.

And so I came here to my grandpa Danny O'Neill's place. A very good place to take it easy. Nobody in Doon remembered my grandpa, which was disappointing.

They knew the line of little cottages he came from but these had all been long knocked down because they had fallen into disrepair. And it was all so long ago, and O'Neill was a very common name in Ireland anyway.

So I decided that he *would* be remembered. I would see to this. I would make a monument to him, but not something vain, something that would be of great use in his home town. I asked around for suggestions. They were many and varied. People thought of a little theatre. Or an art gallery. Or maybe a small park where the children could play and the old people sit in the evening. Or a church hall or a museum. There were as many ideas as there were people offering them.

One old lady said I should go to pray at the well in the woods outside Rossmore and then I would see as clear as daylight what I should do. So I drove in and parked my car near the edge of the woods and went in. I met a big friendly dog that accompanied me and seemed to know his way to the well as he made the correct turning at every little wooden signpost. Then he sat outside respectfully while I went into the damp dark cave.

The well was extraordinary. That was the only word. I'm as religious as the next man, I mean, as the son of an Irish Catholic mother and a Polish Catholic father, I wouldn't have much chance of escaping it, would I? But this was beyond anything I had ever seen.

People had put their petitions on the walls of the cave for all to see, they had left children's tiny shoes and socks with notes attached, praying for a recovery from rheumatic fever, or rosary beads with notes begging for the recovery of a beloved mother.

It was grotesque in many ways and yet so touching in others. Such a collection of frail hopes all gathered in one little space. It didn't give me any sense of well-being, holiness. There was no wisdom coming towards me from that statue. Instead I felt uneasy and wanted to be away from there. Yet as I came out I found the big dog again – a kind of sheepdog or a collie, I guess; he had been waiting for me as if I were his long-lost friend. I scratched his ears and walked back through the woods deep in thought.

Then an idea formed in my mind.

I would build a health centre so that the people of this area wouldn't have to be on their knees in this cold wet place praying to a saint who was two thousand years dead that a cure would be found for a loved one. Maybe, I thought to myself, this is the way the well worked: you got your problem solved once you left it.

The dog trotted along beside me happily.

He was never going to leave me now.

I took him to the nearest Garda station. They looked at him thoughtfully. He had no collar and he wasn't well kept. Someone had brought him to lose him in the woods.

I was shocked.

A lovely, friendly dog like that.

'You might give him a home yourself?' suggested the young Garda.

'Come on then,' I said to the dog and he leaped eagerly into the car.

I decided to call him Zloty. It was the old Polish currency. He answered so readily that you'd think it was his original name.

Back home again in Doon, I was determined that the place would have some kind of medical centre. If anyone needed specialist treatment, or a scan, or an X-ray, they had to take the bumpy road into Rossmore. Yes, I had heard all about this bypass road that was meant to be built. But it could all be just dreams for the next decades. And anyway in Rossmore they didn't have all the facilities that patients needed – sometimes they had to make the long journey to Dublin, adding to their stress and strain.

Wouldn't it be great to have all these opportunities on their doorstep?

The people in this place were all very nice and easy to talk to. I stayed in the local hotel, and Zloty slept in a big outhouse. I met Ciaran Brown from the bank, and Sean Kenny the local attorney, and the Foley family, and Maggie Kiernan who told everyone how desperately she wanted to have a baby and eventually she did. There was a very lady-like woman, Hannah Harty, who was a bookkeeper and the soul of discretion in a very gossip-prone place. So when I bought a plot of land through Sean Kenny, he suggested that I should ask Hannah to look after the paperwork for me, and nobody would know my business.

And there were two doctors in the town, a very crabby sort of fellow, Dermot, and a much younger smarter lad called Jimmy White. Unfortunately I had registered with Dr Dermot before Jimmy White came to town so I had to stick with him. He was a slow, lazy guy, just looked at my prescribed medication and told me to continue with it. Then he went off on a vacation. After a bit I felt short of breath. I consulted Jimmy White who sent me for a stress test and an ultrasound. And a heart specialist changed my beta blockers and I was fine again.

That was a bad time for everyone. Old man Foley died, then Sean Kenny's mother and Ciaran Brown's father died, all within ten days. We had a path worn to the churchyard for funerals.

Poor Jimmy White was distraught.

'It would have to happen on my watch,' he confided to me one night. 'The people here think that the sun shines out of Dermot's arse and that all those old people wouldn't have died if he had been here.'

'But that's impossible,' I said. 'I mean, they were old and frail, their time had come.'

'Tell that to the Foleys, the Browns and the Kennys,' he said glumly.

'That was certainly bad timing,' I sympathised.

'Yeah, or maybe – as I think in my more paranoid moments – it was planned,' he suggested.

I gave him a look and Jimmy White said hastily that no, of course it wasn't possible, even Dr Dermot couldn't have killed them off by voodoo from his vacation. I thought about it myself for a while. Maybe that weaselish little doctor did actually wait until all those old folk were going to take their last journeys.

Was I becoming as paranoid as Jimmy?

Anyway I had plenty to keep me occupied. I had a building firm in Ireland, which was fairly relaxed. Very relaxed. Finn Ferguson often said that when God made time he made plenty of it. Planning permissions were a nightmare; assembling a team was very different from back home. Everyone seemed to be running several jobs in tandem, I would sigh to that nice Hannah Harty sometimes, and she was always very positive and full of practical advice.

Perhaps I should tell the foreman Finn Ferguson that if his wife liked to go to America on a shopping trip, my sisters would look after her and take her to the right stores. It worked like a dream and the woman came back not only with three suitcases of merchandise but with the news that Mark Kovac & Family Building Contractors were huge in the USA. Finn, the foreman, stopped treating me just as bumbling old Chester and called me sir after that. He still would have a beer with me now and then, and often brought a bone for Zloty as well. He would tell me of his worries about the new road that might or might not be built around Rossmore.

Once one of these huge firms got the contract for building the bypass and established themselves in the town of Rossmore, then a little company like Finn Ferguson's would be edged out of the jobs he already had. People would be seduced by big companies with huge earth movers and cranes, and his living would go down the plughole. I assured him that the thing to do was to specialise. To get a name for doing one kind of building very well.

When the Danny O'Neill Health Centre opened there would be a beautiful glossy brochure about it, which of course Finn could use to get himself more clients.

This galvanised Finn to take a less leisurely attitude to the building, I was very relieved to observe.

'You're a very decent skin, you know, Chester, I mean, sir,' he said. 'A lot of people say that about you. I heard Miss Harty telling Canon Cassidy when he came over here last week, she said you were the angel this place has always been looking out for.'

I liked Hannah and was disappointed that she seemed to fancy Dr Dermot. I asked her once if she had ever been in love, and she said no, but at the age of fifty-two she didn't think it was a luxury that might come her way. Her mother had always said that Dr Dermot would make a good catch and she had invested a lot of time in trying to realise that. But he was a man independent and set in his ways.

'Or a little selfish maybe?' I suggested. Wrong way to go, Chester.

Hannah Harty defended him. He had worked tirelessly for this place. Nobody could think he was selfish.

I said I was just an outsider; I didn't really know. But I did know. And he was selfish. I saw this more and more.

He would accept a drink from me in the hotel, but never buy the other half. I heard from Hannah how she would make him a steak and kidney pie or cook him a roast chicken because men were so hopeless. But the hotel had a perfectly good dining room where he could have entertained her and yet he never did. He was certainly very arrogant to young Jimmy White, so much so that the young man told me he would have to fold his tent and steal away. There was no living for him here.

Meanwhile my own plans were going ahead. Finn the building foreman now loved me like a brother and had recruited people from all over the country to build the Danny O'Neill Health Centre in Doon. It was growing like a mushroom every day before our eyes.

The people could hardly believe that there would be X-ray facilities and heart monitoring machines and a therapeutic swimming pool, all on their own door-steps, with a dozen or more treatment rooms planned for those who might want to rent them. It was the medicine of the future, the newspapers said. Already there had been enquiries from a dental practice, a Pilates class, and a yoga class, as well as several specialists interested in the possibility of having a clinic there twice a week. It was all a matter of bringing health care to the people rather than letting patients travel great distances, adding to their distress. I had been hoping Jimmy White would be part of it, but no, he was gone before it was up and running.

Hannah Harty had obviously handed over the bulk of my work to a firm of accountants by now but she still did my own personal books for me. I enjoyed our sessions together.

Finn would come for a Friday drink at the hotel around six and bring me up to date with what had happened during the week, then Hannah Harty would join us, countersign some cheques for Finn, and then she and I would have dinner.

She always had her hair nicely done at the beauty parlour for our meetings. She liked to talk about Dr Dermot and because I'm basically easy going I let her chatter on. She used to meet him on Saturday, so I think the fancy hairdo was really in his honour. But I noticed that there were more and more occasions when Dr Dermot wasn't going to be able to make their Saturday meeting.

He had a case conference about a patient. He had a golf game where they were depending on him. He had friends from overseas passing through. Friends who were never named or introduced.

Hannah had begun to wonder whether Dr Dermot might be avoiding her. I tutted and said surely not, which was just what she wanted to hear.

'And of course you still do his books for him?'

'Well, yes, but he just leaves the material there in a tray nowadays, he's not there himself.' She was very troubled.

'Maybe he's busy, on urgent cases.'

'Ah, Chester, you know Dermot,' she said. 'There's never anything very urgent. I think he's afraid our names are being linked.'

'But he should be proud of that surely?' I said.

She bit her lip, her eyes filled with tears and she shook her head sadly. I wanted to go down and take that annoying Dr Dermot by his thin shoulders and shake the life out of him. Why should he upset a decent woman like Hannah Harty? A woman that any normal man would be proud to escort around the place. And maybe share a life with.

And as that thought went across my mind, it was followed by another thought. Hannah Harty is much too good for that little weasel. She's the kind of woman that I personally would be happy to spend much more time with. I wondered why I hadn't seen this before.

I hoped that she didn't think she had confided too much in me and therefore could never learn to see me as a person. Well, I would never know unless I moved things on a bit. So I suggested that when she had picked up Dr Dermot's papers tomorrow, she and I might take a drive together.

'That's if he's not there of course,' Hannah said.

He wasn't there, so we drove off to see an old castle that had a waterfall in the grounds. And the next week we went to an art exhibition, and the week after that we went together to the wedding of Finn Ferguson's daughter. By now she was talking a lot less of Dr Dermot, and her name was most definitely up with mine or linked with mine or whatever the expression they used around here.

The three months' visit had turned into six months. And despite the best efforts of Finn the foreman, the building seemed to take for ever. I thought less and less about going back to Kovac's in America. Lots of things were keeping me here. The need to make our grandpa's name connected to a centre of excellence, a place that would be at the heart of the community he had loved so much and mourned so long in America.

I told my brothers that I probably saw this as a permanent position. They were pleased for me and assured me that they could well manage without me and they had long realised that I had found a life that involved me deeply back in Ireland. They didn't realise how much I was involved.

And they hadn't heard of Hannah Harty.

She was such a help to me in so many ways: she found a designer to do a restful decor for the Danny O'Neill Health Centre, she got Finn's new son-in-law to do the landscaping, she gave little dinner parties and invited Ciaran Brown from the bank and his wife, and Sean Kenny the lawyer, and his wife. And Maggie Kiernan and her husband when they could get a baby-sitter.

She did ask Dr Dermot from time to time but he never was free to accept. And then she didn't ask him any more.

One day he cornered me about the new centre. He hadn't changed at all, he was still very pleased with himself. He had heard it was going to be opened by a government minister. He was laughing at the thought. Hadn't they little to do with their time?

I reminded him that on several occasions I had invited him to take rooms there. I thought that if he had all the referral places on the premises, he finally might actually start sending people for the tests and scans they needed. But he hadn't listened.

He had even ridiculed the idea, saying that he had his own perfectly good surgery, thank you very much.

I explained that I would then be offering the rooms to other doctors, and he said he wished me luck taking money from eejits and losers. But of course I hadn't done that. The Danny O'Neill Health Centre was going to make sure that the people of this place got proper medical treatment, not like my grandpa and his great number of brothers and sisters scattered all over the globe, each one of them in poor health as they headed for a new life in a new land.

But it was only now, when he realised that a real live government minister was going to come and open the premises, that Dr Dermot showed any interest in it.

'I suppose that place will be a licence to print money for you, Chester,' he said to me with his usual sneer.

It was hardly worth arguing with him. He wasn't the kind of man who would understand that I had put my own money into it, invited others to contribute and gathered a team. The notion that I wasn't in it for a profit would have been beyond his grasp.

'Ah, you know the way it is.' I shrugged. I had learned a few of these meaningless phrases since coming to this land.

'I don't at all know the way it is, I'm the last to know anything around here,' the doctor snapped. 'And a patient told me this morning that you have notions about Miss Harty, that was news to me too.'

'I am a great admirer of Hannah Harty, that is true, your patient was not wrongly informed,' I said pompously.

'Well, as long as it's only admiring from afar, no one would quarrel with that.'

He was actually warning me off, staking his claim to a woman whom he had ignored and humiliated. I felt bile rise in my throat. But I had got as far as this in life by keeping my temper. I wouldn't risk everything now. And I realised that I really did feel a primeval rage against this man as a rival.

But I have seen too many people lose things over rage. I would not give anger its head.

'I have to go now, Dr Dermot,' I said in a voice that I knew sounded choked.

He smiled his superior and hugely irritating smile. 'Well, sure you do,' he said raising his glass at me. 'Sure you do.'

I walked across the square shaking. Zloty came with me to keep me company or to give me courage – I didn't know which. I had never felt so hostile to a man before. Not ever. So that meant that I had never felt so strongly about a woman either. But I had no idea whether she felt anything remotely similar. Calm, gentle, ladylike Hannah, maybe she thought of me just as a pleasant acquaintance.

What a poor specimen of a man I must be. No idea whether this woman liked me, even a little bit.

I found myself walking straight towards the elegant ivy-covered house where she lived alone. Her grandparents would have lived in that house when my poor grandpa was packing his few belongings and leaving the wretched hovel that would now be a tiny part of the Danny O'Neill Health Centre.

She was surprised to see me. I had never called unannounced before. But she welcomed me in and poured me a glass of wine. She looked pleased rather than annoyed to see me. So that was good.

'I was wondering, Hannah . . .' I began.

'What were you wondering now?' She held her head on one side.

I'm just *hopeless* at this sort of thing. There are men who just know what to say, who have words at will. But then Hannah wasn't used to such men, I mean, she had fancied that poisonous doctor. I must just be honest, straightforward.

'I was wondering if you would ever see a future with a person like me.' I said it straight out.

'Someone *like* you, Chester – or you?' She was teasing me now.

'Me, Hannah,' I said simply.

She walked away from me in her elegant drawing room. 'I'm much too old for you,' she said sadly.

'You're two and a half years older than me,' I said.

She smiled as if I were a toddler who had made an endearing remark.

'Ah yes, but before you were born I was waddling around here taking notice.'

'Maybe you were waiting for me to come and join you?' I said hopefully.

'Well, if I was waiting for you, Chester, then I waited a long time,' she said.

And then I knew it was going to be all right. And the rage I had for Dr Dermot died down in me. What had I to be enraged about?

If it **hadn't** been for him I might never have

crossed the street and spoken aloud to Hannah, I might have let it slip away as other possible relationships had slipped away in the past.

'Will I have to go and live in America?' she asked.

'No, I'd prefer to live here. I'd like to see the Centre up and running, I want to know if the big road around Rossmore ever gets built, if the well to St Ann is taken down. I'm fascinated by this place now, and to live here with you would be . . . well, it would be better than I ever dreamed.'

She seemed very pleased.

'But I hope you'll come over and meet my family,' I said.

'They'll be horrified with me,' she said, nervously patting her hair.

'They'll love you and my mom will be so pleased. She said that maybe I'd find a colleen over here,' I admitted.

'Oh, a bit of an ageing colleen,' she said.

'Please, Hannah . . .' I began and she went to draw the curtains of her big bay window that looked out on the square.

Before she closed them I saw Dr Dermot coming out of the hotel. He paused and looked at Hannah's house and then turned and went back to his own lonely place. He had only a short working life ahead of him. Once the Danny O'Neill Health Centre opened in Doon, there would be little demand for Dr Dermot's old-fashioned, blundering medicine. And now he had lost the woman who might have made his last years bearable.

I know that everyone always said about me that I was over good-natured, and always thought the best of everyone.

But truly I felt sorry for the guy.

CHAPTER 8

The Road, the Woods and the Well – 2

Father Brian Flynn went to the station to meet his sister Judy. She hadn't been home for ten years and the time showed very definitely on her face. He was shocked at how pale and drawn she looked. Judy must only be thirty-nine or forty. She could have been in her late fifties.

She saw him and waved. 'Aren't you very good to come and meet me!' She gave him a hug.

'I'm only sorry that I can't offer you somewhere to stay. It seems terrible for you to have to pay for a hotel when you have a mother and two brothers in Rossmore.'

'Will Mam recognise me at all, Brian?'

'Ah, she will in her own way,' he said.

'What does that mean exactly?'

He had forgotten how direct Judy could be. 'I don't know what it means, Judy, it's just something I say to avoid saying anything really, I suppose.'

She squeezed his arm affectionately. 'You were always a pet,' she said. 'I'm sorry I stayed away for so long. There was always one foolish thing or another keeping me over there.'

'But didn't you always write, and you were very good to our mother,' he said.

Judy cheered up. 'Now, take me on a tour of Rossmore showing me all the changes and point me to the best hairdresser.'

'There's a very smart place called Fabian's, though that's not his name at all – I was at school with him, and he was called something else altogether, but apparently they go to him from far and near.'

'Good. I'll remember that. You see, as well as relying on St Ann, I think I should bring up the second line of attack, get some new clothes and a hairstyle as well. A bit of grooming as one might say.'

'You're looking for a husband *here*?' Brian Flynn was astounded.

'Well, yes. Why not? I didn't do too well in over ten years in London.'

'You got a career for yourself.' Judy was an illustrator of children's books.

'Yes, but I am not asking St Ann for a career.' Judy was brisk. 'Lord, would you look at the traffic – it's like Hyde Park Corner.'

'It might not be for much longer. There's great talk of a new road, to take all the trucks and lorries out of the town for one thing. And let the through traffic pass without clogging up our little streets.'

'And will it happen or is it only talk?'

'I think it will happen. That's if you can believe half what you read in the newspapers. There's a lot of debate about it – people coming down heavily on one side or the other.'

'And is it a good thing or a bad thing in your opinion?'

'I don't know, Judy, I really don't. It's meant to be going through the Whitethorn Woods and possibly through St Ann's Well.'

'So I got here just in time,' said Judy Flynn, with a sense of grim resolution that made her brother Brian feel very uneasy.

Judy was astounded at the way every second person seemed to greet Brian as they parked the car and walked along a crowded Castle Street towards the Rossmore Hotel.

A woman came down the steps of the local newspaper office and her face lit up in a smile.

'There you are, Lilly,' Father Flynn said.

'This must be your sister, Father,' she said, pleased.

'It's just as well he hasn't a fancy woman,' Judy said. 'They'd have her identified in ten seconds.'

'No fear of that, isn't Father Flynn a walking saint?' said Lilly Ryan, shocked.

And then Judy recognised her. The woman whose child had disappeared all those years ago. Judy remembered how hundreds of people had gone into the Whitethorn Woods to hunt for a body or to pray at the well. There had been no result from either quest. She felt awkward and she supposed it must have shown on her face. But Lilly Ryan would be used to this after twenty years. Two decades of people shuffling and being unable to mention the great loss for fear of saying the wrong thing.

'I'm trying to get up the courage to visit my mother,' Judy confided. 'I'm afraid our family leaves all the hard work to Brian here.'

'Do it before you do anything else,' Lilly advised. 'If you face the hard thing first it makes it easier.'

'You might well be right,' Judy agreed. 'Brian, can you leave my case in the hotel? I'll go and see her now.'

'I'll come with you,' he said.

'No, I'll do this on my own. Good luck to you, Lilly.'

And they watched as Judy turned into the small side street where her mother lived alone.

'I'd better go after her,' he began.

But Lilly reminded him that Judy wanted to do this alone. So he shrugged and carried his sister's suitcase into the hotel. He would wait in one of their big armchairs until she came back and then he would buy her the stiff drink she would undoubtedly need.

Mrs Flynn had indeed no idea who Judy was, and no amount of reminding seemed to bring any recognition. She thought that Judy was a health visitor and was anxious for her to leave.

Judy looked around in desperation but there were no photographs on the walls or in frames on the old desk. Poor Brian had done his best to keep the place in some kind of order and would take his mother's washing to the Fresh as a Daisy once a week, but Judy noticed that the place still smelled bad and her mam was very uncared for. Every month for years now Judy had sent a cheque to her brother Brian, and she knew he had spent it on items for their mam. But the iron sat there unused, the easy chair was half hidden under a pile of newspapers. Mrs Flynn didn't believe in making herself comfortable.

'You must remember me, Mam, I'm Judy. I'm the middle one. Younger than Eddie, older than Brian.'

'Brian?' Her mother's look was blank.

'You remember Brian, surely, he comes in every morning to give you your breakfast.'

'No he does not, that's from the Meals on Wheels.' Her mother was definite.

'No, Mam, they come at lunchtime. Brian comes and gives you an egg every morning.'

'That's what he says.' Her mother wasn't convinced.

'Do you remember Eddie?'

'Of course I do, do you think I'm cracked or something? He wouldn't be told, married that Kitty, no good she was, nor any of her family. No wonder what happened happened.'

'What happened was that Eddie left her for a young one.'

'May God forgive you, whoever you are! Saying such things about my family! It was Kitty who threw my son out and kept his house, you'll note.' Her mother's mouth was set in a hard line.

'And what does Brian say about that?'

'I don't know any Brian.'

'Don't you have a daughter?'

'I do, a young one over in England doing drawings of some sort, she never gets in touch.' So that was the thanks for the weekly letter or postcard, the monthly contribution to Brian. She never gets in touch!

'I'm your daughter, Mam, I'm Judy, you must know me.'

'Would you get away out of that, my daughter's a young girl – you're a middle-aged woman like myself.'

As Judy walked back to the hotel she decided that a visit to this smart hairdresser called Fabian's might be well overdue. She even paused outside a new beauty shop called Pompadours. A course of facials and manicures might not go amiss either. She had put aside a fair sum of money for this visit and St Ann might need a little help to place her satisfactorily on the marriage market.

Brian was a splendid guide. As well as going with her while she made appointments in Fabian's and Pompadours, he showed her a very smart boutique.

'Didn't Becca King work there?' Judy asked.

'For God's sake, don't mention Becca King,' Father Flynn said, looking left and right.

'Why on earth not?'

'She's in jail. She got one of the van men in the shop to murder her boyfriend's new lover.'

'God, and they say you take risks living in London!' Judy said in amazement.

He brought his sister back to meet the canon. Josef and Anna had made little sandwiches in honour of the guest. They kept everything in the priests' house gleaming and the old man himself looked pink and clean. Unlike Judy's mother, he remembered her well. He had been there for her first communion, had looked on when the bishop came to confirm the girls of St Ita's, and although he had long forgotten her infant sins, he had heard her confession.

'I haven't had the pleasure of assisting at your marriage yet,' Canon Cassidy said as he drank his tea and ate his dainty sandwiches.

'No, but it won't be long now,' Judy said. 'I'm going to do a novena to St Ann. I'm going to pray at her shrine for nine days so that she will find me a good husband.'

'And no better woman for doing that than St Ann,' the canon said, his simple faith and certainties all intact.

Father Flynn envied him with all his soul.

'I'd better go and see the sister-in-law,' Judy said with a sigh.

'Don't raise your hopes too high,' Brian Flynn warned her.

'What would annoy her least, do you think, as a gift?' Judy wondered.

'Let me see, flowers would be a woeful waste of money, sweets would rot the children's teeth. Magazines are full of rubbish, a book could have been got in the library. Get her a loaf of bread and a half-pound of ham, she might make you a sandwich.'

'As bad as that, is it?' Judy asked.

'Worse,' said Father Brian Flynn.

He was not in a good humour. He had discovered that there was going to be a public meeting in ten days' time, a big protest meeting, and he was going to be invited to address it. Many of the townspeople had told him that they were eagerly waiting for his words. And he literally didn't have any.

He simply couldn't find it in his heart to stand up and condemn a possible scheme that would improve traffic and the quality of life for a great many people just because it would mean taking down a perfectly awful statue that was beginning to produce dangerously idolatrous feelings amongst the parishioners.

Had life been easier for Canon Cassidy when he was a curate? Or was this the way things always were? If you were a priest maybe it all went with the territory.

But with his usual optimism, he comforted himself that it was still only a rumour about the road. There had been no statement as yet. And also he still had ten days before the meeting. There was plenty of time to work out what to say. In the meantime there were a lot of problems to be faced nearer home.

Like how to deal with Judy if St Ann didn't come up with a husband. Like how they should face up to their mother's failing health. Like how much longer Canon Cassidy could reasonably be expected to stay in the priests' house with the title of parish priest.

Or how he could go to see Aidan Ryan yet again in the jail tomorrow and try to tell him that his wife Lilly was not a villainous person who had sold their baby.

And, most immediately, what was going to happen at the meeting this afternoon between the anger-filled Kitty and the tense, strained Judy.

He sighed a heavy sigh and ran his hands through his red spiky hair until it stood up around his head like a mad punk halo.

As it happened Kitty and Judy got on perfectly fine. Eventually.

Judy decided to offer her as a gift a hairdo at Fabian's. At first Kitty laughed a sneering laugh and said Fabian's wasn't for the likes of them. Then Judy said she was asking her to come for solidarity.

'Just to patronise me, you mean,' Kitty had scoffed.

'Not at all. Just because Eddie treated you disgracefully it doesn't mean that Brian and I would. I haven't been back here in years and I wanted to give you a big box of chocolates, then I thought you might just think that they would be bad for the children's teeth, so I decided to get you something you wouldn't go out and buy for yourself.'

'You must be made of money.' Kitty was still grudging.

'No I'm not, but I do work very hard and I saved hard for this trip home.'

'And what brought you home eventually?' Kitty was not yet won over.

'I want to get married, Kitty. It's as simple as that. I can't find anyone in London except married men, and I don't have to tell you what a foolish road that is to go down. You've experienced it from the other side. So I was hoping that maybe if I went for nine days to St Ann's Well . . .' She let her voice trail away.

'You're making fun of me – you're just having a jeer at us, you and your London ways.'

'I'm not as it happens, but honestly, life is too short. If that's the way you want to see it, then there's nothing I can do.'

For some reason it worked. Kitty said in a tone that she hadn't used for a long time, 'If the offer's still open I'd love a hairdo. That young slut Naomi that your brother has gone off with has hair like rats' tails. It would give me a great boost altogether . . .'

Father Flynn had another deputation waiting for him when he got back to the priests' house. A request for support from the other side of the increasingly great divide. A group of concerned citizens were going to have a candlelit procession through the town, campaigning for the rumoured new road that would bring an end to the dangerous traffic that roared through Rossmore. This traffic had already caused numerous accidents and the death of a five-year-old. They wanted Father Flynn to march at their head.

Great, he said to himself, absolutely great, and I haven't even answered the other lot yet.

Then his brow cleared. Maybe this was the answer. He would say that the Church must not be seen to enter local politics. Was this the wisdom of Solomon or was it in fact the refuge of a weak man? He might never know.

In a way he wished the whole thing were out in the open. These shadowlands of rumour and counter-rumour were very disturbing. Each day new fuel was being added to the flames of speculation. People said that big builders had been seen dining in the Rossmore Hotel. That meant that the road had been agreed – it was simply a matter of who would build it.

Farmers with land adjoining the woods were giving themselves airs. The land from which they had once scraped a living might now be worth something in the end. The trick would be to sell now to some speculator. Especially if you had a few acres that might not come under the compulsory purchase order when it happened but would be highly valuable for access. It seemed that everywhere you went, you heard voices. Voices with something to say.

The man that ran a garage was very doleful. If the road came it would kill his business stone dead. It was hard enough for people to park in his premises as things were, and getting back on the road was like Russian roulette.

A woman who had a small guest house on the edge of the town was reported to be putting in new bathrooms and extending her breakfast room, once the new road was given the go-ahead. She would have an unending line of engineers, advisers and consultants looking for accommodation near the site.

There were debates on television about the parlous state of Irish roads; the newly rich country would not remain rich for much longer if European exporters found only Third World crowded lanes and endless delays in delivering their goods to the right destination. Tourism would suffer if visitors couldn't get from one place to another without crawling in their rented cars behind a tractor or some huge lumbering bit of farm machinery.

Places like the Fresh as a Daisy Launderette just couldn't wait for the road to arrive. They had never got any business from visitors anyway. And Fabian's the hairdressers thought they would do better if their clients had room to park their cars.

But the garden centre on the edge of town didn't want the new road. They had a nice little business where travellers from east to west would stop, stretch their legs, visit the café and maybe fill the car with bedding plants or gift-wrapped azaleas for whoever they were visiting. If the new road came no one would need to pass this way any more.

And there were those like the Rossmore Hotel, Skunk Slattery and Miss Gwen in Pompadours who just didn't know.

It was swings and roundabouts of course.

They would lose the passing trade because nobody would pass through any more. But it might mean that there would be more incentive for local people to come out and shop, get beautified, or have a lunch in the hotel, once they knew there would be room to breathe and they wouldn't be mown down by impatient truck drivers on the roads.

And there were the hundreds who had been helped by St Ann. They couldn't believe that their fellow countrymen and women were prepared to turn their backs on the saint, allow her shrine to be dismantled. There was talk of people lying down in front of the bulldozers if they came to the woods, and obstructing all the earth-moving machinery.

It was the least they could do to thank their saint for all the miracles that had been worked through her well. It didn't actually matter that these miracles had not been acknowledged and recognised by Rome like Fatima and Lourdes. People round here knew. And people from far, far away knew.

Didn't they come in droves from miles across the sea?

And still, greedy, money-loving people were prepared to ignore this great blessing, which had given so much to so many, just to get traffic moving faster and earn even more money than they already had.

The canon was completely unaware of the issues and said only that we must pray for guidance in these as in all matters. Josef and Anna confided in Father Flynn and said they thought that the old man needed full-time care.

'It's not that I am looking for more hours, Father,' Josef said. 'It's just that you should know. And of course I am always afraid that one day you will tell me he is going to a nursing home and there will be no job for me any more. I hope I am not being selfish but I want to be prepared.'

Father Flynn said he understood very well and it was indeed a grey area. The canon seemed very happy where he was and it would be a pity to move him. His life had no purpose if he wasn't in the priests' house. Yet of course if he really needed more care, then he would have to have it.

'It's just I was thinking of getting a job helping to build the road,' Josef said.

'You mean it's really going to happen?' Father Flynn was astounded.

'I have Polish friends and they say that it will. They are going to stay with Anna and me, and Father Flynn, you would not believe the great money they will earn building it.' Josef's face was full of hope and dreams.

'Yes, but it's only money, Josef.'

'It's money that will buy a little shop for my brothers back home in Latvia. We have everything we need here but they have so very little.'

For no reason at all, Father Flynn thought of his friend James O'Connor who had been ordained the same day as he had. James had left the priesthood, married Rosie, had two little sons. James worked in computer technology of some kind, he said it was great, easy work, and when you came home from the office you could put it all behind you.

Not at all like parish work. No more of this standing up for the indefensible, or staying silent on matters you cared about. Father Flynn thought he would have loved it.

Just loved it.

Skunk Slattery looked up as Kitty Flynn came into his shop with a good-looking woman he hadn't seen before.

'How are you, Skunk?' asked Kitty. 'We're getting ourselves a few glossy magazines and going off to Fabian's for a makeover.'

'More power to you, Kitty. It's never too late, I say,' Skunk responded, not very gallantly.

'Always the man to flatter you,' Kitty said.

'Are you going to introduce me to your friend?' Skunk asked.

'That's not my friend, Skunk, that's my sister-in-law – don't you remember her?' Kitty said.

'Kitty is another person who'll always flatter you!' Judy said. 'I'm Judy Flynn, by the way. Brian and Eddie's sister.'

'Pleased to meet you, I am Sebastian Slattery,' said Skunk.

'You are not!' Kitty would argue with her shadow. 'You're Skunk – you always were and always will be.'

Skunk and Judy exchanged glances of despair as Kitty burrowed amongst the glossy magazines.

'I'm amazed I never met you before. Will you be around for long?' Skunk asked.

'For as long as it takes,' Judy Flynn said mysteriously.

*

Naomi approached Father Flynn. Normally she steered well clear of him. Naomi was used to steering clear of people, there were a fair few she had to avoid. Like Eddie's wife Kitty, like Eddie's children, like his mother, and most certainly his brother Brian, the local priest.

'Excuse me, Brian?' she began.

Father Flynn nearly dropped to the ground in shock. 'Yes . . . um . . . Naomi.' What on God's earth could the girl want?

'Brian, I was wondering if you could explain to me how Eddie could get an annulment of his marriage.'

'With great, great difficulty, Naomi,' Father Flynn said.

'No, I mean, it *can* be done obviously, it's a question of how.' Naomi turned her big nineteen-year-old eyes on him.

'It can't be done,' Father Flynn said. 'Annulment is saying that no marriage existed, and I have to tell you that a marriage did exist between Eddie and Kitty, and they have four children as a result of it.'

'It wasn't a real marriage,' she began.

'It was, Naomi. You weren't born at the time. I was there. It happened, you can't say it didn't happen. Now have I said one word to you about your living with Eddie? No, I have not. It's your business, yours and his, but don't go dragging the principles of canon law and the Church into it. Please.'

'He didn't know his mind then, he was only twenty, for God's sake, what does a young fellow of twenty know about taking on a wife and having children? He shouldn't have been allowed to do it.'

'What brought all this on, Naomi?' Father Flynn's voice was level. It wasn't much worse than anything else that was happening around him in his life these days. But it would at least be nice to know why after two years this girl wanted respectability and the approval of Church and State.

'It's just that I want things to be fair and open . . .' she began.

'Really?' Father Flynn was doubtful.

'And, you see, my parents have discovered that I'm not a student any more, they thought I was going to college and they're being a bit troublesome . . .'

'Yes, I'm sure.'

'And so, you see, I told them that I was going to marry Eddie, and now they're all delighted again and getting ready for the wedding, so that's what we have to organise, you see.'

Father Flynn looked at her wildly. He thought that he had become master of the meaningless comforting cliché. But on this occasion he could not summon up one single word to say.

Neddy Nolan brought his father in to see the canon once a week. The two old men used to play chess together and Josef would serve them coffee and biscuits.

'Tell me, Canon, shouldn't we all be voting against this road if we get a chance?' Marty Nolan asked.

'I don't think we do get a chance.' Canon Cassidy's grasp on it was tenuous.

'But you know what I mean, Canon, voting with our feet. Going to the meeting in the square and everything, having banners maybe. Don't we owe it to St Ann?'

'Why don't you ask Father Flynn, he's the brains of this parish,' the old man said.

'I did ask him, Canon, but he just went on about doing what our consciences told us to do.' Marty Nolan shook his head in disappointment. 'That's no use at all, suppose everyone's conscience told them something different. Where would we be then? It's guidance we need.'

'Do you know, Mr Nolan, I think the days of guidance are long gone. I never thought I'd live to hear myself say this but it appears to be true.'

'It's a great worry for us,' Marty Nolan said. 'You see, people are making us offers for the land. Unmerciful sums of money. And I know it has Neddy awake at night wondering what to do.'

'But nothing has been agreed yet. Why would people be offering to buy your land?' The canon was bewildered.

'I'm not sure, Canon, maybe they know more than we know. But you see the problem for Neddy. I mean, his own mother was cured at that well. No amount of money could ever pay for that.'

'Where is Neddy at the moment?' the canon said, possibly trying to change the subject. It worked.

'Ah, you know Neddy, Canon, always the dreamer,

he's wandering round Rossmore with his hands in his pockets, interested in everything, understanding nothing.'

'Well, we'd better get on with our game of chess then,' the canon said. 'Was it my move or yours?'

Neddy Nolan was in fact in Myles Barry's law office. 'I've always been a bit slow, Myles,' he began.

'I wouldn't say that at all. Haven't you done very well for yourself, married a grand girl? Aren't you a friend to everyone in Rossmore?'

'Yes, but, Myles, I might not be for much longer. All kinds of people are coming to me and suggesting we sell our property to them.'

'Well, isn't that good?'

'Not really. They must have inside information or whatever it's called. They must know that the road really is coming and will go over our land.' He looked very troubled.

'I know, Neddy, but isn't that the luck of the draw? It couldn't happen to a better family.' Myles couldn't see where the problem lay.

'But I can't sell our land to speculators, people who are buying up bits here and there for no reason, except that they can hold the authorities to ransom by cornering all the available acres. Then when the time comes they can hold out and eventually sell it on again at a huge profit to the government and the builders. That's not the kind of thing we want to be involved in.'

'Well, no . . . no . . .' Myles Barry wondered where this was leading.

'It's just a few of them have told me they are approaching you about it,' Neddy said anxiously.

Myles Barry played for time. 'That's a fact, Neddy. But it's not illegal, you know, to make an offer for someone's land. You name a price and they pay it, and you put the money in the bank, and they sell the land on later for more money, because they'll have lots of little bits here and there to offer. Or you refuse it and take less from the government when the time comes and that's that. It's the system. Where's the problem?'

'The problem is that it's all just about making money,' Neddy said.

Myles sighed and decided to be very direct. 'Yes, it's true some clients have asked me to put in an offer to you but I said you'd need to get a solicitor of your own, and maybe an estate agent to advise you and I couldn't be acting as a sort of an intermediary and twisting your arm over it all.'

'Could you be our solicitor, Myles? I've known you for ever, you were at school with my brother Kit.' Neddy's face was without guile.

'I could indeed be your lawyer, Neddy, but I suggest you get someone more high-powered than me. A big firm from Dublin maybe. There's serious money tied up in this. You'd want a really professional team working for you.'

'Is it that you don't want to let the other people down, Myles, by changing horses and representing me?' Neddy wanted to know.

'No, there would be no conflict of interests. Nobody has mentioned any sums involved. I have seen no papers or proposals. I just said I wouldn't do anything until you got representation, that's all,' Myles said.

'So you could do it if you wanted to?' Neddy was distressingly direct.

Of course Myles Barry could. But there would be much more money in it for him if he were to represent a consortium of local businessmen. He couldn't charge Neddy Nolan and his father proper fees. Especially if things were as they looked and the Nolans were going to hold out. The land would be bought eventually if the road went ahead, which it looked very likely to. Those particular businessmen who had approached him would not have sought out the Nolan farm unless they knew something from the council. Myles Barry had been given to understand that any reasonable demand from the Nolans would be met.

Of course it was speculation. But that's how an economy worked. People took risks; they won or they lost. Only Neddy Nolan would see anything dubious about the whole system.

Myles sat and looked at the gentle man on the other side of the desk. A man who had worked very hard for what he had. It would be great to see someone like that being dealt a winning hand.

Myles Barry was only too aware that the rumours were going to become a reality and the heat was about to be turned on. Cathal Chambers in the bank had told him about two local councillors, they were fellows who hadn't a bone to throw to a dog, and yet they were coming into the bank these days with large wads of cash which they wanted lodged in savings accounts. It was so obviously vote buying that Cathal was amazed.

Yet what could he do except invoke the law about banks needing to know where any lodged money came from. They looked him in the eye and told him that it was from poker games. The vote about the road when it came would be first at local council level, and then nationally. And it looked like a foregone conclusion.

Myles Barry looked at Neddy. He needed someone to look after his interests. These were dangerous waters that he was entering. But Neddy Nolan didn't want the big boys in Dublin, the firms that would frighten off anyone trying to cheat him. No, he wanted the man who had been at school with his brother Kit – now serving time in an English prison at Her Majesty's pleasure.

'Sure, Neddy,' Myles Barry sighed. 'I'd be honoured to be your solicitor.'

Judy Flynn walked up to the Whitethorn Woods on her own. She wore her best outfit, a navy silk dress with a navy and white scarf. Her newly streaked hair was elegant and shiny. She wanted to show St Ann the raw material for her quest.

In the cave were half a dozen people muttering

and praying near the statue. Judy kneeled down and got straight to business.

'I'm going to be completely honest with you, St Ann. I don't really know whether you exist or not, and if you do exist whether you deal with cases like this or not. But it's worth a try. I am going to come here and pray for peace on earth, or whatever you yourself think may be needed, for nine mornings in a row. That's a fair bank of prayers we're building up. And in return you are going to guide my steps towards meeting a man I can marry and have children with. You see, I do drawings all the time for children's books and yet I have no children of my own. And because of doing these drawings I sort of believe in magic, well, a magical world where marvellous things happen. So why shouldn't I find a husband in this place?

'Oh, and you'll want to know why I didn't find one already. That's easy. I looked in the wrong place. I looked in publishing and advertising and the media, that kind of world. Not the right base. What I would like is someone maybe from this town so that I wouldn't feel so alienated and guilty about not being here. And then I could help my brother Brian to look after our mam, I could help Kitty – I'm sure she's been up here asking you to get my brother Eddie to go back to her. Don't do it, it wouldn't work.

'I don't think that marriage is all about appearances and dressing well, but it's only fair to tell you that this is the best I can look. I am inclined to be a bit impatient and short-tempered but I think that I am keeping it under control. And that's it now. I'll say a rosary for your intentions and I'll come again tomorrow. I can't say fairer than that.'

Eddie Flynn came out of the bar in the Rossmore Hotel. Times were very worrying. He had a good business deal possibly going ahead with a gang of people who knew what they were doing. It should bring him in some very badly needed money. And did he need money just now!

Young Naomi had been telling her parents a pack of lies, saying she was a second-year student above in Dublin. Now she was telling them more lies, saying that Eddie's marriage was going to be annulled and that he was going to marry her. It would never happen, not in a million years. The girl was soft in the head.

In many ways it would be easier to have stayed with Kitty. At least there was always a meal on the table when he got home in the evening, there were the children to entertain him. It was all a bit awkward and artificial nowadays, they seemed to think he was some kind of rat who had deserted them. Then Kitty would let him take them to the pictures in the middle of the week, and young Naomi wanted to go out at weekends. And everyone was on his case about not going to see his mam enough.

He was weary of it all. If he went home now, Naomi would be there with pictures of wedding dresses and lists of the people they would invite. Apparently she had had a highly unsatisfactory conversation with Brian about it all and now thought they should go straight through the canon who would surely have a more helpful attitude. And anyway wasn't he technically Brian's boss?

On the other side of the road he saw Kitty. Or was it Kitty? She wore Kitty's anorak certainly but her hair was totally different and she was wearing make-up. He pulled back into the shadows and watched. It was Kitty. But she had done something to herself. Dyed her hair, maybe?

She looked years younger.

He saw her talking animatedly to that poor Lilly Ryan, the one whose baby had been stolen all those years ago and then her husband had turned violent. Eddie watched as Kitty moved along the street. He wouldn't even admit it to himself but life would be a great deal easier if he were going home to Kitty for his tea.

The march against the new road was held right through the town and up to the Whitethorn Woods. Some people carried posters with 'Save Our Saint' on them, others had 'No to the New Road'. Television teams and journalists from national newspapers came to cover it.

Father Brian Flynn knew he would have to make some kind of statement to someone. He couldn't sit like a dummy looking on. But he hated the thought of himself on national television.

'I have such desperate hair, I look like a lavatory brush,' he confided to his sister.

'Go to that man Fabian, he's brilliant,' Judy advised.

'Are you mad – you'd feed a family for a week on what he charges.'

'You don't have a family to feed, go on, Brian, it's my treat,' she said and that was that.

He went into the salon feeling more foolish than he had ever felt in his whole life. He couldn't see what the guy who called himself Fabian actually did to him but he did look a lot more normal afterwards.

So he was interviewed and said that the Well of St Ann was a place of local piety and it was always sad to see parishioners upset and their sensibilities offended.

Then a week later he was interviewed again at the candlelit meeting calling for the introduction of something that would take the heavy traffic away from Rossmore. This time Father Flynn told the interviewer that the death of a child was to be deplored and that the authorities had a duty to do all in their power to make sure that a young life was never lost again in this way.

'I'm sure that anyone who saw both of those interviews will think I am a complete clown,' he said to Judy.

'No, they'll think that when you're in a hole you're right to stop digging,' Judy said.

She was proving to be a much more restful companion than he had feared. She said she knew it was barking mad but she was getting a lot of comfort from that crazy old well. She had also painted her mother's kitchen and got her a kitten, which had cheered the old woman up – but not yet to the extent of admitting that she recognised Judy.

The brother and sister would have a drink together each evening in the Rossmore Hotel. Once they saw Eddie there and waved him to join them. Nobody mentioned Naomi, Kitty or Mother.

It was a perfectly pleasant chat.

'I think we're all getting seriously grown up round here,' Judy Flynn said afterwards.

'Oh, if only, if only,' said Father Flynn. He saw really immense problems ahead once the council's vote was known, which would be any day now.

The voices for and against the road, the voices from the woods, were only gathering their strength – they had seen nothing yet.

CHAPTER 9

Talking to Mercedes

Part 1 – Helen

Ah, there you are, Mercedes. I was having a little sleep there. I dreamed I was back in Rossmore, walking down the crowded main street. I often dream that. But you wouldn't know where it is, it's over in Ireland across the sea from here. Ireland is only fifty minutes on a plane from London. You should go there sometime. You'd like it there, you're religious and it's very Catholic.

Well, it was anyway.

I've always liked you, Mercedes, much better than the day nurses – you have more time for people, you'll make a cup of tea. You listen. They don't listen, it's sit up and wake up and get up and cheer up. You never say that.

You have a nice cool hand, you smell of lavender, not of some disinfectant. You are interested.

You say your name is Mercedes and that you would like to marry a doctor. You would like to send your mother more money. But it took me weeks to find even that out about you, Mercedes, because you only want to talk about me and how I feel.

I wish you would call me Helen rather than Madam. Please don't call me Mrs Harris. You are so friendly, so interested in my family who come to visit. My tall, handsome husband James, my gracious mother-in-law Natasha, my wonderful, beautiful daughter Grace.

You ask me all kinds of questions about them and I tell you, it's a pleasure to tell you things. You smile so much. And you aren't curious and don't act like the police, always asking questions. That's what David seems like to me. You know David, he is Grace's boyfriend. I think you sense that about him, you often move him gently on when he is here. You know that he distresses me.

But you I could talk to for ever.

You love the story about the night I met handsome James Harris twenty-seven years ago when I borrowed my flatmate's dress to go to a party. He said that it was the same colour as my eyes and that I must be very artistic. In fact it was the only dress between the three of us that was smart enough for me to wear.

I told you the truth about that, and about how fearful I was about meeting his mother Natasha for the first time. Their home was so big and impressive, her questions so probing. I had never eaten oysters before – it was such a shock to me. And I told you the truth about a lot of things, about how kind they always were to me in the orphanage where I grew up and how they insisted on making my wedding cake. Natasha had objected at first because she thought it would be amateurish but even she was pleasantly surprised.

I went back to see them often at the orphanage. They told me I was the only child in the home who didn't ask about my parents. The others were all very anxious to know details and if it would ever mean their mothers would be coming back to collect them.

But I wanted to know nothing. This was my home. Someone had given me, Helen, away, no doubt for good reasons at the time. What more was there to ask? To know?

I haven't told the Sisters that I am so ill, Mercedes. They couldn't bear it. Instead I told them that I'm going abroad with James and will be in touch later. I have left them something in my will and a letter of thanks. It's important that people be thanked for what they do. Really it is. Otherwise they might never know how much they are appreciated. Like you, for example. I thank you a lot because I am truly grateful to meet someone who will listen to me so well and be so interested in my story.

You who have worked so hard and saved so much would understand how hard I too worked when I did my secretarial course here in London.

The others in the class spent ages having coffee and going window shopping, but I studied and practised very hard.

I lived in a flat with two other girls who loved cooking so they taught me how to enjoy it too.

On Saturdays I worked at a cosmetic counter in a big store and I got makeovers and free samples as well as my wages; on Sundays I worked in a garden centre which taught me a lot and so I did flower arranging and window boxes for people who lived near by. By the time I had landed a good job in the City with a really proper salary I was much more accomplished than many girls who had left the orphanage with me. They always told me when I went back there that I looked like a real lady, they were proud of me and I could marry a duke if I put my mind to it.

But I put my mind to marrying James Harris.

I used to read novels about people like James, but I didn't believe they really existed.

He was such a gentleman in every sense. He never raised his voice, he was always courteous, he had a way of smiling that lit up his whole face. I was determined to marry him and I worked hard at that like I had worked at everything else. I hid nothing about my past. I did not want his mother Natasha investigating and discovering things about little Helen from the orphanage, so I was totally up front about everything. And it paid off. She finally agreed to the wedding and I think that in a way she sort of respected me.

I was a beautiful bride. Did I show you the pictures? Of course I did. I just wanted to look at them once more.

All we were waiting for was a child.

Someone to inherit Natasha's large estate. You don't call it money if you're very rich, Mercedes, you call it an 'estate'. So we were married for three years and no sign of my becoming pregnant. I was anxious, James was concerned and Natasha was incensed.

I went to a doctor in a completely different part of London and had an examination.

I wasn't ovulating, it turned out, so I would need fertility treatment.

I knew only too well how much James would object to this. If it were proven that he was well capable of fathering a child but that his wife could not conceive, things would change between us. If Natasha knew, then the world as we knew it would end.

So I realised there was no way James and I could go together like normal couples who had problems conceiving and could have *in vitro* treatment. There was no way that I could go alone and get a secret artificial insemination. It didn't work like that apparently.

James wouldn't consider surrogate parenting, so there was no point in discussing it. Nor adoption, even if there had been any children to adopt. And I didn't even want to think of Natasha's face on the subject of an overseas baby being brought to our home. A little African Harris! An Asiatic Harris! Don't make me laugh.

No, Mercedes, you are very kind but I'm not upsetting myself, no, not at all. I know that you are always sensitive to my getting upset especially when Grace's David keeps interrogating me about things. But this is not like that. I'm just trying to explain it all to you. You see, I want to tell you this, I need to tell you. Can you think of it as if I am writing you a letter? A letter to Mercedes from Helen.

Yes, I will have a sip of tea, thank you so much, my dear, you are always there when people need you.

So, as I was saying, I had to think what to do next.

Now this was twenty-three years ago, you were only a little toddler then, running around in the sunshine in the Philippines. It is sunny there, isn't it? But I was here in London, worried out of my mind.

I had always been good at finding a solution; I would not be beaten by this. One of the girls at work had been on a holiday in Dublin, over in Ireland, and when they were there they had gone to this place, Rossmore. It was a small town but was very beautiful, it had an old castle and a forest called Whitethorn Woods, and even a wishing well. A saint's well it was, actually. You'd know about that, being Catholic, Mercedes. People went to pray to a saint and they got their wishes answered. They left things there to thank her.

What did they wish for? I wondered.

Everything apparently, the saint had a big job on her hands. People prayed for husbands and for cures from illness. And a lot for babies. There were lots of little baby bootees and things tied to the thorny bushes from people wanting a baby of their own. Imagine!

Well, I did imagine. Day and night I imagined. That is where I would find our child.

These people wouldn't have gone on praying unless there had been some results. So next time James went away on a business trip, I took a couple of days off from my office and sneaked over to Ireland and took a bus to this place Rossmore.

It was extraordinary, the whole thing. It was really very strange. Quite a modern town with nice shops and good restaurants, I even got my hair done in a smart salon. But just a mile out on the road there was this real scene of Third World superstition. Sorry, Mercedes, no offence but you know what I mean.

There were dozens of people, each one with their own story. There was this old woman praying to St Ann. That's who it was, St Ann, the mother of Mary who was the mother of Jesus, but you'd know all that. We used to have a statue of her back in the Home.

Anyway this woman was asking that her son who was a drug addict would get cured, and then there was a girl praying that her boyfriend would not hear that she had had a stupid fling with another man. A boy saying he simply had to pass this exam as the whole family were depending on him. A fourteen-year-old girl was asking that her father would go off the drink.

So I closed my eyes and I spoke to this saint and I said I'd go straight back to my religion, which I had sort of forgotten about since I met James and Natasha, if she would arrange for me to get pregnant.

It was very peaceful there, and anything seemed possible. And I was so sure she would arrange it. Until the afternoon bus came I spent the day looking around Rossmore. There wasn't much traffic back then, you could walk about easily. I believe it's changed utterly now. Everyone seemed to know each other, greeting half the people in Castle Street, which was the main street. They were all families, I noticed. But, I thought, when I came back to this place with my child one day, I would be part of a family too. I would come back to Rossmore and thank St Ann for her help.

A lot of these people left their children sort of parked outside shops since the prams were too big and bulky to bring in. Passers-by would pause to admire the chubby babies in prams. Dozens of them. Soon I would have our baby in a pram, James's and my baby. Natasha's grandchild. And when we did, we would never leave the child out of our sight.

But the months went on and on, with no sign of any intervention on St Ann's part. I looked back with great rage at my useless trip over to her well and I got very annoyed. I kept thinking of that town where the women just left their babies for all to see in the main street without anyone to mind them. They just left their babies out in the street so casually while so many of the rest of us were aching for a child.

That's when I got the idea.

I would go to Ireland, find a pram and bring our baby home. It didn't matter if it was a boy or a girl. If it were our own child we couldn't choose anyway so this made it all the more natural somehow.

It needed a lot of planning.

You didn't need passports to go to Ireland or anything but still there was more chance of being spotted on a plane or at an airport than on a ferry. So I made my plans to go by sea.

I told James that I was pregnant, and that I had gone not to his and Natasha's family doctor but to an all-women-doctors clinic and that I preferred it this way. He was totally understanding, and gentle with me. And of course utterly delighted with my great news.

I begged him not to tell his mother yet. Said that I needed time. He agreed that it should be our secret until we were sure that everything was on course. After three months I said that I now preferred to sleep alone. He agreed reluctantly.

I read all the symptoms of pregnancy and acted accordingly. I went to a theatrical costumier and got a special mould made to simulate a pregnant stomach. I explained that it had to look good under a nightdress for my stage part. They were very interested in it and I had to be more and more vague about the whole thing in case they wanted to come to the theatre and see me act!

Natasha was overjoyed. When she came to lunch every Sunday she even helped me clear the dishes instead of sitting there like a stone.

'Helen, my dear, dear girl, you have no idea how happy this makes me,' she said, laying her hand on my stomach. 'When will we feel the baby kick, do you think?'

I said I would ask them at the clinic.

I realised that I would have to go away around the time of the so-called birth of the baby. This would be a problem but I solved it. I told James and Natasha that there was something about approaching motherhood that made me nostalgic for the orphanage, the only home I remembered. James wanted to come with me but I said that this was a journey I wanted to make on my own. And this was a busy time in his antiques business, he needed to be in London. I would be back in a week, long, long before the birth was due. It took a lot of persuasion but they let me go.

I had already begun my maternity leave from the office. I was in charge, I could do what I liked.

I did go to the orphanage where they were delighted with my pregnancy. They were particularly delighted with the timing because apparently my birth mother was in a hospital dying and she wanted desperately to see me just once. To explain.

I said I wanted no explanation.

She had given me life, that was fine. I needed no more. I had just got on with it.

The Sisters and staff were shocked at me. Here

was I, with a good job, a wealthy husband, a beautiful home, and now expecting my own child. Why could I not open my heart to a poor woman who had not been so lucky in life?

But I would not be moved. I had too much on my own mind. I was about to go to another country, steal a baby for myself, a child for James, an heir for Natasha Harris. Why should I get involved with the ramblings and remorse of some stranger, which had come far, far too late?

Then I drove on and left my car near the ferry terminal. I wore a wig and whipped out my false tummy and put it in the boot of the car. I had bought a cheap raincoat, a rug and a lifelike doll and then I was ready. They didn't have closed circuit TV so much in those days but I wanted to make sure that if there was a hue and cry nobody would be able to call attention to a woman with a baby boarding a boat for the UK – someone else would be sure to mention having seen her going in the other direction. I sat out in the open air cuddling the doll.

One or two other mothers approached me to have a look at the baby but I said apologetically that she didn't like strangers. You see, I was already thinking of her as my daughter.

Then I got the bus to Rossmore, cuddling the doll very close to me. It was a busy Saturday in the town – I walked the length of Castle Street until my feet were sore.

I did some shopping as well, talcum powder, napkins, soothing creams. There were indeed many prams outside stores on this visit also. Innocent, trusting people in a safe town, some might say. I didn't say that. Criminally careless, neglectful parents who didn't deserve children, was what I said.

I had to be careful.

The bus that I must get would leave at three. It would be two hours to the ferry. I must take the child just before the bus left, not earlier, no point in giving the authorities time to search.

It's strange. I could almost draw a picture of the people in that crowded street that day. There was an old priest, you know, wearing a soutane, the sort of black dress they used to wear, right down to the feet. And he was shaking everyone's hand. Half the population seemed to be out shopping, and greeting each other. I was standing on the steps of the Rossmore Hotel when I saw a little baby in a pram. Just lying there asleep and with a small Yorkshire terrier tied by his lead to the handle of the pram. I crossed the road and it was over in seconds, the doll was in a litter bin and the baby was in my arms wrapped in my rug. The eyes were tightly closed but I could hear a little heart beating close to mine. It all felt totally right as if it was meant to happen. As if in some curious way St Ann had led me to this child.

I got on the bus and looked back for a last time at Rossmore. The bus bumped across the country to the ferry and then I moved with my daughter on to the boat. I must have been well away long before the alarm was raised. And who would have thought to search the ferries at once anyway? I was settled in my car by the time they realised that this was a full-blown child abduction.

I had done what I set out to do: I had got my child.

A little girl who would be called Grace Natasha. She must be between two and four weeks old. It was despicable, leaving a child that age to fare for herself, I told myself. She was better by far that I had come along to claim her, to give her a better life. No one could find me now, I told myself, as I prepared her first formula bottle on a spirit stove at the back of the car.

And the wonderful thing, Mercedes, was that nobody ever did.

I had it all very well sorted out, you see.

I reinstated my false tummy, and left the baby in the car while I checked into a shabby guest house. During the middle of the night I pretended to wake with labour pains and insisted on driving myself to the hospital. In fact I drove back to my orphanage.

I told them that I had delivered the baby myself and needed them to look after me for a couple of days until I recovered from the shock.

One of the staff said that I couldn't possibly have had this baby since I was there a couple of days ago. This was a baby who was two weeks old, not three days. Another wanted to get me a doctor. But these were people I had lived with for seventeen years of my life. I could manage them. And they loved me, don't forget. I had been no trouble all those years there. I had remembered them and come back to visit. I had even sent contributions to their building fund. They weren't going to question poor little orphan Helen, whose own mother was dying.

They knew – of course they knew. These were women who lived with children all day and all night. Maybe they should have reported it, I suppose you could say that. But then they thought that I must have bought the baby. And they knew I was hiding it from my rather grand husband and mother-in-law. So they went along with the fiction.

I burned the false stomach and the wig and the cheap raincoat in their incinerator when nobody was looking. They called James to tell him he had a daughter, and he called Natasha to tell her she had a granddaughter. They even registered the birth. James cried on the telephone. He told me that he loved me more than ever and he would look after us both for the rest of his life. And Grace slept on, delighted with herself and everyone, and never caused anyone any trouble for twenty-three years.

She is so like me, not physically, I know, but the way she behaves. You've seen that for yourself. She is my daughter in every sense of the word.

She is a strong girl with a forceful character. She is just like her mother.

Just like me.

No, Mercedes, I did not enquire about the family who lost her in Ireland. You see, they have different newspapers and everything over there, so I didn't have to read about it.

They all have so many children over there anyway. I don't think about that side of things at all.

No, of course I would never tell Grace, never in a million years.

She's got a boyfriend now, David, of course you know. James isn't crazy about the boy, he doesn't say it but I know. I don't like him very much but he's Grace's choice and so I say nothing, I just smile.

David is Irish as it happens. Extraordinary, isn't it! And Grace has never been over there. Since. Not yet anyway. But I had a real scare yesterday when suddenly out of the blue David started saying that there is this big drama going on in Ireland about a roadway that's going to bypass Rossmore. Huge protests about it, apparently.

'Rossmore?' I said with my blood turning into ice.

'Yeah, a one-horse town back of beyond. Much better bypassed. No one would have any call to go there.' He dismissed the place.

I raked his face in case he knew. Suppose he was actually from Rossmore? Suppose for one terrible moment that it was his sister who had disappeared from her pram? Could it have happened that he and Grace were brother and sister?

I felt very faint. Remember, you were there for me as always.

I didn't pass out as I thought I was going to. I could feel myself coming back to reality. I asked myself, why would he mention that town of all towns unless there was some connection? Perhaps he had been tracking me down for years. I had to know.

'Have you ever been there yourself, David?' I asked, hardly daring to think what he might say.

But no, he said he probably passed through it on the way to the West of Ireland but he had never stopped. He and Grace had been talking about it, because of something there that might be of interest or might not. His voice trailed away. He had only been trying to make conversation.

Grace looked at him adoringly.

'I'll tell you what we were talking about, Mother – David was telling me that there's a sort of shrine there, a wishing well or something. And, you know, people get cured there . . .' She looked at me hopefully.

'No, Grace, and David, thank you, but really I'm fine,' I said. 'Just fine. Those places don't really work, you know.'

'But they say that they work in some fashion, Mother, you know, people get strength, confidence, they feel better. People who go there take what they can from them.'

'I took what I could . . .' I began and then I saw all of them looking at me. 'I took what I could from everything and it made me very strong. I feel absolutely fine,' I said firmly.

And Grace lifted my thin hand and kissed it.

Her grandmother is settling all this money on her in two years' time when she's twenty-five. She will have the whole Harris estate. What would she have had if I had left her in that pram with the dog tied to the handle? I won't be here then of course to see her inherit everything, but that doesn't matter. I gave her a very good start in life. I did everything for her: everything a mother could do. For her, for her father, for her grandmother.

I have nothing to blame myself for. I never told James a lie in my life except this one, and I did it from love. We have had such a wonderful marriage, I know in my heart that he has never told me a lie. Not ever. But as I say, I have nothing to blame myself for.

Stop crying, Mercedes, please stop. You're meant to be helping us to feel strong, not the other way around. Things are hard enough without having the nurses getting all weepy on us.

That's better.

That's the smile I like.

And maybe if there's a little more tea, do you think?

Part 2 – James

Mummy always telephones me at 9 a.m. A lot of people think that's rather odd but I find it quite reassuring. It means that I don't have to remember to phone her and that I am kept up to date with all that's happening in her world, which is always interesting. Full of writers and lawyers, bankers and politicians.

We have always lived a very quiet life, Helen and

I, so it's entertaining to hear first-hand about the kind of people you might read about in the newspapers. Helen never answers the phone at that time because we both know it's Mummy. Not that Helen doesn't like talking to Mummy or anything, they get on very well and Helen is utterly charming to her. From the beginning she was the one who decided that we must make Mummy part of our lives, invite her to lunch or dinner with us once a week. Then of course she has always known exactly how to handle her. If Mummy has a fault it is that she's slightly snobby but Lord, does Helen cut straight through that!

She looks at Mummy with big china-blue eyes.

'I'm so sorry, Mrs Harris, but you're going to have to help me here. We didn't ever eat oysters at the orphanage,'. . . or we didn't have fingerbowls or *amuse-bouches* or whatever nonsense Mummy was indulging in at the time. It was completely disarming, Mummy came round to her very quickly – after some initial doubts, shall we say. She was genuinely admiring of someone so direct and unaffected as Helen.

She also knew that I had never loved anyone before and would never love anyone again. I had made it very clear that Helen would be my wife very soon after I met her first, wearing a dress exactly the same colour as her blue eyes. She wears that colour a lot, in silky scarves, in tunics. And also in robes and negligees. Which is all that anyone sees her wear nowadays.

The family, all my uncles and cousins, had always wanted me to work in the City like Father had. But I hadn't the stomach for it. I hated the whole idea. Instead I insisted on serving my time with an antiques dealer. I did the history of art courses and shortly after I married Helen it all took off like a rocket. Helen taught me to dress smartly, rather than in the slightly fuddy-duddy clothes I used to wear, to present myself more forcefully. To give little talks on eighteenth-century furniture. She encouraged me to let the press know when I had something interesting to sell. And the rest, as they say, is history.

My antique shops are all over the country and I am regularly on television, consulted as an expert.

I made my own way and I was very proud of that. As I was proud of marrying Helen. We had our twenty-sixth wedding anniversary a few days ago. Helen even pretended to drink a little champagne tonight in the hospital. We brought in some crystal champagne glasses. She looked quite as beautiful as the day we were married.

And then after that we went to dinner: Mummy, Grace and I. Fortunately Grace didn't insist that the loutish David come with us. We went to a small French restaurant that Helen and I used to go to a lot before she became ill.

Mummy proposed a toast: 'To one of the happiest marriages I have ever known,' she said in one of her tinkly voices. I smiled a gentle, knowing smile.

This was the same woman who had railed and wept at me over a quarter of a century ago, begging me not to marry a girl of whom we knew nothing, a woman with no history, no past, except that she had been given away to an orphanage.

Grace agreed about our marriage. She said her dream was to have a marriage even half as good with David. She said that all her friends reported that their parents were constantly bickering and scoring points. This had never been a part of her life. She never remembered there being any arguments at all.

'Nor do I,' I said simply.

I didn't taste the food, it could have been chopped-up cardboard. The sense of unfairness welled up in me again. Why was this marriage drawing to a close? Next year we would be talking about my late wife, next month even. What reason could there be that Helen who had never hurt a fly was dying, and others whose lives had been full of malevolence and greed were allowed to live on? Why was I here at this table mouthing clichés to my mother and daughter, when I wanted to be by Helen's bed holding her hand, telling her that it had been a magical time and that I could remember no past before her and contemplate no future after she has gone?

And we would talk about inconsequential things, like planting geraniums near each other in clusters, and I was to send my jackets to be dry-cleaned every week and my shirts to be done at the Chinese laundry, and how I was to wear expensive cufflinks even if it did take three minutes to put them in. I loved her so much and I had never thought of being with anyone else. That's true – I never even thought of it.

But that Filipino woman, Mercedes, the one with the big, sad eyes, kept assuring me that Helen was happy tonight. She had talked about her family a lot apparently and took out pictures of our wedding day, and snaps of Grace when she was a little girl. Helen wanted me to try and live what she called a normal life. To go out and have a happy dinner with my mother and my daughter. As if that were remotely possible. I saw them looking at me, sideways glances, Mummy and Grace, it was a warning sign. I must be more cheerful. I'm tired of being cheerful for other people.

Yet that's what Helen wanted most. She had said it was the one thing I could do to help her, I must keep the show on the road. I must remember to invite my mother around regularly, I must be polite to David, Grace's irritating boyfriend, and not say that she could do better for herself even if I thought it. So with an effort I put my shoulders back, forced myself to identify what I was eating and started to keep the show on the road again.

They were both such handsome women. My mother did not look her seventy-something years, even I didn't know exactly how many. Yes, my mother Natasha Harris was a credit to her hairdresser, her beauty salon and her own good taste in clothes. She wore a lilac dress and jacket, something that had been designed for someone forty years younger, yet suited her perfectly.

Grace with her blonde hair and dark eyes was always striking. But tonight in a scarlet dress with those little straps she looked dazzling. Much too good for that David fellow, too beautiful and too bright, but I was not to go down that road.

She was still talking about David. When was she not? He worked in the City too.

People said he was bright. Bright in the sense of having native cunning. Like a bookie at a race track, not like the accountants, bankers and financial experts with whom Grace moved with such ease.

No, indeed, young David was a different breed.

But there was no doubt that Grace loved him. She had never brought anyone home before this and now it had to be this young lout.

'David was in to see Mother today.' Grace rolled his name around as if she loved saying it. 'He said, wasn't it extraordinary that I looked so different from both of you, that I couldn't sit out in the sun for two minutes without getting burned and yet you both could sit out for a month and just turn golden brown. He's the image of his father, of course, they are like twins, same nose and mouth, same way of pushing his hair out of his eyes.'

I restrained myself from saying that this must be unfortunate for both of them. I managed a weak little sign of interest to encourage Grace to go on speaking about the love object.

'Yes, he was asking Mother, didn't she think it was strange that I was so unlike either of you.'

'And what did your mother say?' I asked, trying

to put some warmth and interest into the question. I was barely able to speak. How dare this punk interrogate a dying woman? How dare he confuse her last weeks, days even, with his inane questions?

'Oh, you know Mother, she said she agreed with him, then she wasn't feeling so well so she called for Mercedes.'

'It wasn't the boy's fault, the pain comes and goes for Helen, we were told that,' my mother said. Astoundingly Natasha has always stood up for the young pup.

'And she was fine later, Dad, for the little anniversary ceremony, wasn't she?' Grace's big, beautiful, dark eyes looked at me questioningly.

'Yes, she was fine,' I managed to say.

I managed a lot of things in the next hour. Like smiling at my mother and my daughter, and telling them little stories about happier times. I managed to look as if I cared whether we had an Armagnac or a Cognac as a treat after dinner. And then finally my mother was back in her tall town house, and my daughter back in her flat where undoubtedly that David who looked so like his father would come and sleep in her bed.

And I was free.

Free at last to go and see Helen.

They let you in at any time.

That was the great thing about having enough money for private medicine. I could just push through those big quiet doors into the lobby which looked more like a grand hotel than a hospital. The night receptionist greeted me pleasantly.

'If she's asleep I promise you that I won't disturb her,' I said with my practised and barely sincere smile.

Helen and I had often talked about how life was basically an act. How we have to pretend a lot of the time in life. We sighed over it and told each other that at least we never pretended with each other. But we did. Of course we did. The biggest pretence of all was between the two of us.

She never told me about Grace and I never told her that I knew. That I had always known.

I had known since the day I went into her room that time during the so-called pregnancy when she said she preferred to sleep alone. She was tossing in her sleep in the middle of yet another bad dream, I put my hand on her forehead to reassure her and I saw it, the white garment she was wearing under her nightdress. I lifted up the sheet and saw the beautiful cream and gold negligee pulled to the side and the foam artificial belly attached to it.

The shock was overwhelming. Helen, my wife, lying to me. But it was followed by an aftershock of sympathy and love. The poor, poor girl, how terrified she must be of my mother and, indeed, of me that she would go to such extremes. And what was she going to do when the time came, or rather when she told us that her time had come?

Possibly she had arranged to buy a child from somewhere. But why hadn't she told me? I would have shared anything, everything with her. Why could she not have told me?

I went back to my room that night full of alarm. What did she intend to do without me by her side? I knew that she wouldn't be able to manage it without me, bring to term whatever half-crazed plan she had dreamed up.

But I also knew I had to wait. I had to let her go ahead. Nothing could be worse than the humiliation of letting her know I had discovered her deception.

The time went on; Helen looked pale and anxious, Mummy put it down to her pregnancy. Only I knew that there was a greater reason. I was very relieved in the end when she said that she wanted to go back to visit her old orphanage, the place where she had been brought up. That was where she would find a baby and pretend that it was ours.

It surprised me, even shocked me, that a place like that, a really respectable institution, would go along with her in such a subterfuge. It was against the law, it was against everything they stood for. They had always been meticulous about the children in their care. Surely they would have found a legal way for Helen to adopt a child rather than be a party to all this deception? But I knew they would always look out for Helen.

There were still women there who had been on the staff when she was a baby herself.

They would have nothing but compassion and pity for her.

So when I heard the news that our baby had been born suddenly, a little girl, strong and lovely, and that everyone was being so helpful, I started to breathe again. I glossed over the whole birth registration business, easily filling in documents here and signing my name there, asking no questions, raising no issues.

I held someone else's little girl in my arms, and even I, a mere man as people would say, realised that Grace was older than the tender age that Helen claimed her to be. I helped to keep people away from the mother and child until it was too blurred and late to know the difference. I reminded everyone that I too had been a very big child at birth and, amazingly, my mother – who is inclined to fight with me on issues like this – agreed and said that I was quite mountainous.

Helen gave no descriptions of the delivery, not even to people like my mother and her close friends who begged her for details. It had all passed in a blur, she said, but now that she held her little Grace to her it didn't seem important, and wasn't she lucky that she had been with people who knew how to help her. Nobody thought it was unusual.

Nobody.

Well, why would they?

They had seen Helen over the last six months swelling gently, planning the birth of her child. Only I knew and I would never tell.

I walked along the carpeted corridors to Helen's room. I had only one more thing to tell her, which was that her secret would be safe with me for the rest of her life. That it didn't matter one damn what that foolish, insensitive boyfriend David said, no one would ever know that Grace wasn't our daughter. But I couldn't tell her straight out. That would be letting her know that I knew.

I would sit and look at her and it would come to me.

I would know what to say.

The room was dark, just a small light and the big shape of the Filipino woman, Mercedes, sitting beside her. Mercedes was holding Helen's hand. Helen's eyes were closed.

'Mr Harris!' Mercedes was surprised to see me.

'Is she awake?' I asked.

She was asleep apparently; she had just had her cocktail of drugs. The palliative care nurse had been half an hour ago.

'I believe that David upset her today.'

'She didn't say, Mr Harris.'

But I knew in my heart that David had made her uneasy, her face had shown great alarm when he was droning on about some place over in Ireland with a wishing wood or a magic well or something. I can read Helen's face like a book. The nurse was impassive.

She saw and heard everything but said very little. I had to know.

'Did she mention anything? Anything at all?' I knew I sounded unhinged but I had to know if that boy had made her anxious. Now at the very, very end.

'No, no, she told me only of you bringing in champagne for her wedding anniversary.'

Mercedes was looking at Helen in the bed as if

she might still hear in spite of all the medication.

So it hadn't turned her whole world around in the fear that her long secret would be discovered. I could breathe again.

I asked could I sit with her alone. Apparently not. She was to be watched all night. They were worried about her chest.

'Please, Mercedes, I want to talk to her when she wakes,' I begged.

'Mr Harris, when she wakes I will move across the room and you can talk to her where I don't hear you,' she said.

And that's what I did – sat by her bed for two hours, stroking her thin white hand.

They must expect her to die today or tomorrow if there was a twenty-four-hour watch arranged.

Then she opened her eyes and smiled at me.

'I thought you were at dinner.' Her words came out with difficulty.

'I was, it was wonderful,' I said.

I told her we talked about lots of things: that everyone was very happy, and I was happiest of all. I reported Grace telling us that David said, wasn't it odd that Grace had dark eyes while we were both fair and I told him how my father had dark eyes too. Black as soot, so I told Grace that she must have got them from him. And Mummy had agreed and even added that Grace could also have got the dark eyes from Helen's side of the family. It was just that we didn't know them. So David had agreed. And shrugged and gone on to something else.

Helen looked at me long and hard. 'You still don't like him,' she croaked at me.

'I do,' I lied.

'You can't fool me, James, we never lied to each other, not once, remember?'

'I know.'

And then I told her the last lie.

'I don't really *dislike* him, my darling. It's just that I love my little girl so much nobody will ever be good enough for her. She's my daughter, my flesh and blood: nothing can make me think any other man will make her happy like we did.'

And Helen's smile was wonderful. I could have looked at it for ever but something changed in her face and Mercedes was about to go for the Sister.

Before she left the room she said to me: 'You are a wonderful man, Mr Harris, you made her very happy by what you said.' And even though it's utterly ridiculous – when you come to think of it – I felt for a moment that she knew our secret. That she knew all about Grace.

But, of course, that's not possible.

Helen would never have told her.

Not in a million years.

CHAPTER 10

June's Birthday

Part 1 – June

Well, it was obvious from the word go, wasn't it? I was going to be sixteen on 16 June and my name was June. Where else would we go except to Dublin for Bloomsday? It was going to be a magic day, she said.

I didn't really believe in magic days but she was so excited about it that she told everyone she met. 'My daughter's going to be Sweet Sixteen on the day that Leopold Bloom met Molly.' Most people hadn't an idea what she was talking about, but when has that ever stopped Mom?

The planning began almost a year in advance, with hours on the Internet looking for good-value tickets and low-cost accommodation. I swear we must be the only Irish Americans who don't seem to have any relatives in Ireland. I really don't know what Mom did with all her family. Alienate them, maybe. Talked too fancy about how well we were all doing across the Atlantic – which was far from true.

She had been born in this place called Rossmore, miles from anywhere. But most of the family had gone to live in Dublin. Over the years we had prised this much out of her. When she was a child she used to play in these woods and they all went to a holy well to pray for husbands.

'Was it a real wishing well?' I asked.

It had delivered my papa to Mom as a result so she obviously didn't think much of it. Apparently people went there to this day.

Mom had lived in Ireland until she was eleven, for heaven's sake, she must have had some cousins, friends, aunts, uncles. There hadn't been another potato famine since then to wipe them all out or anything. Why couldn't we be normal and go and stay with them?

Oh, no use asking Mom! She would shrug and flutter and say everything was so difficult these days, what with everyone being dispersed and all over the place. But it was never clear who had gone and where and why. It always seemed to me that we were the only ones who had left, everyone else had stayed.

No point in trying to pin Mom down, asking her serious questions. She knew nothing about Rossmore, and didn't really remember her years in

Dublin. She brushed it all away, and became more vague and restless and anxious.

It was like mentioning dates and ages and things. It always made Mom uneasy and in the end wasn't really worth it. Mom is forty-four. She says to everyone around here that she is thirty-five, which means that she was meant to be eighteen when she had me and only seventeen when she got pregnant. I don't know how that leaves time for all the college education she says she had, in places far from here where all the co-eds and sorority friends once lived. But it's better not to ask.

I see my papa twice a year when he comes east. He is Italian, very over-excitable, married again and has two little boys. He shows me photographs and calls them my half-brothers. He doesn't meet Mom when he comes to collect me and take me to the motel where he stays. If she's at home she watches from the window upstairs. But she's usually at work. People who sell water features and garden pools are at work all the time, it would appear.

Papa is no help when I ask him about things back in Ireland.

'Don't ask, Junie, don't ask, you just get a different story every time,' he would beg me.

'But, Papa, you must know something, I mean, when you and she got married weren't there guests from Ireland at the wedding?'

'A few, but, hey, Junie, you don't want to look back on the past, look to the future, I always say.'

He was about to show me the pictures of my half-brothers again so I headed him off at the pass.

'Okay, this birthday I'm having in Dublin. Did you meet any of Mom's relatives when you were in Dublin?'

'Nope,' he said.

'But why? She met all yours when you went to Italy, didn't she?'

'I never went to Dublin, June honey,' Papa said. 'I always wanted to but we didn't go there. Apparently your mom's grandpa and her father had words one day. Bad words, and her father was a proud young man, so he took his family off to the United States and wouldn't let anyone give a backward look.'

'But wasn't that all years ago, Papa?' I was bewildered that any row on earth could go on this long.

'Oh, you know the way things snowball, they just grow,' Papa said, forgiving everyone as usual.

'But when Mom's father died, when Grandpa was gone, couldn't it have been made up then?'

'Perhaps she felt it would be disloyal to her father's memory. Anyway I never got to see the place, Rossmore, or Dublin. So I'm no help to you.' Papa shrugged.

'I'll tell you all about it, Papa,' I promised.

'Gina and I are giving you a camera for your birthday, June. Take pictures of everything you see and show them to me next visit. You'll have a great trip. Honey, your mom will be so proud of you whoever you meet. She'll show you a really good time.' He is so good, Papa is, wants everyone to like everyone else.

I could feel sudden tears in my eyes.

'You never really told me why you and Mom broke up?' I began without much hope that I'd hear anything.

'Oh well, you know, these things happen, they're nobody's fault,' he said with a big smile. 'And you know, Junie, nothing was ever gained by looking back. We'll look ahead, to your wonderful trip to Ireland and then one day you'll come out to the Midwest to see your little half-brothers and . . .'

I owed him some support. 'I'd love to meet Gina, Papa, and get to know little Marco and Carlo,' I said and saw his face light up that I had said their names.

'How was your father?' Mom's voice was clipped and strained. It had obviously not been a good day selling garden pools. I longed to tell her how kind and generous he was, so open to hearing good news from every quarter. But it wasn't worth it, not if it made her restless and upset. So, like Papa had given in all those years ago about not visiting Dublin, I gave in too and said very little.

'He was nice.' I shrugged. 'Didn't have much to say.'

'He never had,' Mom said, pleased. And she was humming a little tune as she went to get out the big file of info about our trip. The file she had labelled 'June Sixteen' in big green felt-tip pen letters.

'What will you do there?' they asked me at school. I didn't know how to answer for I simply didn't know what we were going to do. But unlike

263

Mom I didn't care what they thought I was going to do.

'Will there be a party there for you?' my friend Suzi asked.

I said I didn't know – there might, as a surprise; there might not.

I'd have a party anyway when we came back. I was hoping we would go to this place Rossmore where there was a wishing well, but I wouldn't mention it to my mom until we got there. The only thing I knew we were going to do on 16 June was to go on this James Joyce walking tour. Mom had signed us into this group.

We were to begin out on the coast at a tower, and go to a museum, then have a huge breakfast of kidneys and liver and things, and then go into Dublin City on a little train. It sounded weird but my mom hadn't been happier for a long time so that was good. Anyway after all the fussing, the packing, unpacking and repacking of suitcases, the day came and we went to Dublin.

The flight was crowded, and the bargain economy hotel was okay – not great, just okay. And the stores were all small compared to at home, and the money was different, and I kept asking Mom did she remember it all or even anything about it, and she said she didn't really know, it was all so long ago.

'Not so long, Mom, you're only thirty-five, remember?' I said and for once she didn't rise to it.

'I feel a hundred and thirty-five compared to all

the young faces I see around me here, this has turned into a country of teenagers,' Mom grumbled. Her face looked tired and anxious. I decided not to tease her any more.

'You look as good as any of the youngsters, Mom, really you do.'

'You're a good girl, June, you have a lot of your father's Italian optimism in you, I will say that.'

'And what about the O'Leary side of the family? Do I have any of that?' I asked. It was walking on egg-shells but if I couldn't mention them in their own home town, where and when could I bring their unspoken name up?

'Mercifully, no,' she said. 'They forget everything but the grudges.'

'Is that why we won't see them?' I was as brave as a lion.

'They are strange people, those O'Learys. We all came originally from this one-horse town called Rossmore and settled in Dublin. Then I'm afraid *words* were said in a house on the North Circular Road.' My mom's voice was clipped. 'But let's get back to Joyce.'

She had arranged that we see the doorway of number 7, Eccles Street, which she said was the most famous address in English literature, and we could go to Davy Byrne's; on the way there we could familiarise ourselves with some Joycean culture and be prepared before the great tour on Bloomsday itself.

'You do know what it's all *about*, June?' Mom fretted.

I did.

One Thursday in June 1904 a whole lot of Dubliners went walkabout and kept meeting each other and criss-crossing and somehow even though it was only a fictional story it sort of drove everyone mad, and now they all dress up and do it again every year. I'd have preferred to do a tour of Dublin looking for my cousins, the real-life O'Learys, myself. But that wasn't on offer.

On Bloomsday, my birthday day, the city was in fancy dress. They were all dressed like Edwardians in boater hats and tottering on fancy old-fashioned cycles – it was half silly and half fun. I tried to be like my father and see the good side of it all. I tried to be like my friend Suzi who sees every gathering as a source of magnificent and yet undiscovered boyfriends. I tried to take my embarrassed gaze away from my mom who was being deeply foolish, showing off her very limited Joycean knowledge to all the others on the tour. We went from place to place and everywhere there were press people taking pictures of it all and camera teams. Eventually a girl with a microphone who was doing interviews for a radio programme came over to me and asked me some questions.

I told her it was my sixteenth birthday, that I was called June Arpino, half Italian, half Irish, and yes, I did know a bit about James Joyce and I was fairly interested in the tour but that actually I'd prefer to find my cousins the O'Learys.

The reporter was a nice girl with big dark eyes

and a friendly manner and seemed interested in my story. Why did I not know where my cousins were?

I told her that they came to Dublin originally from a place called Rossmore miles away in the country. Words had been said, I explained, at a wedding thirty-three years ago in a house on the North Circular Road. My mom had gone to America with her parents shortly after that. Maybe even because of that.

She was really so fascinated about everything I said, this interviewer was, so I told her that I was just reasonably interested in what had happened to Stephen Dedalus and Leopold Bloom and Molly a hundred years ago, but I told her that truthfully I was really much more interested in what had happened to the O'Learys thirty-three years ago and did any of them remember my mom, and was there any chance that the words that had been said that day could possibly be forgotten by now.

She seemed very pleased with this conversation and asked me afterwards for the address of the bargain economy hotel. She told me that it had been a pleasure talking to me and that she wished me good luck, she said sixteen was a great age to be and who knew what could happen before the day was over. I didn't expect all that much to happen actually, just more of the tour, but Mom was having a good time and told everyone that it was my sixteenth birthday.

But it was an okay day. They were nice people on the tour – Swedes and Germans and fellow Americans. They bought me ice creams, they got photos taken with me. My mom smiled all day long. When we paused at the Joyce Centre and bought postcards I sent two to my half-brothers Marco and Carlo. It wouldn't hurt anyone, not a bit, but it would cheer them and Papa and Gina.

Then it was over and we went back to the bargain economy hotel. Mom's feet were very tired, she said she would soak them in cologne before we went out somewhere for my birthday pizza. When we went in the door everyone at the desk was very excited.

They had been having phone calls and messages all day. Never had this bargain economy hotel had such attention. Dozens of people called O'Leary, saying that they were originally from Rossmore and more recently from the North Circular Road, had been looking for us for hours now, and there were a dozen numbers for us to ring. Some of them were in the bar already having a reunion and they wanted to give June Arpino a sixteenth birthday she would never forget.

I looked at my mom in terror. I had done the unforgivable. I had got in touch with people who had Said Words.

I had also, by saying she had left Ireland thirty-three years ago, admitted on Irish radio how old she was. This was as bad as it could get.

Amazingly though, there do seem to be magic days.

'I've been thinking about words all day,' Mom said. 'Joyce was all about words when you come to think of it. Some words are worth remembering for a hundred years, some are worth forgetting much

sooner. Come on, June, let's go meet your cousins,'
she said and led me to the bar.

Part 2 – Lucky O'Leary

Well, I *know* it's a ludicrous name, but tell me how
to get rid of it. I mean, you can't ring a bell and say
from now on I am to be known as Clare or Anna or
Shelley or something you'd like to be called. But no.
It's always been Lucky, and it will always be Lucky
O'Leary. That's my curse.

My parents called me Lucretia after an old aunt
who had money. She didn't leave them any so it was
useless, but Dad always called me his little Lucky
because he thought Lucretia was too much to saddle
a child with, no matter how great the inheritance
might be.

You should have heard the way they used to tease
me at school about it.

If I got a bad mark for an essay, if I didn't know
the answer when the maths teacher pounced on me,
or if I missed a pass in hockey, someone always said,
'Not so lucky, Lucky, now,' as if it was the first time
I had ever heard it in my life.

Anyway, I was far from lucky in my hopes of
going to work for the summer in a diner in New
York. You'd think they'd have been pleased. I didn't
want to go and get smashed and have sex with
everyone out in a Mediterranean resort like half
my class at school wanted to do when we finished
our exams. I didn't want a big expensive university

career that would bankrupt them. I wasn't asking for my fare out to a place that they would consider wild and dangerous.

All I wanted to do was to wear white socks and support shoes and a pink gingham dress in Manhattan. I wanted to serve pancakes and maple syrup; I wanted to put eggs 'over easy' framed with hash browns in front of the customers. And for them to say, 'Hi, Lucky.'

Or maybe I might even change my name out there and call myself a normal Irish name like Deirdre or Orla.

It wasn't such a mad dream, was it? Earning my own living, doing something respectable, worthy even, like getting people their breakfast. It wasn't as if I wanted to dance naked on tables. But you'd think I wanted to fly solo to the moon. How could I even consider living in a dangerous place like New York City? The matter would not even be discussed. I couldn't understand why we had no relations in America – some marvellous family of cousins where I could go at weekends and have barbecues and clambakes and go to ball games and all the things I loved about America from the movies.

But no. Alone in Ireland the O'Learys seemed to be without any emigrant wing of the family. No parcels of amazing American clothes ever came our way. No uncles and aunts with funny accents and permanently worn cream-coloured raincoats. And my mum and dad didn't even begin to realise what a treasure they had in me. They wanted me to come to this place called Rossmore.

They should have been on their knees thanking God that I was seventeen, a virgin, a non-smoker, only a very occasional drinker. And that all this was fairly rare in my crowd. I would pass my exams, I wouldn't have screaming matches at home. I was even reasonably pleasant to my poisonous sister Catriona even when she prised open my dressing table drawer with a knife to get at my make-up. And to my very annoying little brother Justin who used to bring potato crisps into my room and stink the place out because he thought he had less chance of getting caught there.

So what did they really want as an eldest daughter? Mother Teresa of Calcutta?

Anyway things were pretty glum in the O'Leary household this particular June because of everything. I said very politely, no thank you, I did *not* want to join everyone on a lovely family holiday in Rossmore. I said even more politely that I did *not* think this was throwing their generosity back in their faces, just that I did not fancy walking along a river bank or going through thorny woods or ensuring that Catriona and Justin didn't break their necks at the amusement park. And no, I didn't think that I would make lovely friends of my own during two weeks there. And if they just said yes I'd be right out of their hair and into a lovely New York diner up to my elbows in pancakes and bagels.

And they asked me please not to mention any of this again since it simply wouldn't happen.

So I went up to my room, locked the door against Catriona and Justin and looked at my face in the mirror. I wasn't bad-looking, not gross or hairy or full of spots or anything. I wasn't good-looking either but I had a friendly face – one that would have pleased all the clientele in the diner, specially because I had a good memory and I'd remember people and know instantly if they wanted a cappuccino to go or extra jelly on their toast.

I don't normally listen to the radio, I play CDs to myself. I'd really love a cheap television set in my bedroom but Dad said we're not made of money and not to be ridiculous. But anyway I turned on this radio programme and there was some ancient one solving problems. You know, the way they pretend to be young and hip and with it and get all the words wrong. So some crazy girl had written in saying that her mother was a mad suspicious old bat and she couldn't go anywhere or do anything. So I yawned to myself and said, 'Tell me about it,' but I did wonder why she thought the old one on the radio would have anything to say that would be remotely useful.

The old one said, yes it was desperate that old and young people didn't understand each other but there *was* a solution. Oh yes, I thought, of course there's a solution. Give in, give up, lose the argument, lose hope.

I waited for her to come out with this but instead she said: 'Your mother is lonely, dear, lonely and confused, confide in her, make her your ally.'

Sure, really great idea. I start making my mum my ally and in two minutes she'll say, 'You're not getting round me, do you hear?'

'Tell your mother about your concerns and your worries about the world, ask her about hers. She may not respond immediately but, my dear, she will respond in time. Mothers of teenage girls may look confident but in fact they are often anxious and beached creatures. Be interested, pretend an interest at first and a real interest will follow. You are on the eve of making your mother your great, great friend. Act at friendship first and then as time goes by it will become real . . .'

What kind of a world do these old ones *live* in? Imagine – she's paid serious money to go on the radio and talk all this nonsense. I mean, give us a break here.

Then the old one went on to talk about two best friends who had a fight and she told the one who had written in to make the first gesture to hold out her hand and say, Look, I don't want to fight . . . Which was of course the right advice but she'd probably read it somewhere. Mothers lonely and beached. Huh.

They had had a row, Mum and Dad, we all knew that, it showed itself by over-politeness at supper. I didn't know what it was about and I didn't really care.

'Take your elbows off the table, Catriona, and show some respect for the great meal your mother has made for all of us . . .'

'Don't all talk at once, children. Your father has had a long and *very* tiring day . . .'

I didn't know what it was about, honestly, I didn't care. They sometimes had these coldnesses. But it would pass. I pretended to take no notice. Catriona and Justin, of course, who have the brains of a flea between them, did notice and commented on it.

'Are you having a fight with Daddy?' Catriona asked.

'No, darling, of course not,' Mum said in an awful tinny voice.

'Are you going to get divorced, Daddy?' Justin wondered.

'No, Justin, eat your supper,' Dad said.

'Which of you will I go with?' Justin asked, looking from one to the other anxiously.

'Nonsense, Justin, how could a couple with such a wonderful son as you *possibly* get divorced?' I said. I was being sarcastic but Justin doesn't get irony.

'Oh all right then,' he said happily and attacked the rest of his supper.

I helped Mum stack the dishwasher.

'That was good of you, Lucky,' she said.

'Oh you know. Men!' I sighed.

She looked at me suddenly and I thought I saw tears in her eyes. But I didn't want to get soft in the head and make her my great, great friend like the old one on the radio said.

Next morning Dad said I was a terrific daughter, and since he had been saying I was a scourge from on high for the past few weeks I got worried and thought maybe they *were* going to split up.

So I said nothing. I'm getting good at shrugging.

Dad wasn't home for supper next day and Mum was locked up with her sister in the dining room. I tried to listen until I saw Catriona doing the same so I ordered her to go upstairs and not to be so appalling as to listen to other people's private conversations.

Dad came home very late. I tried to listen at their bedroom door but there was nothing to hear. Just total silence.

The next day I decided to do something different. The days were tedious now because we had reached such a stand-off.

Mum had a job working in a children's boutique: it was mornings only, so that she could be home to police us all in the afternoons. I had nothing to do so I went along to the boutique (we were never allowed to call it a shop). She was alarmed as old people always are when they see someone from home. She thought something was wrong.

I told her that *nothing* was wrong, just that there was a new pasta bar near by and that maybe she might feel like us having lunch there together. And her face lit up like the Kish Lighthouse.

During lunch, Mum said, 'It's hard on you, Lucky, having to come to Rossmore with us this year.'

I hadn't told her yet that there wasn't a chance I would go on such a dreary holiday with them. But for some reason I remembered the old one on the radio talking about mothers being beached and lonely. It was worth a try if I could get what I wanted.

'It's probably not all that easy for you either, Mum,' I said.

She looked at me with a long look. 'No, sometimes it's not, Lucky,' she said. She paused as if she were going to say something very important. So I waited. I wondered, would she tell me that Dad bored her to death or she had a toy boy or that I could go to New York, but actually she said none of these things.

'Things have a way of working out, you know,' was what she said in the end. It was so dull and so useless I hadn't an idea what to say.

So I said, 'You might be right, Mum,' and she smiled at me and patted my hand and knocked all the linguine off my fork. I felt like life was over if this was all she could say and I kicked a stone the whole way home, which was stupid because I took the whole front off my fairly new shoes.

Mum was going shopping but I said I had things to do, I was afraid I might kill her stone dead in the supermarket if I went with her. Instead I went home and lay on my bed and wished that I was forty-three, or something ancient with all my life behind me. I turned on the radio and it was some awful thing about James Joyce and all the mad foreigners who come over here.

There was this girl interviewing some Yank girl who was spending her sixteenth birthday traipsing round with her mother, following the whole journey they made in *Ulysses*. Well, I thought, bad as Mum is – and she is pretty barking mad – she'd never make me do that.

And this one, June, with an Italian name – Arpino or something – said she had had Irish relations called O'Leary and they were originally from the dreary Rossmore, which we were too, from the North Circular Road, which is where Dad's family is from. And suddenly I got this thought. Could she be my cousin?

Could June Arpino and her family get me out to New York to work in a diner?

I listened like mad for more information. She was staying in that budget hotel, the place that looked like a prison in Eastern Europe. I rang the radio station and they told me she, this June Arpino girl, wasn't there, that it was an interview done earlier in the day; but they gave me the phone number of the hotel and said that half the country seemed to have been phoning in and they were all heading for the hotel.

Imagine! Maybe they all wanted her to get them jobs in a diner. People are so odd.

So I might go as well, it would be a laugh.

Mum knocked on the bedroom door. She said she had been looking at skirts for herself but none of them fitted her for some reason so she had bought one for me instead. It was nice actually, pink velvet – not like the things she usually gets which a child in an orphanage in the nineteenth century would be ashamed to wear.

'Did Dad ever have anyone who went to America, anyone from the North Circular Road?' I asked.

'Yes, his uncle went over an insult or some cracked thing, no one can remember what it was. And no one knows where they are, so they're no use to you, love, for your diner plans, I'm afraid.' She genuinely did look sorry.

'I think I've found them,' I said and told my mum. Amazingly she seemed interested, and pleased. Excited even.

'Let's go,' she agreed.

The hotel was as awful on the inside as from outside. Absolutely full of people, and would you believe it, some of Dad's dreadful cousins were there too, and they were all roaring at each other with excitement, and there in the middle of it all were two Americans who had to be June and her mother.

June was the image of me, we were like sisters. And she was wearing a pink velvet skirt. Mum and the others were screeching away, with Mum telling all kinds of terrible personal details about how she had a fight with Dad and he never apologised and she was sick of always being the one who ended up saying sorry.

So June's mother suddenly weighed in and said that if she had her life all over again she would certainly have made some kind of apology to June's father rather than letting him go off with a trashy young woman and having two more kids . . .

June and I talked to each other so that we wouldn't have to listen to all this historical stuff. She was a whole year younger of course, but with her being American it sort of levelled out – they mature more quickly over there. And we thought, wasn't it *extra-ordinary* that we were related and had never known the other existed.

Mum rang Dad on her mobile and he turned up half an hour later and the first thing he said was to Mum, that he was sorry he was so difficult and Mum kissed him in front of everyone. And in minutes there he was shaking hands with all of his cousins and telling them Mum was the best wife in the world.

June was just great.

I told her I had two beds in my room if she wanted to stay with me. We might even go down to this mad Rossmore place which had a wishing well never known to fail. My mum said she'd like to have a word with the saint at that well because the first husband she had sent had not turned out to be that great. Maybe he was only a rehearsal, maybe the real husband might be still out there waiting. It was hugely embarrassing at her age of course but June and I could cope.

And June's mother said that of course they could change the air ticket and after their holiday here with us, and the visit to this Rossmore place, I could go back and stay with them in New York. They knew a terrific diner where I could work. A really respectable family place.

Mum and Dad weren't so sure at the start but June whispered at me that I should remind them that the alternative was going to Cyprus or Majorca and throwing my knickers away at the airport. So that sort of concentrated their minds. It wasn't definite yet. There was still a journey to go down that road. But with my new cousin June I was sure I'd swing it.

I caught Mum looking at me a bit soppily.

'You're not drunk, Mum?' I asked her anxiously.

'No, not remotely. Do you remember what I was saying to you this morning, Lucky?' she asked in an awful Mary Poppins voice.

June and I had been talking about how easy it was to keep mothers happy if you just talked their language. They didn't know you were parroting it back.

'You said things have a way of working out,' I said.

And Mum's face lit up with pleasure. 'You see, you remember! You really are my greatest friend, Lucky,' she said. 'I'll miss you so much when you go to America.'

And I smiled back. It was a complicated smile, built on many layers.

First it was the smile of huge relief. I had won the battle, I was going to work in a New York diner. My mother had admitted as much.

Then it was the smile of a friend as the old woman on the radio had advised us all. She had said that it would work wonders. She had said in her talk that at first it would be an act, but after a time we would find that we actually meant it. That was an amazing thing about being grown up, time passes quickly.

I was beginning to feel that it wasn't a pretence any more.

When I said all that bit to my mum that she was my greatest friend too, I meant it. I wasn't acting any more. I did mean it.

Maybe I *was* very lucky and didn't need to change my name after all.

CHAPTER 11

Tell Me Why?

Part 1 – Emer

Tell me, *why* did I have to get one of those huge digital clocks where you could see the figures from the other side of the Rossmore Hotel? Why couldn't I have had a small travel clock like normal people instead of this big thing the size of a dinner plate beside my bed with red numbers changing every minute?

I have been watching it now for four and a half minutes while it changed from 9.08 and a bit to 9.13 a.m. I vaguely remember setting the alarm for 9.30. I have a sort of cloudy memory of doing that. My thinking was that if I got up at nine-thirty I could be showered, dressed, have a coffee and be on the road by ten.

It's really important that I be on the road in good shape today. I have an interview for the job that

I've wanted for years: director of the Heartfelt Art Gallery, a marvellous outfit where I have yearned to work for ages. I had a lot of the right qualifications but there was always someone else in the job. Now the guy who had run it for the last three years was off to Australia. Today I have my interview.

So, tell me *why* had I not gone to bed early, sober and alone?

I can't move, you see, because it would wake him up.

And then he might think I was signalling that I wanted it all over again. I must lie here motionless until I sense the alarm is going off and after one quick blast of its horrific noise I will quench it and leap out of bed all in the same movement and run to the bathroom.

I've got nothing on, obviously, so I'll have to move quickly. There will be no lovely luxurious time while the fizzing drink cures the head and the coffee sends out soothing noises and smells from the percolator. No, it has to be very brisk and businesslike. As if this is the most normal thing in the world to have invited the taxi driver in and gone to bed with him.

Tell me, why didn't I leave him in his taxicab like ninety-nine per cent of the population would have done? *Why* couldn't I have done that too?

I suppose I could blame it on the reception I was at. They had this absolutely rot-gut wine – it practically tinkled down your throat it was so rough. And no food, of course. Not even a biscuit or a crisp to soak it up. It just went on down there in my stomach doing its evil work, sloshing about into every vein and gut and bit of muscle tissue, gradually moving its way remorselessly up to the brain to paralyse it completely. There was that, and of course the fact that I really hated Monica, the woman whose paintings were being shown.

I had always hated her, long ago back at art college, long before she made silly fluttery eyes with Ken on my birthday, at the meal I was paying for. When she knew that I liked him.

And now I hate the way she smiles with her mouth but not her eyes. I hate the way she gets noticed and fêted and admired, and how everyone was standing in line to buy her paintings. There were red dots everywhere to show that they had been sold. Like measles all over her awful chocolate-box paintings.

Well, why did I go? you might ask me. Why did you not stay away and prepare for your interview? Why indeed.

But at the time it made sense to go. I wanted to show Monica that I wasn't going to be frightened away, let her think I was envious, let her think I had cared about Ken and she being friends. Or more than friends possibly. Or anything.

Also, I had got a new hairstyle in preparation for my interview and a new linen jacket which I could wear under my good suede coat. So I thought I should give them an outing. It would do no harm to let Ken see me looking fabulous.

What a bad idea that turned out to be. If Ken feels anything about me this morning it's a huge sense of relief that his cautious Canadian practical streak had triumphed over any tendency he might have had to fancying me. Ken is wrapped in relief this morning. Unlike me. I am wrapped in my own bed with a taxi driver.

From where I'm lying at the edge of the bed I can see the linen jacket with what looks like half a bottle of red wine down the front of it. And my expensive haircut – well, I haven't seen a mirror yet this morning, but it's obviously like a wild bush.

Apart from the terrible wine, it was altogether a dull opening. I mean, the pictures were terrible, anyone could see that. When I get my job in the Heartfelt gallery (that's now *if* I get my job there) I wouldn't countenance hanging an exhibition like that. Nobody liked them – they murmured and said the right things and bought them because they wanted to be well in with Tony who runs the gallery. Tony who might give *them* an exhibition too one day if they play their cards right.

And Monica was so awful to me, so plain rude and insulting, no wonder I took to drink. She seemed to have trouble remembering my name. It's not hard to remember, even slow learners could get to grips with the name Emer. It's not as if the name Emer is challenging or hard to pronounce or anything.

But Monica couldn't manage it somehow. She had to rack her brain when introducing me to people.

'I was at art college with this lady, believe it or

not,' she would coo. As if somehow I was so old and decrepit and she was so young no one could possibly believe us to be contemporaries.

Come on, Monica. We are all thirty-one years of age, you, Ken and I. None of us are married.

Ken teaches art in a school, you paint awful sugar and spice pastels, I work in art administration. This very morning I might well land a terrific job in one of the best art galleries in the country. I will be called a director though actually it's a job that could even be described as a curator.

I want that job so much. Tell me, why did I get myself into this mess?

You see, I can't even move to get up and repair myself, try to limit the damage. Find something else to wear. Oh my God. I've just seen that there's spaghetti on that jacket as well as wine!

Yes, naturally we had to go to a pasta bar afterwards. Instead of coming home on the bus like any normal human, I had to cry with delight when Ken suggested a few of us go to this place. And of course Monica came too, said it would be a fun thing to do and brought Tony from the gallery and awful shrieky people. Well, as it turned out I was probably more shrieky than all of them. And one of the waiters came up to me and gave me a bottle of wine because I had painted the sign for his father's bicycle repair shop. And Monica had thought that was a scream. Imagine – Emer does signs for repair shops, how marvellous, isn't she something else?

At one stage I thought Ken whispered to me not

to take any notice, that she was only winding me up.

'Why?' I asked him.

'Because she's jealous of you.'

Or that's what I think he said. He might have said that but then again I might have imagined it. To be honest the evening isn't at all clear. There's a heavy bit of mist over the bit where the waiters stood in a line and sang 'By the Rivers of Babylon' and I joined them. And I thought everyone thought I was great. But they might not have thought that at all.

And how did we pay? Did we pay? Oh God, tell me we paid.

Yes – I remember it. Ken said that he'd take a tenner from everyone, and everyone thought that was terrific except I seemed to have a window of sobriety and said that he'd need to take fifteen to cover the bill, and I *think* he said, nonsense, that it would be all worth it for the pleasure of seeing me again. And Monica heard and wasn't at all pleased and she put on that vomit-making little baby voice that she does and said that surely nobody expected *her* to pay because she had been feeding them lovely wine all night at the gallery. And Tony got a bit bad-tempered and said that actually *he* had been giving them wine at the gallery all night. And I'm afraid that I said neither of them should fight to claim responsibility over the wine since it was so terrible. And Ken paid hastily with his Visa card and got us all out on the road.

I felt very dizzy when I faced the fresh air and I would have just loved it if Ken had come home with me, not for anything except just to take care of me, make me drink milk or water or whatever I should have drunk. But no, of course, Madam Monica insisted he see *her* home and we all lived in different directions. He got me a taxi, buttoned up my smart suede coat for me and asked the driver to take care of me because I was a very special person.

Boy, did the taxi driver take care of me all right.

But I can't blame Ken, much as I'd like to. He didn't ask the taxi driver to come home and get into bed with me. No, sadly I can't say that that was his fault. It must in some sense have been mine.

But why? Tell me why? I don't normally go to bed with strangers, in fact I never have before in my whole life. Was it something to do with disappointment about Ken? Was he persuasive? Did I fancy him?

Think, Emer. Think and try to reconstruct the journey home. Think silently. Don't wake him.

He was young, early twenties, I'd say. Thin pointy face, a bit like a fox. An evil cunning fox waiting for his opportunity.

'You look as if you had a good evening,' he said as I fell into his taxi, picked myself up hastily in order to wave Ken goodbye and to pretend I was more sober than I was.

'Actually I had a shitty evening if you must know,' I said coldly.

'What would you have preferred?' he asked.

'Not to have gone at all. Not to have drunk that cheap wine, not to have talked to that tiresome woman, not to have looked at her horrifically bad paintings.'

'Sounds terrible all right,' he said. I didn't like him pitying me.

'So what kind of an evening did you have?' I asked him loftily. I think he said it had been an evening like any other really – he was sort of shruggy and resigned over it. I said he had the wrong attitude to evenings.

God, why had I said that, why couldn't I have let him have his own kind of evening like any other instead of going to bed with the passenger? But maybe he did this every evening. What do I know? Very little.

He said something about needing to earn money for a living, and I asked him, did he have a girlfriend? I think he said he had, someone called Hissie or Missie or some awful name. Anyway he can't have liked her much if he ended up here.

He said she was a modern woman, she knew about relationships because she worked in a flower shop, and it was all about guilt and anxiety and lies. She didn't want to get tied down, she let him go his way and he let her go hers. That they both had their eyes open or some such crap.

I said that it was all a heap of lies – that Hissie was mad to settle down with him but she had to pretend not to be, that's how it worked nowadays. I said I knew this for a fact, that I pretended to be cool with Ken but I loved him and if I thought it would work I'd give up any job. But you can't win them all.

'Did you win any part of the evening?' he asked. He was trying to cheer me up.

'Yes, I did, I sang a song with the waiters.'

I sang 'By the Rivers of Babylon' again for him to show him how good I had been, and he joined in at the chorus. Then he asked me if I knew 'Stand by Your Man'. I said I did know it but I didn't entirely agree with the sentiments. But to be a sport I sang it with him, then I suggested 'Hey Jude' and then we were home.

And why, oh why, tell me, could I not have said goodbye to him and thought of it as a good singsong to end a lousy night? Oh no, never do anything the easy way. Instead I must have invited him in with me, and shamefully I can't remember what happened next.

Did I get out my CDs? Was it possible that I could have had more drink? You see, he must have been sober, I mean, he was driving a cab, of course he was sober. Did we go straight to bed?

Oh, if only I could remember what made me do it! Then I might be able to get us out of this situation with marginally less embarrassment than I felt it would involve.

I reached for the huge digital clock just before it burst into sound. Thank God I hadn't woken him. He lay there, a dead weight on the other side of the bed. At least he wasn't snoring or thrashing about.

Where did he park his cab? There's nothing but double yellow lines around here – the traffic is appalling. They are going to build a bypass and the sooner the better. But they haven't built it yet, he'd have had to go miles to find a place to park. Or maybe he left it outside the door in the white heat of passion.

Either way it was his problem.

Did he even give me his name? He must have at some stage. I wouldn't think about that any more, it was too horrifying. Instead I would think what I would wear to the interview. Suppose I were just to button up my suede coat, and drape a scarf over it.

My God, my coat!

Could I have left it in his taxi? It wasn't on a padded hanger on the back of the door where it always lives. Oh no – God, I know you can't be pleased with me. I know it was a wrong thing to take the taxi man to bed with me, very silly and wrong, but I don't do much sinning, not in the great scheme of things. And I had gone to pray at St Ann's Well. I asked the saint to make Ken love me, which she hasn't yet, and I don't suppose she will now. But listen, God, I feel like death, I'll make a dog's dinner of this interview, I've ruined my new linen jacket and now, *now* you tell me that I've lost my suede coat as well.

I was so upset about my coat that I forgot about the taxi driver and not waking him up.

I sat straight up in bed and turned my tortured, hung-over face towards him.

There was no one there.

On the bed beside me was my big suede coat all rolled up. Heavy and obtrusive and taking up an inordinate amount of room in the bed. Pretending to be a taxi driver and frightening me to death.

I leaped from the bed in delight. I had a future, a lot of showering and gargling and finding whatever else in the flat might be clean enough to wear. Then I had to get this job at the Heartfelt gallery, then I would go to the dry-cleaners with all my ruined clothes, then I would call Ken and ask him out to celebrate and I would get him back.

Really, that cheap wine does terrible things to you. Gives you hallucinations even.

As if I would take an unknown taxi driver home to bed with me!

Part 2 – Hugo

It's not that there's anything wrong with driving a taxi. I mean, it's a great job in many ways and you can put in the number of hours you want to. If you're tired you can knock off early, or if you're saving for a holiday you can stay out for an extra three hours a night to help pay for it. There's different people get into the back of the cab every time you stop and you'd need to be a right old curmudgeon not to meet someone you liked a few times a day.

I've driven a woman who was going over to a garden party at Buckingham Palace in London and she was so nervous she had to get out of the cab to be sick twice. I drove an actor who was having trouble learning his lines and we recited them together for forty minutes with the meter still running. I drove a couple who had just got engaged to be married and I had to try on the ring four times and say it was the biggest diamond I had ever seen.

So what's not to like about driving a taxi for a living?

My Uncle Sidney, who drove a taxi and sort of steered me into the business, said he always tried to get one nugget of information from every fare he picked up; that way you got yourself a fine and varied education all while doing a day's work. He came home with information about forecasting the weather, about where to get vegetables half-price when a market stall was just closing down, about how to meet ladies for bridge and other activities through the Internet.

Chrissie, this girl who works in a flower shop, nice girl, I see her around from time to time, she says I'm very funny about the whole taxi driving thing and I should write a book about it. Me, write a book? Me, Hugo? No, that wasn't what I wanted at all.

If the truth be told I would prefer to have been a singer, I fancied myself out on stage in front of the crowds. I'm not afraid of people or shy or anything, this job knocks any nerves out of you anyway. I can read music and play the guitar, but I never got a break, I never made it.

I tried, mind you. I entered talent competitions, I sent sample tapes, then sample CDs. But no one took them. I'm not any worse than a lot of people who did get a chance. I wrote my own songs, I did versions of other people's songs. Nothing worked.

I didn't run with a musical crowd. I know that sounds odd. After all, if you're interested in something, then why not have friends who share the same interests? But somehow I remained pals with the fellows I was at school with.

They liked going to clubs, sure, and liked dancing with birds to good music but they weren't really musical. They never wanted to play it, to be part of it, to be in there making it. So the matter didn't come up much.

They have different jobs here and there and some of them drive cabs too. When we got together we'd talk about that, and about holidays and what teams we support, and sometimes we'd all promise to jog or go to the gym because we're all developing big bums and bellies from sitting in a cab all day. And we'd play football on a Sunday morning and go for a few pints. But one by one they paired off and got married and now when we are all twenty-five or twenty-six I am the only one who hasn't settled down.

So now there's not all that much for me to talk about with them. They go on about raising a house deposit or re-roofing or grouting or laying a decking system. In some ways I envy them because they are all so very interested in it all, and spend the whole of Saturdays fixing up their places. Some of them have had kids who all look exactly the same as each other.

One day I'll marry and have kids but not yet, not till I meet someone right – someone I'd do anything for.

I hope it will be someone involved in the music industry because I haven't quite given up on my dream yet. Nearly, to be honest, but not quite. When you hear these star interviews there was always a bit of luck along the way, they met someone who knew someone who gave them a break.

I still live at home but that's not as wet and wimpish as it sounds for a man of twenty-six.

Well, there's living at home and there's living at home, isn't there? In our house we have a microwave, and a big fridge with three separate shelves marked 'Dad', 'Mum' and 'Hugo'.

My sister Bella, who lives in her own place with two feminists, she said she thought it – our home – was the saddest thing she had ever seen, sadder than a documentary about disabled people because it was only their bodies that were disabled and in our cases it was our minds. We were three sad, sad, dysfunctional people trapped in a pathetic lifestyle. It made her shudder to think of us, three adults who could have had a real life.

Well, I never really knew what she was going on about, to be frank. Our life functioned just fine. I put a nice little sum into the post office for them every month, it was their rainy day fund. My dad worked for a small animals veterinary practice, he was an assistant. That's what he had always been, not a veterinary nurse – he didn't have qualifications

– but they relied on him utterly. He could hold the kittens for injections or calm the dogs, or clean up when the hamsters crapped over everything. He just adored animals but sadly Mum was allergic, came out in a bumpy rash and sneezed and got watery eyes. So he kept the animals for work time, and walked other people's dogs in the park most evenings.

My mum worked in a travel agency, she spent her whole day finding cheap holidays for people, she was quite good at it now. She could get great discounts for all kinds of vacations. The West Indies for half-nothing at short notice, a long weekend off-season in Venice . . . But Dad couldn't fly, he had tried once and his ears went funny so he never did it again. Mum had to go on trips with her colleagues, which wasn't quite the same. But they were happy, they were really quite happy compared to most of the world.

Dad was a vegetarian and Mum was always on some kind of nutter's diet so it made sense to have a shelf for each of us in the fridge. And we arranged everything else in the house very well.

We had two television sets, one in the kitchen and one in the sitting room, so there were no heated debates about what we watched. Every third week we each did the washing; there was no ironing, we had everything drip-dry. My sister Bella found that sad too. As if her life with these two dull women who all wore organic clothes and ate organic food and talked organic talk was somehow less drear.

Mum and Dad are just fine and I'd been driving a taxi for long enough to know they were better off than a lot of people of their age. You can see a lot of human misery from the front seat, let me tell you.

Anyway this morning my mum had said she was going to Dubai next weekend for eight days and my dad said that was great, she'd love it, and he might go to a sanctuary for injured animals – he had always wanted to give the time to poor donkeys with their bones coming through their skin and to frightened dogs who often had only three legs and haunted eyes. They both asked me would I be okay and I said I'd be fine. It was my weekend to do the washing anyway so they could just leave everything for me.

'You're a very good boy, Hugo,' my mum said.

'A man really,' my dad said.

'Maybe you'll be off getting married when we get back,' my mum said.

She said it as a joke but I know she was serious. She'd have loved to see me married. I felt a failure to them in a way. When they were my age Bella was five and I was four. I had nothing to show for anything but a reasonable bank balance.

'No, I think I'll be around here until you are old and grey,' I said.

'I hope not, son, it would be nice for you to meet someone you chose rather than living with us, people you didn't choose at all,' my dad said.

And I got a sudden chilly feeling that I never

would meet anyone I knew was right for me because I realised I could never make up my mind.

I just went with things that fell into my lap. Like Uncle Sidney getting me to drive a taxi and going with this girl because she was someone's sister or that girl because she was the mate of some pal's girl-friend. I played football on a Sunday because some-one else had set up the team and booked the place to play, I bought my clothes in a place where Gerry, a friend of mine, worked. He always held a few things back for me when they had a sale.

'You could look really well, Hugo, if you tried,' he said to me a couple of times. 'You have that thin pointy face that women go for. You should wear good leather jackets.' But then Gerry is a very cheer-ful fat guy who says nice things to people all of the time.

He wouldn't know whether I looked good or like the back of the Rossmore to Dublin bus. So I don't go out much testing my so-called good looks.

And oddly, apart from Chrissie, I never really met anyone I'd like to get to know a lot better. And even with her. Well, I wasn't sure.

It would be foolish for us both to get our hopes up if we weren't really sure. I mean, Chrissie was great fun and she was fascinating about flowers and everything, but for ever? All day and all night? I don't know.

And neither did Chrissie, to be honest. We had both told each other that nothing was worse than people trapped in loveless relationships. Chrissie saw that all the time. She said that a good sixty per cent of the brides that she dealt with over wedding flowers were all wretched.

I knew that so many of the people I drove were miserable too and seemed to fight all the time. Particularly those going on vacation. They often actually seemed to hate each other.

Anyway the night after my mum had gone off to the Gulf to get a tan and buy a gold bracelet, and my dad had gone to feed little broken fawns with bottles of warmed milk and bind up the wounds on donkeys' backs, I worked an extra shift. I was thinking it would be really nice to have someone who just adored you and would fight your corner, like happens in the movies.

And then I was going past this Italian pasta place where people were coming out into the street, most of them fairly drinky as it happened. You want to be careful of a fare like that. Uncle Sid always said, turn off the meter but slow down to see if they can stand and pay what they will owe you and especially to keep a beady eye out for those who might get sick in your cab.

A nice young fellow came out and hailed me, he was sober anyway, American or Canadian maybe. Very polite.

'I wonder if I could ask you to take this young lady home?' He gave me a tenner, well above the fare to where she was going.

The *young lady* was weaving round the place, but she didn't look like a barfer – you get the feeling when they're going to throw up – she hadn't that kind of aura about her, if you know what I mean. Anyway she fell into the taxi on her knees, which was a poor start.

He climbed in and straightened her up, very tenderly.

I asked him, was he going to come with us possibly? I was thinking he might be useful at the other end hauling her out again.

'No, I wish I could but, you see, Monica . . . is there . . . and it is Monica's night really and we do live in the same direction. You're all right, Emer – wake up, darling, wake up and talk to the nice driver.'

'I don't want to talk, Ken, I want to sing to the driver,' she said mutinously.

'Is that okay, driver?' he asked me anxiously.

'Sure, Ken,' I said. 'I'll sing too.'

'I *hate* Monica, Ken, you're much too good for her, she has a face like a marshmallow and she paints as if she dipped another marshmallow into pinks and blues and yellows. She's a really terrible gross person, Ken, it's just that you can't see that.'

Ken seemed anxious for Monica not to hear this description and he looked at me wildly. I often think this job is a bit like being a diplomat and a marriage counsellor all rolled into one.

'I'll be off now,' I said.

'Take care of her, she's very special,' he said to me. And we were gone. She sat grumbling in the back, asking why if she was so special was he going to take home that Monica who had a face like an almond bun.

'More like a marshmallow really,' I corrected her. She was delighted with me.

'That's exactly what she's like. Exactly. How clever you are to notice.' She smiled happily to herself and repeated it over and over: 'Like a marshmallow', as if she had not come up with the phrase herself. 'Hey, Ken asked me to sing to you – what would you like?' she asked eventually.

'Why don't *you* choose.' I was polite as always.

She was a nice girl, late twenties maybe, long straight fair hair. She had drunk far too much wine but seemed pleasant about everything except Monica with the flat face.

'Ken is very nice, you see, he knows taxi driving is a dull job and that you might want to be entertained on the way back, that's why he suggested it. I'll sing "By the Rivers of Babylon".' And she did, quite well as it happens.

I suggested we sing 'Stand by Your Man'. She told me that men were foolish and didn't need people to stand by them, what men needed was a wake-up call. But we sang it anyway, and a few more.

Then I was afraid she was going to go to sleep and we might have trouble identifying her house or if it was a flat which one it might be. So I made every effort to keep the conversation going, by asking her, what did men need to be woken up to.

'To the fact that they usually have perfectly good women just within an arm's length and they never

301

seem to see them,' she said crossly. She told me at confused length about this guy Ken and how he had been taken in by Monica's sheer silliness and had wrongly believed that that stupid woman needed looking after. She didn't think that they were sleeping together but you never knew with men. And tonight could be the night. Tonight could be the very night they might do it. In Monica's horrible house at 35 Orange Crescent. She was pretty glum about that.

'Maybe he's too drunk to do it tonight,' I said, thinking that would help.

'No, he hardly drinks at all. He was the sober one who paid too much for the meal for everyone.'

She was brooding heavily about it all. She said she had been to pray at St Ann's Well and St Ann hadn't bothered at all. St Ann had let the truly awful Monicas of this world prowl round and destroy people. Taking them home to ravish them on the way.

'Well, I imagine he just saw her home, you know, and then went home himself,' I soothed her as best I could.

'But he doesn't see me, that's the problem. What's your name by the way?'

I told her I was called Hugo.

'Hugo – that's a bit fancy, isn't it?'

'Is it? I don't know. I always thought it would look good on a CD or outside a gig where I would be playing. I had my dreams, you know.' I didn't usually talk about myself. I was surprised at myself.

But what the hell, she was one drunken woman, I might as well have been reciting the Highway Code.

She was prepared to fight with her shadow. 'Well, why didn't you do something about your dream then?' She was like a small angry terrier dog on the back seat. 'My family wanted me to be a teacher or a nurse, they didn't want me to do arty things, but I fought for it, and tomorrow I have this interview for a huge job, and I hoped that Ken would come home with me tonight and pat me down instead of going to 35 Orange Crescent and patting down that stupid marshmallow as you so rightly called her.' She was near tears now.

I had to stop that at all costs.

'Listen,' I said, 'I suppose men are a bit hopeless, cagey . . . whatever. It's just that we don't want to get into something which may be wrong and there will be a load of grief and aggravation getting out of it. That's all it is really.'

'That's such bullshit,' she said. 'I bet there's some nice girl who has hopes of you, Hugo, some foolish insane girl who thinks you could be a singer if you weren't so cautious, who thinks she might make you happy if you'd let her in. The world is full of women like that. I don't know where we'd stretch to if you put us all in a line. Really I don't.' She shook her head at the tragedy of it all.

I thought I saw her eyes beginning to close in the rear-view mirror.

'I do have a friend, Chrissie,' I shouted, trying to keep her awake, 'but I'm not certain that it's the real thing and I don't think she's certain and it would be silly to get into something we might have to get out of.'

'Oh for God's sake, Hugo, you are one dumb fool. Who can be certain of anything on this earth? I ask you. I never met such a ditherer. In about forty years I'll meet you again and you'll be exactly the same as you are now, older of course, and bald, and you won't have one of those sharp thin faces that would look so well on a CD, you'll have a fat cautious face and wear a greasy checked cap. But basically you'll be the same.'

I wasn't going to get annoyed with her. I asked her what she thought that I should do. Oho, she knew that too.

I was to go round to Chrissie's house tonight and say I was prepared to give it a go, that life was short and love was good and that we would both give it our best try.

'I might,' I said.

'You won't,' she told me.

'Why don't you say all these things to Ken?' I asked her with some spirit.

'Because I just couldn't bear it if it didn't work,' she said very truthfully.

Then she got out of the taxi and teetered about a bit. I got out to steady her up and help her up the few steps outside the hall door. There was a bit of fumbling with her key but eventually I got her into her flat.

'You're quite a good singer,' she said as she left

me. 'Yes, quite good. You'd need to work on your repertoire but you can certainly hold a tune,' she said before she crashed indoors.

It was a quiet night as I was driving around when I saw I was near Orange Crescent. I remembered what she had said about my being a ditherer. I'd show her.

I rang the doorbell.

Marshmallow Monica came to answer it. She wore no shoes but she did have all her clothes on. Maybe I was in time.

'I've come for Ken,' I said.

Ken came out, bewildered.

'You ordered a cab,' I said.

He was very polite but confused, there must have been some mistake. I was adamant. How else would I have known the name and the address, I had come specially, a long way, to collect him.

'Well, perhaps, Monica, since the driver has come for me . . . I should really go with him.'

There was a poutish display of bad temper from the Marshmallow, but I had him in the cab. I would now drive him home.

'Emer loves you,' I said.

'No she doesn't, she loves her career,' he said sadly.

'You're wrong,' I said. 'You're so very wrong. When she wasn't singing she was telling me how much she loved you.'

'She's drunk as a lord of course,' Ken said.

'I think it's the same drunk or sober,' I said. 'And

she's going to have some hangover tomorrow, maybe you should go round and straighten her up for that interview she's going to.'

He looked thoughtful. 'Are you into therapy or crisis intervention in your spare time?' he asked me.

'No, I'm into singing. Do you know anywhere I could get a gig by any chance?'

It's a funny old life. It turns out that Ken's students were having a disco in the art college the following night. Their live guy with a guitar had let them down. We had an audition in the cab. I sang three numbers for him and Ken said fine, I was hired and he gave me the address where I should show up. He asked me if I had a girlfriend because there would be a nice do afterwards.

I said I had a nice girlfriend called Chrissie, and maybe he could take Emer to celebrate her having got the job in the gallery. He looked as if he had never thought of doing anything like that.

You know, Emer was right.

Men don't need women to stand by them, that's not what they need at all. They need someone to give them a boot up the bum when all is said and done.

And magic well or no magic well, I'd have been unlikely to get that from St Ann.

CHAPTER 12

The Anniversary

Part 1 – Pearl

I've always loved looking up things, silly facts, useless information. If I only had a computer I'd be at it all day. If we were the kind of people who would go to a pub quiz I bet I'd do well, even win prizes. If I only had the nerve to try and get on *Who Wants to Be a Millionaire?* I think I'd do quite well. Honestly I do. I've often got all the questions right when the real contestants didn't know them.

Brainbox Pearl, they used to call me at school, but that was just at school. Girls in my street didn't go on for what was called further education. My family had come over from Ireland to make a fortune in England like so many Irish did during the 1950s and 1960s. We were originally from a place called Rossmore, which was a very poor sort of place back then. But it had changed utterly now.

You wouldn't believe the style some of my cousins lived in back there now. My Bob was originally from Galway, we had met at an Irish ceilidh dance.

My dad worked on the roads and we all got jobs in factories or shops, and were considered dead lucky not to have gone into service in houses like our mothers had back in the old country as they called it. We all married at nineteen. By the latest. It was just what you did.

Just like everyone else here we had two children by the time we were twenty-one. We all went out to work automatically, none of the men we married could earn enough to run a household single-handed. Nobody complained.

We were much more English than Irish. We supported English football teams, Bob and I did. Once a year we took the train and the boat and then another train back to Rossmore. My first cousin Lilly was exactly the same age as I was. They were very poor in those days and she used to envy me what she called my smart clothes.

Smart clothes! My mam had a catalogue on our street, that's how we were dressed. They used to laugh at our English accents when we went back to Rossmore but we didn't mind. Our gran was very nice, she used to make Lilly and me go up to this well in the woods where they had a statue of St Ann and pray that we got good husbands. It was even more important for me to pray hard, because of living in England, where I might meet someone outside the faith.

And it must have worked, the holy well, because of course I met Bob which was great, and Lilly met Aidan which was also great. Back in those days we didn't have the money to go to each other's weddings, but we were both very happy and we wrote each other letters a lot about our lives.

I was expecting Amy at about the same time as she was expecting her first baby, Teresa, so we had a lot of things to write about. Then the most terrible thing happened.

I mean, it's like something that happens to other people, not anyone you'd know. Someone stole Teresa right out of the pram and she was never found and never ever brought back. The poor little dog was barking away and there were hundreds of people in the street but nobody saw anything.

Nothing was ever the same after that. I mean, I couldn't keep talking to her and telling all about Amy after all she had been through. Then after Gran died we didn't go back to Ireland any more. We lived a very happy life here in the north of England and when John was born everything seemed complete.

We did the Pools first every week, and then the Lottery, and we planned how to spend all that money when we won it. There would be a cruise of course first, then a villa on the Mediterranean and a big house on the posh side of town here; there would be a nice small house with a garden for our parents. As for the children! Well, all the plans we had for them!

They were going to go to the most expensive

schools, have music lessons, dancing classes, learn to ride ponies, to play tennis. They were going to have everything we never had. And more still!

To be fair to us we did more than dream for our children, certainly Bob and I did. We knew that the big win just might not happen and we desperately wanted them to have more chances than we did. So we had a fund and every week we put aside a sum for them. Ever since they were born. In the post office a nice little sum grew for Amy and John.

I had read in a book that you should give children plain classic names if you wanted them to get on. The names that we liked might be dead give-away, working-class names later on. So Amy and John they were. Two gorgeous children, but then everyone thinks that about their own.

They got a brand-new bicycle each when the time came, not broken-down reconstructed ones. We took them to theme parks and on their birthdays they could ask friends round to the house and we got them burgers and a video. We got John a computer which he kept in his room. I would love to have used it but John was a very knowledgeable fifteen-year-old and I didn't want to mess it up on him.

We sent Amy to a very expensive secretarial college. The fund was stretched greatly for these two things because I worked on the checkout at a supermarket and Bob was a van driver and these are not jobs that pay hugely well. But in fact it was a great investment for the children.

John turned out to be very gifted in technology and got a great job in what they call IT so it had been well worth getting him that computer at an early age. Amy's expensive secretarial course was a great investment as well; she got a very fancy job as a receptionist in a big company and then moved even further upwards to be somebody's personal assistant.

Both of them in London! Imagine!

They came to see us the odd time but of course they didn't bring their friends home any more. They lived their own lives, independent, successful, that's what we had struggled so hard for. I mean, we knew they couldn't bring people back as a matter of course, not to our little terrace. And by the time Amy was twenty-four and John was twenty-three they were both living in flats with other young people, which was as it should be.

A few of our friends asked Bob and myself what we were doing for our twenty-fifth, for our silver wedding. We said we didn't know because we knew the children must have planned something for us. They knew the date well, 1 April, because we always used to celebrate it when they were young.

April Fool's Day!

Imagine, we made the biggest promise of our life on that day, wasn't that typical, we would laugh. We would get them a big ice cream cake, enough for everyone to have second helpings. Our friends in the street and Bob's sister and my cousin had all organised big silver wedding parties when it was their anniversaries. These had been great gatherings where we played the records of songs that were popular back when we were first married.

I wondered where John and Amy would choose.

The family and friends already knew and I realised that they were only asking us about it to make the surprise even greater for us when it happened. Because we were so used to saving for the children's fund anyway, we had put a bit away and I got Bob a new dark grey suit and a smart white shirt, and myself a navy crêpe dress and a matching handbag. Surely we would be smart enough for anything they could spring on us.

The time was getting nearer and there was no hint about what they had planned. In fact Amy was keeping up the fiction in a big way, saying that she and Tim, that was the man she was personal assistant to, if you know what I mean, would be going to Paris that weekend. I pretended to take her seriously. Just as I pretended to think John was going deep-sea diving with some of the guys in his office, he told me that he had bought a new wet suit and all the gear.

Two days before, I began to worry. Two couples we knew had asked us to have supper with them, one in an Indian restaurant, one in an Italian.

They said the day should be marked. And when I said that it would be, I got a look I didn't like. I decided I had better clear it all up one way or another before Bob got too disappointed. He was trying his suit on every second day and admiring himself in the bedroom mirror. I rang Amy at work.

'Oh, Mother,' she said – she used to call me 'Mam' but it was 'Mother' now.

'About your weekend,' I said. 'Are you really going away, love? I mean, this weekend?'

She was on her high horse at once. 'Now, Mother. Please. Up to now you never interfered, you always let me live my own life, don't tell me that now you've joined in the general hue and cry about Tim. His marriage is dead, Mother, there's nothing hole in the corner about our going to Paris. Please don't join in the general chorus against it all . . .'

I told her that I hadn't intended to criticise her trip to Paris, I hadn't even known whether Tim was married or not. That wasn't why I was ringing, certainly not.

'So why *were* you ringing then, Mother?' My daughter could be so sharp. So very hurtful.

I blurted it out. 'Because I wondered, had you forgotten our silver wedding on Saturday?' I said before I could stop myself.

'Your *what*?'

'Your dad and I will have been married for twenty-five years. We thought that maybe you and John were going to . . . well, had arranged something for us, like a party. It's just that the neighbours keep asking and you know . . .'

I heard her catch her breath sharply. 'Oh, Mother, yes. April Fool's Day. Oh God, yes . . .' she said.

And I knew then that she really had forgotten. And that John had forgotten. And that there would be no party.

And it was Thursday, too late for us to invite anyone and make a celebration. Bob's heart would be broken, he had always found it harder than I did that his little girl didn't come home that much and see her parents these days. He had so looked forward to wearing his new suit and he was going to sing 'You Make Me Feel So Young'. He had speculated that they might have rented the room over The Yellow Bird pub because he had heard there was a function there next Saturday.

I thought about Bob's sister, who was always inclined to be a bit critical of our children, and my big-hearted cousin, and the marvellous parties they and their families had arranged. And I thought about my navy crêpe dress and the matching handbag. About the years of sitting in a draught at the checkout at the supermarket to make more money for the fund. I thought about how the fund had paid for that good jacket when she was going to the interview for her first job, and how their friends had always been invited into this house to have birthday feasts for Amy and John. I thought about the long hours Bob had put in on the road when his eyes were red and tired and his shoulders stiff in order to get the bicycles and the radios and then the CD players. I thought about all those journeys to Legoland and the wildlife parks. I remembered the day trips across the Channel to France.

And I felt for one dangerous moment as if I didn't care if I never talked to either Amy or John again.

Then I pulled myself together sharply. What had

it all been for, a quarter of a century of saving and working and holding a home together to give them more than we had ever known? It couldn't end in a petulant sulk like this. I had to get them out of this big failure on their part, reassure them that it didn't matter. I must speak quickly before Amy started to apologise.

So I interrupted her just as she was assembling her speech. 'You see, your dad and I are going away together for the weekend so we wanted to be sure that you hadn't made any other plans . . .'

'Mother – I'm so sorry . . .' she was interrupting now. But I must not let her apologise.

Everything would change if she did.

'So, that's absolutely fine, then, and if you are sending flowers could you send them to your dad's sister for us, as we'll be away.'

Amy gulped. 'Yes, of course, Mother.'

'And we'll keep the real celebration for the pearl.'

'The pearl?'

'Well, that's what we always thought, your dad and I, the silver wasn't important for us. But what with my name being Pearl and everything, the big showy party would be on our pearl anniversary . . .' I beamed goodwill and anticipation down the phone.

'Which is . . . um . . . ?' my daughter asked.

'The thirtieth, of course,' I said cheerfully. 'Only another five years, so you and John had better get planning. We'll make that the party of all time.'

Her voice was full of gratitude. 'Thank you, Mam,' she said. Not 'Mother', I noticed.

Then I thought of where I would take Bob for the outing and booked us a weekend in Blackpool. Bob's sister would be impressed with the flowers. I knew the bouquet would be guiltily enormous. When all was said and done it was much better than allowing myself to wallow in self-pity.

They didn't call me Brainbox Pearl at school for nothing.

Part 2 – Generous John

In the office they used to call me Generous John.

It all had to do with a silly tradition I established; it was just that every Friday I offered everyone a drink of fizzy wine and some smoked salmon on a biscuit at my desk. It started the weekend off well. People who had nowhere to go enjoyed it; those who were going somewhere always stopped by for a while and it was much better than getting smashed in a pub like a lot of other offices did. And for the cost of two or at the most three bottles of something not too pricey. For this and one packet of Marks and Spencer's smoked salmon, a few water biscuits and a chopped-up lemon I got the reputation of being one really generous guy.

We are a good group in our office anyway. It's not an earth-shaking place – most of us think we might like to be somewhere more glittery by the time we're thirty.

But come on, it's a job and the place has a good name in the business, so what the hell.

I like it, and I share a big bright flat with two of my colleagues.

My sister rang the office one day and asked to speak to John. 'Do you mean Generous John or the other John?' they asked. She said she thought she must mean the other but she was wrong.

Amy was surprised. 'You're not generous,' she said accusingly.

'No, but I'm not mean,' I said. She admitted that was true and we talked on easily.

Are we close as brother and sister? Not really. Well, there's the bond of course that we survived our upbringing. And we've lots of shared memories. But we have lived very different lives.

Amy went to one of those fancy secretarial colleges that teaches women to dress well and social skills as well as office procedure. And she learned well, she's as slim as a pencil, wears very smart designer jackets. Very groomed and cool looking. She has only one blind spot – that guy Tim.

Tim has a wealthy wife, a huge house, a couple of kids at ruinously expensive schools. He has a demanding job as CEO of his company, so he wasn't going to risk the package by going off into the sunset with my sister, glamorous as she may be and trophy wife material as she undoubtedly was. But Amy couldn't or wouldn't see this and by the time she did see it, it would all be too late.

I tried to tell her this one night when we had supper together but boy, did it fall on stony and unwelcoming ground. I was told pretty sharpish that it was none of my business, that I didn't understand the first thing about it.

I was also reminded rather firmly that when I looked at myself in the mirror I would realise that I was no great advertisement for true and undying love. I had never had a proper girlfriend at all.

This was not strictly true and I was annoyed by what she said. But Amy and I papered over the cracks and never talked to each other about our private lives again.

Then I met Linda. After that of course I wanted to talk about my private life to everyone.

Linda was a fantastic-looking girl who had been transferred from head office to us for six months. She never actually went back. She was Irish actually but very together – none of all that drippy Irish colleen thing. She was bright as a button and very popular.

And of all the guys she could have had, which was most of them, she actually fancied me. Which was very pleasing.

One Friday over the smoked salmon she actually asked me straight out how did Generous John spend the rest of his Friday night, and I heard myself saying in this awful voice that whatever Lovely Linda suggested would be fine with Generous John, and we went out to an Italian restaurant. And then we saw a lot of each other.

She took me home to meet her parents. Her father was an Irish banker with some huge job and they lived in a big house with a garden, and an orchard and Labrador dogs.

They didn't quiz me about my family – but Linda did.

'When am I going to meet them? Ever? In this century maybe?' she kept asking.

Now I wasn't so stupid as to pretend that my people were classy like hers were or anything, that sort of thing is only laying up heartache ahead. No, indeed, I had told her that I was born in a small terraced house, and my parents were working class. But I couldn't bring her to meet my mother and father. Not yet.

Dad's awful sister Dervla would want to come in and inspect her. My mother's noisy cousin would find an excuse to come round. They would be talking about places back in the Old Country and trying to find links with Linda's family. It would all be too awful.

I would be apologising for them and then hating myself for feeling that way.

No, keep them apart as long as possible. That was best.

Now, meeting my sister Amy, that was another thing. I invited Amy to a sushi bar to meet Linda and she brought the dreaded Tim. He kept running his hand through his hair and saying he had to be at the next place. Amy was looking at him as if she had suddenly been turned into a spaniel dog instead of a highly efficient personal assistant, which is what she was.

When they left I shrugged at Linda and apologised for him. 'I don't know why she puts up with him.'

'I do,' Linda said.

I was amazed.

'Because she loves him,' said Linda as if it were obvious.

And to my huge regret Linda didn't stay with me in my room in our big airy apartment. Girls often stayed overnight; with my room-mates I would have been so proud to see Linda drinking freshly squeezed orange juice for breakfast, wearing my dressing gown.

But no, she was adamant, and I couldn't stay in the flat she shared with another woman either. We could spend the odd overnight in a hotel when we were away somewhere, so it wasn't sex itself that was out. No, it was what Linda called 'dreaded domesticity'.

We must wait until we were sure, she said, and then get our own place.

I kept saying that I *was* sure but she said, nonsense, I couldn't be yet, and meanwhile, could she meet my parents? I wondered, would they be worse at home or if I brought them here to London? It was a puzzler. At least in London awful Aunt Dervla wouldn't be around and half the street would not be peering and examining us. But then they would be so lacking in confidence in London.

I put it off and off.

One day Linda rang from a business trip to say she was only fifteen miles from my home town and she'd love to call and see my parents. I lied to her, I told her they were away. When she came back, I began to bluster about what a pity it was they had missed each other, but she cut straight across me.

'I didn't miss them, John, I went to see them,' she said.

'But they were away,' I gasped.

'They must have come back,' she said.

'And?' I asked.

'And we had tea and cheese on toast and I told them a bit about what kind of work we do, you and I, and your Aunt Dervla came in and she said maybe we would all meet at The Silver sometime. What's The Silver, John? Is it a hotel or a pub or something?'

'I don't know, I suppose so,' I muttered.

Linda had met my parents, been to my house, met Aunt Dervla and survived it. This must be love.

I tried to tell Amy but she was very worked up about a visit to Paris with Tim and she didn't really listen. I wondered, should I ask my parents to London sometime. After all, they had met Linda now so the worst bit was over. And they might not be so ill at ease as if she was a complete stranger. But there was never any real time for it, and there was a lot else going on.

We worked long hours and then on the weekends we windsurfed all summer long. Some of us were planning deep-sea diving in the autumn. And okay, I did feel a bit bad sometimes when I thought how little they had and how much I had. But honestly, that's the way things are. Look at people out in Africa, they have nothing at all. And we can't cure it. So what's the point about feeling bad all the time?

Linda was always going home to see her family, but it was different for her. And not so far away. She was always telephoning them, telling them nonsensical things. I didn't ring them at my home because Bob and Pearl were really the kind of people who would panic when there was a phone call. Always thought it was bad news, and they'd be warning me to save my money even though I was phoning from the office. And I did mean to book them a show, some musical, you know, that they'd like and an overnight in a hotel. But as I say, the time just passed.

And then I get this phone call from Amy completely from left field, saying that we were meant to have arranged some awful silver wedding party for them. So that was what they meant when they said to Linda that they would be seeing her at the silver. It wasn't a pub at all. It was a bloody twenty-fifth wedding anniversary.

'Shit!' I said several times to Amy, and she was in total agreement.

'If they had only said,' she repeated over and over. 'They never say anything and expect us to be inspired about everything.'

I thought for a moment about the big birthday cards they sent me every year with a linen handkerchief tucked inside or a bookmark or something useless. But then of course people would remember their children's birthdays – when I have children, when Linda and I have a son and daughter, we'll remember birthdays too. Though I must say she's always dashing off for something for people's anniversaries or birthdays at home. But then girls are different.

Which is why it's so annoying about Amy, that *she* should have remembered this goddamned silver wedding. I said, okay, okay, damage limitation, let's do something for them in London, have a dinner, champagne or something, send a limo for them. But oh no. Amy can't be there. She and Tim have some weekend in Paris that just can't be cancelled. She is so selfish, Amy, at times, and foolish. Very foolish.

There was some kind of psychobabble about making the pearl wedding Mum's big celebration, because of her name and everything. A pearl wedding is thirty years apparently.

God knows where we'll all be by then. Linda and I will be married, that's for sure, and Tim will be on to a newer younger model than my sister, that's also for sure.

So I said, let's send a bouquet each to awful Aunt Dervla's house, and I said that maybe they were better off in Blackpool on their own, and I said we'd do a big number for the pearl wedding but somehow I didn't entirely convince either Amy or myself.

I told Linda all about it that evening. She listened to me very quietly. She looked at me as if she had never really seen me before.

I didn't really like the look. It was as if there was some kind of notice on my head.

'What's wrong?' I asked her anxiously.

'Nothing, nothing at all,' she said. 'Go on, tell me more.'

So I went on talking and told her that my mother and father were of course – as she knew because she had met them – the salt of the earth. But what they were was too easily satisfied. It was pathetic, the way they set store by little things. And my mother liked looking well in front of her cousin, of all people, a dreadful woman with no grace, no style, no standards. And they were in awe of Aunt Dervla, my father's bossy elder sister who thought she knew everything but had only been south of Watford twice.

They were perfectly happy with their little house up there instead of finding somewhere proper to live. Times had changed, people had moved on, they just didn't realise it. If the world had been full of people like them we would still be living in caves.

Linda's face showed nothing. Normally she was animated and she agreed or she disagreed. But she sat there blankly and you know the way it is, the less somebody talks the more you talk? I heard myself telling about how my parents had thought chicken and chips was a great treat, how they put up big coloured paper chains all over the house at Christmas so that we could hardly move.

And still Linda said nothing so I told her all about Mum working extra hours to get us new bicycles and awful Aunt Dervla coming to give us milk and biscuits. Little by little I saw Linda moving her feet down from the sofa and slipping them into her shoes, which was odd because we had the flat to ourselves and it wasn't nearly time for her to go.

And then she said she had to be off.

And I said, 'You can't possibly go now – what about the guinea fowl I bought for us to eat with a bottle of really good claret?'

And for no reason at all Linda asked me, had I ever cooked guinea fowl for my mother and father, and I explained that you couldn't cook in their kitchen and anyway they liked such awful things that they would be sick if they had guinea fowl. Her face looked so different somehow.

So I said stupidly, 'What's wrong, Linda? What is it?'

And she looked really sad as she sort of touched my hand before she left. 'Oh, John,' she said. 'Generous John, you really don't know, do you?'

And she left.

And I didn't know and I don't know.

I mean, that's what's so difficult about people – you never really know, do you?

CHAPTER 13

Going to the Pub

Part 1 – Poppy

When I was young our gran lived with us and we adored her. She was far more entertaining than our parents and she understood things. She was much more interesting to listen to, having been around for so long and having seen so much. She used to take Jane and myself on long rambles through Whitethorn Woods, always finding something interesting to show us. Like a treehouse built years ago by her brothers, or how to press flowers in a book, or best of all St Ann's Well. She said we must never laugh at the people praying there because one day we would undoubtedly come here to pray ourselves.

That's what happened. When she was young she thought they were all mad to mumble and mutter and leave mementoes but oddly it became comforting once you got older. She taught us to listen to people. Well, she taught me anyway. That's probably where I got the idea of working with older people.

There wasn't much enthusiasm at home.

'You'll have to get some kind of qualification first,' my dad said.

'Old people can be very demanding,' my mum said.

'You'll never meet a fellow if you get stuck in geriatrics,' said my elder sister Jane.

Jane had turned out to be very different from me – she wore blusher and eyeshadow properly and had a steam iron for her own clothes. She took great care of her shoes, always stuffing them with newspaper, and polishing them with shoe cream. My friends and I used to call her Elegant Jane.

So even though they were all against the idea at home I took no notice because to be honest they were pretty negative about everything. I trained as a nurse here locally in Rossmore in St Ann's Hospital and I asked to work in the wards with older people.

And there I met marvellous people and got huge advice about life from them all.

One man taught me all about stocks and shares, another all about planting window boxes, one old lady who had had seven proposals of marriage told me how to attract men and another taught me how to polish copper. So I was well advanced in the ways of the world by the time I saw the advertisement for a matron in a place called Ferns and Heathers five miles outside Rossmore.

It was an old house owned by two marvellous dotty old dears who were obsessed with gardening. When they died it became a nursing home. I was thirty-seven and I had put all the advice I got to good use. I had a small but satisfactory portfolio of shares. Men had certainly fallen in love with me, but unfortunately I had married a man called Oliver who fell in love rather too easily and too often, so I had actually left him after a year of marriage.

I had copper saucepans that shone like jewels. I could make anything grow in a window box and had very successful year-round colour. None of these things were really qualifications for the job of matron at Ferns and Heathers, but I am a well-qualified nurse and enthusiastic so the four directors liked me at the interview and I got the job. A little cottage went with the post. A place with an entirely neglected garden but I'd soon sort that out.

As soon as I was appointed I went to meet the staff and the people for whom Ferns and Heathers was home. They seemed a happy enough group. They had liked the previous matron who had left to work in television apparently.

'I hope that you're not going to use this place as a jumping-off ground to a media career like she did,' grumbled Garry who, I could recognise in ten seconds, was going to be the mouthpiece of any discontent.

'No. If I'd wanted to go that route I'd have gone it,' I said cheerfully.

'Or go away and get married on us?' a frail

woman called Eve asked fretfully. I put her down in my mind as a worrier.

'Married? Oh no, I've been there and done that,' I said.

They looked at me open-mouthed. They had probably been used to a more genteel approach.

I asked, would everyone mind wearing name badges for the first three days and that if I didn't know everyone by then, well, it meant I wasn't up to the job. I told them my name was Poppy. I agreed it was a deeply silly name but there's a worse one on my birth certificate so, if they could get their heads round it, Poppy it would be. I said I loved to listen and learn and if any of them had any ideas to add to my store I'd be thrilled.

They seemed to like that. I could hear them saying that I was unusual anyway, as they went off to their tea. I looked around the place that was going to be my new home with some pleasure. It was going to be a real home for me, I realised. The home that I grew up in was becoming ever more remote.

I realised this when I didn't feel any need to ring my dad and mum about the new job. I didn't feel like listening to all the negative things they would say. They would tell me what a huge responsibility it all was and that if any of these people broke their hips it would be my fault.

I certainly didn't ring my sister Jane because she would tell me yet again that there was nothing wrong with Oliver, who was handsome and wealthy, and that I had been foolish to throw him out, and that I should take on board the fact that all men wandered a little. It was in their nature.

I didn't ring Oliver because I never rang him.

I rang my best friend Grania who was also my lawyer who had helped me do the contracts, and I told her that the place was fine and she must come and see me.

'I might be coming sooner than you think,' Grania said. 'My dad has been told he can't live on his own.'

Grania's father, Dan Green, was a marvellous man. I had always enjoyed going to their house. He was unfailingly cheerful with a big red face and a loud laugh.

'I would love to have him in Ferns and Heathers,' I told Grania. I said I'd make a room ready for him as soon as she wanted.

'That's the problem,' she sighed. 'He says he hasn't a notion of going into any kind of home, he's staying put and going to the pub every night for a pint. The problem is that he can't do it any more. That's the problem, Poppy.' She sounded very upset.

'There's got to be a way round it,' I said. Grania's father couldn't be abandoned but then he must not be harassed either. 'Invite him here for tea some day – I won't do the hard sell,' I said.

'I'll try.' Grania didn't have much hope.

One of my first acts at Ferns and Heathers was to reclaim the garden. It had been very neglected.

'A happy matron is a good matron,' I told them. 'And I am deeply unhappy with our garden. I'm getting in a few raised flower beds but I need help planting them.'

Garry said that they paid good money to be in this place and he had no intention of working with earth and dirtying his hands. So I said, fine, of course he must do as he pleased. But when he heard all the laughter and the reading of seed packets and examination of bedding plants, not to mention the glasses of iced tea I prepared for the gardeners, he changed his tune.

As a reward I gave them each a window box and supervised their planting. It became highly competitive and they all asked their visitors to bring them something exotic from the garden centre. By the time the board had its first visitation we were seriously discussing a little fountain which we called a water feature. It was all going very well.

Then Grania brought her father to visit. He was still a jolly happy man, Dan Green was.

But he had been weakened by illness and he was not a fool. He realised that he couldn't live alone for much longer, though he couldn't live with Grania and her big family. We walked together, he and I. I showed him all the planting and said that when the winter came we were going to have painting classes and maybe an exhibition of our work.

'You want me to come and live here, Poppy, don't you?' he said.

'No, I wouldn't be able to swing it for you – it's very hard indeed to get in here, Dan,' I said regretfully.

'I can read you like a book, you've been Grania's friend since you were ten. If I were to go anywhere it would be here but I can't. I really am not able to give up what I like best in life: going to the pub for a drink every evening.'

'You can drink here, Dan. I do, believe me, you could come and have a glass of wine every evening.'

'No, it's not the same,' he said, really testily as if this was an argument he had fought many times before. 'Women never understand about going to the pub. It's the beer, the draught beer, the whole ritual of the thing.'

And he was right, you know. I don't understand it. I don't get this thing of going into a place where you might be bored to death by people telling jokes, or wearied by the barman mouthing clichés at you, or regulars telling endless tales, where you might be assaulted by drunks or feel lonely and isolated because everyone else has a gang and you are on your own. Why not get a few drinks and go to a friend's house or invite them to yours? But it wasn't the time to argue this down to the bone with Grania's father.

I moved to safer waters. I told him about the new big flat-screen television we had and how we were going to make a room into a real old-fashioned cinema, with popcorn and one of the staff with a torch showing people to their seats. I told him how we had set up the library with a huge notice saying 'Silence' and the daily papers laid out there for all to read. People's relatives and friends brought books of every kind and they were properly catalogued too.

I explained that every week a minibus came and took us up to Whitethorn Woods and how I told them my gran's tales, and those from round here shared their own memories, and we collected bark and leaves and flowers. I introduced him to Maturity, the marvellous shaggy dog that had been given to us by Skunk Slattery who had needed to find a home for the animal. Maturity was the perfect old people's home dog, allowing everyone to fondle him and pat his head equally, favouring nobody above anyone else.

I showed Dan the hens in the backyard which were my pride and joy – seven White Leghorns each with a name and a laying record, clucking about happily in a coop. He was quite interested in all this but still he assured me that no inducement would work – Ferns and Heathers was too far from a pub. Nothing wrong with the place apart from its location. It was five miles from Rossmore and civilisation.

'Grania could drive you to one when she comes to see you,' I heard myself begging.

I would love to have had her father here. But no, apparently Grania didn't understand the psychology of a pub either. And a man needed to be able to wander in when it suited him, find his own level. He seemed almost regretful as he was leaving. He had got a smell of some interesting food from the kitchen.

On Thursdays we had a cookery class and a different group each week prepared supper. Tonight it would be nasi goreng after the basic Indonesian food lesson in the afternoon.

So anyway I was very busy, it's always busy here. I didn't think of Dan for a couple of weeks until Grania told me that he had had a bad fall and when he came out of hospital he would need looking after. Please, Poppy, she begged me, would you take him? Just for a couple of weeks until she could see what could be done.

There was only one big corner room available. I had been going to make it into a music room. So now I fixed it up for Dan when he arrived. He was very down, and he showed no interest whatsoever in meeting any of his fellow residents at Ferns and Heathers. There was no sign of his loud laugh and his big red face seemed smaller and more grey. But as it happened I couldn't give him much attention anyway, I didn't have time to worry about these changes in a friend's once happy father. There was too much else happening.

Garry, the voice of any dissident opinion, had led a protest against Dan getting a bigger room than anyone else. Eve who worried about everything said that some of the new books for the library included real hard-core pornography. Oliver my ex-husband said that on mature reflection he had decided that women didn't understand about being free souls and he was happy to return to me on a strictly monogamous one-to-one basis. My sister, the very elegant Jane, said that I was of course insane not to take him back. But that it was clear I had never made a wise decision in my whole life. The board of Ferns and Heathers announced that one of their number was going to cash in his shares and they needed to do a detailed examination of the home in order to establish its worth.

So I sent Garry in to talk to Dan face to face. I knew Dan would explain very forcibly that he had no intention of staying permanently and that this would calm Garry down.

I went to the library with Eve and examined the hard-core pornography, which turned out to be a few innocent bodice rippers. I wrote to Oliver and said that I wished him well in his insights and spiritual journeys but that I would not contemplate a reconciliation. I reminded him politely of the various barring orders that prevented him from visiting me to discuss the matter any further.

I told the board that I would be very happy to bid for a quarter-share in Ferns and Heathers once they had done their valuation. I also said that they were free to come and look at any time just so long as they didn't disturb the residents. And that they would see a fair picture. After all I might want to make the place look rundown so that I could buy the shares cheaply, but then I had to make it look good otherwise I would not keep my job as matron.

It all worked really well. Dan and Garry became fast friends. Eve started a feminist group in Ferns and Heathers to see could anyone understand the psyche of men since they were basically decent, just confused.

Oliver went to my sister's house and droned on and cried on her shoulder so often and for so long on each occasion that far from telling me that I had been idiotic to throw him out she remained fairly wordless about the situation.

And the board came on a secret inspection to see Ferns and Heathers one day when we were out at the woods and pronounced themselves very pleased and asked me for an enormous sum, for twenty-five per cent of the business.

But I was ready for them.

I explained that my buying into it would ensure my continued presence here. I listed the improvements I had made and hinted at further planned developments. I asked them to speak freely to the residents to enquire how they would view continuing to live here if I had moved on. Grimly they agreed that as I had contributed so much already to the whole project, my financial input would be considerably less than they had originally suggested.

'You are quite unorthodox, Poppy,' they said. 'Just make sure that Ferns and Heathers keeps its licence, that it doesn't break any of the rules.'

I didn't think we had broken any rules. The hens were very hygienic, there was no pornography in the library. But there was something niggling at the back of my mind.

It had to do with Grania's father.

Dan was somehow too cheerful.

I would keep an eye on him.

There was no way that he could go out to a pub.

The nearest pub was four miles away and if he were to take a taxi I would have known in ten seconds. And yet he had returned to his previous good form and florid complexion.

When he had decided to stay he had gone back to his own place for his possessions.

We had offered to help him install them but he had said no. If he were to have any dignity he must be allowed to put his own few bits and pieces around the place himself.

His new friend Garry would help him, he said.

We believe strongly that our residents should indeed have as much independence and dignity as possible so of course we agreed. There was a bit of hammering but nothing seemed to have knocked down the walls. He had an old sideboard with a mirror at the back of it, some hunting prints, a notice board, a dartboard on the back of the door. Some vague furniture shapes covered with rugs and velvet cloths. Cupboards, chests of drawers possibly?

But his room was so big there was plenty of space for them all. And he said he had brought a few fold-ing chairs in case he invited people in to his room, and two high stools which he used as stands for vases of flowers. I noticed that before lunch several people would drop in to Dan's room for half an hour, and again in the evening.

The women had started to dress slightly better. They had their hair done more regularly by our vis-iting stylist, even put on jewellery and perfume. The men wore cravats sometimes and slicked down their hair.

Something was up.

It took me longer than it should have to work out that Dan had set up a pub in his room.

He had optic measures which he fitted into his sideboard. The rug-covered furniture turned into a counter. The vases were taken off the high stools, the chairs were assembled around occasional tables.

Eve would have a small dry Martini, some of the other ladies had thimble-sized glasses of sherry, and the men mainly had beer taken from a metal barrel, well disguised during non-pub hours as a giant magazine stand.

How did I discover this?

By spying on them.

And what I discovered looked a very happy scene. They were never drunk and it was doing nobody any harm. But of course they were breaking the law. You are not actually allowed to sell intoxicating liquor without a licence. Anywhere. And certainly not at a nursing home where there are all kinds of rules and regulations and none of them include allowing the residents to have a cash bar.

But they were enjoying it so much. It would be a shame to end it. I resolved that I must never know about it.

So whenever any member of the staff began to tell me that maybe I ought to know something, I managed to avoid hearing it. Lord knows what else I might have inadvertently closed my eyes to! Anyway the board continued to visit and I always managed to let Dan know what day they were coming well in advance as they sometimes called on residents to know how they were getting along, and I didn't want them to arrive when the cocktail hour was at full throttle. Eventually another board member sold out and I now owned half the place.

My sister Jane was awfully sulky and not a bit pleased for me when I told her. I wanted to take her out to dinner to celebrate. But Jane was full of shrugs and raising of shoulders and saying it was so odd that a nurse who was more or less trained by the State should have risen so high. I was too busy really to worry about it, I had to make sure not to schedule painting classes at an hour that would cut across Dan's opening times and on the day we had our art exhibition a lot of them went for Dutch courage to Dan's.

The very next day I went for a walk by myself in the woods, accompanied only by the dog.

Maturity loved the woods and found something interesting at every turn. We were near the well so I went in to inspect it.

There were notices around it about the intended road.

'We won't let them take you away, St Ann,' said one of them. Another had a pencil attached and asked people who opposed the huge highway to add their names to a list below. I was going to put my name on it. Most of my people back at the home were against the change. Then I wondered, might it in fact mean that some of them would get more visitors if all that traffic congestion was eased.

At that very moment my mobile phone rang. There was a bit of sighing around me as if to say that nowhere was sacred these days.

It was the home. Three inspectors from the Health Board had arrived unannounced.

I had to think quickly.

I looked up at the statue for some advice. 'Come on, St Ann, you didn't do much for me in the husband stakes,' I said. 'Get me out of this one anyway.' Then I asked to be put through to Dan's room.

'Mr Green?' I said with as much authority as I could muster. 'Mr Green, there's been a little change of plan. I won't be able to join you and discuss your artwork with you as arranged. I wonder if I could ask you all to go almost at once to the dining room. You see, some health inspectors have arrived and I'm not in the building. I'll be back shortly and I want to show them around. It would be a great ease to me if I could know that everyone was heading for lunch. Having of course cleared up all your artwork before you leave, if you know what I mean. Thank you so much for being co-operative, Mr Green.' I hung up.

Dan would do it. Maturity and I raced back to the car and I drove like the wind back to Ferns and Heathers. The inspectors were having coffee and shortbread in the hall. They were looking at the exhibition of local flora in glass cases. They were studying the notices on the wall about upcoming cookery demonstrations, a matinée showing of *Brief Encounter* which was a regular favourite, and a debate on the great new road.

I apologised for not being there and suggested a tour of the premises. As I was leading the inspectors along the ground floor I saw the little line of lunchtime drinkers full of giggles heading for the dining room. Not even the flappers who drank bathtub gin during Prohibition could have had as much fun as they were having.

All I had to do now was make sure that Dan never acknowledged what I had done, how I had saved his little pub enterprise and my home.

'Afternoon, Poppy,' he said cheerfully. Then he nodded at the inspectors from the Health Board. 'Fantastic place this, but my God, she's a stickler for law and order, every by-law has to be observed, fire drill, hygiene, you wouldn't believe it. Still we all like it and that's saying something, isn't it?'

The inspectors were impressed, the gigglers went to their lunch and I knew that we could go on like this for ever.

Part 2 – Elegant Jane

They used to say about me when I was young that I was a perfectionist. I liked the description actually, it meant that I wanted things to be perfect, which I did. But as I got older they stopped using the phrase. Probably thought it meant finicky, picky, hard to please.

And eventually old maid.

Nobody ever said Poppy was a perfectionist. Dear me, no. She always had cut knees or scabs on them. Her hair was constantly falling over her face, her clothes ripped or torn from climbing up in the Whitethorn Woods or sliding down things. And yet amazingly people always liked Poppy. Quite disproportionately in fact.

The house was full of her friends, that loud noisy Grania practically lived in our house for heaven's sake. Oh and crowds more. And it was the same with boys when the time came – which was very early really – she had dozens of them around the place too. When she left St Ita's school in Rossmore she could have gone to university as I did. I have a degree and became a librarian but no, Poppy, who always knew her own mind, had insisted on nursing.

Mother and Father were, I suppose, relieved that it didn't cost them anything but still. What had they worked for and saved for if it wasn't to give us an education? Poppy would come home with hair-raising tales of life on the ward. Honestly, what she had to do all day! How people trusted human lives to my half-crazed sister was beyond me.

When she was qualified (against all the odds; I must say I never thought she'd see it through) she went into a ward for the elderly, most of them mad, poor dears, and completely wandering. Poppy found them fascinating and hilarious. You'd swear she was working with Einstein and Peter Ustinov, not a lot of elderly people who were totally confused and barely knew what day it was.

Amongst the seemingly endless series of young men who all wanted to be with Poppy there was one called Oliver. His people owned a lot of property all over Rossmore. Very, very good looking, a bit of a philanderer, I suppose. He didn't really work because he didn't really need to. And his family were all torn between relief that he was settling down at last and concern that he had chosen as his bride a nurse called Poppy with no background. I warned Poppy that he might not be the entirely utterly faithful type and she said that life was all about taking risks, and after all she might find herself attracted to another man so marriage was just a giant optimistic step.

I didn't see marriage like that. I saw it as something you thought about rather a lot and made sure it was the right thing to do. Oddly, I had never really been close enough to consider seriously marrying anyone, except that time with Keith who was also a librarian and we were really quite well suited but there was a huge misunderstanding there. I don't know what happened.

We were actually talking about getting engaged and I explained about the small square-cut emerald I would like for my ring. It wasn't extraordinarily expensive or anything but it seemed to upset him that I had already chosen it and tried it on. When I was telling him we must have a walk-in closet in the house because otherwise our clothes would get crushed beyond belief he felt . . . well, I don't know what he felt really. But he said he needed more time and then he sort of faded away.

Oliver and Poppy's wedding was just what you'd expect. Haphazard, disorganised, everyone laughing. Lots of champagne and little chicken sandwiches. And a wedding cake. That was all. No proper banquet with place names or anything.

Mother and Father enjoyed it. I didn't.

That loud Grania was braying all over the place, brought her dreadful red-faced father with her. Mother and Father said that Poppy had never been a day's trouble in her whole life.

I thought that was rich.

Poppy? No trouble?

What trouble had I been, I might ask? I lived in my own flat and I did go to see them. Not as often as parents like, but enough. From time to time anyway. Poppy and Oliver had a marvellous house, well, compared to my small flat it was marvellous, but of course hopelessly neglected, what with Poppy still out slaving away in a geriatric ward.

I'll tell you, if I had married Oliver and all his money I would have stayed at home, done up that house and invited people in. Then he mightn't have wandered so much.

I knew about his wandering quite early on actually. I saw him nuzzling a girl in a wine bar. Naturally he saw me too and disengaged himself. He came over full of charm.

'We're adults, you and I, Jane,' he said.

'Indeed, Oliver.' I was icy.

'So adults don't run home with silly tales, do they?'

'Unless they see other adults doing silly things in wine bars,' I said, proud of myself.

He looked at me for a while. 'I suppose in the end, it is your call, Jane,' he said and went back to the girl.

I paid my bill and left.

As it happened I did not tell Poppy.

I had tried to warn her before she married him and she had been shruggy and so dismissive – let her find out herself.

She found out about six months later when she came home unexpectedly and opened her bedroom door to find Oliver and an old flame having a nostalgic whatever. She asked him to leave. That very day.

Of course he made a fuss.

She was being doctrinaire, he had said, which indeed in many ways she was. She wanted no explanations, excuses, no promises of a faultless life from then on. She said to him that she just wanted the house, no maintenance, that it was actually a good deal he had got, which he would realise when he came to talk it over with the briefs and his own divorced friends.

And then as if that wasn't all bad enough losing this great catch, Poppy threw up her dull but safe job in the hospital and went to work at a crazy retirement home called Ferns and Heathers.

I mean, what a name! But Poppy, being Poppy, said she liked it. It was better, she said, than calling it St Something as a lot of these places were called, and it made the people who lived there feel they were not being hurtled rather too swiftly towards the next world. And some of these homes for the elderly were called remorselessly jolly names, she said, so she was happy with Ferns and Heathers, and was always down on her hands and knees planting both to make sense of the silly name.

Really, Poppy defied every rule in the book.

Against all the odds the damn nursing home took off and became very successful and Mother told me that Poppy owned a great deal of it nowadays. They said they would like to go and live there when they were old. And Poppy said they should go in nice and early while they still had all their energy for the marvellous things that the residents all did.

I hated going there actually.

I went of course out of solidarity from time to time but really it was looking at the old people's crêpey skin and thinking of their table-tennis tournaments that upset me.

Sometimes Poppy would say in that idiotic way she spoke like an eleven-year-old, 'What exactly is it that you do, Jane, which is so exciting compared to all this?' And of course nobody can answer a question like that.

Mother and Father said there was no stopping Poppy. I don't know why but they seemed to say it with some admiration.

Lots of the old mad people in the home felt very strongly about the bypass that was going to be built around Rossmore. Some of them welcomed it, saying it was progress when they went into town on their occasional visits. It would be easier to cross the road as the traffic would be less. Others were against it and said that their relatives would now fly by and not come to see them at all. Poppy began to organise debates on it at the home and then bring both sides into Rossmore to let them protest on different sides. Is that mad or what? And even Oliver when he called to visit me from time to time said she was a bloody marvel.

I took to keeping big juicy olives and little slices of salami in my fridge in case Oliver called. And I always dressed up anyway so he never found me looking like a slattern. Poor Poppy often looked as if she had been doing hard manual labour all day . . . which in a way she had on those nursing wards. Before she went to that home. And I liked Oliver coming to call, yes I did.

And of course we went to bed together. I mean, Oliver is that kind of person. I mean, there was nothing serious in it. I was his sister-in-law after all or his ex-sister-in-law to be strictly accurate. And I didn't really see him as husband material. No, if St Ann were going to answer my prayers, I don't think it was going to be with Poppy's ex.

He talked rather a lot about Poppy, which was irritating. I said once that we had gone beyond Poppy as a topic of conversation but he looked puzzled.

He always wanted to know if she was seeing anyone and I said, you know Poppy, seeing everyone, seeing no one. This puzzled him further and he asked did she want to know about him?

Now the truth was that if I mentioned Oliver, Poppy would raise her eyes to heaven and sigh. But I didn't pass this on. He seemed to think we were much closer than we were, asking me little titbits about when we were girls. As if I can remember!

I decided to go over to this idiotic place, Ferns and Heathers, to see Poppy, well, really so that I would have something to tell Oliver about her. I wanted him to think we were more loving and bonding than we actually were.

The first thing I saw when I arrived was Poppy's bottom up in the air as she dug at some hole in the ground. Beside her were assorted geriatrics including of all people that loud Grania's red-faced father, Dan. What was he doing here? They were all laughing hysterically at something. I felt that when my shadow fell on them they stopped laughing.

'Why it's Elegant Jane!' cried the awful Dan. And the others looked at me without much pleasure. Poppy came up from the hole in the ground, her hands filthy and streaks of mud on her face.

'Oh hallo, Jane, what's wrong?' she asked. As if there would have to be something wrong for me to come and see my only sister.

'Why should there be anything wrong?' I snapped at her.

They all understood, the old folk, and Dan understood better than most.

'Fasten your seat belts,' he said. They laughed.

'Light the touchpaper and retire,' said another old man with hardly any teeth. A man who must have retired thirty years ago.

I hated them for seeing our coldness and recognising it for what it was. I hated Poppy for letting them see it.

'Right, folks, I have to go away for a short while. Please stay well away from the hole, for God's sake, I don't want to be digging you all out with broken hips,' Poppy ordered them and led me to her little house in the grounds. She washed her hands, poured me a sherry and sat down to talk to me.

'You still have mud on your face,' I said.

She ignored me completely. 'Is there anything wrong with Dad?' she asked.

'No, of course not, why, should there be?'

'Well, his blood pressure was up last week,' Poppy said.

'How on earth do you know?' I asked.

'I take it every week when I go round on my half-day,' she said.

Poppy goes to Mother and Father every week on her half-day? How extraordinary!

'So what is it then?' Poppy asked, looking wistfully out at the garden where she wanted to be, not in here talking to her only sister.

'I was talking to Oliver,' I began.

'Oliver?' She sounded bewildered.

'Yes, Oliver. Your husband, the man you were married to.'

'But I'm not married to him now, Jane,' Poppy said as if she was talking to someone retarded. She talks to those old bats outside on much more equal terms than she talks to me.

'No, but he was making enquiries about you,' I said, wondering how this had got so out of control.

'Like what kind of enquiries?' She was totally uninterested. I so wished I hadn't come.

'Oh, I don't know. Things. Like were you good at games at school, like what we did on your birthday at home.'

'Oliver wants to know all that? Lord, he must be madder than we thought,' Poppy said cheerfully and looked out the window again as if she were dying to get back to digging holes.

'I don't think he's mad at all, I think he is very sane. I really believe that he wanted it all to work, you know, when you were married.'

'Yes, of course he did, that's why he brought his old girlfriend back to my bed,' Poppy said in a matter-of-fact way.

'Well, it was his bed too,' I heard myself say idiotically.

'Oh well, of course, that makes it all right then,' Poppy said.

There was a silence between us. I tried to fill it. I wanted to show some interest in this mad place where she worked.

'What were you digging the hole for?'

'Mass burial ground, cheaper than funerals,' Poppy said.

For a moment I believed her. Well, we don't go round making these silly jokes in the library.

'Sorry, it's for a giant palm tree. It's arriving this afternoon – we wanted to have its space ready for it.'

'Then don't let me detain you.' I stood up huffily.

'Don't go – finish your sherry.' She sat there tousled and untidy. I sipped it in silence.

Twice she looked as if she were about to confide in me and then stopped at the last moment.

'Say it,' I ordered her eventually.

'All right, well, item number one, I don't fancy Oliver remotely, so go right ahead if you do. You aren't stepping on any toes. But item two, he's really very boring, clinging and boring. You'll find that. So he's rich and good looking but actually that's not very important in the long run. The rich can often be tight with spending their money and the handsome are often vain. And you end up feeling guilty because you encouraged him. And he hasn't the remotest notion of being faithful. You told me that years back and I didn't believe you. So why should you listen to me now?'

Poppy sat there, assured and mud spattered, with a sherry in her hand and a lot of mad old people outside the window waiting for her to come out so that they could get on with digging a hole.

'And this is better?' I said, indicating the garden,

the residents and the whole set-up with a nod of my head.

'Vastly,' she said.

I knew then that I had never understood her and never would. My efforts at friendship and trying to get close, admittedly late in the day, were being thrown back in my face.

As I was getting into my car I heard them cheer at the reappearance of Poppy. Well, it was what she wanted. And she had said the coast was clear.

I got my hair done and bought some smoked salmon – in case Oliver came round.

As it happened he didn't. But he came next evening.

He never brought a gift and he did look at himself in the mirror quite a lot. And he always stayed just a little too long for me, because I had to get up early for work. Sometimes he would stay the night but that was rather disruptive too.

He never suggested that we go out anywhere. And there *was* something a bit clinging about him. But we weren't married so I couldn't divorce him or get a barring order against him. Even though at times I would have liked to. For a little peace.

There was very little laughter around at the library or at home. The days often seemed long. Compared to that madhouse at Ferns and Heathers where there was never a spare moment in the day and the inmates were laughing all the time.

Was it at all possible that Poppy could have been right? Poppy whose skin had never been cherished, whose hair had never been styled and whose wardrobe was a joke, a bad joke. Surely Poppy couldn't have discovered the secret of life? That would be too unfair for words.

CHAPTER 14

Your Eleven O'Clock Lady

Part 1 – Pandora

I hope it's going to be busy today at the salon. When you have to hang about between clients, time seems to drag a lot. I didn't need any free time to think about the conversation at breakfast.

I was in at 8.45 as usual. Fabian, who is a legend not only in Rossmore but for four counties around, likes to have what he calls 'grooming control' before he opens the door. His salon sinks or swims, he says, by what the staff look like. No grubby fingernails, no down-at-heel shoes, and our own hair must be perfect. We had been warned about that at the very outset. Fabian expected us to have shining, well-conditioned hair every morning, any snipping or trimming he would do. It was one of the perks of the job.

Our uniforms were laundered on the premises so

they always looked bandbox fresh. That's a funny word, bandbox. I wonder what it means. Fabian insisted that we all smile a lot and look pleased to see customers. The salon wasn't the place to be if you were going to look glum. Worries had to be left outside the salon. That was an absolute.

Fabian said he could only charge the top prices he does if people felt they were in a special place. No one with hangovers, headaches, difficult children or unhappy love lives had any place on the staff.

Unreal, you might say. And Fabian would agree.

But he said that going to an expensive hair salon was an escape for people, they didn't want to hear of the dull or problem-filled world of ordinary people. So there was to be no talk about the traffic, or illness, or being mugged. An expensive perfume was sprayed around the salon just before opening time and several times again during the day. This was to set the tone of the place. Glamour, peace, elegance, a palace with the power to transform all who came in and paid big money.

The tips were good too, and you could work any-where you wanted to if you had been a few years in Fabian's. But usually you set up your own place. If you said that you were 'late of Fabian's' people would come to you from far and wide.

Not that I was going to be in a position to set up my own salon. Once I thought I might – and Ian had been behind me all the way, assuring me that I was management material.

But breakfast today had changed everything.

Stop it, Pandora. Smile. Teeth and eyes, Pandora, we are nearly on show.

Pandora is my salon name, and that's what I think of myself as being while I'm here. At home, I'm Vi. Don't think of home. Smile, Pandora, the day is starting.

My nine o'clock lady was in the door like a greyhound out of a trap. She came every Thursday without fail, attached almost surgically to her mobile phone. Fabian was very strict about this. He only allowed phones that vibrated to show there was someone looking for you. No ring tones to disturb the other clients.

My smile was nailed to my face. Her conversation was quickfire and one way; she wanted agreement, nods of affirmation and acknowledgement, all in the right place.

You couldn't let your mind wander here and so no thoughts of Ian and his guilty, shifty account of where he had been last night was allowed room in my head.

The nine o'clock lady was always in a lather about some aspect of her work. Some fool had done this, some idiot hadn't done that, some bloody courier had been late, some bloody sponsor had been early. Rossmore was the boondocks of the world. All that was needed was immense sympathy, a litany of soothing sounds – and speed. The nine o'clock lady had to be out screaming at a taxi at nine-forty-five.

My nine-thirty lady had been shampooed and

was deep in a magazine story about Princess Diana.

'It's a shame they can't let her rest, isn't it?' she said. 'Do you have anything else about her that I could read, do you think?'

She was a regular also, trying out a different style every week until she found the perfect way to look at her daughter's wedding which was going to be a huge affair. The nine-thirty lady had not been invited to get involved in the planning of it all. There was a wedding organiser. Nothing in her whole life had ever hurt her so much. Her only daughter had turned her back on her on this the most important day of her life. Mighty soothing was called for here also. Huge reassurance that it had been a kindness rather than a rejection on the daughter's part. Useless bleatings that it gave her much more time now to concentrate on her own hair, her own outfit, her own enjoyment of the day. The nine-thirty lady had wanted to be in the centre of it, fussing, bossing and driving everyone mad.

'Don't marry, Pandora,' she warned me as she left. 'It's never worth it, believe me, I know.'

I had told her many times in answer to her absent-minded questioning that I *was* married, to Ian. But she didn't remember, and as Fabian said, we mustn't expect them to remember anything about us. They are centre stage when they come in here. We are just a well-groomed, charming set of props. Certainly not the occasion to tell her that she was spot on about marriage. It was indeed, judging by the way this morning was going, far from worth it.

The ten o'clock was an out-of-town person who had seen a write-up of Fabian's in a magazine. She had come to the town to get fabric for soft furnishings. She had decided to have a hairdo as well. No, nothing new, thank you, she knew what suited her, like she knew what fabrics she needed. The tedium and monotony of her life seeped all over me. I wondered: if possibly my life with Ian was at the moment anxious and unsettling, it might be better than the living death that the ten o'clock lady seemed to be living.

My ten-thirty was a model. Well, actually she was a glamour model, for a photo catalogue for underwear, but she called herself a model. She was nice actually, she came in every six weeks to have her roots done.

'You look a bit peaky today,' she said.

I suppose it was good that she even saw me, most of them didn't. But to be seen and identified as peaky wasn't good. It was a funny phrase, something people said in British soap operas to someone who was about to die or who was pregnant or getting dumped.

Peaky.

Not a good thing to look. I hoped that Fabian hadn't heard. I smiled more brightly than ever, hoping to beat off whatever dull, dead sort of vibes I must be giving out.

'I know, I know. I have to smile like that every night,' the ten-thirty said sympathetically. 'Sometimes I feel like a big bawling session and that's when I have to smile most.'

She was very kind, interested and made me think she cared. I'm sure she's very good at her job, making ladies feel confident about lingerie – I bet they all confide things to her at her work because she sounds interested in other people. I looked around to see whether Fabian was in earshot. We had strict rules about not burdening the clients with our own personal problems.

'It's just my husband, I think he's seeing someone else.'

'Believe me, he is,' she said, applying her lip liner.

'What?' I cried.

'Sweetheart, I work for a place that is packed to the gills every night with people's husbands getting the catalogues just to ogle over them. That's what husbands do. It's not a problem unless you make it into one.'

'What do you mean?'

'Listen to me – I know this, they like to look at the pictures and chat up birds. They don't want to leave their wives. They're not sorry they married them, it's just that they hate to think that it's all over and that they are missing out on whatever else is on offer. They sometimes feel that they've been filed away under "Married Man". Cross-reference, "Dull Man". A sensible wife would make nothing of it; the problem is a lot of them make a great, useless fuss about it – weakening everything as a result.'

I looked at her in amazement. How did she get such wisdom? This woman whose modelling name was Katerina but who was probably called Vi, like myself at home.

'You mean, put up with infidelity and cheating and pretend it isn't happening? You seriously mean that?' I asked her.

'Yes, in a way I did mean that, for a bit anyway, until you know definitely it's true – and even if it is you must know definitely if it's going to be the end of the world if he has a bit of a whirl. Soon it could be nothing but a confused memory.'

'But suppose it's not just a bit of a whirl. Suppose he really does love her and not me. What happens then?'

'Well, then he walks,' said Katerina. 'And there's nothing any of us can do. I'm just saying that the very worst scenario is to make a fuss now. Right?' She looked as if she had finished with the subject so I went on to autopilot again, got her hair rinsed and blow-dried it to perfection. As she left she gave me a big tip.

'You'll survive, Pandora, see you in six weeks,' she said and glided like a lithe panther out of the salon.

'Your eleven o'clock lady not in yet, Pandora?' Fabian had a control of the salon that would have been envied by any military leader in a war room. He knew what was going on, or not going on, in every corner. Together we looked at the appointment book. New client. A Ms Desmond. It meant nothing to either of us.

'Find out how she heard of us, won't you,

Pandora?' he said, on the ball about work twenty-four hours a day.

'Yes, of course, Fabian,' I said automatically.

Actually I would spend the time trying to find out how this had happened, my five-year-old marriage to Ian unravelling.

First I had accidentally seen the bracelet in his drawer. 'For my darling, to celebrate the new moon, all my love, Ian.' I had no idea what he meant. We hadn't seen any new moon together recently or that I could remember at all.

But it might be referring to something that was about to happen. I checked the diary: there would be a new moon on Saturday next. Possibly he was going to take me away somewhere to celebrate it. I wouldn't spoil the surprise. But there was no mention of an outing on Saturday, instead the rather depressing news that Ian would be away for the weekend on a conference. Still it didn't dawn on me. I must be very foolish. Thick? Trusting? Apply which word you choose.

But last night Ian was very late home from the office and I went to bed at eleven because I was exhausted. I woke at four and he still wasn't back. Now this was worrying. He has a mobile phone, he could have called me. I tried calling him but he had the phone on voicemail. But at that very moment I heard his key in the door. I was so angry with him that I decided to pretend to be asleep and avoid a row. He took ages to come to bed, but I never opened my eyes. At one stage he went to his sock drawer and took out the bracelet. I opened my eyes just wide enough to see him smiling at the engraving and then he put it away. Deep in his briefcase.

Ian always left the house earlier than I did. It took him ages to get to work in his car but he needed it for work. And for who knew what else? He could only have had three hours' sleep. He asked me what time I had gone to bed.

'Eleven o'clock, I'm afraid I was dropping. What time did you come back?' I asked.

'Oh, early hours of the morning, you were sleeping so very peacefully I didn't want to wake you. Such a bloody great fuss on at the office . . .'

'Still, think of all the overtime,' I reassured him, trying to force the suspicion out of my mind.

'Not sure they'll pay anyway and listen, love, I have to go away for the weekend, there's a conference, bit of an honour really – I suppose I should be pleased but I know it's your weekend off so I'm so sorry.' He put on his little-boy face that I used to find endearing. Until this morning when I found it sickening.

He was having an affair.

Lots of things fitted into place now. I had made a list of all these things when he left.

I had an hour before I needed to go out myself but I did not feel like washing up after Ian's breakfast, cleaning Ian's house, preparing Ian's dinner. I put on my coat and headed out the door as soon as I heard his car leave. I got on the first bus that came to the stop. It wasn't going to the part of

Rossmore where Fabian's was but I didn't care. I just wanted to get away from the house where I had once been so happy. Once. But it was now like a prison.

The bus stopped at the far edge of Whitethorn Woods and then was going to turn round and go back to wherever it had come from. Like a zombie I walked up through the woods. People said that they were going to be dug up to make a new road but that might just be a rumour. Anyway if the woods did go it would be nice to have a look at them now.

I walked on fighting back the sick feeling of dread in my chest, the feeling that it was all over and Ian loved someone else. Some horrible, scheming girl.

He had been taken in by her, bought her a bracelet and was going to see the new moon with her.

I had followed the wooden signs to the well. We used to come here when we were kids but I hadn't been since. Even at this early hour there were people praying. An old woman with her eyes closed. Two children with a picture of someone, their mother probably, asking for a cure. It was unreal and kind of sad.

Yet, I thought, now that I'm here, it can't do any harm. I told St Ann the situation. Quite simply. It was amazing what a short story it was really. Boy loves girl, boy finds other girl, first girl heartbroken. There must have been thousands and thousands of similar stories told here.

I didn't feel any sense of hope or anything. In fact

I felt a bit foolish. I didn't know what I was asking her.

To afflict this new woman with some awful illness maybe? St Ann wouldn't do that.

To change Ian's mind, really, I suppose that's all I wanted.

Then I walked briskly to the gates of the woods and caught a bus to work.

I travelled with a grim face into Rossmore and all morning I kept remembering more damning proof of the affair. The way he had refused to go bowling last week – normally he couldn't be kept away from it. How he had changed the subject twice when I asked him to do a business plan on buying that corner newsagents near us out in our suburb which was for sale and making it into a salon.

'Let's not be too hasty,' he had said. 'Who knows where we'll be in a year or two?'

Suddenly my thoughts were interrupted.

'Your eleven o'clock lady is in,' one of the juniors called.

Ms Desmond was waiting at the desk. She had a nice smile and she asked me to call her Brenda.

'What a lovely name, Pandora!' she said wistfully. 'I'd love to have been called that.'

Fabian didn't encourage us to tell clients that these were made-up names, in fact he actively discouraged it.

'I think my mother was reading an over-fancy book at the time,' I said, taking the grandeur away from it to reassure her.

I liked this woman. Brenda Desmond handed her coat to the junior and sat down while we looked at her in the mirror.

'I want to look terrific for the weekend,' she said. 'I'm going off to a really gorgeous place in the country to look at the new moon with a new fellow.'

I looked at her reflection in the mirror and told myself that all over this town there were people going away for the weekend with new fellows. It didn't have to be Ian. My pleasant interested smile was still there.

'That's nice,' I heard myself say. 'And are you serious about him?'

'Well, as much as I can be, he's not entirely free, alas, he says that's no problem but, you know, it does throw a wrench in the works. Funny phrase, that, I wonder where it comes from.'

'Probably it's quite a literal thing, like, you know, if a wrench falls into the works of some machine or is thrown into it, it sort of wrecks the whole machine,' I said.

She listened, interested.

'You're right, it's probably quite straightforward. Are you interested in phrases and where they come from?'

She was treating me like a real person with views, not someone who would crimp her hair. But I had to be sure that she was the one before I pulled every tuft of her flat, greasy hair out by the roots.

'Yes, I am interested in words, I was just thinking about the word bandbox this morning. Do you know where that came from?'

'Well, oddly I do, I looked it up once: a bandbox was a light box that held bands, like hairbands, I suppose, caps, millinery, that sort of thing.'

'Does it now?' I was actually interested. Imagine her knowing that! And why should a bandbox be so fresh and clean? But enough speculation. Back to work.

'What do you think you'd like done?'

'I don't really know, Pandora, I'm not much good about hair, I have to work so very hard, you see. We are flat out all the time. So this is a real excitement for me; I called in a sickie this morning, I can't go in tomorrow with a new hairdo or they'd suspect and then on Saturday I'm off for my wicked weekend with a colleague.'

'Where do you work?' I asked her. I could hear the words booming, resounding, echoing in my head.

Please may she not say Ian's company.

She said Ian's company.

My hands were on her shoulders. I could have raised them and put them around her neck and choked her until she was dead. She wouldn't have been expecting it, you see, so it would have worked. She could be lying dead in the chair now.

But I resisted it. There would have been too many repercussions.

Instead I talked about hair.

'You wear it fairly flattish,' I said, amazed that I could function at all.

'Yes. Do you think I should have it higher, and

maybe some more shape? What do you suggest?'
She didn't want to know what I would have suggested.

I thought of my Ian running his hands through this woman's horrible limp hair, telling Brenda she was beautiful as he so often told Vi she was beautiful. It was almost too much to bear.

'It's quite stylish the way it is,' I said thoughtfully. 'But let me ask Fabian, he always knows.'

I tottered on unsteady legs to Fabian.

'New lady just loves her hair the way it is, think she could be a regular, can you come and tell her she looks fine.'

He peered across the salon.

'She looks ludicrous,' he said.

'Fabian, you asked us to use our initiative to second-guess people, I'm doing that and suddenly now it's wrong.' I looked offended.

'No, you're right.'

He glided over and touched her head in that way he does. 'Ms Desmond, Pandora, who is one of our most esteemed stylists here, asked me to give my opinion. I think the classic style you have chosen is perfect for your face, complements your features and I feel that all you need is a little, tiny trim.'

'You think it's nice?' she asked foolishly and the great Fabian closed his eyes as if to say it was almost too nice to describe. It also prevented him from having to lie to her face.

'Lucinda,' I called to a junior. 'Take my lady and give her a very good, thorough shampoo,' I called. I hissed to Lucinda – who in real life was called Brid – to beat her head on the basin and get lots of soap in her eyes. The child not unnaturally wondered why.

'Because she's an evil tramp and is sleeping with my best friend's husband,' I hissed.

Brid-Lucinda obliged. Brenda Desmond was brought limping, near blinded and aching back to my station. Brid-Lucinda had kicked her for good measure, pretending to fall over her feet. I put the greasiest gel I could find into her already greasy hair and dried it until it looked like rats' tails on either side of her head. I cut it so that it ended up wispy and uneven. When any of the others looked over at it, I shrugged as if to ask, what could I do when these were the instructions I got.

When I had finished and made her as awful as I could, she looked at herself doubtfully in the mirror.

'This is classical, you say?'

'Oh very, Brenda, he'll love it.'

'I do hope so, he's very stylish, you know. What with being French and everything.'

'He's *French*?'

'Yes, didn't I say, they sent him over from the Paris office! Imagine! And yet he does seem to fancy me . . .' She looked childishly delighted.

I looked at her in horror.

'Do you know Ian in your office?' I said suddenly.

'Ian? Ian Benson? Of course I do. He's a great guy, Ian. How do you know him?'

'I know him,' I said glumly.

368

'He's married to Vi, he's always talking about her.'

'What does he say about her?'

I was so wretched now that I nearly threw myself on the ground and held her around the knees, sobbing out my apologies for making her look like a madwoman.

'Oh everything, he was hoping to take her away this weekend and then they sent him on a conference. It's an honour and everything but he said he'd have preferred to take Vi to this place with a lake and they could have watched the new moon. And made a wish.'

'What do you think he's wishing for?'

'He didn't say but I think he might have been thinking they'd have a baby sometime soon. And that he would get Vi a salon much nearer home. He's been doing endless overtime recently. He's definitely saving for something . . .'

And then she was gone, out there with her horrible hairstyle, about to make a total mess of her weekend with the sophisticated Parisian man.

I think they told me that my eleven-thirty was in but I didn't hear. Like I haven't really been hearing much of anything lately.

You're meant to give something to charity if St Ann grants your request. But she didn't really, did she? I mean, Ian had never stopped loving me at all so we were praying for something that had already been granted. But on the other hand, it had all turned out the way we wanted.

Oh, go on.

It's only money for handicapped children.

It's not the end of life as it had been five minutes ago.

Part 2 – Bruiser's Business

My real name is George. Not that anyone would know it. I have been called Bruiser since I was two. And in the salon I'm called Fabian.

So when anyone calls out 'George Brewster', like at an airport if I am on standby and they are reading my passport, I take ages to answer. Then I leap up guiltily as if I am travelling on forged documents.

At our school, the Brothers in Rossmore, everyone had nicknames and sadly they heard my mum calling me Bruiser so that was that. I wasn't colossal or anything but I was a sturdy thick-set boy, I suppose, so they leaped on that name. In a way it wasn't a bad name to be called. New people I met thought that I had some terrific reputation with my fists and so they kept away from me which was a relief.

I was ten when my mate Hobbit told me that my dad was running around. I was so stupid I thought he actually meant running around, you know, like in circles or up and down the road jogging. But he didn't, he meant going after the ladies. He said he had seen my dad in a car with this blonde one who was much, much younger and they were going at it like knives.

I didn't believe Hobbit and I hit him. Hobbit was annoyed.

'I only told you so that you'd be ready for it,' he complained, rubbing his shoulder where I had thumped him. 'I actually don't care if your dad runs from here to Timbuktu.'

So I gave him two KitKats from my lunchbox as a consolation and everything was all right.

I always had a terrific lunchbox because my mum knew I loved chocolate and peanut butter sandwiches. Poor Hobbit had awful things like apples and celery and cheese and bits of very dull chicken.

Shortly afterwards my mum discovered that Dad was running up and down or whatever I called it in those days and everything changed.

'It's all our fault, Bruiser,' she told me. 'We are not attractive people, we haven't been able to hold your father's attention and interest. Everything must change.' And everything did.

First, she kept dragging me up to St Ann's Well to discuss the matter with a statue.

Then I got horrible lunchboxes, worse than Hobbit's, then I had to jog four bus stops every morning before catching the bus. After school I went to the gym with my mum. It was very expensive so we both had to work there in order to be allowed to use the machinery. She used to man the reception desk for two hours and I went round picking up towels.

I actually liked it, I liked talking to the people there, they told me their stories, and why they were there. There was a fellow who had hoped to meet birds but hadn't met many, there was a man who had had a heart scare and a woman who wanted to look well for a wedding, and a singer who had seen a video of herself and said that her backside was the size of a mountain, which it more or less was.

Because I really was interested in their stories they talked more and they told the people who ran the gym that I was a great asset. And though I wasn't really meant to be working there at all, what with being way under age, they gave me more hours. They were afraid to give me money because of the law but they bought me nice things like a good brand-new school blazer from the shop and a camera and it was great.

My mum lost a lot of weight and apparently Dad stopped running all over the place and said that no one should ever underestimate the power of St Ann and a healthy diet. And everything was fine again at home.

It was fine at school too because I had got a lot fitter and when we were thirteen and I went to the disco, Hobbit said that most of the babes there thought I was a fine thing. Which was terrific for me but not for Hobbit.

Neither Hobbit nor I knew what to do as a job, a career, whatever. My dad was a sales executive for electric goods and I sure as hell didn't want to do that. Hobbit's dad and mum ran a corner shop and he hated even the thought of working in it. My mum worked full time in the gym now, she had done a course and she taught aerobics there. But none of that made it any easier for Hobbit and myself to know what we would do. Even Miss King, the careers teacher who came to the school as a consultant, seemed hard pushed to advise us.

She said to me that I was interested in people, I should take that into account. I told her straight out I wouldn't be a social worker, I'd hate it. No, she didn't mean that, she said. Nor teaching. I couldn't *stand* teaching. She nodded sympathetically. She was always nice, Miss King was.

'Some job where you'd be talking to people and making them feel good?' she suggested.

'A gigolo?' I wondered. I just wanted to tell Hobbit that I'd said it.

'Yes, that sort of thing, certainly that's the area where we should be looking,' she said agreeably.

So I didn't tell Hobbit about it after all. Then amazingly Hobbit said that we might do hairdressing, there were loads of babes at the classes in college and we'd be stroking women's heads and all kinds of things all day in the salon.

'*Hairdressing?*' I said.

'We've got to do something,' Hobbit said reasonably.

Nobody liked the idea except Hobbit and myself. My mum said I could have done something more intellectual, my dad said it wasn't for real men. Hobbit's parents said they wouldn't be able to hold their heads up again in the corner shop.

It wasn't bad at all as it turned out. Hobbit got

a job at a ritzy salon where he was called Merlin.

Merlin!

I had to remember that when I went in to see him or called him on the phone.

I got a place in a family-style salon way out in the suburbs of Rossmore called the Milady Salon. I liked the owner, Mr Dixon. We all called him Mr Dixon, even people who had been there twenty years.

It was a very middle-aged, middle-class, once-weekly shampoo-and-blow-dry brigade, and a nervous request for a cut, which they called a trim, once every six weeks, discreet colour twice a year. Nothing innovative, no experiments, no chance to show off any style. But basically good people who wanted to look better.

Their eyes seemed big with anxiety as they looked in the mirror. Every hairdo was some kind of dream. A woman might be giving a dinner party, or another might be going to an extravaganza on ice, or to an old girls' reunion. A lot of them were very lacking in self-confidence, which was why they never tried anything new. Sometimes I noticed that they didn't really look all that much better when they left the salon but they felt better and so they walked straighter with more purpose and half smiled at their reflection in the shop window rather than scuttling past it as they had done on the way in.

It had been a bit like that with my own mum.

She didn't look hugely changed after her first weight loss at the gym. She just had more confidence, that was all. She felt better about herself and she didn't bite the head off Dad and ask him where he had been and accuse him of ignoring her. She was just a nicer person to live with and so he was nicer to her. It was as simple as that.

And that's just the way these women at the salon felt too.

I think they liked me, they gave me nice tips, they loved my name, Bruiser. They asked about my family and my holidays and if I had a girlfriend. A good fifty per cent of them said I should settle down and the other half said I should take my time. Some of them said I could do worse than visit St Ann's Well, that she was the last word on matters of the heart.

I was taking my time as it happened. Hobbit and I would go out clubbing but we only met awful screeching girls, not settling down material at all. Hobbit, now that he was called Merlin, was full of confidence and ambition. He said to me that I would end up an old man who only knew how to do tightly permed grey heads unless I moved. We needed to branch out, go somewhere that there might be a bit of action, where we might win competitions.

In my head I knew he was right but I hated leaving Mr Dixon and the Milady Salon. It seemed like a betrayal. Mr Dixon said he had five really difficult clients who just loved me. Could I see it in my heart to come in once a month? Merlin said I was raving mad to make a lash for my back like this, but I couldn't not. Mr Dixon *had* taught me everything and paid me well, and I don't think it's right to walk over people who helped you.

So anyway Merlin and I put our savings together and opened our own salon. Rossmore had certainly changed over the years. New affluence meant people had to have the best. There was a young and apparently endless line of clients with money. Girls with tigerish manes, girls with close-cropped, plum-coloured hair, ladies with such heavy frosting that no one could guess at the original colour.

They were leggy and languid and came to the salon twice a week. I marvelled at their wealth and their interest in their hair. It made Milady's seem light years away.

Naturally, my name was changed as well. I was Fabian now. And though Merlin laughed at me for going back to Milady's on the last Friday of every month, I think he half admired me for it as well. Mr Dixon smiled at me as if I were his long-lost son who had come back to the family farm.

They still called me Bruiser there and admired my own very different hairstyle and smart waistcoats. I told them that people were totally mad in the zany salon in Rossmore and liked us all to dress up. They loved hearing these stories and felt safe in their own place. I had more confidence nowadays and so I suggested a little adventure for some of them. Mr Dixon even accepted some of my ideas about slightly more up-to-date decor.

They all asked me about my love life and I told them truthfully that I had been working too hard to find anyone to love. Better not wait too long, they advised, and I nodded gravely.

What I didn't tell them in Milady's was that everyone in the zany place, everyone except Merlin, that is, thought I was gay. Now I had no problems with this, in very many ways it actually worked to my advantage. Women confide in gay men more, as if they were somehow the best of both worlds. Not predatory and about to pounce, not thick and male and wordless; like a girlfriend, really, but not in competition.

It didn't do me any harm; in fact it did me a lot of good. The clients seemed to like it; it helped them to confide in me. They confided. Boy, did they confide. Like that amazing girl Hazel who told me about all her one-night stands and how lonely and used she would feel afterwards. She would never have told me if she had thought me to be a hetero male and possibly a contender.

I did my best for her by toning down her extremely tarty image and making her look somehow more dignified. I suggested a more classy look, and less in the way of bare midriffs. She told me that it was working a treat.

And there was Mary Lou who couldn't get her fellow to commit. He was very happy with her but he wouldn't let her move her things in. And of course no mention of a ring or anything. I said I thought she should be more independent and go on a holiday with girlfriends. No, definitely not a sun, sex, sleeping-with-the-waiters holiday, on the contrary a cultural kind of thing. She was very doubtful but of course it paid off. He was very worried when she looked as if she could survive without him.

So there I was as happy as anything. I was beginning to fancy a beautiful girl called Lara, a designer who came to have her hair done regularly. All the time I went back to Milady's to Mr Dixon, who had after all started me off in the business. Sometimes I brought him a fancy mirror, a turbo hairdryer or a bale of new towels as a gift but I always took my wages from him even though I didn't need them.

Mr Dixon was the old school. You wouldn't want to offend him.

He had come to visit me in our salon once and he took in the whole scene. He said to me later that I was a good lad, the best he ever had, and that he didn't care about my personal habits; it was up to me. My personal life, so to speak.

And I just couldn't explain it all. It was too complicated. Mr Dixon died shortly afterwards and he left me the salon.

I couldn't believe it. But he had no close relations and he didn't want his life's work wound up and sold off to someone who would open a fast-food outlet on the premises.

I had no idea what to do with the place, it was ludicrously old-fashioned and losing money but I knew it had to be kept on as a salon. And I didn't want to dispossess all the old ladies who had been going there for years, by turning it into a proper

Fabian salon with all that that involved. Anyway I wasn't giving it much thought at that time. I had other things on my mind.

By then I had fallen totally in love with Lara but she thought I was gay and I couldn't convince her otherwise.

'Nonsense, Fabian, you can't fancy me, sweetheart, you're as gay as a carnival!' she would laugh. 'We're *friends*, you and me, it's only some silly hissy fit you've had with some gorgeous guy and you want to tell him, "I'm going out with a girl, so look at me!".'

'I am not a gay man, Lara,' I said in a level voice, 'I am one hundred per cent heterosexual.'

'And so are Gerry and Henri and Basil in the salon, I suppose,' she mocked.

'No, of course not. But I am.'

It was no use. I told her my name was Bruiser, and she laughed even more. Or George, I suggested in desperation, and she told me to make my mind up.

The nervous woman who was running Milady's kept telephoning me to know what to do about the electricity bill, or whether or not to order more conditioner. Now to top it all off one of my best stylists was having some kind of hysterics in the staff room, roaring and bawling and totally incoherent about having ruined someone's hair and not having understood that her husband was desperate to have children, and about people not trusting other people.

It was all we needed on a busy morning.

Gerry and Basil, who were usually great with tantrums and nervous breakdowns and people howling, couldn't make head nor fist of it. Henri said we should call the paramedics. I went in and sat with her.

'Pandora,' I said gently.

'Vi, my name is Vi,' she cried. I had forgotten. She was always Pandora in the salon.

'I'm Bruiser – that's my real name,' I said. I thought it might help. It didn't.

'Bruiser?' she said in disbelief.

'I'm afraid so,' I confessed.

'Oh my God,' she said. 'That's all we need – you're called Bruiser.'

I decided to get down to the problem. She started to sob again so I got about one word in four: there was Ian who was her husband, there was her eleven o'clock lady, there was poor Brenda Desmond and the Frenchman, and there was the new moon.

I wondered if Henri was right. Maybe she had just gone mad and should be sectioned and locked up. I got her a drink of water and patted her hand.

I was told that Lara was in the salon. I said she'd have to wait. And I went on patting the weeping woman beside me.

'You don't want to annoy Lara,' Pandora-Vi blubbed at me.

'I don't care if we annoy Lara. Lara has annoyed me, she persists in thinking I'm gay, she makes fun of me and sends me up. Let her bloody hair extensions wait until I'm ready.'

Vi looked up with a tear-stained face.

'But that's idiotic, Fabian, just to look at you, anyone would know you swing both ways.' She was red-faced and earnest.

I wanted to give her a good slap, but this was not the moment to argue my sexuality down to the bone with her. She saw the look on my face, however.

'It makes sense to be bisexual when you think it through,' she gulped. 'Less chance of making a mess of things, always another option open.'

'I am not bisexual, Vi. I have sex with women, do you hear, women, girls, birds, babes, broads, whatever. Not enough of them, I have to say, not nearly enough. From now on I'm going to sleep with any woman who has a pulse. And that will show those know-all Laras out there. That will teach them . . .'

I saw Vi's mouth in a round O of horror. She was staring not at me but over my shoulder. I knew it before I turned. There was Lara, listening to every word. Looking very disapproving indeed.

'How dare you make Pandora cry,' she began. 'Big bully. Poor Pandora, what did he say to you?'

Pandora was of course in floods of tears again, triggered by this sympathy. Again I heard a few key words: babies, new moon, Ian, eleven o'clock lady, Frenchman, bracelet. Totally disjointed, completely off the wall. Yet Lara understood at once. There was no problem, she said, we were all to pretend we knew nothing about anything.

Well, that would be easy for me. I mean, I did know nothing about anything.

The eleven o'clock lady could be given a voucher, Vi was to stop taking the contraceptive pill, Ian loved her, the bracelet was for Vi, not the eleven o'clock lady: all was well, nothing to cry about. Main thing was to avoid stress.

It was complete gibberish.

Yet Vi had dried her tears, blown her nose and was actually smiling.

'Hard to avoid stress in a salon like this,' she said ruefully to Lara.

'Go somewhere calmer, somewhere nearer home,' Lara suggested.

'Where?' Vi asked.

'Oh, I'm sure Tiger or Bruiser or whatever he's called here will have a master plan for you,' Lara said but she was smiling at me. A different kind of smile, as if she saw me properly for the first time.

And I did have a plan there and then.

Vi as it happened lived fairly near Milady's, out in the farthest suburbs of Rossmore near the Whitethorn Woods. She could be manager there. She could have babies and bracelets, and new moons, whatever she wanted, and the eleven o'clock lady would be kept away from her. Whatever they wanted. Was that all right, could we all go back to work now? Please?

And we did and I looked at Lara's eyes in the mirror and told her she didn't need hair extensions, her hair was beautiful as it was.

She said, she wondered was there something a bit unprofessional about the way I was stroking her neck. Was it rather like a doctor and a patient and

382

maybe I could be struck off for unprofessional behaviour?

I said I thought not, I thought that different rules entirely apply in a salon and she laughed a warm enthusiastic laugh and said I was not to dream of sleeping with every woman who had a pulse.

She had been there for that bit too . . .

CHAPTER 15

The Intelligence Test

Part 1 – Melanie

You know the way it is: people think that because you're deaf, you're slow. In fact nothing could be further from the truth. If you're deaf you're often as sharp as a tack because you have to pick up so much from the other senses. I look at people's faces all the time and I watch to see what kind of mood they're in. I mean, if you look at the way people can clench their fists, or bite their lips, or just fidget, you know exactly what's going on. I could walk the whole length of Castle Street and Market Street in Rossmore and tell you what kind of a mood the town was in.

So when they all started talking about the intelligence test, well, of course I knew it was important. And the more they said it was nothing to get worked up about, the more I knew it. I'm not a fool, profoundly deaf, yes, but not at all stupid. It was all about this school for girls like me called St Martin's.

'You'd love it there if they have room for you, Melanie,' my mum said over and over. 'It's a kind of legend in education, their girls do so well in life. But if they don't have room then no problems, we'll just go and find another place. There are lots of places.'

But I knew it had nothing to do with St Martin's finding room for me, and I knew that there weren't lots of other places. If I managed to get the questions right on this intelligence test I'd get in, it was as simple as that.

I had already met a girl who was at school there so I knew all about it, it sounded a great place. This girl who was called Kim said they had fantastic food, and you could be a vegetarian if you liked and even though it was a girls' school there were dances with fellows at them. They would even teach us to dance properly by getting us to recognise the reverberations in the floorboards. They had art classes and an exhibition every year and played a whole rake of games like netball, and hockey, and rounders, against hearing schools as well as other deaf schools. All the girls wore a sort of uniform, any kind of cream-coloured blouse and a navy skirt or navy jeans.

They had all kinds of flashing lights instead of bells, and make-up lessons as well as lip-reading and ordinary things.

I was desperate to get into St Martin's.

But my mum and dad were even more desperate. It would be free, you see, on top of everything else. Some rich deaf person had left a fortune to provide an education for girls with hearing problems. Now the money wasn't the main reason they were so keen on it. They mainly wanted it because girls from St Martin's got everywhere. They got to go to university and had great jobs. But it would be a help because my mum and dad hadn't much money and they had Fergal and Cormac to look after too. I know they're not deaf. But they need schooling too.

Dad's business is always threatening to close down. My mum's back is bad and she has to do long hours at the supermarket to keep things going. I knew that Mum used to go up to the well in the woods to pray that I would get my hearing restored, which was kind of ridiculous really. How could they reverse something that had already happened? And if they were able to, then there were a lot of people worse off than I was.

So even though they were doing their best not to pressurise me, they were sick with anxiety in case I wouldn't pass this test.

The test itself didn't really worry me. I didn't think it was going to be very hard. It was going to be general knowledge and fitting shapes into spaces. That wasn't hard. And there would be identifying objects from pictures or drawings. Kim, the girl I knew who was already at St Martin's, said it wasn't too hard. She had problems with a picture of a kite, she said, she never saw one in real life because she hadn't been allowed to go out running after kites in case she didn't hear traffic and might get killed, so she didn't know what they looked like. But she knew everything else so she got in okay.

On the day of the test, I've never seen my mum and dad so worried. My mum kept changing her clothes – the suit was too formal, she said, the frilly dress made her look like a poodle, the jeans made her look as if she hadn't bothered. What was the right thing to wear?

I didn't think it mattered all that much what she wore or indeed what I wore. But she was dead nervous and their bedroom floor was covered in clothes like it never was before. So I didn't say what I was thinking, which was that she could wear a black plastic sack for all I cared – I said that I thought the suit was the best and she could wear a pink scarf to make it look kind of lively. Mum stopped fussing and started kissing me and saying I was a treasure and that I'd obviously get into the school no matter what anyone wore.

My dad cut his face three times shaving and I said it was like going out with someone who had been involved in a massacre. Suddenly his eyes filled with tears.

'You're so bright, Mel. You know marvellous big words like "massacre". They'd be mad as wet hens not to take you in that school.'

We were nervous wrecks when we set out for the place.

We took a train from Rossmore to the town where

the school was and then a bus to the gate and we walked up the long avenue. Well, the school looked terrific: as I said, there were these huge sports grounds and there was this walled garden that Kim had told me about where every pupil had a flower bed and they could all grow what they wanted, and I saw through the windows a terrific art room – I could see girls painting a mural and I longed to be part of it all. The school where I was at now seemed so dull compared to it, and it was so hard to get the teachers to remember I was deaf, and so tempting to stop paying attention. But if I were here in St Martin's I'd work so hard, I really, really would. I must not tell them that though. It would sound like pleading or begging.

It would all depend on the test.

When we got in, both my parents had to go to the loo as soon as they got in the door and I stood in the big hall and looked around me. I could just see myself here for the next few years. I imagined having friends that might come and visit me at home and I would go to their homes. They would hate my brothers Fergal and Cormac of course but I would probably hate their brothers and sisters too. My parents would come and visit me here during term time, and see my flower bed, and my exhibit in the art show.

A woman came up to speak to me. She was obviously used to dealing with deaf people. She didn't speak until we were looking at each other.

She was very glamorous looking, with long, dark,

curly hair and a big smile. She was very elegant in a tight black skirt and a yellow blouse with a black and yellow brooch on it. She had a book bag over her shoulder and both her hands were free so as well as speaking to me she signed.

This was unexpected.

You see, I thought they didn't sign at this school. I thought they would disapprove of it, and believe it was holding us back. When I went to my lip-reading classes three times a week I was told over and over that if I wanted to live in the real world I shouldn't sign.

But then she had signed, and she looked like a teacher. It might be a test. A trick even? It was so hard to know what to do.

But then maybe she might be deaf herself? Courtesy demanded that I should reply in sign language but I decided to speak aloud as well to show I could.

She had asked me, was I lost?

I said, using both ways of talking, that no, thank you, I was waiting for my parents who had both gone to the bathroom and that then we were going to go for an assessment. She said that was fine and she'd see me later because she was going to be taking part in it all.

She looked around the big hall and gave a sort of a little sigh.

'You must like it here,' I said.

'I do. Very much,' she said and there was something sad about the way she spoke as if she was going to be leaving soon. You have to try so hard when you're deaf to pick up the words, you end up picking up loads of other things as well.

My mum and dad were so nervous and they kept getting confused, answering the questions they had to answer, which were just ordinary things for filling in a form. I wanted to scream that *I* was the one being tested, I was the one meant to have the language problems, and that if they could see my mum at the checkout in the supermarket, she was so fast she was like a wizard, and my dad was so reliable in his company that he had the keys to everywhere and if people got locked out they had to come to him. They didn't look like reliable people – they looked like people who couldn't remember if they owned their house or rented it, and they seemed to have trouble remembering what age Fergal and Cormac were.

Anyway the woman with the black curly hair came in to join us and she said her name was Caroline and she would go through a few things with me. She would ask me some questions.

Well, first I thought it was a kind of a joke. They were things a five-year-old would know about – the colours of traffic lights and who was the Taoiseach of Ireland and who was Prime Minister of England and the President of the United States and what animal did St George get involved with; then a little harder like in what part of your body would you find a cuticle or a retina. And then a few puzzles about the speed of a train or the length of a platform.

They asked me to tell them about Rossmore and so I told them about all the fuss about the bypass road which would cut through Whitethorn Woods. I said I was in favour of it really because it is so hard to cross the street there at the moment with all the huge lorries, and that really places should want progress rather than looking back. They seemed interested but of course it was hard to know.

Caroline asked, did I want to ask anything myself, so I asked about the signing and what was their policy on it, and she said that a lot of deaf people liked talking in sign because it made them relaxed so St Martin's didn't discourage it, they just used it as a second language. And that seemed fine to me.

Then she said she had a hard question: if a house painter was going to paint the numbers on a housing estate from one to a hundred, how many times would he paint the number nine. I looked at her waiting for the real question. That was it.

I kept looking at her, waiting.

'That's it. There's no catch,' she said. But there had to be a catch. Anyone would know the answer to this one. They couldn't let you into a great school like this or keep you out over something like this.

She asked me to write down the answer on a piece of paper and I did. When she looked at it she nodded and folded it over and involved everyone else in the room.

'What do *you* think?' she asked the Principal.

The Principal said nine. The Assistant Principal said ten. My mother said eleven. My father said definitely eleven, because there would be two nines in ninety-nine.

Caroline smiled at them all and asked, 'Do you know what Melanie said?'

They all looked at me and I felt my cheeks go scarlet.

'I'm sorry,' I said, 'I thought you meant every single time he painted the figure nine . . .'

'I did,' said Caroline. 'And you were quite right, the only one in this room who did get it right.'

They all started playing with their fingers: 'Nine, nineteen, twenty-nine . . .'

Caroline put them out of their misery. 'Melanie said twenty times, the rest of you all forgot ninety-one, ninety-two, ninety-three, etc. Well done, Melanie.'

My mum and dad were beaming at me and giving me a thumbs-up sign. The Principal and the Assistant Principal, to give them credit, were laughing and a bit ashamed of themselves.

Then they came to the identifying objects bit.

They were all on cards and to be honest it was very easy at the start: rabbits and houses and sunflowers and buses and things. And we moved on to what might have been the slightly harder things. Now I didn't want to get too confident but these weren't too bad either. Things like a truck, or a food mixer, or a violin, or a saxophone.

But there was one I couldn't work out at all.

It was shaped like a triangle. I turned the card round a bit until I could get a better look at it. No, I still couldn't see what it might be, the drawing was very simple, too simple; there were no real clues.

'I'm afraid I have no idea,' I said apologetically.

Caroline looked disappointed. I could see it in her eyes.

'Take your time,' she said.

But the longer I looked at it the more confused I felt. Who would know what it was? I glanced at my parents and to my amazement I saw they were holding hands very tightly. My dad's eyes were closed and my mum had that slightly exasperated look she sometimes had at the checkout when people were being stupid or fumbling in their handbags for their money. I realised that they knew what this thing was. I couldn't believe it, how did they know? You'd need to be inspired to know.

'No hurry,' Caroline said again. She had big eyes, and she was willing me to know what it was. The others were startled that I didn't know, I could see that.

They shuffled a bit as if to say that maybe my good performance so far had all been sheer luck or getting questions I knew. They couldn't even work out a simple problem about how many nines the guy painted and yet they knew what this thing was.

I stared at the triangle until my eyes hurt. Was this what was going to keep me out of a great school? Did this stand between me and a terrific education? Would I be back in my old school, peering and straining and missing a lot of it? Would I be back in the concrete school yard and not here going to play hockey three times a week and with my own flower bed? I had been planning what to plant in it, tomato plants up against the wall and lots of dwarf conifers and winter pansies in the front for all the year-round colour.

'No, I'm sorry, it really has defeated me,' I said to Caroline.

'Just guess,' she begged.

'Well, it is only a guess,' I warned her.

'That will do fine,' she said.

'It *could* be Cheshire,' I said doubtfully. 'A slice of Cheshire taken from the block but it might be Cheddar. I'm torn between the two of them.'

And then everything changed. They all seemed to be dissolving into tears and shaking each other's hands and hugging me. Caroline had as many tears on her face as Mum and Dad had. Apparently after all my nearly killing myself trying to work out what variety it was, the word 'cheese' was all they had wanted me to say. Imagine. They didn't even know what kind of cheese it was, they just wanted the word. And the fact that I thought this was too easy a question had just settled everything.

They showed us the dormitories and the dining hall, and my mother and father had stopped being nervous and were acting like normal people again.

Caroline said, 'See you at the start of next term then.'

I said, 'You are coming back then?'

She looked at me astounded that I seemed to know there had been a doubt about it although it had been written all over her face and she said yes, she was, that she had just decided it this very day. About ten minutes ago. And she looked a lot less troubled somehow.

As we went home on the train Mum and Dad got out a paper and pen to work out why the painter painted nine twenty times, and I looked at the card with the silly triangle of mousetrap cheese drawn on it, which Caroline had given me as a souvenir of the day.

Part 2 – Caroline's Career

When we were young we had this aunt who came to the house all the time. She was my mum's younger sister but we never called her Aunt or Auntie because she said it made her feel ancient. We always called her Shell.

She was a real glamour puss, Shell was, and she told me and my sister Nancy all kinds of things that our mum wouldn't ever have told us, like that men just loved girls to wear very high-heeled black shoes and to have very big shiny hair and wear bright red lipstick. Shell kept all these rules herself and she was gorgeous and there were always men around her. But never the same man for any length of time, as my mum said, because apparently Shell was a bit flighty. She was always heading off somewhere for a while and always coming back.

Flighty or not, she was dead interested in us and plucked our eyebrows and got us push-up bras. She told Nancy and me that the world was full of opportunities and we must grab them all, which was so different from what everyone else told us. Our mum and dad were always telling us about studying hard and keeping our heads down, and that was what the grannies said too and they said it at school.

But Shell was her own woman. Life was full of promise, she said, and we must be ready to seize whatever came our way. She made us feel great and excited but only one thing worried me.

Shell often said to me, when we were on our own, that I shouldn't bother getting a career or anything. I was a looker, she said, and I'd marry when I was twenty, just let me be sure to get a decent fellow with plenty of money. I didn't like any of this, well, you don't when you're twelve, do you? I mean, saying that because I had a prettier face than Nancy, that I shouldn't study and she should . . . it was a bit . . . I don't know . . . making looks out to be everything or nothing.

But you don't argue with Shell so I said nothing, just nodded and agreed with her.

When I left school I got a place in a training college and learned to teach the deaf. Nancy went to university and studied Economics and Politics. Shell was with a very rich guy at this stage and she gave us both a holiday; Nancy went on an art appreciation tour to Italy and I went on a skiing holiday in a posh resort, which was where I met Laurence.

Laurence was a lawyer in a very well-known law firm. He was a big, handsome, warm man with dark curly hair, and a great smile. And he had everyone around the dinner table in fits of laughter every night. The girls who ran the ski chalet said they would give him a free holiday any time, he was such fun.

He told me the very first night that I was just *ravishing* – that was the word he used – so often I almost began to believe it . . .

Shell had always said that some men were too perfect to be true and that the wise thing to do was to look for their flaws at the beginning, then you wouldn't get so let down later.

Okay, let's look for his flaws, I said. He was very handsome and they say handsome men are vain. He didn't appear to be, but I had to remember that as a possible flaw. He was a little impatient with people who were slow on the slopes or who didn't get the drift of the conversation at dinner. But for me he had all the time in the world, and he was interested in everything about me, my studies, my family, my hopes and dreams – and very interested in going to bed with me.

I told him that I didn't do that on holidays.

'Why did you come on this holiday then?' he asked, irritated.

'To ski,' I said simply.

Surprisingly he accepted that and stopped bothering me about sex. I assumed that I would never hear from him again so was very surprised when he called two weeks after we returned from our holiday.

He lived only fifty miles away from me in a place called Rossmore so we had dinner a few times, and then he brought up the matter of whether I might come away with him for a weekend to a hotel in the Lake District of England.

I said, that would be great, thank you, that I'd love it.

It was great and I did love it.

He brought me to meet his family and they were posh but not overpowering.

And I brought him to meet my family and naturally Shell turned up to inspect him. Out in the kitchen she put her fingers in a bunch up at her mouth and blew a kiss in the air.

'Exquisite, Caroline, that's what he is. Didn't I always tell you you'd be married before your twenty-first birthday and not to bother with a career?'

I looked at her open-mouthed. I *had* a career. I was going to teach the deaf, beginning with my probationary year the following September. What did she mean that I was not going to bother with a career?

But as usual with Shell, you say nothing. So nothing was what I said.

And as it happened things turned out differently. Laurence and I got married in September and there was such fuss getting the house and doing it up, everyone considered it better if I didn't start my probationary year at once. The next year I was pregnant so I couldn't start then.

After that, well, I was looking after Alistair, so it would have been idiotic to try and fit in teaching hours with that. Then when he started going to his first school and I looked for some morning hours teaching, I just couldn't find anything around home. Around Rossmore.

I don't want you to think that I was aching to get out there and be at work or that I was bored, because truly that wasn't the case. There weren't enough hours in the day. Often Laurence would ring and say, could I escape and meet him for lunch; he always told me I was ravishing and he was always admiring me. I loved being with him and making a good life for him.

Money was never short. I had full-time help in the house and a gardener. I went to the gym regularly and to get my hair done at Fabian's and had a manicure; every week we would have people to dinner on a Friday.

Always eight people – like the senior partners at Laurence's work, and business people, and sometimes if there was an extra man we might ask Shell who, according to Laurence, performed very well at a dinner party. I had learned to be a very accomplished cook: I knew ten different starters and ten different main courses and I actually wrote down what I served people so that I would not give them the same thing over and over again. And across the candlelit table Laurence would raise his glass at me.

'Lovely, Caroline, thank you so much,' he would say and the other women at the table would look at me with envy.

We had decided from the start just to have one

child but after I held Alistair in my arms I wondered, should we have more. Laurence was against it and he reasoned it out gently with me. We had always said that one child was fine. Alistair was very happy and had lots of friends – it wasn't as if he pined for a brother or sister. We could have time on our own together, which was what we wanted most. It made a lot of sense, I agreed with him. I didn't think I was being talked into it or anything.

Before I knew it Alistair was eleven and it was time for him to go to boarding school. Now this I didn't want, it seemed inhuman really. But Laurence was very anxious that our son should go to the same place that he had been and his father had been. He brought me to the school several times and we saw where he had smoked his first cigarette, and played his first game of rugby and the library where he had studied hard to get his A levels. He said he had been very happy there and it had made him grow up and he had met most of his friends there, people he still knew. We could come up every second weekend and stay in the hotel and take Alistair and his friends out for a super lunch.

I asked Alistair what he really wanted. I asked him when we were on our own in the garden. I said he could tell me the complete and total truth because it was his life.

He looked up at me with his huge brown eyes and said he would love to go to the school.

So that was that.

That's when I set about getting a job teaching.

I would have loved to get a job in St Martin's. Well, anyone would have. The place was out on its own. They performed miracles there, better than any miracle ever worked at St Ann's Well up in the woods where I took Alistair to play and the dogs to walk. But they had no openings.

Here in Rossmore we did not have a school specifically for the deaf, but there were facilities in St Ita's and in the Brothers. The kids were terrific and like every teacher starting out I made all my mistakes on them and learned a great deal that first year.

I learned how to delegate at home so that the house and garden were in fine shape without me, and I arranged for the shopping to be delivered every Friday and kept up with the dinner parties.

When my mother-in-law said that I was wonderful to be going out to work – in a tone that meant she thought it anything *but* wonderful – I deliberately misunderstood her and thanked her for her praise.

I tried getting my hair done in Fabian's at lunchtime, and transforming a small dark room which we had once used just for storage into a study for myself so as not to have all my papers and laptop and things strewn around the house. It meant there were no more sudden lunches with Laurence in smart little Italian places, and no long shopping trips with my charge card. I learned like every working wife has learned that if you stay up late and don't do the clearing away, then it's going to be bloody hard in the morning getting it all sorted before racing off to work.

Every second weekend we went to see Alistair and he was making lots of friends and was in a chess club and a birdwatching group, so I became reconciled to the idea that it was the right thing to do for him. We couldn't have found these activities for him at home.

I used to listen to the women at work talking about their husbands and their partners or about the guys they were involved with. Every word that came out of their mouths made me realise just what a jewel I had in Laurence. A warm enthusiastic man, who told me all about his work, who shared everything with me, who told everyone I was lovely or even *ravishing* – he still used that word about me – to my embarrassment when he said it in front of people. I don't even know why I needed to hear their stories to convince myself that he was marvellous.

I listened to their stories of how unfaithful they had found men to be. Many of them, even sophisticated women, had been to St Ann's Well hoping for some kind of magic that would improve their marriages. I just knew that Laurence wasn't unfaithful. And he was just as loving and eager as he had been all those years ago when we were out in the skiing chalet and I was keeping him at arm's length. Sometimes when I was tired, or had to study my notes, or get up early, I wasn't really able for his loving and sort of hoped that he might be tired or sleepy or lose interest for a bit. But when I heard the

tales of my colleagues I realised this was a dangerous road to go down.

My sister Nancy often told me that I must be the
luckiest woman on earth. As did my aunt Shell. So
did my mother, and Laurence's mother.

And so I was.

I just wished he was a little more interested in my
job. I was very interested in his. I asked him about
cases, and helped look things up in law reports for
him. I knew all the partners in his office, the possible partners, the rivals, the allies. I had discussed
with him for ever the date of his own possible partnership, which would happen within the next eighteen months.

I persuaded him not to tell Alistair that there was
a room with his name on it in the office. He thought
it was something that would make Alistair feel
secure; I thought it might be something that might
make him feel trapped.

Laurence discussed it all with me over a bottle of
wine – it was a discussion, not an argument. He was
always very reasonable and tried to see my point of
view. Possibly I was right and that our son needed
more freedom in his life, more chance to have hopes
and dreams like we all had. When Laurence talked
like that I asked myself why on earth I woke most
nights at 3 a.m. and worried.

Surely I had nothing to worry about?

But suddenly when I was thinking about St
Martin's School I realised what was upsetting me.
Laurence just didn't get it about teaching. He didn't

know all the wonderful things they could do there for deaf girls. He tried to be interested when I told him about the school records and how they had placed so many of their pupils in positions that hearing children would have been so glad to reach.

He tried. I know he tried because he knew it meant so much to me, and he wanted to be part of my enthusiasm. If he said once he must have said one hundred times that the more he heard me tell him about my work, the more he thanked the Lord that our Alistair wasn't deaf. And that was not what I was saying, hinting or even thinking.

If Alistair had been deaf I knew that with today's techniques he would still have been able to have a great life. Laurence didn't know this. He thought it was a matter of head shaking and tut-tutting and counting our blessings. Which drove me mad.

A chance came up for me to do a further degree. I needed to do practical work as well and St Martin's School, the crème de la crème of deaf schools, was willing to take me on for six hours' work a week. Suppose, just suppose, that I made a success of that . . . then they almost definitely would offer me a full-time job.

I couldn't have been more excited and was impatient for Laurence to come home so that I could tell him. He was full of some happening at the office, one of the chief partners was resigning. It was completely unexpected and, indeed, out of character. Some story about going to Arizona to find himself. A likely story. The man was off his head.

I remembered him. A dullish sort of person with an equally dull wife who was probably not going to Arizona with him in this search. I listened restlessly to the ramifications of all this, and people moving up and moving over, and someone taking over conveyancing and someone coming in from the cold.

Eventually I began to realise it would be the long-desired promotion for Laurence. He would be a partner at last. I tried to be pleased for him, I assured him that it wasn't like stepping into a dead man's shoes since the boring man going to Arizona to find himself was almost certainly going with someone twenty years younger than his wife and of his own free will.

'It will mean a lot of changes in our lives,' Laurence said sonorously. 'A lot more entertaining for one thing, but you're so brilliant at that, Caroline, and you'll like it, you must be lonely with Alistair away at school.'

I don't know what you would have done but somehow I decided not to tell him about the degree and the practical work at St Martin's. Not that night. This was to be his night. Instead I ran him a nice bath with some sandalwood oil in it and brought him a Martini to drink while he was there. Then I got some fillet steaks from the freezer and opened a bottle of wine, dressed myself up in a little black dress and lit the candles. He must have told me twenty times that I was ravishing and that he adored me and that he was the luckiest man in the practice and indeed in the world.

It was four days before I could tell him, and when I did he was astounded.

'But you can't possibly go to St Martin's, Caroline, it's sixty miles away,' he said.

'I have a car, and there will soon be a new road so it won't take long,' I said lightly while beating down my huge disappointment at his reaction.

'But darling, those distances! I mean, I thought . . . I would have thought . . .'

'I'll be well able to do it,' I said, trying hard not to cry.

'But why, Caroline my angel, *why* would you want to take on all this when there's so much for us to do here together?'

I managed to say nothing, which was a very great achievement. What was there to do together? Nothing.

For me alone in the house there might have been overseeing further decoration, repainting, new upholstery. The building of a conservatory, possibly the extension of the paved patio for more guests to drink kir royale at one of our summer dinner parties.

'Why aren't you speaking, Caroline my angel?' he asked me, mystified.

'I feel a bit dizzy, Laurence, I'm going to bed,' I said and pretended to be asleep when he joined me full of concern and a lot of face and arm stroking.

Next day he brought the subject up at breakfast.

But I had had seven sleepless hours thinking about it all and so I was ready for him.

'I'm going to get my qualifications and do my six

hours a week in St Martin's, Laurence, and at the end of the year we will discuss whether I shall work there full time or not. It may indeed turn out that they don't want me. Or that the distances are indeed too long. But this learning year is something I can't and will not give up.'

And then I moved on in a seemingly effortless way to talk about a barbecue that we were having the following weekend when Alistair would be home from his school.

I thought I saw Laurence look at me admiringly as he might look at a fellow lawyer who had made a good point at a case conference.

But maybe not. I'm always hopelessly optimistic.

And the year was indeed hard, there is no denying that. I have to say that I remember hours of night-driving in wet weather, with the windscreen wipers clacking and my being on the mobile phone barking instructions about the meal.

Laurence did become a partner and the man who was finding himself in Arizona did indeed go on the quest without his wife but with a very young temp from the office.

My work at the school was magnificent, we taught people to speak. Over and over, we actually gave a vocabulary and a life to the wordless and it was the most exciting thing I had ever done in my life. I loved it in St Martin's and they appeared to like me, and as the exhausting year ended they told me that they would definitely offer me a full-time post there.

They wondered, would I like a bedsit in the school as several teachers had, just in case the weather was bad and the travelling distance, traffic jams and long hours on the motorway were too much?

I said I would let them know. Very soon.

We had a sort of super-glitzy dinner party for the partners and wives, and I must have got in the door twenty minutes before the first guests arrived. I had just time to change my clothes, leave the extra cream that I had bought on the way home in the kitchen, rearrange the place names, and set out the shop-bought canapés on big oval dishes with wild flowers from St Martin's gardens scattered amongst them and flat leaf parsley sprinkled on top.

'Isn't your wife a genius?' one of the partners said to Laurence.

'Lovely, lovely, Caroline.' He raised his glass at me.

'And she has a worthwhile job as well,' one of the wives said in a tinny voice.

'Yes, I can't think why she does it,' Laurence said.

I looked at him, shocked.

'I mean, all it really does is make sure that my income tax situation is even worse than it was. I mean, when they see "wife's earned income" they are all of a flutter and come down on me like a ton of bricks. And I mean, for what in the end? But she will do it. Won't you, darling?' He looked at me indulgently.

I smiled back at him.

I didn't hate him. Of course I didn't. You couldn't

hate Laurence. And there were ways in which he was right. Maybe I was just trying to show him I had a life of my own. Possibly it was all a waste of time.

There were plenty of people to teach the deaf. Maybe the deaf were even happier when they were called the deaf-and-dumb; when we weren't trying to get them to breathe properly and force sounds out of them.

Who knows?

I would make up my mind next week. I would put it out of my head for now.

We talked about the new road. Voices were raised. Some said it was all barbarous, others said it was totally essential. I mentioned the old well in Whitethorn Woods. Voices were raised still higher.

Some said that it was a ludicrous and dangerous superstition, others said it was part and parcel of the old tradition of the country. So I moved them seamlessly on to something we would all be agreed on, like the price of property. I also produced the truffles that I had bought during my lunch hour and brought home and bashed up slightly to make them look uneven, then rolled in cocoa and chopped nuts. Everyone thought they were home-made.

'Lovely, Caroline.' Laurence raised his glass to me again.

'Laurence,' I said, raising my own glass.

My heart felt like lead.

It had probably been a lot of running round after nothing, when I had thought it was a great career. I managed not to sigh at the thought of a dream that had not been achieved. The world is full of people who don't get their dream.

I wouldn't do all the clearing-up tonight. Tomorrow was not a particularly busy day.

Next day when I had left the house gleaming, I drove slowly to St Martin's. I had been asked to sit in on an assessment of a scholarship child. A girl called Melanie who sounded very bright.

It wouldn't be very demanding and what's more I would enjoy it. It might after all be one of the last assessments that I would ever do.

Funny, isn't it, the way you never know when something is going to happen. When I saw what that child Melanie had done already and how much more we could do now with her, there was simply no decision to be made.

We would take her in St Martin's. I knew this as clearly as I knew I would be here to watch her grow in confidence. This is what I wanted to do and would do.

Just as Laurence wanted to run a law practice.

There were no more grey areas. It wasn't going to be the end of the world. There would be no argument, no confrontation. All over the country people were following a dream and having a marriage. It didn't have to be one or the other. We would work it out. Of course we would.

Strangely the bright little girl seemed to understand, it was just as if she could see the machinery in my mind clicking into place.

'You are coming back then?' she asked me casually, just moments after I had decided.

And I smiled the first real smile for weeks. Because now I knew it was settled.

CHAPTER 16

The Road, the Woods and the Well – 3

Eddie Flynn waited outside the church after Mass until he saw his brother leaving.

'Brian, can I have a word?' he began.

'Not if that word is "annulment",' the priest said without stopping in his progress towards Skunk Slattery's for the paper and then back to his house.

'You know it isn't.' Eddie was almost running to keep up. 'Hang on a bit, this isn't the four-minute mile.'

'I'm going for my breakfast, I'm hungry, I have a lot to do today, talk away if you want to . . .' Father Flynn continued to move purposefully along the road, greeting parishioners at every turn.

'You're so well-known here you should go into politics,' Eddie grumbled as they paused for Father

Flynn to wish this one success at an examination and that one good luck with his new greyhound.

'Right. A cup of coffee?' he said when they got back to his kitchen.

'I thought you'd have someone to cook your breakfast. Haven't you got a Russian or something working for you?' Eddie seemed disappointed.

His brother had put three pieces of bacon and a tomato in a frying pan and was turning them expertly. 'Josef, who is Latvian actually as it happens, not Russian, looks after the canon, not me.'

'The canon should be in a home for the bewildered,' Eddie said.

'Naomi didn't have much luck with him either, is that right?' Brian Flynn smiled.

'Leave it, Brian. I wanted to ask you about the well.'

'The well?'

'The well, man, it's in your territory, for heaven's sake, the holy well, the sacred well, whatever. I'm asking, will they let it go?'

'Will who let it go?' Father Flynn was confused.

'God, Brian, you're getting very thick, will your lot let it go, the Church, religion, the Pope, all that?'

'Oh, my lot, I see,' said Father Flynn. 'The Pope has never mentioned it to my certain knowledge, or if he has, the burden of what he said hasn't trickled down to us here. Are you sure you don't want a piece of bacon?'

'No, I don't want any bacon, and you shouldn't be having any either, clogging up your arteries.'

Eddie Flynn was very disapproving.

'Yes, but then I don't have so many social demands on my life, I don't have to keep so many ladies happy.'

'I'm serious, Brian.'

'So am I, Eddie. The best part of my day is often sitting here peacefully at my breakfast reading the paper. And here you are in my kitchen picking on everything I say or do . . .'

'Some people asked me to join up with them in a syndicate,' Eddie said in a tone of great gravity. He seemed to be waiting for an admiring response.

'But isn't that what you do, Eddie? You're a businessman, you're always joining up with people over this or that.'

'This is my chance to make real money, Brian. And boy, am I going to need real money. Do you know what this wedding is going to cost?' Eddie seemed agitated.

'A simple registry office wedding? Not much surely?' Brian suggested.

'Oh no, we have some dissident priest or other, and somebody is lending him a church to give a blessing in, there are going to be bridesmaids, groomsmen, a huge reception, the whole works. And then all the while I have Kitty sending me notes about school fees. God, I need this break, that's why I have to know about the well.'

'Listen to me, Eddie, I may very well as you say be thick but *what* do you have to know about the well?'

'All right. I'll tell you but it's for your ears only, seal of the confessional and all that. The new road is all ready to go bar the shouting, and we've bought up a lot of land in little bits here and there. Everyone will have to negotiate with us when the compulsory purchase order goes out so we are sitting on a fortune. There's only one snag: some of the lads are afraid the bloody well in the woods is going to balls things up.'

'You may not approve of the well but I wouldn't use that kind of language about it,' Father Flynn said disapprovingly.

'No, okay. But you know what I mean. And I know for a fact that you aren't that convinced by the well either. But is it going to be an issue? That's what we need to know. Nobody wants to take on a crowd of religious nutters.'

'I know nothing about it.'

'Of course you do, Brian.'

'No, I don't, I have managed to stay out of everything. Deliberately. I would not support either side in the issue. I got out of any involvement so you're asking the one man in Rossmore who doesn't have a view.'

'But you're the one who *knows* whether it will blow up and cause a fuss or if it will just die down. You have the feel for these things and we have to know. Now . . .'

'We being the syndicate who are investing money in land?'

'Don't sneer at it, *Father* Flynn. Plenty of money

418

was spent educating you as a priest, wasn't it? And if I am financially secure that's a weight off your back too.'

'You're not a weight on my back, Eddie, you never were.' Father Flynn was extremely annoyed but he tried hard not to show it. 'Now if that's everything I have to go about my work.'

'*Work?* What work?' Eddie scoffed. 'Sure, nobody is bothered about God these days, you have nothing to do. You've never really done a proper day's work in your life.'

'Fine, Eddie, I'm sure you're right.' He sighed wearily and packed his briefcase.

He was going to visit his mother in her home with a series of old photographs which the counsellor had told Judy might jog her memory about the past.

He was going to take Lilly Ryan and one of her sons to visit Aidan in the jail. Aidan Ryan apparently in a window of calm had relented enough to agree to talk to his wife.

He was going to take Holy Communion to Marty Nolan and another old man out on that road; he was going to open a multicultural World Food Day in aid of world famine at St Ita's; he was going to throw in the ball for a match between the Brothers School and St Michael's; he was going to go out to Ferns and Heathers and admire their new prayer and meditation room. They didn't call it a chapel but that's where he said Mass on a Sunday for them.

Maybe Eddie was right and it wasn't really a proper day's work. But it sure felt like it.

Judy Flynn had done eight days of praying at St Ann's shrine. Just one more left.

She had enjoyed her visit far more than she had ever expected she would. It had been a pleasure getting to know Brian again, he was such a good-natured young fellow, as he had always been, and the people here loved him. Her mother was lost in a strange, half waking, half sleeping world but had become markedly less hostile. Poor Eddie was being well and truly punished for having strayed from home – Judy and Kitty had many a laugh over the amazing problems he had on his hands with young Naomi. Kitty said she wouldn't have him back if he crawled the whole way through Whitethorn Woods to ask her.

Judy had tried to assist St Ann in the search for a man by going to the local bridge club in the Rossmore Hotel. She met two handsome men called Franklin and Wilfred. Con men, both of them, talking dreamily about a mobile phone service they were going to set up.

Some day.

They lived with an older lady who never went out because of some scandal, it was too complicated to work out, and anyway they were too shallow for her, so she left them to their plans.

Judy worked out a satisfactory routine to her day. Visiting her mam, spending three hours in her hotel room doing her drawings with no distractions. She would have a cup of coffee with Kitty and then dress herself up for her walk to the well. On the way she would buy a newspaper and then later in the evening she would have a drink with Brian and he would tell her the business of the day. It was a restful way to live. She didn't know why she had been in such flight from it for so many years.

She got her hair shampooed at the smart Fabian's. The young man who seemed to own the place told her that he was in love and hoped that he would marry before the year was out. This surprised her. She had been certain he was gay, but she had learned since coming here that nothing was ever as it seemed.

'I'm hoping to get married too,' she confided to him. 'I've hired St Ann above at the well to help me find a husband.'

'I'd say you'll have no problem there.' Fabian was flattering. 'Beating off the offers is what you'll be.'

She was smiling as she thought of beating off all the offers. She picked up the newspaper in Slattery's and brought it to the counter.

'Just the usual, Sebastian,' she said.

'You're very beautiful when you smile, Judy.'

'Well, thank you,' she said, surprised.

The man they all called Skunk Slattery wasn't known for little pleasantries like this.

'I mean it. I was wondering, would you be free perhaps any evening to have a . . . I mean, to . . . go . . . maybe we could have a meal together?'

'That would be very nice, Sebastian,' Judy said, trying to work out his matrimonial status. She hadn't heard Kitty saying anything about Mrs Skunk but then you never knew.

'If you're not sick of the food at the Rossmore Hotel, they do a very nice dinner,' Skunk said eagerly. There couldn't be a Mrs Skunk if he were taking her somewhere as open as that.

'And what night would you suggest, Sebastian?' she asked.

'Should we strike while the iron is hot? Tonight at eight maybe?' he said anxiously. 'In case you have second thoughts or anything?'

Judy walked up to the shrine with a spring in her step. Everything was going very well. She must ask people why they called him Skunk.

Neddy Nolan said to Clare that eventually he must get in touch with his brothers in England about the land and see that they get something from it.

'I don't see why. Kit's in jail, it can't matter one way or the other to him, the other two haven't been home in years either; we don't even know where they are.'

'But they have a right to share in whatever there is to share if we do have to sell,' Neddy said.

'What right, Neddy? Honestly now, what right? They never gave anything, never kept in touch, never knew or cared what happened to your father.' Clare was very firm on this.

'But things didn't work out well for them, like they did for me.' As always he saw the very best in everybody else.

'You did it all yourself, Neddy, and you never

forgot your father. Now your father is a man who wouldn't have any such sentimentality about the rest of the family,' Clare said. 'They didn't get up to deal with foxes in the hen-run, a sick cow having her calf in the upper field, rebuilding all the hedges and walls. They were never any part of getting your father's meals, clearing up after him and bringing him out to see his friends.'

Her face was full of loyalty to him and Neddy wondered again as he did so often how she could possibly love him so much.

'Anyway, it may all come to nothing, this business about the road,' he said, rather forlornly.

'I wouldn't rely on it, Neddy,' said Clare, who had heard a great deal in the staffroom at St Ita's, at the bridge club in the Rossmore Hotel, and when she left the big bag of laundry in for a service wash at the Fresh as a Daisy. Nowadays nobody was saying *if* the road came, they were saying *when* the road came. There had been a subtle change over the last few weeks.

One of these days her Neddy was going to have to make up his mind. She was not going to influence him. This was something he had to decide on his own. Would he sell his father's farm for a small fortune to that syndicate of gangsters which had people like Eddie Flynn in their number? Or would he hold out in case he alone could stop the march of progress and save the woods and the well that in his big innocent heart he really believed had cured his mother for so many years?

'You're never going to dinner with Skunk?' Father Brian Flynn was astounded.

'Are you going to tell me he has a wife and ten children?' Judy asked in a slightly brittle tone.

'Lord, no, who'd marry Skunk?' Brian said and then wished immediately that he hadn't said it. 'I mean, he's never been married so you think of him as always being single,' he said lamely.

Judy was brief and crisp in her response. 'Why do you all call him Skunk?'

'I can't tell you,' her brother said truthfully. 'He was always Skunk as far back as I remember. I actually thought that was his name.'

Lilly Ryan couldn't believe the change in her husband Aidan over the last eleven months. He was very gaunt looking, with a drawn face and large dark circles under his eyes. Their son Donal, who hadn't wanted to come, seemed to shrink back from the man with the wild look.

'Please Donal,' she begged in a whisper. So the boy stretched out his hand unwillingly.

'I hope you are looking after your mam properly.' Aidan sounded very stern.

'Yes, I'm trying,' Donal said.

He was eighteen and wanted to be a million miles from here. He had seen his dad beat his mam in the past. He couldn't bear that his mam was pathetically grateful that they had been allowed to come.

'You can't make a worse job of it than I did,'

Aidan Ryan said. 'In front of Father Flynn and you, Donal, I want to apologise for the way I treated Lilly over the past time. I simply have no excuse so I am not going to struggle to find one. Alcohol and the grief over our lost baby is a sort of explanation but it's no excuse.' He looked from one face to another.

Father Flynn said nothing because this was family business.

Lilly was completely lost for words. So Donal answered. In a very grown-up voice he said, 'Thank you for saying all this publicly. It can't have been easy for you. If it were just myself and my forgiveness you were asking for, I would never give it to you, not for a hundred years. I have seen you take the leg off a chair to beat my innocent mother. But life goes on and if my mother asks me to forgive you, I will consider it. We will go out now, Mam and myself, and leave you with Father Flynn and we'll see do you still feel the same next week at visiting time.' He stood up to go.

Aidan Ryan pleaded with him. 'Of course I'll feel the same, son. I'm not going to change my mind.'

'You used to change your mind within half an hour before they locked you up here.' Donal spoke flatly, without emotion. Then he made to leave.

'Don't go!' Aidan Ryan cried. 'Don't go away and leave me for a week not knowing where I am before I know if you'll forgive me.'

'You left my mam for years not knowing what she had done to make you so violent. You can wait a week.' He was propelling his mother out before she spoke, they were nearly at the door.

Father Flynn admired the boy so much he wanted to cheer aloud but he kept his face impassive.

'It was grief, Donal,' said Aidan Ryan. 'It takes everyone in different ways. I grieved so much for your sister who disappeared.'

Donal spoke calmly. 'Yes, it does take people in different ways. In my case I didn't ever know Teresa but I envied her because whoever took her had taken her far from you and your furious drunken rages . . .'

And then they were gone.

Outside in the corridor Lilly said, 'Why didn't you let me speak to him? He's so sorry . . .'

'Speak to him next week, Mam, if he's still sorry.'

'But think of him sitting there all that time . . .' Her eyes were full of pity.

'You sat there all that time, Mam,' he said.

In the visiting room, under the eyes of the warders, Father Flynn sat beside a weeping Aidan Ryan.

'Do you think she'll forgive me, Father?'

'I'm sure of it.'

'So why didn't she say something?'

'She was in shock, Aidan. She needed time to think. You see, how does she know if she can forgive you or not? A year ago you landed her in the regional hospital and then you wouldn't let her come in here to see you. I think that takes a bit of thinking about, don't you?'

The man looked frightened, Father Flynn was

pleased to see. This was good. Father Flynn knew that Lilly Ryan would forgive her husband next Tuesday. Donal Ryan probably knew it too.

Let him sweat a little.

Myles Barry, the lawyer, went out to the Nolans' farm. His face was grim.

He had a communication from one of Her Majesty's prisons in Britain. A Mr Christopher Nolan (otherwise known as Kit) had read of the compensation about to be offered to farmers near Rossmore whose land might be acquired in the scheme for the new road. Mr Christopher Nolan wished it noted that his father Martin Nolan was elderly and unable to make any real decision on the matter. And to add that his younger brother Edward Nolan (otherwise known as Neddy) was in fact mentally handicapped. He had not ever been able to hold any position of responsibility or trust. In fact he had proved himself unable to work even on building sites in London. It would therefore not be in the interests of justice if either of these men were to reach a decision that would affect the Nolan family. He, Christopher Nolan, would like his interest in the property recorded and acknowledged.

Myles Barry had never been so angry.

The worthless criminal Kit, having read in some tabloid paper in jail that there was money to be made out of the home and family he had long abandoned, was coming in for the kill.

Myles Barry had to show them the letter or tell

them its contents. It wasn't something he looked forward to.

He met Father Flynn who was just leaving the Nolan farm.

'Nothing wrong, is there?' Myles asked.

The priest laughed. 'No, it's not Last Rites or anything. Marty likes Communion brought to him now and then, he's not able to get into the church for Mass as well as he used to.'

'I suppose he should be in care?' Myles suggested.

'Hasn't he the best care in the world here with Neddy and Clare?' the priest said, unaware that Neddy had come out behind him. 'If I was an old person in Rossmore I'd much prefer to have that couple looking after me than anyone else. It would be desperate to be left there, like my poor own mother and the poor old canon who are determined to stay independent but who are really just struggling to keep going . . .'

Neddy, who had come out to greet the lawyer, joined easily in the conversation.

'Isn't the canon just fine, Father? Josef was telling me that he loves being near the centre of the town and in the heart of everything.'

'Yes, Neddy, but Josef wants to leave and go to work full time on the new road when it comes.'

'If it comes,' Neddy said.

'No, I'd say it's when it comes,' Myles Barry said. 'That's what I'm here to talk to you about.'

'Oh well, there go my hopes that we wouldn't have to make any decisions.' Neddy laughed at himself.

The priest got into his car and drove off and the lawyer came into the kitchen. Neddy kept this house in shining condition. Myles Barry noted the gleaming surfaces, the scrubbed table, and the blue and yellow china neatly arranged on the open shelves.

Neddy said his father was having a rest in his own room, poured the lawyer a big mug of coffee and offered a plate of home-made biscuits. He had seen a cookery expert do them on television last week, he said, and thought they looked easy enough.

He was an innocent, certainly, but he was not a foolish man.

Suddenly Myles Barry decided to show to Neddy the hurtful, greedy letter written by his brother Kit from an English jail. Neddy read it slowly.

'He doesn't think much of us, does he?' he said eventually.

'Wasn't I at school with Kit? He was always a bit dismissive of people, you know the way he went on, it really meant nothing . . .' Myles Barry began.

'Was he ever in touch with you since he left school?' Neddy asked mildly.

'No, but you know the way it is, people's lives are different. They go in one direction or another . . .' Myles Barry was wondering why he seemed to excuse Kit Nolan when really he wanted to punch him in the face.

'He never writes to me either. I send him a letter every month, always have, telling him what's happening here in Rossmore, how Dad is and everything else that might interest him. I told him all about the road of course. But I never hear back.'

'Maybe he has nothing to tell,' Myles Barry said.

His anger over Kit was now at boiling point. Imagine, the decent Neddy wrote to that ungrateful brother of his every month for years and what was the result? Kit stirred himself to write to a lawyer to say that Neddy was a halfwit.

'That's true. Every day must be like the day before in there.' Neddy shook his head sadly.

'And you heard from Eddie Flynn's syndicate, did you? I believe they were coming to see you.'

'Oh yes, a confused sort of visit.'

'And what did you say to them, Neddy?' Myles Barry held his breath.

'I told them I couldn't possibly deal with them, and that we would never take that huge sum of money, it was just outrageous.'

'And what did they say to that?' Myles's voice was only a whisper.

'You won't believe it, Myles, but they just offered me more money still! Like as if they hadn't been listening.'

Myles wiped his brow. Never again in his life would he have a client like this. Mercifully.

'So what exactly happens now, Neddy?'

'We get it sorted out when the time comes – when the compulsory purchase order comes.' Neddy was calm about it all.

'You do understand, I mean, I did explain to you, the government won't pay nearly what Eddie Flynn's pals will. You see, those syndicate people are operating from strength – they've bought up little bits of land everywhere.'

'Yes, I know all that, but if I sold it to them it would be theirs and I'd have no say in what happens.'

Myles Barry pondered over whether he should say that Neddy Nolan wouldn't ever have any say in what happened once he sold the land. But it hardly seemed worth it.

'So what will we say to Kit?' he asked despairingly.

'There's no need to say anything to Kit – he doesn't have any rights to anything from this place, only what I choose to give him.' Neddy looked around him proudly at the refurbished kitchen in what had been his father's broken-down farmhouse.

'Well, I agree it sounds as if it would be hard for him to prove any legal claim but of course as your father's son he might be able . . .'

'No, Myles.' Neddy was again very calm. 'No, when I bailed him the second time, I had to go across there to do it. And I found an English lawyer, a very nice old man he was too. But anyway, he made Kit sign a document saying that in return for the bail money he would relinquish his claim on the family estate. I mean, I told this lawyer it was only a few acres of poor land, but still it was an estate technically.' He smiled, thinking of it all.

'And do you still have that document, Neddy?'

'Oh I do. You see, Kit skipped bail that time, so I never got our money back, and when he was back in again they wouldn't even give bail so there was no point in his even asking.'

'Could I see this document, do you think?'

Neddy went to a small oak cabinet in the corner. Inside were neat files that would have done credit to any company. Within seconds he pulled out the right piece of paper. Myles Barry looked back into the filing drawer. He saw files marked 'Insurance', 'Pensions', 'St Ita's School', 'Medical', 'Household Expenses', 'Farm' . . . And all this from the man whose brother said he was not the full shilling.

Sebastian Slattery was proving to be an excellent companion. Judy found it very easy to talk to him and he was very interested in her work too. How she set about illustrating a children's story. Were there some stories that she didn't enjoy and did she find them harder to do?

He asked her, did she ever go to France on the Eurostar train? It was something he had always promised himself that he would do when he was next in London. He told her that he had hardly any family himself. He was an only child and his parents were dead. He did have cousins some miles out, in a small village called Doon – a nice place actually. He had been invited to the opening of a building out there called the Danny O'Neill Health Centre, in memory of some Irishman who went to America, and his grandson who was half Polish was doing it in his honour. Maybe Judy might like to come with him as his guest.

'Why do they call you Skunk?' she asked suddenly.

'I don't know, Judy, to be honest. They did at school and it stuck. Maybe I smelled awful then. I don't smell awful now, do I?'

'No, Sebastian, you do not, you smell fine to me,' she said.

At that moment Cathal Chambers the bank manager walked by.

'Evening, Skunk, evening, Judy,' he said affably.

'Oh Cathal, we were actually just discussing this. Sebastian is going to be called his real name from now on,' Judy Flynn said as if she were addressing a class of unruly ten-year-olds.

'Sure, I'm sorry, Skunk, I mean, Sebastian, no offence ever meant.'

And Skunk Slattery, who had been called that for over thirty years, graciously forgave him.

Next day Judy got an extensive grilling from her sister-in-law Kitty as they made Mrs Flynn's bed and settled her in a chair. They had got a good routine going now. Mrs Flynn had eventually and grudgingly recognised her daughter, and equally grudgingly got over her unreasonable dislike of her daughter-in-law, which was a considerable advance.

Of course she complained as usual that someone had stolen all her clothes and was not at all comforted when Judy briskly unpacked the clean items from the Fresh as a Daisy.

'Well, come on then! Did Skunk lay his hands on you?' Kitty asked.

'His name is Sebastian and he was quite delightful,' Judy said primly.

'Skunk? Delightful?' It was beyond Kitty's comprehension.

433

'I told you, he's not answering to that silly school-boy name any more.'

'It'll take a while to get that message across, Judy.'

'Well, he's starting this morning, he's painting a new sign over his shop,' Judy said.

Mrs Flynn looked from one to the other. 'You could do worse than Skunk, you know, he has plenty put by,' she said.

'You don't choose a man just for what he has put by,' Judy said, reprovingly.

'For what reason would you choose then? Because he's a good tap dancer?' her mam asked and for some reason that they couldn't quite understand they all found this very funny.

Cathal Chambers at the bank was concerned because Neddy Nolan had borrowed so much money. Of course he had put the farm up as collateral; still it was a heavy sum. And this from a man who would think twice before buying a pair of shoes in the charity shop.

'Could you let me know what it's all for, Neddy?' Cathal asked.

'It's for my advisers,' Neddy explained.

'But God above, what kind of advice are you getting that could cost all this money?' Cathal was bewildered.

'Experts in their field charge high fees,' Neddy said as if that was any kind of explanation.

'It's just that you wouldn't want cowboy advisers

who might bleed you dry or anything.' Cathal was sincere. He was as much out for Neddy Nolan's good as for the bank.

'No, indeed, Cathal, highly professional,' Neddy said with a calm little smile.

Cathal went to see the lawyer, Myles Barry.

'Myles, I don't want to get into the lawyer–client relationship but who are all these advisers Neddy Nolan has?'

'Advisers?' Myles Barry was confused.

'Yes, people he's paying huge fees to apparently.'

Myles scratched his head. 'I don't know who the hell they are – I haven't even sent him one bill, he can hardly have retained another firm of lawyers without telling me. I don't know what you're talking about, Cathal, I really don't.'

Lilly Ryan and her son Donal went to the prison on visiting day. This time they wanted to go without the priest.

'I'll be there visiting someone else in case you need me,' he said.

Father Flynn had an entirely unsatisfactory conversation with poor Becca King, who seemed to be getting madder all the time. She had got a very long prison sentence for being involved in the murder of her rival in love. She showed no repentance at all, just kept repeating that it had to be done. He hoped that she wouldn't ask him again to arrange a prison wedding with that young man she was obsessed with. A young man who wouldn't even come to visit her in jail, let alone marry her there. But no, today it was something different. She had a petition for St Ann, a card that she wanted pinned on to the shrine for all to see.

She showed it to the priest. It was a photograph of Gabrielle King, her mother, and underneath was written: 'Please, St Ann, punish this woman severely for having destroyed her daughter's life. And if any of your loyal followers should see her in the streets of Rossmore, they should spit at her in your name.'

Father Flynn felt very old and tired. He gravely said he would go there this afternoon and do it, he would give it priority.

'It must be in a place where everyone can see it,' Becca called as he was leaving.

'Pride of place, that's what I'll get for it, Becca,' he promised.

As he left, Kate, one of the warders, laid her hand on his arm.

'You are a kind man, Father, not to upset her.'

'You do know that I'm going to throw it away, don't you?' Father Flynn said.

'Of course I do, but you'll wait until you get home and burn it rather than leaving it round here for anyone to pick up,' Kate said.

Brian Flynn put the card in his wallet beside a cheque that had come from London that morning. It was money left by a lady who had died, a Helen Harris. She wanted to thank the shrine of St Ann for having answered her prayers for the safe delivery of a baby twenty-three long years ago. Perhaps the priest could spend it as he thought best to honour the saint.

As he sat there on a wooden bench in case Lilly Ryan might need him later, Father Flynn speculated to himself about the role of a priest in today's society. He hadn't come to any satisfactory conclusion when Lilly and Donal came out.

'All well?' he asked anxiously and felt annoyed with himself at the very question. How could all be well in a family where the father was in jail for domestic violence, a family that had lost a child nearly a quarter of a century ago?

But surprisingly Lilly nodded as if it were a normal thing to ask. 'Just fine, Father. I realise now he's a very weak man. I didn't know this, you see, what with him being so big and strong, and hurting me for being stupid. But he's actually weak and frightened, I see that now.'

'And my mam realises that just because she is understanding and forgiving to him, the State will not be forgiving and allow him to go home. He will have to finish his sentence,' her son said.

'Yes, and Donal was very good, it's not really in his heart but to please me he shook hands with his dad and wished him courage.' Lilly's tired face looked less strained than before.

'So would you say we have a result then?' Father Flynn said.

'Best result in the circumstances,' Donal agreed.

'That's all any of us can hope for,' Father Flynn said.

Clare was taking her pupils to the Heartfelt Art Gallery to do a project. Emer, who was the director there, was a friend of hers. They would let the girls wander round the gallery and try to answer the questions on the form while the two women had a cup of coffee.

Emer was getting married shortly to a Canadian called Ken whom she had always fancied but thought she had lost. Then suddenly out of the blue he had come to her with bunches of flowers and everything had been perfect.

Father Flynn was going to do a nice speedy job on the service. Emer supposed that the priest was so glad that anyone came into a church at all these days or married anyone of a different sex, he'd agree to anything.

'He's his own man,' Clare said.

'He is indeed,' Emer agreed. 'Did he marry you and Neddy?'

'No, the canon did, but he was there kind of rescuing the canon and bringing him back if he started to wander down too many byways . . .'

'I see your Neddy often these days, he has some kind of business in an office near Ken's up here in the old flour mills they converted,' Emer said.

'Neddy? Business?'

'Well, I assumed so, I saw him today when I was bringing Ken some lunch in his office. And yesterday . . .'

Clare was silent. Neddy had mentioned nothing

of any business. She felt a cold lump of dread in her heart. But not Neddy. No, never.

Emer realised what was happening.

'I could have been mistaken,' she said lamely.

Clare said nothing.

'I mean, it's all offices here, little suites they rent out as offices, you know. It's not as if it was flats, apartments. No, Clare, not Neddy. He worships you, for heaven's sake.'

'I think these girls have had enough time, don't you?' Clare said in a very brittle voice quite unlike her own.

'Please, don't jump to conclusions . . . you know men,' Emer begged.

Clare knew men better than anyone in Rossmore.

'Come on, girls, don't take all day,' she said in a voice that was not going to be disobeyed.

She was getting into her car when she met Cathal Chambers from the bank. He greeted her warmly.

'You and Neddy must be making great plans up in that farm of yours,' he said.

'Hardly, Cathal, it's still very uncertain whether there will be a road running through the middle of it or not.'

'So what are all these advisers then, the ones that cost all the money?'

'I don't know about any advisers costing lots of money.'

'Maybe I got it wrong. But you do know you have huge borrowings, don't you?' Cathal's round face was anxious.

'Huge borrowings? Oh yes, yes indeed, I know . . .' Clare said in a voice that would be obvious to anyone that she had absolutely no idea.

There was a time she had thought that Neddy was just too good to be true. Maybe she had been right.

When she got back home her father-in-law was having a siesta out on the porch they had built together. She remembered handing Neddy the nails one by one. Marty was asleep in a big wicker chair with a light warm rug on his knees. This place had meant peace and refuge to Clare, and now it was all over.

Neddy was sitting at the kitchen table surrounded by papers.

'I have something important to ask you, Neddy,' she began.

'And I have something very important to tell you, Clare,' he said.

Judy Flynn stood back to get the full effect of the new sign over Slattery's newsagents. It looked very splendid.

'It may take time for them to stop calling me Skunk,' he said anxiously.

'Well, we have time,' Judy said.

'You don't have to go back for a while yet, do you?' Sebastian Slattery asked from the top of his ladder.

'No, I'm my own boss, but I'm not made of money, I can't go on staying in the Rossmore Hotel for much longer.'

'What about your mam's house?' the newly named Sebastian suggested.

'No, she would be found killed dead with a bread knife in her if I stayed there.' Judy knew herself fairly well.

'Kitty's?'

'Something similar. These are people I can meet just for very short periods of time.'

'Well, what about my place then? You could stay here over the shop for a while until . . . until . . .'

'Until what, Sebastian?'

'Until we get married and look for somewhere nicer for you and for me, for us, I mean . . .'

'Are we going to get married? We barely know each other,' Judy said.

'I do hope so,' Sebastian said, coming down the ladder.

'Right. I'll move in tonight,' she said.

'Um – I'll have to do up a room for you . . .'

'You mean, we aren't going to sleep together? In your room?' she called across the street to him to the entertainment of passers-by.

'I'll have your terrible Druid of a brother after me, saying I am the wages of sin and all that sort of thing.'

'Don't be ridiculous, Sebastian. Brian will just be delighted to see us happy. He won't go on with all that kind of stuff. You've been away from the Church too long . . .'

*

Brian Flynn was surprised to see Chester Kovac, the big American who had financed the Danny O'Neill Health Centre in Doon.

'I was wondering if I could prevail on you to marry Hannah Harty and myself quietly, you know, no big ceremony . . .'

'Well, of course I will, and my warmest congratulations. But why won't you be getting married out in Doon where you live? Father Murphy is in charge of the parish there.'

'No, we'd have to ask everyone if we had it in Doon, and we're a bit advanced in years to be making a big show of it. And anyway there's Dr Dermot there – we don't want to be sort of showing off in front of him. It's complicated.'

Father Flynn knew Dr Dermot – a mean, crabbed man. He could well believe that it was complicated.

'I just didn't want you to miss out on a big day, that's all,' he reassured Chester.

'Oh, don't worry about that, Father, we'll miss out on nothing. There will be plenty of people at a big do when I go back to the States for a honeymoon. In fact we will be bringing my mom back here with us for a vacation. Her name is Ann, too, so she is very anxious to visit the well here.'

Father Flynn thought to himself that she had better come fairly quickly if she wanted to see the well and he examined his diary to get a suitable early date for the wedding.

*

Eddie Flynn was nowhere to be found when the decision to build the new road was announced. The vote in the council had been satisfactorily in favour of building the bypass. Eddie's syndicate had bought every piece of property that might have been central to this plan except the Nolans' farm. The plan said the road would go straight through this property and up through the woods in a straight line, taking the well and the shrine with it.

Eddie had assured the others that buying land from Neddy Nolan was like taking candy from a baby. Yes, true, it was Neddy who was the loser. The compulsory purchase order would not pay anything like what he had been offered by the syndicate. But Neddy had always been soft in the head. The real problem was that Eddie Flynn had not delivered. So he had disappeared.

Kitty and the children barely noticed that he was gone. Naomi, however, was very distressed. She had fabric for bridesmaids and flower girls, and she needed to talk to him about it. Why had he done this now? And he had left her no money to be getting on with, and the flat was only paid for for the next two months. It was vexing in the extreme . . .

Lilly Ryan had heard from her cousin Pearl over in the North of England. Pearl was married to this really nice fellow, Bob, and they had two grown-up children. It appeared that something nice had happened in their lives. Their children, who used to be quite cold and distant and maybe a bit ashamed of them, had been much nicer of late. Pearl always wrote very honestly, not pretending or putting on airs. She wondered, could she and Bob come and spend a long weekend in Rossmore. Now Lilly was to say if it was difficult, and she would quite understand.

So Lilly sat down and wrote everything, all about Aidan and his accusations, and how he couldn't cope and that despite his violence he was a weak man, and that he would be in jail for another eighteen months and how she, Lilly, would just love them to visit. When she posted the letter she felt much better, as if she had needed to write out the whole story to make some kind of sense of it. She said that she and Pearl would go up to St Ann's Well for old times' sake when she arrived.

Clare and Neddy sat one on either side of the table. Clare didn't even look at the papers spread out all over the place. She was about to have her first and last row with Neddy Nolan on the day she had been going to tell him that her period was three weeks late and they might possibly be looking at the pregnancy they both longed for. Now it was too late.

Neddy spoke very quietly.

'The permission for the road has been given today, Clare. As we thought it's going straight through here and on up to the well.'

'We knew that would happen, but you refused to sell to Eddie Flynn just at a time when you might actually need money more than any other time of your life.' Clare's voice was cold.

'But I couldn't sell to them or we'd have had no control,' he said as if explaining it to a toddler.

'And what control do you have now? Less money, that's all . . .'

'No, Clare, that's not true, we have all this . . .' He waved at the papers and maps on the kitchen table.

'This?'

'I took advice, I got experts to draw up an alternative plan, another way the road would go so that it wouldn't take away St Ann's shrine. It involved architects, engineers, quantity surveyors, and cost a fortune. Clare, I had to borrow from Cathal Chambers and he thinks I'm into heroin or gambling or something.'

Suddenly she knew that this was indeed what he was doing with the money, rather than feathering a little love nest for himself in the converted flour mills. Her relief was followed by a wave of resentment.

'And why didn't you tell him and tell me, for God's sake?'

'I had to keep it very quiet, have meetings where no one would see me.'

'In the old flour mills?' she guessed.

Neddy laughed sheepishly. 'There's me thinking no one knew!'

He patted her hand and kissed her fingers as he often did. The resentment had gone. Clare felt only the relief that he still loved her. She hadn't known until now just how much she would dread the thought of losing him.

'Will it work, Neddy?' she asked weakly.

Neddy Nolan had hired all these people to make maps and surveys. It was unbelievable.

'I think it will,' Neddy said calmly. 'You see, I hired a public relations expert as well to show us how to get public sympathy. And he will get us a media coach for the two of us for television.'

'For television?'

'If you agree we can go on a big news programme and debate it with the developers.'

'We can?' Clare whispered.

'Oh yes, we can explain how so many people here feel grateful to St Ann and want to keep the well and the shrine. It would make no sense now for anyone to oppose us.'

'But Neddy, couldn't we have done that without you having to hire all these experts?'

'No, that's just the point,' Neddy cried. 'Then we'd only have been pious, old-fashioned, superstitious people standing in the way of progress. We'd only have looked like the old Ireland rooted in history and traditions against the good modern Ireland which wanted to improve life for everyone . . .'

'And now?'

'Now we have a perfectly possible alternative plan. A plan which you and I paid for with our own money, refusing huge financial offers from syndicates and the like.' He nodded over at the little oak cabinet. 'I have every detail of it recorded there. They'll know we are telling the truth and putting our money where our mouth is.'

'And where will the road go?'

She bent over the map with him and he stroked her hair with one hand as he pointed with the other. The new road would still go through the Nolan farm, but would then follow a route that would allow a sizeable part of the woods to remain, the part that held the shrine. There would be a big car park there and a side slip road from the new road to bring visitors directly to the shrine instead of going through Rossmore. And yet the local people could walk there through what remained of the woods as always.

Clare looked at him with admiration. It could well work. A government heading for a General Election, a local council fearful of being accused of taking backhanders, might well want to take this chance of avoiding the huge confrontation that seemed to be brewing. Neddy's solution seemed a perfect way out for everybody.

'I wish you'd told me,' she said.

'Yes, I was going to, but you looked tired, and you have to go into a classroom every day. I just stay here. I have a much easier life.'

She looked around the gleaming house that he kept so well for the three of them. It was not such an easy life, and she knew it. But Neddy never complained.

'Hey, you said you had something to tell me – what was it?' he asked.

She told him that there was an outside chance she might be pregnant. Neddy got up and held her in his arms.

'I was up there at the shrine today and I know it's

nonsense but I did say that it was something we both wanted badly,' he said into her hair.

'Well, she had to do something for the man who saved her well,' Clare said.

They were still standing there, arms around each other, when Marty Nolan came in.

'Father Flynn arrived and he couldn't get any answer so I came in to see were you two all right.' He was indignant that he had to be woken from his chair.

As they had their tea and home-made biscuits, the birds started to gather on the trees for the night. And the sun began to set over the woods that Neddy Nolan had almost certainly saved.

And the priest knew that his sister Judy was up there at the well, thanking St Ann and saying she hadn't expected that it would all work so quickly.

So Father Flynn listened, as it got dark, to Neddy's plans.

He was going to buy a house much nearer Rossmore, and then maybe Father Flynn's mother and the canon could come to stay. It would not be like moving too far from the town, he had seen a grand place with a garden that the canon would like. Neddy would look after them all.

And if by any chance they were to get a little baby he would look after the baby too. It would be nice for older people to have a new young life around the place.

And for once Father Flynn could find nothing to say. What he liked to think of as his comforting supply of meaningless clichés had dried up.

He looked at the good honest man in front of him and for the first time for a long time he saw some purpose in a life that had recently been confused and contradictory on every front.

He looked back up at the ever darkening woods.

And it wasn't fanciful to think of them as a very special place, where so many voices had been heard and so many dreams answered.